Steve Martini, a former trial attorney, has worked as a journalist and capital correspondent in the California State House in Sacramento. He has been engaged in both public and private practice of law. He lives on the US West Coast with his wife and daughter. Steve Martini is the author of the highly acclaimed thrillers *The Simeon Chamber, Compelling Evidence, Prime Witness, Undue Influence, The Judge, The Attorney, The Jury* and *The Arraignment*, also available from Headline.

Praise for Steve Martini's electrifying bestsellers:

'Sensationally good' *Los Angeles Times*

'The best debut, in my opinion, is *Compelling Evidence*' John Grisham

'The exchanges between the opposing lawyers and their witnesses are often riveting and the eventual exposure of the guilty party comes as a genuine surprise' *Sunday Telegraph*

'A dazzling climax . . . Martini has written the courtroom novel of the year' *Kirkus Reviews*

'A fine courtroom drama . . . with a believable plot, a sympathetic hero . . . and a little bit of downbeat humour stirred into the pot' *Irish News Belfast*

'Crisp dialogue and tart observations' *Publishers Weekly*

The List

and

Critical Mass

Steve Martini

headline

THE LIST
first published in Great Britain in 1997
by HEADLINE BOOK PUBLISHING

CRITICAL MASS
first published in Great Britain in 1998
by HEADLINE BOOK PUBLISHING

First published in this omnibus edition in 2004
by HEADLINE BOOK PUBLISHING

A HEADLINE paperback

10 9 8 7 6 5 4 3 2 1

ISBN 0 7553 2258 4

Printed and bound in Great Britain by
Clays Ltd, St Ives plc

Papers and cover board used by Headline are natural, recyclable
products made from wood grown in sustainable forests. The
manufacturing processes conform to the environmental
regulations of the country of origin.

HEADLINE BOOK PUBLISHING
A division of Hodder Headline
338 Euston Road
LONDON NW1 3BH

www.headline.co.uk
www.hodderheadline.com

The List

To Leah and Megan

PROLOGUE

He held it to his right eye and searched for the telltale signs of heat, a wavy thermal image of someone hiding in the shadows on deck.

The old starlight scope was a relic from the '60s. He wished he had his night-vision goggles, but he didn't.

Vapors of hot steam coming from a pipe at the side of the ship threw up a ghostly green haze, its own kind of fog. He lowered the scope from his eye to re-orient himself for a moment. Then he picked up the search, starting where he left off, under the hundred-and-eighty-ton derrick that thrust skyward from the foredeck.

'Do you see her?' His companion hovered over his shoulder.

'Not yet.' He kept looking.

'Maybe she made it inside already?'

'No.' She would have had to cross the open deck, and he would have seen her. 'She's there somewhere.'

He kept looking, scanning along the deck. Occasionally he hit a bright light on the ship and the image through the scope flared out. He would have to squint, pick it up, and start scanning again.

'You think he's on board?'

'Why else would she come here?' The man with the scope didn't want to talk. It made the instrument move in his hands, turning his search into a maze of jittery phosphorous lines.

'Let's just get her and go.'

'It's not that easy.'

'You think he's armed?'

'I don't know.' He doubted if the man would be armed. He couldn't have been expecting them. Still, if he was armed, they would deal with it. 'What's that?'

'What?'

'There.' He stopped scanning and focused in on a sliver of luminous green, like a fingernail moon, sticking out from the edge of a canvas tarpaulin just aft of the derrick.

Abby Chandlis was exhausted. The instinct for survival was strong, but it was not boundless. She was tired, and tired people make mistakes. She had made one at the airport, and they had seen her. Abby was running for her life.

She was pressed against the cold steel plates on the main deck, soaked through from the moisture of the fog and her own perspiration, hiding in the shadows created by the ship's heavy equipment. Her eyes searched the dock for movement.

Out there, somewhere among the pallets and giant steel containers, she knew they were waiting, searching for movement, listening for sounds. It was no delusion, she had seen them. Worse, they had seen her.

She moved just a few feet, slowly, crouching, hands in front of her, feeling along the steel deck until she was behind a stack of webbed life rafts covered by a canvas tarp. To move beyond this point would put her out on the open deck in clear view where they couldn't miss her. Sooner or later she knew she would have to chance it. She had to reach mid-ship and the superstructure that led inside.

Morgan was here on this ship. She had to find him. She had to warn him. She knew that they would kill him, just as they'd tried to kill her. Only now without intending it, she had led them to him.

Her hope lay in the fact that Morgan knew ships. He would know his way around this one, perhaps a quick way off, some avenue of escape they wouldn't be able to observe. Abby was sure of it. Together they would lose the men on the dock. As soon as they delivered the documents, it would be over. The two men would have nothing to gain by killing them. Once the information in the documents was known, the contracts and the copyright, it would all be over. The documents were what they wanted, their entire purpose in killing Morgan. Without realizing it, Abby had made him a target.

'Got her.' He zeroed in with the scope.
'You sure?'
'Yeah.' He pointed to the gangway stairs that led from the dock up onto the forward deck. He looked up at the bridge to see if there was anyone in the wing. He checked it with the scope quickly. It was clear. 'Let's move.'

They scampered down the ladder. He put the scope in his pocket and followed the other man, behind a line of steel containers. He felt in the back of his pants, the checkered handle of a nine-millimeter Beretta.

There was a line of cargo carefully stacked, two containers high beneath the huge dock crane, waiting for the stevedores in the morning to be loaded on another ship. The cargo was conveniently between themselves and the *Cuesta Verde*. If they stayed behind it, Abby would never see them. They would be on her before she could make a sound. Surprise was critical.

Silently they moved to the corner of the last container. From there it was a hundred-foot dash to the base of the stairs, all of it in the open. For the first fifty he estimated she could see them from the deck, that is if she was looking in the right direction. After that they would be too close to the side of the ship to be seen. From there it would be easy; up the stairs and slip in behind her.

'You first,' the other man looked at him and whispered.

This was his job and he knew it, so he didn't argue. Instead, he slipped off his shoes. Even rubber soles made noise on asphalt. He looped the laces together in a single knot and hung them over his shoulder. His companion did the same. Then without hesitating, he darted out from behind the containers, his heart pounding. If she saw him or heard him, she would take off. There were a million places to hide on a ship.

He made it soundlessly to the stairs, then stopped and listened. He heard nothing except the monotonous internal rumblings of the ship at rest, a motor here, and a generator there, distant rhythmic sounds unbroken by the patter of feet on the deck overhead. He looked back, then signaled for his companion to follow.

Twelve seconds later they were huddled together at the base of the stairs. Now they didn't talk. He went first, two steps at a time up the metal staircase, gripping the railing as he went, carefully so as not to rattle the metal scaffolding supporting the stairs.

He was just ten steps from the top, the gate in the

ship's gunnel, when he heard the clatter behind him, turned and looked. It hit two more times on the metal stairs before it fell with a thud to the dock below. The knot on his companion's shoes had come loose. The man was juggling the other shoe and finally managed to catch it.

She had been lost somewhere in the past when the noise brought her back to reality. She whirled and looked at the stairs behind her.

It could have been nothing, the creaking of the ship against the dock, but Abby didn't wait to investigate. In her heightened state she bolted, instincts taking hold, running headlong toward the ship's looming super-structure, her shoes echoing on the iron deck. She raced into the open companionway along the side of the ship and tried the first door she came to. It was locked. She tried pulling on the metal latch handles. She couldn't move them, frozen solid.

Now she heard footsteps behind her, muted heavy heelfalls on the iron deck, and they were coming closer.

She ran on, down the companionway. The next door was open, a dim corridor illuminated only by a single overhead bulb, underpowered. She stepped over the threshold and reached behind her to pull the door closed. It didn't move.

The footfalls came closer. Abby stepped outside and looked behind the door; a large brass hook fitted through a welded eye held the door open against the steel wall. She unhooked it, and as she did, she turned and saw them, two silhouettes against the glare of lights from the dock coming toward her, running full speed into the companionway.

Abby stepped over the threshold pulling the door

closed behind her. She fumbled with the metal latch handles on the watertight door and finally managed to close one of them, then another until she had all four shut. The problem was they could open them just as easily from the outside.

She held two of them closed in the down position at the top of the door by hanging on them with the weight of her body, then watched in horror as they opened the bottom two and pulled on the door. Three hundred pounds of iron, it flexed only slightly as long as she held the two latches closed. She felt them pull and fight to turn the upper latches.

Her strength ebbing, running on adrenaline, her arms ached. She couldn't hold much longer and she knew it. She turned her head to the side and rested it against the cold steel. Looking through blood-shot eyes she wondered what it would feel like to die. With this thought in her mind, her eyes focused on an object in the corner, a push broom, its long metal handle propped against the wall. Her feet dangling off the floor as she hung on the latches, she tried to hook the broom with her foot but couldn't.

They fought with the door latches, lifting her halfway to an open position before gravity set in and they let go. She dropped with a jarring thud, all of her weight hanging on her arms. The latches settled back into a full locked position as they concentrated their energies pulling on the door.

This gave her an instant of reprieve. She released her grip on one of the latches and instantly they turned it. The door was held shut by a single latch, and that was beginning to turn now that the weight of her body had been removed. It was now her strength against theirs, a losing battle having given up the leverage of gravity.

She reached for the broom, grabbed it with her free hand. Then turning it, lifted the broom head toward the ceiling, wedging the handle between the steel latch and the door, jamming it until it stuck. The latch was now held closed by the broom handle.

They pulled from the outside and the handle flexed but held. Slowly, Abby stepped away, her gaze glued to the latch.

They fought with it. She could hear them swearing, a string of expletives on the other side of the steel door. But it held.

She turned and ran down the dark corridor not knowing where she was going.

He fought with the handle. Something had jammed it.

'Let's find another way in.' They headed down the companionway. Two more doors were locked, their latches bolted on the inside. They came to a lighted porthole and could hear voices on the other side. He peered through near the bottom of the thick glass ellipse and saw two men talking in a small cabin. The one with his back to him was wearing oil-spattered coveralls, a crew member from the engine room, he guessed.

They slid under the porthole and kept going.

Halfway down the superstructure there was an alley that traversed the center of the ship from starboard to port on the main deck: broadway. He knew the term from his time on shipboard in the Marines. He watched from outside for several seconds before entering. This would be a main thoroughfare on the ship. The crew would use it regularly to move from one side to the other. Tied to the dock, with a skeleton crew, this passage way was now dark and abandoned. They entered and ran quickly, emerging seconds later on the port side of the ship. They retraced their steps toward the bow and seconds later found an open door. The two men disappeared inside.

The first explosion sent Abby to her knees in the dark passage way. A bright flash of fire lit up the corridor, and smoke began to billow from somewhere below decks. Klaxons and alarms sounded. She got to her feet, just as the second blast bounced her off of one of the steel walls and sent a stabbing pain through her shoulder. The shock wave set her ears ringing and finally threw her to the floor like a rag doll. She lay there stunned, her senses paralyzed, mind numbed, as heat from the metal deck embraced her in the folds of its comforting warmth.

In Abby's mind, images danced like a time-lapsed film. She hovered in the dim shadows of consciousness, shaking and exhausted, wondering if this was death, and searching in her mind to remember when it was, the precise moment that this obsession to surrender her identity had taken hold, and what had possessed her to do it.

CHAPTER
ONE

Abby Chandlis was approaching her middle years and suffered the anxiety of nearly every woman – that she would not age gracefully.

This morning the image in the mirror did nothing to diminish this fear. Her hair looked like something left in the aftermath of a tornado, spikes in every direction. Even with the fine features of her face, a few lines had begun to creep under her eyes. She was a candle burning at both ends.

She stood five-six, slender, and approached mid-life with the velocity of an earth-bound meteor, sharing a sense of its common destiny. Abby was beginning to feel like a burnt offering in a culture where youth is the state religion.

On top of it all, this morning she was late for work. By the muted light of the bedside lamp, Abby groped in her dark closet for something to throw on. She grabbed the first thing that felt warm and long. She had no court calls today, just a pile of paper on her desk.

She flung the flowing peasant dress over her head and slipped the Birkenstocks on over a thick pair of red cotton socks. It wasn't stylish, but it kept out the chill of

9

the cold winter winds of western Washington – short days and long dark nights.

It took her nearly forty minutes to traverse the seven miles between home and work during rush hour. She huddled in her office on the seventeenth floor, a sky-scraper pitched on a hill over Elliot Bay. She had a partial view of the Seattle skyline to the south, and if she leaned with her face close to the glass she could see the edge of the Space Needle in the distance.

She was pushing papers on her desk when the com-line rang.

'Yes.'

'A woman out here to see you.'

'I left a message not to be disturbed.'

'She's very insistent. Something about a book.'

Suddenly Abby felt the blood drain from her head. Who would come to her here at her office?

'Who is it?'

'I didn't get a name. You want me to ask?'

Abby thought for a moment. 'No. Give me two minutes, then send her back.' Abby didn't need them talking about the book at the firm. She glanced down and realized that she wasn't dressed for this.

She grabbed the small mirror and lipstick from the second drawer of her desk.

A few seconds later there was a light rap on the door and it opened. Abby ditched the lipstick and mirror.

'Ms Chandlis?' The female voice that inquired was not familiar, but still it raised tiny hairs on the nape of Abby's neck.

'Yes.'

The woman was tall, well dressed, and carried an expensive leather briefcase. She made her way across the office and held out her hand. 'I'm Carla Owens. You spoke with my office last week.'

Abby's jaw went slack. She stood there staring at the woman with a vacant expression. It took her a moment before she collected herself.

'Oh yeah. Sure.' She smiled brightly as a wave of apprehension washed over her. Then absently she wiped her hands on the skirt of her long peasant dress and reached out to take the other woman's hand.

'Can we talk here or is there somewhere else?' said Owens.

'This is fine. Please. Sit down.' Abby pointed to one of the client chairs.

As Owens adjusted herself in the chair, Abby fidgeted with her appearance. The premature graying wisps at her temple, and the long shapeless dress over Birkenstocks, offered the picture of some earth mother off the prairie. Abby smoothed her hair in hopes that somehow this might improve the image. She wished that perhaps she'd had a court call so she'd dressed better.

'You probably think I'm foolish to have come all this way especially after the call from my office?'

Abby said nothing but gave a tilt of the head, an indication that the thought had crossed her mind.

In her most frenzied fantasies Abby had never imagined that Owens would show up here. Five days ago her office had called Abby's house looking for Gable Cooper. Abby had told them that he was out of town and that she would have him call as soon as he returned. She figured she had bought some time, at least enough to find Cooper. Now what she had set in motion was suddenly careening·out of control, and for Abby there was no way back.

Carla Owens was one of the most powerful literary agents in New York. She performed marketing magic for the written word. The hottest book deals on earth passed through her fingers. She represented presidents, people who wrote romances, and more recently the pope, of whom it was said it was easier to obtain an audience with than with Carla herself.

Protruding from the top of Owens's briefcase was a package that Abby recognized, a large FedEx envelope that had traveled many miles and showed the wear.

'Actually I was traveling in the area. So I thought I'd stop in and say hello.'

'Where are you headed?' asked Abby.

'Oh, just up from L.A., on some business. On my way back to New York.'

The woman's idea of traveling in the area was a triangle that spanned the country. She was in hot pursuit of Cooper and Abby knew it.

'I just thought I'd take a chance and drop in,' said Owens. She looked around as if she was half expecting to see some sign of the man.

'I didn't know you were a lawyer,' said Owens.

'Hmm. I guess I forgot to mention it.'

'Is Mr Cooper a client?'

'Just a friend.'

This seemed to please her.

'Is he in town?'

'No.'

This did not.

'I told you on the phone he's traveling.'

'I took the chance that he might be back by now.'

'I'm sorry you went out of your way,' said Abby. 'I told your office he would call.'

Owens offered a deep sigh as if her trip was for naught, spread her elbows on the desk, and smiled at Abby.

'How about some coffee?' said Abby. 'The least I can offer you after coming all this way.'

'Sure.'

Abby went outside and got two cups of coffee. When she came back in Owens had removed the large package from her briefcase and had it on the desk in front of her, still in the bright red and blue envelope that Abby had used to send it off nearly two weeks before.

'It's magic,' said Owens. She looked up at Abby.

'There's something absolutely beguiling about a man who can write in such a seductive voice. And the way he gets inside the female mind,' said Owens. She rolled her eyes. 'It's very important that I talk to him. The sooner the better.'

Owens wasn't exactly sure how much to tell this woman. As little as possible was the general rule. The agent's credo.

'I take it Mr Cooper asked you to send the manuscript to me?'

Abby swallowed hard. In her mind this was the literary equivalent of war, and in every war truth was the first victim. 'Right,' said Abby.

'If you don't represent him, do you mind my asking what you do?'

'Some typing. A little editing. Sometimes we talk about ideas.'

Owens was fishing. She was trying to find out if Abby was someone important in Gable Cooper's life. If she wasn't his lawyer, where did she fit?

She measured the woman. Abby was to the late side of thirty, but not unattractive. There was a possibility for beauty, but she had obviously taken no pains with her appearance. Owens was forming a picture in her mind. A little editing, the occasional back rub, a long night of work that might turn into an indolent morning of slumber. It was possible that they were lovers.

'Then you collaborate with him?'

'I don't know if I'd go so far as to say that.'

Owens offered a smile that made evident what she was thinking.

'Let's just say we're friends. We spend time together. When he leaves he tells me where he's going, and he usually comes back.'

'I see.' Suddenly Carla's face was a curling smile. Abby was someone to contend with. Perhaps the trip wasn't wasted after all. If she couldn't bend Cooper's ear, Abby was the next best thing.

The two women huddled over their cups taking stock of each other.

'Do you know where Mr Cooper is?' Maybe Owens could run him down herself.

'Last I heard Mexico.'

'Big area.'

'Somewhere down by Cancun.'

That was smaller. Should she try for the name of a town? Owens wasn't sure. 'Is he at a resort?'

'No. Gable hates those places. People around pools all baking on cement. He's into remote areas. He's out in the Yucatan someplace. Beating the weeds.' This clearly put him out of touch.

Owens took a sip of coffee and considered the next question.

'What's he doing down there?'

'Gathering color for the next book.'

'He has another in the works?'

Abby nodded.

'Like this one?' Owens touched the package on the table in front of her as if it possessed healing properties.

14

Abby nodded again.

'It's vital that I talk to him,' said Owens. 'Could we try to reach him? Maybe tonight? I'd be happy to hold over. Pay for the call.'

Abby shook her head. 'No. No. That would be a waste of time. It'll take a number of phone calls to run him down. If he's where I think he is, there's no phone in the area. Besides, when he's working, he doesn't like to be disturbed.'

'Believe me,' said Owens, 'when he hears what I have to say he'll want to be disturbed.'

Abby looked at the woman over her coffee mug.

'Is there a publisher interested in his manuscript?' The lawyer bearing down.

'You might say that. But the details I have to give to Mr Cooper directly.'

'I see.' Abby had blown it, deviated from her planned cover story. Owens had surprised her by showing up here in her office. If Abby represented Cooper as a lawyer, she could have demanded answers. Now Owens had smoked out of her that they had no legal relationship. It was as if Abby were being denied a key to her own safe deposit box. She would have to produce Gable Cooper before she could find out what was in it.

'Does he do this often?' asked Owens.

Abby gave her a questioning look.

'Mr Cooper. Does he disappear like this very often?'

'Sometimes.'

'How long is he usually gone?'

'Depends. Sometimes a month, sometimes more.'

Owens said something under her breath that sounded a lot like 'shit.'

'Somebody must be able to get in touch with him.' Owens should have been the lawyer. Every answer gave birth to another question. 'What if there was an emergency? Doesn't he have family?'

Abby raised her eyes in thought. Shrugged her shoulders. 'I think there's a sister somewhere down in California, but Gable never talks about her much.' If Abby had a special gift, it was the ability to create.

'Do you have her name or number?'

Abby shook her head.

'You think her name might be on his Rollodex.' She was now suggesting prying into Cooper's private places.

'Gable keeps all his notes, including phone numbers, on scraps of paper in his pockets. Organization is not his middle name.'

Owens seemed to accept this without question.

'Is *that* real?' she asked.

'What?'

'His name?'

Abby considered for a moment, then fessed up. 'It's a pen name.' She shrugged. 'He likes classic movies. The golden age. His two favorite actors.' She offered an expression that said, 'Childish, but what can I say?'

'I thought so. What's his real name?'

'Oh no.' Abby started to shake her head, first gently and then with more conviction. 'I can't tell you that. Not until after I talk to him. I know he would be very angry if I did.'

Owens had checked *Books in Print* and a number of other sources to see if the name Gable Cooper showed up as authoring other works. It didn't.

Abby's reluctance to tell her his name fed a theory that Owens had been nurturing, a reason why the author might not want his true name to be known. If the theory was correct, the manuscript was worth vastly more than any of them figured.

'Tell me a little about him?' Owens played for time and information, a slip of the tongue.

'What's to tell?'

'How old is he? Is he good-looking?'

Though Owens didn't notice, Abby's eyes for a fleeting instant drew a dark, cold bead. The agent had wandered onto dangerous ground. Abby now knew with certainty that she had done the right thing.

'Is that important?'

'Oh, don't get me wrong. The book is wonderful. I'm sure we can find an enthusiastic publisher.'

'But if Gable is good-looking it helps?' said Abby.

Owens's face was a million expressions, all of them adding up to the word 'yes.'

'For television, and protein ads, it's a consideration. It helps,' she said. 'Please don't misunderstand, we're interested in talent, and the book's a great read . . .'

'But a little beefcake doesn't hurt.' Abby said this in a frank fashion, smiling, woman-to-woman. She might dress like a peasant, but she wasn't one.

Owens gave her a face of concession, winked at her over the coffee mug, and they both laughed. The ridges in Abby's cheeks as she did this were hard as steel.

'You know I'm not exactly sure how old he is. It's not something he talks about. We've had a couple of birthday parties for him, but he'll never tell us how many candles.'

'Sounds like a state secret,' said Owens.

'Chalk it up to vanity,' said Abby.

'What do you think, fifty?' Owens dipped her toe in this pool of uncertainty hoping she wouldn't have to go deeper.

'No. No. Late thirties, early forties tops.'

Relief blossomed on the agent's face.

'Has he ever been married?' She was nibbling around the edges.

'Twice.' This would mean that at least two women thought he was enough of a catch to go after.

'Good-looking?' Finally she stepped in it.

'Very. In fact, he's done a little modeling, years ago,' said Abby.

Owens's eyes grew like two oval saucers. 'Any pictures?'

Without thinking, Abby had dug herself another hole.

'I'm sure there are some. Unfortunately, I don't have them. I'm sure as soon as he gets back he'll be happy to send them to you.'

Owens probed for a little more description.

'Dark. About six feet,' said Abby.

'Sounds like a Ken doll,' said Owens.

'Ken dolls don't look dangerous,' said Abby.

'Really?'

'And very well spoken. Articulate,' said Abby.

'Speaks as he writes?' says Owens.

'You could say that.'

A growing satisfaction spread across the agent's face. The trip was not in vain after all.

'I can't wait to see the real item,' said Owens.

'In the flesh, so to speak,' said Abby.

'So to speak.'

Both women laughed. Abby a little louder this time.

By now, Owens was running up a dead end. No Cooper, and no way to get in touch with him, except through this woman who wasn't telling her much.

'Abby. Can I call you Abby?' Owens suddenly had one hand across the desk on top of Abby's as if to impress upon her the significance of the moment.

'I assume that you know a little about my agency? I mean, being a lawyer and all, you checked us out?'

In fact, Abby knew a lot – everything she could find on the Internet. She knew, for example, that the agency had ties with one of the institutional talent shops in Hollywood, which in turn had under contract some of the largest box-office stars in film. Mass entertainment had become a vast communal meal served up in package deals by agencies that controlled every aspect of the business. If you could get your nose under that tent, you could draw up a chair and sit at the table. The manuscript had not landed at Owens and Associates by accident.

'I know a little,' she lied.

'We're very selective. We take only a very few clients. I usually have fewer than a dozen. All very big.' She dropped some names, authors who if they sneezed left the entire publishing industry with a cold.

'Ordinarily we don't take people unless they already have a proven track record. At least three or four major bestsellers to their credit.'

'That must be very nice for you,' said Abby.

Owens gave her a smile. The two women were talking the same language.

'Because of our contacts, the influence of my agency, we are usually able to take these authors to that next higher level.' What Owens meant was into the stratosphere where books sales and movie deals grew by geometric progression.

'What I'm saying is that based upon what I've read –' Owens tapped the package on the table – 'we might be able to leverage your friend into an extremely favorable position.' Owens arched an eyebrow, waiting for a reply.

'I see.' Abby sat sipping her coffee contemplating the

good fortune of her friend, leverage being what it is in life. Owens fished in her briefcase for something.

'I'm going to be back in my office tomorrow, in New York.' Then she reached across the table and pressed several business cards into Abby's hand as if she should paper the walls of her office with these lest she forget the agent's number.

'My phone number.' She pointed to it on one of the cards.

'Do you think you might be able to find Mr Cooper for me quickly? Time is of the essence. There are opportunities being offered, and if we don't act quickly they may be gone. Do you understand?'

What Owens was worried about were her opportunities, the stream of sharks, other agents, who would swim in if word got out that Cooper was unrepresented.

'I can try,' said Abby.

'Do better than that. You've got to find him. It's important. To his career. To his life. From this moment on we're a team, Abby. You and I. You find him, and I'll represent him.'

Rah, thought Abby. Am I in for a commission? If Owens had an article of Cooper's old clothing, she would have rubbed it under Abby's nose at this moment.

'Oh, he'll come back,' said Abby.

'Yes, but will it be in time?' said Owens.

'Maybe if you told me what this was about? How long do I have?'

'Every moment is important. I can't tell you any more than that. But believe me, it's the biggest deal of his life. I hope you understand.'

Having fanned anxiety, Owens buckled up her briefcase and slipped out of the chair. 'It is important. You know that much.' She shook Abby's hand and headed for the door. When she reached it she turned and waved, a big glossy smile.

'Your Mr Cooper sounds fascinating. I can't wait to meet him.' With that she was out the door, closing it behind her so that she didn't hear Abby's last comment.

'Sweetheart, that makes two of us.'

CHAPTER
TWO

Jack stood in front of the mirror in the bathroom off his study scratching the little cleft on his chin and looking at the dark stubble. Something in the image troubled him. A single wisp of gray hair had slipped out from the sea of dark brown at one temple. At his age he could have a mass of these. But Jack led a charmed life in all ways but one, the only one that seemed to matter to him at the moment.

He was bare to the waist, trim and athletic, with a tan that he'd added to on a five-day trip to the Bahamas, an excursion to kill the frustration and pain of continued failure. A hot beach and the warmth of the sun always gave Jack the lift he needed in low moments. And the young girls in thong bikinis with tans to match didn't hurt.

But now he was back at Coffin Point and the realities of life, which at this moment in his mind were dismal.

He plucked the gray hair from his temple and washed it down the sink, put his body on the scale and weighed it. Lost three pounds. He always did in the tropics. Life was not fair, and Jack was on the winning side more than he had a right to be. He had the wild consolation that if he went to hell, a prospect that given his diversions in life was not entirely improbable, even in that hot place he could debauch himself, attract all the best looking women, and still lose weight.

He checked the luminous dial of his diving watch. Seven-thirty. He shaved, combed his hair, pulled a white polo shirt on over his head, and wandered in front of the dormered windows of his study. Beyond the yard and the marshes, a twin-masted ketch plied its way through the winding channels using its engine to buck the tide as it motored in the direction of Hilton Head.

He looked at the yard and the peeling white picket fence that separated it from the marsh. The old plantation house had seen better days. Jack had the money for repairs but not the inclination.

He walked to the desk and for a long moment simply stared down at the surface. There in the center on top of the leather-edged blotter was the letter with its envelope, ragged edge torn open across the top. It had arrived yesterday morning, the fifth such letter in two months.

He picked it up and read the words one more time, only five lines long, then folded it neatly and slipped it back into the envelope, headed out the door and down the stairs.

In the hall he paused long enough to open the center drawer of an antique secretary, reached inside and removed the nine-millimeter Beretta. He fished in the back of the drawer and found the loaded clip heavy with fifteen rounds. He slammed the clip into the handle and tucked the pistol into the belt of his pants at the small of his back. Now he moved quickly without hesitation down the hall, through the kitchen, and out the back door to the yard.

Salt air and sea breezes hit his nostrils as he paced across the yard, a hundred feet, past the brick patio with its chairs and umbrella-covered table; another fifty feet to the picket fence where he stopped, nearly in a daze. A bead of sweat trickled from the hair at the nape of his neck down his shirt. He looked at the boat in the distance, and for several moments stood alone, still, his hands resting on the pickets of the fence, his mind absorbed in thought. Then almost absently he slipped the envelope with its letter into the crack formed by the fence's top railing and one of the pickets. Trapped in this crack, the envelope's loose left end in the gap between pickets fluttered in the breeze. Jack looked at it in a trance, and slowly moved away as if he were making one final attempt to distance himself from the letter's bad news.

At the patio, he reached behind his back, removed the pistol, and laid it on the table. Then he slumped into one of the chairs and stared off into nothingness. He sat there still and silent for more than five minutes.

Finally he reached for the gun, kicked off the safety with his thumb so that the red dots appeared at each side. He pulled the slide back and let it go, slamming a round into the firing chamber. Carefully he held the muzzle up close to his mouth, until he could easily reach out with the tip of his tongue to flick the white dot on the front site.

In a flash he leveled the muzzle and pulled off five quick rounds. The roar of gunfire sent birds billowing into the air from the trees. He realigned the sights and fired ten more shots, emptying the clip.

Fifty feet away, little punched-out pieces of paper fluttered to the ground where they joined a small but growing pile – the fractured trademarks and names of a dozen book publishers. With rejection letters Jack always concentrated his fire on the company logo in the left-hand corner.

CHAPTER
THREE

'You have a minute?' Abby poked her head inside his office door.

Morgan Spencer sat behind a large oak desk, its surface swept clean. He dropped the document he was reading, lifted his glasses, and smiled.

'Come on in and shut the door.' He reached into his desk drawer and pulled out a large bundle of paper held together by a rubber band.

'As they say in the trade, you owe me a night's sleep.'

'What did you think?'

'Good stuff.'

Spencer was one of Abby's few sounding boards. He couldn't write, but he had a good ear.

'Who is this guy Cooper, anyway?'

'That's what I wanted to talk to you about.'

Morgan had a sparkle in his eye and a quick word for every circumstance. He loved Irish limericks and any film featuring Peter O'Toole. In fact, there was something in the aspect of the man that reminded Abby of the actor in an earlier day. He was eight years older than Abby but a generation wiser. He was Abby's Father confessor, the uncle she never had.

They had worked together on several cases. In the increasingly competitive atmosphere of the office, he had taken her under his wing and offered her protection from the slings and arrows of the corporate climbers. The problem was that of late, Morgan's ability to protect anyone, including himself, was beginning to fade. The firm had been caught up in the disease of corporate downsizing.

She noticed that he was looking at a firm management document known as 'The Book.' In essence, it was a partnership agreement that governed the internal workings of the firm.

'What's up?'

'Just had a battle with Cutler.'

Lewis Cutler was African American, the firm's new managing partner installed by a group of young turks hell-bent on control and increasing their own profit margin. He had gotten the nod from the management consultants and in turn been elected by the partners in order to deal with the secretaries and clerks, many of whom were minority. It made it harder for these laid-off employees to argue they had been dealt the race card from the bottom of the deck. 'The twit wants to cut my bonus,' said Spencer. 'Can you believe it? Twenty years they wanna treat me like an associate. The policy's carved in stone. Right here.' He pointed to the place on the page. 'A pro rata share. That's what it says, in the Queen's English.'

'Actually it's Latin, Morgan.'

'What I hate about lawyers. Always want to get technical.'

The power group in their late thirties had all come out of a single law school in Washington State. In business they acted like a social fraternity, tight and exclusionary.

There was nothing benign about it.

Like Abby, Spencer had gone to school out of state. Though he had been in the firm for more than twenty years, the guys he'd practiced with had all retired or left the firm, and the economics of law practice had changed. His speciality, honed over two decades, was Admiralty, and it had fallen on hard times.

'I'll be damned if I'm gonna let 'em get away with it. I've got a surprise for that bastard.' He was talking about Cutler. 'He just doesn't know it yet.'

Spencer didn't have much of a temper, or if he did he concealed it well. This was as angry as she had seen him, a little red in the face and thumping the surface of the desk with a purposeful finger. He was the kind who was slick and quiet. Abby had never gotten cross-wise with him so she'd never felt his sting, though she'd seen it demonstrated in court on a few occasions. It wasn't until Morgan enveloped you with his affable smile that you felt the point of his sword.

'Maybe I should come back later?' said Abby.

'No. No. What is it?'

'You've got problems of your own.'

'Yeah, but yours are always smaller. God, you're looking good today. Why don't you move in with me and I'll make an honest woman out of you?' Morgan was kidding but only partly.

She smiled, and he twinkled. It was the one problem with their relationship. Morgan always hoped for more than friendship. Abby didn't.

Early on she had taken herself out of the running for a partnership in the firm. In college she had studied what she loved – literature – but everybody she knew told her that writing words didn't pay. In a job market racked by increasing uncertainty, Abby made a deal with the devil and went to law school. Now she was paying the price.

She had grown to hate the practice of law. The best lawyers loved a good fight. The constant rancor with opposing counsel, judges, and at times one's own clients was the stuff to spike adrenaline in a good trial lawyer. For Abby it only produced ulcers.

Her only reprieve came at night when she pursued her dream with a missionary's zeal. Toward that end she worked for more than eight years and penned three novels. They were good stories with a literary edge. She won an award with one of them. Published by a small company in New York, they garnered solid reviews and kudos from her editor. But without marketing or promotion they suffered the fate of the vast bulk of general fiction in this country. They died on the shelves.

When lawyers became hot in fiction, all her friends told her to pen a legal thriller. They were the same friends who told her to go to law school. Abby ignored them. Writing was her own way of running from the law.

'You took that seminar last year on intellectual property and entertainment law?' she asked.

'Down at USC,' he nodded. 'They give me the exotic locales. Cutler gets four days on Taxation in Belize, and comes back on the "S.S. Lust." I get two days in L.A.'

'Would you like a client?'

'Sure.' He looked at her over his shoulder, still searching for the materials. 'I have them here someplace.' He swung around in his chair and started pawing through the drawers of the credenza behind him. 'The syllabus and some books, if I can find 'em. What do you need?'

'A registration of copyright. I've never done one.'

'Oh hell, I can do that.'

'Have you done one before?'

'Simple form,' he said. 'I think I even have one in the materials. Who's it for?'

'Me.'

He swung around and looked at her from under arched eyebrows. 'Writing again?'

She nodded.

'Well, good for you.' He went back to the credenza. 'I wish I had the gift.' He was talking about writing. 'You write lies and they pay you. All of mine are in the courtroom, verbal, and they call it perjury.'

'They aren't lies. It's called fiction, Morgan.'

'Right.'

A year ago, Abby's publisher was bought out by a larger company. In the shuffle of reorganization, they fired her editor and rejected her next manuscript, offering a number of vague reasons, all of which added up to a single fact – in the publishing business Abby had become used merchandise, a name with a failed track record. In today's publishing world it was better to be a virgin author, someone who had never seen print, than to have committed the mortal sin: producing a book that didn't make its way onto the bestsellers list. The list was everything. It was all that mattered. The message was clear. What Abby needed was to reinvent herself.

Her former agent, a small-time operator who worked alone from a brownstone in Manhattan, took Abby's manuscript to two other publishers. One checked her record of sales and passed. The other came back with an astonishing request – before they decided whether to publish they wanted to see a photograph of the author.

Abby was dumbfounded. The agent explained that this was becoming increasingly common. Publishers, if they were going to put money behind a book, wanted to know if the author could carry their load on the television talk show circuit if the book caught on, whether their likeness could be used to advantage in print ads. Or, thought Abby, whether it might be a detriment on the dustcover.

Abby didn't like it. More than offended, however, she was scared.

Faced with no alternative, she finally submitted. A week later, after the photograph was sent, her manuscript was rejected. Of course she could not be certain of the reason, whether it was her work or her looks, but for a woman approaching middle years, personal insecurities weighed heavily, and in Abby's mind, she knew.

'At least one of us is doing something we enjoy,' said Morgan.

'You enjoy the practice. You complain a lot, but you enjoy it,' she told him.

'I'd enjoy it more if somebody would nudge a few of these supercilious pricks out of some windows.' He was talking about Cutler and his entourage.

While Morgan fumbled in the drawer, Abby looked about the office. In the corner stood a large object, a hunk of brass the size of a lectern with a handle and gage. It was an engine room telegraph. It had come off an old ship salvaged by one of Morgan's clients, now no longer in business. Even the position of the telegraph's handle said volumes about Morgan and his career. It was set at 'Stop.'

'I thought your publisher usually did the copyright?'

'I don't have one yet.'

'Why don't you wait until you sell it? Let them deal with it.'

'It's a little more complicated than that. I'm doing this one under a pseudonym, a pen name,' said Abby.

'Hmm?' Morgan swiveled around in his chair and looked at her.

'Gable Cooper,' she said.

'You wrote this?'

'Don't act so surprised. I *can* write.'

'No. No. That's not what I meant. It's just I would never have guessed. Your other books were so different.'

'You mean no action. Not much plot,' she said.

'Yeah. Well, that's part of it,' said Morgan. 'But this one. It grabs you by the gut and keeps you turning pages. I'm not kidding. I was up all night two nights running. Cutler owes you his life. If I wasn't so tired I'da killed the son of a bitch during our meeting this morning.'

She laughed.

Over time, Abby's agent had drifted away, no longer returning her calls. The process made a lasting impression. There had always been something secure about writing. She had the talent. Her age and how she looked didn't matter. There was a certain comfort in the knowledge that you could write until you were old and frail, and all that mattered was the quality of your thoughts strung together in words and sentences. Now all of that had been swept away.

But Abby was no quitter. She was angry and made no pretense. In the fickle business of fiction she was tenacious, and in her own way a risk taker. She had been all of her life. It was something that her father, now deceased, had instilled in her at a young age, a fierce independence, and a willingness to take a chance. It was what kept her writing, engaged in a long-shot venture on those cold dark nights – and what caused her to do the crazy thing she was now doing.

'Why not just do it under your name?' said Morgan.

'I have my reasons.'

'And they are . . .?' He looked at her.

'*My* reasons.'

He shook his head.

Abby was wondering if she'd come to the right place for help. A stranger might have asked fewer questions.

'The publisher will still do a copyright.'

'I know they will. But I want a separate one, in my own name.'

He studied her for a moment.

'I want you to do it off the books.' Abby meant that there would be no record of the services performed on the firm's billing records. 'I'll pay you.'

'Don't be silly.' He fumbled in the files for a second, looking for the materials again. Then he looked up at her. 'No, actually you can pay me, but not with money. I want to know why you're doing it? Using a pen name?'

'Because I don't want anyone to be able to find out that I wrote it.'

'It's a fine piece of work,' said Morgan.

'It's a shamelessly commercial manuscript, written in a shamelessly commercial fashion,' said Abby. 'I know what it is.'

'You talk like it's a bastard child,' said Morgan. 'It may not be fine art, but I couldn't put it down. You shouldn't be ashamed.'

'I'm not ashamed. I have my reasons. Can we leave it at that?'

'Only if you want to stiff me on the fee.'

Abby was a thousand pained expressions. 'Alright. I'll tell you. But it can't go any further than this room. Do you promise?'

'Lawyer-client,' said Morgan. 'All the privileges.'

'Fine. I don't intend to identify myself as the author to

34

anyone. To the agent, the publisher, or anyone else. I'm convinced the book will do better without me.'

'Being pretty hard on yourself,' said Morgan.

'I'm not. They are.' The *they* in this sentence were the giant publishers in New York. 'If my name's on it they won't buy it. They certainly won't push it. And I want the book to have a chance.'

'At some point you're gonna have to meet with them. Don't they get a picture for the cover?'

'Yes.'

'What are you gonna do then?'

'I'm gonna give them someone else's. A man's photograph,' said Abby.

Morgan sat there shaking his head. He couldn't believe what he was hearing. 'You're a good-looking woman.'

'I'm almost forty. Besides a man, a good-looking man, is more likely to catch their attention.'

'Who?' said Morgan.

'I haven't found him yet.'

'You're out of your mind. Please tell me you haven't done anything about this yet? I mean, you haven't talked to a publisher?'

'Just an agent. But I think she has a publisher lined up.'

'What did you tell him?'

'It's a her. And I told her that Gable Cooper was out of town. On business. I'm busy locating him now.'

'And she believed you?'

'I told her he has dangerous looks. She wants the book. She wants Gable Cooper. She wants the whole package. And I'm going to deliver it.'

Spencer sat with his head in his hands, shaking it.

'There's nothing illegal, Morgan. There isn't.'

'Just a little friendly fraud,' said Spencer.

'People do it all the time. Pen names.'

'Oh yeah. People use pen names. But this. You're gonna trot this guy out?'

'They want beefcake. I'll cut 'em a slice. Young and juicy. And they'll pay through the nose.'

'You actually think they're gonna pay a man more than they would a woman?'

'A young man. Good-looking. You bet your ass.'

'Why?'

'Ask them. Besides, it's not just the gender. I've got a blemished track record. Books that never came close to the list. They don't make a star out of somebody like that. It isn't done. In this business, you get one shot at being discovered. They want a fresh face so they can tell the world it's their discovery.'

'But this?'

'So I'm giving them tight buns to go along with it,' said Abby.

'They'll sue you nine ways from Sunday,' said Morgan.

'For what?'

'For fraud. Try that on for starters.'

'No they won't.'

'Why not?'

'Because to prove fraud you have to prove damages. And to prove damages they would have to prove that they would have paid less to me, a woman, than they would have to the hunk I put in front of them.'

Like a riddle, Morgan thought about this for a moment, then smiled. 'Title Seven.'

Abby nodded. 'They'd have to admit to discrimination.'

'They'd be on the horns of a dilemma,' said Morgan.

'With a prong in each cheek,' said Abby. 'Besides, if the book is successful, why would they want to sue? If the book isn't successful, who cares? There'll be nothing to fight over.'

Morgan admired the ingenuity. She had thought it all through. She was not all writer after all. There was more lawyer there than he had credited.

'Doesn't it bother you that somebody else is gonna take the credit for your work?'

'Only until the paperback publication,' said Abby.

'What then?'

'Then I intend to go public.'

'You think they'll let you?'

'How can they stop me? If we put it together the right way, with a copyright to prove that I wrote the work. Maybe a contract with whoever I get to do Gable Cooper. They won't have a choice.'

Morgan had to admit it sounded like fun. More fun than he was having practicing law. 'Maybe I could do it. Be Gable Cooper, I mean.'

Abby didn't know how to tell him. Morgan could read it in her eyes. She didn't have to.

'I know. Things are sagging in all the wrong places,' said Morgan. 'And the hair's starting to get a little thin.' He reached up and mussed the shaggy top knot.

'Now who's being hard on who?' said Abby. 'But I don't want to get you involved.'

'I see. You just want me to help you plot this fraud, not perpetrate it.'

'Can it be done? Can you copyright it in my name and can you keep them from finding it?'

Morgan paused, thought about it. 'I think so. Does anybody else know what you're doing?'

Abby thought for a moment. 'Just three people.'

'Who?'

'You and I, and Terry. She's staying at my house for a while, so she knows.' Abby and Theresa Jenrico had been tight since grade school.

'Is he hitting on her again?'

Abby nodded.

'What an asshole.' Spencer was talking about Joey Jenrico, Terry's estranged husband. The two women and Morgan had socialized after work a few times at a bar around the corner.

'What Joey deserves is a shot in the head,' said Morgan.

'Are you offering your services?'

'I know some people.' He pushed his nose off to one side with a finger like some busted prize-fighter. 'Could be done very discreetly. Drive over him in his bed with their Mack truck. I mean, what's a little mayhem when we're already doin' fraud?' He winked at her.

She looked at him and laughed.

He made a few notes. 'You haven't told anybody else about what you're doing on the book?'

'There will have to be one other person.'

'Who's that?' said Morgan.

'Gable Cooper.'

He was not bad-looking, dark with a shadow of a beard. But then it was late afternoon. The clerk eyed him sort of sheepishly, a young girl at an older man, good-looking at that.

'Can I help you?' she asked.

'I'm lookin' for Abigail Chandlis.'

'I don't know if she's in. What's your name?'

'Joey Jenrico.'

'And what does this regard?'

'That's what I wanna talk to Chandlis about.'

'No, I mean does this regard a case in the office?'

'Yeah. My divorce.'

'Are you a client?'

'No. You guys represented my wife.'

'Oh. Just a moment.' By now red lights and alarms were going off in the brain of the receptionist. There had been enough shootings in law firms by irate husbands in the last few years that clerks in the big firms had undergone more training in emergencies than the National Guard. She hit the button under the desk that signaled security on the first floor, the yellow button that told them to come up without guns drawn. She looked for bulges in the man's coat but didn't see anything, all the while smiling.

'They'll be right out.'

Then she hit the com-line. But it wasn't Abby that she called. The security pros had told them that the lawyer involved in the case was the last person you wanted. If Abby came out, she might as well be wearing a big bull's-eye.

A second later, a young guy, suit and tie and about seven feet tall, came into the reception area from an office in the back.

'Can I help you?'

Dan London was a former cop turned lawyer. Before that he was a tight end for the University of Washington team that went twice to the Rose Bowl and kicked ass each time. He was the firm's pick for internal security.

'Yeah . . .' The guy's dimensions alone were enough to slow Joey down. 'I'm lookin' for one of your lawyers.'

'I'm a lawyer,' said London.

Joey didn't realize they made them in that size.

'Yeah, but I'm lookin' for Chandlis.'

'I'm afraid Ms Chandlis isn't in right now.'

'Right.' Joey wondered if this was the one Theresa was seeing. He'd been told by a friend that some lawyer was seen partying with Theresa at a restaurant downtown. He was intent on kicking somebody's ass. But if this was the guy, Joey was gonna have to come back with a fork lift.

'Maybe I could wait.'

'I don't think so,' said London. 'She's not coming back today.'

'Where is she?'

'Out.'

'Oh.'

By now there were two guys in blue caps and white shirts wearing forty pounds of hardware around their waists outside the door. Joey turned and saw them through the glass.

'Maybe I could come back.'

'I don't think that would be a good idea.'

Joey gave him arched eyebrows as a question mark.

'Are you represented by counsel?' asked the lawyer.

'Why? Am I under arrest?' Joey thought maybe this was a form of Miranda. He was a loser. He'd spent a lifetime passing 'Go' and he hadn't collected two hundred bucks yet.

'No. I mean, did a lawyer represent you in your divorce?'

'Oh yeah.' Joey was relieved.

The lawyer was laughing. Joey didn't like it. Still it was better to be laughed at than arrested. So he laughed, too.

'If you want to talk to Ms Chandlis, have your lawyer call her.' He stuck a business card in Joey's hand. 'She can't talk to you, anyway.'

'Why not?'

'Professional rules. If you're represented by a lawyer, she's not supposed to talk to you.'

'I didn't know that.'

'Well, you do now.'

Just like a cop, thought Joey. If he had a hammer and got behind the guy, he'd show him.

'Nice to have met you,' said the lawyer.

'Yeah.'

The two guards collected Joey outside the door and escorted him to the elevator. Downstairs they put his name in a book; the equivalent of Wyatt Earp posting you out of town. Joey would never get through security and upstairs again. If he wanted to see Chandlis, he would have to do it someplace else.

As he passed through the big glass revolving door, he felt the chill wind off the Sound hit his face. It turned his cold sweat icy. Joey knew he'd dodged a bullet. He felt his stomach at the belt line and rejoiced that the two guards hadn't done the same. Because he had a record, he couldn't get a permit. But whenever he went looking for his wife, Joey Jenrico always carried a gun.

He answered on the second ring and before he could say hello, Abby was on him.

'Where in the hell is the check?' It seemed like she was always exasperated when she talked to Charlie.

'Abby?'

'I'm flattered,' she said, 'that you could recognize my voice from among the throngs you must owe money to.'

'They haven't paid me in two months,' he said.

'And you haven't paid me in five.'

'Listen, I'm having a hard time.' It was the story of Charlie's life.

Charlie Chandlis was Abby's ex. They had been married for eight torturous years during which Abby saw him mostly on weekends, and then only between legal briefs and trips to Walla, where the state's maximum security prison was located. Charlie was a criminal appellate lawyer in Seattle who lived on the edge along with most of his clients, several of whom were on death row.

He owed her a total of nine thousand dollars, half of their credit-card obligations at the time of the divorce. The cards had been in Abby's name, but Charlie had racked up most of the debt. The court had ordered him to pay it in installments over twelve months. He was now four installments behind.

'What's the story this time?' she asked him.

'Indigent defense panel. What else?'

None of Charlie's clients could pay the freight, and so the taxpayers did it for them. They hired Charlie to tie the system up in knots, or at least that was Charlie's self-avowed mission in life – endless appeals. The money for fees was never enough to go around. There was always more crime than public dollars to pay for lawyers.

'They cut my fees. They hold my money. What am I supposed to do?'

'Tell them you have bills.'

'Right. Only welfare recipients get their checks on time from the state. You know that,' said Charlie. 'Mine they hold for at least ninety days. Sorta like the aging of good meat on a hook so that when it arrives it'll be ripe, and properly appreciated.'

It was a good story, but it didn't solve Abby's problem. She had taken sixty days off of work to finish the book once she was in striking distance. She had also taken a loan and factored Charlie's payoff into her budget. Now the bank was calling and the piper had to be paid.

'Charlie, I've got my own problems.'

'They took my car last week,' he told her. 'Repossessed it. Right out of the lot behind my office. Now I'm hoofing it, and taking the bus,' he said.

Charlie was his own kind of loser, well educated but hell-bent for poverty.

'Charlie, you've got a law degree, you passed the bar, why don't you . . .'

'Let's not get into that again.'

It was a good part of the reason their marriage had broken up. Charlie was a true believer, part of the pony-tail set from the sixties who believed that feeding the root of every crime was some social injustice. It was Charlie's sacred mission to get things right. Somewhere in the quest for ultimate justice, Abby and what was left of their marriage had gotten lost.

'It's five months since I've seen a check,' she told him.

'Can't pay if I don't have it,' said Charlie. He said something about blood out of a turnip and then she heard his hand over the mouthpiece and part of another conversation.

'. . . it should be hand carried. Have it messengered,' said Charlie.

'What? My check?' said Abby.

'No. No. It's some documents we need to file with the court before five.'

Always on the edge, Charlie's life was one big statute of limitations.

'You could go to jail, you know.' Abby was no fool, so she'd hired a lawyer in the divorce. She reminded him that her lawyer had threatened to get an order to show cause why Charlie should be held in contempt when he missed the first payment. The lawyer also told Abby that it probably wouldn't work. Charlie lived in the courthouse. He was on a first-name basis with all the judges. He would blame the system and they would buy it, giving him only a stern warning. In the meantime, Abby would be stuck with a bill from her own lawyer. So she spent her time and money on long-distance calls, jerking him around on the phone, with virtually the same result.

'You got ten days,' she said.

'Then what?'

It was a good thing he couldn't see the vacant expression on her face over the phone, though he could read it in the crackling silence on the line. It was an idle threat and they both knew it.

'Listen, I'll get you the check as soon as I can. Really.' His voice dropped an octave like he was about to impart some state secret. 'I haven't told her yet, but I'm not even gonna to be able to pay my secretary this month.'

'Why don't you put her on the phone so I can tell her,' said Abby.

'Gotta go,' said Charlie.

'How do I pay my rent?'

'Tell 'em to wait.'

'Right. I guess I don't eat this month,' she said.

'I'll come over and take you out to dinner,' he told her.

'You have enough money to take me out to dinner, but you can't pay your bills?'

'New credit card,' said Charlie. 'They keep sending these applications in the mail.' He laughed. Good-time Charlie.

It was another sore point. Abby couldn't get a credit card if her life depended on it. Charlie had ruined her credit rating. Now he had a new card in his own name.

'Why can't you borrow against it?' she asked him.

'Can't do that. They'd take it away faster than I could flash it. The secret of credit is not to need it,' said Charlie. 'Listen, why don't I come over?' He changed the subject on her.

'Don't bother.'

'Why can't we get together? For old times' sake.'

'Old times weren't all that good,' she told him.

'They weren't all that bad, either. Not as I remember.'

'I guess it all depends where you were sitting,' said Abby.

There was some pained silence on the phone that was quickly filled by Charlie. He always seemed to be the first to rebound after a fight.

'Listen, I gotta run,' he said.

'Charlie?'

'I'll get the check to you. I will,' said Charlie.

'Sure,' in the next life, thought Abby. As Charlie hung up, she wondered if she would be eating cat food by the end of the month, or if the bank was into restructuring personal loans, and if so, at what level of usurious interest rates.

CHAPTER
FOUR

It was one of the jagged teeth in the Manhattan sky-line, a mammoth tombstone facing the East River – a hundred and twenty stories of steel and glass known to those who inhabited it simply as 'The Towers.'

It was home to one of the three networks, along with a publishing consortium that had euphemistically and otherwise become known over the years as Big-F. Together the package made up an entertainment and news conglomerate that along with the building that housed them was now owned by an Australian tycoon.

In the lobby there was security as tight as anything in the White House. No one got past the armed guards to the elevators without a call upstairs, a visitor's pass, and an escort who came down to collect them.

Today that honor was performed by Alexander Bertoli's secretary, who greeted Owens on a first name basis.

'Carla. Nice to see you. How was your trip to the coast?'

'Just fine, Janice. Wonderful.'

'Alex is waiting for you upstairs.'

Owens would give the details to Bertoli himself.

In the past two years, Big-F had fallen on hard times.

It had suffered restructuring, downsizing, and layoffs after a leveraged buyout, and had slipped from second place in annual profits among the giant publishers to fifth. There had been three changes at the helm in the last decade, and Alexander Bertoli, C.E.O. and publisher of Big-F, was worried that a fourth might now be in the works.

He was pacing the carpet of his palatial office on the hundred and fifth floor when the door opened and the secretary admitted Carla.

'Sweetheart. How was your trip?' Bertoli traversed twenty yards of deep wool, to touch cheeks. 'Let me take your coat.

'Harold, get Carla a drink. She's frozen.' Bertoli snapped his fingers at his man, who took Carla's order and disappeared behind the large bar next to the fireplace.

'Are you asking about the trip or the business?' said Carla.

'Both. You know me, darling. I'm always concerned for your welfare.'

'Of course. Well, in a word, the trip was hell. What can I say?' said Owens.

This was not the part Bertoli was itching to hear, but he put up with it.

'Air travel is not what it used to be,' said Carla. 'Even in first class, it's a lottery to see if you get a seat. Overbooked every flight. And the service.' She rolled her eyes. 'Your bags get better treatment. A thirty-five-hundred-dollar ticket and they give you corn flakes for breakfast and a stewardess with an attitude.'

Bertoli laughed. 'I told you. You should have accepted my offer. I could have had the Gulfstream pick you up at Santa Monica, take you north, a little business, and then home. I offered,' said Bertoli.

'I know you did, and you're a sweetheart for it.' Carla had her own reasons for not wanting the intrusion of Bertoli's corporate jet. The thirty-million-dollar ego container had been leased for him two years before as part of the compensation package to lure him from another house. She suspected that if he sent the plane it would come with strings – in a word, Bertoli on board with contracts ready. Ever since he read Gable Cooper's manuscript, Bertoli was hot for the property. Carla had plans, and while they might include Alexander, she wanted other options. Business was business.

Twenty tongues of blue-tipped flame licked the air from a large gas log in the fireplace, and Carla moved to warm herself in front of them.

'Well, tell me what happened? Did you meet him? Talk to him? What's he like?'

Bertoli was a bundle, every nerve poised for good news. God knows he'd had enough of the other kind lately. His predecessors had made the classic mistake in publishing; one big egg in a single basket. Another publisher had stolen it.

For the last four years Big-F had spent millions on a high-risk gambit building a single author. His first book rocketed into the stratosphere and stayed at the top of the bestsellers list for over a year. Each successive book followed. There were motion pictures and mammoth book sales until the author's name was a household word.

For three years money flowed into the coffers of Big-F like water over Niagara, and during this time the company did little to balance its publishing list. They had a few other mid-bestselling writers, but no one approaching the stature of The Author. This was the lopsided fountain of prosperity that Bertoli inherited when he took over – a leaning Tower of Pisa pouring out money.

What The Author didn't know is that his own agent had been seduced in a sweetheart deal by Big-F. They were paying him more than a million dollars a year under the table to shackle The Author to the wall at Big-F, to prevent him from shopping his wares to other publishers.

A few lesser authors in the agent's stable were thrown into the pot for seasoning and treated as hors d'oeuvres; their contracts picked up for a fraction of their value, they became tasty morsels for Big-F. These were the halcyon days of deception.

Then six months ago it happened. The earth shook. The Author's agent died. If timing is everything in life, the agent couldn't have picked a worse time for his to end. Bertoli and Big-F were involved in intense contract negotiations with The Author, contracts that were not yet signed.

Cut adrift in corporate seas at a critical time, swimming with the sharks, The Author was getting nibbles like monkey bites from half the agents in North America. In this chaos he turned to the only person he felt he could trust – his lawyer.

Bertoli considered his options. Maybe the lawyer would take the same deal as the agent. There was a problem. Lawyers had a written code of ethics, not that Bertoli thought it meant much to most of them. But they also had state bars and courts to enforce them. That was a problem. In a fit of morality, the lawyer might set him up. Big-F could end up in a monumental law suit. Worse, Bertoli could end up in jail.

He negotiated as best he could. He made a huge offer, an offer he thought The Author couldn't refuse. He tried to ingratiate himself, extending the prestige of his office and his own services as word meister to edit The Author's books. But the lawyer had a point. If Big-F was willing to offer thirty million for three books, maybe somebody else was willing to offer forty. The company had created its own version of Kong, an eight-ton literary gorilla – and his lawyer was about to manipulate one of the giant's fingers in an obscene gesture of farewell. Bertoli hated lawyers.

When they didn't come to terms over dollars, the lawyer found the door and The Author followed him. In a single blow, Bertoli lost the top of his list, and about fifty-five percent of Big-F's annual profits. It was a move likely to put Alexander Bertoli on the shelf with other moguls of business – right next to the Ford Division Chief who signed off on the Edsel. The departure left a huge hole on Big-F's Summer list. It was something that Bertoli was back-pedalling fast, trying to fill. Carla's new client looked like the answer to a prayer. If he could only get him signed and move the manuscript toward publication fast enough. The book had all the signs of a blockbuster.

'What did he say? Did he know about the film stuff?'

'I didn't see him.' Carla had uttered only four little words. But given the look on Bertoli's face, one might have thought she'd injected hot lead into his veins.

'What do you mean you didn't see him? Why the hell not?' His courtly manor evaporated like steam. Carla looked at him as if perhaps he wanted to take back his kiss. 'Is he represented by somebody else?' The first thought that entered Bertoli's mind, somebody had out-hustled her. Though in the pit of his heart Bertoli knew that it would be easier to reverse the laws of physics than to beat Carla to a hot client. Still, if this was the case, Carla wouldn't be staying for supper even though her place was already set at the small table in front of the window. Alex was not one to squander a business meal. He would be working his Rolodex for a quick substitution.

'He's not represented by anyone as yet. But you're looking at his future agent. I have a lock,' said Carla. When she wanted, Carla could drip confidence, and at this moment it was staining the carpet of Bertoli's office.

'You said you didn't see him?'

Carla dropped into one of the large club chairs facing the fire.

'Yes, but I saw the next best thing. The woman he lives with.'

'Ah.' Bertoli moved closer.

'And we have an arrangement,' said Carla. 'He's as good as signed.'

'I knew you could do it.' Bertoli was back in her camp.

'When are you gonna sign him? Is he coming to New York?' For the moment, everything waited for the agent. Until Carla could get her leash on him, Gable Cooper would not be doing tricks for anyone.

'As soon as he gets back in town. Now from your side,' said Carla. 'Any word on how the manuscript got out to Hollywood?' This had been a mystery since the book had gone nowhere except Carla's office and Bertoli's shop. It had to be a leak in one of these two places.

'No. But if it works, I'll kiss 'em,' said Bertoli.

Carla wasn't telling him the other part of her plan. Not until she had Gable Cooper signed on the dotted line. Then Bertoli could piss and scream all he wanted.

'Do we know anything about him – this guy Cooper?'

'We know it's not his real name,' said Carla.

'What's his name?'

'I don't know. She wouldn't tell me.'

'Why not?'

'I'm not sure.'

'What's her name? This woman?'

'Abby Chandlis.'

Bertoli took a pen from his pocket and made a note.

'What's she like?'

'She's a lawyer.'

Bertoli looked at her like this was a clock-stopper.

'Don't worry. I don't think it's exactly lawyer-client that we're talking here.' Carla looked at him and smiled.

'Ah. He's into fucking lawyers,' said Bertoli. 'A man after my own heart. What does he look like?'

'According to her, if she's telling the truth, he's done some modeling. He's supposed to be very good looking.'

Bertoli's eyes perked up. A movie deal and good looks to boot.

'Why wouldn't she tell you his name?'

'That wasn't real clear. She said he wouldn't like it.'

'But you have a theory?'

Carla gave him a whimsical look, and an equivocal bob of the head that could pass for a nod. For reasons known only in the demented minds of artists, bestselling authors had been known to craft novels under a pseudonym and sell them to publishers, attempting to conceal their true identity. It was crazy. In many cases their names would have propelled a book on the *New York Times* list before it was even published. But their egos had taken hold and they actually started to believe that it was the art of their words rather than marketing that sold their books. They were looking for confirmation. It rarely worked.

'It's possible he has a track record under his real name,' said Carla. 'Doesn't want us to know.'

'Maybe the man has a contract with another publisher and he would rather be free?' Bertoli had a more devious mind. 'You think he might be a big name?'

'It's a possibility.'

This appealed to Bertoli's mercenary side, the opportunity to raid talent from another house. Then it hit him. What if it was The Author? It was just the kind of game his lawyer might play. Chinese water torture. String him along and pull the book from Bertoli's reach at the last moment. He uttered this concern to Carla.

'Give it a break. You worry too much,' she told him.

'I get paid to worry,' said Bertoli.

'Then they aren't paying you enough. Besides, think about the upside, the fun we'll have if this guy's hot property. Gee, how did his name leak to the press two weeks before pub? And why is this mystery man hiding?' This was Carla's kind of game.

'He might not like it,' said Bertoli.

'Oops,' she laughed.

'You're awful,' he told her. In their minds they were both counting the money such a move might bring in.

'Are you ready to have dinner served, sir?' Harold nosed in.

'I think we'll wait awhile.'

'Yes, sir. Is there anything else I can get you?'

'No.'

Harold returned to his status as a potted plant in the corner.

'When's Cooper due back?' asked Bertoli.

'In a few days,' Carla lied, but she was hoping that in that time Abby could reach him. 'Gimme a week, I should have him signed.'

'Wonderful. Great.' Bertoli was up off the couch, rubbing his hands together. He didn't need the flames of the fire to warm him. The thought of another hot book, somebody to replace The Author, was enough to stoke the coals of his particular furnace.

Bertoli was looking at something more than the vague hope of success. There were many formulae to break out an author. Most of them involved risk, and each one could produce success in varying degrees, none of them guaranteed to work.

Most authors made it the old-fashioned way, one book at a time, slow incremental growth over a period of years. In the course of a dozen books, with modest investments for marketing and promotion, very limited risks on the part of the publisher, you could buy an audience. But to Bertoli's thinking, Big-F didn't have time for this. The company might still be around when it began to pay dividends, but Bertoli would not.

Then there was the way The Author did it; pure luck – a strong commercial story and great timing. Gable Cooper, though he couldn't know it yet, was on the same course. The fuel firing this particular engine was a movie deal brewing in Hollywood. Ordinarily it would have taken Big-F at least a year to plan and promote the debut of a big new author. But Bertoli didn't have that kind of time, not with a hole the size The Author left in his Summer list. With a film sporting a box-office star, Gable Cooper and his book were now on a fast track.

Success, fame, and fortune appeared to be right around the corner for this budding writer, and like The Author before him, he had backed into it.

'So what did they say out there?' Bertoli was talking about the first part of Carla's trek, to Hollywood, or more accurately Wilshire Boulevard in Beverly Hills. 'Is it true? Is he cast in the role?'

'Like concrete,' said Owens. 'He's read the manuscript and wants the part. Subject, of course, to script
approval and somewhere in the neighborhood of
twenty million in payment from the producers. But if
they can buy the book for him, my people are telling me
it's a go. Green light all the way to production.'

'Oh my God. Then it's true.' Bertoli rubbed his hands
together in glee. 'I'm his biggest fan,' said Bertoli.

'No, his biggest fan is his banker. You come second,'
said Carla.

Bertoli looked at her, wondering if he should argue
the point, then laughed. 'Fine. I can live with that.'

'What you can live with is the fact that he's gonna
save your ass,' said Carla.

'That too.' Bertoli made no bones about it, and instead
lifted his glass and drank to Carla's words as if they
were a toast.

Carla guessed that Alex was already doing some
money changing in his head. If the movie brought in
two hundred million, the initial book rights could be
worth anywhere from a third to half of that, maybe
more, and that was being conservative. The paperback
tie-in when the film came out would start the money
flowing all over again.

'He opens this thing, and word gets out, the hard-
back's gonna fly off the shelves.' Bertoli did his own
little dance, a pirouette in place in front of the sofa. 'You
know time is tight, but we could do something at ABA.'
Bertoli was talking about the American Booksellers
Association convention held in late spring. Usually it
was reserved for books being promoted on the Fall-
Winter list, but in this case you could kiss the rules
good-bye. 'A beach book at the ABA,' said Bertoli. 'The

presses will be smoking. We won't be able to keep this thing stocked. And the book, it's good. It'd sell itself. But with this . . .'

What Bertoli meant is that the film deal removed all the risk. It came as close to a guaranteed result as you would find this side of the pearly gates. Alex and his company wouldn't be flying alone. They'd be in the embrace of one of the major studios where marketing with smoke and mirrors was an art form. With a box-office star cast in the lead role, given the sums of money they would have to pay to get him, the studio couldn't afford to let Cooper's book fail. More than a year before the movie's release they would be bankrolling the marketing of Gable Cooper's hardcover book. It was what every publisher dreamed of, an unlimited budget using somebody else's money.

CHAPTER
FIVE

A month had passed since her meeting with Owens at the law office and Abby was now getting desperate. Owens was calling her daily. She needed to find Gable Cooper. To keep the agent off her back and buy time, Abby agreed to Owens's representation. She told Carla she was authorized as Gable Cooper's lawyer to do this. Carla didn't ask any questions.

This morning she used a pair of scissors to rip open the top of the large envelope and then removed the catalogue-sized loose-leaf binder. It contained at least two hundred pages with the name of a talent agency stenciled on the cover. It had taken several weeks and all of Morgan's efforts, but he had finally done it. A contact he had met during the entertainment law seminar had loaned him a copy of the directory, and Morgan had it sent directly to Abby.

Theresa hovered over her as she set up at the card table in the living room. It was cluttered with papers, the remnants of notes from the last manuscript. In the center was the old Underwood manual, built in the fifties and now nearly an antique. It wasn't that Abby shunned computers. She used one at work. But the manual typewriter was her forty-pound lucky charm when it came to fiction. She had written four novels on it including Gable Cooper's. There was a certain therapy in beating on the heavy keys. Abby was afflicted by the disease of over-writing. The old typewriter exacted a cost for revisions in the form of retyping, and so it served as a restraint.

'You know,' said Theresa, 'people go to jail for this kind of stuff.'

. 'You worry too much,' said Abby.

'No, I mean it. Remember the guy who wrote the book about Howard Hughes? The unauthorized biography?'

'Where did you ever hear about that?'

'Hey, I read.'

'But that was years ago.'

'Don't change the subject. He did prison time,' said Theresa.

'Stop worrying. Gable Cooper isn't Howard Hughes.'

'My God, woman. He's a figment of your imagination. How do you know he isn't Howard Hughes? You haven't found him yet.'

Theresa Jenrico liked to laugh at her own jokes even with a bruised cheek. Theresa's husband Joey had used her for a punching bag for the umpteenth time just before their divorce five weeks earlier and, according to Theresa, she was now residing permanently with Abby, though how long this would last was not certain.

Joey was manipulative and chronically violent. Theresa had him arrested four times, and to date he had a perfect record; four busts – no convictions. She dropped charges each time, after Joey professed his love and vowed he would never hurt her again.

It was Abby who'd finally convinced her to go for the

divorce and then represented her in the ordeal. She also tried to talk her into a restraining order to keep Joey away, but Theresa told her it would only make matters worse.

'You're telling me that I'm being stupid,' said Abby. 'Look at yourself in the mirror.'

'Hey. I left him, didn't I?'

'Yeah. For the fourth time. What was it last time – two broken ribs? And the time before that a detached retina?'

'They only thought it was detached,' said Theresa.

'Well, lucky you.'

'I'm only telling you this cuz I don't want to see you get in trouble,' said Theresa.

'I'm not going to get in trouble. I talked with Morgan and he agrees.'

'Did you tell him everything?'

'What he needed to know,' said Abby.

'I'll bet. And the agent?'

'So far I'm managing to hold her off. I've told her he's on a junket, a trip into the jungles of southern Mexico for more color.'

'Sooner or later that's gonna wear thin,' said Theresa. 'What then? Hmm?'

'By then I'll find somebody.'

'Right.'

'You should have heard her,' said Abby. She was talking about Owens.

' "What does he look like?" "Does he have big baby blues?" "How tall?" "How thin?" "How young?" "Does he have hair halfway to his ass and cleavage of the chin?" Listen. If she wants a dimple on his pecker I'll find one – and if I can't, I'll make one,' said Abby.

Theresa looked at her, bright eyes. 'I got it.'

'What's that?'

'We can use Joey. You can hold him down and I'll do the honors. On his pecker, I mean.' The thought of circumcising Joey with a meat cleaver offered a certain sense of comic justice.

'He's too stupid,' said Abby. 'Besides, if he wrote the book, all the characters would speak with a slur.'

'Hey, I will say, Joey did kick the bottle.'

Abby wondered if it wasn't in Theresa's teeth at the time.

'Good for him,' said Abby. 'Call me when he kicks the bucket.'

'No, I mean it. He stopped drinking.'

'And the pope's gone over to Scientology,' said Abby. They'd had this discussion before. Abby had warned her that if she didn't leave Joey, he would eventually kill her. The relationship had all the classic signs. Joey was a drunk out of control, a paranoid fueled by alcohol, with a raging temper that knew no bounds. If he killed and dismembered her, he would no doubt be too drunk to remember where he put the parts. He would beat the charges on a plea of diminished capacity.

'Don't change the subject. We're talkin' about you and this stupid thing you're gonna do.'

'It isn't stupid.' Abby centered the binder in front of her on the card table so that it was upside down to Theresa.

'Look at it this way. How often have you had a chance to play Pygmalion?'

'Pig who?' said Theresa.

'Greek Mythology. Pygmalion was a sculptor who hated women until he carved a statue of a gorgeous woman and promptly fell in love with his own work.'

'Sounds like some of the men I've known.'

'He called the statue Galatea and when he got tired hugging cold stone Pygmalion went crying to the gods, in this case Aphrodite, and asked that she supply him with a woman as beautiful as what he'd created. Aphrodite took pity and brought the stone to life.'

'So what are you telling me, that this Gable Cooper, this dream boat with a dimple on his dick, is your statue?'

Abby laughed. 'Not a statue, but he is my creation.'

'All I can say is I hope to hell you're praying to the gods. Cuz you're gonna need all the help you can get.'

Abby opened the cover and popped open the rings of the binder, removing the first page and holding it up for Theresa to see.

'The gods help those who help themselves.'

There, pasted to the page, was an eight-by-ten color glossy of some male hunk, blond, blue-eyed, pearly whites smiling at Theresa across the table.

'Who's that?' Suddenly she was all interest.

'Somebody from a talent agency in L.A.' Abby pointed to the binder in front of her. 'This is full of the same.' She fanned some of the pages with her fingers. It was an endless array of photos, all great-looking men.

'Spencer got it from somebody he met at a seminar in L.A. This guy was dating a woman who works at the agency. I'm going shopping,' said Abby.

If anyone found out she had a copy of the directory, the woman who palmed it from the talent agency would lose her job. So Abby had to be discreet.

Each entry contained a photo with the name of the actor, followed by a résumé including acting credits, address, and telephone numbers for their day job and home. Abby thumbed through the binder quickly. Most appeared to be waiters or sales clerks by day, all of them with looks to stop time.

Theresa moved around the table for a better look. 'Lemme see.' She picked up the photo.

'Oooo. He's nice. Michael Chapen. Redondo Beach. Do you know him?'

'Nope. But he's not my type.'

'I knew it,' said Theresa. 'You're sick. Lemme take your temperature.'

'I told the agent that Gable Cooper was dark. Mr Chapen doesn't fit the bill.'

'Ah.' Theresa pulled up a chair and sat down for a closer look. She was convinced Abby was nuts, but as long as she was going to do this thing there was no harm in indulging fantasy.

'So tell me. What are you gonna do?'

'I'm going to go through this and find the ones who come sufficiently close to the description I gave to the agent. Then I intend to call and set up auditions.'

'You're kidding me?'

'No.'

'You're gonna meet these guys?'

'Until I find the one I want.' Abby made it sound like buying salami in a store.

'You actually think they'll do this? What you're asking?'

'It's acting, isn't it? They're actors. Listen, for most of these people it's the opportunity of a lifetime. The chance to play a real live author. Who knows, they might even become famous.'

'Yeah, right. Their picture in every post office in America. Listen, the only possible silver lining in this cloud is if you both get convicted and they put you in the same cell with him.'

'What's wrong? I'm gonna pay the guy.'

'With what?' asked Theresa.

'A percentage of the advance and royalties on the book. Whatever I can negotiate.' Abby turned the page and suddenly Theresa swallowed her protests.

'Now he's tall and dark,' said Theresa.

'He might do very nicely.'

'Listen,' said Theresa. 'You need help? I could carry your luggage. Take notes.'

Abby thought she was joking, looked at her for a moment, and realized she was not. Suddenly they both started laughing.

Ron Sidner took the call directly. It came in on his back line, somebody he knew.

'Ron here.' He was typing a memo to the front office, coverage on a movie script sent to him by an agent.

'More news from Big-F,' said the voice on the phone. It was clear and precise, the words clipped with a certain air of formality and very businesslike.

'I have been told that the author's operating under a pseudonym,' it said.

'We figured that much,' said Sidner. He was cool, good-looking, and twenty-two. Good looks were a must in the industry, where deals were increasingly driven by kids in their twenties. Sidner had originally aspired to become an actor but had come to his senses when he realized there were better odds for success in the lottery. Since then he'd worked as a tour guide for one of the major film studios in L.A. before graduating to its story department. He was now bitten by the film bug and craved a spot in the executive suites.

'Yes,' said the voice, 'but did you figure the reason for the pen name?'

Sidner was all ears.

'Word has it, he's a bestselling author. A major name.'

Sidner suddenly stopped pecking away at the computer keyboard. 'Are you sure?'

'My information is from well-placed sources.'

'Gimme a name?' said Sidner. 'The author?'

'That I don't have, at least not yet. Give me awhile and I can probably find out.'

'How long?'

'I don't know.'

Silence from Sidner as he thought. 'There's an extra thousand in it for you, if the information is accurate and we get it before anybody else.'

'I'll see what I can do.' The voice was on retainer, part of a stable of film scouts maintained by studios in New York to keep an eye for potential hot properties in the book world. Most of these operated above-board, out of offices in the publishing district of Manhattan. They routinely combed the files of literary agents and publishing houses on the make for stories that might be scripted for film. A few of them, like the voice on the phone, were moles, secretaries and office assistants, who could be used when the need arose for inside information. This could run the gamut, from the price a publisher was paying for a book, to the scope of their advertising budget, and, most important, whether another studio might be interested in the property for film rights. People heard things in offices and passed them as gospel. Film was an industry fueled by rumors. Nothing was hot unless someone else wanted it, in which case the sky was the limit. It was an industry that operated on the premise that perception was reality, or if it wasn't, it soon would be.

'There's more,' said the voice. 'Owens hasn't signed him yet.'

'What are you talking about? She's had a month. She went out to Seattle.' This did surprise Sidner.

'She never saw him. He was out of town. And he hasn't come back. Off someplace doing research – on another book. From what I am told, it picks up where the first one left off.'

They didn't own the property, hadn't cast the star, weren't in production yet, and a sequel was already looming. Sidner buffered out of the coverage he was writing on the screen and quickly started a new memo while he talked.

'You mean after her visit here Owens struck out?'

'Not entirely. She made contact with a woman who supposedly lives with the author. The woman knows where he is, and according to my information is now working with Owens to contact him.'

'Got a name?'

'Abby Chandlis.' He spelled the last name and gave Sidner the address of her place of employment and what details were known about Gable Cooper and his whereabouts.

Ten minutes later Ron Sidner was centered in front of the huge oak desk, hand-carved in deep relief, a quarter-inch of plate glass protecting its surface. It was rumored that the desk once belonged to David O. Selznick, and that on one of its corners Clark Gable inked his name to the contract to play Rhett Butler.

Behind it, in a tufted wing-back maroon leather chair, sat Mel Weig, cool and detached, impeccably attired, the Armani suit coat buttoned even as he sat.

In another chair across the desk from Weig sat Stanley Salzman, head of production and Weig's number two at the studio. One never moved without the other.

Weig read Sidner's memo as he toyed with the twelve-thousand-dollar gold-braceleted watch on his wrist.

'Anybody else seen this?'

'No, sir,' said Sidner.

'Let's keep it that way.' He passed it to Salzman, who did a quick reading. Weig knew that just as his mole had penetrated Big-F it was possible that other studios had eyes and ears in his own. The fewer people who knew the contents of the memo the better. Weig had been responsible for hooking the actor interested in Gable Cooper's book. But if some other studio bagged the film rights, the deal would be gone, like a moveable feast. Box-office stars were no longer in bondage to the studios. They were free agents, signing contracts on a film-by-film basis. Studio execs had to crawl on their knees to get the hot ones, as Weig had on this deal. In the end, the actor came only because he longed to play the character created by Gable Cooper, and Weig knew it.

The com-line on his phone rang and he picked it up.

'Sir, I have Carla Owens for you on the other line.' It was Weig's secretary who had placed the call at her boss's directive moments before. He punched the line.

'Carla, darling. Mel here. How are you?' Some silence while she chatted.

'Oh good. Listen, do you mind if I put you on the speaker phone. Stanley Salzman, you know Stan, head of production? He's here with me, and I think he'd like to hear what's happening.'

An instant later Weig hit the speaker button and laid the receiver down.

'Carla, can you hear me?'

'Oh yes.'

'Hi, Carla, it's Stanley.'

'Stan, how are you. It's been a long time.'

'Too long.'

'Listen,' said Weig. 'We're very interested in what's going on with your man Cooper.'

'Oh, it's going great. Just fine.'

'Then you have him signed?'

'Done deal,' said Carla.

Weig looked over at Salzman whose dark eyes revealed the deception.

'Listen, what's he like?'

'I think your gonna love him.' She avoided direct answers. 'He's very good looking. I'm told that, in fact, he did some modeling. He's a marketer's dream.'

'That's good. That's great. When can we talk about numbers for the film rights?'

'Oh well, give me a few days. He's just getting back from a tiring trip to Mexico, so we should be on the phone in the next few days. I'd like to talk to him in more detail before we get down to specifics. Is that O.K. with you?'

'As long as you aren't talking to anybody else,' said Weig. 'Another studio or a producer?'

'Mel.' She made his name sound like a cat in pain. 'How could you think such a thing? No. No. As soon as he gets his feet back on the ground and we have a chance to talk, I'll be back to you.'

'Right,' said Weig. 'Take care, Carla, and I'll wait to hear.'

'Ta ta, be in touch,' said Carla and the phone went dead.

Weig said it all with his expression. 'We obviously can't rely on Carla. When will your source have more information?' he asked Sidner.

'We're not sure. He thinks maybe a few days.'

'What do you think, Stan?' Weig looked at Salzman.

'It looks like Carla's having difficulty lining him up,' said Salzman.

'Or playing games,' said Weig. He had a more sinister agenda in mind. 'She could be trying to buy time, to jack the price up. Get us into a bidding war with another studio.'

Though Gable Cooper couldn't know it, Weig's studio was already prepared to offer a million dollars for the film rights to the book. The hint that he might be a bestseller, and their inability to reach him to talk dollars that might bring a smile to the author's face, left them in doubt as to whether it would be enough. Anxiety in Hollywood always had a predictable and singular effect – a higher price.

'Where are we on the budget?' asked Weig. 'Can we go higher for the rights?'

'Looks like we may have to,' said Salzman. 'We could take a little off casting, some of the minor characters. That could take us up to three million for the rights.'

'Do it,' said Weig. 'If somebody else gets the book, it won't matter how much we reserved for casting.'

Sidner marveled at the exercise of power; two million more just like that – 'do it' – a million dollars a word.

'What else?' said Salzman.

'We can't wait,' said Weig. 'There's too many wagging tongues in this town. Get Ackerman and his agency to find the woman.' He looked at the memo. 'This Abby Chandlis. Have them contact her.' Weig thought for a second. 'No. No. On second thought, you better make the contact.' He looked at Salzman. 'And take Zitter here with you.'

'Sidner,' said the kid.

'What?'

'The name's Sidner, sir.'

'Whatever,' said Weig.

'So what do you want? Ackerman or us?' said Salzman.

'Both. Have the Ackerman Agency trail the woman. If Cooper, whoever he is, comes back to town, I want to be the first to know it. But I only want them to surveil.'

Salzman nodded.

'Then I want you to put yourself on a plane to Seattle. Get your ass up there and talk to this Chandlis woman. Romance her. Wine and dine her. Do whatever you have to do, but tell her we're interested in the film rights and we'd like to deal directly. Not through an agent. I'm tired waiting for Carla. She wants to bullshit us, she's gonna learn there's a price.'

'Is that smart?' said Salzman. 'I mean, Owens has already talked to her.'

'Tell her whatever you want, that an agent's gonna slow things down. That we don't like to do business with this one. Whatever gets us to Cooper. But get us there.'

'What if we get halfway through and they think they can find a better deal someplace else?' said Salzman. It was the concern in every agentless deal: people who fancied themselves artists could be notorious flakes – agree to a deal today and renege tomorrow. To the studios, agents weren't professionals representing talent. They were animal trainers with a leash and a whip. Their principal value was client control.

'Owens hasn't signed him. If we can get to him before she does, maybe we can limit this to one player, ourselves. If not,' said Weig, 'I'm afraid the price is gonna get very steep, in a hurry.'

CHAPTER
SIX

Jack had learned the art of origami from a woman he'd lived with in Thailand during the war – from his days in the Corps. She was young, as he was at the time, and sweet and had taught him many things from the Asian art of love to the construction of ornate Buddhist temples in miniature from folded pieces of paper.

The one in front of him at the moment stood more than two feet tall on top of the table. Terraced and decorated like a wedding cake, it had taken him more than two weeks to build. Soaking the paper in the solvent and letting it dry is what consumed most of the time. Still the fact that the temple progressed faster than his writing may have said something about his creative aptitudes, though if it did it was lost on Jack.

The upper six levels were constructed of plain paper, the early discards of his current work in progress, the fourth in a series of now unpublished manuscripts for novels. Maybe he had lost the touch. His last published work was a piece of non-fiction, a technical work for a small publisher in the southern states: *The Ragged Renegades Resource Book*. It was more of a pamphlet than a book, an epistle with a little humor added by an editor, on how to home brew your own explosives and incendiary devices. Jack was slipping and he knew it.

The base of the paper temple, the first two levels, were braced on the outside by heavier paper, light card stock with printing and handwritten words evident only on close inspection. The writing gave a unique appearance to the structure, as if the surface had been carved by the midgets who made it in some exotic script. These cards Jack had collected over a period of months.

Sometimes editors didn't even take the time to type a letter. Instead they hastily scrawled a note, often illegible, on stock printed with their name at the top, each one a variation on the same word: 'NO.' They would send these like postcards in the open mails. This practice in particular pissed Jack off, because the postman and anyone else who happened to touch his mail saw them.

He lifted the piece of plywood on which he'd constructed his masterpiece and carried it out the back door to the yard, Jack's place of special mischief.

He placed the sheet of plywood with the temple on top of an old tree stump sixty feet from the house.

Attached to the straw fuse, which disappeared under one edge of the little temple, he used a twenty-two caliber rimfire cartridge emptied of its powder as a detonator. Jack replaced the smokeless gunpowder with a carefully prepared solution, chemicals from a hobby shop, and a little black powder packed in around a single filament of fine steel wire. This in turn was connected by a tiny clamp to a length of lead wire that ran to a small battery near the rear of the house.

Years ago he'd been told about this. A common solution for soaking paper. It was said that a newspaper properly prepared and left to dry was virtually undetectable, except by sophisticated Neutron Vapor Analysis not used at most security checkpoints including airports. Carried under the arm with an outer covering of today's front page, it would look like any other newspaper. Tightly compacted it would also carry the explosive force of three sticks of dynamite.

He marveled at the things his own government had taught him, survival techniques and ways to wreak havoc, and wondered if this one would work.

There were no neighbors within a quarter-mile. The fact that the little paper pagoda had a lot of space for air inside meant the force would be muffled, more of a whoosh than a bang – so that when Jack touched the wire to the battery lead and the force of the explosion threw him against the side of the house and shattered a window over his head, he was for a moment at least stunned. A million tiny shards of paper, many of them singed, some still on fire, floated to the ground like golden leaves of autumn.

'Damn. It works.' Jack now knew how he would destroy the airliner, at least on the mythic pages of the manuscript he had not yet started.

CHAPTER
SEVEN

A bby rattled along I-5 in the slow lane at fifty miles an hour. She had to stop once to put oil in the old Plymouth. The odometer had quit working at a hundred and sixty-seven thousand miles, but the car still ran. Abby, ever frugal, babied it along. Theresa kept complaining that the springs were poking her in the ass. There was no doubt the car needed work, but Abby's resources were stretched to the breaking point. And at the moment she had more pressing matters on her mind. It took them a half hour to get downtown in the mid-day traffic, and she was worried that she would be late.

Abby was in the middle ranks of the baby boom. The leading edge of this demographic wave was now inching toward fifty. The boomers were being pushed along by the twenty- and thirty-somethings. Most of the men in her own age group who weren't married hung out in restaurants and bars that catered to younger women. The message to the woman over forty was 'get lost.'

It was an attitude that plagued the business world as well. For a woman involved in any form of entertainment, even at the fringes, in commercial literature, life beyond forty seemed a wasteland of lost opportunities.

Abby had no intention of accepting this, gracefully or otherwise. She covered the few wisps of gray in her hair with a rinse.

She was attractive and when dressed she could still turn male eyes as she did today, walking west on James Street, toward Pioneer Square. In three-inch heels she offered the illusion of height with a sassy walk, and a skirt that ended three inches above her knees. She was bare on the shoulders except for a light shawl, and freezing to death. But it all had a purpose; to keep Charlie's mind off the reason for her visit.

Gritting her teeth and coming up with new excuses for Gable Cooper's long absence, Abby had given Carla the run-around while she cleared her calendar at the law firm and narrowed down the list of possible candidates from the talent agency directory. Carla was now calling twice a day, and Abby was worried that the whole thing might fall apart. Somebody named Bertoli, a publisher, was pounding the agent. Carla gave her a deadline. Three more days and if she couldn't find Cooper the whole thing was off. Abby was desperate. Now all she needed was some money, a small stake to carry out her plan.

She called and accepted Charlie's earlier offer for lunch. He gave her directions to a small restaurant not too far from his office. He was surprised by the call but anxious to see her.

She hoped that he still had a penchant for the use of initials. Everything Charlie owned was always labeled 'C.W.,' 'Charles William Chandlis,' from printed stationery and business cards to his monogrammed handkerchiefs. She prayed that this habit hadn't changed. Somehow, knowing Charlie, she knew it hadn't. He was a creature of habit.

When he saw her a half block off, the way she was dressed, his face lit up like a Japanese lantern. He nearly sprinted the distance.

'Babe. Good to see you.' Charlie was all hands, first on her shoulders, then around her back. He aimed a big kiss at her lips, but Abby managed to turn her head enough so that it landed awkwardly on one cheek.

Since their divorce, on the few occasions when she saw him, Abby wondered increasingly how she could have ever loved this man. It was not that he was vile or evil, but they had nothing in common. Even now she sensed that to Charlie she was nothing but an object of gratification; something to wear on his arm for the world to see, and if he was lucky, to maneuver back to his apartment when they were done.

'It's good to see you, Charlie,' she lied.

'Yeah. Yeah.' He looked her up and down, like some kid on a first date. 'You look great! Really great! Lost some weight.'

Cat food will do that for you, thought Abby.

'You're looking good yourself, Charlie.' He always dressed well, though he'd aged since she'd seen him last. No doubt the result of a faster single life.

She managed to untangle herself from his embrace and they walked the few feet to the restaurant, where Charlie held the door and then followed her inside.

'Mr Chandlis. Good to see you again.'

'Oscar, how are you?' Charlie might not be rolling in it, but he had enough money to be on a first-name basis with the maître d'.

'I have your table in the back.' Oscar turned and led the way, menus in hand, threading his way between tables until they came to a booth in the rear of the restaurant, almost to the kitchen. Charlie was looking for something cozy.

Abby surveyed the terrain, a quick glance down the corridor where there was a sign overhead that read RESTROOMS. The phone she assumed would be in that direction. She couldn't see it. That was good.

'This O.K.?' asked Charlie.

'Fine.' She smiled and scooted in behind the table.

There was a chair on the other side, but Charlie didn't take it. Instead he slipped into the booth next to her so that their bodies were now touching. Abby felt uncomfortable.

A waitress showed up and Charlie ordered scotch and soda. Abby passed.

'I'm freezing. I should have brought something heavier to wear.'

'I was wondering about that.' Ever the chivalrous Charlie.

'It's really cold in here, don't you think?'

'No. Not especially.'

'Well, you're wearing a jacket, no wonder.' She looked at him and finally he got it.

'Oh. Here.' Charlie took off his suit coat and draped it over her shoulders.

Finally.

'Thanks.' She shivered as he wrapped it around her shoulders. It was no act. Oblivious as he was, the first part of her plan had worked, little thanks to Charlie.

'They have a great menu. I thought we could do lunch and then maybe head out.'

'Where to?'

'Oh, I don't know. Maybe over by Seattle Center. Take a walk. Then I thought maybe over to my place for a visit.'

'Oh, did you?'

'Why not?' Charlie was all innocence. No doubt he had a bottle of wine already chilled and two glasses back at his apartment somewhere close to the bed – ever the conniver.

'We'll see,' she said.

'Good.' Charlie took this for 'yes.' He picked up his menu and started to peruse. 'I can recommend the rack of lamb, it's very good. And, let's see. The lobster.'

'That's market price,' said Abby. 'Are you sure you can afford it?'

'Don't worry about it.' He laughed.

Abby felt better about what she was doing.

'Sir?'

Charlie looked up from his menu. It was Oscar, the maître d'.

'Telephone call for you.'

Charlie gave him a quizzical glance, then looked at Abby, a question mark. 'I didn't tell anybody at the office I was coming here.'

She shrugged her shoulders.

This was not a first for Abby. Through their marriage, on the few occasions when they went out to dinner, Charlie always spent his time on the phone while she amused herself and dined, for all intents, by herself.

'Just take me a minute,' he said.

'Sure. Take your time.' She turned back to the menu.

He slid out of the booth, and as expected Oscar pointed down the corridor toward the area by the restrooms.

She watched him go, hugging the jacket of his suit coat to her bare shoulders. A few seconds later she heard his voice, faint but still audible.

'Hello.'

Abby now worked quickly.

'Have we met? I mean in the office? I don't recognize the name. Could you speak up? I'm having trouble hearing you.'

She didn't have much time. But then it didn't take long. A second later she dropped her napkin on the table, and carefully laid Charlie's jacket on the bench seat, everything back in place. Then she slid out of the booth and took a quick glance down the hall. He was buried in a little corridor off to the side, leading to the restrooms, and couldn't see out.

She wound her way through the tables, and out the front door of the restaurant, and merged with the heavy noonday foot traffic on the sidewalk. A half block down she turned the corner. There at the payphone she saw Theresa still talking into the receiver. Abby gave her the high sign that all was well.

'Jeez. I think I got the wrong party,' said Theresa. 'You're not the Charlie Chandlis who does windows and rain gutters?'

'Who the hell is this?'

Abby could hear Charlie's voice over the phone from where she stood.

'Wrong number. Sorry.' Theresa hung up. She turned to Abby. 'Did you get it?'

Abby held it by the edges like a photograph for Theresa to see; Charlie's shiny new credit card, lifted from the wallet in his suit coat pocket.

She hoped he had enough cash to pay for his drink, or maybe Oscar would just put it on the tab.

After eight years of marriage, Abby knew Charlie like some people know the flu. Whenever he was around her bones ached. As she suspected, he still used initials on everything from luggage to stationery – including his new credit card. At the airport she signed the credit card slip for the two tickets to Los Angeles in the name of 'C. W. Chandlis.'

The ticket agents wouldn't check picture I.D.s until they got to the gate the next morning and then only to see if the last name on the ticket matched the passenger's driver's license.

Abby knew that Charlie would never call and report his card lost or stolen, at least not for awhile. He might do a lot of things, but he would never have her arrested. As a criminal defense lawyer it was against his religion.

Still she didn't abuse the privilege. She used the card to book a cheap room for herself and Theresa, clean but cut-rate, in one of the single story motels on Route 99 across from the airport. She decided to stay there because she knew Charlie would be looking for her at the house once he missed his credit card.

She got Theresa to come along by telling her she valued her judgment. Abby liked Terry, but this was a lie. Abby was afraid that in her current state Theresa, in a weak moment, might go back to Joey if only to try to talk things out. Joey seemed to have a hold on her that was messianic, like voodoo. He would beat on her, but in the end she would always come running back. Whether it was Joey's manipulation, or Theresa's insecurity, he always had the ability to make her think it was her fault.

At the motel, Abby brushed her teeth and got ready for a shower while Theresa lay on the bed and continued to fondle the photos in the talent agency directory.

'Come to Mama, blue eyes.' Terry rolled over on her back on the bed and hugged the picture to her breast, nearly bending the hard covers of the binder.

'Be careful. I may have to return that thing,' said Abby.

'Can I have the ones you throw back?' said Theresa.

'This is business,' said Abby.

'Just give me Conan the Barbarian here. He's blond. You can't use him anyway. You already said your guy's gotta have dark hair and big baby browns.'

'I didn't say anything about eyes. I told her Gable was dark, that's all.'

'Fine. I'll take all the blonds,' said Theresa. 'Line 'em up, turn out the lights, and tell 'em we're auditioning for a nude scene.'

'Why don't you just take a cold shower?' said Abby.

'What's wrong with a quick roll in the hay? I say if we're gonna check 'em out, we oughta do it right. Why go halfway? Besides, before you turn your guy over to this Carla, you might want to make sure all the equipment works. I mean, what if she gets him in a compromising position and he goes limp?'

Abby laughed.

'No, I mean it. You don't think it happens?' said Terry. 'I'll bet it happens all the time. I'll bet those literary types hump like bunnies. I mean, if your guy doesn't put out, that could blow the whole deal,' she said.

'Contrary to what you might think, we're not buying a male hooker,' said Abby.

'Right,' said Theresa. She turned another page in the directory. 'God. Look at the pecs on this one.'

Abby sighed and shook her head, but she didn't look.

'The way he stretches that shirt. I've seen more wrinkles on Roman body armor. You think there's any hair under there?' asked Theresa.

'I wouldn't know.'

'You like 'em with hair, or bare breasted?' Theresa

made it sound like white meat or dark, thigh or breast.

'Never really thought about it,' said Abby.

'Listen, sweetheart, every woman thinks about it. Now it's true you may never have thought about it up front. Maybe it was –' she rolled her hand at the wrist searching – 'what's the word I'm looking for?'

'Subliminal,' said Abby.

'What's that?'

'Means subconscious.'

'Yeah, that's it. Subconscious. I'll give you that, subconscious. But you've noticed,' said Theresa. 'It's like a tight rush. It never goes unnoticed. Now you may either be a fan or you're not. Me I'm a bona fide pec and bun lady. Into cheeks and chests. Give me something hard I can put my head against and sink my fingers into and I'm a happy camper.'

Abby said, 'You're awful.' With a mouth full of tooth paste this sounded like 'You owl.'

Theresa surveyed the picture again. 'I'm board certified in cheeks and chests. I can tell just by looking at this guy's pecs – the distance, the broad expanse like Montana, between his tits – that he probably has a prong the size of a titan missile.'

Abby looked wide-eyed at her friend through the open door, a mouth full of toothpaste. 'What?' But Abby couldn't hold a serious expression. She broke up laughing and spat toothpaste all over the sink and choked between laughs.

'You think I'm kidding?'

'No. I think you're sick,' said Abby.

'Listen. Studies have proven there's a direct correlation. Distance between tits divided by the surface area of the tush squared, equals length of the dingle dangle. Unless of course it's a full moon in which case gravity is neutralized, and the sky's the limit.' As she said this Terry's big brown eyes rolled in their sockets. Abby started laughing and finally dropped her toothbrush in the sink which was filled with water.

'Now look what you made me do.'

'Look for yourself.' Terry held up the picture. 'He's built like a pile driver,' said Theresa. 'In case you hadn't guessed, I like men and I'm not afraid to admit it.'

'I hadn't guessed,' said Abby.

'You know these're good pictures but next time you oughta tell 'em to put in a rear view. Sorta round out the whole picture as they say, so we don't have to waste our time.'

'Yeah, our time's so valuable,' said Abby.

'Yeah, but cheeks are important. I'll bet Carla's into buns. It's a power thing,' said Theresa.

Abby reached behind her with a hand and swung the door to the bathroom closed before she got another lecture on the attributes of the male body. Still, she could hear the voice outside in the other room as Theresa took it up another octave to account for the closed door. Now the people next door could probably hear as well.

'Here. Here we go. This one's really got a *tight* ass,' she hollered. 'Come take a peek. He's lookin' over his shoulder.'

'Hold it down,' said Abby.

'I'd like to hold him down. *Come out here and take a gander at this guy's ass.*' Terry was now shouting, for the world to hear. '*What's a matter, you afraid to look at titanium glutes?*' Theresa was now giving her a bad time and Abby knew it. She enjoyed her ability to embarrass Abby, to take it up a notch in a crowded situation.

Abby turned on the shower. The sound of water hitting hollow fiberglass was too much even for Terry to overcome. She finally gave up, drowned out by the noise. A few seconds later, Abby adjusted the water temperature and climbed into the tub, pulling the curtain closed behind her.

She took a long hot shower, shampooed her hair, and stood for several minutes with the warm water running against the nape of her neck and down her body. She wondered what Charlie was doing at that moment; whether he might have a way of checking the credit-card charges so that he would be waiting for them when they got to the airport in the morning. This she quickly dismissed. Charlie would have to tell them the card was lost or stolen to get any information. They would cancel it. He couldn't be sure they would reissue the card. No. Charlie would be camped at her doorstep when she got home demanding his card back. This was as predictable as his initials on the plastic.

She went over in her mind the handful of candidates from the directory. She winnowed it down to the best three. She would start there.

Abby had to be careful in terms of what she said. She couldn't just go barging in and ask them if they would be willing to pull the wool over some New York publishing house. They would think she was out of her mind. She would have to feel them out. Theresa would love the sound of that.

She finally reached around and turned off the water. As the sound died, Abby could hear a male voice in the other room. Terry had finally tired of the book and turned on the television. That was good news, though it was louder than Abby would have liked.

She grabbed a towel and started to dry herself. The speakers on the set were really good. Must be stereo, she thought.

Then there was a loud vibration, something heavy and hard bouncing off a wall.

'Where is he? Is this the one? In the fucking book here? Open your mouth, sweetheart. Eat some more paper.' There was a loud smack, the sound of flesh and bone hitting the same.

'That's it. Now I know you can eat and talk at the same time. Tell me.' Another smack. 'Hungry? Have some more. Take your time. I'm enjoyin' myself. Ain't had this much fun since last time.'

It wasn't television. It was Joey Jenrico, his voice a little slurred – liquid fury.

Abby reached for her jeans, had one leg in, was bent over with the other foot up searching for the pant leg, when the thin wooden panel of the bathroom door splinted in her face. The only thing she saw were shreds of wood and Joey's foot. Fortunately for Abby it got caught in the splintered opening as he tried to pull it out, and Joey went down on his ass.

'Who the fuck?' He had a look of fright in his eye. Joey, in his current state, couldn't be sure if there was some brute on the other side of the door who had done this to him. Visions of Goliath at the law firm had caused Joey to leave the door ajar when he entered; just in case a quick exit was needed. It was the thing about taking courage from a bottle. If Theresa lived long enough and got lucky, some lover he stumbled in on might one day beat the crap out of Joey. That's if there was any justice in the world.

He pulled his leg out through the opening and saw Abby, and all that God had given her on the naked half of her upper body. There was a quizzical look in his eye as if at first it didn't register. Then he collected himself through the alcohol haze.

'Goddamn. My lucky day. The lawyer bitch. Kick the door and hit the fuckin' bull's eye.'

He was looking at Terry on the bed, her mouth full of paper, the torn and folded remnants of one of the photographs from the book.

'Two for the price of one,' said Joey. 'Well. They told me you was datin' a lawyer. But I figured it was a guy. Stupid me.' He looked over at Theresa, who was bleeding from the corner of her lip.

'Son of a bitch. I shoulda' known. Away for awhile and you go dyke on me.' He grabbed a heavy metal lamp off the dresser, a base the size of a bowling ball, and with both hands he flung it at Theresa on the bed. It sailed over her, hitting the headboard. The shade twisted and the bulb shattered, but the bulk of the massive lamp bounced harmlessly to the end of the bed.

'Goddamn we're gonna party tonight. Come here, bitch.' Abby was trapped in the bathroom, so Joey turned on Theresa again. She was paralyzed with fear.

With one arm in the sleeve of her blouse, Abby opened the bathroom door. By now Joey was on top of Theresa, slapping her face with both hands.

'Here, want some more to eat?' He grabbed the book and tore out another picture, poked his finger into the image's midsection so that if the photo was double-sided, the rear-end would have stuck out on the other side. 'You like asses so much. Eat this one.' He stuffed the picture whole into her mouth, then grabbed the electric cord from the broken lamp and looped it around her neck. He was beginning to take up the slack and pull when Theresa went for his eyes. She managed only to reach one cheek with her fingernails.

'Damn you.' He punched her full force with his left fist on the side of face, blood spattered from her nose onto the pillow. She was out cold.

By now Abby was through the door. She flung herself onto Joey's back, both arms around his neck pulling hard.

Joey rose up on his knees, throwing a shoulder toward the top of the bed. Abby went headlong over the top, landing on the pillows, the small of her back across the broken lamp, her feet up against the head of the bed and the wall. It knocked the wind out of her.

He grabbed the blouse and tore it off her arm, then pulled her down onto the bed like a rag doll. He tried to force his tongue into her mouth. Abby could smell alcohol like a distillery. He threw his body across her until he was straddling her on his knees at the edge of the bed. For a drunk he was amazingly agile.

He groped her breasts roughly. He put his hand on the waist band of her pants and ripped. The button shot off like a bullet. He tore the zipper open. As he raised up to reach inside, Abby thrust her hips high, as hard as she could. His knees went over the edge of the bed and gravity did the rest. His hands came out of her pants and Joey tumbled to the floor.

By now he was raging, though for a moment he was lost under the curtains from the window, looking like the headless horseman. He rose from his knees to his feet, still draped in the curtains.

With one hand he pulled down his zipper, with the other he fought to get the curtain off of his head. His pants went down around his ankles, underpants and all, fully exposing his bottom half, the curtain still over his head.

'Come here, bitch. Lemme show ya my cruise missile.'

Abby reached down and grabbed the lamp Joey had thrown at Theresa. It made a sound like a Chinese gong as hollow metal struck his head on the side. Joey's face had just cleared the cloth of the curtain so that his eyes looked like two glass marbles that had been scratched on concrete.

Abby wondered whether she should hit him one more time just for good measure. She was winding up as his bony knees buckled and he went down, dick first. Joey hit the floor with a thud.

She kicked him and pushed with her foot to make sure he was out. He went belly-up like a beached whale.

'Cruise missile, hell,' said Abby. 'More like a rain-soaked fire-cracker to me.'

CHAPTER
EIGHT

The evening air hung heavy with the odor of the tropics, in this case rotting bananas on the dock and the buzzing things that feasted on them.

He looked across at the *Cella Largo*, powdered his body with talcum, and donned the blue-black wet suit. Then he checked his equipment one last time: regulator and tanks. He checked his wrist compass for headings. Once in the water he would be blind.

Stripped to its essentials, a large ship is nothing but a floating power plant. The one he was looking at at the moment was an old oil burner, a stick ship with its cargo booms jutting to the sky, lit like a tree at Yuletide.

He possessed every piece of information available on this particular ship, courtesy of the voice on the phone, no doubt some drone. The people at the top always operated the same way using underlings and middle-men to distance themselves from the deed and any risk of incrimination.

According to the information, there were only two men on board, an officer and an engineer below decks to operate essential equipment.

He checked the pressure gauge on his tanks. They

were full. The device itself was not sophisticated or large. Its genius was simplicity. The object was to inflict just enough damage, and to leave nothing behind. It contained just enough explosives to do the job, an accelerant that would dissolve completely in salt water. The firing mechanism was a wooden clothes pin on a pull string. At the other end of the line was a small open parachute designed to be caught in a current of water. It was a variation on a car bomb he had once seen devised in Columbia to deal with a recalcitrant drug dealer who did not want to share territory. It blew the man's wife through the moon roof of her Mercedes.

The magic of the device was that the ship itself would detonate it the moment the engine started, like clockwork. The stirring of the giant diesel would muffle the blast. Anyone looking, after the fact, would think only one thing: a massive failure of the condenser head. Sea water streaming in and no way to stop it. The schedule was fixed. At precisely twenty-one hundred hours, the *Cella Largo* would fire up her engines to charge a bank of batteries used to power the inverter, which in turn provided electric power to certain circuits when the ship was in port. They would allow the engine to run for exactly forty minutes. Only this time they would not have nearly that long.

He checked his watch and realized that he was already four minutes behind schedule. He entered the water through a thick bank of reeds, and a minute later was engulfed in black murky waters.

The wheels touched the runway at LAX. Twenty minutes later the plane connected to the jet-way and they off-loaded like livestock down a shoot, everything but the mooing and cattle prods.

After being jumped by Joey at the motel, Abby and Theresa changed their plan and went stand-by on an evening flight to L.A. Joey was crazy, and the two women wanted to distance themselves as quickly as possible.

The departure lounge was already overflowing with the progeny of a canceled flight and another one delayed. People were standing in the aisles while others slept on chairs. The two women had to shoulder their way through the gathering crowd, hauling their luggage. Abby, swinging a nine-ton piece of Samsonite, nailed some guy in the leg. The man winced noticeably and groaned.

'Sorry. You O.K.?'

The guy rubbed his leg and gave her a dirty look.

'I'm really sorry.'

'It's alright.' He waved her off as if any effort on her part to minister to his wounds would only make it worse. She might drop the thing on his foot.

'Hold up,' Abby called to Theresa, and tried to catch her as she got lost in the crowd.

'Jeez, whadda they carry in their suitcases?' Stanley Salzman rubbed his leg while he held the fishing pole and trout net in his other hand. He wondered how he would explain the bruise to his wife when he and Sidner got back. Salzman was not much of a traveler. In fact, he hated it.

'What are those for?' Sidner pointed to the pole and the net.

'I got clothes to go with 'em,' said Salzman. 'For both of us, from wardrobe.'

'What for?'

'Let's hope we find this guy Cooper first thing. Maybe we get back tonight.' Salzman ignored the question.

'At least the woman Chandlis,' said Sidner. 'There's a chance we can cut a deal with her.'

'Carla didn't have much luck,' said Salzman.

'Carla didn't have a three-million-dollar budget.'

'I wish you'd quit saying that.' Salzman looked around as if somebody might hear. 'Three mil is tops. We don't start there. And we have to be careful. They get a whiff of that kinda money and suddenly they're gonna start thinking there's more where that came from, that we got pockets down to our ankles. Especially the woman, the lawyer. They're trained to think that way. There's only one way to buy rights, kid. Make 'em think you don't need it. Carla's first mistake.'

'Oh yeah. That's going to work. Two guys from Hollywood traveling to the back of beyond in search of an author nobody's ever heard of, and they're supposed to think we're only casually interested.'

'That's what this is for.' Salzman held up the pole. 'The Great Northwest. The home of the Sockeye. We're goin' fishin'. We just happened to be in the neighborhood. Thought you might be interested in selling your book to a major studio. Mixing a little business with pleasure. But we can take it or leave it.'

Salzman figured he was dealing with hicks. Open for a few thousand and grudgingly move toward six figures. Somewhere along the way Gable Cooper would cave like a card table, and give them an option on future works that would make slavery look charitable.

'You heard Mr Weig. Get the book at all costs.'

'Believe me, Mel Weig will understand if we erase a few zeros off of the check he has to write.'

It took him more than twenty minutes to cross the channel before his eyes glimpsed the ominous presence looming above. Forty feet up was a massive dark outline, a ceiling of steel plates curving at one edge toward the surface.

He came up slowly underneath the center of the ship near the keel. Using his flippers, he glided along the chine of the ship's curved bottom. Bubbles from the regulator's exhaust rolled off the barnacled plates and expanded as they floated toward the surface like shimmering silver balls.

He had only twenty minutes left by the time he found it; the entrance to the raw water intake. Here cold sea water was taken in and washed through the condenser to cool the engine. On most small trawlers a man could fit his hand into this opening. On the *Cella Largo* it was the size of a small cave, large enough to maneuver his entire body inside. But there was a problem. The opening was blocked by grillework. With all of the planning he'd never been told about this. He had not brought tools nor had he built time into his schedule to deal with it.

Quickly he pulled his diving knife from the sheath strapped to his ankle and poked at the rusting metal. He tried the screws that held the grille to the hull. They were frozen with rust. He pried at one of them and the head of the screw snapped off. A corner came loose. He checked his watch: nineteen minutes.

He slid the stainless-steel blade of the knife under the edge of the grille and lifted. Part of it, a sizable section, ripped free from around the screws, leaving a jagged edge of rusted metal like the rotting teeth of some sea denizen to guard the opening. Pulling and straining, he clawed his way inside. There was no time to waste. Seventeen minutes. Rusted metal ripped a gash in his wet suit and tore into the flesh of his thigh. He didn't even feel it, such was the rush of adrenaline.

He pushed himself free and swam deeper into the pipe. Using his arms he clawed his way along the water-filled duct until he was ten feet inside the ship's hull. He flipped on the flash light. The massive pipe took a turn. He followed it, careful not to bump the metal sides, something that might alert the watch in the engine room. Ahead he could see the fanlike blades attached to the impeller motor.

Gingerly he flipped around so that his head was now facing the opening in the pipe, the avenue of escape. Sixteen minutes to go. Now he worked frantically.

He removed the device from the bag and checked it under the light. The plastic covering was intact. It was taped to a small magnetized piece of metal. Carefully he lifted and placed it against the inside metal of the pipe until the magnet snapped and clung. With tremulous fingers he uncoiled the cord leading to the detonator. In his sojourn across the channel, part of it had knotted. It took some time to work these out. All the while checking his watch, time ticking away. He stretched out the line. With the small white nylon parachute open at the end floating free in the still waters of the pipe, the device took on a curious aspect. It looked like nothing so much as a dreaded Portuguese-man-o-war trailing a single deadly tentacle.

Inside the engine room Henry Handle looked at the clock pinioned on the pipe overhead. The second hand twitched, but it didn't move. It was frozen at eight forty-three. Henry wondered how long it had been stopped. He crossed the companionway and tapped the clock overhead with the back of his knuckle. It didn't move. He reached up and lifted the clock off of its hook. Suddenly it came to life. The sweep hand began to move. Henry looked at it. He couldn't be certain how long it had been stopped. He hung it back on the bolt and instantly it quit. He took it off, it started, put it back and it quit. Henry wasn't a whiz with machinery, but he knew what stopped clocks. He lifted it off again and instantly it started. He took a small metal pen knife from his pocket and raised it up toward the pipe, near the bolt. A half an inch away it jumped out of his hand and stuck fast to the metal of the conduit overhead.

'Son of a bitch.' Henry'd heard about salt water doing strange things to metal, oxidation in the form of rust, and worse, electrolysis that eats through it. But this was a first. He wasn't sure what was going on, but his principal concern at the moment was that he was late with the engines. He had no way of knowing how much time had passed since the clock quit. He walked back to the control panel and reached for the switches.

He was done. Using the flat of his palms against the smooth inner surface of the pipe, slowly, an inch at a time, he pulled his body toward the exit. He was careful not to kick with his fins. This might create a current in the pipe. He wasn't certain exactly how much force it would take to dislodge the firing pin and detonate the device. Given his present circumstance, he wasn't anxious to find out. He rounded the bend in the pipe and maneuvered his head out and past the grillework and into open water when the strap on one of his tanks hooked on a jagged piece of metal. He turned his head but couldn't see it. He gave a jerk with his body. Nothing. Somehow one of the straps to his tank had looped over an exposed edge of the grille. He reached around, tried his knife, but couldn't get it. He checked his watch. He had less than eight minutes to put distance between himself and the doomed ship. He offered up a lunging breaststroke with his arms in an effort to break free. The flippers on his feet hung like dead weight on a paralyzed man. He couldn't use them without stirring a current inside the pipe.

The upper part of his body protruded through the opening to the raw water intake like a man in the jaws of a giant whale. He was struggling to free himself when he heard it; an electrifying high-pitched hum magnified by the density of the water. It was an alarm transmitted through the steel hull overhead. Instinctively he knew what it was. Somewhere inside the bowels of the engine room someone had turned on the blowers, the fans that expelled diesel vapors. It was a prelude to the start of the engines. They were six minutes early.

It started as a deep rumble in the water, vibrations at the wide band of the sound spectrum, like some giant's phlegm-driven cough. The engine turned over but didn't start.

Frantically he tore at the strap. He tried to free the buckle on the belt to swim out of the tanks. The buckle caught. His hands fumbled with it.

Another cough of the engine. This time it kicked over twice and died. He owed his life to the cold-blooded diesel, notoriously hard to start. Finally the belt came free. He shrugged his shoulders out of the harness and swam. Just as the rumble began once more he hooked his foot. The strap of his fin caught on the metal and suddenly he stopped dead in the water. He looked back, his eyes bulging behind the glass of his mask. He reached down and freed his foot from the swim fin just as the blast hit.

The tempered steel of the pipe fractured like glass. Chunks of iron the size of a car door fell on top of Henry along with a shelf covered with heavy machine parts. It was strange, almost surreal, as if time had stopped. Henry lay on the iron bulkhead dazed, staring at the gaping hole over his head and wondering why nothing came out of it. There was only a thin spray and a few drops of salt water. His ears popped, and a second later the bubble from the blast dissipated out the end of the tube and rose along the hull of the ship toward the surface.

Then he heard it. Henry's eyes widened. Like the rush of Niagara, the water hit him with the force of a hydraulic cannon. He struggled with the weight across his lower body but couldn't budge it. Henry's legs were trapped. He called for help but his cries were drowned in the briny rush. Diesel fuel floated on the surface. Within seconds, the level had risen over his stomach to his shoulders. An instant later only his head remained above the water. He stretched and craned his neck to borrow a few seconds of life, when something hard and black hit his face in the rush of water. Henry looked in dazed wonderment as water rose above the level of his mouth and overtook his nostrils. His eyes bulged. He reached out a dying hand and with his last breath grasped the dark object that had slapped his face.

Like a bullet shot from the barrel of a gun he was expelled through the dark, soundless void like a body through rapids. Somewhere in the distance behind was a vague rumble. The resistance of the water finally stopped his headlong tumble, and he lay dazed, floating listless near the bottom. His first sensation was of choking. Hands reflexively to his mouth, he kicked hard for the surface. Swimming hand over hand, his frantic eyes probing the darkness, wondering if he was heading in the wrong direction. The senses of the inner ear were scrambled by the blast. He was out of breath, his lungs bursting as if on fire, as his outstretched hand met humid air. His head burst through the surface. He coughed and sputtered, grabbed his stomach with both hands, and retched up bubbles of sea water. He reached down and felt for his legs, uncertain whether both limbs would be there. Sculling the surface with his hands, he did a lazy circle with his body in the water. Behind him, perhaps two hundred feet away, there was an eerie incandescent glow from beneath the water at the side of the ship, a dozen points of shimmering light spanning the length of her hull. The *Cella Largo* settled into the water, the glimmering lights from its submerged port-holes streaming to the surface like a murder victim giving up its soul.

CHAPTER

NINE

The first two were dead ends. One of them had moved to Las Vegas a week before where he was doing stand-up comedy while he doubled as an aerobics instructor in a resort hotel.

They were down to the man Abby thought was the best-looking, but too young. His name was Jess Jermaine. He was twenty-six, dark hair, square jaw, a face chiseled from stone, and sparkling green eyes. When he opened the door to his apartment, Abby knew she was on the right track. If looks can be said to be magnetic, Jess Jermaine was the north pole, almost too good-looking. She guessed he stood just under six feet, with broad shoulders and a tan like a bronze god.

Standing in the open doorway to his apartment she explained that she was getting ready to audition several candidates for a role and that someone had given her Jess's name.

'It's a little unusual,' he said. 'Normally I get casting calls by phone from my agent.'

'It's an unusual situation,' she told him. 'A bit of a rush. But we're willing to pay for it.'

He opened the door and invited them in. Jermaine

studied Theresa, who was still wearing the oversized dark glasses.

The place was one big room, a studio with a fold-out bed in the couch.

He moved an old pizza box from a chair and offered Abby a place to sit. Theresa without asking flopped onto a large bean bag in the corner. It was the only thing left besides the bed, which Theresa considered for a moment, but it was covered with clothes waiting to be folded.

'You caught me doing laundry. I'd offer you something to drink, but I haven't done the weekly shopping.' He offered them a glass of water instead.

'We're fine,' said Abby.

'Looks like you could use a woman around here,' said Theresa.

'That's what my girlfriend keeps saying.' He pointed to her picture in the frame sitting on top of the television.

'Beautiful child,' said Theresa.

Abby shot her a dark look.

'Don't mind me. You guys talk. I'll just amuse myself,' said Theresa. She looked at the arm of the couch a foot away, some skimpy article in fake leopard skin that the hunk had not gotten around to. 'I'll just make myself useful.'

'What's the part?' Jermaine was ignoring her, talking to Abby. He was curious though he didn't give the impression that he was hungry.

'It might require some travel.'

'Film, television, or live stage?' he asked.

None of the above, thought Abby, but she would have to tread carefully or risk scaring him off. She was down to her last best shot for a Cooper stand-in. 'I think you'd have to characterize it as a live performance.'

'At least until they catch you,' said Theresa.

Jermaine looked at her, a little confused. 'I've done a little off Broadway,' he told Abby. 'A couple of years ago, before I came out to the coast.' He dropped onto the bed and draped a long leg in tight jeans over the arm of the sofa while he folded some socks. The T-shirt he was wearing was cut short, in the style of a college football jock. It showed a midriff, tanned, with abs rippled like a washboard.

'What we have in mind is not exactly Broadway,' said Abby.

'Yeah. Right town, wrong street.' Theresa was examining the leopard G-string she'd plucked off the arm of the couch. 'Do these things bind?' She smelled it like a connoisseur might a fine cigar, then pulled the pouch back and let it snap like a slingshot while holding onto the thong.

Abby gave her a look to kill.

'Can we cut to the chase?' said Jermaine. 'I've got an appointment in Studio City in an hour. An audition for a part in a commercial, and I don't wanna be late.'

'Then I take it you've done commercial photo shoots?' said Abby.

'I thought it was a part you guys were talking about. You're looking for a model?'

'Not exactly.'

'Well, what is it, a part or a shoot?'

'Your picture would be required, but there would be some acting as well,' said Abby.

'Where is it, how many days, and how much?' Just like that he was down to the dollars.

'The job's mostly in New York, I'm not precisely sure how long it will take, and the money – well the money is somewhat negotiable.'

Jermaine smiled as if perhaps he liked the sound of that. 'For photo shoots I get twenty-five hundred dollars a day, all expenses paid, accommodations in a four-star hotel or better, first-class air fare both ways, and I don't do anything in the buff.'

Theresa whistled low and long.

In fact, he never got any of these things, but he figured he might as well ask. He got up from the couch and crossed the room to where a calendar hung on the side of the refrigerator in the tiny kitchen.

'Let's see. I gotta be back in L.A. in a week, cuz I have another audition.' He had his back to them as he checked the calendar.

Abby looked over to see Theresa with the G-string over her head, the pouch arranged so that it covered her nose and mouth like an oxygen mask while she inhaled through the fabric, deep breathing. Then she laughed at Abby, who offered her an expression of fury.

Before Jermaine could turn around Theresa pulled the item from her head. 'What exactly defines the buff?' she said, dangling the G-string by its thong on a single finger.

'Underwear ads I do, as long as they're discreet, no cheeks.'

'Hey. Absolutely,' said Theresa. 'Do we look like ladies who'd come here and ask you to do something cheap, tawdry?'

'You'd be surprised at the things some people will ask you to do.'

'I'll bet I wouldn't,' said Theresa.

'I could tell you some stories,' said Jermaine.

'I'm all ears,' said Theresa.

'The man doesn't have time, *Terry*. Remember he has an audition.' Theresa had seen gargoyles with a more kindly expression than Abby's at this moment.

'I think we need to get to business,' said Abby. 'Cut to the chase as you say.'

She pulled one of her business cards from her pocket and handed it to Jermaine. 'I'm a lawyer. I have a client who shall remain nameless. This client is an author of some talent. For reasons that you don't need to know, the author has opted to write a major book, a novel, perhaps a bestseller, under a pen name. He does not want to be identified either to the public or the publisher. He's looking for someone to act as a stand-in.'

'Is that legal?' asked Jess.

'Yes. You can take my word. It's been thoroughly checked out. The job would include still photographs for the book's dustcover and if successful, public appearances. Perhaps television, and book autographing around the country if it comes to that.'

Jermaine made a face like he was impressed by the possibilities.

Theresa sat dumbstruck watching Abby and the ease with which she pulled it off, this final piece of subtlety, the ultimate lie: 'I have a client.' She didn't intend to tell Jermaine the truth until she thought she could trust him.

Jermaine's eyes lit up. 'You're kidding?'

'No.'

'Who pays for all this?'

'If there's any travel, the publisher.'

'I imagine there could be some good publicity,' he said.

'Yep.'

'And I get paid too?'

'A percentage of the advance.'

'How much?'

'We'll talk about that after I know whether you're interested.'

'I don't get it. What's the downside?'

Abby shrugged her shoulders as if there were none. 'Are you interested?'

'I don't know. Sounds good. I don't know anything about writing or publishing.'

'I need a decision.'

'What I don't understand is what's the point?' he asked. 'I mean, why is the author doing this?'

'From what we understand, the publisher's prepared to pay a lot of money to a man who wrote a novel that caught their attention. If he's good-looking and comes across well in the media, it feeds their confidence that they can market him. That makes the book more valuable.'

'You're kidding?'

'I wish I were,' said Abby. 'Are you interested?'

Jermaine started thinking. 'How much more valuable?'

'What do you mean?'

'You said if the author's good-looking, the book's more valuable. How much more?'

'We haven't entered negotiations yet. But you can forget any value-added formula. The author spilled his blood on this one.'

'Well, at least give me some guess as to what the book is worth?' he said.

'If I had to . . .' Abby considered for a moment. Owens didn't take clients unless they were worth multiples of six figures on a book. She wouldn't cross the country on a lark unless some publisher, maybe more than one, had an interest. It was always possible that the book could end up in an auction which would drive the price even higher.

'If I had to venture a guess, I would say maybe two hundred thousand by way of an advance, perhaps more.' She was being conservative. But it was better to be on the low side than to disappoint him later and have him walk out in the middle, after Owens had met him.

'And my portion?'

'Five percent?' said Abby. It was more of a question than a statement. She was desperate and Jermaine could smell it.

'Ten.'

'You'd have to sign a contract.'

He nodded.

'Done.'

They had to ring the bell twice and wait for more than a minute before the door opened. It had taken them two hours to find Abby's house in the University District.

A guy with a grizzled growth on his face who looked about six feet tall peeked out through the crack in the door left by the security chain.

'Whadda ya want?'

The glance exchanged between the two men on the stoop outside was one of amazement. Perhaps there was a God in heaven after all.

'Am I speaking to Gable Cooper?' Stanley Salzman already had a business card in his hand.

'Depends who's asking.'

'Someone with a business deal for you if you're Mr Cooper.'

The eyes that had looked out from under sleepy-hooded lids suddenly lifted.

'You are Mr Cooper?' Salzman slipped the business card through the crack in the door. In blue raised letters was the name of the studio and the logo that anybody who wasn't from Mars would recognize in an instant from the wide screen of a thousand movie theaters.

'Can we come in?'

They were wearing strange clothes. One of them had a tan cap with a bill that must have been a foot long. The thing had ear flaps. The other was dressed in some kind of canvas pants that looked like mildew had gotten to them in places. He had a canvas strap across his shoulder holding a straw basket on his hip. The entire affair looked like some kind of an antique fishing rig.

'Just a second.' Joey Jenrico closed the door, then walked down the hallway where he closed another. The second door led to a back room that Joey'd been trashing when the door bell rang. He'd already smashed all the dishes on the kitchen floor and emptied the contents of the refrigerator on top of them. Then he moved on to what he assumed was Theresa's room where he broke up most of the furniture and was working on Theresa's clothes with a knife when he was interrupted.

Joey would have told the two guys to get lost, except for the business card, and the mention of a deal; that and his mean curiosity. Joey was wondering if this guy Cooper was the one who was seeing Theresa. If so, he'd find the son of a bitch and either kill or cripple him, but not before seeing if there was a dollar in it. He wondered what the guys at the door were talking about. He could smell money, but how much?

He hustled back to the front door and opened it. Salzman came in first followed by Sidner, who asked where Abby Chandlis was.

'She's out,' said Joey.

'Then this is her house? We've got the right place?'

'Yeah. You were talking about a deal?' said Joey. First things first.

Salzman looked about and then suggested maybe they could sit in the living room to discuss business.

'Whatever.' Joey hesitated to give directions. He wasn't precisely sure where it was. Fortunately he hadn't had a chance to tear up the living room yet.

Salzman nodded toward what appeared to be the front room.

'Make yourself at home,' said Joey. 'I'd offer you drinks, but right now the kitchen's a mess.'

'We understand. We were just passing through,' said Salzman. 'On our way north for a fishing trip. You just get in yourself?'

Joey misunderstood the question and looked at them with a blank gaze. For a moment he thought maybe they'd been parked outside and had seen him breaking the screen and climbing through the side window.

'We heard you were down in Mexico,' said Salzman.

'Oh. Yeah.'

'A good trip, I hope?'

'Yeah. Had fun.'

'I thought you were working?'

'That too. What's this all about?'

'One of our colleagues at the studio heard we were taking a trip up here to do a little fishing, so he asked us if we could stop in and talk to you for a few minutes.'

Joey peeked through the blinds in the front window. He'd heard about cops gaining entry with some bullshit story when they suspected a crime in progress. Maybe a neighbor had called them. But he could see a fishing pole in the back window of the car parked out front.

'Talk about what?' said Joey.

'Your book of course.'

'Oh.' Joey thought for a moment. 'That,' he said. Joey gave them a lazy nod as if he knew what they were talking about.

'He thinks your book is pretty good. This friend of ours.'

'Then he already has it?' Joey was hoping he wouldn't have to find it. Given the state of the house, it was probably under the rest of the shit he'd already dumped in the back room.

'Oh yeah. I guess you're wondering how we got it?'

Joey shook his head like he could care less.

'Well. We have our sources. I hope you don't mind?'

'Why should I mind?'

'Precisely,' said Salzman. 'We were thinking maybe there's some film possibilities in the story. Nothing certain, mind you, but it has potential. We option a lot of things. Very few of them go into production, actually get made, you understand. But we like to keep the pipeline full of ideas.'

Joey raised his eyebrows in thoughtful contemplation. 'This pipeline, it must cost a lot to fill up? How much you willing to pay?'

Salzman smiled. Direct. He liked that. 'The kind of author I like. A bottom-line man,' said Salzman. 'A few thousand maybe. We understand that you're at work on a second book at the present time. A sequel?'

'I suppose,' said Joey. He didn't know what a sequel was, but it sounded like the movie man did so he went along.

'If we could package the whole thing, both books, tie them up at the same time, get a solid option on future works,' said Salzman. He sized Joey up in his mind and the picture came to pocket change. 'We might be willing to go as high as twenty, maybe twenty-five thousand.'

It was more money than Joey had ever seen at one time in his life. Dead or alive, this guy Cooper was valuable. Maybe he wouldn't kill him right away even if he was bonking Theresa, at least not before he did whatever this sequel thing was.

'You have to understand,' said Salzman, 'we only do this, go this high, because the studio likes to encourage a promising new writer. Feeding new talent so to speak.'

'Right. And when would this happen? This feeding of talent.' Joey was no writer but he knew bullshit when he heard it.

'As soon as our lawyers can put the contract together.' Salzman couldn't believe how smoothly this was going.

'How long would that take?'

Usually it took weeks, but under the circumstances they could use the standard form, the one they used with screen writers that gave them nothing but the money. They would grab off character rights and plant an option in the agreement that would guarantee that they owned all screen rights to Cooper's next three books. Before he knew it, he'd be on the studio planta- tion picking cotton out of his navel.

'I could make a phone call and have it back to you overnight express, three days tops,' said Salzman.

'Twenty-five thousand,' said Joey.

'I said twenty, maybe twenty-five.'

Sidner almost jumped on Salzman when he heard this.

'But since you've been so reasonable, twenty-five it is.' Salzman looked at his partner and winked.

Joey would have sold them whatever they wanted for a tenth of that, particularly if he could have it now, in cash.

'When do I get the money?'

'As soon as you sign the contract, we'll send the check.'

'No check,' said Joey. 'I want cash.'

'The studio doesn't deal in cash. What are you worried about, you saw the card. We're good for the money. Just give us the name for the check.'

'The name?' said Joey.

'We were led to believe that Gable Cooper was a pen name. You give us your real name, and we'll make the contract out and the check as well.'

Sometimes you live right, and the sun shines on you, thought Joey.

'I want it to go to a P.O. box. That alright?'

'That's fine. Anything you want.'

'The name's Joey Jenrico.' He spelled it for them while Sidner took notes.

'You wrote a wonderful book, Mr Jenrico. You keep it up,' said Salzman, 'and you'll have a big future in front of you.' It's what publishers, studios, and agents told every writer in order to keep their nose to the stone and their eyes off of business.

Sidner wrote down the name and mailing information along with Joey's social security number for reporting the payment to the IRS. Mel Weig was gonna love the price, though he would be disappointed by the fact that Jenrico was clearly no bestselling author. But then, what did he expect for twenty-five thousand – the fucking moon?

CHAPTER
TEN

Bertoli looked up the unlisted number and punched the buttons on the phone. It rang once before she answered.

'Carla. Alex here. You got problems.'

'What's the matter?' Carla Owens was sprawled on her bed with a pile of manuscripts, stuff culled by her staff that showed promise for new clients. Unfortunately none of it came up to the commercial quality of Gable Cooper's book. She saw one of those every ten years, if she was lucky.

'I'm hearing some troubling stories out of L.A.,' said Bertoli. 'Information that your friend Mel Weig has picked up the film rights on Cooper's book for peanuts.'

'What are you talking about?' Owens dropped the manuscript she was reading and lost her page.

'I'm talking about a screw job, that's what I'm talking about.'

'No film rights have been sold,' said Owens.

'Then somebody's dealing behind your back. I thought we had a deal, Carla.'

'I don't know what you're talking about. Slow down and tell me what's going on.'

'Somebody from the studio – I don't know who yet – got hold of Cooper.'

'Where did this happen?'

'I don't know.'

'When?'

'Yesterday. Maybe the day before. It wasn't clear.'

'What happened?'

'What do you mean what happened? They cut a deal directly.'

'They wouldn't do that,' she told him. 'I talked to Weig the other day. He gave me his word. I was getting ready to negotiate a deal. Just waiting for the right moment.'

'Well, they aren't waiting any more. And it gets worse. From what I'm hearing they tied the thing up for pocket change. Stole it,' said Bertoli. 'Not only the current book, but the new one he's working on.'

'What do you mean?' asked Carla.

'I'm hearing twenty-five thousand.'

'You're out of your mind,' said Owens. 'Weig knows it's worth more than that.'

'Yes, but the question is, does Cooper?'

'Who told you this?'

'You think we're the only ones with a leak in the pipeline? I've got my sources.'

'Who?'

'*My* sources,' said Bertoli. He no longer trusted her. He couldn't be sure whether she had been duped, or if maybe there was some devilish plan here and Carla was part of it.

In fact, she hadn't told him everything, including the fact that Abby had called her that afternoon to tell her that Cooper was on his way home and would be in New York in two days. The timing of Abby's call and now

Bertoli's information set off alarms in Carla's head.

'It's probably garbage,' she told him.

'No. I don't think so. It comes from somebody in a position to know. And if it's true, I'm not sure we'd still be interested in publication rights, certainly not for anything approaching the dollars we've been talking about.'

'Listen, Alex, don't panic. If something's going on I'll find out what it is.'

'It's a little late to find out, don't you think?'

'Are you telling me Cooper's already signed a contract?' There was actually cold sweat forming on her upper lip as she asked the question. If Cooper had signed away film rights for twenty-five thousand, they could all fold their tents and go home. Mega-bucks bestsellers and blockbusting films were not made in the bargain basement. The studio could recoup this kind of investment with something shot over a weekend in somebody's garage. Cooper's career would be over before it started.

'He hasn't signed yet. But I'm told that the terms are already agreed to verbally.'

'Any money change hands?'

'That I don't know. But I don't think so.'

'Then you know what they say about verbal agreements,' said Carla.

'What's that?'

'Not worth the paper they're written on. Let me look into it. I'll get back to you.'

The dial tone barely had time to stutter and Carla was punching buttons. It rang once, twice, three times and the taped message came on. She waited. The message beep lasted for several seconds. Abby hadn't cleared the earlier messages. Carla tried to piece it together. Abby must have called her from somewhere else – the studio in L.A.; Carla's devious mind.

'Abby. This is Carla Owens. If you're there, please pick up.' She waited for a moment. No answer.

'There's something that's come up that we have to discuss.' She waited again. Still no answer.

'Listen, it's urgent. If you haven't left already or if you clear this message, please call me. I repeat, it's urgent. It doesn't matter what time it is, just call.' She left phone numbers for her home, cell phone, and office on the tape.

She waited several more seconds hoping someone would pick it up. All she heard was the hiss of the tape as it turned inside the answering machine. What she couldn't have known was that it lay buried under broken glass and the rotting remnants of food from Abby's refrigerator. Still the message wasn't without an audience. Sitting in the corner killing time, playing mumblety-peg with a pocket knife into one of the kitchen cabinet doors, Joey Jenrico was waiting for Theresa.

Abby stayed in L.A. the next day and worked with Jess, briefing him on the book. She would take the red-eye from L.A. to New York.

Theresa was staying with friends in southern California. She would be there for at least a week. Terry was treating it as a vacation with Abby's encouragement and blessing, especially after their row with Joey at the motel. For a few days at least, Abby wouldn't have to worry about her friend.

The plan was that Abby would meet Carla alone in New York and that together the two women would pick up Jess at the airport the following day, presumably coming in from Mexico. Jess would transfer planes in Dallas so there would be no way for Carla to trace his point of origin.

Abby was the advance team. Meeting Carla alone would give her time to find out if Owens had any surprises in store. She and Jess had set up a signal; she would get sick if there was something he should know. They could regroup at the hotel for strategy and meet with Owens again once they'd made adjustments to their story.

He seemed to have it down pat, all the answers on how he wrote the book, how the story line came to him, how he selected the pen name and the title, what he was doing down in Mexico and where. For this Abby had brought some maps and travel brochures. Jess was even prepared to offer a few titillating details about the sequel, the follow-up book that Abby was now working on.

Jess was a quick study and by the time she left for the airport Abby was confident that he could pull it off. On the way to LAX she took care of a little business. She made a telephone call to Charlie's answering service and dropped an envelope in the mail. In the phone message she told Charlie that his credit card was in the mail. What she didn't tell him was that before she mailed it, she booked two round-trip tickets to New York as well as rooms in a modest hotel not far from Carla Owens's office using Charlie's card. Then she took a cash advance against the card to pay for the rooms and meals. In terms of expenses, she was not yet even with Charlie for the marital debts, but it was a good down payment. She told him this in a note that she sent along with the card. He would be wasting his time if he tried to file charges. There were some things the criminal law did not handle well, among them ex-spouses fighting over money. Prosecutors usually wouldn't get involved, and Charlie would know civil court was a loser. She'd clean his clock. After all, while the method of collection may have been unusual, the debt was valid.

Abby slept for most of the flight. She didn't arrive at the hotel in Manhattan until after two in the morning. She paid cash for the room, followed the bellman with her bags upstairs to her room, and was asleep within twenty minutes.

The wake-up call came at seven the next morning. Abby rose and showered. She didn't see it until she passed the closed door to her room the second time on her way from the bathroom to dress; a small white envelope on the floor. Someone had slipped it under the door in the middle of the night.

She opened it. Inside was a note on a hotel message slip scrawled in the hand of what she assumed was the clerk.

'Ms Chandlis: Sorry to do this to you at the last minute, but I won't be able to make it to New York. Something has come up. I've made arrangements. Trust me. Everything will work out.

Jess.'

The adrenaline raced through her body like molten lead. If he had been there at that moment, she would have killed him. 'Trust me. Everything will work out.' He had the brains of a banana.

Abby had been warned by Morgan and Theresa, and even that little voice inside her conservative lawyer's mind, not to trust a piece of beefcake with the dreams of her life. Now she was paying the price.

She had told Carla that he would be there the next day. If he didn't show up, Owens would start to suspect that something was going on. If Abby came clean and told her that she had in fact written the book, Owens would never believe her. It's the problem with coming clean after a lie, even the truth takes on the tinge of deceit.

Abby made a beeline for the phone. She called Jess's number in Los Angeles. It rang four times and was cut off by the mechanical voice of an operator: 'Your party is not answering. If you wish to leave a message, press the pound sign.'

Abby hit it so hard she broke a fingernail.

'Leave your message at the sound of the tone.'

'Listen, you son of a bitch. You made a deal. If you don't get your ass back here I'll wrap a law suit around your head like an iron mask. You won't live long enough to pay off the judgment. Do you understand me? And don't give me any excuses, just get your ass on a plane and get back here.'

Then she wondered whether by scaring him he might simply avoid her. It was something Charlie had told her in dealing with his special breed of clients. The first instinct of every flake is to run. She softened her tone a little. 'Wait, Jess. I'm sorry. I'm upset. I just want you to call me. I mean it. If there's a problem, we can work it out, but call me.' She left the phone number at the hotel and hung up, then sat by the phone and waited.

An hour went by. There was no response. She rubbed sleep from her eyes and looked at the red light on the phone. She cupped it with her hand to make sure. Maybe he'd called and left a message and they hadn't put it through. But the light was not on.

She called the front desk. No messages.

By now his plane would have left L.A. Jess was not coming, and Abby knew it. She saw her life going up in flames. She had spent two years writing a novel to die for, and now all of her work as well as her dreams were being undone by some Hollywood jock. She had visions of Jess lying in bed with some starlet bimbo, figuring ways to convert Abby's plane ticket into a trip to Vegas for two.

There was nothing she could do. She looked at her watch.

It was now eight o'clock. She was scheduled to meet Owens downstairs in half an hour for breakfast to talk, before they went to pick up Gable Cooper at the airport. Gable who was not coming.

There was no sense in prolonging the pain. She picked up the receiver and punched Carla's office number. If she couldn't get her perhaps her staff could head her off before she got to the hotel. Abby had no desire to meet with her, or to talk.

The phone was answered almost before it had a chance to even ring. The voice was exuberant, high-pitched.

'Hello.'

'Who is this?' Abby thought she'd dialed the wrong number.

'Who are you trying to reach?'

'I was calling Owens and Associates.'

'Abby, is that you?' It was Carla herself. 'I'm glad you got in. Did you get any sleep?'

'Not much.'

'Listen, if you're tired we can push everything back a few hours.'

'That's what I wanted to call you about. There's been a problem. It's Gable . . .'

'Oh, listen, darling. He's everything you'd said he would be, and more. We've been having a wonderful time here in the office talking.'

'What?'

'We've been visiting for the past hour. I guess you guys must have messed up on the flight arrivals. He came in by taxi early this morning and my service called me. We've had breakfast and have been talking ever since. Oh. And by the way, disregard that message I left on your answering machine. Somebody got their wires crossed. We'll get to the bottom of it when you come in. How long are you going to be?'

Abby was dazed, confused. Maybe the note was a mistake. It felt like a reprieve from the hangman. She looked at her watch, and then at the mirror. She was a mess.

'Give me forty minutes.'

'Good. See you then, darling.' With that, Owens hung up in her ear. It seemed Carla had what she wanted.

CHAPTER

ELEVEN

In New York it had been the winter from hell, and it looked as if it would never end. It was officially spring, and several inches of snow blanketed the sidewalks of Manhattan. People huddled in doorways emitting vaporous breath.

In the congestion and snow, it took Abby nearly an hour to reach Owens's office. It was on the fortieth floor of a skyscraper, a suite that took up most of the corner of the building. For a literary agent it was flashy. Abby had seen agent's offices before. The ones she had known were usually in brownstones or office buildings in the lower rent districts.

Carla's was on Madison Avenue, nestled among law offices and the executive suite of a major insurance company. Her name was emblazoned in silver script, letters a foot high across the black glass double doors.

OWENS & ASSOCIATES
LITERARY AGENTS

Abby counted nine names underneath Carla's stenciled on the sidelight.

When she pulled the brass handle, the door gave way like a bank vault opening, slow and hushed. A receptionist in a sky blue silk dress sat behind a sweeping black lacquer counter taking phone calls. The outer office looked like the flight bridge from a star ship, all curved symmetry and geodesic forms. She sank into the maroon carpet as she crossed the room, a cushion of plush to her ankles. There were walls of smoked mirrors so that she couldn't tell where room ended and the private corridors began. The reception area was cloaked in muted light from overhead canisters.

As soon as Abby reached the counter, the woman behind it looked up and smiled. 'Can I help you?'

'I'm here to see Carla Owens. My name is Abby Chandlis.'

'Oh yes, Ms Chandlis. They're waiting for you in Ms Owens's office. Just a moment. I'll ring.'

Abby looked about as the receptionist punched buttons and talked on the phone. A moment later she heard a voice, 'Ms Chandlis,' and turned. Standing in front of her was an African-American woman, tall and slender, with cheekbones like chiseled onyx and striking oval eyes. She was wearing a soft wool dress that clung to her flowing contours. Abby figured the dress must have cost at least a thousand dollars.

'I'm Jadra, Ms Owens's secretary. I'm pleased to meet you. I've heard so much about you,' said the secretary. 'If you could follow me this way. They're waiting for you.'

Abby walked behind Jadra down a long corridor, a labyrinthine affair of smoked glass walls through which Abby could see the dark outline of minions laboring inside, some on the phones, others hunched over documents and piles of manuscripts.

In the reflection of the walls, Abby self-consciously straightened her dress, anxiously aware of the fact that it was the best thing she owned. She hoped and prayed that Jess had kept to the details they had gone over in their briefing session in Los Angeles, and not adlibbed. She was still troubled by the note that had been pushed under her door and what had led him to change his mind, first not to come at all, and then to come early.

The corridor ended in a massive double door of striking contrast to the rest of the office, a swirling bird's-eye maple with modern brass handles.

As Jadra reached for the door, Abby took a deep breath and tried to compose herself. It swung open and she could see Carla facing her, seated behind a shimmering glass desk with transparent curved legs. It sat on a pedestal a foot above the rest of the office. On the same level were two client chairs facing away from Abby and the door. Jess sat in one of these with his back to her.

'Well, here she is now.' Carla rose from her chair, her arms extended like some high priestess about to slay a sacrifice upon an altar of crystal.

'Abby, darling, it's wonderful to see you again. How was your flight? You look wonderful. Doesn't she look wonderful? Come in. Come in. Would you like a cup of coffee?'

Before Abby could answer, Carla said, 'Jadra, get her a cup of coffee. Cream and sugar?'

Abby didn't feel like it, but it was easier to go along. 'Just black,' she said.

'Just black.' Carla repeated it as if Jadra was deaf to all but her own voice.

Abby took four steps and was halfway to the desk when suddenly Jess rose, turned and in two strides, came off the platform, and covered the distance between them. It was not until she glanced away from Carla and focused for an instant on the form moving toward her that she realized; the man coming at her like a locomotive was not Jess Jermaine.

'So what have we got?' Morgan Spencer sat behind his desk looking at the contents of a small paper sack spread out before him on the desk.

Alvin Cummings stood at one corner and pointed with a ruler. Cummings was an investigator, retired from the military, and a specialist in naval ordinance. He had been brought in by Morgan's client, a maritime insurance company.

'Looks like a scrap of wood,' said Morgan. He moved it around on the blotter with the point of his pen.

'That's what it is,' said Cummings. It was less than an inch long and appeared to be charred at one end.

'The lab believes it's part of a clothes pin. You can see right there it has a tiny hole drilled in one end. If they're correct, this was where the string was attached that ran to whatever was used to detonate it. They found traces of nylon fiber, probably parts of the string.'

'Yeah, and maybe it's something they used to hang a clipboard down in that engine room. Pretty thin basis to deny a claim,' said Morgan. 'Anything else?'

'Some chemicals in the wood. They're not precisely sure what yet. But it appears to contain nitrates. Most of it would have dissolved in the sea water.'

'So final analysis is they don't have squat, but they don't wanna pay off. Is that it?'

Cummings looked at him and nodded.

'I'm gonna have to tell the client it's a no go,' said Spencer. 'They try to stonewall this one, they could be looking at bad faith, the boundless world of punitive damages,' said the lawyer. 'You want to tell them or should I?'

'I think we shouldn't be hasty,' said Cummings.

'There's something more?'

Cummings nodded. 'I think there was a bomb.'

'Fine. Even if there was, they can't avoid payment. Act of war clause wouldn't apply to terrorism or sabotage,' said Spencer. 'The ship didn't go down in a war zone. There's no exclusion for coverage.'

'I'm not talking terrorism or sabotage.'

'What then?' said Spencer. 'The boat's sitting in a harbor in some banana republic, a country with revolutions on alternate Tuesdays. It's what I'd be looking at. Crude bomb with household chemicals. Some guerilla group.'

'I don't think so,' said Cummings. 'Somebody went to a lot of trouble to make it look like an accident.'

'How so?'

'Ordinarily, if you want to send a ship to the bottom, you'd use shaped charges. It's easy enough to get on the open market. Or you just steal the commercial stuff from some construction company. This would be something you mold like putty. C-4 is the military version. You make a rope, as long as you want. Form it in a circle and attach it to the hull, and it'll cut a ring any size you want right out of the steel plates. You want a five-foot hole, make a five-foot circle. But they didn't do that here. You gotta ask yourself why?'

'I was hoping you'd know,' said Morgan. 'All that intuition working overtime.'

'Instead of a hole in the hull, we get massive failure in the condenser.'

'So?'

'So it's made to look like a maintenance problem.'

129

'Probably what it was,' said Spencer. It was easy for the carrier to say 'no – we won't pay' and for the investigator to feed them theories to match their fantasies, but in the end Spencer would have to feed those same theories to a jury. And what he had to work with here didn't look good.

'Except for one thing,' said Cummings. He lifted a black plastic bag from the floor, opened it, and reached inside. What he pulled out he tossed across the desk to Spencer, who caught it almost in self-defense. It was a large black rubber fin, a skin diver's flipper, the expensive kind that a pro would wear with adjustable heel straps to accommodate a diver's wet suit or dry suit. It had a pivoting plane on the front edge for more power in the water.

'We found that in the drowned crewman's hand. Regular death grip,' said Cummings. 'As well as traces of neoprene caught on the screen leading into the raw water intake. You can take my word for it. The *Cella Largo* went to the bottom because of a bomb.'

Morgan looked at the heavy hunk of rubber in his hand. The case had suddenly grown major complications. The file would be with him for years. Authorities would soon be discussing theories of murder.

Abby would have spoken but for the shock of it as the man's arms embraced her, his mouth covering hers. He was powerful and forced the breath from her lungs like bellows. For an instant, she thought his tongue was trying to invade her mouth, and she began to recoil. Then she realized that as he kissed her unresponsive lips, he was in fact trying to say something.

Under his breath and impaired by the crush of their lips it sounded a lot like: 'Hess's mother.'

Abby might have resisted, but at the moment she was in shock. His tongue grazed her closed lips, and he finally gave up the kiss and pulled his head away to the side for a long follow-up hug that nearly broke her ribs. It was an effort to keep her from speaking as he whispered into her right ear.

'The name is Jack. I'm Jess's brother. Keep your cool. We'll work through this. Don't blow it, sweetheart. Now give me a hug like you mean it.'

Abby didn't realize it, but her arms on his back, the only part of her that Carla could see, were limp as a rag doll. Thank God that at the moment her face was lost in his shoulder.

Reluctantly she flattened her hands against the breadth of his shoulders and squeezed. He was several inches taller than Abby and hard as a rock, and while she recoiled at the thought of enjoying the experience she couldn't claim that it was unpleasant, either.

'Good,' he whispered. 'Now smile.'

When he turned to face Carla again, this time holding Abby's hand, he was flashing a mischievous, broad grin. Abby's expression was one of smiling bewilderment. She felt sick and nearly looked the part. They walked hand in hand back to the client chairs, and he held one as Abby sat down. Jack then dropped into the one next to her.

'Abby are you O.K.?' Carla was suddenly focused on her. 'You look a little flushed.'

'Probably the trip,' Jack spoke before Abby could answer. 'She doesn't like to fly.' He pointed to the side of his head and smiled.

For a moment Abby thought he was giving the signal that she was mentally touched. Then he said, 'Inner ear thing.'

'Aw.'

Then he turned to Abby. 'Ms Owens has been telling me that the book is likely to draw a crowd in an auction for rights. She thinks it's quite possible we could get to *seven* figures.' He said the word 'seven' slowly so it would sink in, as if he was telling her to count the zeros before she spoke.

All the while Abby's eyes were on Carla seated across the desk. She heard his words, but what sent the chill down Abby's spine was the fact that Owens was not denying or qualifying them in any way. Instead she was nodding with a confident smile.

For the first time, Abby realized that the book she had written over two years of her life, sweat and toil, could be worth a million dollars. It made the hair on the nape of her neck stand out, and fired the blood in her veins. She smiled and shook, her hands trembling. A million-dollar novel. It was the stuff of dreams.

'I think she's overcome,' said Jack.

Abby nodded, but her voice had left her. As much as she tried, she couldn't speak.

'I think I should get her back to the hotel,' he said. 'I think the trip's affected her a little more than I thought.'

'Of course,' said Carla. 'We can talk again tonight over dinner, sign the contract in the morning. In the meantime, I'll straighten out the mess with this Joey Jenrico guy.'

With the mention of the name Abby's eyes darted. She wanted to ask, but didn't dare.

'I don't know where the studio got the idea that he wrote the book,' said Carla. 'Some interloper. But now I know what happened. Who he is. We'll take care of it. Get to the bottom of it.'

'What studio?' asked Abby.

'Oh, that's the rest of it,' he said. 'I'll have to bring her current back at the hotel. Carla says there's major film interest in the book out in Hollywood. We'll be talking about that tomorrow.'

As the three of them moved toward the door, Abby's knees were actually going weak. He held her hand and finally had to put an arm around her shoulder to steady her.

'It's just great, isn't it, darling?' He was talking to Abby, holding her up like some drunk. 'Ms Owens . . .'

'Carla. Please.' She corrected him.

He smiled, pearly whites that seemed to melt the agent in place. 'Carla thinks my book could be a major bestseller by summer.'

'Trust me,' said Carla. 'It'll be in the hands of passengers on every plane in the world, and around the pools of luxury resorts from Barbados to Bar Harbor, Trinidad to Tahiti. We have a unique opportunity with a publisher on the Summer list.'

'Don't you think it's great?' He was looking at Abby.

She gazed back at him, this stranger, tanned and tall. He looked like Jess, only older, with blue eyes, piercing, and deep as two tropical pools. He was nodding encouragement, a gesture for her to say something. But she was speechless. All she could do was to issue an inane smile.

Though she had planned all of this meticulously for months, the use of the possessive 'my book' by a man she had never seen before was like a sucker-punch in the gut for Abby. It carried her back to sober reality, to the realization that she had written a major bestselling novel, and she could not tell a soul. Abby had buried herself in a sea of anonymity.

'Who the hell are you?' Abby found her voice the instant the cab door closed behind the two of them and the driver pulled away from the curb.

'The name's Jack Jermaine.' He held out his hand for a shake. She ignored it.

'I forgot. We already kissed.' He smiled at her. There was something devilish and infuriating in the curl of his lips and the twinkle of those blue eyes.

Abby shot him a look that might have been something out of a spear gun with multiple barbs. 'Who invited you into my life?'

'I thought you'd be pleased.'

'You're Jess's brother?'

He nodded. 'Older and wiser,' he said.

'Where the hell is Jess?'

'If I had to guess, somewhere in a studio out in West L.A.'

'He made a deal to be here,' she said. 'I gave him tickets and told him I'd pay him.'

'Well, now you can pay me.'

'That's not the deal.'

'O.K. We'll go to Carla tonight and tell her I'm not really Gable Cooper. He's really my brother out in Hollywood, but he had a conflict, and couldn't . . .'

'Shut up,' she said. 'Let me think.' She thought for a moment, picking at the words out of his mouth.

'What conflict?' She was talking about Jess again. She wanted to know the details, the crisis that had led him to back out in order to measure it. Maybe it was true, in which case she might trust Jack a little more. Maybe the man was in the hospital half dead.

'He calls me in the middle of the night,' said Jack, 'and gets me outta bed. "Hey bro, is that you?" Who else would it be at that hour? That's Jess,' said Jack.

'Listen, he says, I got something for you. Now mind you, Jess's voice on the other end is sounding frantic at this point. I ask him what time it is. He tells me ten-thirty. I look at my clock, it's after one in the morning. Jess says it's only ten-thirty out there. I tell him, Yeah well, that's the funny thing about the sun and the rotation of the earth.'

'Has all of this got a point?' said Abby.

'I'm getting to it. He tells me he has got a phone call from an advertising firm late last night, I guess after you guys talked and you'd left. He didn't know what to do, so he calls me. He says this guy, this producer, is putting together a major campaign for a coffee company. One of those continuing soaps. You know the kind. Will she take it straight up or with cream, and will he do her doggie-style while she's loading the Mr Coffee.'

Abby looked at him with disapproval.

'Jess's words. I swear. That's what he said to me on the phone.' He held up two fingers like the Cub Scout salute. 'He's a little crude sometimes.'

'Yeah and you think it's cute.'

Jack gave her a sheepish grin that said she was probably right.

'So what about this thing? This ad?'

'Anyway, he tells me they've offered him the part. He says these kind of ads win awards, make careers. I say, yeah, right, Golden Globe. He says, no, no. The last two, the girl and guy who did these, are now doing appearances on *Good Morning America*.'

'That's why he's not here?' said Abby.

'Yeah. He said they were gonna start shooting in the morning. He had to be there. Then he tells me about your problem. And here I am.'

'My problem?' Abby looked at him like Vesuvius

135

about to erupt. 'My problem is that I trusted that flake of
a brother of yours, some jock who uses fake leopard
skin to floss the crack of his butt. I should have known
better.'

Jack looked at her. 'Flossed the what?'

'Nevermind.'

'Hey listen. If you guys got it on, it's none of my
business.' He gave her that look, a devilish grin, and
then stared up at the cab's ceiling. 'That slippery brother
of mine.'

'We didn't get it on.'

'Whatever you say.' Jack was still smiling, the devil in
his eyes.

'If you must know, he was doing his laundry and on
the couch was this thing, this . . .' She searched for the
right word and then realized what she was doing. 'Why
am I explaining this to you?'

'I don't know. Do you feel guilty?' Jack could take
irritation to the level of an art form.

'Listen, asshole.' She said it with emphasis.

'This from the woman who was offended by the
mention of doggie-style?'

'Shut up.'

He was still smiling, though he did stop talking.

'And what's this about Joey Jenrico?' she said.

'Who is he, anyway?'

'An acquaintance,' said Abby.

'Yeah, well, with friends like that you don't need any
enemies.'

'Why. What did he do?'

'Seems the film people somehow ran into this guy in
Seattle. They were looking for you. From there it gets a
little hazy. All Carla knows is that somehow they came
away with the impression that he was the author, this

Gable Cooper. And it seems he did nothing to set them straight. Now the folks in Hollywood think they have a deal with him for film rights.'

It was Abby's worse nightmare.

'Not to worry. I took care of it.'

'What did you do? What did you tell her?'

'I told her he was some guy I used to run around with years ago who is now off his nut. That he did drugs in another life and had a bad trip. It's a sad story, but the man now has trouble remembering the number of toes on his feet.'

'Wonderful. So now you've got Gable consorting with drug users.'

'Hey, listen, to these folks that would be a major marketing angle. I could have told her this Joey and I were former lovers and she would have smiled, scheduled us for Oprah, and calculated the audience share.'

She shot him a quick glance.

'I didn't,' he said. He held up a hand. 'So where do we go from here?' he asked.

'For the moment I figure some way to get you out of my life.'

'Well, you can think about it, but for right now, unless you want to throw away a good deal, I think we're joined at the hip as they say.'

'You have a high opinion of yourself. Maybe I don't see you as such a good deal.'

'Oh, I have my qualities. But that's not what I was talking about. That's right. I forget. You didn't hear the rest of it.'

'The rest of what?'

'You never told me who he was. This Jenrico guy.'

'Later. The rest of what?'

'You must have written one hell of a book. Someday

you'll have to tell me how you did it.'

'The rest of what?' She was getting angry again.

'Don't bang your head jumping up in the car, but Carla thinks the whole package, the book rights and film stuff . . .'

'Yes?'

'She thinks it's possible the whole thing, the author's take, could be worth as much as two million dollars.'

CHAPTER
TWELVE

Abby had not yet come down from the psychic buzz, the figures laid on her by Jack in the cab, as she was dialing a number in Seattle on the phone from her hotel room.

Abby had put Jack up in a room down the hall in the hotel for a night until she could think of what to do. While he was waiting for his room to be cleaned, Jack sat sprawled in a chair in the corner munching peanuts from a bag he'd taken out of the snack bar near the television set.

The phone rang twice. 'Starl, Hobbs and Carlton, law offices.'

'Katie. This is Abby. Is Morgan around?' Abby looked at her watch. It was early on the West Coast and she was hoping that Morgan would be there.

'Let me check.' The phone went dead while she was put on hold.

'You never told me who this guy Jenrico was?' said Jack.

'He was married to a friend of mine. He beat the crap out of her and she divorced him. I handled the case.'

'So now he has it in for the two of you.'

'You could say that.'

'How much does he know about the book?'

'Nothing.'

'Well, he must know something if he got the film people to buy into the fact that he wrote it.'

'I don't think he knows anything.'

'What about your friend? His wife. What's her name?'

'Theresa.'

'What does she know?'

'She wouldn't tell him.'

'So she knows you wrote it.'

'Yes, but she wouldn't tell Joey.'

'If she did, or if she does, you're gonna have a problem,' said Jack.

'What's that?'

'He has something to hold over your head that could be worth two million dollars, the truth about the book. If it came out at the wrong time. In the wrong way. That could do some real damage.'

He was right, and if he got to Theresa, it wouldn't take Joey long to figure it out. She was worried about something else, too, but she kept it to herself.

'I guess you think I could do the same thing,' he said.

She looked at him and wondered for a moment if he could read her mind. Before she could speak, the receiver came alive at her ear. It was Morgan's voice, the sound of someone rational whom she knew and trusted. She was beginning to wish she had taken his advice and abandoned the charade with the pen name, or used Morgan, regardless of his age. She was beginning to wonder if age was really an issue. Jack was forty-three. She'd demanded a look at his driver's license in the cab. There was only two years difference between him and Morgan. But there was something else. Like Redford, Connery, and Newman, Jack had something special.

'Good to hear your voice,' he said. 'How's it going back there?'

'As they say, there's good news and bad news,' said Abby. 'The good news first. The book is worth a lot of money.'

'How much?'

'Are you sitting down?' she asked him.

'Yes.'

'I'm hearing millions.'

'A million dollars?'

'With an "s" on the end,' said Abby.

There was stone silence from Morgan's end of the line, followed by a long low whistle. 'You're kidding?'

'Not unless the agent is blowing smoke.'

'Well, that's wonderful. Hey, when you're famous, can I tell people that I once knew you when?'

'You can tell them you still know me.'

'Can I borrow money?'

'That we'll have to talk about.'

He laughed and so did she.

'Now for the bad news. Some flake has bulldozed his way into my life and now has Owens believing he is Gable Cooper.'

Jack looked at her from under arched eyebrows. A hurt expression.

'Who?' asked Spencer.

'His name's Jack. The brother of another flake. The guy I talked to down in L.A.'

'The Flake Brothers. I like that,' said Jack. 'It has a kinda ring to it. We could take it on the road. Maybe do a little leopard skin butt flossing.'

Abby turned her back to him. He thought she was

pissed. She was having a hard time keeping from laughing.

'Do you want me to deal with him?' said Morgan.

'No. No. Besides, what can you do from there?'

'I could fly out.'

'No. There's no point. I'm just gonna have to work it out somehow. Did you get the copyright done yet?'

'I'm working on it.'

'When will it be filed?'

'I'll get it finished tonight and file it overnight express in the morning. I'll call the registry at the Library of Congress and see if we can get it expedited. We should have the registration back in a week, maybe ten days.' Ordinarily it wouldn't be a problem. A common law copyright would be in effect the moment Abby typed the manuscript and put her name on it. The problem here was that her name was not on it.

'Good. The publisher won't have time to file in Gable Cooper's name before then. They don't even have a contract yet.'

Given what was happening, the copyright was Abby's life line. Without it, plus dealing with the enormous sums that were now being discussed and with a man she didn't know and might not be able to control, she would have no evidence of ownership. At least she had Morgan.

'Listen, I'm worried about you.' Morgan sounded concerned. 'I shouldn't have let you go back there alone.'

'I'm a big girl.'

'I know. But if anything happens to you . . .'

'What's going to happen? It's fine. It's just that I'm tired.' Things hadn't worked out the way she thought they would. Abby didn't like surprises, and Jack was a big one.

'There's one other thing,' said Abby. 'Do you remember Theresa?'

'Sure.'

'You remember Joey, her former husband?'

'Never met him. But how could I forget?'

'Somehow he managed to get his nose under this particular tent.'

'What do you mean?'

'I mean the book. Somehow he found out about it and managed to hook up with some people interested in film rights.'

'There's a film?'

'There's serious interest. It's part of the millions,' she told him.

'Jesus. This thing really is exploding. Watch yourself with this guy. What's his name?'

'Jack Jermaine,' said Abby. 'But right now I need help with Joey. I've got to get him out of the middle of this and put the fear of God into him. Any ideas?'

'I can put an investigator on him. Have him talk to the guy and tell him if he doesn't stay out of it we'll sue him for interference with contractual relations. Maybe threaten to have him arrested for fraud.'

'The first one won't mean anything to Joey. He doesn't have a pot to piss in. But jail. That's something Joey understands. Your investigator, do you have somebody who's large?' said Abby.

'I can find somebody. Why? Is the guy dangerous?'

'Usually just to women. But you never know.'

'I'll make sure our man has a firearm permit. That he's packing,' said Morgan.

'It's probably unnecessary, but just to be safe,' said

Abby. 'I'll call you tomorrow.'

'Take care of yourself. And Abby. Be careful with this guy.'

Abby looked at Jack, lounging in the arm chair, his leg thrown lazily over the arm, tossing peanuts into the air and catching them in his mouth like a trained seal.

'I will,' she said. 'Good-bye,' and hung up.

'You have a choice,' she told him.

Abby and Jack sat in a coffee shop in the lobby of an office building a block from Carla Owens's office. It was eight o'clock in the morning. They had an hour before she and Jack were to appear in Carla's office and Jack was supposed to sign the agency agreement. Abby had made a decision.

'You can either do as I say, or I'm prepared to come clean with Owens now, tell her everything, that I wrote the book, that I own the rights, and have her throw your ass down the back stairs.'

Before he could speak, she added, 'I know the book may not be worth as much if she finds out. But I'm prepared to take that risk.'

'Are you?'

'Yes.' Abby was going to set the rules now. She had no intention of allowing Jack to call the shots. He had already pushed his way too far into the deal by talking to Owens without Abby being present the day before. She was not going to have it happen again.

'Are you in or out?' she asked. Moment of truth.

He took her measure with a calculating look. 'What's my cut?'

'I thought you talked to your brother?'

'I did. But we didn't discuss money.'

'You came all this way and you didn't discuss money?

144

You're not interested in how much you're going to be paid?'

'Part of me is,' he said. 'The mercenary part.'

'And the other part?'

He thought for a moment. 'I suppose you'd have to call that curiosity, mixed with a little envy.'

She looked at him, a question mark.

'I wanted to see exactly how they publish a big book.'

'How did you know it was going to be big?'

'As soon as Jess told me the story line, read me the opening on the phone, I had a hunch.'

'And where did you gain this remarkable sense for commercial fiction?'

'Maybe I was born with it.'

'Maybe you ought to be a writer.'

'I am. I've got a chest full of finished manuscripts.'

'You'll have to show them to me sometime.'

'I've got a drawer filled with tattered rejection letters that go along with them.' He didn't tell her how the letters came to be tattered.

Abby could have lied to him. She could have told him that his compensation would be five percent of whatever she got; her original offer to Jess. But it was not the figure Jess had finally negotiated. She looked into Jack's blue eyes, the tanned face. If anything, he was better-looking than Jess, rugged and more mature. And there was something else. It wasn't so much an air of mystery as it was a look of danger. Jess was an Adonis, good-looking, but a child. Jack had some wear on him, a sort of lived-in look that you didn't get with a model. It showed in the craggy lines of his face, and the steely gaze with which he held her eyes at this moment. You had to wonder what other things these eyes had seen. Peering out from a television screen, or from the back of a novel's dustcover, it was the look to launch a million-dollar book, and Abby knew it.

'If you do everything I say. Do a good job. Play the role. Become Gable Cooper.' She looked into his eyes. 'I'll pay you ten percent of everything I get.'

'That's very generous,' said Jack. 'And I want you to know that I appreciate your honesty.'

'What do you mean?'

'That you didn't try to cheat me. To pay me less that you offered Jess, cuz maybe you're pissed or something.'

'I thought you didn't talk to him about money.'

'I lied,' he laughed. 'But I really do appreciate your own sense of ethics. That's really special.'

'Give me a break.' She got up and started to walk away from the table.

'Where are you going?'

'To tell Carla that I wrote the book.'

'Wait a minute. I didn't say I wouldn't do it.'

'Well I just did,' said Abby.

'Listen, I'm sorry. It was a joke. I give up.' He held both hands in the air like she had a gun. 'Don't throw this away. You'd be out of your mind.'

'You think you're that valuable?'

'Well . . .' He thought about it for a second. 'Yeah.'

'No one will ever accuse you of modesty.' She was still walking at a good clip. Abby reached the counter of the coffee shop, handed the girl the check and three dollars, and didn't wait for the change. She was out the door with Jack on her heels.

'Listen. You're making a big mistake.'

'No, I made a big mistake when I got involved with your brother and ended up with you.' She stopped and turned and faced him on the cold sidewalk near an intersection. 'Listen. I don't know when you're lying and when you're telling the truth. And when I have to trust somebody in a situation like this, that's a real problem. You may consider it funny. I don't.'

'I was only testing you.'

'Well, I don't like to be tested. I thought maybe we had something in common. That you were a writer. Unpublished, but still a writer.'

'That part was true. Scout's honor. I can show you the manuscripts. In fact I'd love you to read them.'

'In my spare time,' said Abby.

'I mean it. Listen. You can pay me five percent. That's what you wanted to pay Jess.'

She looked at him, wondering where the hook was.

'I don't want to see you lose this,' he said. 'How often does a deal like this come along? You've written an incredible novel. All the ducks lined up. How often do you think that happens?'

Abby had thought about it a lot in the last two days. 'Not very often,' she said.

'Once in a lifetime, if you're lucky,' said Jack. 'Do you think it will happen to you again?'

She looked at him but didn't answer.

'Don't count on it,' he told her. He sounded like the voice of experience. 'Do you think you'll ever be able to produce a book like this again?'

Before she could speak, he put his hand to her mouth. 'Don't answer that. Anybody who's ever put a word on paper would say no.'

He was right. It was the insecurity of the writer.

'Commercial or literary, it doesn't matter,' he told her. 'Whenever you've written something good, that you think is really good, your mind says, "I will never be able to do that again." Now maybe you will. But at that moment of completion, your mind says "no." Until you actually do it again, you will believe it is impossible. And if your mind says no I can't do it, too often and for too long, you never will.

'The good news is that for the moment you don't have to worry about it. What you have to worry about is not allowing these people to squander what you've written. Because that's what they'll do if you walk away from this thing now. Like abandoning a child,' said Jack. 'They will leave it to die.'

'What do you mean?'

'You might have been able to do it before, to come clean, to tell them the truth. But believe me, if you tell them now, they'll be offended that they were taken in, and embarrassed to let the world know it. They will take your confession as a sign of weakness, that you had 'em by the throat and lacked the courage to finish the kill. The law of the corporate jungle,' said Jack. 'They will tell you not to worry. They're gonna blow it out, take it to the top. All the while they'll be movin' on to the next project, somebody else's big book.'

He understood much more than she thought.

'You've been published before,' said Jack. 'How did it feel?'

She gaze him a quizzical laugh. 'Five thousand copies,' she said. 'There were heads of lettuce that had a longer shelf life than my books.'

'Right,' said Jack. 'And they'll do it to you again if you let them. They'll tell you they're doing a two-hundred-and-fifty-thousand-dollar ad campaign, and they'll do ten. They'll put your book on the street and if it doesn't grow legs and walk on its own in three days they'll pull the plug and watch it die. Even if the book starts to take off, they'll cap your press runs to avoid taking returns.'

Returns were the curse of the industry, stores sending back unsold books to the publisher for a refund, an age-old industry practice. Publishers, the smart ones, protected themselves by capping the numbers that they shipped. A store would order twenty and receive five and the author was never told.

'And they're going to do all of this to me because your face is not on the cover?' said Abby.

'No, because you blinked. Because they'll know you didn't have the courage to reel them into the boat when you had your book in their gill. If you pull out now and tell them the truth, oh, they'll publish your book. But they won't back it. You've passed the point of no return, Abby. You've taken a chance. If you don't finish it, they'll finish you.'

He was right, and Abby knew it. The first battle of publishing, the only one that really mattered, was with your own publisher. Win that, and the war could be over.

They stood in silence, the winds whistling through the canyons of Madison Avenue, people milling past them on the sidewalk. Jack held Abby's gaze for a long moment, their eyes locked. She couldn't be sure if she could trust this man, a stranger she didn't even know. But there was an ultimate truth to his words that sad experience had taught her she could not deny.

Jack left New York that day. Before he did, there was a tussel in Owens's office, hard-core dealing between Abby and Owens over the terms of the agency contract.

Carla had given Jack her standard form; in effect a personal services contract for life. Carla would have a piece of all of his future works even if he left her at some point and hired another agent to sell them. It wasn't until they were headed for the door, refusing to sign, that Owens opened another drawer on her desk and pulled out the real thing. It was what lawyers call an 'at will' contract. She was free to leave them and they were free to fire her at any time. It was the only thing Abby would let Jack sign. Beyond this, Carla got ten percent of everything she sold, except for foreign rights where she would take ten, and the foreign agents she employed would get ten. It was standard fare. In the end, Carla learned one thing: Abby knew more than she let on about the business of publishing.

After signing at Owens's office, Jack begged off. He'd had enough of business, told them he had things to take care of from his trip to Mexico, and asked Abby if she would stay behind to work out details with Carla for the sale of book rights. After all, she was the lawyer.

It was their plan. He told Carla he was going back to Seattle to write. Then he flew to Coffin Point. Inside the old plantation house he unpacked his luggage and repacked it with clean underwear and clothing, checked his mail, and dialed a phone number in California.

'Skytell pager. Please leave your message.'

He punched in his phone number and hung up. Then he grabbed his bags and went downstairs. In his study, he gathered a brightly colored box from one of the express overnight carriers. Jack had an account. It was red and blue, about the size of a shirt box. Jack had used them to send manuscripts to publishers and agents in the past, as well as a few other things. He assembled the box, and filled out the packing slip addressing it to himself at a hotel in Seattle for morning delivery the next day. He had made the reservations the night before from New York. As he was finishing the slip, the phone rang.

'Hello.'

'Jack. How'd it go?' It was Jess in Los Angeles. He'd gotten the message from his pager.

'Hey, you know when you called I was a little pissed off,' said Jack.

'Yeah, I know. Interfered with your beauty sleep. You gotta get a life, brother. Come out here and party. We don't hit the sheets 'til the sun's peaking over the mountains. And California girls *are* sweeter.'

'Pop was right. You never would have made it in the military,' said Jack.

'Hey, let me sleep 'til noon with a blonde in my bunk. I don't think that's unreasonable.'

'You're soft, Jess.'

'Well, Semper Fi to you, too, but let's stick to the subject at hand. What'd you think of her, this Abby chick?'

'Not bad. Fix her hair a little and get some decent clothes.'

'That's not what I meant. This stuff with her book?'

'That's why I called. I'm headed out to Seattle. There's a loose end out there I have to take care of.'

'Geez, you're really into this stuff. I hope she's paying you for all this.'

'Some things you do as a labor of love. Someday you'll learn that.'

Jess laughed.

'She went weak on me yesterday. Got scared and wanted to pull the plug on her plan. But I saved her from herself.'

'I'll bet,' said Jess. 'Oh please, Jack. Take me. Ravage me.' His voice played a high falsetto and then he laughed. 'And I thought you were just doing this as a favor to me? You dog. So is she good in the sack?'

'I thought maybe you could tell me.'

'What are you talkin' about?'

'Leopard skin butt flossing,' said Jack.

'What? Aw no. What did she tell?'

'She doesn't kiss and tell.'

'Whatever it was it's bullshit. I never touched her.'

'Don't bother, Jess. She told me all about it.'

'Hey, listen.'

'She even told me about that little birthmark. The one on your thigh.'

'Hey, now I know you're lying.'

'If she's with child, we'll know who to call,' said Jack.

'Right. Well it sounds like you had your chance to pull out . . .'

'You should really watch your choice of words, brother.'

'Cut it out. You know what I'm sayin'. If she wanted to pull the plug on the book, you coulda gotten out. Why didn't you?'

'Don't want to.'

'Why not?'

'Jess. Let me give a little advice. The next time you hand something like this off to somebody else, you might check to see what it's worth.'

CHAPTER
THIRTEEN

'How were we supposed to know?' said Salzman. 'We went to the woman's house and this guy answers the door. You tell me?'

'You get some identification?' said Weig.

'What, you think he's gonna be packing a driver's license in his pen name? He told us he was Gable . . .'

'That's not exactly how it happened,' said Sidner.

Salzman shot him a look, but it didn't deter the kid. Sidner figured he was the fall guy if Weig decided he wanted a head to roll. Salzman and Weig went way back.

The two of them were in front of Mel Weig's desk trying to explain how they'd cut a deal for twenty-five grand with Joey Jenrico who'd never read a book, much less written one.

'As I recall,' said Sidner, 'you asked him if he was Gable Cooper . . .'

'And he said yes,' said Salzman.

'No. He said, "It depends on who's asking." '

'Well, that's as good as saying yes.'

'Stop! Enough!' Weig slammed the desk with his open palm. 'For your information. This Jenrico is a high-school

153

dropout with a criminal record and three misdemeanor convictions. He probably has the I.Q. of a brick. What that says about the two of you I'm not exactly sure.'

'Listen, Mel. No money changed hands. No harm done,' said Salzman.

'Not exactly,' said Weig. 'The harm is that Carla now has the real author signed, and she's on the war path. His name is Jack Jermaine.'

Salzman and Sidner looked at each other.

'I thought you said he was a bestseller.' Salzman tried to deflect a little of Weig's heat toward Sidner.

'It's what I was told,' said the kid.

'Well, that piece of misinformation could have cost us a bundle,' said Salzman.

'It still may. Carla knows we tried to go around her,' said Weig.

'Is she angry?' asked Salzman.

'A hornet with its stinger up your ass is angry. Carla's dripping malice like acid, and looking for some way to get it into my eyes.'

'You don't think she'd try to take the book to another studio?' said Salzman.

'She's making noises about some independent producers. She wants blood, and we may have to pay her the big bucks just to soothe her.'

'Why, if nobody ever heard of this guy Jermaine?' said Salzman.

'It's not gonna matter,' said Weig. 'Word is the buzz is on. Carla's already got the network morning shows,' said Weig. 'They're already lining up for this guy Jermaine.'

Her name was Sandra or Sally, or something else that started with an 'S.' Joey couldn't remember. He didn't much care. All that mattered for the moment was that she was down to a pair of leather bikini panties lined with jade colored beads, standing bare-breasted at the foot of his bed. Joey stood in the doorway to the kitchen watching her from behind.

When she turned and saw him she stuck her finger inside the beaded fringe at the front of her panties and studied him with wistful eyes. 'How do you like them? They've glove leather,' she said. 'Made by Indians in Arizona.'

'Them Indians do some fine work,' said Joey. 'Real crafty, if you know what I mean.' He smiled at her. Joey'd found her at a bar that was a hangout for the Western set, doing line dancing in a skirt that showed her cheeks whenever she stomped to the rhythm. Indian panties or no, in Joey's mind he was about to hang another beaver pelt on his own lodge pole. But before he did he wanted one more beer.

He turned into the dark kitchen and opened the refrigerator door. He was concentrating on the last bottle of Bud at the back of the shelf, his head lost inside the ice box, when suddenly it slammed closed, catching his head like a vice at the ears. If it hadn't been for the rubber insulation on the old door, it might have cracked Joey's head like a nut. As it was, he was on his knees, his head locked inside with the light on, dazed and wondering what he was doing on the shelf next to the mayonnaise.

With his knee still wedged against the door for leverage, Jack reached around inside of Joey's belt and grabbed the revolver. Joey'd worn it in the open for the girl's benefit once they'd gotten home.

Jack looked at it with an appraising eye. Thirty-eight Smith & Wesson.

'Nice piece, but you gotta be able to get it out of your

pants,' said Jack. He tossed it onto the kitchen table. It landed with a thud. Then he pulled his own, the nine-millimeter Beretta, eased up on the refrigerator door, and grabbed Joey by the collar of his shirt.

Before he knew what was happening, Joey was almost standing on his feet, with his ass pushed into the open refrigerator, looking at the cleft in Jack's chin.

'Now this is real smooth. No cylinder to get caught on your belt. And this part fits real nicely up your nose.' Jack pushed so that the half inch of barrel that protruded out from the end of the Beretta's slide was actually stretching one of Joey's nostrils.

'Now shall we talk?'

'Gnu na fuck are gnu?' It sounded like Joey had a truck parked up his sinuses.

'No, I don't think we'll start with that.' Jack turned and saw the girl standing in the doorway wearing Indian craft work and not much else.

'Could you give us a minute, sweetheart?' Jack smiled at her.

Looking into his eyes lighted only by the glow of the open refrigerator door, Joey's ass pushed halfway into it, it was as if she didn't even notice the gun. She offered a lustful look and melted her body against the frame of the door as if she wasn't going anywhere.

'Fine, you can stay if you like, but don't interrupt.' Jack turned his attention back to Joey. 'Now where were we? Oh yeah. We were about to discuss you. Why you like to beat on women, and a certain game you decided to play with my book.'

Joey's eyes got big.

'Oh. I forget to introduce myself. I'm Gable Cooper. I understand you were trying to steal my book?'

Joey started to shake his head and suddenly found it

caught between hard steel, the door of the freezer compartment in back, and Jack's gun up his nose in the front.

'Maybe we should try the other side.' With Joey's head pressed back, Jack had a clear line of sight. 'Looks like you've had some shit up there before. Maybe we should clean it out.' Jack clicked off the safety and cocked the pistol.

'Anyway, where were we? Oh yeah. My book. They were gonna have an investigator talk to you about a law suit or a criminal thing, you know, bring in the lawyers. All that kinda stuff. But you know Joey . . . Can I call you Joey?'

Jenrico nodded, as much as he could with a gun up his nose.

'Joey, it's my view that we're already too heavily lawyered. We live in a society that's far too litigious. What do you think?'

Joey looked at him, wondering what the word meant, and when he didn't nod in agreement, Jack did it for him with the muzzle of the gun.

'I mean look at O.J. A year watching strutting lawyers diddle around on television, and thump their dicks on the table. They put all the afternoon soaps in the toilet, ratings a cat wouldn't shit on, and when it's all over, what do we have? A bunch of unemployed actors, and books out our ass telling us what went wrong with the criminal justice system. Now I ask you, is that any way to run a society?'

Joey looked at him down the business end of the pistol and found himself shaking his head.

'Yeah. That's what I thought. Oh boy. I see you got chocolate-covered macadamias, the kind in the little jar. You know those are my favourites. Do you mind?'

Joey shook his head, the barrel of the gun still up his nose. With his free hand Jack took the jar off the top shelf of the refrigerator. Then not bothering to set the safety on the Beretta, he held the jar of nuts in one hand and fought with the lid, using three fingers of the other while the fourth slid around on the trigger of the pistol. The gun went sideways at a cocked angle and pushed hard so that Joey now looked like some pug-nosed boxer. He winced in anticipation, his eyes glued to the hammer at the rear of gun. Joey's life was at the mercy of a metal spring.

The girl in the doorway was in a trance, watching like it was some drama on the wide screen.

'You know you really shouldn't keep these things in the ice. Tends to make the nuts go soft.'

The only nuts Joey was worried about at the moment were not in that jar, but they *were* shriveling up.

'Oh and you got peppers. The kind in that vinegar stuff. Are they hot?'

Joey nodded.

Jack picked up the jar and was back at it with his fingers. Even with the cold air from the fridge, Joey had pimples of sweat forming on his forehead.

'Anyway, to make a long story short. I thought if we just took the time and talked we'd come to some common understanding here. You know they all told me you were an asshole, but somehow I knew you'd be a reasonable guy. There's something about getting to know someone up close and personal that makes even the biggest shit in the world seem human. What do you think?'

Joey's eyes wandered for a moment to the Smith & Wesson on the table, and then to the girl standing nearly naked in the doorway. Neither offered much comfort at the moment. Sue or Sharon or whatever her name was was actually giggling. Joey would kick the crap out of her when this asshole left. He felt the muzzle press hard against the septum of his nose, bringing his eyes off his dreams and back to Jack.

'You're letting your mind wander.'

Jack held up a pepper from the jar, dripping its juice down the front of Joey's shirt. 'Want one?'

Joey shook his head. Jack stuck it between his lips anyway, and pushed with his finger until it slid all the way inside. 'Chew. That's it. Taste good? Here, have another.' He stuffed two more in.

'I don't like the hot ones,' said Jack. 'They make my eyes water.'

Joey chewed carefully so as not to upset the cannon up his nose. He was getting cross-eyed looking at it.

'You know these nuts aren't very good,' said Jack. 'Maybe next time I come over you could have a fresh jar? Keep 'em in the cupboard,' said Jack.

Joey nodded.

'Oh Jeez, where's my manners? You could probably use something to wash that down.' He put the peppers jar down on the shelf and took the bottle of beer, popped the cap, and stuck the neck of the bottle halfway down Joey's throat, watching the bubbles come up in the bottle as Joey gagged. 'That's it. Close the mouth. Keep it in there.'

Joey inhaled some beer and a little pepper juice and started to cough. Jack pulled the bottle out of his mouth, sticking it upside down in Joey's belt so that the rest of the ice-cold beer ran down in the inside of Joey's pants.

'There, how's that? Cool you down there, too. Now where were we? Oh yeah. I assume we're not going to have any more trouble over this film stuff, are we?'

Joey shook his head quickly. He was getting the hang of it now, like one of those applause signs on a T.V. show. His nose was running and his eyes were beginning to water from the acid in the pepper.

'Want another?'

Joey shook his head.

'No, I wouldn't want to get rust all over my gun,' said Jack. 'And the girls, Ms Chandlis and the former Mrs Joey. What do you think I should tell them?'

Joey gave him a shrug with his shoulders.

'Maybe I should tell them not to worry cuz they're never gonna see you again?'

Joey gave him a look, not exactly certain what that meant.

'Or maybe I could tell them that nobody's ever going to see you again?'

He knew what that meant and shook his head vigorously.

'You know it has been delightful,' said Jack 'but I think we're gonna have to continue this at a later time.' He looked over at the girl and then whispered up close in Joey's ear. 'Joey. I think you must live right. I mean, with the audience and all.' Jack nodded toward the girl. 'Otherwise no telling what could have happened. Good night.'

Lowering the gun from Joey's nose, Jack took him by the lapel of his shirt and pulled him forward hard. At the same time, Jack threw his shoulder with all of his weight into the refrigerator door. The corner of the door caught Joey just above the bridge of the nose and with a thud Jenrico went to the floor, out cold.

Jack turned to the girl. 'You oughtta get some clothes on, sweetheart, you're gonna catch cold. I'd go if I were you. Something tells me he's not gonna be good company tonight.'

'Carla, what are you telling me?' They were on the phone, Bertoli and Owens.

'Alex, it's not like you didn't expect this. Now be honest. Did you really think I would bring you a book this hot for an outright purchase without testing the market?'

'I thought we had a deal?' Bertoli was using his hurt voice, the one he employed to spawn guilt in others. With Carla it didn't work.

'But how do I know what he's worth?' said Carla. 'Unless I test the market.' What she was talking about was an auction for Gable Cooper's book done by telephone after copies of the manuscript were sent to every large publishing house in New York. Bertoli knew that this could drive the price substantially higher. Bertoli had a problem, a gaping hole in his Summer list. The ABA convention was looming. If he was going to move, he had to do it now. Time was running out.

To this point he had been banking that as soon as Cooper signed with Owens, she would deliver him on a platter to Big-F. Though she was right, knowing Carla as he did, Alex figured there would be some expensive detour along the way.

'I told you we would pay a million dollars for the story, advance against royalties,' said Bertoli. 'What do you want? He's not a bestseller. He's untried. It's a big gamble. The book may fall flat on its face.'

'You don't believe that any more than I do,' said Carla.

'You know as well as I do that even the hottest story requires a hundred things to go right in order to reach the top of the list. Most bestsellers get thirty of them, if they are lucky,' said Alex.

'I'm sorry you have such a pessimistic view of things.' She reminded him that of the hundred things, this one already had the big one: the prospect of a hot movie deal with a blockbusting star to open it. Mel Weig had been on the phone all morning pleading for the rights and begging her not to take the book to another producer. He was at three million and counting. It was already a record for an unknown writer.

'I've already told you, Alex. You can set the floor. A million dollars.' What she meant was that if nobody came in above a million, Alex and Big-F would get the book for that price. Carla was busy turning his top-dollar offer into a minimum bid. She would then release the news on the movie millions and the land rush would be on. Bertoli and Big-F would be killed in the stampede and he knew it.

'Never,' he told her. 'Won't go for a floor,' he said.

'Fine, you don't want the floor, we'll go elsewhere.'

'I didn't say that. What do you want, Carla? You want a million and a half, fine I'll go a million and a half.'

'No, Alex. You know I think you truly believe I'm trying to gouge you.'

'Carla, how could I believe that?' His voice dripped with sarcasm.

'I just think I owe it to my client to find out the market value of his book.'

'And your ten percent wouldn't have anything to do with it?'

'Business is business,' said Carla. It was true that agents and publishers were there every day. The authors came and went. Usually in the tussle of business, the thought of future deals on other books and the requirements of good will would bring an agent to their senses, cause them to stop before they pushed for absolute top dollar. But it wasn't often that an agent saw a manuscript as hot as this one – perhaps once, twice if you were lucky, in a lifetime.

'Fine. Two million,' said Alex.

'Alex, you make me feel awful, but I told you. I can't.' It was going better than she'd expected. But then Bertoli knew as well as she did that the Cooper manuscript had one other thing going for it. If it worked, it would establish a new genre. If there was a way to reach the big time, that was it. Ludlum did it in the '70s with the international thriller; Stephen King in the '80s with horror; and Grisham later with legal thrillers. Each in their own day had put a new twist on an old genre and ridden the wave of their invention to the top. Now it was Gable Cooper's turn. The irony was that the mania of female revenge, the new genre, should be coined by a man. Carla had thought about this and whether it was a problem. She dismissed it when she saw Gable Cooper in the flesh.

'What do you want, Carla, my blood?'

What is it worth? she thought.

'It's against my better judgment,' she said, 'but four and it's yours.'

'Four million! You're out of your mind.'

'I guess we'll have to see.'

'That's crazy.'

'Fine, we'll see what it brings on the open market.'

'Three,' said Bertoli. 'And we get a solid option on his next book.'

Like a game of chess, it was the price Carla already had in mind. 'We keep foreign rights.' She spoke before Bertoli could collect the rest of the pieces. She would sell these, translations rights around the world, for another cool million.

'You really want to cut the heart out of me,' he said.

'Do we have a deal, Alex?'

'Deal.'

'Then smile.' Even though she couldn't see him through the phone line, she knew his face was a grimace at this moment. The acid would be churning in Bertoli's stomach for the next year until he earned back his three-million-dollar nut. The two-million-dollar package for book and film rights that she'd told Jack and Abby about was suddenly looking like six. Carla had learned the art of the deal. First rule: never oversell your own client.

A bby hadn't heard from Theresa since arriving in New York, and there was a lot of news. She wanted to tell her about the sale of the book rights. She was burning up inside. She had to tell somebody. Theresa and Morgan Spencer were the only ones who knew the truth, the only ones she felt she could share it with. Morgan wasn't home.

She dialed the number of Orange County, the friends Terry was staying with somewhere out near Anaheim. A woman answered the phone.

'Hello.' It wasn't Terry's voice.

'Hello. I'm looking for Theresa Jenrico.'

'Oh, Terry's not here.'

'Is she out?'

'No. She left this morning.'

Abby was surprised.

'Where did she go?'

'Home, I think. Said she had some things to take care of back in Seattle.'

Now Abby was worried. Theresa was supposed to be there for two more days when they would both return to Seattle and hook up at the airport before returning home.

'Is there a problem?' said the woman.

'No.' Abby thanked the woman and hung up. With Theresa back in town and Joey on the prowl, Abby was worried. She punched in the phone number to her house in Seattle. It rang and rang. There was no answer. She wondered why the answering machine didn't pick up.

CHAPTER

FOURTEEN

It was dark and drizzling by the time the cab driver dropped Theresa and her luggage at the curb in front of Abby's house. The driver slammed the trunk closed, pocketed his fare, and before she knew it she was standing there alone staring at the shimmering red of his taillights as they turned the corner. One of her suitcases was resting in a puddle.

'Thanks, dickhead.' She got a grip and started lugging toward the front door. If she was twenty with big tits and a skirt to her crotch, the driver would have hauled them up the steps with his tongue hanging out. To Theresa, men were all the same: interchangeable assholes. It was just that she couldn't live without them.

She trudged across the wet grass toward the small dark house with its shuttered windows and overgrown lawn. There was something not quite right with the scene she was seeing. It took her a moment, then it dawned; the front porch light was out. She remembered that Abby had made a point of mentioning it. She'd flipped it on when they left for Seattle to get Charlie's credit card. Abby never liked to come home to a dark house. The bulb must have burned out.

She was soaked by the time she reached the porch, her coat flapping in the wind. Once under the cover of the small portico, she took the time to stop and look. There were a few cars parked on the street, but she didn't see Joey's truck. She figured it was safe.

She fumbled with her key in the front door. In the dark it was hard to find the right one and get it in the keyhole. When she finally did, it turned, and the door swung open.

It was pitch black inside. Terry hesitated. For an instant, she thought she saw something move at the far end of the hall. She strained her eyes and tried to cut through the dense blackness. Nothing. Must have been her imagination. Ever since the motel at the airport her nerves were frayed. There was something wild in Joey's eyes that night, something even in his most violent moments she had never seen before, and it scared her. Theresa sensed that if Abby had not been there to stop him that night, Joey would have killed her.

She moved inside the door, lugging the two heavy suitcases. She tried to get beyond the entry in order to close the door behind her. With both hands full she had no chance when her feet hit an immovable object. She went down hard on the wooden floor. Something sharp cut deeply into her knee. She felt a searing pain and lay there shaking as the cold wind from the open door blew up her skirt. Crumpled on the floor she bent to examine her knee, her feet toward the open door. It was then that she saw it; the motion of a shadow on the porch behind her.

It was a late-night session on the speaker phones juggling the numbers, Bertoli at his end, Salzman for the studio in L.A.

Bertoli had made a name for himself not because the books he picked were all successful but because he had a knack for making people remember his successes and forget his failures.

Bertoli already had his people brainstorming. 'The thing with the booksellers convention,' he told Salzman. 'We got an angle. If you can get your network to do a piece on one of their magazine shows to include a segment on books and how they're sold.' The studio was part of a conglomerate that owned a television network.

'Not bad,' said Salzman. 'Maybe we do something like *Forty-eight Hours* with cameras following our author. We could get it to air the week the book hits the stores,' said Salzman. It was a glimpse of the corporate octopus scratching its own back. Both Bertoli and the studio were heavily invested in the book, but Bertoli wanted to control the early publicity to the greater glory of the book. The studio could worry about their film later. The question was how much Bertoli could get them to pony up.

'We do television,' said Bertoli. 'Fifteen- and thirty-second spots in major markets.' The ads would not be long, but they would saturate the airwaves in an opening blitz to drive the book onto the bestsellers list. Then they would pace themselves, clustering ads when the book started to slip to keep it in the public eye and on the list.

'National print ads in New York and L.A., *P.W.*, *Entertainment Weekly*, *People*, maybe *Time* and *Newsweek*,' said Bertoli. 'Not once, but maybe eight or ten times. We'll do teasers in some of the smaller papers. We hit the two coasts hard, and we do a T.V. satellite tour. On the day of publication we do insertions, the first two chapters into selected home editions of the *New York* and

L.A. Times.' What he was talking about was hitting the opinion makers where they lived to create buzz. It didn't matter if they read it, only that they talked about it falling out of their morning papers.

It was a pie-in-the-sky campaign. Why not? As far as Bertoli was concerned, L.A. was paying.

Salzman whistled. 'That's gonna cost a fortune.'

'I figured you guys for a million,' said Bertoli.

'A million!' Salzman was screaming on the other end.

Bertoli reminded him what would happen if the book fell flat. There would be no film. Besides, the studio was getting by cheap. It was going to cost the studio twenty million just to get the star to put his big toe on the set. By Hollywood standards, the book promotion was chump change.

'That reminds me,' said Bertoli. 'Can we use his name? "A major motion picture starring . . ."'

'I don't know.'

'What do you mean you don't know? I thought he was committed?'

'To these people, commitment is an endless courtship. He's a star.'

'So?'

'So they want to be perpetually wooed. The minute they sign on, all the noses in the Western Hemisphere pull out of their assholes. So why sign?'

They thought for a moment, then Salzman spoke. 'Whadda you want to do?'

'We'll use his name, but you don't know about it.'

'He'll sue the shit out of you.'

'Not if it works.'

'And if it doesn't?' said Salzman.

'If it doesn't, you and I are gonna be looking for work. What fool sues the unemployed?'

Theresa exploded in a string of expletives when she saw the cat center itself in the doorway out on the porch. Its long moving shadow cast by the street lights took five years off her life.

It mewed in the open doorway, begging, a plaintive cry about the foul weather.

Theresa let go a huge sigh and started to scratch. She looked at the mangy thing. 'Go. Scat.'

The cat took one look, then moved before she could, slipped through the door, and into the darkness down the hall.

'Shit.'

She reached down with her hand and touched what felt like broken glass. Her knee was bleeding, a jagged edge embedded in it.

She rubbed her fingertips gently over the area and the piece of glass came out. She thought she got most of it. In the dark, she couldn't tell, but there was a warm trickle down her leg to her ankle. She didn't dare crawl. Carefully she got to her feet, one knee bent a little in pain. Then an inch at a time, sliding her shoes on the floor, first one foot then the other, she made it to the wall. Using her hands, she felt around until she found the light switch, flipped it on. Nothing.

She shuffled with her feet down the dark hallway, the cat meowing ahead of her, a feline procession. At one point, it rubbed up against her leg and Theresa kicked at it hard. It wailed and slid halfway down the hall on the hardwood floor like a fluffy hockey puck.

Theresa left the front door open. She could feel the steady breeze down the hall. For some reason it was a source of strength, the open door, an avenue of retreat if she needed it.

Every few steps she was interrupted by objects on the

floor until her feet felt like two ice-breakers moving through a heavy flow. Someone had trashed the place, and Theresa knew who. She was wondering how she would tell Abby.

A few more steps and she was in the kitchen. There was a strong foul odor here and in the dark it took Theresa a moment to place it; rotting produce like a garbage dump. To the cat it was the smell of opportunity. It disappeared.

Theresa found a broom. 'Here kitty.'

A light from the house next door filtered through a window over the sink, and as her eyes adjusted Theresa could see the extent of the damage. There wasn't a dish or glass left that was not in pieces on the floor. Cabinet doors were pulled off their hinges and scattered. The drawers were all pulled out and dumped on the floor. The refrigerator was open, its light either smashed or out, and the contents spilled in a gooey mess. She stepped in what must have been juice. Her shoes clung to the floor like suction cups.

She felt inside the cupboard for the flashlight that wasn't there, then looked on the floor but didn't see it. Theresa tried the light switch on the wall. She knew it was no use. She was right. In the light from next door, she could see that the overhead fixture was still in one piece. It was the only thing in the room Joey had missed. He must have pulled the fuses or damaged the service box. But he'd also screwed up.

There on the floor on top of a pile of refuse was the box of spares, screw-in fuses for the ancient system. She picked it up and carefully stepped over the trash, around the overturned kitchen table. The place had a look of rage about it, like some crazed animal had gone on a rampage.

She kicked a few things out of the way, and the cat scurried out in front of her again. She almost threw the box of fuses at it but stopped herself.

She made her way across the kitchen, and opened the door to the basement. The stairs down were pitch black. She flipped the switch on at the head of the stairs. Sure enough, Joey got them all. She looked back one more time toward the kitchen in hopes that maybe she would see the flashlight or at least a box of matches, anything to light her way down the staircase. There was nothing. She stepped down into the black void, a few more steps, clinging onto the hand railing. She was halfway to the bottom when she looked back and saw the silhouette of the cat staring down at her from the top step.

She felt with her feet as she went, counting the steps. At twelve she hit the landing. She felt her way around the turn and it hit her. There, she could see something, a glow like a red beacon. Theresa froze. At first she thought it was a cigarette. She stared in stark silence for a moment. But it didn't move, and the glow was steady. She couldn't tell how far away it was. She reached out to touch it. In the pitch darkness, with nothing else but the beam of red light. There was no sense of depth.

Then she realized, took a deep breath. It was the tiny light on the lid to the old chest freezer. Joey hadn't gotten all the fuses after all. It didn't illuminate the basement, but still it was a comforting glow.

She felt her way along the concrete wall, and then down again, another smaller flight of stairs. Finally she reached the cement floor of the basement.

Now that she was around the turn in the stairs she couldn't even see the scant light from the open door to the kitchen up top. The electrical service box was mounted somewhere on the wall of the basement near a small wooden work bench. She'd helped Abby change a fuse during a lightning storm a few months earlier.

She felt with her hands, iron tools, a saw hanging on a nail over the bench. She was close. She moved along the bench, ran into the vice bolted to the edge and it drove into her side. Theresa groaned.

She rubbed her ribs, then suddenly felt something press against her leg. She jumped to one side, threw herself against the edge of the work bench, and felt it again. The cat meowed.

'Son of a bitch.' Her heart was pounding. She lashed out with her foot but missed the cat. They could see in the dark. Or was that a wives' tale?

She worked her way to the center of the work bench one more time, leaned over and felt a sharp metal edge with her fingers, a corner. Maybe it was just another tool. Then she felt the small hinged door. She'd found it. It was open.

Blind in the darkness she was afraid to feel inside the box with her hands. She couldn't quite reach. If Joey had removed fuses, her fingers might find an empty socket. Knowing Joey, it was probably what he had in mind.

She felt along the top of the bench. It was clear. Carefully she put one knee onto it and boosted herself up. She opened the box of fuses and removed one. Then, using it like a probe, she found an empty hole and screwed it in. A solid stream of light flickered on somewhere above. It wasn't much, but now she could see the gray outline of the box.

She grabbed another fuse and threaded it in.

The phone rang. She could hear it up in the kitchen. She had just found another empty socket.

Second ring. Third ring. Theresa wondered why the

answering machine didn't pick up. Then she realized its fuse must still be out.

The door above at the head of the stairs suddenly slammed closed.

Plunged into darkness, the noise of the slamming door echoed through the empty basement, the ringing phone upstairs. She nearly fell off the bench. Theresa was shaking, terrified. For an instant, before all light vanished, she actually thought she saw Joey. Tricks the mind will play.

She knelt stone still on top of the bench for several seconds, her hand glued to the fuse already one full turn into the socket. She listened but heard nothing.

It was the wind. It had to be. She should have closed the front door. She could go back up now and do it, but she was so close. The phone stopped ringing. A few fuses and the lights in the basement would come on.

She turned and it seated out, but nothing. She tried another, still no light in the basement. She picked one more fuse. Now she had to reach to the top of the box on the wall. It was awkward from the wooden work bench. Abby could have done it standing on the floor, but Theresa was several inches shorter. She sprawled with her stomach at the edge of the bench, legs dangling, her feet a few inches off the floor. She seated the fuse in the socket. The cat was at her again, rubbing against her feet.

She lashed out kicking, slipped on the wooden bench. The electric flash lit up the basement with an eerie blue glow, the smell of ozone, and the odor of burning flesh.

CHAPTER
FIFTEEN

Salzman was in his office pushing paper and picking sleep from the corner of one eye when the com-line rang.

'Yeah.'

'A Mr Jenrico on one for you.'

'Who?'

'Says his name's Jenrico.'

Salzman thought for a moment. 'I don't know any . ... Wait a second.' The idiot was looking for the contract. Salzman couldn't believe it. What balls.

'Do you want me to tell him you're out?'

'No. No I'll take it.' He sat for a second, then punched the button for line one. 'Hello.'

'This Mr Salzman?'

'Mr Jenrico, how are you?'

'I thought maybe you forgot.'

'How could I forget.' Salzman was smiling so the phone would catch the proper tone, beefing it up.

'Where are you?' He was hoping that Joey was at the studio's front gate where he could let him in, arrest his ass, and charge him with fraud.

'The airport. L.A.,' said Joey. 'I was wondering where

the contract was? Thought maybe we could have a meeting.'

'That's what I figured. There's been a little problem.'

'What's that?'

'Just a slight technical matter,' said Salzman.

'Tell me,' said Joey.

'Seems someone else claims they wrote the book.'

There was a long silence on the other end.

'You there?' said Salzman.

'Yeah. Yeah, I'm here.'

'We don't know what to do about this.'

'They're lying,' said Joey.

'That's what they're saying about you. Lemme ask you a question. We know you've never written a book, but have you ever read one?'

'What are you talkin' about?'

'You can read?'

'Yeah, I can read.'

'Then read my lips,' said Salzman. 'Go fuck yourself,' and he hung up.

'Stupid son of a bitch.' Salzman went back to his papers. Thirty seconds later the com-line rang again.

'Yeah.'

'He's back,' said the receptionist.

Salzman punched the button on line one. 'What part of the message didn't you understand? Lemme explain. You take your dick. You can find that?'

'*You* don't understand. I got somethin' I think you might wanna see.'

'No, you don't understand. I'm not interested in seeing you or anything you have. Whadda you think, we're stupid?'

There was some silence while Joey considered the matter.

'That mean you ain't gonna pay me?'

Salzman couldn't believe it. 'That means if you bother me again I'm gonna take personal pleasure in hunting your ass down and having it committed.'

'That would be a mistake.'

'And why's that?'

'Because you don't know who wrote the book.'

'Oh, we know. You don't have to worry about that.'

'No, you don't,' said Joey.

'The author's name is Jack Jermaine, alias Gable Cooper.' Salzman knew because Weig'd put Jack's picture under the clear acetate cover on his desk blotter as a reminder of how he'd screwed up.

'You're wrong,' said Joey.

'Listen, I'm sorry, but I don't have time for more bullshit.'

'No. It's the truth. He didn't write the book and I can prove it.'

'And how would you know that?'

'Because I have the original copy,' said Joey. 'The thing. The manuscript. At the house after you guys left. I looked and I found it. Somebody else wrote it.'

Salzman had visions of Joey typing, hunt-and-peck. 'Now lemme guess. You want to sell us this piece of shit manuscript?'

'I was figuring if you didn't mind.'

'Blow it out your ass,' said Salzman.

'Guess I'll have to take it to the magazine,' said Joey.

'What are you talking about?'

'He was real interested. Just as soon as I told him your studio was involved. I sent 'em your card.'

'What magazine?'

'*The Intruder*.'

The mention of the name raised bumps on the back of Salzman's neck.

'They're interested. They want to meet with me,' said Joey. 'That's why I'm down here.'

The Intruder was the kind of magazine that hung on the fringes of entertainment, pissed off stars by reporting that they gave birth to cosmic aliens. To call it a tabloid was an insult to yellow journalism.

'They pay pretty good,' said Joey.

'What did you tell 'em?'

'Nothing. Yet.' It was Joey's turn to smile.

Salzman was already in the dog house with Weig. He was responsible for Jenrico getting in the middle. Maybe it was bullshit. But what if he was telling the truth? What if he did have information and they were being scammed? It was the kind of story *The Intruder* would love, and not the kind of buzz the studio wanted. If there was substance, other papers might pick it up. The star would get cold feet. Three million bucks for film rights down the tubes. And Weig would blame it all on Salzman.

'How do I know you're telling the truth?'

'Show me the color of your money,' said Joey. 'We can meet and I'll show you what I got.'

Shit. Salzman thought it but didn't say it. Another meeting with the idiot.

'How much?'

Joey thought for a second. 'Same as the last time. Twenty-five thousand.'

'That's when you were writing the book,' said Salzman.

'How much you willing to pay?' said Joey.

'Two thousand, if your information is good and what you have is real.' Salzman was going to have to dig into his personal savings. He had no intention of telling Mel

Weig anything, not until he had a chance to look at whatever it was Jenrico was peddling.

'O.K., I'll come to the studio.'

'No.' Salzman thought for a moment. 'I want to meet with you, but only in Seattle.' He had no intention of letting Joey anywhere near the studio.

'Why do that? I'm already down here,' said Joey.

'I'll wire you some money. A couple hundred. Show of good faith,' said Salzman. Anything to keep Joey at arm's length. 'The Red Lion by SeaTac airport. You know where it is?'

'Yeah.'

Salzman looked at his calendar. He was booked solid with meetings. He would have to juggle. 'Next Thursday afternoon. Two o'clock. Come to the white courtesy phone in the lobby and ask for me by name. They'll put you through to my room. And bring the stuff. The manuscript. And don't even think about copying it.'

'You bring the money,' said Joey. 'And wire me something.'

He never got an answer because Salzman hung up.

Abby went stand-by on a late night flight, New York to Seattle with a stop in St Paul.

She tried to snooze, propped her head against the window on one of those little pillows, and covered herself with a blanket. The rumble of the engines would ordinarily put her to sleep, but tonight she was immune. She closed her eyes and saw only one thing, Jack Jermaine's face in Owens's office. He might have had the looks to stop time, but there was something else, something in the eyes that caused her to be cautious. The way he'd forced himself into her life was unsettling. She wondered where he was at that

181

moment, and what he was doing.

With her head against the plane's inner curve, her nose pressed to the Plexiglas counting clouds out the window, she tried to sleep, but it wasn't working. Abby's mind was in overdrive. She tried to regroup. Things had gone dangerously out of control since leaving Los Angeles. She took some solace in the fact that the basic elements of her plan were still in place, though she wondered if she was deluding herself. How much control did she really have? How long before Owens tried to go around her directly to Jack, to get more books or some other concession?

There were serious legal questions here. Jermaine was for all intents and in the eyes of the law, her agent-in-fact. She had cloaked him with apparent authority by pushing him up front as the author. In their ignorance, Owens and Bertoli had a right to rely on this. If Jack signed further contracts without her knowledge, Abby would be bound by his actions. Jack had all the signs of a loose cannon. Abby would have to lash him to the deck and do it quickly.

She thought about Morgan. At the moment he was her psychic safety net, the only one she could run to with problems. She had confided in Theresa, but Theresa was useless when it came to business.

Morgan was a lawyer with a good mind. He was cool under pressure. She would sit with him in the morning in his office and go over the events of the last several days, Jack's insertion into her life, and work out her next move. Morgan would have answers. In his own way he had a calculating mind. She was unwilling to allow a stranger to control her. If need be, if Jack pushed her, she would come clean with Owens, tell her the truth about the book.

Six million dollars. How much of it would vanish with Jack if she told the truth? Would they still want the book without his face on the dustcover? It was a good story. It had driven intense interest in Hollywood. By now Abby had created certain expectations. Would they accept it with a woman as author? It was a strong male part, written in a male voice. Part of her wanted to know. Part of her didn't. How many novels got this far – unless you had a gimmick, a celebrity? It was a sad commentary. She consoled herself with the thought that she was not playing by any rules she had made. It was a deal with the devil and he had made all the rules.

It cost Abby nearly eighty dollars to get her car out of hock at the airport, almost more than the vehicle was worth. She was caught in the early rush hour and labored up I-5 in the slow lane stop-and-go until she passed the business district. Then traffic thinned and she moved at a break-neck forty miles an hour to her turnoff just beyond the bridge and the University. She was in a daze, half asleep, car on autopilot as she rolled through the stop signs and took the curves leading to her house. Her sleepless night was catching up.

As she turned onto her block all the anxieties that had been lapping at her subconscious suddenly crested and crashed. There in the middle of the street were flickering blue and red lights, a fire truck, and police cars. Abby wanted to think a dozen things, a kitchen grease fire, a car crash, a neighbor's heart attack, but in her mind she knew what it was. The only question was how badly he'd beaten her this time. And from the lights on the street, it didn't look good.

A lone cop in uniform was stringing yellow tape from the trunks of trees in front of her house.

Abby parked haphazardly at the curb. Left her purse and her luggage in the car, the door half open, and ran the distance toward the house. She was stopped at the tape.

'I live here. It's my house.' She tried to push her way through, but the cop stopped her and called another.

'Wait here.' The young cop held her at the line while a sergeant talked to somebody in plainclothes. The young cop went back to his tape but kept an eye on Abby.

'Can you tell me what happened?' she asked.

He shook his head. 'Lieutenant will be here in a minute.'

When the older cop returned he was with a taller man in a gray suit, slender with dark silky hair and looks that reminded her of a film star she couldn't place. There were wisps of silver at his temples, and a devious smile on his lips. *Kiss of the Spider Woman.*

'I'm Lieutenant Luther Sanfillipo.' He spoke with a Latin tilt to his voice. 'You are?' he looked at Abby.

'Abby Chandlis. I live here.'

'Of course.' He lifted the tape and Abby slipped underneath. By now a camera crew for one of the local television stations had found the action. Seeing the cops and Abby headed for the house, they trained their camera, the reporter shouting something barely audible from a distance as a uniformed cop held them back. It was the same question Abby had: 'Can you tell us what happened?'

The detective ignored them. 'Get those people off the grass,' he told the young cop. 'I'm sure Ms Chandlis here does not need to have her garden trampled.' He smiled at her and they walked on a few more steps.

'Tell me what's happened,' said Abby.

They walked far enough to be out of earshot of the

camera crew and stopped on the path that bisected the lawn at the front of the house.

'Do you live here alone?' he asked.

'I have a friend staying with me.'

Knowing looks passed between the cops.

'What's happened? Is Theresa alright?'

'Theresa?' said Sanfillipo.

'Theresa Jenrico.'

'She is the friend who lives with you?'

'Tell me what's happened?'

'Can you describe Ms Jenrico for us?'

'Are you going to tell me what's going on?'

'A description. It's a simple request,' he said.

'Five-five. Dark hair, shoulder length.'

The detective's eyes grew a pained expression. He turned around to one of his subordinates. 'Do we have a Polaroid?'

They looked at one another, a lot of shrugging shoulders; the cop's universal reply to the unknown.

'Well get one.' Sanfillipo snapped his fingers a couple of times, and in that gesture Abby placed his looks, the cutting image of the late Raul Julia. Tall, dark, with Latin good looks and the perpetual enigma of a half-smile.

They stood awkwardly for several moments, Abby, Sanfillipo, and his entourage.

'May I ask you where you've been?'

'Traveling,' said Abby.

'I can see from the state of your house that you have not been here. Pleasure or business?' he asked.

'What do you mean, the state of my house?'

'Please just answer my questions.'

'Business.' She handed him a card, the last one from her coat pocket.

His brows arched as he read the card.

'What type of law do you practice?'

'Mostly business, some bankruptcy and domestic relations. What has this got to do . . .?'

'Nothing criminal?'

'No.'

'No clients you have ever represented who might want to vandalize your house?'

'Is that what's happened?'

He gave her a look that was something just short of confirmation.

'May I ask you the nature of your business trip?'

'No, you can't.'

'Then perhaps you can tell me where this business took you?'

'Los Angeles and New York.'

'And how long were you there?'

Before she could answer, Sanfillipo was interrupted by one of the uniforms coming toward him holding two wet Polaroid prints out to dry.

'It's about time. Let me see.' He looked at the pictures, then shook his head grimly trying to decide which one.

. 'This is difficult.' Sanfillipo made his pick. 'It is not pleasant. You might want to prepare yourself.' He held the two photographs like a poker player, close to his vest.

Abby steeled herself.

'Do you recognize this woman?' He finally handed her the one in his right hand.

For a moment her eyes refused to focus on the picture and instead looked over the top at the detective and the cops hovering at his shoulder.

'Please,' said Sanfillipo.

When she finally looked it didn't appear real; skin the pallor of blue-gray and bulging eyes. The face was swollen, tongue protruding, bitten through in one place. There was no word for it. Grotesque was too mild. There was something about one of the eyes, Theresa's beautiful eyes. The lens was fractured like a piece of glass.

'Oh God!' Abby slumped and one of the cops caught her. She was gasping, trying to fill her lungs with air, uttering the only question she could think of. 'What happened?'

'Perhaps an accident,' said Sanfillipo. 'Get a chair.'

Abby's knees went weak. She stumbled a little but didn't fall. Sanfillipo grabbed her by one arm.

Abby stiffened. 'I'm O.K.'

He gave the order for a piece of lawn furniture on the porch, a light wicker chair, to be brought down.

'No. I want to see her,' said Abby.

'Now is not the time,' said the detective. 'For identification I must know. Is that your friend?'

Abby looked one more time. She nodded but couldn't speak, evaporating denial mode.

'The woman in the picture is Theresa Jenrico?' He pressed for unequivocal identification.

'Yes.

'How did it happen?' She wanted answers.

'Electrocution,' said the cop. 'For now we are investigating. Do you know anyone who would want to vandalize your house?'

Abby shot him a look. 'One person.'

'Who?'

'His name is Joey Jenrico. They were divorced.'

Sanfillipo had one of the other cops now taking notes.

'He'd beaten her several times. He wouldn't let go. Check your computer, you'll find a record. He was arrested and charged. More than once,' said Abby. 'No convictions.'

Sanfillipo raised an eyebrow.

'Theresa wouldn't prosecute,' said Abby.

He nodded like he understood. 'Do you have an address for Mr Jenrico?'

'She has a little book in her purse. It's in there.'

'That may be a problem,' said the detective.

Abby looked at him.

'We are having some trouble finding things inside.'

'I don't understand?'

'You have not yet seen your house,' said the cop.

They couldn't find the directory, Theresa's purse, or much of anything else. Everything was in pieces.

The coroner had removed Theresa's body in a black bag, but not before Abby had insisted on one last look. In her mind she prayed that perhaps she had leapt to conclusions with the photograph. Lying on her back on the gurney, as deformed as death had left her, the features of Theresa's face were now burnished in Abby's mind. It was an image she would carry to her grave.

Morgan Spencer had arrived. Abby had called the office.

Spencer took charge while Abby slumped in a chair on the front porch. Forensics was still picking through the belongings in her house. Abby could see some of the damage through the windows, though they wouldn't allow her inside. Morgan confirmed for Sanfillipo and the coroner the identification of the body.

'Then you knew her as well?' asked the cop.

Morgan nodded. 'Socially,' he said. 'We'd met a few times.'

'You will have to find other accommodations for

tonight,' the detective told Abby.

'She can stay with me.' Morgan spoke before Abby could answer.

'Are you sure?' She looked at him.

'I insist.' Morgan was halfway to having Abby move in. What he'd always wanted, even if it was separate rooms. He'd work on that later.

'Any sign of the purse or the victim's phone book?' Sanfillipo had stuck his head in the front door and directed this to one of the officers. They were now pawing through the carnage in the living room. There were a lot of stooped backs and shaking heads. The detective stepped back out.

'How are you feeling?' Luther asked Abby if she was up to a little walk.

'Where to?'

'Around back.'

Abby and Morgan followed the detective through the side yard to the back of the house.

'Mr Spencer, if you would wait here.' Sanfillipo took Abby by one elbow and ushered her through the door, down into the basement.

'Where are we going?'

'Show you in a minute,' said the detective.

There were two forensic technicians dusting for prints near the work bench. The surface of the bench was scorched, an arc of charred wood.

'Is this where it happened?'

Sanfillipo nodded.

'When is the last time you changed a fuse in the service box?'

Abby thought for a moment. 'Maybe a month ago. It didn't work very well. An old system,' said Abby.

'Yes. Do you remember this?' he pointed down to a

heavy piece of wire that ran out from under the work bench several feet.

Abby shook her head. 'What is it?'

'It's attached to the back of the fuse box. There was water in a puddle under the bench. When she turned the fuse in the right socket, it completed the circuit, pressed the wire to make contact. Two hundred and twenty volts,' said the detective. 'She must have been standing in the water. Touch the box and you're dead.' He turned to Abby. 'You've never seen this wire before?'

'No,' said Abby. 'It wasn't there.'

'It appears someone was arranging an accident,' said the cop.

'Joey,' said Abby.

He looked perplexed. 'How would he know that his wife would replace the fuses?'

'He wouldn't,' said Abby. 'He wouldn't care. I represented Theresa in her divorce.'

Suddenly Sanfillipo got big eyes. Things were starting to make sense.

CHAPTER

SIXTEEN

Twenty-four hours turned into seventy-two before the cops let Abby back in her house. When she got there, she remembered Sanfillipo's words about its condition. Still she was not prepared for what she saw. From first impressions it was beyond repair. She wandered with Morgan aimlessly for nearly an hour, from room to room, trying to figure where to start.

The police were still looking for Joey. Abby knew he was on the run. When he sobered and realized what he'd done, no doubt panic set in and he took off.

The police had left their yellow tape up outside around the trees as a courtesy, a barrier against the curious. Still, a few neighbors, people Abby recognized, could be seen jaywalking in front of her house, purposeless strolls, looking as they passed at the place where the woman had been killed. Within an hour, Abby knew she could no longer stay there.

In the afternoon, a man she'd hired came by to board up two windows at the back of the house. Joey had smashed them out of their frame. The police might not have found his prints, but to Abby, Joey's fingers were on every article in her house. His odor fouled the place.

She had never been an advocate of the death penalty, but in Joey's case she would make an exception. Lethal injection was too humane.

She could hear the workman pounding nails into plywood, sealing out the weather from her bedroom. It was raining again, somber light to add to her melancholy mood.

Late in the morning, Morgan had to return to the office. Now she was alone in the house. The workman finished. Abby busied herself straightening up, packing her possessions into cardboard boxes, whatever she could salvage. The rest went into large plastic trash bags, which Abby stacked at the curb until she had a sizable pile.

Morgan found her phone. The cops had taken her message machine to copy its tape and returned it. Morgan put the phone back on the kitchen countertop and hooked the machine up so that it worked again.

Abby hadn't been near the office since returning from New York, though she had called once to collect messages. There were none. This troubled her. She was told that one of the younger associates had been assigned to handle her workload for the time being. Abby saw Morgan's hand in this, easing her load while she dealt with Theresa's death. It was like him.

She was just about finished straightening in the kitchen when she noticed that the message light was flashing on her machine. She stopped and pushed the button. The first two were hang-ups. There was a message from Carla. It was more than a week old. She assumed it had been left on her machine before her house was vandalized. The final message was left by Lewis Cutler's secretary. The firm's managing partner wanted to talk to her. Abby called the office. Cutler's secretary answered.

'Hello, Marcia.'

'Abby.' The woman sounded startled when she recognized the voice. 'How are you?'

'You sound surprised,' said Abby.

'It's just that I didn't expect to be hearing from you. With all that's happened, I mean. How are you doing?'

'Cleaning up.'

'I heard about it. Your friend,' she said. 'Terrible. Terrible. If there's anything I can do?'

'There's not much anyone can do at this point,' she said.

'I suppose not.'

'Reason I was calling, I was going through my messages and found yours from Mr Cutler.'

There was silence at the other end. Abby thought Marcia was having trouble remembering.

'Something about his wanting to see me.'

'Oh, that.' There was another long pause. 'Let me see if he's in. What he wants to do,' she said. Then the line went dead while Abby was put on hold. She listened to elevator music piped over the phone while she tapped her fingers on the wall next to it and looked at her watch. It was taking longer than Marcia needed to find her boss, unless he'd disappeared. There were no chairs left to sit on in the kitchen so Abby stood, looking down the hall into the bedroom over the top of her mattress cut to its springs by a knife. Idle thoughts for an idle mind. Why, if Joey had a knife, had he taken the time to fashion an accident in the basement? She thought for a moment, then dismissed it. Who in their right mind would try to analyze Joey? On his best day he was psychotic. It was something for the police to consider. They probably already had.

Her gaze down the long hall wandered toward the

corner of her bedroom, now looking nearly normal. The
small folding table that was her altar of work, the place
where she wrote, rested upright again under the window covered by plywood. Abby had even managed to
salvage a few of her reference books, a dictionary and
thesaurus. But she still hadn't found her typewriter, the
old manual. Morgan had scoured the basement looking
for it. She wondered why Joey would take a typewriter.

'What are you doing this afternoon?' Marcia was back
on the line.

'Cleaning up,' said Abby.

'Were you planning on coming by the office?'

'I wasn't, but I can. What's it about?'

'Mr Cutler would like to talk to you.'

'What time?'

'About two o'clock.'

'I'll be there.'

The offices of Starl, Hobbs and Carlton were subdued,
a mirror image of Abby's own mood at the moment.
She was the author of a book worth millions, but Theresa's
murder had thrown a cloud over her life. New York and
the meeting with Carla Owens seemed like something
from another age.

In the confusion after the murder she had never had
time to talk with Morgan about Jack and her problems
with the book. It would have to wait until things
calmed. She wondered if things would ever be the same
again. Abby was beginning to regret that she had ever
written the book. Most of all she rued the day she'd
hatched the scheme to use a male pen name and supply
it with a human face.

Today Abby had dressed the part for her meeting
with Cutler. She wore the same gray wool business suit

she had taken with her on her trip to New York and matching heels. It was the extent of her work wardrobe after Joey had dumped all of her clothes on the closet floor and poured bleach and vinegar on them.

She wandered down the long corridor toward her office. A few heads came up, eyes of sympathy acknowledging her presence. Still no one came out to say a word. It was like she had the plague. Violent death does strange things to people.

She didn't realize until she'd already passed the little cubicle outside her office that Marla, the paralegal who doubled as her secretary, was not at her desk. She was hoping she could pick up the loose ends of her business life starting with the messages and notes from her assistant.

She flipped on the overhead light and walked into her office. She had left papers and files on her desk when she went to New York. Her in-basket was full. Now it was empty, and the top to the desk dusted and clean.

She wandered out to Marla's station expecting to find everything there. She didn't. Marla's desk was cleaner than her own. The carousel with phone messages rested on the counter of Marla's desk. There was only a single small white envelope in Abby's slot on the carousel, marked personal. She opened it. Inside was a pink telephone slip: 'Call me at this number. It's important.'

It was from Jack Jermaine, dated two days earlier. More troubling was the fact that the return telephone number bore a 206 area code. Jack was in Seattle. Now he was shadowing her, intruding further into her life. She would call him alright, and give him a piece of her mind. She looked at her watch. One forty-five. No time like the present. She went into her office, closed the door, and dialed.

What she got was the operator at the Four Seasons, one of the swank downtown hotels. One thing was clear: Jack didn't stint when it came to money. She wondered if it was her own he was spending, perhaps part of an advance wheedled out of Carla.

'I'm looking for a Mr Jack Jermaine. I believe he's a guest.'

'One moment, please. I'll put you through.'

Jack picked it up halfway through the second ring.

'Hello.'

'What are you doing here?' Abby didn't bother with preliminaries.

'I read about your friend. Saw it in the paper, your name in the story. Are you alright?'

'I'm fine.' Abby didn't want to talk about Theresa's death. Not with Jack. She was angry. He'd followed her to the coast. 'I asked you what you're doing here.'

'This is probably a bad time, but we gotta talk,' said Jack.

'What's so pressing that you had to come out?'

'Things have changed,' he told her.

'How's that?'

'We have work to do.'

'What are you talking about?'

'I'm talking about the sequel. Carla called me the night you left New York. Put on the full court press. She wanted to talk about the next book in the series.'

'What series?'

'Seems they're assuming I'm going to write a series, using the same characters.'

'Who led them to that assumption?'

'I thought you did,' said Jack.

'It wasn't me.'

'Well, it wasn't me. Anyway, they're looking at a replay,' said Jack.

Carla and Bertoli were at it. Abby had smelled it in the first meeting. One or both were control freaks. If she had to guess, it was Owens. Before they were finished, they would be rejecting story lines and dictating their own plots, turning her into a ghost writer, using Jack's name and face.

'Well, call her back and tell her you won't do it.'

'What reason do I give?'

'I don't know. Artistic. Tell her you never intended to do a series. It cheapens the message.'

'This book contains a message? I must have missed it,' said Jack.

'Nevermind. Just tell her you won't do it.'

'Before I do, you better listen to the rest of it.'

'Rest of what?'

'Got your calculator?'

'Why?'

'They're talking doubling the deal on the second book.'

'What do you mean?'

'As in six million just for book rights.'

'You're kidding?'

'No, I'm not. We would still hold the film stuff and all the foreign rights. Maybe get another six for those.'

'*We*?' said Abby.

'Fine. You. But they want to hear from *me* with an answer as soon as possible. Carla won't let me sleep. She's called me three times in the last twenty-four hours. Once in the middle of the night. The woman's manic. Gotta give Alex an answer, she says. He won't wait forever. She says we need to do this in order to set the hook.'

'Bertoli's a eunuch,' said Abby. 'The only hook we have to worry about is the one Carla's trying to put through your nose. He'll do whatever she tells him.'

'My take, too,' said Jack. 'Why I didn't worry too much about getting back to her.'

'We haven't even published a book and they want more of the same, with the same characters. They call it publishing. They're creating swill,' said Abby.

'Question is do we want to belly up to the trough?' said Jack. It was an open line. He was waiting for an answer.

'Tell them to wait.' Abby thought for a moment. Where was Morgan when she needed him?

'Why don't I come down there and we'll talk.' Jack wanted to go for the deal. Abby could smell it. But he didn't have to write the book.

'No. Just stay where you are.'

'We need to talk,' he said. 'I'll come by there.'

'No.' Abby couldn't tell if he'd heard her or not, because Jack had already hung up.

It was a strange feeling, like winning the lottery. Suddenly, if Carla was right, there was a six-million-dollar payday just waiting to be collected, and another one in the offing. For the first time since traveling to New York, the thought actually settled on Abby: she did not have to practice law any longer. She could do whatever she wanted. There was no question she hated her job, but it was an anchor to the normal world, where real people lived. Abby didn't like to think of herself as rich. She had never been there, done those things. She came from working-class parents. Her father was a warehouse foreman. Somehow the thought of being rich ripped her from her roots.

In every way commercial publishing was a game of chance; the right book at the right time with the right publisher and the right budget. Writing a novel was like pulling the handle on a slot machine. If you were lucky enough to line everything up at one time, you won. If not, you went to work on the next book.

Abby had seen them on T.V., winners being handed checks the size of bill boards, all uttering the same mantra – 'It won't change our lives. We'll continue to work, cuz we love our jobs.' A week later they would disappear like dust, off to the south of France. No one would hear from them again. The insidious thing that memory did.

Lewis Cutler's office was a show place, the kind of digs designed to make a statement. In Cutler's case, the message was 'I got the power.'

When Abby arrived at the secretary's station outside, there was no small talk. Instead she was ushered in immediately. It was the first time she didn't have to wait.

Cutler sat behind the desk in a cushioned high-back leather chair, hunched over a pile of papers.

'Come in. Sit down.' He motioned Abby toward one of the client chairs without looking up. 'With you in a minute.' Still not looking at her.

He ignored her for several more seconds while he issued instructions to Marcia, handing her some papers he had finished. She turned to go.

'Take the stuff in the basket, too.'

Marcia came back, and as she reached over to grab the stuff in the out-basket her eyes drifted toward Abby sitting in the chair. It was Abby's first glimmer that something was wrong; a look that you would give only to the terminally ill.

Marcia left the room, and Cutler put his pen down.

'You've been away for several days.'

'Personal leave,' said Abby.

'Personal business as I understand it.' He made it sound like an accusation, like anyone in the firm with a personal life had to apologize.

'I heard about your friend. I'm sorry. Have they figured out what happened?'

'Not yet.' It was not something Abby wanted to discuss with Cutler. 'They're still investigating.' She left it at that. She guessed that if Cutler had concerns about this it was limited to the possible fallout on the firm. Two women living together, one of them found dead, could be a matter of cruel speculation among the small-minded in Cutler's circle.

'It makes what I have to do particularly painful,' he said.

Abby raised an eyebrow.

'As you know, there have been a lot of changes in the firm over the past several months. What you might call a restructuring.' The use of the code word was abrupt, just like that, no preliminaries. It caught Abby flat-footed and sent her into an adrenaline rush.

'We've had to do some downsizing,' said Cutler.

'I hadn't heard.'

'That's because you've been away. Much of it was announced last week.'

'Announced?'

'Layoffs,' said Cutler. 'Fourteen positions.'

'I didn't know. Am I . . .?'

He nodded.

It wasn't that she cared about the job as much as the message that it seemed to convey; that she wasn't good enough for them.

'You're not alone.' This was supposed to make it easier.

'I understand,' she caught herself saying it even though she didn't know why.

'I know what you're thinking,' he said.

In fact he didn't have a clue. Abby sat in the chair with a smile on her face. Cutler figured shock. Abby was thinking that if he'd waited two more days he probably could have had her resignation without asking.

'You're thinking why you?' said Cutler. 'There's nothing personal in it. It's just that you hold one of the positions affected by the restructuring.'

He was prepared to respond to questions she didn't even ask. Cutler no doubt had taken a course on how to do this.

'I want you to know that before we made the decision we looked at all the possible alternatives. I'm sorry to say that there's no possibility of part-time work in the firm. We've already considered that and it just doesn't fit into our plans. Nor is there a chance for some form of reduction.'

She looked at him quizzically.

'Reduced pay,' he said.

Abby started to open her mouth to tell him that she wouldn't consider it. Cutler anticipated. 'Nor can we delay the decision,' he said.

She hadn't asked for a thing. In fact, she was enjoying his discomfort, wondering why he was running off at the mouth.

'May I ask how the firm is restructuring?' said Abby.

'That's confidential, at least at the moment. It would be easier,' he said, 'if you were to tender your resignation.'

Now she raised an eyebrow. 'Easier on who?' She

knew where he was headed, cutting her off from unemployment benefits. If she quit, she wouldn't get them. This would help the firm's bottom line.

'It would look better on a résumé,' he said. 'We'd be prepared to offer you a letter of recommendation.'

'Are you saying that if I don't resign you don't give me one?'

'That's not what I said.'

Abby felt a rush, thought for a second. He was talking to the six-million-dollar woman and the prick didn't have a clue. She wasn't about to tell him. She thought for a moment, looked at him, and said: 'Why not?' Just like that she'd quit.

Cutler looked up from his desk, an expression like he'd missed something. No one went this easily.

She wondered what the partners would do with her pay. No doubt divvy it up into bonuses for themselves.

'I'd like to say good-bye to Marla.'

Ah, finally there was something he could deny her. 'That's not possible.' Now he felt more in charge.

'Why not?'

'Ms Evans resigned last week.' He said it almost with a smile.

Marla Evans had two kids and a mortgage. Without notice, without any warning, they'd waited until Abby was out of town and fired her. She wondered why Morgan hadn't told her. Then it hit her. Maybe he was on the hit list as well. But how could they fire a partner?

'I'd like to say good-bye to Mr Spencer.'

'Not on the premises,' said Cutler. 'Now that the decision has been made, we'd prefer that you clean out your desk and be out of the office quickly. Say an hour,' said Cutler. It was one of the rules fashioned by the canning consultants. You didn't want the canee hanging around the water cooler poisoning the labor pool.

'We can provide assistance if you need it,' he said.

Abby looked at him.

'To clean out your desk.' It was almost as if he was trying to provoke an argument, searching for a normal reaction, some anger. She wasn't going to give him the satisfaction.

'That won't be necessary.' Instead she offered a smile. 'And I want to thank you.'

He hesitated but couldn't resist. 'What for?'

'For being such an asshole. It always makes it easier.' She got up and headed for the door. There was no apology. No 'sorry this had to happen,' no justification or cause. Just 'clean out your desk and disappear in an hour.' Modern American business etiquette.

He had done this three times in the last two days, and in each instance Cutler had returned to the papers on his desk before the person he sacked made it to the door. With Abby he watched her go, until the door closed behind her, wondering if perhaps she might have gone around the bend, and whether she might be coming back with a gun.

On the way out she passed Marcia's desk.

'Oh.' The secretary looked up. 'I have to ask you for your keys to the office.'

Abby reached in her purse and pulled out her keys. She broke a nail sliding them off the ring. She was angrier than she looked. She dropped the two keys on the secretary's desk.

'And your parking pass?'

'That I paid for through the end of the month,' said Abby. 'I think I'll keep it until then.'

Marcia looked at Cutler's door as if she didn't quite know how she would break this to him.

'Tell him to sue me,' said Abby. When she turned,

there was a uniformed security guard standing in front of her.

'What do you want?'

'He's supposed to stay with you until you're finished. Then escort you from the building,' said Marcia.

'Is that really necessary?'

'It's the procedure,' said Marcia.

Now she knew why no one would make eye contact when she showed up in the office. It had nothing to do with Theresa's murder. It had to do with another killing, the one Cutler had just performed in his office.

It was like a parade of humiliation down the hall, Abby and the security guard, the hardware on his belt squeaking and jingling like some jailer. Every eye in the office came up for a glance as she passed by the phalanx of open doors down the long corridor. She wanted to scream 'I'm worth six million dollars' but couldn't even whisper it. By the time she reached her own office, Abby felt like the scarlet woman. She had difficulty restraining herself when she saw him sitting behind her desk with his feet propped up.

'Are you comfortable?'

Jack looked at her and immediately removed his feet. 'You look awful.'

'Thanks.'

He uncoupled his hands from behind the back of his neck and got out of the chair. 'Who's he?' he pointed to the security guard.

'Didn't get your name,' said Abby.

'Harold,' said the guard.

'Harold, meet Jack. The two men in my life.'

'How you doin'?' said Jack.

The guard actually waved, not exactly certain what he should be doing.

Abby could not remember a moment when she'd felt so low.

'Your timing, as always, is impeccable,' she told Jack.

'Why's that?'

'I really don't feel like company right now.'

'I understand. But I thought we could talk.'

'Not just now.' Abby started going through the drawers of her credenza, taking things out and stacking them on top of her desk. She was exhausted, emotionally and physically, at the end of her string. Jack sensed it, rolled the chair her way, and Abby slumped, almost falling into it.

'Are you alright?'

'Fine,' she told him.

'You want some water?' Jack looked at the guard. 'Get her some water.'

Harold hesitated but only for a second.

'Now.' It was the thing about dominance. Harold disappeared down the hall.

'What's wrong?'

'What isn't,' said Abby. 'My best friend's been killed. I've just been fired. A security guard is standing over my desk while I clean it out. And when I come back to my office you're sitting in my chair with your feet on the desk.'

'One out of four ain't bad,' said Jack.

Even in her present mood, Jack got a smile. 'Don't you ever take no for an answer?'

'No.'

'Maybe I should have Harold throw you out.'

'Let's see if he can find the water cooler first.' He fanned her with some paper from one of the drawers.

'Do the cops know what happened to your friend?'

'Theresa?'

Jack nodded.

'They're not sure. Still looking into it. You never told me what you're doing here,' she said.

'What I said on the phone. They want another book.'

'No. I mean what are you doing in Seattle?'

'Bringing you the news.'

'You could have done that on the phone. In fact, you did.'

'I thought it would be better if we worked out the details in person. Don't want to mess anything up,' said Jack.

'God forbid,' said Abby.

He eased her back in the chair until she was reclining, then spun it around so that her back was to him. Then he began to slowly rub her shoulders and the nape of her neck.

'What are you doing?' she asked.

'Keeping up appearances. You never know when Carla might have somebody watching,' said Jack.

It wasn't lost on Abby that he'd never answered her question; what he was doing in Seattle.

'Right. And who would be watching us?'

'How the hell do I know. Want me to stop?'

'No.' His hands on the back of her neck melted the tension in her spine like snow on a hot day.

'By the way, how did you get in here?' Abby looked up at him, an inverted image overhead.

'Nobody out front. I let myself in.'

'Just like that?'

He nodded.

'But there's an electronic lock on the door.'

'And a button on the secretary's desk,' said Jack. 'Laid a book on it. Does the trick.'

'You really don't take no for an answer, do you?'

Harold was back with the water. Jack used a little on Abby's forehead. She sipped the rest from a paper cup.

'Got any boxes?' He turned to Harold.

'Some out by the stairs,' said the guard.

'Well what are you waiting for? Get 'em.'

The guard was wondering if this was in his job description. Jack shot him a look and Harold disappeared down the hall one more time. He was back a minute later with two boxes.

It took Jack ten minutes to empty the drawers of Abby's desk and credenza, and a couple more to load her books and a sweater off the coat tree in the corner. He taped the tops of the boxes closed and handed one to Harold. 'Here, make yourself useful.'

The guard found himself stooped over with the weight of the box. The bottom rested on his can of pepper spray in its holster on Harold's two-hundred-dollar webbed belt. Just when he figured Jack was going to carry the other box, Jermaine picked it up and slid it on top of the first one, wedging it under Harold's chin. Then he turned to Abby. 'Ready to go?'

'That's mine, too.' She pointed to the coat tree.

'No problem.' Jack picked it up, slipped it under the crook of Harold's arm, pushing the guard's elbow down like a clamp to hold it in place. 'There. How's that?'

Harold couldn't talk. His chin was jammed with boxes and if he moved his arm the coat tree would fall out.

'Gotta be careful of that,' said Jack. He tapped the can of pepper spray hanging on Harold's belt. 'Move too quickly, it could go off. That stuff'll burn the pupils right out of your eyes.'

Jack took Abby by the arm and they headed out the

door, followed by Harold the thirty-eight-caliber bellboy.

Out front, Jack opened the door from the inside. The two women were back at reception. They looked at the strange entourage. Harold in uniform with boxes. Jack opened the outer door for him.

'It's the white Ford, up front. Third floor parking garage.' He would have stuck his keys in Harold's mouth, but the guy would have broken a tooth, he was that angry.

'Ladies,' Jack gave them a casual salute.

They looked at Abby as if they'd never seen her in quite this same light before.

They couldn't take their eyes off of Jack, his steely blue gaze and bullshit grin, like where in the world did she get him?

CHAPTER
SEVENTEEN

It was like central command, the war room, Jack and Spencer seated at the dining room table at Morgan's house. Jack had already signed contracts put in front of him by the lawyer. He wasn't happy about it. The documents were intended as insurance, proof to the world that Abby wrote the book and that Jack was a stand-in. Morgan at work. Jack didn't read them and Morgan kept all the copies. It wouldn't do to have them floating around.

'Is that everything?' said Jack.

'No. We have a problem,' said Abby. With her departure from the firm and the annihilation of her house, Morgan's was the only place they could meet.

It was a spacious Georgian on Queen Anne Hill, a sweeping staircase, Tara on a movie set. The kind of place a middle-aged lawyer owned when he wanted to make a statement. In this case, it was a message Spencer could no longer afford. Property taxes were breaking his back. He was fighting for his life at the firm. Cutler was withholding his annual bonus, telling Morgan to sue him. And on top of everything else Spencer owed alimony to his wife. He and Anne had divorced after twenty years. She was claiming a part of his practice as community property. The man was being steamed, rolled, and pressed.

'What's the problem?' said Jack.

Abby flung her coat over the back of the chair. It fell on the floor and she didn't bother to pick it up. Her hair looked like smoke in a wind storm. She was wearing jeans and a soiled work shirt from packing the last boxes at the house. She felt around inside her briefcase and pulled out a yellow legal pad with some notes on it.

'The guy's name is Robert Thompson. He called this morning about nine-thirty. I'm only guessing as to how he got my number. Said he works for *The Intruder* and he's doing a feature piece on novels and the people who write them. Immediately bells started going off,' said Abby.

'Why is he calling you?' said Jack.

'I have been published.'

'Don't take offense,' said Jack, 'but not that anyone would notice.'

'At least she's in print. Not like some people I could mention.' Morgan had picked Jack's brain. Found out he was a frustrated writer, unpublished, and now he was using it. It was one of Morgan's less endearing qualities, the talent to find a flaw and exploit it. He had taken an instant dislike to Jack. Abby knew what it was. He was jealous.

Privately Morgan told her that it burned him that Jermaine was about to be crowned king of pulp fiction on a book he had no part of. But Abby knew it was more than that. He didn't want Jack working with her, on the book, or anything else. It was awkward. Abby didn't know how to tell Morgan that she was only a friend.

'Cool it, guys.' She didn't need a fight at the moment.

'The thought had entered my mind. I mean, I'm not exactly at the top of anyone's list.

'Anyway he gets into it. Wants to know if I'll answer a few questions. I ask him how he got my number. He says he has his sources. I tell him I'm busy. He says it won't take but a minute. Then he tells me I don't have to answer any of this. That I can hang up anytime I want.'

'Journalism's answer to Miranda,' said Morgan.

'Exactly,' said Abby. 'By now the adrenaline is leaking out of my ears. Why would I want to hang up? I ask him. It's killing me. I'm wondering what he knows. Seems this feature piece is about manipulation of the market place. The games authors and publishers play to push books. How they use the media.'

'But why is he calling you?' said Jack.

'I'm getting to that. It seems someone has told him that I have a client who is posing as the author of a soon-to-be big novel.'

'Oh shit,' said Jack.

'My thoughts exactly,' said Abby.

'How much does he know?'

'I don't know. I stonewalled him. Told him I didn't know what he was talking about.'

'And?'

'And he folded. He didn't have any names. Didn't seem to know the title of the book or the publisher. If I had to guess, all he knows is what he's been told, which was just enough to get to me.'

'You think he believed you when you told him you didn't know anything?' said Morgan.

'If incredulous tones on the phone are any measure, he didn't buy it. He starts asking me what I'm afraid of. Tries to give me legal advice. Consoles me by telling me that whatever it is I'm doing, it can't be a violation of any law. So why not just tell him the truth?'

'Right. So he can stick the hot poker of journalism up our ass,' said Jack. 'The ultimate cleansing experience. Every reporter's form of absolution.'

'So what do we do?' said Spencer.

'I got a better question for you,' said Jack. 'What if he finds Carla or Bertoli and starts asking them questions?'

'I've thought about that,' said Abby.

'If they start thinking about the money they're paying, and wondering if they've been had, it's all over,' said Jack. 'They'll flush the book. To say nothing of six million.'

'Which brings us back to what do we do?' said Abby.

There was a long silence around the table.

'He may not call back,' said Spencer.

'He may show up at her front door tomorrow,' said Jack.

'That would seem to depend on how much information he has, and how big a story it is.'

'Do I have a vote?' said Jack.

'Let's hear it.' Abby looked at him.

'You should leave Seattle. The booksellers convention is next week. Go to Chicago. See what Bertoli is doing on the book.'

'I was planning on going anyway,' said Abby.

'Good. Then don't come back.'

'What are you talking about?'

'Disappear somewhere. We'll find a place. That way you can write undisturbed,' said Jack.

Abby considered it.

'Make yourselves scarce. I mean, if this guy doesn't have anybody to talk to, he has no story. We cut down his sources.'

'Still, somebody's been talking to him,' said Morgan.

'Who?' said Jack.

'Only one person we can think of,' said Abby. She was looking at Spencer. 'Joey.'

'Why would he?'

'I wasn't sure,' said Abby. 'Not until this morning when I finished packing. There was something missing from the house. I haven't found it and I've looked everywhere. There was an early copy of the manuscript. It was typed on the back of some old letterheads, reams of paper they were throwing out at the firm. I figured the back side was perfectly good. I could do a draft. I knew I was going to have to retype anyway. Nobody would ever see it. I threw it in a box under the table in the bedroom. It's not there. I've turned the house upside down.'

'That and the typewriter,' said Morgan.

'Your typewriter's missing?' said Jack.

Abby nodded.

'What the hell's Joey gonna do with a typewriter?' said Morgan.

'Probably write ransom notes,' said Abby. 'You want your papers back, it's gonna cost. If I know Joey, he's looking for the highest bidder. Wait long enough and he'll come to us.' She reminded them that he'd already tried to mess with the film stuff.

'He wouldn't do it again,' said Jack.

'You don't even know him,' said Abby.

'Call it intuition,' said Jack. 'I think he can be persuaded.'

'I think he smells money,' said Morgan.

'We could pay him off,' said Abby.

Both Morgan and Jack gave her the same look. 'That would be a huge mistake,' said Spencer.

'I agree,' said Jack. 'Lemme talk to him.'

'Why you?' said Morgan.

'Because I think I can be more persuasive.'

'This is business. It should be handled in a business-like way.'

'I know the kind of business he's in,' said Jack.

'Maybe he found the copyright,' said Abby.

Morgan shook his head and gave her a dirty look as if to say, what was she thinking about?

'What copyright?' said Jack.

'Nothing.' Abby realized she'd blown it. Jack didn't need to know about the copyright. Morgan had taken care of it, with a registered copy now tucked away neatly somewhere in his files. Abby was wondering if maybe the reporter would be looking for it.

'So how much does he really know?' Spencer changed the subject. 'Joey, I mean.'

'We have to assume he has the manuscript,' said Abby. 'It doesn't take a mental giant to figure if it's on the back of law office stationary that Jack didn't write it. It's got my handwritten notes all over the margins. He could hold it over our heads.'

'He's running from the cops,' said Morgan.

'Yeah and he probably needs money,' said Abby.

'But the only players he's aware of for the moment are the film guys,' said Jack.

'That we know of,' said Spencer.

'Let's assume his access is limited,' said Jack. 'Besides, Joey would be dazzled by thoughts of dealing with Hollywood. Let's assume for the moment that's his play.'

'Let's assume,' said Spencer. 'How do we stop him?'

'We reason with him,' said Jack.

'You don't know Joey,' said Abby.

'It's all a matter of persuasion,' said Jack. 'Or there is

another possibility. You could come clean.'

They looked at him.

'Why not? Tell them the truth, that you wrote the book. What? Don't look at me like that. I think the problem is you don't have enough confidence in yourself.'

'It's not just that,' said Abby. 'There are forces here that you can't fight. Mindless rules of marketing that govern every book that is printed. I've been published three times. They don't break people out who have been published three times, no matter what they write.

'They won't break you out unless you're a fresh new discovery. Haven't you noticed? They're publishing bilious piles of commercial shit, but all of the authors are prodigies. I give you Gable Cooper.' Abby motioned toward Jack, who wasn't sure if he should take a bow.

'You can see the headlines,' she said. 'Record money paid to first-time novelist. That's the hook,' she told them. 'Why do you think Bertoli stepped up to the dollar mark so easily?'

'It's a good book,' said Morgan.

'There's a lot of good books,' said Abby. 'I checked. To this point the largest sum paid for a first novel was two million dollars. He now owns the record at three. He's gonna ride it like a horse all the way to the winner's circle if he can. He'll flog it 'til it dies in every press release and feature piece they can muscle. It'll be what Jack's introduced with on every television talk show. "We have with us the author whose first novel earned him a record six-million-dollar payday." The IRS will be waiting outside in your limo,' said Abby. 'I can read Bertoli like a book, and follow his spin like a gyroscope.'

Spencer'd never fully understood her cunning mind.

Abby knew the game they were playing. She bore the scars to prove it.

'If I'd written only one book before, maybe they could bury it, treat this as number one and hope nobody found out. But three. No chance. So we're going to do it my way. Let them blow Jack through the roof. Then we'll step up and tell the world what really happened. Who did what. They can lick the egg off their face when we're finished,' said Abby.

'So that's it?' said Spencer.

'That's it.' She offered no apologies and didn't tell them the rest of it. There was a risk involved in the one big book path to stardom that Abby hadn't mentioned. If it didn't work, the author's career was over. It had happened before, more than once. No one would ever push such a writer again. They had marketing leprosy. It was the genius of Abby's plan that she had hedged this bet. If it didn't work with Gable Cooper, there was always another story, another pen name, and another face to put behind it. Sooner or later she would seduce the publishers at their own game. She had confidence in her ability to write and to invent high concept stories. It was where every blockbusting book had to start; with a good idea. All she needed was a pencil and a mailbox, and she was in business. In a way, Abby was her own form of the literary terrorist – a force they couldn't stop.

CHAPTER
EIGHTEEN

The phone rang once and Salzman grabbed it. He was sitting on the edge of the bed, his overnight bag still packed, ready to go. He had no intention of staying in Seattle if he didn't have to.

'Hello.'

'Is that you?' It was Jenrico's voice.

'It's me.'

'What room are you in?'

'Nevermind. We'll meet down there. In the bar. Five minutes.' Salzman didn't trust Joey beyond the line of sight. He'd brought the two grand, but he wanted to keep it in his room until he saw what it was Joey had.

He took the elevator down. Jenrico was standing at the bar. He was wearing a tank top and a dirty pair of jeans with a hole in the ass. The corner of a worn leather wallet was sticking out of this from the back pocket. Hooked to his belt was a ring of keys hung on a cheesy chrome chain. Joey might have passed for a biker, except he was too sleazy.

'Hey, Mr Salzman!'

'Keep your voice down,' said Salzman. He looked for

a box or a large envelope, something big enough to hold the manuscript.

'Where is it?'

'What?'

'The manuscript. What do you think, I flew up here to have drinks?'

'I got it. You brought the money?'

'Don't worry about the money. Where is it?'

Joey reached into one of the tight pockets at the front of his jeans, pulled out a folded piece of paper, and handed it to Salzman. It was moist with sweat.

'What the fuck is this?'

'A piece of it,' said Joey.

Salzman looked for a place, somewhere away from the lights and the bar. He saw an empty table and made for it, Joey right behind him. They sat down and Salzman opened the paper, flattening it out on the table with his hands.

'So what the hell is this?'

'First page,' said Joey.

'I can see that. Where's the rest of it?'

'Outside.'

What he'd given him was the title page to the novel with Gable Cooper's name typed underneath it.

'Look at the other side,' said Joey.

Salzman turned it over. There at the top was the letterhead:

STARL, HOBBS & CARLTON
ATTORNEYS AT LAW

The names of associates and partners was in small print running down the left-hand margin like snot off a kid's nose.

'So?' said Salzman.

'It's what I was telling you,' said Joey. 'Your guy didn't write the book. Otherwise it wouldn't be printed on the back of that.'

'Anybody could have typed this. One page. Doesn't mean a thing. Why didn't you bring the rest of it?'

Before Joey could answer the bar maid came over. 'Can I get you gentlemen something to drink?'

'A beer,' said Joey.

'No. We're not gonna be here that long.' Salzman started to get up. The waitress drifted off.

'I got six hundred pages, all typed on the back of that stuff,' said Joey. 'Some of it's got hand-written notes all over it. And like I say, if you don't want to look at it, I can take it to the magazine.'

That stopped Salzman. He'd come this far.

'Why the fuck didn't you bring it?'

'Where's the money?' said Joey.

'You'll get paid.'

'Yeah, right. The check's in the mail,' said Joey. 'We already did that one, remember? Cash or you don't see any more.'

Salzman reached in his pocket, took out two hundred dollars, chump change, and slid it across the table. 'The rest is here in the hotel. But I wanna see what you got before I pay anything more.'

Joey got up, pushed the two bills down into his pocket, and headed for the door. Salzman followed him. When they got outside the hotel's front entrance Joey turned. 'Wait here.'

Jenrico crossed the parking lot to a point about two hundred feet away, to an old rusted-out Chevy pickup. Salzman watched as Joey slid between two vehicles, his truck and the car parked next to him, a tight squeeze.

Joey couldn't get the door to the trunk open. The other guy had him jammed in. The driver was still there stooped over in his trunk. Salzman guessed he was busting his hump with some luggage that Salzman couldn't see from where he was standing.

Joey said something to him. From where Salzman was it sounded a lot like 'hey shithead.' He couldn't hear the rest of it. Still the guy didn't pull his head out of the trunk.

A second later an airport van rolled up under the portico in front of the hotel and Salzman couldn't see anything. The van started to unload passengers and Salzman had a mind to step around so he could keep an eye on Joey.

Then something caught his eye. A pretty young thing in a micro-mini came down the steps of the van, all knees and thighs. To Salzman it was the kind of dress stewardesses used to wear back in the golden age of flight when the boomers were young, before they got sanctimonious and defined everything above the knees as hostile work environment. The driver got her bags. The bellman tried to keep his eyes on his work. Salzman took in the rear view as he drifted toward the back of the van. He watched as she headed up the stairs and into the lobby.

Where the hell was Jenrico? He took a walk around the backside of the van. Joey's truck was still parked there. The other car was gone. The door to the truck was wide open now, but he couldn't see Joey. Salzman headed out into the parking lot. He was getting strong vibes that Jenrico was screwing him around. He threaded his way between cars and made it to the back of the truck. When he stepped around he could see that Jenrico wasn't leaning over into the seat, what he'd thought when he looked from under the portico. He was gone.

Salzman looked inside on the seat. There was nothing. No box, no envelope, just two empty beer cans on the floor on the other side. The fucker had given him a single piece of paper with a dozen words that anybody could have typed on the back on a letterhead that anybody could have gotten. Jenrico had taken his two hundred bucks and stood him up. Salzman slammed the truck door hard, rattling the window in its metal frame. Then he noticed; Joey's keys were in the lock, and dangling from them was a broken piece of chrome chain.

CHAPTER

NINETEEN

Along with his contracts Spencer had Jack sign a power of attorney, listing Morgan as the agent for receipt of money on book advances and royalties. This way Abby maintained control of the money, keeping it out of Jack's hands. Morgan would cut a check paying Jack his share. The rest he would deposit in an account in Abby's name. Spencer was now playing a bigger role, for which he finally accepted a retainer from Abby for his services.

Abby stopped at the cemetery on the way out of town and put fresh flowers on Theresa's grave. She found it hard to believe that only a month before the two of them had clowned over the photographs in the agency's modeling directory. Now Theresa was dead. Of the small circle of friends, intimates that she trusted, only Spencer was left.

She flew out of Seattle on a Wednesday evening and hooked up with Jack at the airport in Chicago. They were destined for the Virgin Islands, to hole up while Abby wrote the sequel. But first Jack's presence was required at the American Booksellers Convention. Jack and the book were now on a fast track, speeding toward an early publishing date. Abby wasn't about to let Jack go alone. She still didn't trust him.

She had never heard of a manuscript brought to publication this quickly. Nor had she ever been to an ABA convention. The event was larger than she had imagined. It had started the day before and took up the entire floor of the Chicago Convention Center.

There were acres of gargantuan booths, many of them opulent, some with two-story columns in faux marble. One of them took on the appearance of a Southern plantation mansion, columns and ivy-covered lattice. The booths dotted the convention center floor, forming broad aisles that were jammed with people. Every major publisher was represented, even some from Europe and Asia. It was the largest gathering of publishers in the world, a part of publishing that most authors never saw. Only the cream were usually invited, and only the biggest names were asked to autograph books.

This year they were expecting thirty thousand people, by invitation only, professional booksellers from around the world, everything from mom-and-pop books stores to the mammoth chains. There was an air of carnival about the place with sales people manning booths like barkers at a county fair. The din of the crowd milling up and down the aisles merged with music from the convention center's speaker system. This occasionally broke from the music with announcements, usually about authors signing their books in a separate wing of the center that had been set up for the purpose. It was an eclectic mix, film stars and other pop celebrities alongside artists who had illustrated children's books. Everywhere there were posters, magical art work from the covers of books from around the world.

At one point, Abby and Jack nearly got trampled by a

crowd fighting for free canvas book bags being given out by one of the publishers. Carla had picked Abby and Jack up in a limo at the airport and was now running interference to the Big-F booth where Jack was expected to make an appearance.

For some reason, people seemed to be looking at him as he fought his way through the crowd. Abby figured it was just his good looks, until several of them began to point and finally a woman broke the ice.

'Would you sign my book.' She pressed her way in. The woman wore a name tag that read 'The Tattered Cover – Denver.'

Jack looked bemused. She handed him the book. Abby had not seen it before. It was an advance reader copy with paper covers, Gable Cooper's name on it, and Abby's title underneath. Jack's picture was on the back.

Jack took the woman's pen and started to sign his name. Abby jammed him in the back with an elbow. He scratched out 'Jack' and instead wrote 'Gable Cooper.'

Before he could give the woman her book back, a line started to form in the aisle.

'Not here.' Carla waved them on. They headed for the Big-F booth, Carla, Abby, and Jack, followed by a growing crowd, an ever-increasing line snaking its way across the convention floor like the Carioca.

By the time they got to the booth, Jack had his work cut out for him. Two of the sales reps took up positions alongside of him, opening covers and marking the place to sign. They could no longer see the end of the line, hundreds, perhaps a thousand, standing with books in their hands. Jack went to work, under a mammoth poster of the bookcover with his picture, a beaming countenance six feet tall smiling out at the convention throngs.

There was a crew with television cameras taking pictures.

'Local news?' asked Abby.

'Part of their marketing,' said Owens. 'T.V. magazine piece to air at the time of the publication. Jack will have to sit for a few interviews.'

They were leaving nothing to chance. Abby marveled at the campaign.

Carla leaned into her ear so she could be heard. 'Alex brought twenty thousand advance reader copies. They put out eighteen thousand of them yesterday morning. On pallets over there.' She pointed to some wooden pallets near the corner of the booth that were now bare.

Abby looked at her.

'They were gone in an hour,' said Carla.

Abby knew that her book had the legs to walk. But she never expected this. She wondered if people had read the advance copies the previous night, or if the mob was simply propelled by Big-F's promotion and Jack's picture on the back cover. Whatever it was, one thing was certain: the tidal wave had begun.

Jack signed books for nearly three hours but the line never ended. Finally Bertoli put a stop to it. They were late for a private reception back at the hotel. Jack and Abby were ushered out through a back service area and into the limo for the mile-and-a-half ride to the Hilton.

When they arrived the reception was already underway, several hundred people in a large banquet room. Bertoli led the way, making introductions as they went and talking to Jack in a seamless stream.

'It's wonderful news,' he told them. 'The film is now green lighted.' After signing their star, the studio had named a top notch director. The script was already into revisions. This would now be an endless task rewriting lines to stroke the egos of the stars until the film was in the can.

Bertoli asked Jack if he wanted to take a cut at the screen play. Jack's eyes lit up, but Abby said no. There wasn't time if Jack was going to finish the next book.

'Good thinking,' said Bertoli. 'Casting for support is proceeding at full pace. They'll be in production within four months. It's timing to die for,' said the publisher. 'The film will be out with the paperback.'

Bertoli had received a half-dozen phone calls from *Variety*, *Entertainment Weekly*, and the trades in a single afternoon following the star signing.

He also knew something else he wasn't sharing until he had what he wanted. The novel had just been sold in a hotly contested auction to one of the book clubs for the highest price ever netted on a first-time novel. It was the kind of outside confirmation that caused the ground to swell. Bertoli was beginning to sense an eruption, and he wanted to move on Jack before it happened.

They popped more corks, poured more champagne. A waiter passed among them with trays of hors d'oeuvres. Most of the executive staff of Big-F was present along with representatives from the chains and many of the independents, owners and managers of large and small book stores from across the country.

For Jack the introductions began to pile up, name overload so that Abby had to whisper in his ear as they mingled. Some of the guests took Abby for Jack's wife until he introduced her as his lawyer.

Bertoli presented him with a crystal champagne glass, bigger than any of the plastic cups the other guests were using. It had a red ribbon around the stem and the title of Abby's novel etched in the glass.

A waiter with a magnum bottle seemed to follow Jack wherever he went, filling his glass. Abby had to wonder how embarrassed and angry Bertoli would be when she went public. He would look like a fool. But if it worked, she didn't care. After seeing the lines forming on the convention floor, mostly doe-eyed women gazing at Jack, Abby was convinced she'd done the right thing. She hadn't made the rules, but she'd learned to bend them.

A few seconds later Bertoli told Abby someone wanted to meet her. He dragged her across the room and introduced her to another lawyer, a woman on their staff. It was ham-handed at best, an excuse to separate Abby from Jack. When she looked back she found herself supplanted by Carla, who'd taken charge shepherding him through the crowd.

Within three minutes the other lawyer drifted off. She'd done her job. This left Abby to sip from a plastic cup quietly in a corner, virtually ignored. She noticed that in one of the small conference rooms off the mammoth reception area everything had been carefully laid out for a meeting. She stuck her head inside and looked. The place had all the signs of a ritual sacrifice, including name plates. The only thing missing was the offering. Abby didn't like it. Across the room Bertoli kept swilling champagne into Jack.

It was all very sociable, but a few minutes later Jack was herded into the little room. Bertoli and Carla and a couple of the other executives from Big-F followed them. When they started to close the door, Abby made her move.

'What's going on?'

One of the minions barred the way. 'Private meeting,' he told her.

'Not without me. I'm his lawyer,' said Abby.

The guy holding the door looked over at his shoulder at Bertoli for direction.

Abby was prepared to make a scene and they knew it.

'Oh sure. She should be in here,' said Bertoli. He scolded one of his subordinates for the oversight and offered Abby a big beefy grin. 'Come on in.'

Like some bouncer in a bar, the man released his iron grip on the door and let her pass. There were knowing glances exchanged between Owens and Bertoli like a quarterback giving audibles on the line, changing the signals. The end run would now have to be a power play up the middle, over Abby's body.

'Get Miss Chandlis a chair.' Bertoli issued the order to one of his associates, a guy at the far end of the table, who immediately rose to offer his chair.

'I'd like that one.' Abby pointed to the man sitting next to Jack. Grudgingly the guy got up and Abby took his place.

'What's this all about?' she asked.

Owens took the lead.

'Alex thought we should have this meeting, that it was essential before we went any further. Everything is moving so fast,' she said.

'Light speed,' said Abby.

'Green-lighted film. Fast track to publication,' said Carla.

'Unscheduled meetings,' said Abby.

'Yes. Well. There is one problem.' Carla broke the ice.

'And what's that?' said Abby.

'The promotional budget on the book is ballooning,' said Bertoli. 'The marketing costs are out of all proportion to the probable return.'

'Oops. Maybe we should put this back in the bottle,'

said Jack. He held up his glass. Jack looked a little drunk.

Nervous chuckles from Bertoli. Maybe they'd gone too far with bottle diplomacy.

'There's no crisis,' said Bertoli. 'It's just that there are formulae in the industry that determine a sound marketing budget. And on this book we've thrown them all out.'

'I appreciate it.' Jack threw his head back and swallowed half a glass of champagne like it was a shot.

'I think what Alex is trying to say is that he can't continue to do this without some assurance that he'll be able to recoup that investment in the future. Isn't that what you're saying, Alex?'

'That's what I'm saying.'

'What kind of assurance?' Abby didn't like the sound of it.

Bertoli cleared his throat. 'Let's say, five books under contract.'

'Five books?' Jack had a look like Bertoli'd lit him up.

'Of course we can negotiate the terms,' said Bertoli.

'Bullshit,' said Jack.

'Surely not that many.' Carla ignored Jack as if he'd sneezed. This was polite New York bullshit. 'Perhaps the sequel you're working on and one or two more.' She looked at Abby, who to this point hadn't said a word.

'That wasn't the deal,' said Abby.

'Everything must be negotiable,' said Bertoli. He was looking at Abby, the mellow one without the drink in her hand. They had played it wrong and Carla and Bertoli now knew it. They'd plied him with booze, but Jack had the signs of a mean drunk.

'Could it be you have a little inside information?' Jack

raised his voice. He was looking at Bertoli through an intimidating alcohol haze.

'Well, I don't think there's anything material that you don't know,' said Bertoli. He looked at Carla. 'I couldn't think what it might be?' he said. 'I'd have to talk to my people. Look at the numbers.' Bertoli started to yammer, all the things that come out of a guilty mouth.

'Perhaps we should continue this at a later time.' Carla stepped in to save him. It wouldn't do to have this turn ugly with three hundred buyers standing outside the door.

'No, I think we should resolve it now,' said Abby. She liked the idea of crazy Jack and the crowd. It gave her leverage. They made a mistake, and now they were going to have to play on her field.

'It's just that Alex loves Jack's work,' said Carla. 'He wants to publish everything he writes. Isn't that right, Alex?'

'Absolutely,' said Bertoli. 'All we're talking about is good faith negotiations.'

Carla was dug in, almost more than Big-F. For Bertoli, it was the price. He wanted to get the books before the cost doubled or tripled. Abby guessed that for Carla it was control. She wanted Jack, Gable Cooper, under her belt for more books. If she had to, she would savage Bertoli later, renegotiate the price upward to keep the author happy. The cost of renegotiation to the author would of course be the perennial demand for still more books. There was a downside to everything in life. For the successful author, it was the agent working both ends.

'You have the one book,' said Abby. 'Publish it. Do it well, and we can talk. That's good faith.'

'But you don't seem to understand. I can't continue to

spend in this fashion,' said Bertoli. 'To, to, how do I put it . . .?'

'Lavish,' said Carla.

'Thank you,' said Bertoli.

As an agent in the trenches, Owens was worse than worthless. She was her own fifth column.

'I can't continue to lavish money,' said Bertoli, 'unless . . .?' He held his hands palms-up and smiled. The message was clear. They were holding hostages in the form of Abby's book.

'So you figure it's a good time to hold us up,' said Jack. He took another drink from his glass, more powder from the keg.

'You're being very unreasonable.' To Carla, all things were made possible by the agent; the deals from heaven. Books were just an incidental bi-product of her power. If she could, she would have skipped the writers completely and allowed the readers to gain their enjoyment from her glow.

'It's extortion.' Jack moved on to other crimes and took another drink.

'Extortion.' Carla smiled and tried to regain her composure. She and Bertoli laughed and tried to dismiss it, the ravings of a drunk who would not remember the next day.

'No one is engaging in extortion,' said Carla. 'This is business.'

'Only if you're Al Capone,' said Jack. He looked at her over the top of his crystal champagne glass.

Jack had driven them into a defensive crouch and now Abby took over.

'What assurance do we have if we give you more books that you'll use your best efforts to market this one?' said Abby.

'What do you mean?' said Bertoli.

'If we give you more books, how do we prevent you from climbing the list on our back, from doing it in marginal increments instead of one big push?'

'Why would he do that?' Carla looked incredulous.

'To conserve his budget. There's only so many dollars. Once we give you more books, we don't exist. You can afford to ignore us.' And Abby knew they would.

'No tours. Your publicity people use their chits with the networks to put other authors on the talk shows. You cut the corners on our print ads. We get the teasers. They get full pages. Squeaky wheel gets oiled,' said Abby. 'And without the ability to negotiate future contracts, we can't squeak. Not so that you'll be able to hear us anyway.'

Bertoli laughed. He looked at Carla. He'd never heard of anything so ridiculous. 'We're in the business of making money,' he said. 'We'd never cut Jack's budget. He's a valued author. We're gonna take him over the top,' said Bertoli. 'Pull out all the stops.'

'But how do we know that?'

'Because I'm telling you.' Bertoli gave her a big grin, something like Boris on Rockey and Bullwinkle.

'There,' said Carla. 'See, you have Alex's word on it.'

'Tell you what,' said Abby. 'You take us over the top, pull out all the stops, and you have my word. We'll give you more books.'

There was a dead beat of stone silence in the room. Bertoli hated lawyers.

'We should hire this woman. Brassy,' he said. 'I like that. You, guy down there. You could take some notes.' Bertoli was talking to his two underlings. 'Still,' he said. 'I have to have something.'

'Or else what?' said Abby.

Bertoli made a face, followed by a long pained silence. It was the kind of expression that left Abby to wonder about the consequences.

'We need to cooperate on this,' said Owens. 'We're a team. We're working together.'

'Oh. We can all see that you're cooperating with him,' said Abby.

Jack actually laughed.

'Tell you what.' She ignored Owens and dealt directly with Bertoli. 'You want security for your investment. We want assurances that you won't squander the book you already have. I think there's an easy answer,' she told him.

Bertoli was all ears.

'We sign a contract,' said Abby.

'You're gonna let these people bulldoze you?' said Jack.

'Hear me out,' said Abby.

'More books?' Bertoli was a smile.

'Not yet,' said Abby. 'We do an agreement to sign a future contract on certain terms and conditions.'

'What do you mean? What terms and conditions?'

'We agree to give you more books in the future, if you carry out your promise to take the current manuscript "over the top." "To pull out all the stops," as you say.'

'How are you going to put something like that in a contract?'

'By defining what you mean by "over the top," and "pulling out all the stops." '

'Just a turn of speech,' said Bertoli.

'So you don't mean it?'

'Oh sure. We're gonna try. But we can't guarantee anything.'

'But you want us to guarantee more books,' said Jack.

'Now that's a double standard if I ever saw one.' He pointed an accusing wobbly finger at the publisher and tried to get up but slumped again into the chair. 'You don't have to do a damn thing, but we have to provide good books. Blood from my veins,' said Jack.

Abby had a hard time keeping a straight face.

'So what do you want?' said Bertoli.

'Two things,' said Abby. 'I want this book to go high on the bestsellers list and I want it to stay there a long time.'

'What? Number one?' said Bertoli.

'For at least ten weeks,' said Abby.

Bertoli actually fell back in his chair.

'That's absurd,' said Owens.

'In addition, you'd have to agree to hold it on the list for an additional five months, inside of number seven.'

Bertoli was flabbergasted. 'That's ridiculous.'

'Fine. Inside of ten. That's the "pull out all the stops" part,' said Abby. If he was going to throw terms around and make idle promises, she was going to nail his feet to the floor.

'Why the hell should I have to do more books?' said Jack.

'Quiet,' said Abby.

Unless Bertoli had a superman complex or was blowing coke on the side, it was a deal he couldn't accept, and Abby knew it. She didn't want him to. It was designed to do one thing: take the wind out of his sails for more books.

'That's outrageous. I can't guarantee placement on the list.'

'I'm not asking you to guarantee anything. I'm offering you a performance incentive. Perform and you get more books,' said Abby.

'It's unheard of,' said Bertoli.

'Not, it's not. You do it to authors all the time,' said Jack. Suddenly he wasn't as drunk as he'd made out.

'What are you talking about?'

'Your bonus clause,' said Jack. 'You put it in my contract. You know the one. Says if we get on the *New York Times* bestsellers list you release the advance a little faster. You aren't paying us any more, you're just paying it out a little quicker.'

Abby was stunned. Jack had actually read the contract.

'That's different,' said Bertoli.

'I know,' said Jack. 'We're offering you something real.'

The silence from Bertoli filled the room.

'What's the problem? Is it that the mark's too high?' said Jack. Now he was taunting Bertoli.

'Where exactly is this "over the top" you've been talking about?' asked Jack.

'It's just a manner of speech,' said Carla.

'Ah, so now we're getting down to it. So it's just a lot of loose talk?' said Jack.

'That's not what we're saying,' said Owens.

'You've got a problem,' said Abby. 'You either have to define it or forget it.'

'I can't do that,' said Bertoli. 'I just can't guarantee a result on the list. You don't understand.'

'Oh, I think I understand.' Jack made it sound like a measure of Bertoli's manhood. What he was afraid of was failure. Reduce the test to writing in a contract and the entire industry would know about it. If Alex failed and lost future books and the author with them, he would be legend. It would follow him to his grave in business hell.

'Do we have a deal or don't we?' said Jack.

'Maybe we should consider the terms?' Carla was pitching Bertoli now, but it was a little late. 'Maybe a few weeks less on the list,' she said. 'How about if he takes you inside of three, instead of one?' She looked at Jack.

'I can't do it. I won't do it.' Bertoli cut her off.

Jack shrugged and looked at her like the sensible drunk that he was. 'You heard him. We're trying to be reasonable,' said Jack. This after Abby had just capped Bertoli's knees.

Jack smiled and stood, looked at his watch. 'Geez, it's getting late. Don't we have the gala dinner tonight?' The producers were flying in the star of the film to meet the author and talk with the book buyers in one of the big ballrooms. The studio had a big stake in the success of the novel, and Abby and Jack knew it. They now had a big stick.

'We'll have to continue this,' said Carla. 'After all, everything in life is negotiable, right?'

'I suppose you would think that,' said Abby. 'Now that we know what you are, all that would be left to discuss is your price.'

Owens shot her a look to kill.

CHAPTER
TWENTY

Lake Washington had the big houses. It was where
Bill Gates, the Microsoft magnate, had a mansion.
Lake Union, its little sister to the west, had a few
apartments and condos, but for the most part it was
commercial, boat yards and brokerages, a few restaurants at the south end.

The fire had occurred a few days earlier, but the acrid
odor of smoke hung over the water like a guest who
wouldn't leave. With the window of his car rolled
down, scents of burnt wood and chemicals tickled Sanfillipo's sinuses as he drew closer.

He could hear the constant buzz of tires on the iron
spans of I-5 two hundred feet overhead.

He found a place and parked in front of a canvas shop
that advertised dodgers and bimini tops for boats,
locked the unmarked car, and walked. A dump truck
was backed up on the dock being loaded with debris,
piles of charred, water-soaked wood. A floating crane,
its boom four stories in the sky, drifted in the current off
shore. Workmen in hard hats scurried about. Luther saw
one of them with a clipboard, symbol of authority, and
got directions.

Sanfillipo made his way around equipment and down the paved incline of a driveway toward the water. The breeze suddenly took the smell in another direction. He could see the ridge line of a small building, what was left of it, poking a few feet above the surface of the water about fifty feet out from the docks. There was a small army standing around. Everything had been shut down since they discovered the body two hours earlier. As he approached, they turned and Luther introduced himself.

'Lieutenant Sanfillipo.' He flashed the foreman his badge, and the guy shook his hand. 'I understand they have some business for me?' He saw some uniforms down by the water, but he wanted to talk to the workmen first.

'Coroner's down there right now,' said the foreman. He pointed to a small work barge where several men, some in uniform, were huddled over a dark bundle.

'They're not sure if it was an accident or what,' said the foreman. 'Our drivers found the body at first light. He was tangled in some lines. Looks like maybe something heavy might have fallen on him during the fire.'

'Like half the building,' said one of the other guys.

'How did the fire happen?' asked Sanfillipo.

'We don't know yet. Fire department thinks it could have been arson,' said the foreman. 'With all the paint and other stuff inside, it's hard to tell. We're raising it so the fire marshal can find the point of origin.'

'Guess it burned all the way through the dock,' said the detective.

'No. No. It was an old wooden ammunition barge. Makeshift boat yard,' said the guy. 'Told it dated to World War One. Wonder it floated anymore.'

'Is the owner around?'

The foreman shook his head. 'City's been chasing him around. A lot of complaints filed on the business. Code violations. That sort of stuff.'

Luther nodded like he understood.

'They think he might have started it?'

'I don't think so. Apparently he lost everything, tools, the works. No insurance. Three generations in business down the drain. Just like that. Tough break,' said the guy.

'A tragedy,' said Sanfillipo. 'But not as bad as what happened to the guy in the bag over there. What about him? Didn't anybody miss him when the fire broke out?'

'He wasn't an employee.'

Luther offered up arched eyebrows.

'People from the boat yard don't seem to have any idea what he was doing there.'

'Maybe he set the fire?' said one of the other workmen. 'I suppose it wouldn't be the first time an arsonist got caught up in what he was doing.'

'Yeah. Sort of consumed by his own work, you might say,' one of the other guys chimed in and they all laughed at his joke.

'A lot of gallows humor in this business,' said Luther.

'Yeah, regular Robin Williams,' said the foreman. 'Let's get back to work.' The group sauntered away unhappy that they couldn't stay where the action was.

'It's possible,' said Luther, 'that your arsonist is in the bag out there. Though without insurance you wonder why.'

'Firebug,' said the foreman. 'They don't need a reason.'

'True,' said Luther. 'Any identification?'

'I think they found a wallet. Coroner's got it.'

Luther wandered down toward the work barge, one end of which was tied up against the dock, stepped down into it, and wedged his way into the group. There was a diver in a black wet suit, his mask propped on top of his head, his feet in the water sitting on the edge.

'Harmon.' Luther recognized the deputy coroner.

'Lieutenant.' As soon as he said it, the other men moved aside, giving Luther a little more room and a lot more deference.

'What brings you out here so early?' said the coroner.

'The smell of napalm in the morning.' He looked at the zipped-up body bag on the deck. 'Burned?'

The coroner shook his head. 'Fire burned through the wooden hull pretty quick. Sank like a rock.'

'What can you tell me?'

'May have drowned. It's also possible he may have been dead before it went down. Took a little fluid out of the lungs, but not much. Body's pretty bloated. Been down there over a week. Won't know more 'til I get him on a table.'

'Any name?'

The coroner showed Luther a clipboard with a county form, some notes on it, and pointed. Luther looked at it and thought.

'Did he work in the area?'

'Got me. If he did, you'd think somebody would have noticed that he was missing.'

'You would think so,' said Luther. 'You pretty sure he went down with it at the time of the fire?'

'Oh yeah. He was buried under fire debris. I would say he was there before it started. Also there were some burns. The divers didn't even see him 'til one of them grabbed his foot in the dark.'

'I suppose that might cause a mess in your wet suit,'

said Luther. The diver didn't look at him.

'They tell me you found a wallet?' Luther asked the coroner.

'Yeah.' The man reached for a water-sodden paper bag resting on top of the barge's winch and poured the contents out on top of a flat area on the machinery. There was a ring, some change, and a black wallet. The leather of the wallet was soggy and soft. A piece of green lake weed had worked its way inside the plastic window with the driver's license, but it was still readable. Luther pawed through the contents of the wallet. Inside one of the flaps was the stub from an airline boarding pass showing a flight from LAX, the date and time.

'Lotta possibilities, I suppose,' said the coroner. 'If he wasn't one of the employees, he could have been a customer. Maybe had a boat in the works.'

'Hmm,' said Luther. 'But how did this customer get here?'

'Whadda you mean?'

'Without any keys,' said the detective.

The coroner looked at the items spread out on the rusted metal surface on top of the winch. Luther was right. Among the objects found on the body there were no keys, to a car or anything else.

Luther compared the name on the coroner's notes with the name on the driver's license, then looked at the picture on the laminated license.

'I don't think this man was a customer,' he said. 'I don't think this guy was into yachts.'

They took an early morning flight to Atlanta and from there to Savannah. Abby tried to catch a few winks but the stewardesses kept fraternizing. It was the thing that happened with Jack. He was a magnet for women; even the old lady he helped with luggage in the overhead compartment kept looking at him with eyes of wonderment. To Abby it was getting tiresome. He was good-looking, but he was only flesh and bone. If she was right, the warts were all on the inside; boils of arrogance the size of oranges. Jack didn't seem to mind the gaping looks. She guessed that he'd had a lifetime of it and had grown accustomed to the stares of women.

They landed, grabbed their luggage, picked up the car, and headed for Coffin Point. To Abby, never having seen it, the name conjured ominous thoughts.

As they drove north, in the direction of Hilton Head, the area served up a generous offering of serenity; white clapboard houses against green lawns, towering oaks overgrown with moss, cricketlike sounds, and the smells of the country. It wasn't as lush as western Washington, but it had its own kind of beauty. It reminded her of places in the Delta near San Francisco Bay. Only it seemed much larger. They passed through Beaufort with its stately old homes, picture-card perfect.

They stayed on Highway 21 out of Beaufort, crossed the channel to Lady's Island, and from there to St Helena Island and toward Frogmore. A few miles on they turned off and within minutes the road turned to dirt.

The thought had crossed Abby's mind as they left the state highway and headed down the sandy loam road; she didn't know Jack Jermaine from Adam. She had expected a call from Morgan in Chicago. It never came, and she wondered why. They were supposed to coordinate before she left. Still Morgan had her number at Jack's house. Maybe he'd left a message there.

They rattled along in the Landcruiser on the dirt road, past picket fences and small houses, a few mobile homes.

The inside of Jack's car was clean, meticulous, military, though the outside could have used a wash.

'You took a real chance,' said Jack. 'What if Bertoli had decided to pull the plug when you told him no more books?'

'He wouldn't.'

'Why not?'

'You saw the line on the floor of the convention center.' Abby didn't mention the star-struck gaze of many of the women standing in it. Jack's ego didn't need any feeding. 'They tried and they lost,' said Abby. 'Round one.'

'He seemed pretty angry to me.'

'People in New York like to argue,' said Abby. 'It's all part of the Great Manhattan Mindfuck.'

Jack laughed.

'Look at it this way,' she said. 'Bertoli gave us his best pitch, at least for this inning. We made him eat it. Now he has something more to play for. If I'd given him the books without a fight, Carla and Alex would have had to go home and take depression meds.'

'Then you intend to give them more books?'

'We'll see.' She had no intention of tipping her hand to Jack.

'They didn't just want the books, they wanted bondage. They wanted to own me.'

'They were looking at me,' said Jack.

'You. Me. For now it's all the same.'

'I saved your ass.'

'You saved nothing. My ass was about to walk out of the room.'

'That would have been a mistake,' said Jack.

'Why?'

'Because that would have left me in there alone.'

Abby looked at him and couldn't tell if he was kidding.

'Hey. I wanted to find out what they were willing to offer for four more books,' said Jack. 'Aren't you at least curious?'

'Whatever it is, it's not enough.'

'I saw something recently. An author got twenty-four million,' said Jack.

'That was for three books,' said Abby.

Jack looked over at her. She *was* interested after all.

Abby brushed a string of hair out of her face and then said casually: 'I saw it in the paper last week.'

'Oh right. Next to the stock quotes and obits.' He laughed. 'There's nothing wrong with being interested in money.'

'No. It's just the questionable things it makes you do,' said Abby. She thought, like get in a car with a man I don't know and head down some lonely dirt road.

'Five months on the *New York Times* list,' said Jack.

'I wanted to give him a challenge,' said Abby.

'More like a coronary. Did you catch the look? Like you lit him up. I've seen people touch high tension wires with less effect,' said Jack.

'You're the one got drunk.'

'Putten him on. That's all,' said Jack. 'Who in their right mind argues with an angry drunk. You think I went too far?'

'You were fine. Just your average obsessive author.' She looked at him and they both started to laugh.

'Artsy-fartsy me,' said Jack. 'Make me God or I won't play. The look on his face when you said ten weeks, top of the list, was worth the royalties. Train-struck deer.'

'Carla's probably still peeling him off the ceiling,' said Abby.

'I could have given him the books,' said Jack. 'But then I suppose we would have been in trouble.'

'We wouldn't have been in trouble,' said Abby, 'I would have been in trouble. You forget. You're my alter ego. In the eyes of the law, you stand in my shoes.'

He looked at her feet. 'Now that would hurt.'

'Get serious,' she told him. 'You agree to something and I'm obligated to perform.'

'In that case we should visit the red light district in Atlanta,' said Jack.

'Very funny.'

'I could get you a little bustier, some lace on the thigh. Buy myself a purple fedora.'

'Is that the kind of work you do?' said Abby.

'Do I look like it?'

'Looks are deceiving,' said Abby.

'On a dusty road with a man you don't know. It's a little late to be asking, isn't it?' It was something that her father might have said when she was a teenager about getting into cars with strangers. Jack didn't look at her when he said it. It was also the kind of thing a killer might ask a hitchhiker just before he plunged the knife in or jumped her.

She studied him for a long moment. There was an awkward silence. Abby wasn't sure if she should treat the question seriously. It would only feed her anxieties or, she thought, lead to something worse.

'I was only kidding,' said Jack. 'You're perfectly safe.'

'Right.' Abby didn't look at him.

'Relax.' Jack looked at her and laughed. 'Listen, you want me to stop?'

'No,' said Abby. It was the one thing she was sure of. She didn't want him to stop on a deserted road in the middle of nowhere.

'You never told me how your friend, what was her name?'

'Theresa?'

'Yeah. You never told me what happened. The article in the paper was a little vague. Was it an accident?'

'I don't know. I don't think so.'

'Someone killed her?'

'It looks that way.'

'Her husband?'

Abby looked at him trying to figure how he would put this together so quickly

He caught her glance. 'Well, it makes sense. An angry husband. Bad marriage.'

'The cops don't think he did it.'

'Why not?'

'It's a long story.' Abby didn't want to talk about it. 'Can we discuss something else.'

'Sure. Let's talk about more books. What's your take? You think Bertoli will bury us now that we've turned him down?'

'I don't think he can afford to.'

'Why not?'

'We're into him for three million. He's got to get it back somehow. Plus the film thing. True, we don't get the big bucks there until they get to principal photography. Just the same, the studio's on the hook with the star. They have to keep him happy. Why do you think I got three million for books rights?'

'It's a good book,' said Jack.

'Oh, it's a fine book,' said Abby. 'Marvelous read. But take it from me, the payout wasn't based on my excellent prose. This has all the signs of a deal driven by the stars,' said Abby.

'And you think that gives us leverage?'

'On this book, yes. The only way we lose is if they get more books. Then Bertoli can spread the risk. Make it back over the long haul and let the studio worry about their star. Right now we need to keep Bertoli on a short leash, and keep him hungry. If he makes us big . . .'

'Us?' said Jack.

'Speaking metaphorically,' said Abby. 'Then maybe it's time to talk about more books.'

'So if he brings us to the prom, your theory is why not dance with him,' said Jack.

'As opposed to a sock-hop,' said Abby.

She was right and Jack knew it. The tail wagging the dog. It was the movie deal that had the book on a hot burner.

'There's something else,' said Jack. 'Plain as the nose on your face.'

'My nose is plain?'

'Poor choice of words,' said Jack. 'That's why you're the writer.'

'Not that anyone would notice,' said Abby.

He looked over at her. 'In fact, you have a very nice nose.'

She touched it self-consciously with the tip of her finger like maybe it was running.

'Anyway,' said Abby. She didn't trust him enough to flirt.

'Anyway. There's another dynamic.'

'What do you mean?'

'What I said at the meeting. There's something Bertoli's not telling.'

'What?'

'I don't know,' said Jack. 'Early orders for the book. Something from the big chains.' He shook his head in puzzlement. 'Something's turned the buzz up a notch for him to come after more books that way. Kinda frontal, don't you think? No finesse. I would have figured Carla for finesse. One thing for sure. The books they wanted are worth a lot more than we know.'

Abby thought about this for a moment. 'It does make me angry. The garbage about the forces of the market-place. That he had to recoup his investment. Couldn't continue to lavish money.'

'Don't get mad. That's business. You gave him a price,' said Jack. 'His house, his soul, and his first born. As soon as Carla rubs his ego down they'll be back. You gotta think there's one rule in the jungle. We come and go. The agents live in the sandbox with the publishers. The writer's always the odd man out. Still, she brought you the deal. You couldn't have gotten here without her.'

'She cut herself a piece of cake,' said Abby. 'Question is, can I trust her now?'

Jack looked at her straight across as he gripped the steering wheel. 'Who ever told you you could trust anybody?'

To say that cops have suspicious minds is like saying cats land on their feet: an article of faith.

When Luther Sanfillipo called Abby's house and discovered that her phone has been disconnected he began to wonder. When he drove over and found a For Sale staked in her front lawn and the house empty he began to worry. And when he called her office and was told that she'd quit her job and left no forwarding address he began to act.

He parked his car in a commercial garage. In this neighborhood Luther figured it was the price of keeping his hub caps. He hiked the two blocks, mostly up hill, to the dilapidated three-story office building. The outside was covered with tattered posters, and a lot of graffiti that would have required decoding by the gang unit.

Downstairs was a video store and a small grocery. In between the two was a single glass door with an address in metal numbers over the top that somehow the neighbors hadn't managed to pry off and steal. Luther entered and made his way to the top of the stairs over the soiled carpet.

At the top a hallway formed a *T* going in two directions, with separate doors at the end of each. 'Marcia's Relaxation Center' was painted on one of them. The other bore the name:

'C. W. CHANDLIS, COUNSELOR
&
ATTORNEY AT LAW'

Luther heard the patter of typing on the other side of the door, opened it, and went in.

'Can I help you?' A man, fairly well dressed, was seated at a desk in an outer office; what passed for reception.

'I'm looking for Mr Charles Chandlis.'

The man continued to hunt-and-peck at the typewriter.

'You found him.'

Luther looked at him sitting at the typewriter. 'You're the attorney?' said Luther.

'My secretary's out for a few minutes,' said Charlie.

It was a bad omen, Luther hadn't even introduced

himself and he was being lied to. He'd done a little checking, including employment records. Chandlis's secretary had filed for unemployment two weeks before, along with a labor claim for unpaid wages. The lawyer was on the financial edge, one more reason why Luther thought he might want to talk to him.

'Who are you?' said Charlie.

'Name's Sanfillipo.' He took out his badge and showed it to the lawyer.

Instant hackles. If Charlie had been a dog, the hair on the back of his neck would have stood up.

'If this is about one of my cases, you can forget it. I only deal with your bosses,' said Charlie.

Luther flexed his eyebrows in question.

'The county prosecutor's office,' said Charlie. Then he looked at the door as if Luther might want to use it again, to leave.

'Oh. No. No. It's not about one of your cases. It's about one of mine.'

The way he said this caused Charlie to pause for a moment and look at him.

'I am looking for your wife,' said Luther.

'I'm not married.' Charlie went back to his typing, and looked at his watch like he was on some deadline. He hit some wrong keys, several letters, and had to back over two of them with the correcting ribbon.

'You should get yourself a computer,' said Luther.

'Yeah, right. And spend six months learning how to use it,' said Charlie.

'Your secretary should be able to do that,' said Luther. He did the kind of Raul Julia smile that so intimidated.

'What do you want?'

'I told you,' said Luther. 'I'm looking for Mrs Chandlis. Abigail Chandlis.'

'My former wife,' said Charlie.

'Yes.'

'As the title implies, we don't live together anymore,' said Charlie. 'You might try her house.'

'I did. It's empty,' said Luther.

For the first time, Charlie stopped typing and swiveled around in his chair to look up at the cop, more questions in his eyes now than on his lips.

'Do you have an interest in it?' said Luther.

'What?'

'Your wife's house.'

'No. Why do you ask?'

'Because it's for sale.'

Chandlis considered this for a moment, and unless Luther had lost his ability to judge body language, the lawyer was hearing it for the first time. He returned to his typing.

'Why are you looking for her?'

'An investigation,' said Luther. 'Just routine.'

'Did she do something wrong?'

'Not that we know of.' Luther made it sound like a question.

Charlie didn't bite.

'We would just like to talk to her,' said Luther.

'Did you call the firm?'

'Hmm.' The cop nodded. 'She quit last week.'

There was no pause in typing, but several mistakes. Luther might have asked him if he knew about this, but he didn't have to.

'I thought you might know where she is?'

'I don't.'

'When was the last time you talked to her?'

'Can't remember. We're not that close,' said Charlie.

'Oh. I was under the impression that you kept in touch.'

'And what gave you that impression?'

'The fact that you received six thousand dollars from her ten days ago,' said Luther.

Charlie didn't say anything but stopped his typing in mid-word and looked at Luther, clearly angry that the police were prying into his financial affairs.

'Do you mind telling me what it was for?' said Luther.

'Why should I? You seem to know everything already.'

'Am I safe in assuming a private debt?' said Luther.

'Not anymore,' said Charlie.

'I can assure you . . .'

'You can fuck your assurances,' said Charlie.

'That would be an interesting trick, but somehow I don't think it would make them any more acceptable to you,' said Luther. He thought Charlie sounded a lot like one of his clients. Perhaps it was contagious.

'How long have you been divorced?' he asked.

'The records are in the courthouse,' said Charlie. 'Why don't you go look?'

It was a possible theory that whoever killed Theresa Jenrico had done so by mistake; that the real target was Abby Chandlis. If so, she might be on the run. Or maybe they'd already gotten her.

'You heard about her friend Mrs Jenrico?' said Luther.

'Yeah. I heard. Tragic,' said Charlie.

'How did you hear about it?'

'The papers,' said Charlie. 'I can read.' He waited for the next question, what he was doing that night, but it didn't come. Luther wasn't that frontal.

'You must admit it's a rather peculiar way to pay a debt?'

'What do you mean?'

'I mean Mrs Chandlis paying it to your credit-card account like that.'

'It's the way she wanted it. For convenience,' said Charlie.

'I see. I'm sure the credit-card company thought it was convenient.' Luther smiled at him. He knew that Charlie was over his limit. The only thing that saved his card was his wife's payment.

'What business is that of yours?'

'Oh none. But I am curious why she would pay you such a large sum of money and then disappear without telling anyone where she was going?'

'You'd have to ask her that.'

'If I could find her I would.'

'Can't help you. Now if you're finished, I've got work to do.'

'Do you know where she got the money? To pay you, I mean?'

'No.'

'That's a lot of money. She isn't a wealthy woman.'

'No.'

Charlie wasn't the only one whose financial life was now under scrutiny.

'And the nature of the debt?' asked Luther.

'It was a loan,' Charlie lied.

'What for?'

'That's private. You wanna know anything more, get a subpoena. And I don't appreciate your fucking around in my financial affairs.'

'Oh, I assure you there was no fucking around,' said Luther. 'We merely called your bank and told them it was a homicide investigation.'

Charlie's eyes lit up.

'They were most anxious to help,' said Luther.

'Wonderful.' Now all the tellers would be looking at Charlie as if he were an ax murderer.

'We have been very discreet,' said Luther.

'I'll bet. Now just you and a few hundred of your asshole friends downtown know my credit rating.'

'I had never considered my colleagues in that light before,' said Luther. 'But I will tell them when I see them.' He headed for the door.

'Do that.'

Luther turned. 'All of this hostility, I assume, comes from your work?'

'I hadn't noticed,' said Charlie.

'That's the problem with job stress,' said Luther. 'It tends to creep up on you and kill you without your noticing.'

CHAPTER
TWENTY-ONE

What was once a grand entrance to a great planta-tion was now spotted by several houses and a few mobile homes. In the distance, a half mile off through a tunnel formed by a tree-lined lane, Abby could make out the white-washed walls and double staircase of an old plantation home, its columns reaching skyward.

The long drive leading to the house was overhung by ancient oaks, their broad branches merging in a canopy overhead. They nearly shut out the sunlight. To Abby, the drive looked like the vaulted ceiling of a Gothic cathedral hung with moss.

The road itself was soft sand, in places puddled with standing water from the recent rain. The rear end of Jack's car fish-tailed a little as it hit one of these.

'You own all of this?' said Abby.

'Don't look so impressed,' said Jack. 'You haven't seen the inside yet.'

As they drew closer she could see that he was right. Jack's house was like the man, well built, but showing signs of wear. It could have played well on a movie set; plantation house sans slaves, fallen on hard times. It stood three stories if you counted the flood basement set up on white pillars and shielded behind a mass of shrubbery. Heavy postered beams supported the covered porch that ran the length of the house and the picket-railed balcony at the top level.

Abby guessed that the place dated to the early part of the nineteenth century, something Sherman missed on his march to the sea.

They pulled up in front of the twin staircases and stopped. Jack got out and stretched. Abby joined him and felt the warmth of the dappled sunlight on her face. The smell of early blossoms was in the air. It was a setting as far removed from Seattle or any other big city as was possible; peaceful without a hint of traffic or the bustle of modern life. Without Jack's car parked in front, it could have been a picture from the last century.

'I'll get the luggage later,' he told her. 'Come on inside.'

On the way to the house he took a detour toward a little kiosk under the stairs, went inside, and a second later came out with a stack of letters in one hand, and a red, white, and blue express package in the other, the size of a shirt box.

It seemed the mailman and delivery trucks left mail and packages for Jack in the little building when he was gone. 'An informal agreement,' he told her. 'One of the perks of country life.'

Jack started picking through the envelopes as Abby followed him up the stairs. The front door wasn't locked. Another perk of country life, she assumed.

The entry hall was like something Abby had seen only in museums: broad-planked floors scarred and heavily polished by a century of wear. In one corner was an antique hall-tree, its beveled mirror blotched by missing silver in a few places.

Jack headed into a large central hall and Abby followed.

'Make yourself at home. I'll be right down.' He went up the stairs, a grand sweeping affair with a carved railing, the mail in one hand, the box under his other arm.

Abby wandered toward a large parlor. The interior was dark. Heavy curtains that looked like velvet with fringe, dated like the rest of the house, hung from the windows behind panes of bottle glass and long shades. The parlor was at the front of the house and was separated from the dining room by two twelve-foot pocket doors that rolled back into the walls for entertaining. Each of the rooms offered high-coffered ceilings. An immense crystal chandelier hung over the polished mahogany dining table and its surrounding high-back chairs. It looked like a setting for a war counsel.

In the parlor the museum decor continued; cut crystal dishes and bowls behind curved glass in a French cabinet. There were open shelves of leather-bound books, floor-to-ceiling. Some of the titles were in gold leaf, the histories of great battles and the thoughts of great minds: Cicero, *On the Republic*, and *Reflections on the Revolution in France* by Edmund Burke. She took a book down and looked at it; a first edition. Abby carefully put it back.

There were certificates and diplomas framed on one wall, something from Annapolis conferred on Joseph Jermaine, and a glass cabinet filled with trophies, several of them with little bronze men on top pointing pistols. Three of these had Joseph Jermaine's name on them. Two more dated thirty years later bore the inscription 'Joseph Jermaine, Jr.'

She studied these for a moment, then walked, hands coupled behind her back, toward the fireplace. The fire pit itself was the size of a small room, with giant andirons bearing twin bronze horse heads staring out at her. Over the fireplace was an immense mantel carved from a single piece of walnut.

There were military medals in a display case on top of this. Abby recognized one of these, a purple heart. Several others appeared to have inscriptions in foreign languages, one of them in French, and a case of battle ribbons, all the colors of the rainbow.

In a box off to one side, by itself, was another medal. It was not larger than the others but had a distinction. It was set off by the broad blue ribbon from which it hung. The medal itself was a bronze five-pointed star inverted with a single point down. The star was surrounded by a wreath. In this case the pendant was supported by an anchor. It was the Congressional Medal of Honor.

She picked up the box and looked at it, holding its wooden lid with her fingers.

'Most of them belong to my father.' Jack had come into the room behind her and caught her touching things.

'I'm sorry.' Abby put the box back on the mantel.

Jack was carrying a thick sheaf of papers held together by a rubber band in one hand. He came around her, took the box with the medal, and put it in a drawer in a cabinet in the corner.

'What can I get you?' said Jack. 'Are you hungry?'

'No. I'm fine.'

'Something to drink?'

'Anything cold and wet,' said Abby. 'Your dad was in the military?'

'Marines,' said Jack. He drifted toward the kitchen and she followed him.

'Who's Joseph, Jr?'

'I confess,' said Jack.

'You?'

'Jack's my nickname. Joseph Senior was my father.'

'Was?' said Abby.

'He's dead.'

'I'm sorry.'

'Don't be. He had a full life. Lived to be over eighty.'

'Was he a professional soldier?' said Abby.

'You could say that. Others prefer to think of him more as a professional son of a bitch.' He smiled as he said it.

'You make it sound like a term of endearment,' said Abby.

'In these parts? You bet your ass. Camp Perry's right over there.' He pointed casually in the direction of the sound that she could see through the kitchen window. 'Its own kind of hell,' said Jack. 'Among the officer corps, only sons of bitches live there. The rest die or retire early.'

'Besides being a son of a bitch, what did he do?'

'Oh, he wasn't just a son of a bitch. He was *the* son of a bitch of sons of bitches. The Great Son of a Bitch. The Commandant at Perry.'

'You make it sound like a concentration camp.'

'In a word,' said Jack. 'His ghost spends half its time over there, and the other half here in this house.'

She looked at him.

'Oh yeah. He haunts this place. If you hear any salty words at night, it'll be the old man. Any smacking of flesh, you know he's thumping somebody.'

'Sounds like a wonderful guy,' said Abby.

'People who knew him when he was younger tell me we look a lot alike.'

'So are you a professional son of a bitch, too?' she asked.

'Who me? No. I'm a pussycat. Just a little chip off the block. In my case, you could call it more of a splinter.'

Jack rummaged through the refrigerator. 'Cold and wet,' he said.

The kitchen was institutional. The sink was stainless steel as were all the countertops, and a large island in the center of the room. You could have cooked for an army on the commercial gas range, though it looked like it was forty years old.

'Let's see. I've got milk.' He smelled it. 'Scratch the milk.' He put it on the countertop. 'I wouldn't recommend the orange juice. Not exactly USDA,' he said. When he took it out in the clear glass pitcher the orange juice had a brown tinge to it. It looked like maybe it had been there since the previous Christmas. Jack wasn't fastidious about his refrigerator.

'Looks like wine, beer, or soft drinks.'

'Anything diet?' said Abby.

'You got it.' He took out the can and popped the lid, grabbed a glass, and put it under the ice dispenser in the refrigerator door.

'Did you follow in your dad's footsteps?'

'Hmm?'

'Marines, I mean?' said Abby.

'Oh yeah. You heard of the X and Y chromosomes. The things that make little boys and little girls. Well somewhere in my blood is a G chrome.'

'What's that?'

'For grunt,' said Jack. 'My grandfather had it. My great-grandfather had it. You could strop a razor on our necks. Hidebound leather. But it looks like it's gonna end here.'

Abby gave him a questioning look.

'No little Jacks,' he said.

'Ah,' she nodded. 'I thought maybe you'd been married?'

'That's not a good subject,' said Jack.

More questioning looks from Abby.

'Let's just say they weren't fruitful relationships.' He took a swig from a frosted bottle of beer and put the glass, fizzing with soda, in front of her on the stainless-steel island right next to the thick sheaf of papers he'd brought down from upstairs.

'And the house?' said Abby.

'That's inherited,' said Jack. 'Just like the genes. I got the house and nine hundred acres of bottom land, all leased out. Jess. You remember Jess – the leopard-skin flosser?'

Abby nodded and laughed.

'He got most of the family trust. Some stocks and bonds.'

'He must be frugal,' said Abby. 'From the looks of his apartment.'

'Frugal? Jess? Right. Pissed through most of it is more like it,' said Jack. 'Jess likes the fast lane. Life's just a big party. He found L.A. and never stopped.'

'He didn't go into the Marines?'

Now it was Jack's turn to laugh. 'Jess was a throw-back. Someone in the wood pile, I think. He and the old man used to come to blows.' He looked at the ceiling and thought, like maybe this brought back memories, not all of them pleasant.

'Lucky for Jess he came along so late in life. If the old man'd been ten years younger, Jess would have never made it out of childhood. But that's another story. Are you tired?' They were leaning on separate sides of the stainless-steel island.

'Wired's more like it,' said Abby. She often got that way after long trips.

'Well, good. Maybe you'd like to sit down, relax, read something,' said Jack. 'We got lots of things here in the house to read.'

'I know. I saw your library.'

'That's not what I meant.' He gave her a coy smile and slid the pile of papers under the rubber band toward her side of the island.

'What's this?'

'Oh. Just something I wrote,' said Jack.

'Is that what was in the box you got outside?' Abby was thinking a rejected manuscript.

'Oh no,' said Jack. 'I stopped making submissions several months ago. The box contained something else.' This was at least good news. Abby had been concerned that Jack might be sending stuff over the transom in his own name, unsolicited manuscripts to publishing houses in New York. If so, and an editor put his name together with Gable Cooper's, it could lead to questions. It could also sully Cooper's name if Jack produced garbage.

She flipped the corners of the pages, a few of them dog-eared, with her thumb. It was a long manuscript. Abby guessed a thousand typed pages. 'You try to sell this by the pound, do you?' she said.

'You think it's too long?'

'Not if you're going to print it in multiple volumes,' said Abby.

They both laughed.

'I can't guarantee I'll read it tonight,' she said.

'Oh, take your time. Take tomorrow. Take it with you when we go. No rush,' he said, though there was a gleam in Jack's eye, like he couldn't wait for her critique.

THE LIST

It was four in the morning and Abby couldn't sleep. She heard noise downstairs and figured Jack was an early riser. He had put her up on the top floor of the house in one of the ornate four-poster beds with a full canopy. There was a porcelain bowl and pitcher for washing in the room, and a bath down the hall. Jack had given her privacy upstairs and taken one of the rooms down on the main floor for the night. Abby's room was bigger than some hotel suites, and filled with antiques.

She had gone to bed about ten, and had slept for nearly three hours when she woke with a start. For a moment she seemed dazed, disoriented, wondering why the window was on the left instead of the right, then suddenly realized that she wasn't in her old room at home.

She rolled over in bed and sat up. Abby didn't know what woke her. Perhaps it was dreams of Theresa. She had thought a lot about it the past several days. She had visions of Theresa's lifeless body on the gurney that morning outside her house. These images haunted her, especially at night. She wondered if the cops had caught up with Joey, and why Morgan hadn't called. There were a lot of things turning over in her mind.

She laid down and tossed restlessly for two more hours, then finally flipped on a light and tried to read. Abby hadn't written a word since going to L.A. with Theresa. She had worked on an outline for a sequel but hadn't actually broken ground on the manuscript. She would do that in the islands. Jack wanted to know the story line, but Abby wasn't talking, not yet anyway. He already had too much control over her life, and she didn't like it. The sequel and its details were her leverage. Publishers were never satisfied with just a single book, especially if what you wrote held the prospect of money. They expected creation on demand, constantly shortening the time between manuscripts. The halcyon days of publishing as part of the arts were over. Books were now just another product, and the people who wrote them were viewed by the industry as an eccentric but necessary evil. Abby knew that sooner or later Carla and Bertoli would be demanding details on the sequel. They would want jacket copy and art for the cover before the manuscript was written. Jack would have to come to her for bits and pieces to keep them happy. It was how she would keep him on a string like a puppet. The sequel was Abby's ultimate source of control.

Lying in bed she read a little Elmore Leonard from a paperback she'd bought at the airport. Leonard was the king of dialogue, and after Jack's manuscript, he was like a dish of sorbet on the heels of a course of raw onions; something to cleanse the reader's palate. If Jack's manuscript contained a message it was that the man couldn't write.

His story was one of those male thumping things, high tech hardware wrapped in a cartoon of global dimensions. It was peopled with an army of evil politicians and bureaucrats, and heroic soldiers. The protagonist was amazingly handsome and had graduated at the top of his class from Pedigree U. All the women were amazingly beautiful but hadn't gone to college. That didn't matter because they all had big tits and long legs. The amazingly beautiful women couldn't keep their hands off the amazingly handsome man. When all of these amazingly beautiful people weren't otherwise occupied humping, they could be found disarming nuclear bombs, and uncovering plots to kill the president. The protagonist was ageless and single, and driven by a purity of duty matched only by Superman.

The only thing faster than a speeding bullet was the hero's dick. All things taken together, Abby guessed that the invention was a lot like Jack himself, unbelievable, except that Jack was the incarnation in the flesh.

There was a degree on the wall downstairs in Junior's name. It didn't come from Annapolis. Jack had taken a degree from Stanford in Latin American studies. She wondered where he'd stood in his class, if he'd ever disarmed a nuclear bomb, or met the president. She had little doubt that he liked long legs and big tits. She wondered how all of this, especially the stint at Stanford, had sat with the old man, as Jack had called him. She could imagine a lot of shouting when Jack stepped out of the military mold.

By now she was reading words, her mind distracted by other thoughts. She heard the sound of gravel under wheels in the driveway, got out of bed and walked to the window just in time to see Jack's car rolling down the lane. By the time the engine started, it was too far away to hear it. The car disappeared into the tunnel of trees. Abby wondered where he could be going at five in the morning.

Wherever he had gone, he would be back. She returned to bed and her book. She read half a page without a single syllable denting her consciousness. She closed her book and got out of bed, considered for a moment the fact that she was now alone in the house.

'No. I shouldn't.' She said it to herself but without much conviction. Then she remembered how he'd bulldozed his way into her life. Without further thought she slipped her jeans on, pulled a sweater over her head, put her running shoes on over bare feet, and slid quietly from the room.

The hall outside was dark, lit only by the dim light of

an early dawn that spilled in through a skylight over the staircase.

She tiptoed down the hall to the door at the far end. She had seen Jack come and go from here, gathering a few things for sleep the night before. She figured it had to be his room. She turned the door handle and it opened. Abby stepped inside and closed the door behind her.

It was a large room, larger than the one she slept in, and cluttered. There were clothes folded neatly on the bed. It was not a postered antique like her own, but a metal frame which, like Jack, had a military hardness to it.

A door on the other side led to a small sitting area. This opened onto a wall of windows, a shed dormer that looked out on the yard, the marsh, and the sound beyond.

Under the small-paned windows was a large antique partners desk inset in leather with a large computer and an array of electronics on top. Crude pine shelves supported on cinder blocks flanked the desk on each side to a height just below the windows. These sagged under the weight of books. Not the uniform leather and gold spines of the library downstairs, but an assortment of cheap covers, many of them stapled instead of bound, what to Abby appeared to be technical monographs.

The surface of the desk was littered with paper, some of it still sprouting from the top of the laser printer.

The bouncing blue globe of an earth careened off the inner edges of the computer's color monitor.

Abby didn't know much about computers. She had purchased a small used notebook just before leaving Seattle. This was to replace her old manual typewriter that had disappeared in Joey's wake. Spencer had turned the basement upside down looking, but there was no sign of it. She could not figure why Joey would have wanted to take it.

Jack's desk-top computer was cutting edge, a million graphical interfaces hooked to the buttons on a mouse; a joystick that looked like it had been ripped from the cockpit of a jet fighter. And games, an entire shelf of games, helicopters and planes, tanks and missiles.

She reached down and without thinking touched the joystick. Instantly the globe on the screen disappeared, replaced by the inside image of a cockpit careening through space at high speed. Abby took her hand away and watched while whatever was flying was shot at by other faster moving things. The pinging sounds of an arcade resonated from speakers somewhere inside the desk. She tried to push the stick away, hoping that the screen would return to the tranquil blue globe. Instead, the horizon on the screen flared up. An instant later there was an orange flash on the monitor and the gargled sound of a crash from the speakers. Large red letters appeared: GAME OVER. Abby could only pray that Jack didn't keep score.

She turned her attention to his collection of books. There were the usual writer's references, dictionaries and an assortment of synonym finders, a volume of famous quotations, and books on how to write novels. Jack had cornered the market on these. *How to Write*; *How to Plot*; *How to Craft Characters*. They were propped up on his desk between a single bookend and the computer as if by osmosis the machine itself could absorb their contents. It was clear that Jack had failed. What he really needed was what he'd found in Abby; a ghost writer. The question now was how she would maintain control until it was time to go public.

She turned her attention to the stack of books next to the desk. These were not the usual reference texts: *Household and Recreational Use of High Explosives*; *The Anarchist's Armory*; and *The Art of Strangulation*. Some of these were stapled and clearly produced by copying machines, all the signs of an underground press. Abby opened one of them. Inside were explicit recipes for explosives and directions on making bombs, everything from fire jars to road mines. It was a veritable encyclopedia of terror. She had heard of such things but had never seen them. She put it back on the shelf.

A slender trade paperback was open-spined, printed page down on top of a stack of other books; *Making a New Identity*. Underneath the book was a small dark blue note pad. To Abby it looked like a pocket address book. Abby picked it up and turned it over:

Passport

United States of America

She opened the cover and turned it sideways, the way a Customs inspector might to read it. Jack's photo was crystal clear, under plastic laminate on the bottom page. Next to it, typed on the passport form, was the name Kellen Raid.

Jack had an arrangement with the NCO, an old buddy, who ran the commissary at Parris Island. Once a week Jack would drop by in the early morning and leave a list of groceries pinned to the back door of the commissary. An hour later an enlisted man in a jeep would deliver them to the house at Coffin Point. There was nothing particularly wrong with this. Being retired, Jack had commissary privileges and always paid the freight. Besides, he hated to shop.

Dew was still dripping from moss in the trees as Jack drove back toward the big house at the end of the road. He checked his watch. He had been gone only a few minutes and figured she would still be sleeping. A hundred yards from the house he pulled off and parked near a small locked shed, got out, and opened a padlock from the shed door. He went inside. Against one wall was a wooden work bench with two metal presses bolted to it. One was primitive, probably fifty years old. His father had bought it second-hand after the war. The other one was larger, newer, and more sophisticated, what people in the trade called a progressive loader. With brass, primers, and powder it could load a thousand bullets in an hour, any caliber you wanted, depending on the dies that were threaded into the machine.

Against the other wall were four old metal gym lockers each with a combination lock on the door. Jack went to the second locker, worked the dial, and opened the door. Inside, stacked from the bottom nearly to the top, were plastic ammunition boxes with several different calibers of loaded rounds, each box holding a hundred bullets. If he had to guess, there were probably five thousand loaded rounds in the locker. The other lockers contained gun powder, cases of primers and barrels of new brass casings. There were boxes of lead and jacketed bullets. The loaded bullets were mostly copper jacketed, the kind that slide and eject easily from semi-automatic weapons. All of this was stored a good distance from the house. Though Jack's heroes were all invulnerable, he had no desire to become a human skyrocket. What a bullet did in fiction was one thing. What it did to a real body was another. Jack had more potent things besides gun powder in one of the other lockers. The firearms he kept at the house along with a handful of rounds for personal security. In Jack's mind, you could never be too prepared.

He looked for the boxes marked nine millimeter, found one and grabbed it, closed the locker, and spun the dial. He walked outside and locked the door to the shed, then headed toward the house. He left the car parked where it was. There was no sense in taking a chance. He might wake her up. Besides, he would have to drive right up to the house to get the gun that was inside.

Abby was studying the date and place of birth on the passport, scribbling notes on a scrap of paper from Jack's desk, when she heard it; an indistinct creaking somewhere in the distance beyond the door to his room. It sent an adrenaline rush through her body. She stopped the pencil scratching on paper and listened. Maybe it was just the settling of the old house, the creaks and groans of age. She heard it again. This time she dropped the pencil on the desk and literally flew to the window. She looked out on the side of the house. She could see a part of the gravel drive as it disappeared, sweeping in front of the house. But she could not see the area directly in front where Jack had parked his car the day before. Still, she hadn't heard the sound of tires on gravel or the motor. She pressed one eye close to the old bottle glass window but still she couldn't see anything.

Then she heard it again. This time there was no question. Someone was coming up the stairs. Frantic, her eyes scanned the room for a place to hide. First instincts, the closet on the far side of the bed. Then she realized the passport was in her hand. There was no time. She took two steps toward the closet and stopped. It would be the first place he would go if he needed a change of clothes for the day.

Abby hit the floor with an easy motion. A second later she was under the bed, sliding on her stomach on the dusty hardwood floor, just as the door opened and two male feet shod in dark high-top Nikes entered the room. She thought they were Jack's, but she wasn't sure.

Abby held her breath, fearful that the sound might give her away. Her eyes focused on the passport still in her hand. She prayed that he hadn't come looking for it. Until she had seen the passport, getting caught would have been only a major embarrassment. Now she wasn't so sure.

Whoever he was, Jack or Kellen, he strode across the room confidently. He was standing in front of the desk rummaging through papers. Cold sweat dripped down Abby's forehead and mingled with the dust to make mud under the bed.

She wondered if she'd left anything else out of place. Then it hit her; the screen on the computer, the game she had interrupted. If the large red letters were on the screen, he couldn't miss them. He would know instinctively that someone had entered the room.

She craned her neck but still couldn't see the monitor. His body was in front of it. Now he was looking through drawers. Maybe he was looking for the passport. Perhaps he'd forgotten where he'd left it. If so, he might check another room, giving Abby time to drop it someplace and get out, to slink to her own room.

He was in the second drawer at the level of his knees

when his hand disappeared inside. When it came out he was holding something black and hard. It flashed quickly and then disappeared from Abby's view. She'd seen it for only a fleeting instant, but Abby knew what it was; a matt-black pistol. She was breathing in little gasps now. Her hands spread flat, one of them on the floor, the other holding the passport. She heard the sound of metal sliding and clinking. He was doing something to the gun, perhaps loading it. Abby's heart began to pound.

When he finally moved, she could see the monitor on the desk. It was aglow – with the blue bouncing globe. But how long had it been there? She knew it was on a timer. Was it there when he'd entered the room or not? She couldn't be certain. Was he loading the bullets for her?

She took a deep breath and then heard the slam of metal against metal. She didn't have to be told. It was the sound of a clip being jammed into the handle of the gun.

He walked over, closer to the bed now, and stood silent. Abby's body tensed. She slid a few millimeters away toward the other side of the bed. The only advantage was the dust on the floor. It made her body glide. He inched closer. Now the toes of his shoes were actually under the bed with her. Something heavy bounced on the bed and rattled like pebbles in a box. She heard noises but couldn't tell what he was doing. The sound of a spring, but it wasn't coming from the bed. Then he slapped something shut, like the lid on a plastic box. He moved around the bed and a second later he was out the door, closing it behind him.

Her heart pounded. Her temples throbbed. Then she wondered; would he check her room? She listened to his footsteps as they receded from the door. She couldn't be sure which direction he'd gone, whether down the stairs or toward the other bedroom.

Abby lay there for a long time, silent on the cold hard floor, unable to move. When she finally did, she didn't hesitate. She went to the desk first and pushed the passport under a pile of loose papers so that if he came back and looked he might think he'd simply missed it the first time. Then she went to the door, opened it a crack, and peered out. She could see the staircase and down the hall toward her room. He was not there. She listened for sounds. Nothing. She waited a second longer. It was now or never. He might return any moment. She slipped out, closed the door behind her, and tiptoed down the hall. She was four steps from her room when he nailed her from behind.

'Did I wake you?'

Abby gasped and whirled, hand to her breast. Her heart exploded in her chest so that she jumped.

'Sorry. I didn't mean to scare you.'

Jack was standing there ten feet away, in the doorway to another room, the pistol in his hand and what looked like a box of bullets in the other. She couldn't be sure how long he'd been there, whether he'd seen her coming out of his room. Abby was petrified, her eyes focused on the gun that he made no effort to conceal.

'Ah . . . I . . . ah . . . had to go to the bathroom,' she said. She pointed to the door a few steps behind her. 'I got lost,' she said.

'Ah.' He nodded like he understood.

They stood, two adults in the dark hallway, one of them holding a pistol, and the other covered in dust, and said nothing about it. Their own versions of the emperor's clothes.

'Are you feeling alright?' he asked.

'Oh yeah.' Her gaze was monopolized by the pistol in his hand.

'Does this bother you?' He held it out.

'No. No.' But she couldn't take her eyes off of it.

'Good. I was just going to do some targets. Why don't you come with me?'

'I have to take a shower,' said Abby.

He came closer, his eyes on her. Abby wanted to back up, but her feet wouldn't move. Frozen in place.

A step away he stopped, reached out with one hand, and rubbed a smudge of dust from her cheek.

'I can see,' he said.

Nervously she rubbed her face with her hand.

'You can take a shower later. There's plenty of time,' said Jack. It seemed more an order than a suggestion.

'Let's go shoot,' said Jack. He stepped toward her and put his arm around her shoulder so that she felt the weight of the pistol against her breast under the cotton sweater. There was no saying no to Jack.

'Well maybe,' said Abby. She wasn't sure if she was under duress or not. But she wasn't going to press the point. They headed down the stairs. In the service porch he grabbed some targets, orange with a bull's-eye and a cross in the middle. He picked up two sets of ear protectors, the kind of mufflers that ground crews wear at the airport. He handed one of these to Abby.

She started to put it on.

'Not yet,' he said. 'We don't start shooting 'til we get outside.' He laughed a little. 'You've never done this before?'

She shook her head.

'Never fired a pistol?'

'A rifle. Once,' said Abby. 'When I was a kid with my dad.'

'A twenty-two?' said Jack.

'I don't know.' Abby was still shaking. Unless it was an elephant gun fully loaded and pointed at Jack's head, Abby couldn't have cared less what her father's rifle might have been at this moment.

'Relax. It won't hurt,' said Jack.

Abby wasn't sure what he meant: shooting, or getting shot.

They crossed the yard to an area on the far side near the marsh. Here there were several pieces of heavy wire strung between two poles. Jack hung two of the targets from metal clips on the wire.

He then walked to an area near a little wooden table. Abby guessed they were a good fifty feet from the target.

'You want to get a little closer to start?' he asked.

'Whatever,' said Abby. 'Why don't I just watch?'

'Nonsense. You'll enjoy it. Ever written about guns in your books?'

She shook her head.

'Then it'll be a good experience for you. Broaden your horizons. Grist for the mill,' said Jack. 'You can put those on now.' He pointed to the ear protectors. He put his own on and Abby followed suit.

'I'll shoot a couple so you can gauge the sound and see how it works.' He shouted a little so she could hear him. 'Then you can try.'

Jack took aim with two hands, one braced underneath steadying the other, clicked off the safety, aimed, and fired a single round.

It happened so quickly that by the time Abby's body jerked from the shock wave the empty brass casing was on the ground and the slide was back in place with the hammer cocked for the next round. The pistol worked with the speed of light.

He fired again. This time she jerked, but a little less, and she kept her eyes on the target. It didn't seem to move. She was sure he'd missed.

He clicked the safety on, ejected the clip still with bullets in it, pulled the slide to eject the round in the chamber. Without a clip in the handle it stayed open. He put the pistol on the little wooden stand.

'Let's take a look.' Jack walked toward the target. Abby followed along. About twenty feet out they came into focus, two small holes. As she drew closer she could see that they were actually touching, each no more than half an inch from the center of the target.

'What you look for is a pattern,' said Jack. 'Bullet strikes that are close together. You can put a quarter over a good pattern and cover three holes.'

He walked her back to the wooden stand and the gun, coaching her all the way. 'Don't worry right now about hitting the center of the target. Try to keep a tight pattern. Aim for the same place each time.' He picked up the gun, loaded it, and handed it to her.

It felt awkward, too big for her hand. She was still shaking, but she held it out. Abby's hands clasped the pistol between them as if she was in prayer.

'No,' said Jack. 'Like this.' He moved behind her, put his arms around her, and placed his hands over hers. Then he directed them, the left hand underneath, the flat of the palm open so that the heel of the pistol grip rested on it for support while she held the gun with the other hand.

'Don't squint. Keep both eyes open. Line the sights up and aim with your right eye.'

Abby wasn't squinting. She had her eyes closed tight. She opened them for an instant and jerked the trigger. Nothing happened, though the gun waved all over the place.

Jack started laughing.

Abby was starting to calm herself. If she had an emotion stronger than fear, it was anger. She didn't like to be laughed at. If he wasn't careful, the next time he saw the gun it might be pointed at him.

'You have to take the safety off first,' said Jack. 'And don't jerk. Squeeze the trigger. You want to be surprised when it goes off.'

Abby didn't need any more surprises this morning.

He reached up with his thumb, his body braced up against hers, and flipped off the safety, then cocked the hammer with his thumb. Amazingly for a woman whose body had been quaking only moments before, Abby was now stone steady.

'Ready.' Before the words had cleared his lips the gun exploded in her hand. When the recoil stopped, it was aimed somewhere up into a tree out near the marsh.

'It's alright. Try it again,' said Jack.

With the recoil measured from the first shot, she held it down, lined the sights up on the target, and squeezed. It exploded with a sharp crack, only this time she controlled the gun. It didn't jump nearly so much.

'Good. Again,' he said.

She fired four more times before she put the gun down and they checked the target. She had actually hit it three times, twice inside of the big outer circle, each time moving closer in the direction of the bull's eye. She was getting into the challenge of this, competing against herself to improve with each shot.

A few minutes later, she looked at the box of a

hundred rounds and noticed that it was more than half empty. Abby had shot most of them. For many of the shots Jack was standing behind her, holding her steady, giving her pointers.

The fear had drained from her body. His touch up against her wasn't an entirely unpleasant experience. His hard body against her back, the low whisper of his voice in her ear, had a calming, almost mesmerizing effect. She fired four more shots, emptying the clip, when he tapped her on the shoulder and pointed in the other direction.

'We'll take a break. Breakfast is here.'

An old military jeep was rumbling down the road toward the house, a man in fatigues behind the wheel. The jeep pulled up in front of the house, and when the driver got out he gave a lazy salute to Jack.

'Captain. You want me to take it into the house?'

'Appreciate it,' said Jack.

The man carefully handed Jack a big brown paper bag, the wafting warm odors of which escaped and ran under Abby's nose. Suddenly she was famished.

'I hope you like eggs and hash browns,' said Jack.

'Smells delicious,' she told him.

The enlisted man was busy unloading the groceries, lugging them up the stairs.

'So where did this come from?' she asked.

'Officer's mess,' said Jack. 'An old friend who takes pity, especially on my guests. Cooking is not one of my finer arts. You'll appreciate this more if you ever have to eat my cuisine,' he told her.

They headed up into the kitchen, where Jack set two places at the table, and opened a large container of orange juice from one of the bags. He had put up a pot of coffee earlier in the morning, and as Abby sipped she had no complaints with his coffee. She nibbled at her eggs now removed from their plastic container and spread on a china dish.

'Outdid himself today.' Jack dug into what looked like Potatoes O'Brien.

Abby had to admit they were delicious. All the terrible things she had heard about food in the military was a lie if this is how they ate.

She was exhausted. The lack of sleep, and the adrenaline rush of the morning were catching up with her. Though she had to admit she enjoyed the shooting. It had actually taken the edge off of the earlier events, but she still wondered about the books and the passport in Jack's room. Who was he? Had he lied to her about his name?

'Is this how you always get your groceries?' She nodded toward the soldier who had just left the last package on the sink and retrieved a check in payment from Jack.

'Sometimes. Sometimes a lady stops by and leaves things in the fridge for me.'

'Oh.' Now Abby felt like she was prying. A woman in his life.

She tried to change the subject by scanning the little morning paper that lay on the table. There was a lot of country news, but nothing to spark a conversation.

For Jack's part, between scoops of eggs and potatoes, he was writing on a small form with a pen. It looked like an express label. There was a box to match, like the one he'd retrieved the day before when they arrived. The box was on the counter behind him. Again it looked like a manuscript box, and Abby shuddered with the thought.

'Excuse me.' Jack realized that he was ignoring her

and that her eyes were on him.

'It's alright. Finish what you're doing.'

'Be done in a minute. I hope you don't mind if we stop on the way to the airport. I need to drop this off for delivery. I'll just take a minute.'

'That's fine.'

'What did you think of the manuscript?' asked Jack.

'Oh.' She thought for a moment. What could she say? 'I was pretty tired last night.' A lame excuse, but it avoided an awkward subject.

'Well, you can take it with you,' said Jack. 'I don't need it right now.'

'Oh. Great,' said Abby. 'Thanks.' If he kept pushing, sooner or later she would have to tell him that it wasn't only his cooking that sucked.

'Tell me about yourself.' Maybe this would be a more pleasant subject. 'You must have friends?'

'Oh. A few.'

'The lady who drops your groceries off?' Now she was prying. She was also smiling across the table at him.

'Oh yeah. A great woman. We've known each other for a long time. She used to change my diapers.' Jack smiled back. 'An aunt in failing health. Maybe you'd like to meet her?'

'I doubt if we have time,' said Abby. She took another sip of coffee. 'You're going to tell me that there's no one in your life, that writing is a jealous mistress.'

'I don't know if she's jealous or not,' said Jack. 'But she is a bitch.'

Abby laughed. At least he made no bones about it.

'There was somebody. Once,' he said.

Abby gave him a look, like go on.

'Her name was Jenny. She was beautiful. And young. Though not as young as I was.'

'Ah. The older woman,' said Abby. 'Were you in love?'

'Who knows. Never been able to define love,' said Jack. 'But I know I had a fire in the pit of my stomach whenever I was around her. And my heart thumped like a cement mixer. Probably more lust than love.'

'What happened?'

'She caught me looking at another woman.'

'Just looking?'

Jack nodded.

'And?'

'I blinked. Looked a little guilty, I suppose. Started making excuses. What you do when you're young and stupid,' said Jack.

'What did you say?'

'I told her, "What am I supposed to do? I enjoy looking at women." '

'And what did she say?'

'She said, "Gee, that's funny. So do I." ' He gave Abby a kind of smile that made her think this might be the setup to a joke, then sipped his coffee, leaving her to wonder.

'You're pulling my leg?'

He raised his hand with his mouth full of coffee, like honest Injun.

'Swear to God,' said Jack. 'I was eighteen. She was twenty-two. Last I heard she was living in Atlanta with three cats and a woman named Alice.'

'I don't believe you. You're putting me on.'

'Yeah, I am.'

She laughed and gave him a look of exasperation.

'I was exaggerating,' said Jack. 'There were only two cats.'

She looked at him for a moment, waiting for him to laugh again. But he didn't.

'You know, I don't know when you're telling me the truth and when you're lying,' said Abby.

'That's what makes life interesting.' Without missing a beat, he smiled, took a sip of coffee from the mug in front of him, and returned to his address label.

CHAPTER
TWENTY-TWO

'Starl, Hobbs and Carlton, law offices.'

'I'd like to speak to Morgan Spencer,' said Abby.

'Ms Chandlis, how are you?' The receptionist recognized her voice on the phone. There was a totally different attitude toward Abby in the firm now that she was a client and no longer an associate. She had learned from Spencer that even Lewis Cutler, the man who had fired her, was now asking after her welfare. He had discovered that she'd come into a large sum of money and had hired Morgan to handle some business affairs. A well-heeled client was something that every partner in the firm wanted, and Cutler had the audacity to believe that if he played it right, perhaps he could mend things with Abby. Spencer enjoyed tantalizing Cutler while keeping him in the dark. He stored all of Abby's business files at home.

She waited for a moment and Morgan's secretary came on the line.

'Jenny, Abby here. Is Morgan in?'

'He's been trying to reach you for two days. Just a second,' said the secretary.

When Morgan hadn't called her in Chicago, and then

failed to contact her at Jack's house, Abby began to worry that something was wrong. At the airport she slipped away and found a bank of payphones. She looked at her watch. It was almost noon out on the West Coast and she hoped that Morgan hadn't left for lunch. She breathed easier when she heard his voice on the phone. 'Where are you?'

'Atlanta. I have to be on a plane for San Juan in just a few minutes. We'll have to talk fast.'

'I've been trying to reach you for two days,' said Morgan. 'I just missed you in Chicago. The front desk said you checked out fifteen minutes before I called.'

'Jack wanted to get an early start,' she told him.

'Eager beaver,' said Morgan. 'Tell him when you see him that he gave me the wrong phone number to his house. When I tried to call it I got a disconnected number. And he's unlisted.'

'Are you sure you wrote it down right?'

'I didn't have to. He wrote it down for me,' said Morgan.

Abby thought about this for a moment. 'Don't worry about it now. I'll call you when I get into San Juan, and as soon as I get to St Croix. I'll give you the number to the beach house.'

'I don't like it,' said Spencer. 'I don't trust him.'

'Relax,' said Abby. 'Everything's going to be fine.'

'We've got a lot to talk about,' he told her.

'What's up?'

'Good news and bad. Money is starting to pile up.'

'What's the bad news?' said Abby.

'That cop, Sanfillipo, he's been nosing around the law office. In fact, he just left a few minutes ago. His second trip in two days.'

'What's he want?'

'For starters, to know where you are. He wants to talk to you.'

'What about?'

'He's not saying. Only bits and pieces. He's been to see your husband.'

'Why would he want to talk to Charlie?'

'I'm not sure. But he knows you've come into some money. He wants to know where it came from.'

'Damn.' Abby was angry with Charlie. She figured he had a big mouth. That's what she got for being nice, for repaying the money on his credit card when she didn't have to. She was flush with money. She felt bad about stealing his card and knew Charlie was broke. Never again, she thought.

'What did you tell him?' she asked.

'That I didn't know anything about any money.'

She worried now that she was drawing Morgan into some kind of a criminal web, lying to a cop in a murder investigation.

'What else could I tell him?' said Spencer. 'If I told him about the book and where you were, we may as well put it up in neon outside of Bertoli's office.'

He was right. The cops would check it out, and within hours she would be getting calls from Bertoli's lawyers.

'You did what you had to,' said Abby.

'There's more,' said Spencer. 'They found Joey.'

'Great.' Given his penchant for drink, Abby knew Joey couldn't stay ahead of them for long.

'Did they arrest him?'

'Not exactly,' said Spencer.

'Why not?'

'He's dead.'

There was silence on the phone from Abby's end.

'Are you there?' he asked.

'I'm here.'

'I didn't think you'd be that shaken,' said Morgan.

'It doesn't take the edge off my day,' said Abby. 'I'll light a candle when I get around to it. But I am surprised. How did it happen?'

'A fire. The cop didn't give me many details. But from what I gather, the problem is not how he died, but where he was when Theresa was killed.'

'What do you mean?'

'I mean that according to what they've uncovered so far, Joey was in L.A. when Theresa was murdered.'

Now there was silence on the phone and Spencer could smell mental rubber burning on the other end.

'How do they know that?'

'Found a ticket stub in his pocket and checked with the airline. He spent three days down there.'

'He could have wired the box before he left,' said Abby.

'Not according to the police.'

'How would they know?'

'Your telephone answering machine. When the fuses were pulled, the machine quit. Problem is the time and date of the last message. Joey was in L.A. when it was recorded.'

'You're telling me that they've excluded him as a suspect?' said Abby.

'That's what it sounds like to me.'

Her mind was now racing. It threw a whole new light on why the police might want to talk to her.

'Could it have been an accident?'

'I don't know. They aren't sharing that kind of information. At least not yet,' said Spencer. 'But they have a lot of questions. They found his truck abandoned in a hotel parking lot out near the airport, miles from where they found the body. They dusted the truck for prints and they threw a name at me. Hang on, I got it here on a piece of paper someplace.'

Abby could hear the rustle of papers on his desk.

'Here it is. Stanley Salzman. Mean anything to you?'

'No.'

'He's an executive with one of the film studios in L.A. The cops are trying to figure what his prints are doing on Joey's truck.'

'Oh boy.' Abby had one hand to her forehead now as if a migraine had set in.

'Do you want to come back?' said Spencer.

If Abby returned to Seattle, there was no telling when or if she might be able to leave again. The reporter, Thompson, would no doubt be waiting for her. If he found out she was being questioned in a murder investigation, it would only add fuel to the suspicion that he was on a hot story. The cops couldn't seriously consider her a suspect. She had an alibi. She was forty-thousand feet up, on a plane between New York and the coast, when Theresa was killed. She was so sure that Joey had done it.

'Are they certain about Joey? That he was in L.A.?' she asked.

'Sanfillipo didn't seem to be hedging on the issue,' said Morgan. 'He did have a lot of questions about the money you paid to Charlie.'

'What does he think, that the two are related? Theresa's murder and the money?'

'You have to admit, to a suspicious mind it offers a lot of possibilities,' said Morgan. 'Your roommate is killed. Suddenly you have cash to pay off debts and you disappear.'

'If Charlie hadn't told him about the money . . .'

'I don't think he did,' said Morgan.

'Then how did he find out?'

'Probably a subpoena for financial records.'

'If that's the case,' said Abby, 'it won't take him long to find the rest of it.' What she meant was the balance of the six hundred thousand dollars that Spencer had deposited in the account in her name, the signing money for the advance on the book, and whatever else had come in since then.

'If he finds that kind of money it'll fan the flames,' said Abby.

'Yeah. He'll be thinking drugs, and looking for you in Columbia. What else pays that well?' Morgan had a point. 'The check you drew to Charlie was on your old checking account?' he asked.

'Yes.' She had closed out the account the day she left Seattle, after paying for her airline tickets and withdrawing two thousand dollars in cash for expenses.

'Have you used any credit cards?' he asked.

'I don't have any, remember?'

'Right.' Spencer had forgotten.

For the first time in her life it might be an advantage. There was no trail of receipts for the cops to follow.

'It may take them awhile to find the new account,' said Spencer. 'They would have to know where to look, what bank. You haven't drawn any checks on it?'

'Not yet.'

'Good. Don't.'

'I'm going to need money pretty soon,' said Abby. 'Besides, the longer I stay away, the worse it looks.'

'Don't worry about it for now. I can wire some cash to the island. What's the name of the town down there?'

'Christiansted. St Croix.' She could hear his pencil scratching paper on the other end.

'I'll check and see if there's a Western Union Office. If not, I'll figure some other way. That will hold you until I can open something offshore. An account on one of the islands and set you up with an ATM card. In a foreign bank, it'll take them months to find it. By then it won't matter,' said Spencer.

He was right. Once the book was published and Abby came out of the weeds, she would be more than happy to go back to Seattle and answer their questions.

Morgan was rock solid, the kind of person you could depend on in a crisis. Even his enemies in the firm referred to him as the fireman, for his ability to deal with disasters.

'Sooner or later I'm going to have to come back,' she said. 'I'm going to want to come back. I'm starting to feel like an exile.' She had been away less than a week, and she was already getting homesick. Abby was no world traveler. 'I already miss you,' she told him. She might not work at the firm anymore, but in Seattle they could always do lunch.

'I miss you, too,' said Spencer. 'But it's only for awhile. When it's over, once the book is out there, when the paperback's in the works and you go public, it won't matter anymore. You've got an alibi. We can tell the police why you did what you did, where the money came from. They can check it out, and it'll be over.'

He was right. All she needed was time. Abby heard the public address system announce her flight.

'I've got to go.'

'Are you sure you're alright?' he asked.

'I'm fine.'

'Where are you staying tonight?'

'I don't know. Jack made the arrangements.'

'Let's hope he did a better job than with his telephone number,' said Morgan.

'There's one thing,' said Abby. She'd almost forgotten.

'What is it?'

For a moment she hesitated, wondering whether she should tell him. 'I don't want to alarm you,' she said, 'but Jack has a passport in another name.'

'What?'

She could tell by the tone of Morgan's voice that it was a mistake to have said anything.

'I found it when I was wandering around his house the other day. It's a U.S. passport in the name Kellen Raid.'

'You're sure it's his?'

'His picture's in it.'

'Listen, I want you to catch a plane and get back here right now,' said Morgan.

'Why?'

'If he's got a false passport, God knows what else he's into.'

Abby felt almost guilty about mentioning it, prying into a man's private papers. After all, Jack had never threatened her, and he'd had plenty of opportunities. 'It's probably nothing,' said Abby.

'What are you talking about?'

'A lot of people have false IDs,' said Abby.

'Passports?' said Spencer.

'How do I know?' said Abby.

'Precisely,' said Morgan. 'How do you know he's not dealing drugs?'

'I didn't find any paraphernalia,' said Abby.

'You're telling me you searched his house?' Morgan's voice went up an octave.

'Wasn't exactly a search,' said Abby. 'I couldn't sleep. So I took a walk.'

'And the passport was just lying around?'

'It was on his desk. In his bedroom,' said Abby.

'What were you doing in his bedroom?'

'He was someplace else at the time.'

Morgan was already worried about her. Now he had other reasons to be concerned. It was the kind of thing a woman could read in a man, on the jealous edge.

'Are you sure you won't come back?' he said.

'What for?'

'You're traveling with a man who's committed at least one serious violation of federal law. If you don't know I can't tell you,' said Spencer.

'He's not using the passport now.'

'How do you know?'

'Because he used his real one when we boarded the plane, at the counter in Savannah.' While Abby wasn't particularly worried, she wasn't stupid, either. 'Besides,' she said, 'unless you've forgotten, he has another false identity besides the passport. The one we invented.' She was talking about Gable Cooper.

Morgan reminded her that the use of a pen name was not a federal offense.

'How do we know he's ever used the passport?' said Abby.

'Did you look for entry or exit stamps?'

'No. I didn't think to look. I didn't have time.' Abby wasn't used to the formalities of foreign travel. She'd had a passport for five years, but it sat in a drawer; a kind of flight of fancy. She wanted to be ready in case the opportunity for travel ever arose. Until now it never had.

'Check the passport out,' she told him.

'I will.'

'Discreetly.'

'You bet.'

The P.A. system made a second call. Her row was now boarding.

'Listen, I have to go. I'll call you at home tonight from the hotel.'

'Wait a second. We need to talk.'

'From the hotel,' said Abby. 'Wish me luck.'

'Wait . . .'

Abby never heard Spencer's last word. She'd already hung the receiver in the cradle.

CHAPTER
TWENTY-THREE

Jack delivered his package to an office near the airport for express delivery somewhere the next morning. He and Abby flew from Atlanta to Miami and spent the night in a hotel near the airport. The next morning they caught the flight for Puerto Rico.

The 737 coasted in over azure seas, bleached white beaches, and acres of ramshackle tin-roofed huts. In the distance, Abby could see verdant forests and mountains sheathed in tropical jungle. The plane dropped its wheels and two minutes later the tires smoked the runway at Puerto Rico's International Airport.

It was Abby's first time in the Caribbean, and as the door to the plane was opened the humid smells of the tropics ignited her senses.

'We'll get the luggage and go to the hotel,' said Jack. 'You may want to freshen up before we look up Enrique.'

Enrique was a friend of Jack's. He was supposed to help them find a place for Abby to set up, a quiet writer's retreat somewhere further to the south in the islands so that she could work undisturbed on the sequel. According to Jack, Enrique knew the territory.

'Your friend, does he live here in Puerto Rico?'

'You could say that. His family's been here awhile.'

'How long?'

'About three hundred years,' said Jack. He left her standing there looking at him for a moment as he moved on along the concourse.

The terminal reminded Abby of a movie set from the '40s. Casablanca in disguise. She expected to see Bogart in his trench coat and Bergman in her hat around the next corner. While dated and in need of some remodeling, the place dripped of nostalgia and perspiration, not necessarily in that order. The lobby was air-conditioned, but the areas off of it were not.

By the time they hit the sidewalk out front, Abby was bathed in her own sweat. People jostled in the hot humid air heading for cars or taxis. Several school girls in parochial uniforms clustered like flies near one of the windows waiting for friends or relatives to emerge. Security was tight. Except for those with tickets, the public was excluded from the main building by police.

Businessmen in suits with briefcases mingled with tourists trying to read signs and directions, all of which were in Spanish. If life was slower in the tropics, the message hadn't reached this place.

They found a line of taxis, and Abby slid into the back seat of one of them while Jack and the driver loaded the luggage.

'Condado Plaza,' said Jack.

A few seconds later Abby felt the comforting breeze on her face as the taxi sped out along the highway, its windows down to compensate for the lack of air-conditioning in the old Chevy. They rode in silence, Abby taking in the sights as the road wound its way through densely populated San Juan. Abby noted that the most prominent feature on some of the buildings were the security bars over the windows. There were low-slung complexes of apartment buildings, brightly painted in myriad colors behind high cyclone fences; projects, Caribbean-style.

'Some of the best beaches are over there.' Jack pointed beyond the tenements that flanked the highway. 'Condado has some walled villas on the water that are very nice.'

'Is that where we're going?'

'We'll stay at the Condado Plaza. I think you'll like it.'

The snarl of traffic grew thick as they approached the center of the city. The smells of hot food from roadside restaurants invaded the car. They passed over the Puente Esteves and the Puente Dos Hermanos, concrete bridges with sculpted balustrades over the Condado Lagoon. On the left was a strip of sandy white beach. Abby could see brown-skinned girls in thong bikinis lying next to bronze lovers, sunning themselves on towels. A half mile out the open Atlantic crashed on reefs just off shore.

The taxi stopped, made a left turn across traffic, and pulled under the covered entrance of an immense high-rise hotel. Behind walls of glass Abby could see the sprawl of the lobby and beyond that to the other side of the building and the cresting rollers of the Atlantic.

A young man in white livery replete with a spotless pith helmet opened the taxi door.

'Welcome to the Condado Plaza.' He was tall, young, and dark, with a flashing smile to slay any teenage girl. 'Do you have luggage, sir?' His words emitted a thick Castillian trill. He snapped his fingers and a bellman wheeled up with a cart to the trunk of the taxi, and without a word unloaded the bags.

'Will you be staying long?'

'Two nights,' said Jack. He gave the kid a five dollar bill and it disappeared like a flame under water.

'Fernando will take your bags.' The doorman led them to the main entrance and opened the door wide. 'Thank you for staying at the Condado Plaza.'

Inside Abby was beginning to wonder if she had packed the right clothes, or for that matter whether she owned them. Most of the women were dressed elegantly, basic black with tasteful jewels, pearls and diamond necklaces. A young Latin woman, tall and stately, wearing an evening gown that clung to her curvaceous contours, stood with a small group of men each elegantly attired in thousand-dollar suits. The woman was on the arm of an older gentleman six inches shorter than she. He had hair like spun silver. As Abby passed she could hear them speaking in Spanish.

Jack caught her gawking. 'They come up from Rio, and Argentina,' he told her. 'Bring their oil and cattle bucks, sometimes narco dollars. They do a little business. Bring their mistresses along and drop a bundle in the casinos. Then they go home to their wives and ten children. You know,' said Jack. 'Traditional old-world values.'

It was Abby's first look at the upper crust of the Southern Hemisphere, and she was feeling like the ugly American.

'Jesus, you're a cynic,' she told him. 'How do you know it's not his daughter?'

'Because she's too young.'

'Maybe it's his granddaughter,' said Abby.

'Well, there you have me.'

'Maybe you'd like to ask them?' said Abby.

'I'm not the one getting whiplash,' he told her.

'Besides, I don't judge them. As far as I'm concerned, there's nothing wrong with a good mistress. It's why Catholics have fewer divorces. It also makes abstinence easier.'

Abby started to laugh, shook her head, and gave up.

The few U.S. tourists in the lobby stood out like vagabonds, a couple of the men in baseball caps and tourist-trap T-shirts. The women did no better, some in jeans with fanny packs.

Abby nervously rubbed the wrinkles from her own slacks, and adjusted the collar on her blouse, which was soiled and wet with sweat.

'I'm going to need some clothes,' she whispered to Jack as they approached the registration desk.

'Go ahead. Take your time. The shops are down there.' He pointed toward an arcade of boutiques, richly dressed mannequins behind glass and windows of glittering jewelry.

She hesitated while Jack dealt with the woman at the counter. He passed her his credit card.

'Ah yes, Mr Jermaine, we have your reservation. We also have a message for you.' The clerk handed Jack a small envelope.

He opened it and read. 'Henry's found us.'

'Henry?'

'Enrique.'

'Did you tell him we were staying here?'

'No.'

'How did he find us?'

'There is very little that happens on this island that Henry doesn't know about. Seems his limo missed us at the airport. He's sending it by in a few hours to pick us up.'

'Limo,' said Abby. 'Pretty generous of him to rent a limo.'

'Oh, he didn't rent it,' said Jack.

The clerk took an impression from Jack's credit card and a moment later handed him two electronic card keys and hit the bell for their luggage to be rolled upstairs.

'We're on the ninth floor, adjoining rooms.' Jack handed Abby one of the keys in a little envelope with a room number written on the outside. 'Go ahead. Go shopping. I'll take care of the bags and meet you upstairs. Oh, and we'll need to dress for dinner.' He turned and started to leave, but Abby just stood there.

'I . . . ah . . .'

'What's the problem?' he asked.

'I don't have a credit card,' said Abby. Six hundred thousand dollars in the bank and no way to spend it.

'They'll cash a check at the desk,' said Jack.

'I can't do that, either.' Abby remembered the warning from Morgan not to tap her account while the police were trying to find her.

Jack leaned over the counter and whispered something to the clerk on the other side. The woman nodded and pointed to the shops down the way.

'Not a problem,' said Jack. 'You can use that.' He pointed to the key in her hand. 'Charge it to the room.'

'I can do that?'

'It's probably how she got the dress she's wearing.' Jack nodded toward the young Latin woman on the older man's arm. 'Mistressing has its benefits,' said Jack.

'And what's that supposed to mean?'

He smiled and moved quickly toward the elevator before she could grab him.

'It's on your credit card,' she hollered after Jack.

'Don't worry about it.'

'I'll pay you back,' she said.

'We'll figure something out,' said Jack.

'Wait a second.'

Before she could catch him, Jack and his infectious grin disappeared into the elevator and the door closed behind them.

Abby stood alone in the lobby looking at the young woman in the shimmering black evening dress, then down at her own wrinkled slacks. She closed her hand around the card key. It seemed no matter how much money she made, she could never come out on top.

Thrift was a word the shop keepers at the Condado had never heard. Abby hoped Jack had a high limit on his credit card. She bought only two outfits; a casual change of clothes, slacks with a blouse and a light sweater, and a pair of matching navy loafers and handbag. She also found an evening dress. The dress set her back half a month at her former salary. Still it looked better on her than anything she could remember wearing in years. It was a kind of flowing feminine tuxedo. Simple, but with the appearance that it could magically complicate the intrigue of an evening. She purchased a pair of three-inch heels to go with it. It was the most expensive shopping spree she had ever taken. Abby was used to waiting for season-end sales and buying from some of the cut-rate catalogs. People who thought all lawyers were rich were nuts. She would tell Spencer to wire the money immediately, the next time she talked to him. She didn't like the idea of owing Jack money.

Two and a half hours after leaving him in the lobby, the phone in her room rang. The limo was waiting for them downstairs.

Jack was waiting by the elevator when Abby stepped out of her room, dressed in her new evening clothes. He gave a low whistle of appreciation. 'You look great.'

Abby flushed. 'So do you.'

With a genuinely pleased look he took her hand. 'Come on. Let's go see how the other half lives.'

They emerged from the elevator and were greeted by a tall man in a chauffeur's uniform. He was not Hispanic but Anglo.

'Mr Jermaine, good to see you again.' He spoke with a clipped British accent.

'How are you, Zeke? It's been a long time.'

'Too long,' said the driver.

'Zeke, I'd like you meet Abby. Abby, Zeke.'

The chauffeur tipped his hat. 'Ma'am.'

Abby smiled at him. He led them to the car parked at the hotel entrance. It was not the usual stretch limo, but a sleek black Rolls-Royce.

'I see you're still driving the Phantom,' said Jack.

'Wouldn't have it any other way,' said the driver. 'They can keep the stretch Lincolns and Caddys. They just don't have the ride.'

'You ought to talk Henry into buying you the Silver Ghost.'

'He's talked to them about it,' said the driver. 'Rolls won't let it go.'

The driver held the door while Abby and Jack got into the back seat. The driver went around to the other side.

'What's the Silver Ghost?' said Abby.

'The first car Rolls-Royce ever made. Nineteen-oh-eight. They say it's worth forty-four million.'

'Must have been quite a year,' said Abby.

'But as you heard, Rolls won't sell it.'

'And that's the only thing stopping your friend from buying it?'

Jack looked at her and smiled.

'Right.' Abby gave him a skeptical look.

The engine purred softly as the Rolls pulled into traffic.

'I've kept the receipts for the clothes,' she told him. 'I'll pay you in a few days. Just as soon as some financial affairs are straightened out.'

'Don't worry about it,' said Jack.

'But I do worry about it.' Abby didn't like wearing clothes bought for her by a man with whom she had nothing but a business relationship.

'These financial affairs, are they being handled by your friend Spencer?'

Abby looked at him but didn't respond.

'Are you sure you can trust him?'

'I can trust him.'

'As I remember, there were a lot of zeros on that check I endorsed over to you,' said Jack. 'There's an old saying. When you have that much money you should put it all in one basket, and watch that basket very carefully.'

'I'll watch it,' said Abby. 'And I'll pay you as soon as the money is available.'

'No hurry.'

The car breezed along narrow streets, some of the worst slums Abby had seen. These slowly changed to small houses. Another mile and the houses grew walls around them. As they moved on, the buildings inside of the walls got progressively larger, until some of them rivaled the size and stature of art museums, what Jack called Mediterranean villas. The Rolls took a turn toward the coast. Now the traffic was much thinner.

'Where are we headed?'

'Out along the ocean,' said Jack.

'Your friend lives on the beach?'

'Sometimes. He has a couple of different places on the island. Sorta splits his time between them.'

They drove along a rocky shore interspersed with beaches until all of the houses seemed to disappear behind them. A few miles out, the car turned out onto a point of land and a quarter of a mile down the road slowed just a little. An armed guard in uniform stepped out of a stone kiosk, recognized the Rolls, and waved them through a large iron gate that opened and then just as quickly closed behind the car.

They drove further. It seemed like forever to Abby until finally out of the canopy of trees a large house could be seen in the distance across a rolling verdant lawn. Below it swept a broad beach and the azure blue sea. It was evening and the sun was etching the underside of a cloud at the horizon like mother of pearl.

The house itself was unique, unlike anything Abby had ever seen. It was made up of a number of circular pavilions, each with a massive thatched roof. The front door was carved mahogany, and the small-paned windows were framed in teak.

'Henry saw something like it in a village in Bali a few years ago,' said Jack. 'He liked it.'

'I can tell.' Abby stepped out of the Rolls as Zeke held the door open.

'Of course the one in Bali wasn't this big. Still, he had his architect fly over there and take a look. This is the result.'

'I'd hate to have him take a fancy to the Taj Mahal,' said Abby.

'Yeah. It's amazing what a little creativity and five million dollars will do,' said Jack.

Abby was wondering what anyone with that much money would be doing living here, and more to the point, where he got his money. The thought crossed her mind: drugs.

They walked to the front door and Jack pulled a woven silk chord that rang a bell somewhere deep in the interior of the house. A moment later a house-man in a white linen coat opened the door.

He smiled broadly. 'Ah, Mr Jermaine. We have been expecting you. Please come in.'

Abby walked into the entry, a lavishly appointed room with carved and painted native masks hanging from terracotta walls. The furnishings were all Polynesian, dark hardwoods, and heavily carved. It was cool, and Abby wondered how it was possible to air-condition a dwelling with a high-thatched ceiling.

'He is anxious to see you.' The house-man showed them the way. They passed through several large rooms until they came to what appeared to be a library with a heart-stopping view of the ocean. A ship with lighted portholes stood just off shore, a cruise liner that appeared to be anchored in the lee of the bay.

A man was seated at a large carved desk. He looked up as they entered the room.

'Jack, you scoundrel.' He laid his pen down and was immediately out of his chair. 'You did not tell me where you were staying. It was the devil trying to find you.' He was a big man, tall and rangy with dark hair and eyes and an infectious smile, the kind that deceives you. Abby sensed that it could turn cold in an instant if he were displeased. He crossed the room in five easy strides, and his arms embraced Jack in a bear hug.

Jack was clearly uneasy with this display of affection. He patted Henry on the back with one hand while the other hung limp at his side.

'Henry,' he said. 'It's good to see you.'

Abby watched, laughing at Jack and his embarrassment.

'Goddamn, it has been a long time,' said Henry. 'I keep telling you, you must come down and visit more often. What has it been?'

'I've lost track,' said Jack.

'Precisely. It is how you lose track of friends. You know,' he said, 'I would have sent the Gulfstream to pick you up in Atlanta or Savannah. All you had to do was pick up the phone.'

Then Henry realized there was a stranger in the room. 'Where are your manners?' he told Jack.

'Excuse me. Henry, I'd like you to meet Abby Chandlis.'

The man named Henry backed away from Jack and for a moment took in Abby with deep-set dark eyes. Then he extended a hand and a warm smile.

'Abby, meet Enrique Ricardi.'

'Henry's fine,' said the man. 'Everybody on the island calls me Henry, except my mother. She gives me no end of grief. She tells me I'm becoming Anglicized or Anglophiled or some damn thing.'

As he spoke, Abby's jaw hung open. She knew the name. Anyone who had ever entered a bar knew the name. Lamely she took his hand and shook it. The name Ricardi was synonymous with rum, the largest distiller in the world, with plants in the United States and Europe. There were signs with the name on half the roads in America and all over the island. It was no wonder, as Jack said in the hotel lobby, that nothing happened here without Henry knowing about it. For all intents, Enrique Ricardi owned the island. He was one of its wealthiest men, well up on the food chain on the Fortune 500.

'Are you feeling alright?' asked Henry.

'Ah . . . oh, yes,' said Abby. She caught herself staring and diverted her eyes.

'Did you catch the look on her face?' said Jack. 'I've been telling her about my friend Henry for two days, and now you could knock her over with a feather.'

'Well, you didn't tell me,' said Abby.

'Excuse my ill-mannered friend,' said Ricardi. 'May I call you Abby?'

'Sure.' Abby was trying to appear casual in such lofty company.

'Please, have a seat.' Henry called the house-man and ordered drinks, piña colada for Jack, rum punch in honor of her host for Abby.

'You are probably wondering how someone like myself, cultured, and refined, could have ever had the poor judgment to have become involved with someone like this?' He pointed to Jack and shook his head. 'A mean low life.'

'Just a minute,' said Jack.

'Now that you mention it,' said Abby.

'Oh, here we go,' said Jack.

'Well, I had the misfortune, the incalculable poor judgment, to admit him to my fraternity at Stanford.'

'Your fraternity?' said Jack. 'I seem to remember that I was on the membership committee the year you rushed.'

'Goes to show you how clouded your memory becomes with age,' said Henry. 'Ah.'

Before Jack could counter, the house-man came back into the room with a tray of drinks.

'Time for my medicine,' said Jack.

'Yes. To improve your memory,' said Henry.

They laughed and each took a glass as the house-man passed them along. Abby's was tall and frosted, with a small parasol poking from the top, and a slice of pine-apple over the edge. Suddenly it started to make sense; Stanford and a degree in Latin American Studies. Where else would you meet the commercial royalty of the Caribbean?

'You know, you really should be scolded,' said Ricardi. He was talking to Jack. 'You come to my island and reject my hospitality. Of course you will stay here tonight.'

'We have rooms back at the Condado Plaza,' said Jack.

'You *had* rooms at the Condado Plaza,' said Ricardi. 'It seems they have suddenly become overbooked.' A wry smile spread across his face as Henry settled into the couch across from them. 'Zeke has already gone to retrieve your luggage. I have spoken with the hotel manager. There is no charge.'

'What about the charges I put on the room?' Abby said this in a low tone to Jack. She was wearing part of them. Henry picked up on the comment.

'As I said, there was no charge,' said Henry. 'We supply a major staple to the hotel, and their guests imbibe rather generously.'

'What Henry is saying is that he owns a chunk of the Condado,' said Jack. 'Along with every other major hotel on the island.'

'A small family franchise.' Henry grinned, something insidious. She could imagine him owning slaves and giving them away with similar equanimity in another age. It invaded her sense of Yankee independence, which seemed to be eroding like a landslide the further down the road she went with Jack.

'Now we will put you up in rooms in the guest wing,' said Ricardi. 'I understand you are a writer?'

Abby shot Jack a look. She wondered how much he had told Ricardi about their arrangement.

Jack shrugged. Whipped dog. He knew he was going to get a tongue lashing later.

'Yes. Well, Jack has those ambitions,' said Henry. 'I have told him to give it up. To be realistic. That all of that is in the past. But alas, Jack and reality, they are strangers.'

'Really?' said Abby.

'Oh yes. He chases the dream ever since . . .'

'That's enough,' said Jack.

'No, I want to hear more,' said Abby.

'Who am I to interfere with dreams?' said Ricardi. He let it drop. 'I have even offered him a job here, but he will not take it.'

'Nepotism,' said Jack.

'No, nepotism is when you hire your family. God knows I have done enough of that. I think they call it cronyism when it is a friend. Just think, we could travel the world, chase women, and drink.'

'You can do that down the road in your refinery,' said Jack.

'Distillery. Please,' said Henry. 'Anyway. Back to matters at hand. I have a wonderful place selected for you down in St Croix,' he told Abby. 'I think you will like it. Very quiet. Very private. The Kennedy family, Ted, rents the house down the road for Christmas sometimes. But the house I have selected for you is less conspicuous.'

Abby was wondering how much it would cost.

'Now, how long are you going to be on the island?'

'Two days,' said Jack. 'We have a flight out day after tomorrow in the afternoon.'

'Nonsense,' said Henry. 'Certainly you can stay longer than that.'

'I wish we could, but there is a deadline,' said Abby. 'We have to start work immediately.'

'Work,' said Ricardi. 'The nemesis of us all. I myself am off to Europe in the morning. But surely you could stay here. Have the run of the place.'

'Gotta be moving on,' said Jack.

Ricardi understood. 'But you will not fly down to St Croix. Not on that little twin prop job. It is so uncomfortable,' said Ricardi. 'I would give you the Gulfstream, but I need it to fly to London.'

'Not a problem,' said Jack.

'Of course it is not. You will take the *Isabella*.' He pointed to the cruise ship moored in the bay beyond the study window. 'I have already given instructions. Alerted the crew and the captain. And while you are on the island, you will use Zeke and the car.' Henry was the kind who didn't take no for an answer.

Jack made a face, like what could he say.

'I have some last-minute matters to clear away and then we can have dinner. Ah, before I forget,' he said, 'I have the key to the house, and something that arrived for you earlier today,' he told Jack. He reached into a drawer in his desk and removed a small box, an express package that looked remarkably like the box that Jack had dropped off at the office near the airport the day before.

CHAPTER
TWENTY-FOUR

Ever since the cop's visit to his office, Charlie Chandlis had been dying of curiosity. He knew that Abby had come into money. What he didn't know was how much, or where it came from. He thought he knew his former wife, but the episode with his credit card had showed him that he didn't know her as well as he thought. The Abby he was married to would never have had the sand to take his credit card, or to use it.

He didn't show much anger. But underneath he was quietly seething. Abby had made a fool out of him and Charlie didn't like it. Still, there was another aspect to him that was titillated. The thought that Abby had turned over a new leaf, especially one with a slightly shady color, was something strangely intoxicating to Charlie. He didn't know what he would do if he got his hands on her. That was the exciting part.

It had crossed his mind more than once over the past week that perhaps Abby had hidden assets during their marriage, something stashed away that was community property that she had failed to disclose during the divorce. The reason Charlie had a suspicious mind was that he had hidden assets himself, nearly eighteen thousand dollars in retainers, that he had never put on the books of his practice during the months just before they split up. Why she had paid back the six thousand on the credit card Charlie wasn't sure. But if she had that kind of money, maybe there was more.

Abby's law practice wasn't much. For the most part, she was salaried. Still it was possible that she had come into a windfall, maybe a large settlement in a case. It wasn't what lawyers were paid by the hour that made some of them rich. It was the contingent fees when they went to trial or settled a case on the courthouse steps. In a big case, the lawyer's take could be six figures.

Charlie was confronted with the problem of how to find out. There had to be a bank account somewhere. Banks were secretive places. If your name was on the account, they might tell you what was in it. Otherwise you could forget it. If you held a check drawn against the account, they would only tell you whether there were sufficient funds on deposit to cover it. Charlie already knew they were sufficient in the case of Abby's check for the credit-card charges. The card company had cashed it.

It took him a few days to devise a plan to find out more. In Charlie's eyes lawyers were the high priests of society, special people with special powers. They made the laws, so why not use them for their own purposes. Over a two-day period in his spare time, Charlie concocted a civil complaint against Abby, a trumped-up law suit that he filed in the superior court in Seattle. Lawyers did this thousands of times a day all over the country, and no one paid particular attention, unless it was filed against a rock star or some basketball jock.

In the suit he charged Abby with civil fraud, the

failure to disclose assets in connection with their divorce. In fact, he had no evidence at all. But evidence isn't required to file a law suit, only to win one. Charlie had no intention of going to court. In fact, he made no effort to serve a copy of the law suit on Abby either by personal service or publication in a newspaper. Instead, using the court's file number issued by the clerk in the law suit, Charlie then issued a subpoena duces tecum. This was a court order requiring the recipient to produce records. In this case, banking records. Then Charlie started off on a fishing expedition.

The first place he visited was the bank where Abby had written the check to cover the credit-card bill. What he discovered was that she'd closed the account two days after her check had cleared. He wasn't surprised. If she was hiding assets, she would be more cagey than to leave a bundle where Charlie could find it that easily. The fact that the account was closed, however, confirmed in his mind that there was something going on. Abby had something to hide.

He crafted a second subpoena. Calling on the sale of Abby's house and pretending to be an interested buyer, Charlie had gleaned one other vital piece of information. Morgan Spencer, a lawyer with Abby's old firm, was the contact on the sale of her house. If that was the case, it didn't take much to conclude that Spencer might be handling other business matters for her. The question was, where did Spencer and his law firm do their banking?

Charlie combed a back issue of one of the small legal newspapers until he found what he wanted. It was a list of names, young lawyers recently admitted to the practice of law after passing the state bar examination. He ran his finger down the list until he found a likely candidate, then picked up the phone and dialed.

'Starl, Hobbs and Carlton.' It was a woman with a sexy voice on the other end.

'Hello. My name is Daniel Swenson.' Charlie pumped himself up to sound young and naive. 'I'm a new admittee to the bar and I wanted to talk to one of the lawyers at your firm, if I could, about some business advice.'

'What kind of advice?'

'You know. Getting started. Opening an office. Setting up financial records, that sort of thing.'

'How did you get our name?'

As Charlie had suspected, the most difficult part would be getting past the receptionist.

'One of my professors at law school told me that your firm was among the best managed firms in town. A great reputation,' said Charlie. 'So naturally I thought I would start there.'

'Just a moment,' said the woman.

He whistled quietly to himself as he listened to elevator music being piped over the phone.

'Hello. Who am I speaking to?' It was a man's voice, deep and melodious, that came back to him on the line.

'Oh. This is Daniel Swenson. I don't know how much your receptionist told you, but I'm a recent admittee, just getting set up in practice.'

'Yes. How can I help you?'

'I recently attended one of those meetings. You know, sort of bridging the gap between law school and practice. Several of the attorneys who spoke to us mentioned your firm as being particularly well run.' It was the kind of horseshit designed to turn the head of a silk-stocking lawyer.

'They sort of suggested,' said Charlie, 'that more

experienced lawyers wouldn't mind giving a little advice. Just to get us off on the right foot.'

'Absolutely,' said the older lawyer.

'May I ask who I'm speaking to?' said Charlie.

'My name is Lewis Cutler. I'm the managing partner.'

'Oh Jeez, I didn't expect to get the boss,' said Charlie.

'That's alright. What can I help you with?'

'I have to establish some business bank accounts, a client trust fund. You know the sort of thing. I thought maybe you could recommend a local bank that comes highly regarded within the profession?'

'Oh sure. No problem. We've used First National, the downtown branch, for years. Just ask for Jim Hanford. Tell him Lew Cutler sent you.'

'Do all the partners there use the same bank?'

'For business, yes,' said Cutler. 'We use one bank for ease of record keeping. It gets to be a pain when you have accounts spread all over town.'

'Gee, thanks. That's a big help. I'll remember that,' said Charlie.

'Not a problem. Anything else I can do for you?'

'No. I think you've been more than helpful.'

'Listen, I know how it is when you're first setting . . .'

Charlie hung up and left Cutler talking to himself on the phone. He turned to the typewriter and plugged in the name of First National on the form subpoena, then ripped it from the typewriter, signed it, and grabbed his briefcase.

Twenty minutes later he waltzed through the revolving door of First National. He pretended to make notes at the counter in the center of the bank until he found the name plate on the desk he was looking for. He walked up to the bank officer sitting at his desk.

'Can I help you?' The man was middle aged and balding.

'Mr Hanford. My name is Charles Chandlis. I'm an attorney and I have a subpoena for financial records regarding one of your depositors.' He handed the man the subpoena, and the officer looked at it.

'Please have a seat.' He motioned Charlie to one of the chairs on the other side of his desk.

The form was official-looking, bearing the title of the superior court along with the file number of the case.

'It's very specific.' Charlie sat down. 'We seek only information regarding accounts for the named individual. Nothing else. The bank is not named as a party defendant.' He mentioned this in hopes that the banker might see the downside in failing to comply. With Charlie, subtle intimidation was an art form.

'Yes. I see. Our legal department is in another building.' The banker seemed confused as to what to do with the document, whether simply to comply or to have his own lawyers scour the form for awhile.

'You can send it along to them if you like. But I was hoping to get some basic information today. Certainly you can have a reasonable period to produce the records. Ten days. Two weeks. I know you're busy.' First the whip, and now the carrot, thought Charlie.

'I see.' The banker was straining his eyes hoping to find something that might jump off the page at him, some justification for delay. But he didn't find it.

'Your bank comes very highly recommended,' said Charlie.

'Oh really?'

'Oh yes. A good friend. Lew Cutler at Starl, Hobbs and Carlton. Speaks very highly of you.'

'Oh sure. I know Lew.'

'Great guy,' said Charlie. 'Yeah, we go way back. He can't say enough good things about this bank. He keeps telling me I'm going to have to move my business accounts over here. Looks like I'm gonna have to have him up on it,' said Charlie.

There was a budding smile on the banker's face as he looked at Charlie over the top of the subpoena. 'Everything appears to be in order,' he said.

Actually it wasn't. The banker might have asked for a return on service of process. This would have shown that their depositor, the defendant in the law suit, had not been served with a copy of the suit. Without notice of the litigation, Abby had no way to fight the subpoena, to try to quash it. A lawyer in the bank's legal department would have seen this. If Charlie played it right, by the time they did, he would have what he wanted.

'What is it you want to know?' said the banker.

'Very simple,' said Charlie. 'All I need for the moment is whether you have any accounts on deposit for the named individual? And if so, how much is on deposit as of this date? For now, that's all I would need. As I say, you can copy the records at your leisure and send them along later.'

This sounded reasonable to the banker. They didn't have to do anything but look in their computer. 'I think we can do that.'

'Wonderful,' said Charlie. Subpoenas were such wonderful things.

Hanford started punching his computer keys.

'What's the depositor's name?' said Hanford.

'Abigail Chandlis.' He spelled the last name for him. 'It might be under Abby.'

He punched some more keys.

'Yes. We have an account in that name. It's a joint checking account with a Morgan Spencer.' He wrote the account number on a slip of paper and handed it to Charlie.

'May I ask how much is in the account?'

Hanford punched a few more keys and scrolled down on the screen.

He looked at the numbers and had to focus his eyes. He wrote it out on a slip of paper and passed it across to Charlie. It was bank policy when balances got this big, to protect the privacy and the security of their patrons.

Charlie whistled. Abby had a million-two on deposit. He nearly fell out of the chair.

'Can you trace the source?'

'There's only two deposits. But the computer doesn't show where they came from.'

'Is there any way to find out?'

'Just a moment.' Hanford picked up the phone and dialed. 'Yes. I need an account history.' He gave the number of the account and waited a moment. 'Only two items? Could you fax those for me? Great!' He gave the bank's fax number and hung up.

He looked at Charlie. 'It'll be just a moment.'

A couple of minutes later he walked over to the fax machine and collected the pages coming through.

'The most recent check deposited in the account, a little over six hundred thousand, was drawn against the account of Pietros Films, Ltd.'

This meant nothing to Charlie.

The first one, a total of six hundred thousand, was written against a royalty account on a bank in New York. Carla Owens & Associates.

What was strange was that both checks were written to a Jack Jermaine. They were signed over by him and then deposited into Abby's account.

CHAPTER
TWENTY-FIVE

Abby never had the time or the money to travel. Practicing law by day and writing by night left little time for leisure pursuits or for seeing the world. It was the price every part-time writer paid.

She had never seen anything like Old San Juan; buildings that dated to the time of Columbus.

It was early afternoon, the day of their departure from Puerto Rico. Enrique's boat was to pick them up at the docks that evening. Abby and Jack walked through a maze of narrow cobblestone streets and wound past shops whose owners gathered in doorways chatting in Spanish. The historic city was filled with romance and images of an older world. It was rich in color, and Abby considered ways of fitting it into the story for her sequel.

A cruise ship was moored at the docks. Its passengers ambled down the stairs of the terminal building. Like so many fleas they flitted about the streets of the old town, climbing on its monuments and cornering deals on T-shirts. Even Jack looked like a tourist. He wore a tight polo shirt and running shorts and sported a good-sized camera case on his hip.

As they ambled through the plaza, Abby felt strange, almost embarrassed, as Jack fell under the gaze of passing women. Old and young, it didn't seem to matter, his looks were like an aphrodisiac. Even a few men stopped and stared. In a crowd, Jack stood out. Charisma and presence, he should have been a politician. He was taller and tanned with chiseled features. There was something about his thick dark mane of hair and the way he swept it to the side periodically with one hand. And the flashing bright smile, like JFK. Most of the women tried to be cool, subtle glances until they were past. Then they would turn and take a full look, a few of them whispering into cupped ears. For Abby it was a bizarre sensation. She could feel the radiating envy of the passing women like the pings on sonar. It was as if she had somehow cornered the glamour market. The shallow values of the world, she thought. Still she couldn't help enjoying the moment in the sun. Abby was no teenage fashion model, but she was not a bad-looking woman. In a world unpoisoned by the culture of youth, she might have stood out herself. She wondered what it would be like to be dressed to the nines strutting on Jack's arm through some flashy night spot, like the red carpeted walk on Oscar night.

She put away her daydreams as they edged away from the tourists and climbed the steep sidewalks of the town until they found themselves standing on Calle Norzagaray. It flanked the edge of Old San Juan high on a bluff. Jack and Abby stood there looking out at the white capped swells of the Atlantic.

'Over there,' said Jack. He pointed off to the northwest, a mile away. 'That's the fortress of El Morro. It guards the harbor entrance.'

Abby could see the ramparts of the ancient fort,

turreted guard towers and parapets of massive stone, walls that ringed the old city.

'I'd like to see it,' she said.

'Later,' said Jack. 'First let's get something to eat. Do you like Mexican food?'

A block down was a small restaurant with a sign in black letters spanning the second story, 'Amanda's Cafe.' There were two rooms inside, a small triangular bar, and a dining area. Jack and Abby opted for the veranda out front over the street. They ordered margaritas and relaxed, watching the turquoise, white-capped combers blow in off the Atlantic.

The motif of Amanda's was flamingo pink and teal green, the hot colors of the Caribbean. And the food, as Jack had promised, was delicious. They listened to Latin beats, and Jimmy Buffet from the juke box inside, as they labored over sizzling iron skillets of chicken and beef. They built fajitas from flour tortillas the size of Mexican hats, and talked about Abby's book.

Big-F had done a photo shoot for Jack's picture on the back jacket and for publicity. They had also hired a large public relations firm to do screen testing, a kind of briefing for television. Owens and Bertoli wanted Jack well prepped for the talk-show circuit. Abby was nervous about allowing him to go to New York alone. But she had work to do, and sooner or later she would have to trust him.

'What will you talk about in the interview?' she asked him.

'My book.' He gave her a sly grin. 'And how I wrote it.'

'And how was that?'

'With great care. You see, it was a labor of love,' said Jack. 'Every word and comma.'

'And how long did this labor of love take you to create?' she asked him. Questions she anticipated would be asked when they prepped him.

Jack thought for a moment. 'Five months.'

Abby shook her head. 'Longer.'

'Seven months.'

'More.'

'Did you chisel it on stone?' said Jack.

'A good book takes time,' said Abby. 'Like fine wine.' After reading his manuscript, Abby guessed that Jack knocked out a novel a month.

'How long did it take?' he asked.

'Two years.'

He whistled low under his breath.

'It took that long to capture the right voice, to deal with characters and motivation. Even formula fiction takes time,' said Abby. 'If it's going to work.'

'How are you going to have the next one ready in a year?' he asked.

'By working my ass off. Feast or famine,' said Abby. 'Either they don't want you at all, or if you're successful the publishers demand a book every twelve months. Sooner if they could get it.

'The theory,' she told him, 'is that they can addict the reading public like tobacco companies hook smokers.'

'Well, at least the readers don't get cancer,' said Jack.

'I wouldn't be so sure. There's no CAT scan for the intellect,' said Abby.

'So you finished the book in two years,' said Jack.

'Actually I did the first draft in eight months. I spent the next sixteen revising and rewriting.' She could have said dumbing it down, but she didn't.

'Anyone can write,' said Abby. 'The question is, can you rewrite? And when you do, is it better or worse?'

'What do you mean?' said Jack.

'How can I put it? It's like music, only you're not listening for melodies. It's more the cadence of speech and the pattern of prose. Credible writing requires an ear. If you're tone deaf, forget it.'

Jack looked at her as if perhaps she were sending him a message.

'That's a great line,' he said. He reached for a pen in his pocket and wrote it down on a napkin.

'Now what else are you going to tell the vast television audience?' she asked.

'You tell me.'

'You might talk about what you did for a living while you were writing. People are usually interested in that.'

'Ah. The starving author,' said Jack. 'Well, unfortunately I didn't have to work.'

'Independently wealthy, are you?'

'Wealth, no. Independent, you bet.'

'You were in the military.'

'True.'

'Tell 'em about that. What did you do? Remember, you're an instant celebrity. Oprah loves you. The world wants to hear what you eat for breakfast.'

'What does anyone do in the military? Follow orders,' said Jack.

'What kind of a job did you have?'

'Job?' said Jack. 'I was a Marine. Spit and polish, and shining sabers. I trained a lot of boys to become a few good men.'

'A drill sergeant,' said Abby.

'A training officer,' said Jack.

'Better title,' she told him. 'You've got to sell yourself to sell the book. Remember that.'

He saluted with his mouth full of fajitas, like he was taking orders.

'Anything exciting and adventurous?' said Abby. 'What did you do before you were a training officer?'

'What is this, twenty questions?' said Jack.

'No. It's work. It's what you signed on for. Now tell me. What did you do before you were a training officer?'

'I ran a river boat.'

'What, like on the Mississippi? Don't be so mysterious. Inquiring minds want to know,' said Abby.

'Smaller,' said Jack. 'Inflatable.'

'You were the captain of a rubber raft?'

'A twenty-foot Zodiac,' said Jack. 'With a thirty caliber mounted machine gun and a crew of five.'

'Now that sounds interesting.'

'We wore grease paint and black hoods and operated at night.'

'Tell me more.'

'We'd go ashore. Our job was laser painting.'

'What's that?'

'We used a thing called a "mule." It looks like a shotgun on steroids,' said Jack. 'There's a short stock. You aim it just like a gun. It emits a nearly invisible laser beam that illuminates the target for the guys in the sky. You aim at a window or a doorway, sometimes an air duct or an elevator shaft.'

'Like that paint ball stuff?' said Abby. 'For training in war games, right?'

'Like in Panama and Kuwait City,' said Jack. 'We painted targets so that two thousand pound laser-guided bombs could find them.'

Jack stopped talking and looked at her over his tortilla, dripping juice onto his place.

'But you never killed anybody, right?' Abby wanted confirmation of this. Why, she wasn't sure herself.

'I would assume there were people inside those buildings. Besides, you could usually tell.'

She gave him a quizzical look. She didn't want to ask but felt compelled.

'It's the smell of burning flesh,' said Jack. 'There's a real distinctive odor.'

She suddenly lost her appetite, pushed her plate away, and sipped a little of her margarita.

'On second thought,' said Abby, 'maybe mysterious is better.' She had visions of Jack opening his wallet to show pictures of burning babies on the morning shows.

'Hey, you asked, so I told you,' said Jack.

'Why is it so important for you to write?' Abby changed the subject.

'I enjoy it,' said Jack.

Maybe that was the problem, thought Abby. Every good writer she had ever known hated it. What was the line? There's nothing at all to writing. Just sit down and open a vein. She guessed the reason it was so effortless for Jack was that he lacked self-criticism. If you're tone deaf, every click of the keyboard, each scratch of the pen, sounds like Mozart.

'Tell me, does my stuff sound real?' he asked.

'I don't know. I'm not a good judge of what happens in war.' Abby copped out. 'But maybe you're trying too hard.'

He gave her a look. He could tell bad news was coming. 'Here we go,' said Jack. 'Let him down easy. Tell him he has promise, but maybe he should consider another line of work. Ever thought of being an auto mechanic?'

'Did I say that?'

'No, but you're thinking it.'

'Your friend Henry started to say something. That you've had this passion to write ever since, and then you cut him off. What did he mean? Ever since what?'

'Henry talks too much,' said Jack. 'He missed his calling. He should have been a therapist.'

'He seems to think you're obsessed.'

'See what I mean?' said Jack. 'Do I have to have a reason?'

'No.'

'But a little talent would help. Is that it?' Jack finished the thought for her.

'I didn't say that.'

'You don't have to,' said Jack. 'I haven't come all this way without some sense of my own limitations,' he told her. 'Go ahead, say what you're thinking.'

'Maybe you should consider Henry's offer for a job,' she told him.

'Do I look like a charity case? Besides, I don't need the money. Henry doesn't need my help. He's lonely. He wants to buy a friend.'

'So be his friend.'

'I'd rather be a writer.'

'Not everybody can pen a novel,' said Abby. 'Your manuscript needs a lot of work.'

He put his fajita down on the plate and started to sip his margarita. 'That's why I thought we could work on it together.'

'And what gave you that idea?'

'The fact that we're working together on yours.'

'Different definition of working,' said Abby.

'Ah. I see. Flashing a smile and flexing my pecs is not your idea of collaboration. So that I get this straight. You don't want me for my mind, just my body?'

Abby started to laugh. But it was true. It was why she was using him. Men in the field of entertainment always made more money than women. And money was the ultimate measure of success. Of the box-office stars capable of opening a blockbuster film, only two or three were women and they were paid considerably less than their male counterparts. The same was true in the top realms of fiction writing, from legal thrillers to military fantasies. The only place for women was in the genre of romance with a little grudging acceptance in mysteries.

But the heavy guns, the first order, Grisham, Crichton, Clancy, and Stephen King, all were men. Nobody was Chrichtonizing Judith Krantz or Danielle Steele. True, they quietly went about making millions. Still, even with blockbuster sales, they never entered the elite top rung in which every word written was scripted for feature film. The commercial literary coronations were all for men. Abby figured if she couldn't beat them, she would join them – at least until it was time for her grand entrance, out of the shadows to claim what was hers.

'So tell me, in a nutshell, what's the problem with my manuscript?' asked Jack. 'Is the story flawed?'

'It's not the story,' said Abby.

'So it's the writing?'

She made a lot of faces, all of them adding up to yes. Jack was tone deaf.

'We could work on it,' He returned to his meal. 'Like you said, rewriting is the key.'

'If you have a good ear,' she told him.

'We'll use yours. I'm not proud,' said Jack. He had a hide like an alligator. He just smiled and filled his cheeks with food.

'I don't have time,' said Abby.

He ignored her.

'How many of these things have you written?' she asked.

'Manuscripts?'

Applied to Jack's work it was a generous term, but she nodded.

It took him a moment while he counted. The fingers of both hands. 'Eight. So far,' said Jack.

'I would stop there.'

'Quit while I'm ahead?'

Abby waited a beat, smiled, and nodded as gently as she could.

'Actually there's nine, but you don't have to worry about that one.'

'Why not?'

'No reason,' said Jack.

'I don't teach remedial writing, and I'm not a ghost writer,' said Abby. 'I don't do that.'

'Really?' He smiled.

'Don't get the wrong idea. I'm not ghosting my novel for you.'

'Of course not,' said Jack. But he continued to smile.

'Just because you have an unsatisfied obsession,' said Abby.

'And you don't?' said Jack.

'No.'

'I see. You're just a frustrated artist trying to sell her work.'

'That's right.'

'Save it for the depositions if Bertoli sues you,' said Jack.

'I just wanted to improve the book's chances for success,' said Abby.

'Oh, I see. And you aren't interested in the money?'

'Only as a measure of success,' she told him.

'Oh, well. That elevates it to a lofty plane. So if you're not doing all of this – pulling the wool over Bertoli's eyes and the scam with Carla – for the money or for the fame, then what?' said Jack.

Abby looked him dead in the eye. 'For revenge.'

By the time they finished their tour of El Morro, the sun was setting. They didn't notice the two men milling near the gate, looking at tourist maps.

Abby and Jack walked at a brisk pace along the path, more than a quarter of mile across the broad field of grass that separated the fort from Old San Juan.

Jack checked his watch. If they moved they could make it to the docks before Henry's crew began to worry and wonder where they were.

Their luggage had been put on board the yacht that morning from Henry's Balinese palace. The boat then sailed up the coast in the afternoon. Abby and Jack had watched it from the battlements of El Morro as it rounded the point into the harbor. There it would take on fuel and ready itself for the cruise to St Croix.

As they cleared the plaza and began to thread their way through the maze of streets, it became clear to Abby that there was another side to San Juan; the old town after dark. By now the shops were all closed, and the tourists were gone, back to their hotels and cruise ships. In the distance, Abby could see the string of brilliant lights from the superstructure of one of the big boats as it left the harbor with its load of tourists hopping to the strains of mariachi music on their way to the next port of call.

Abby was having trouble keeping up with Jack, whose long legs seemed to devour whole blocks at a stride. He kept asking if she wanted to stop and rest, but

Abby was stubborn. They never noticed the two men walking at a distance behind them.

'How far do we have to go?'

'About ten blocks,' said Jack.

They turned the corner into a street that was too narrow for vehicles. A few children's toys littered the alley. Three figures moving at the far end stepped out of the shadows just as Abby and Jack reached the halfway point along the block. On first glance Abby thought they were just itinerants hanging in the doorways. Then Jack grabbed her elbow and pointed. One of the men, the one in the middle, was carrying something short and stout, like a club in his right hand.

Quickly Jack surveyed the terrain. There were only second-story verandas and doors flush with the street. No doubt these were locked. Even the windows had bars over them. Jack started to pull her back, a tactical retreat.

They'd gone a half-dozen steps when they looked behind them and saw the two men who had been shadowing them ever since they'd left the fortress. The two men entered the alley at the end, sealing off any avenue of escape.

'What do they want?' said Abby.

'Our watches, our wallets, and anything else they feel like taking. Of course that's only a guess,' said Jack.

'They can have them,' said Abby. She started to remove the watch from her wrist.

'Don't be so quick to give away my watch,' he told her.

'You're out of your mind. Give it to them.'

'I paid good money for this. Besides,' said Jack, 'if we give in too easily it may only feed rising expectations. No telling what else they may want.'

The men closed in from the two ends of the alley.

Jack edged toward the shelter of a doorway, and put Abby behind him into the threshold where she was protected on three sides. He put his body in front of her, sealing it off. 'No matter what happens, stay behind me,' he told her.

'Don't be a fool. If we give them what they want, they won't hurt us,' said Abby.

'That's the theory,' said Jack. 'But then I'm not the one they'll probably rape.'

She looked at him, or more accurately at the back of his head, then strapped the watch back on her wrist.

The five men slowly moved in, closing the distance like a pack of jackals until they formed a semicircle ten feet out from their quarry. One of them said something in Spanish and the others all laughed.

Jack forced a smile. 'Do you speak any Spanish?' he asked her.

'Un poco,' said Abby. 'A little.'

'Now's the time,' he told her.

'*Como esta usted?*' Abby looked at the man with the pipe in his hand as she spoke. He was clearly the leader.

'*Oh, muy bien,*' said the man. '*Muy bien.*' He sported a smile like a broken picket fence, a lot of missing teeth.

'*Y usted?*' he asked her.

'*Bien,*' said Abby. She forced a smile as if perhaps she were sufficiently positive it would come true; they would be fine, even though her knees were knocking.

The guy turned to his colleagues. '*Bien.*' They all laughed.

'*No. No. Usted no esta bien. Te voy a robar.*'

'He says we're not fine,' said Abby.

'Why not?' asked Jack.

'Because we're being robbed.'

The man with the pipe motioned with a curling finger, a come-hither gesture. He wanted Abby to step out of the doorway.

Jack told her not to move. 'Fuck you.' He looked the man with the pipe dead in the eye.

By the look on the man's face Abby could tell that it was not the first time he had been told this.

'Oh no, señor, I intend to be fucked, but not by you.' He suddenly dispensed with the Spanish. 'Give me your watch and your wallet and you can go.'

'Let's give it to them and go,' said Abby.

'Who said anything about you?' The man with the pipe gave Abby an appraising look. 'You stay with us for awhile. *Como se dice?*' He struggled for the right words in English. 'We have a party,' he finally said.

'Still want me to give him my watch and wallet?' said Jack.

'Maybe it's not such a good idea,' Abby told him.

'You want it?' said Jack. He pointed to the watch still on his wrist.

The guy smiled, all toothless in front.

'It's all yours. All you have to do is come and get it,' said Jack.

The smile left the guy's face. He swung the pipe in a wide arc and came a step closer. The others fanned out, looking for an opening. One of them pulled a knife from under his shirt, pushed a button, and a four-inch blade snapped out.

They had Jack surrounded in a half circle that began and ended with the wall of the building. Abby huddled in the shadow of the doorway behind him, looking for something she could use as a weapon. Nothing.

Jack took a quick step forward and they all backed up. This left a small gap between Jack and Abby. She stood in the doorway like cheese in a trap.

One of the men on the edge near the wall saw his opening and made a move toward her. In a single fluid motion without even looking Jack ˜lashed out with a foot. Like lightning he caught the man just below the kneecap. Abby heard the crunch of bone. The man shrieked in pain and reached down to grab his knee. As he did, Jack caught him full in the face with the second kick sending the guy sprawling on his back to the ground. His head hit the cobblestones, blood spurted from his mouth. He lay there unconscious. One down.

This seemed to have a mixed effect on the others. One of them backed away. The one with the pipe took another swing but missed. He was now paying a lot of respect to Jack's foot and losing face for it with his comrades.

The man who backed away was talking fast in Spanish, his hands moving quicker than his tongue, a bundle of anxiety. Abby couldn't understand his words, but his body language was clear enough. He wanted to go. This tourista was more than they bargained for.

The man with the pipe shouted something. Orders or encouragement, Abby couldn't tell which. A grim look of resolve came over the others. Reluctantly they closed the circle once more and filled in for their fallen friend.

Suddenly the man with the pipe lunged. Jack caught his forearm on a downward thrust and brought it down over his knee hard.

Abby heard a snap like a branch and realized that Jack had just broken the man's arm. There was a howl of pain and the pipe fell to the ground, sending the echo of metal on stone clanging through the alley.

Using pain for leverage, Jack gripped the broken arm and lifted the man to his full height. Then with a powerful kick he caught him squarely in the groin. With a muffled shriek, the guy crumpled to the ground and lay there motionless, his one good hand groping in his crotch to see what was missing.

One of the others turned tail and ran for the end of the alley.

The other two were of sterner stuff. One of them, the one with the knife, took the lead. He flipped the blade so the point was now between his finger and thumb; in throwing position.

In a reflex, Jack lowered his shoulder and charged. He nailed the man with the knife in the stomach, driving him onto his back in the middle of the street. They grappled and rolled, the knife dropping onto the cobblestones a few feet away. The Puerto Rican lunged for it. Jack's hand closed around his wrist just as the man reached the knife handle and closed his grip. The man had the knife, but Jack had his wrist like a tiger by the tail. They did a deadly dance, rolling to their knees, struggling in a death lock.

All the while Abby and the other Puerto Rican watched. Then suddenly the other man realized there was no one to stop him. He eyed Abby alone in the doorway, then quickly moved on her.

Jack saw it out of the corner of his eye as he fought for his life.

In two steps the man was on her. He grabbed Abby by the throat with both hands and began to press hard.

She scratched at his eyes and got a thumb in one of them. The man merely turned his head and tightened his powerful grip.

Abby felt the pressure building in her head, consciousness waning. She groped in her purse that hung from a strap on her shoulder, frantically feeling in the bottom for the pepper spray she had just remembered.

By now Jack had wrestled the other man to his feet. They struggled for the knife, Jack twirling him, spinning his partner like a top across the alley toward Abby and the man who was choking the life from her body. Like a whirling dervish, Jack and the other man suddenly disappeared behind the human mass in front of her, just as her hand found the tiny canister. She raised it toward his face.

Then suddenly, before she could press the button, the man's eyes went large and round, like two olives floating in mayonnaise. Every aspect of his expression lit up. He stared at Abby like some frozen comic mask. His grip eased, and for some inexplicable reason his hands went soft around her throat. He staggered back a step as if he was about to say something. His mouth moved but nothing came out, nothing but a small trickle of blood that ran down the corner of his lip.

His shoulders seemed locked in a raised position, his hands extended as if he might lung at Abby one more time. She held the pepper spray toward his face just in case.

Instead, he turned, and as he did she saw it. Embedded in his back, near the center of the man's spine, was the handle of the knife now seeping with blood like spigot that ran through his shirt. He took two steps and collapsed in the street.

Abby's hands went to her mouth and she began to shake. For a moment they all stood staring at the body lying in the street, and the growing puddle of blood.

Then suddenly the other Puerto Rican went wild. '*Matò mi hermano.*' He grabbed for Jack's throat, scratching him on the neck. The man went ballistic, as if newly charged with adrenaline. He caught Jack by surprise. They rolled on the street a few feet from the bloody body. The man reached for the knife in his friend's back, grabbed the handle, jerking it out. Halfway to Jack with the blade, the man felt cold steel against his temple. When he looked, a sideways glance, he saw a matt-black semiautomatic pistol, its muzzle pressed hard against his temple.

'Enough,' said Jack as he cocked the pistol.

The man's eyes went big, his hand opened, and the knife clattered to the street.

Jack lifted the man to his feet, grabbing him by the collar, and pushed him down the alley.

'Go. Get outta here. Come back and I'll kill you. Muerto.' Jack pointed the pistol so there would be no misunderstanding. Then he kicked the guy in the ass and the man started to run. The other two, the man with the broken arm and his friend, who now needed dental work, had already made it crawling and stumbling to the end of the alley. In less than a minute Jack had filled the street with carnage.

Abby was shaking in the doorway. For a moment, Jack ignored her. Instead he moved to the man lying in the street, placed a finger on the jugular, and searched for a pulse.

'We should call an ambulance,' said Abby.

Jack said nothing for the moment but continued to feel the man's throat. 'He won't be needing one.' He moved away from the body, pulled a handkerchief from his pocket and with it reached down and picked up the knife. 'I don't think I touched it,' he said. 'Still, can't be too careful.' He wiped the handle and the blade with the handkerchief, then stuffed the bloody cloth into the dead man's pocket.

Then he grabbed Abby's hand. 'Let's get out of here before his buddies find some more friends.'

336

CHAPTER
TWENTY-SIX

'I appreciate your doing this,' said Spencer. 'I know it's not part of your job.' This morning Morgan went to Alvin Cummings's office, a squat single story building out beyond the Lake Union locks near Shilshole on the Sound side of Seattle.

It looked like an insurance office, Venetian blinds with greasy dust on them, and dead flies on the windowsills.

Cummings himself had the looks of an F.B.I. agent, which he had been at one time, before he retired. He had done other things as well for the government, some of which Spencer knew about, and others he could only guess at. His hair was parted in the middle over silver-rimmed glasses, his body lean, flat stomach and butt so that if you saw him at a distance you might not know whether he was coming or going. He was from the old F.B.I., the Hoover days of male WASP agents in gray flannel suits. He still operated with a precision that was quasi-military even if a little worn.

'Listen, it's no trouble,' said Cummings. 'Besides, it didn't take much time. You may be getting exactly what you're paying for.' What Cummings meant was nothing. He had done a freebie for the lawyer who over the years had thrown him a lot of investigative business. Now Spencer had a personal problem and Cummings was eager to help. He handed Morgan a written report, which he'd kicked out of his computer's printer twenty minutes earlier. It contained some information that was confidential, government records that Cummings had acquired from sources better left unidentified. For this reason he did not want to commit the report to a fax, and told Spencer he would have to read it and leave it in the office.

'That's him. South Carolina,' said Spencer.

'Place called Coffin Point. According to the information, old family home,' said Cummings. 'Records show it's been in the family for some generations.'

'Country boy,' said Morgan.

'Except he went to school up north and out west. Degrees from Columbia and Stanford. Then he disappears for awhile, back in the eighties.'

'There oughta be a credit report,' said Spencer.

'Sparse one. Shows income of a few hundred dollars a month. One loan, a car.'

'That's all?'

'Yeah. That's what caused me to look. He was either on welfare during that period or something else.'

'What?'

Cummings handed Spencer another sheet of paper. 'This is confidential. You've never seen it. Understand?'

It was printed on a form with a government department logo and headed 'Department of Defense.'

'His father was deep in the military,' said Cummings. 'Marines. The name Joe Jermaine is synonymous with the Corps. The kid traveled in dad's footsteps. Did a stint as a training officer and then disappeared.'

'Where did he go?'

'Deep cover,' said Cummings. 'Special unit. What they called a "River Rat." He commanded a small boat squadron, riverine vehicles to those in the know. These guys are the first to see action in a conflict. They work with Navy Seals, float up and down rivers in the tules and come ashore at night for reconnaissance. They spot targets for artillery and air sorties, then slither back in the water so you never know what hit you.'

'He did this?'

'Big time,' said Cummings.

'But he's retired now?'

Cummings shrugged a shoulder. 'If the records are to be believed.'

'What do you mean?'

'Shadowy rumors,' said Cummings. 'There was trouble, back a few years.' Cummings settled his butt onto the corner of his desk and talked while Morgan listened.

'Seems your guy Jermaine is the kind who dances to the tune of a different drummer. There had been some scrapes with higher authority along the way, some ruffled feathers, and then trouble.'

'What kind of trouble?' said Morgan.

'One of the men in his squad died under questionable circumstances. There had been bad blood between the deceased and your guy. No charges were brought, but it seems to have put a crimp in his career. Jermaine was passed over for promotion. It was in a period of downsizing in the military and it was either up or out. He was forced into retirement. That's what the papers show,' said Cummings.

'But?'

The P.I. rolled his eyes and made a face that could only be described as a question mark. 'Here's where it gets hazy. There's nothing in writing, nothing anyone would send me, but there's some icy rumors, that he's done some private contracts.'

'What do you mean contracts?'

'I mean hired work for private parties, foreign governments. That from time to time he hires himself out.'

'To do what?'

'Whatever they're paying for. You gotta understand, this guy is heavily trained.'

'No specifics on these jobs?' asked Morgan. He needed something concrete to take to Abby or she would never believe him.

'No specifics. It's the kind of stuff you don't put on a résumé.'

'What about the passport?' said Morgan.

'It's an unusual name,' said Cummings. 'I checked. Passport office has no record of one issued in the name of Kellen Raid.'

'So he made it himself,' said Morgan.

'Or had it done by somebody else,' said Cummings.

'Any record of whether it might have been used to enter or leave the country?'

Cummings shook his head. 'But it's the kind of thing you would do if you had a job outside the country and you didn't want your own government to know you were there.'

Morgan thought for a long time, quietly in the chair, looking off into space.

Cummings got up and headed for the coffee pot, poured himself a cup. 'How about you?'

Morgan shook his head.

'I haven't asked you why you're so interested in this guy,' said Cummings. 'It's none of my business, I suppose.'

Spencer offered him nothing by way of reply. He

wasn't about to tell Cummings about the book and Abby, or Jack Jermaine's part in all of it. Cummings was a P.I. with a good sense of direction. He could keep a secret. Still there was no need to tell him, and Spencer had no intention of doing so.

'Are you thinking that this guy has something to do with the *Cella Largo*?' asked Cummings.

Morgan looked at him, somewhat surprised. The thought had never entered his mind.

'It is his line of work,' said Cummings. 'The kind of thing he would hire out for.'

'I suppose,' said Morgan.

'You sound almost disappointed.'

'No,' said Morgan.

'Do you know this guy?'

'We've met.'

'I understand,' said Cummings. 'You sound like you like him.'

Cummings didn't understand at all.

'It's not that. Just keep it under your hat for awhile. I'll let you know if I need anything more.'

'Sure.'

Morgan got up, grabbed his briefcase, and handed the report back to Cummings.

'What do you want me to do with this?' asked the P.I.

Morgan thought for a moment. 'Hang onto it.'

Cummings nodded. 'Take care,' he said. 'Be careful.'

'I will.'

'Jesus. They could have killed us. There were five of them. Did you count? Did you bother to count? I didn't know what to do. I couldn't think what to use as a weapon. We should go to the police.' Abby was yammering in shock, breathless by the time they reached the sanctuary of Ricardi's yacht.

They got to the cabin and closed the door behind them. Jack took her and held her for a moment while she hyperventilated.

'You're alright. Relax. Take a deep breath. Good. Again.'

'Shouldn't we go to the police?'

'Quit talking and breathe. We would spend the next week answering questions through an interpreter,' said Jack. They were in the master cabin below decks, all teak and mahogany, with a crew to man the boat and an Asian cabin boy.

Jack sat her on the bed and then poured a glass of whisky from the bar while he changed his shirt, which had been ripped in two places and had someone else's blood all over the front of it. Abby was too shaken for alcohol, but Jack insisted. He poured her a shot of brandy and she sipped it.

The crew had just cast off and the yacht made its way slowly down the channel toward the open sea. Their problems, the dead body in the alley, were now behind them.

'Besides,' said Jack. 'If we went to the police, they would want to know about this.' He flipped the semiautomatic pistol from his fanny pack onto the bed, where it bounced twice on the mattress and came to rest.

'They're not the only ones with questions about that,' said Abby. 'I can't believe you carried that through airport security.'

'I didn't,' said Jack.

The way he said it, Abby thought maybe he'd planted it on her. 'Was that in *my* luggage?'

'I had it delivered. I wanted to see if it would work. It did.'

'What are you talking about?'

'If you needed a gun. Just suppose,' said Jack. 'And you had to travel by commercial means. How would you do it?'

'It's not something I stay up nights thinking about,' said Abby. 'Most normal people don't.'

'Most normal people don't write the kind of material I do. If it isn't authentic, if it doesn't work, I don't put it in my books,' he told her.

'Yeah, well, we know how successful that's been.'

'So I thought about it.' He ignored her. 'Do you have any idea how many packages are processed daily by private express delivery companies in the States?'

She shook her head.

'Millions,' said Jack. 'Do you know how long it would take for them to X-ray the contents of every one of those packages?'

'Tell me.'

'I don't know. But I'm guessing it would take more than sixteen hours. And that's the average time they have to deliver an overnight package to most places in the Western Hemisphere.'

'So?'

Jack picked the gun up off the bed. 'So when it absolutely, positively has to be there the next day,' said Jack.

She looked at him dumbstruck. 'You didn't.'

Jack smiled and nodded his head, a proud beaming grin like some college jock who had just pulled off a panty raid. 'I dropped it off when we left my house, remember. The piece was at Henry's before we arrived in San Juan. It traveled through the night. We didn't.'

Abby thought about it for a moment, all the boxes coming and going from Coffin Point. 'And the one that was waiting for you when we got to your house?' said Abby.

'That was the return from Seattle.'

'You had the gun with you out there?'

'I try not to travel without it,' said Jack.

'In Chicago?'

'Especially in Chicago. That's a dangerous city,' said Jack. 'We were there on business.'

'That's what I mean. You're out of your mind.'

'I just believe in thorough research,' he told her. 'Now I know. The express companies don't X-ray their packages.'

'There are other ways of doing research.'

'If I'd called and asked them the question, do you think they would have told me the truth? Not on your life. They would have hemmed and hawed and ultimately they would have lied. They don't want to know what's inside all those packages. But they're not about to tell the public that.'

Abby wasn't sure if he was crazy or merely possessed an eccentric sense of humor. It seemed the longer she stayed around Jack, the more impaired was her judgment. There was a kind of ether that surrounded him. Whether it was his looks or his childlike charm, Abby was losing her critical perspective.

He swept a hand through his dark hair that was now tousled from their street fight and examined his body in the mirror. 'Think about it,' said Jack. 'If you were accepting several million sealed containers from the great unwashed masses and giving them to your employees to deliver all over the world, would you *really* want to know what's inside each one of them?'

'I never thought about it.' Abby studied him.

'I wouldn't. I'd figure ignorance was bliss.'

'What about Customs?' said Abby.

'Ah.' Jack turned toward her with his index finger pointed up like she had stumbled on a subtlety. 'Now that's the interesting part. I figured to be safe I would only send to locations where there's sufficient traffic to keep things humming. Good-sized cities with a lot of parcels coming in. And you always send it priority. Overnight express. That way the delivery companies are pushing Customs to rush things.'

Abby looked at him mystified. In his own inimitable fashion Jack had carefully thought it all through. And he was proud of himself, she thought, like a school boy who had just farted in class. Only in this case he had probably violated a dozen federal laws.

'They probably sniff for drugs,' he told her. 'And X-ray a handful of the packages. Random selection,' said Jack. 'So what are the chances?'

'You took a risk,' said Abby.

'Life's full of risks. You cross the street . . .'

'I know,' said Abby. 'You can get hit by a car.'

'I was gonna say you might get mugged.' He lifted one arm and looked at the back side under his elbow.

'That looks bad.' Abby observed a cut on the underside of his arm. It seemed that not all of the blood on his shirt belonged to other people. 'Let me see what I can find.'

She went into the head, more of a master bathroom, paneled wood and beveled mirrors with gold fixtures. There was a full-sized Roman tub on a platform behind saloon-type swinging doors.

She rummaged through some drawers until she found a roll of gauze and some tape. She grabbed a washcloth and wet it. By the time she came out Jack was bare to the waist, rippled abs and tanned. He was now dressed only in his running shorts and was checking an abrasion on his knee.

It was a hard body, rugged with a few scars on it. Abby remembered how it pressed up against her own that morning when they shot at targets near the marsh at Coffin Point. His touch that day lingered with her, hard body and soft hands and the deep whisper of his voice up close in her ear. Jack's tones carried just a hint of slow Southern drawl almost imperceptible unless you listened closely. It was an exotic cadence.

She remembered how his fingers closed around her own as she held the pistol. Jack steadying her. There was something about him. For all of the bluster and cynicism, there was an edge of softness under it all, a sort of school-boy charm. It was in the twinkle of his eye, and the angle of his head when he smiled, and the flashing white of his teeth against the bronze tan.

While she was attracted, Abby was scared. Of what she wasn't quite sure. To this point, Jack had been every inch the gentleman. He had never hit on her. In this moment, as they looked at one another, it was as if he was waiting for her to give him some signal, to say 'yes.'

Abby started to clean the wound on his arm. In a flash, the moment passed.

'Since we're sharing such intimacies, when are you going to tell me about the outline for the sequel?' said Jack.

'When it's time.'

'When will that be?'

'When I decide.'

'How far along is it?'

'It's coming.'

'When will it be finished?'

'When it's done.' Abby looked at him, a kind of

motherly expression of exasperation.

'It's what I like about you,' said Jack. 'Your candor and openness.'

'Then why do you ask?'

'Because we both know they're gonna press me on it.'

'Who?'

'Carla and Bertoli. When I get to New York. They're gonna want to know how it's coming.'

'They don't own the rights.'

'They have an option.'

'Tell 'em it's going well,' said Abby.

'They may want a little more than that.'

'Tell them it's going very well.' She smiled and Jack laughed.

'I'm sure Carla will accept that.'

'Take my word. The sequel is not a subject you want to get into,' said Abby.

'Why not?'

'For the same reason delivery companies don't look inside their packages.' She offered a sly grin. 'I'm sure you can hold them off. Besides, if we were to tell them anything, they'd only want to know more. Then they'd insist on plotting the story probably over dinner. By the time you finish dessert, they'll change the title three times, invent four new characters, and suggest that you include a dinner fork in the plot because they already have a nice drawing of one for the cover art. And when they're finished they'll claim they have proprietary rights on the book because they've contributed to it.'

'Whatever you want. It's your story,' said Jack.

'Don't tell them that.'

'I forgot. It's my story.'

'And that's exactly what you should tell them. And nothing more.'

Owens and Bertoli weren't the only ones Abby didn't trust. The less Jack knew about the sequel, the better. It was one of those pressure points of control she could use if he became difficult.

'So what do you suggest for small talk?' said Jack.

'Tell them you knifed a guy in an alley in San Juan. That should get things going.'

'It was an accident.'

'Right,' said Abby. 'This Puerto Rican just fell on his own sword. Bertoli should understand that, the corporate jungle being what it is.'

'Ow.' Jack flinched and pulled his arm away. 'What are you doing?'

'Cleaning the wound.'

'Yeah, but you're enjoying yourself a little too much,' said Jack. As he said it, he lifted his forearm to check the wound. As he did, he peeked at her from underneath, their faces less than a foot apart.

Abby's was a smile. 'If you don't like it, you should stay out of street fights.'

'Like I had a choice.' His words were slow as their eyes met.

'You could have given them what they wanted,' said Abby.

'As I recall they wanted you.'

There was something in her look at this moment that told Jack it had suddenly dawned on Abby. He had saved her life.

'I suppose I should thank you.' His gaze was on her lips, moist and parted as she uttered the words. Their thoughts converged like psychic energy, the snap of electricity spanning the distance.

'It was nothing. Besides, they wanted my watch.' Their eyes locked. Somewhere in the ionized atmosphere

Abby's eyes said yes. Their lips met.

He settled back onto the bed and tugged her by the arms down on top of him. The running shorts rode high on his thigh, exposing flesh and a tan line.

Her head went on his chest to the side, her eyes cast down. 'They got you there, too,' She said. She touched him on the thigh, a wound high on the outside.

His fingers covered hers, tugging, pulling her hand to the center of his body, to his stomach that quivered with the touch of her fingernails, to the band of his shorts.

'That's an old one,' said Jack. He shifted, lifted his knee until it wedged between her thighs, lifting her at the vortex. With his hand he tilted her chin until their lips met, gently nibbling.

'Old one,' Abby repeated his words in an erotic daze.

'Hmm. Diving accident.' Teeth closing gently on her lips, his tongue touched the tip of her own, his words the last intelligible sound as they descended into sensuous seas, the gentle motion of the ship, silk sheets, and satin comforters.

CHAPTER
TWENTY-SEVEN

He checked a local bookstore first, where he cruised through *Books in Print* on their computer. It listed nearly every book written in the last five years, cross-referenced by title as well as author. Morgan had the clerk look under two different names; Jack Jermaine, and Kellen Raid, the name Abby had found on Jack's passport. There was nothing.

Morgan was worried. He was in love with Abby and she didn't seem to notice. Now she was off to the ends of the earth with a man she didn't know, a man who, if Alvin Cummings was to be believed, spent his time in the military, slithering out of rivers like a snake to kill people.

Morgan trekked to the county library next. He could be dogged when something bothered him, and this did. It was nothing but a hunch, one of those nagging points that pick at the subconscious in your sleep.

Ever since Abby had told him about Jack's passport in the name of Kellen Raid, it had been turning over in Morgan's mind. Jack's seemingly boundless desire to be published, almost compulsive, and the way he'd inflicted himself on Abby caused Morgan to wonder;

had he used the name for something else?

In the library, Spencer located a volume that defined the origin and meaning of names. The name 'Kellen' was Gaelic. It meant warrior. Raid was only a guess on Spencer's part. But together the first and last name looked suspiciously like an action-oriented pen name, something an author might use who fancied himself a writer of military fiction.

He tried the library's computer catalog next, and struck out. There was nothing under either name. But the librarian pointed him in one last direction. Public lending libraries, even large ones, didn't possess copies of every book printed, especially when it came to popular fiction. Except for the classics there was a short shelf life.

He went back to his office and called the phone number the librarian had given him. Several days passed before they called back. It had taken that long, but they found something. Morgan wasn't sure exactly what it was. But it was enough to cause him to skip lunch and hoof it eight blocks through the noonday traffic.

The shop was small, squeezed in between a café on the corner, and an art studio. It specialized mostly in collector's items, rare editions, and other obscure works. What they didn't have on their shelves they could locate. The store belonged to a national network of used book shops. If a customer wanted something, he could place an order and put out the word. It might take a week, or a month, or a year, but if it existed, sooner or later they would find it.

It was a long shot, but Morgan was a gambler at heart. He knew that while the odds of finding anything might be slim, the payoff, if he did, could be huge. It was the kind of thing you prayed for in the closing days of a trial, that last-minute piece of evidence that showed your opponent was a convicted child molester. It was the kind of dirt you could shovel in front of a jury to tilt the entire case. Only in this case Abby was the jury.

Morgan was worried. For a hard-bitten lawyer, somebody on the jaded side when it came to publishing, Abby had become far too trusting of Jack. To Spencer it was beginning to look as if Jermaine had cast a spell over her. There was something about the man that Spencer didn't like. Maybe it was his good looks, or his quick tongue, a little too quick for Morgan. As far as he was concerned, Jack was the wrong kind of man for Abby. When Spencer's antenna was up, it was unfailing. At the moment he didn't like the signal he was getting. Several times in their telephone conversations Abby had let slip that she was talking to Jack about her work. Increasingly she was turning to Jermaine. Sooner or later she would take him into her confidence. To Morgan that spelled trouble. He should never have allowed her to go off to the islands, especially with Jack.

He breezed through the door of the small shop, setting chimes ringing over his head, shades of Dickens. The place was musty, and crammed with crude wooden bookcases to the ceiling, and as far as Morgan could see to the back of the building. There were narrow dark aisles and an old wooden ladder against one wall for reaching books on the upper shelves.

A young man sat on a stool behind the counter. He didn't look up when Spencer entered but continued pricing a stack of books with a pencil on the inside covers. The kid's hair was dyed a shade of chartreuse and shaved on the sides, the kind of stuff that you saw all over town these days. He wore the single obligatory earring, like a medal of defiance. Spencer wondered why anyone would hire somebody who looked like this.

'Can I help you?' The kid was polite and businesslike, but Morgan had a hard time seeing past the appearance.

'My name's Morgan Spencer. You're holding a book for me.'

The clerk spun around on his stool and thumbed through a stack behind him against the wall. 'Did they call you?'

'This morning,' said Morgan.

'Spencer. Spencer. Ah. Here it is.'

The clerk plucked the volume from the shelf. The title was printed in gold letters on the cloth spine. *Shadow War*. The clerk opened the cover and looked for the price in pencil on the inside. He punched a few numbers into a calculator on the counter next to him.

'With shipping that comes to nineteen dollars.' That didn't include the search fee that Morgan had already paid on a credit card over the phone.

'Can I look first?'

'Sure.'

Morgan checked the copyright for the date of publication. The book had been published nine years earlier by one of the large publishing houses in New York. This alone caused Spencer to suspect that he was barking up a wrong tree. If Jack was as talentless as Abby had said over the phone, how could he ever get published, let alone by a major publisher? Still, nine years. That was enough time for the book to have been forgotten in the perpetual tidal surge of fiction.

'There's no paper cover,' said Morgan.

'The dust jacket,' said the clerk. 'Probably came in without one. We get a lot of them like that. Jackets get tattered over the years, people toss 'em out.'

'Is there any way I could get one? The dust jacket?'

The clerk gave a big sigh, and checked a card catalog behind the counter. 'It's the only copy we found. If you want, I can take it back and try again.'

'No. No.'

Morgan's interest in the dustcover had nothing to do with the book's value. It was purely informational. The dustcover was where the author's picture would be if there was one, along with any biographical note. Without it, all he had was a title, and a name, the author's name: Kellen Raid.

'Have you ever heard of this guy before?' said Morgan.

The clerk shook his head.

'So there's no way for me to find out if he's ever published anything else?'

'If he'd published anything before this they would usually list those titles in the front of the book, right after the title page.' The clerk looked. There was nothing.

'Do you know where I could get a biography, anything at all on the author?'

'There are some literary source books. But I can tell you, he's not going to be there.'

'Why not?'

'They mostly cover classics and maybe some commercial authors,' said the clerk.

Morgan was up against the proverbial rock. It was a unique name. Still, it left Jack enough wiggle room. He could claim it was a coincidence. Maybe Jermaine had read the book and liked it. He could have used the author's name on the passport for that reason. He might even say it was subconscious. Morgan was a cynic. He was sure he had something. But Abby wasn't likely to buy it unless he had proof. She would want to give Jack the benefit of the doubt. Innocent until proven guilty.

'Would the publisher have anything on him?'

'You could try.'

Morgan feathered the pages of the novel. There were more than five hundred. He felt the cloth cover with his fingers and wondered if Jack was capable of writing such a thing.

'Can I have a minute?'

'Take your time.' The clerk turned to other duties. He rolled a cart out from behind the counter to an area a few feet away, climbed a foot stool, and began stacking some new arrivals.

Morgan opened the book and began to read. The writing was O.K., a little clunky in places, but the book opened with a gripper, an action sequence set deep in the jungle, according to a headnote somewhere in Southeast Asia. He read the prologue, eight pages. The story had a good hook, but Morgan was looking for something else. When he finished he was no closer to proving the identity of the author.

He turned back to the title page, flipped to the next page. There was a lot of small print, the name of the publishing company and its address. This was followed by a disclaimer that the characters in the story were all fictional. There was something about the Library of Congress. And after that was the author's name, Kellen Raid, and the designation of copyright in that name. Underneath, at the bottom of the page, were a line of numbers, what looked like three through ten, but printed in a peculiar order, odd numbers to the left, even to the right, with the number ten in the middle.

'Do you know what this is?' said Spencer.

The clerk turned to him from the stool and then down for a closer look.

Morgan pointed to the numbers at the bottom of the page.

'That's the press count. It tells you how many times the publisher went back to press for further editions. This is not a first edition.' If there had been any doubt, the clerk now knew that Spencer was no book collector.

'If it were a first edition, the number one would appear there on the left-hand side,' said the clerk. He checked the numbers. 'This is the third edition. There were two earlier printings. That's why the numbers one and two are missing.'

'What does that mean?'

'What it says,' said the clerk. 'It affects the value of the book as far as collectors are concerned. First editions are usually worth more.'

'Is it unusual that a book would go back to press that many times?'

The kid gave him an expression like he wasn't sure. 'Most books probably only get one printing. They get a small initial run. Unless there's demand for the book, that's it.'

'So this book would have been in demand?'

'Enough for three runs.'

'Could it have been a big book?' said Spencer. 'Commercially successful?'

'Depends what you mean by big. If it had been huge, I think I would have remembered the author. If somebody writes one that hot, they usually do another. Law of the marketplace,' said the clerk.

'But it could have been successful?'

'Possibly. It would depend on the size of the press runs. There's no way to tell that from the information here.'

Again Morgan had nothing to show for his efforts. He

offered the clerk a deep sigh and reached for his wallet. He paid with a credit card, and while the clerk was processing the slip, Morgan continued to scan the page, over to the other side, to the acknowledgments. There were only five paragraphs. Morgan didn't find what he was looking for until he got to the last one. There, buried in a single line, was what he'd been looking for all along.

'Mostly I thank my father, Joseph Jermaine, for an inquisitive mind and the questions that inspired this story.'

St Croix rests on a shallow shelf at the edge of the Atlantic Ocean. It is separated from its sisters of the Virgin Islands, St John and St Martin, by a rift in the ocean's floor more than four miles deep, a canyon known as the Puerto Rican Trench. The chasm divides a chain of islands that define the outer edge of the Caribbean Sea.

But for Abby it was as if somehow a barrier had been bridged. Their time on the ship, the embrace of his arms, the sharing of intimacy, brought her to know Jack in ways she never thought she would. The combination of power and gentleness that was Jack overwhelmed her. For the first time in her life she felt safe. They made love and they talked about things they had not discussed before: Jack's time in the military, his relationship with his father. He wanted to know about her marriage. There was a time when she actually thought she loved Charlie. But now Abby was certain that she had never really fallen in love. She had just stepped in it.

For the first time since Theresa's death, Abby opened up with another human being. In bed, Jack was tender and warm, as warm as the afternoon sun that cascaded down upon them as they stepped off onto the dock at King's Wharf in Christiansted.

Jack had ditched the shorts and fanny pack, in favour of a pair of pleated khaki pants that draped his long legs, and a safari vest with a million pockets. Abby wondered if one of them held the semiautomatic pistol. She was still uncomfortable about this, traveling with a man who thought nothing of being armed.

Up on the docks the first thing that caught Abby's eye was the bright yellow walls of the little Dutch Colonial fort, and the villagelike atmosphere of the town. She heard people on the docks, visitors speaking French and German.

Jack had told her that tourists from Europe spilled over from the British Virgin Islands to the American side for a day of shopping and sightseeing. The place reminded Abby of some exotic port of call, Java in the last century. The calm water of the little harbor was azure blue illuminated by the white sand on its bottom. There was a small island a quarter-mile off the docks, with what looked like a hotel perched over its sandy beach: Protestant Cay.

'We'll have to clear Customs,' said Jack. 'Shouldn't be a problem.' The captain of Enrique's yacht had greased it for them on the ship-to-shore radio coming in. A Customs agent met them at the dock, asked two or three questions while their luggage remained on board unopened. He stamped their passports and left. Being friends with the largest rum dealer in the world had its advantages.

Jack hailed a taxi and they headed out of town, east past Gallows Bay along what was called the East End Road. The taxi driver drove on the left, British style.

They passed lush fields and old stone towers. The island was dotted with the remnants of ancient windmills, their wind-catching apparatus snatched by hurricanes whose names had long since been forgotten. They passed ruins of eighteenth-century sugar plantations where the windmills had been used to crush cane, and drove through a rain squall that seemed to be the width of a cloud so that the hood of the car was awash in water and the trunk was bone-dry.

It was a short drive, less than ten minutes, when they pulled between a pair of pink and white pillars and onto a private drive. It wound a half a mile off the highway, past tamarind trees, some of which Jack told her were more than a hundred and fifty years old. They came to a stop at an old stone building, two stories, with a guard and barrier gate.

'Another of your friend's estates?' said Abby.

'A resort,' said Jack. 'You should get to know it. It's close to where you'll be. We'll just spend the night. We can get groceries in the morning and you can move into the house. It's just down the road, off the grounds.'

In locating the house Jack had thought of everything. 'The resort has a good bar and a restaurant,' he told her. 'A well-stocked wine cellar, all the comforts of home. If you don't want to cook, you can just come over here. It's a little walk, but not that far.'

The resort was gorgeous and private. On the land side were acres of manicured grass, a golf course. The buildings were all flamingo pink and old mortared stone. Most of them looked like they were at least three hundred years old. The place had once been a sugar plantation. The main building of the hotel sat on a promontory overlooking a deep bay of Caribbean blue water.

The taxi pulled up to the entrance and an attendant

got their luggage. Jack headed for the front desk just beyond a pink-and-white-covered portico. Over the entrance was a sign, black letters on old marble:

1653 THE 1947
BUCCANEER

Abby stayed with the luggage. She had no intention of losing her little computer. The outline to the sequel, now nearly completed, was in it. This was becoming an increasingly important document. With the first book presumably worth millions, the outline to the second was like gold, and Abby treated it like a state secret for good reason. She kept one paper copy and a backup on a disc. The notebook computer was quickly becoming her lifeline if she was going to finish the next book on time.

By the time she caught up with Jack at the desk he had a message for her from the clerk.

'Seems your friend Spencer's caught up with us.'

'How?'

'I told him to leave any messages here before we left,' said Jack. 'He's sent you a gift.'

'What is it?'

'It's out in the parking lot, right in front of the building.' Before Jack could speak, the woman behind the counter answered the question with a broad smile. She was convinced they had some luminary staying with them. Gifts like this were unusual.

Abby looked at Jack quizzically.

'Don't ask me.' He shrugged.

She stepped outside to the end of the walkway. There at the curb was a sporty little convertible, a Z-3, with its top down, parked in the shade.

Abby went back inside. 'Did he rent it?'

'Seems he bought it,' said Jack, 'with your money.' He dangled the keys from their ring on his little finger while he read a note from an envelope and then passed them to Abby.

'Greetings from the Home Front.

Knew you were going to need wheels so had this shipped from a dealer in Miami. Don't get mad. You can afford it. Besides, you need to celebrate. Trust me.

Morgan.'

Abby wasn't just angry, she was steaming. It was an act of extravagance, something that brought attention to her on the island, the precise thing that she didn't want. The woman behind the counter was smiling at her. She knew the car had to cost at least thirty thousand dollars. Now it marked her as a rich tourist, making it that much more difficult for her to blend in with the locals. Morgan had no right. He had overstepped the bounds of friendship.

Inside the envelope was another smaller one, this one very stiff and sealed. She opened it. There were two small plastic cards inside with the name of a bank in French, and another note. They were debit cards on a bank in Martinique, two separate accounts, a place where Abby could now draw funds without being found. He would give her the PIN numbers over the phone.

It was like Spencer. With one hand he infuriated you, and with the other he saved your bacon.

Abby and Jack checked into separate rooms in a part of the resort down on the water. The place was dated, just enough to be comfortable, blue tile floors in some kind of Dutch print with a king-sized bed and a large bath. Each room had a private patio overlooking the water. The beach was off to the right a hundred yards away, where it formed an arc and disappeared into a cove.

'Give me your passport and any credit cards you're not gonna use regularly,' said Jack. 'Got any jewelry?'

'What is this, a robbery?'

'Henry told me there's no safe at the house. You have to be careful down here. A U.S. passport is worth a lot of money.'

Abby looked at him wondering whether she should. Then she handed over her passport and one of the debit cards.

'Come in here and I'll show you.' He led the way. 'We'll use the one in my room since I'm gonna keep the room.' They went into the closet in his room through the adjoining door. Inside on a wooden platform was an electronic ElSafe, the size of a large microwave oven.

'What's your birthday?'

'You don't know me well enough for that,' said Abby.

'Lie,' said Jack.

She gave him six digits that would have made her thirty-four. Jack punched them into the electronic combination and removed a metal pin from the inside of the door. 'Now it's set. Unless somebody puts the pin back in and changes it, that's the combination that will open it everytime.'

He closed the door and pushed the lock button. The steel door hummed and sealed itself tight. He punched in the combination. It hummed again and opened. Jack put Abby's passport and one of the debit cards into the safe, closed the door, and pushed the lock button.

'You can put your outline in there, the manuscript, whatever you want. Feel free to use it.' Jack helped her with her luggage, then told her they could get lunch at the bungalow out near the beach.

She looked at her watch. 'I have a phone call to make first. Give me fifteen minutes.'

Jack smiled. He knew she was going to call Spencer and chew his ass. Abby wore her anger on her sleeve, and at the moment she was still steaming over the little car.

'It's beautiful,' said Jack. 'Wish I had a friend like that. You should thank him.' He wanted to stay and listen.

'See you in a few minutes,' said Abby.

'Can I take it for a spin?'

Abby gave him a look that pointed to the door.

'Just kidding.' He left and closed the door behind him.

It was nearly noon. Four hours difference. It was not yet eight o'clock out on the coast. If she was quick, she could catch Morgan before he left for the office.

She tried to dial direct, but it didn't work. The phone system on the island was primitive. She had to go through the hotel operator, who in turn connected her to a long-distance operator who placed the call. The phone line kept crackling. Water in some of the underground lines on the island from the last hurricane according to the operator. Abby listened as the phone rang on the other end, a lot of static. She was hoping she wouldn't lose him.

'Hello.'

She heard Morgan's familiar voice.

'What in the world do you think you're doing?'

'Abby.' Spencer's voice was elevated, almost euphoric. 'It sounds like you're in a tunnel. Where are you?'

'St Croix. I didn't order a car, Morgan. What are you thinking?'

'I know. But I thought you could use it. Besides, I got a sweet deal. Don't be mad at me. Please.'

The pleading tone of his voice and the familiarity of it from thousands of miles away instantly cut her anger by half. It was the thing about Abby. She would flash fury, but she could never stay mad for long, especially with those she liked. The phone crackled again.

'Are you there?' he said.

'I'm here. Everybody in the place knows my name,' she told him. 'The woman with the flashy little car.'

'Have you driven it?'

'Not yet.'

'They're a kick in the ass,' said Spencer. 'I tried one at a dealership here in town before I ordered yours. Stop on a dime, turn on a nickel,' said Spencer.

She could see him, his mane of graying hair streaming in the wind. It was the kind of thing that Morgan lived for, the staid attorney acting like a child.

'You shouldn't have done it.'

'You have to learn to enjoy your success,' he told her. 'I knew it was something you would never do for yourself.'

He was right and Abby knew it. She could never slow down enough to enjoy what she'd achieved in life, whether it was graduating from law school or authoring a novel. She was always too busy working, trying to find the seam of opportunity or to make one; moving on. And now she had managed to cut herself off from any public acclamation on her own book, by putting Jack and his picture up front. She was beginning to wonder if she would be able to reclaim her property. Maybe Jack was right. Maybe the public would never accept her.

'Do you want me to see if they'll take it back?' Spencer was talking about the car.

It would be a graceless thing to do. Besides, the dealer would never take it back and the damage was already done. It wasn't the money. It was the fact that Spencer was asserting control that angered Abby.

'No. I should thank you. But I want you to promise that you won't do anything like this ever again.'

'I promise.'

'Do I have your word?'

'Hope to die,' said Spencer.

She didn't want to humiliate him.

'Then you're not mad at me any longer?'

'I'm not mad at you.'

There was a deep sigh on the other end.

'Then let me give you the good news. First, the car is a business expense, at least part of it is. Think of it as a gift from the tax man,' said Morgan. 'And you're going to need more of them.'

'What? Cars?'

'Business expenses,' said Morgan. 'You better start thinking about setting the next book someplace expensive. Maybe in the South of France, a private villa.'

'Why?'

'Because I'm going to be depositing a lot more money than we thought into the account. Hold your breath,' said Morgan. 'Nearly' – there was a crackle on the line – 'million dollars.'

'Say again?'

'I said three million dollars.'

'We weren't supposed to see that kind of money for almost a year.'

'I know,' said Spencer, 'but the foreign sales are way beyond Carla's original estimate. She says it's the dynamic of the film sale. She didn't have the numbers when you guys met at the convention. There's a feeding frenzy going on in Europe over the book. And she wants to talk to Jack, to give him the good news. You know, agent to author,' said Morgan. 'She's been bugging me for days trying to figure out where you guys went. You'd better prep him. Tell him to act surprised and to kiss her ass when she calls. She'll figure she deserves it.'

Three million dollars. Abby's knees folded like a tent with the news. She sank onto the edge of the bed. She had no idea what to do with that kind of money, how to spend it or invest it. She wasn't sure she wanted to know. She was sure of one thing. It would change her life, perhaps in ways she didn't like.

'What do I do?'

'What do you mean?'

'With all that money,' said Abby.

Morgan told her not to worry. He had it parked in a safe place, growing interest. 'I wish I had that kind of problem,' he told her. 'Cutler and his pals are circling like vultures at the firm. They want my blood. Everyday it's a new move. Always watching my backside, and it's more difficult now that you're gone.'

'If we keep doing this, you won't have to worry about it. You can quit and go to work for me, full time,' said Abby.

It was what Morgan wanted to hear; that he was back in her good graces.

'Did you get the bank card?' he asked.

'Yes.'

He gave her the PIN number and she wrote it down. 'You don't have to worry. There's plenty in the account, and the authorities won't be able to trace you when you use it. They might look in the Caymans, but Martinique, I don't think so. It's a little too far. Besides, it's French and you know the French,' said Morgan. 'They are notoriously difficult to deal with. If the cops go poking around, they'll find themselves in diplomatic hell.'

'Good,' said Abby. 'That should give us the time we need.' In a way Abby wanted to talk to Sanfillipo, to find out what was happening in Theresa's murder. But she knew that if she did, she would be trapped in Seattle, facing questions not only from the detective but from the press. And it wasn't just Thompson anymore. As buzz around the book grew, others were circling, trying to track down Jack and anybody who knew him.

'There's one more thing,' said Morgan. The phone began to break up again.

'I can't hear you,' said Abby.

'Be careful with Jermaine. Don't trust him Abby.' Morgan was shouting into the phone to make himself heard. It was a terrible connection, like talking through a tube underwater. 'Is he there with you right now?'

'No.'

'We have to talk, but not on the phone. I'm taking a few days and coming down there.'

'Why?' More crackling on the line. Abby sensed that she was about to lose the connection.

'I have a briefcase full of foreign contracts to be signed by his majesty,' said Spencer. 'And something else we need to talk about. Very important.'

'Tell me now.'

'I can't. Not over the phone. I'll try to clear my calendar and come down there.' He didn't know how he was going to do it with Cutler on his back, but somehow he would have to figure a way.

'Tell me now,' said Abby.

'Not on the phone.' He didn't know if she'd heard him or not. The line had gone dead. It was just as good. Spencer was a firm believer. Bad news, especially when it was this good, had to be delivered in person.

CHAPTER
TWENTY-EIGHT

Luther hadn't had a break in the case of Theresa and Joey Jenrico in nearly a month. Sanfillipo had to wait in line in the D.A.'s office along with other law enforcement agencies waiting for them to process warrants and subpoenas. It always took longer for the cops than for those with private lawyers. In this case, the wait took its toll. After getting a subpoena, he ran into a stone wall tracing the financial records of Abby Chandlis. After some banking sleight of hand, she'd disappeared. Luther found evidence of large sums deposited into a bank account, but the account was closed.

The lawyer Spencer was uncooperative. He now claimed an attorney-client privilege with Abby Chandlis and refused to answer more questions, challenging the cops to arrest her if they had grounds. To Luther, lawyers were all assholes. They weren't interested in the truth. That wasn't their job. For the time being, he lacked sufficient evidence to bring charges against Chandlis, and Spencer knew it. Even so, Luther was sure that she was either involved in the murders or knew much more than she was saying.

In the weeks of picking through the evidence, forensics

did come up with one piece of information that Luther found intriguing. After finding his body in the lake, authorities sealed Joey Jenrico's apartment for a period of time and combed it for whatever they could find. What they found was a mess. Mr Jenrico was a disgraceful housekeeper. Among other things, they found a lot of fingerprints. It seemed he never dusted.

The police were still running down leads that the prints provided, a veritable who's-who from local topless joints and roadside bars. Joey had a penchant for picking up things late at night, mostly strippers, and if the coroner was to be believed, an early case of herpes simplex B. Whoever killed him did the public health department a favor.

In some cases, forensics was unable to match the prints they found in the apartment with known samples on record. One such set came from Joey's refrigerator door. The state's biggest bank of prints, motor vehicle as well as their department of justice, turned up nothing. But there was something else in the prints that caught the technician's attention. These prints were particularly well formed due to an oily substance left on the enamel of the door. This was not your ordinary set of greasy fingerprints. After lifting them from the door, technicians took trace evidence and had it analyzed. This particular brand was a light machine oil, and not just any kind. It was manufactured by a company known as Hopps. It was gun oil, the type used to lubricate light arms.

Luther suddenly took a keen interest in the unidentified prints. He had them sent to the F.B.I., something local authorities didn't always do. It was expensive and time consuming. But this time it paid off. The prints belonged to one Jack Jermaine and were on record with the military. Luther had to wonder what a man who lived in South Carolina was doing with his fingerprints on Joey Jenrico's refrigerator door in Seattle.

What was even more interesting to Luther was that Jermaine's name showed up on bank records as having endorsed two large checks over to Abby Chandlis before her accounts were closed. Jermaine, it seemed, was the link between Chandlis and Joey Jenrico's death. Maybe she had hired him to do it. The question was why?

Luther considered the possibilities as he pushed the button in the elevator for the ninth floor. It was ten o'clock in the morning, and he was taking a chance that Morgan Spencer would be in his office. Sanfillipo wanted to hit him unannounced. Spencer may have been able to claim an attorney-client relationship with Chandlis, but what about the man Jermaine? Besides, Luther now had what was looking very much like a continuing criminal conspiracy, something that the attorney-client privilege did not embrace. He wanted to see if the lawyer jumped with the mention of Jermaine's name.

The reception area was empty when Luther entered the office. One secretary sat behind a long counter.

'Can I help you?'

'I'm here to see Morgan Spencer.'

'Do you have an appointment?'

'No. But I think he will see me.' Luther fished his badge from a leather case in his coat pocket and flashed it at the secretary.

'Just a moment.' She punched a few numbers on her telephone key pad and spoke with someone in the back of the office.

'Your name?' she asked Luther.

'Lieutenant Sanfillipo.'

A few moments later another secretary came out from the back. 'Lieutenant, if you'll follow me.'

They did a short parade past the rabbit warren of little cubicles to more palatial digs where the partners hung out, offices with views out onto Elliot Bay.

'Mr Spencer's in conference right now, but I'm sure he'll see you when he's finished. Can I get you a cup of coffee?'

'That would be very nice,' said Luther. The woman disappeared and Luther took a seat in one of the two chairs arranged for clients in the small area just outside of Spencer's door. He could hear voices inside, but nothing as distinct as words. It sounded like two men, but he couldn't be sure.

Coffee came and the secretary left him and went to her work station a few feet away. Luther picked up a newspaper from a side table and started to read. The Mariners were on a roll again, maybe headed for the playoffs. Luther scanned the headlines. The voices inside the room were now up a notch. He could now tell it was definitely two men. And things were getting heated. The secretary looked at him to see if he'd noticed, but Luther continued to read the newspaper as if nothing had happened. They were going at it fast and furious behind the closed door. He could now make out words.

'No more time off. Enough is enough.'

'This is business.' Luther recognized the second voice as Spencer's. He didn't know the other one.

'Right. Three days in St Croix is business. Forget it.'

'What is this? I have to ask you for permission to go out of town on business?'

The secretary was now clearly concerned that she had brought a stranger close enough to hear all of this.

'The meeting could last a long while,' she told Luther. 'Are you sure you want to wait? I could have Mr Spencer call you immediately when he is finished.'

'No. No. That's fine. I'll wait,' said Luther. She couldn't have moved Luther with a crane. He went back to listening.

'You're not going. Not on the firm's nickel and not on company time.' It was the other voice in the room. 'And we're not going to cover your court calls while you're gone, either. Look at the calendar,' said the other. 'You've got three appearances on pending cases during that time. Who's supposed to do your work while you're gone? You've been taking nothing but trips and you want to know why the partners are upset. Look at your calendar. You've been out of town four times for a total of more than three weeks in the last four months. That doesn't include vacations.'

'That was business.'

'I didn't see any billable hours.'

'Flat fee,' said Spencer.

'Right.'

'You can assign somebody. One of the junior associates to cover my cases,' said Spencer.

'No. It's not going to happen.' This last must have been intended as the final word because it got much louder as the door opened. Luther glued his eyes to the newspaper that was now held fully open in front of his face so that he assumed the identity of a news rack in the outer office.

'So you want me to tell her that the firm doesn't want her business? Seven figures and growing,' said Spencer.

The other man who was leaving came to an abrupt stop in the doorway. He was now facing Luther but couldn't see him behind the paper. He must have been another lawyer, thought Luther. The only thing that moved him was the sound of money.

The guy turned in the doorway. 'Where did Ms Chandlis come into all of this? And what is she doing in St Croix?' He filled the frame of the door with his back as Luther peeked over the top of the paper. He was doing Luther's work for him. The cop was all ears. Then he walked back into Spencer's office and closed the door.

Luther strained his ears but was unable to pick out anything. Now that it was money, they'd returned to civil discourse, just the mercenary hum of male voices through the solid door. Still Luther had one big piece of the puzzle he didn't have when he'd arrived. He knew where Abby Chandlis was.

Luther got up and folded the newspaper, put it back on the table, and started to go.

'Are you leaving?' said the secretary.

'I think I will come back at a more convenient time,' said Luther.

'Can I show you out?'

'No. No. I know the way.' Luther headed down the corridor. It was not a good time to talk to Spencer. He was hoping that the secretary might even forget to tell the lawyer that Luther was sitting there listening. If he moved quickly he might be able to find Chandlis before she moved on to someplace else. What Sanfillipo wanted was to check with the authorities in St Croix. He would save the information regarding Jermaine for another meeting. For the moment, Luther figured, why reveal anything more than he had to?

In what seemed like no time at all the house on the beach felt like home to Abby. Shoy Beach Road started on the grounds of the Buccaneer and paralleled the ocean for more than a mile where it ended in front of the gates of an estate at a point overlooking the sea.

Abby's house was not nearly as large as the estate at the end of the road. It was a small yellow single-story bungalow about a half mile from the resort.

The house was set back from the road behind a driveway lined with young palm trees. It was surrounded by a sea of Bermuda grass that ran to the sand dunes above the ocean. The beach itself was a tropical dream, deep and crescent-shaped. It lined a cove that was ringed by heavy vegetation and palms leaning toward the ocean. A white froth of waves surged endlessly up out of the blue green sea to spend itself on the powdery fine sand.

Abby had dreamed of such a place all of her life; the smells of the sea and the sound of the surf, black frigate birds with their split tails dancing on currents of the trades, gliding motionless in the sky over a verdant bluff on the coast. At dusk she would walk the beach feeling the breath of the sea upon her face and watch as the fading sun turned the clouds on the horizon from pink to purple. It was as if time had not touched the place. By night, as she worked at the small computer in her room, she could hear the rhythms of reggae as they erupted from the bar at the Buccaneer just one cove away. Jack maintained a room there, but spent most of his time with Abby at the house. It was a liaison that at times and with increasing frequency had its softer moments. For the first time in her life, everything seemed to be going right for Abby. That she was now here, doing what she wanted most in life, writing, and with a book about to explode upon the bestsellers list, seemed too good to be true.

Within two days she was into her schedule, rising

early with the sun to work at the little computer that she'd set up on a table in the living room looking out at the sea. Like clockwork, she broke for breakfast by nine. Jack would return with fruit and yoghurt from the market in town. Then she would return to work.

Abby could usually crank four or five good pages before noon. During these hours, except for breakfast which they shared, Jack kept his distance, a kind of unwritten rule. Abby was disciplined in her work and did not like to be disturbed. Like many writers, she required total concentration. She induced a sort of mental state, a kind of psychic transport that ferried her mind to the fictional world of her creation. Like a camera lens, unless she could see it in her mind's eye, she couldn't write about it.

The islands seemed to favor Abby. In two weeks she had added five more chapters to the new manuscript. She was flying and was now nearly a third of the way into the sequel. The book seemed to be writing itself. It was almost too easy.

In the early afternoon, she and Jack would roam the beach. To a casual observer it might look like two lovers at play. It was actually part of their schedule. Jack required intensive briefing on the details of the book he was going to have to sell. If he was going to New York to stand up to the scrutiny of the press and the glare of cameras, Jack would have to speak with authority.

Commercial fiction might only be a part of the entertainment world, but to people who covered it, wrote about it, and reported on it, it was serious business. They played the game for keeps. Those who followed pop culture still remembered Milli-Vanilli and the scandal that brought them down. One slip by Jack and the entire scheme could collapse. Whatever he said about the book would have to sound real, as if he had written it himself.

They talked about the mechanics of writing, the daily schedule that Abby employed, and the process of creation. She reminded him that she'd written the manuscript on a typewriter.

'You never know what Carla or Bertoli might get into over dinner,' she told him. She knew that the manuscript would speak for itself with X'ed out words and typeovers that could not have come from a computer printer. It was a minor point, but the kind of thing that could trip him up in a conversation over cocktails.

'If they ask, tell them you lost the typewriter in the move to the islands. The next manuscript will be written using WordPerfect, an old DOS-driven version. They'll probably want discs if we sell them the book. Most publishers do. Tell them that if we come to terms we'll supply them.'

Jack wanted to know why she didn't use Windows for her writing.

Abby didn't like all the bells and whistles. They slowed her down and got in the way.

'You have to decide whether you want to write, or play computer games.' She winked at Jack and he smiled sheepishly.

'If they ask, tell them that you keep it simple,' said Abby.

In the afternoons, Abby and Jack would swim in the ocean, Abby thinking of things and talking as they bobbed in the surf. She was increasingly anxious as the time drew short. Jack was scheduled to be in New York in ten days. The lay-down date for her novel, the time when the book would start appearing on store shelves across the country, was rapidly approaching.

'Are you sure you can handle it?'

'You worry too much.' He gave her one of his beefy school-boy grins. Jack was made for the lens of a camera.

'I'm trying to think of anything we might have forgotten,' said Abby. 'Remember the characters are all composites.'

'I know,' said Jack. 'We already went over that. There's no one in the book I've ever actually known. My characters are just bits and pieces, mostly fictional, sometimes little fragments of people I've rubbed up against in life. I'll call it a fictional gene pool,' said Jack.

'Good,' said Abby. 'That's a nice touch.'

She danced over the top of a wave and Jack reached out to grab her. He threw an arm around her from behind, and as the wave passed he rubbed his body seductively against her backside.

'There. Now you can be one of my characters,' said Jack.

'Not now.' Abby tried not to smile. 'This is business. And unless you pay attention, you're gonna get us both in a lot of trouble. These people are not fools.'

He tried to ignore her. Jack was getting bored.

'Where did the idea for the story come from?' said Abby.

'Another pop quiz,' said Jack. He continued to hold onto her tightly from behind. 'Let's talk about something else.'

'What?'

'I don't know.' He thought for a second. 'The sequel,' said Jack. 'Is there a seduction scene in it?'

'No.'

'Why not?'

'I don't talk about work in progress.' She gave him a sideways glance. 'It's bad luck.'

'You don't trust me.' He spun her around in his arms.

She looked at him for a moment, the square jaw and broad shoulders, locks of dark hair glistening under the bright sun.

'That's not true,' said Abby.

'Tell me, does Morgan know about the sequel?'

'Morgan has to know about certain things for reasons of business.'

'Like the copyright on the book,' said Jack.

'Like the copyright,' said Abby.

'But you haven't copyrighted the outline.'

'True,' said Abby.

'So then why does he know and I don't?'

'You'll have to trust me,' said Abby.

'When are you going to learn to trust me?'

She looked into the pools of his eyes.

He smiled that kind of juvenile grin that melts most women, then buried his face in her shoulder and started to nibble. 'I need to know what's going on if I'm going to pull this off. At least give me the story line. Some of the details.'

'No.'

He went back to work on her shoulder and Abby started to giggle. 'Cut it out. Come on, Jack. You can't eat my shoulder.'

'Why not? It tastes so good. A little salty maybe.' He sank his teeth into the soft flesh at the side of her neck, not enough to hurt, but enough to ignite erotic fires.

'Quit it.' She was laughing as his tongue made its way along the side of her neck and up under the lobe of her ear.

'All I want is a little peek,' said Jack. 'Just a peek.' He was talking about the outline, but his fingers toyed with the strings of her bathing suit.

'Stop it.' She tried to sound serious but couldn't. She could feel the warmth of his lower body against her own. Even in the cool water Jack radiated heat like a nuclear reactor. A wave washed over them, and one of Jack's legs found its way between her thighs so that it supported her body, and she rode on it. They floated and bobbed in the sea as one.

He nibbled on her ear, catching the lobe gently between his teeth and she quieted, her arms around his neck.

'That tickles,' said Abby.

'It tastes good. You should try it.'

'I can't reach them,' she told him.

'Not yours, mine.'

'Oh.' She laughed and rested her chin on his shoulder. 'Why is it so important for you to know about the sequel?'

'What if they ask questions in New York?' said Jack. 'Carla may be pretty persuasive.' As he said it, Jack slipped a hand into the bottom of her bathing suit. 'She may have techniques of torture we can only imagine.'

'Cut it out.' She reached for his hand and tried to remove it, but his grip was firm. She wiggled in his grasp, but her movements only spurred him on. Abby looked toward the beach. It was deserted. There was no one there to see them. Jack's hand was soon joined by a second, where they met inside the bottom of her bathing suit. Gently he gripped the cheeks of her buttocks, lifting her until her legs were locked about his midsection.

'She may have ways of getting information that cannot be resisted,' said Jack.

'Steel yourself,' said Abby. Their eyes met.

'What if she forces me to tell her a lie?'

'Make it a good one,' said Abby.

Their bodies were gently raised and rocked by another passing wave as Abby's eyes closed, and their lips met.

'I forgot to tell you. Morgan's coming down next week.' It was Saturday, mid-morning, and Abby and Jack had slept in. Abby was drying herself with a towel after her shower.

'What for? Anything he needs to do he can do over the phone.'

'What's your problem with Morgan?' she asked.

'He's a hard-ass lawyer,' said Jack. He had never forgiven Spencer for his tactics that day when he forced Jack to sign the contract and to play by his rules.

'So what? I'm a lawyer, too,' said Abby.

'Yes, but your ass is much softer,' said Jack. He pinched her as she walked by as if to prove the point, and Abby scampered to the foot of the bed with a towel wrapped around her. She rummaged through the closet for something to wear.

Jack admired the view as he propped himself against the headboard of the bed with a pillow behind his back. 'So what does he want?'

'It's something important, but he won't tell me what.'

'You should tell him no. He's just gonna be in the way. Another distraction,' said Jack.

'God knows I don't need any more of those,' said Abby.

She looked at him with a smirk. Jack had a single sheet covering his body and an erection that was now at half-mast.

Abby selected a pair of pants and a matching top and

headed back toward the bathroom. He grabbed her towel on the way by, and she had to fight him for it.

'Stop it. We've got to get ready.' Abby finally gave up and retreated into the bathroom, covering herself with the clothes in her other hand. Quickly she slipped on her panties and bra and started to fix her hair.

'You better get out of bed. The photographer will be here in twenty minutes. *Entertainment Weekly*,' said Abby. Like Jack had forgotten.

'Let 'em wait,' said Jack. 'I'm an artist.'

The crew from one of the network magazine shows was coming down later in the day to do candid shots of the writer at work at his island home. The piece was scheduled to air the week of publication. Jack the author was about to earn his money.

He got out of bed and didn't bother to cover himself. There wasn't a modest bone in the man's body. He stood naked next to Abby, peering into the mirror over the bathroom sink and plucked a gray hair from his temple.

'Little devils keep showing up,' said Jack.

'Keep pulling them out, you're going to be bald,' said Abby. 'Something tells me you're not going to age gracefully.'

'I'm not going to age at all.' He smiled at her.

Somehow Abby sensed that he might be right. Whoever said that life was fair?

Jack smiled for the mirror and checked his perfectly spaced teeth as if he was looking to see if they might have shifted on him during the night.

'He didn't give you any hint of what he wants to talk about?' said Jack.

'Who?'

'Spencer.'

'No. He said he couldn't discuss it over the phone.'

'Something about the book?' said Jack.

'Possibly. Or Theresa's death.'

Jack suddenly looked over at her. 'What's happening on that front?'

They hadn't talked about it in weeks. It was not a subject that Abby wanted to discuss.

'The police want to talk to me,' she told him. 'Routine. Nothing unusual.'

Jack shot her a look.

'They traced the bank account.' She shrugged like what could she do. 'The advance on the book.'

'Spencer hasn't told them where you are?'

'No. And he moved the funds to where they couldn't find them.'

'That should be giving them food for thought,' said Jack. 'A woman is murdered and her roommate disappears with a shit load of money that keeps vanishing. Yeah, I'd say they might have a few questions.'

'We'll find out when Morgan gets here,' said Abby.

'Let's hope the surprise isn't a warrant for your arrest.'

'There's no arrest warrant. I had no reason to kill her. I wasn't even in town when it happened. I have an alibi.'

'You don't have to convince me,' said Jack. 'I'm not the one with the questions. Personally, I think Spencer's just looking for an excuse to come down here.'

'Why would he do that?'

'Because he wants to check and make sure you're alright. He doesn't trust me.'

'Maybe he has good reason.'

When Jack looked over at her he couldn't tell whether she was serious or not.

Then Abby cracked a smile. 'Morgan thinks he's my father.'

'Be careful he doesn't have his mind set on a little incest,' said Jack.

Abby looked at him. 'Morgan and me?'

Jack nodded.

'You gotta be kidding.' He was Jack's age but a generation older. It was not so much a matter of age as it was a state of mind. It was the reason Spencer was a father figure and Jack was a lover. 'We're friends. Nothing more.'

'Have you told him that?'

'I never had to. Unlike some people he's never put his hands inside my bathing suit.'

'Lacks confidence, does he?'

'He's a gentleman.'

'That's what I mean,' said Jack.

The afternoon was taken up doing photo shoots and staging pieces for the network magazine program. First *Entertainment Weekly* showed up with their photographer and took pictures of Jack dressed entirely in black, set off against the stark white sand of the beach. They seemed to like artsy shots.

An hour later the television crew showed up and began setting up their equipment. Jack did a quick change of clothes, and they did a long distance telephoto shot of him walking on the beach with the female interviewer, and talking about the sacrifices made by the novelist for his craft.

'Of course it's a lonely life. But I wouldn't trade it for any other.' Chatter and prattle.

'How do you write such a good story?'

Jack gave her a thoughtful moment before he spoke.

'Michener probably said it best. He said he was actually one of the worst writers in the world. But one of the best rewriters who ever lived. I'm a great rewriter,' said Jack.

With bullshit like that Jack should have been working in the White House rewriting history, thought Abby.

'Is that where it's at, the revisions?'

'Absolutely. It's like music,' said Jack. 'You have to have an ear. If you're tone deaf, you'll never make it as a writer.'

Abby huddled with the television crew under the shade of a palm tree and listened to the feed-through sound equipment, to the echo of her own words emitting from Jack's lips. She tried to convince herself that she had done the right thing. It was, after all, everything that Abby detested, the glitz and buzz of commercial fiction. It was a world in which the contour of Jack's face and the form of his body took precedence over the content of Abby's book.

But as she watched him on the beach, Abby could not deny the pangs of regret and resentment. She knew that the book was hers, but millions of viewers watching Jack on the tube would not. Would they ever accept her? Maybe Jack was right. She had created a mirage so alluring that it now threatened to consume its own maker.

She had bared her soul to Jack during weeks of preparation. Now as her own words came streaming back through the headset propelled by Jack's voice, there was a sense of loss that she could not explain. She had given up not only the credit and recognition for her work but a part of herself. Listening to him talk as he walked on the beach, Abby realized for the first time that she had surrendered a large chunk of her own identity.

They moved inside to take some shots of Jack sitting at the table over Abby's little computer.

They talked about his childhood as a military brat, and how it felt to be on the cusp of literary fame.

'A fleeting thing,' said Jack. 'It doesn't feel real. It won't,' said Jack, 'until I can see the title of my book squarely on the bestsellers list. Maybe not even then.'

'It takes a lot to convince you,' said the interviewer.

'Only because I know it can slip away. Until the book is firmly established, I know it can always slip away.'

He thought for a moment, one of those wistful expressions that the anchors on the networks do so well. Then Jack looked directly into the camera, nothing shifty-eyed or shy. 'It's like a dream,' said Jack. 'You always know that you can wake up at any moment to discover that it wasn't real.'

He allowed a short beat to pass in silence. Jack's timing was a gift that could not be learned. Then he spoke. 'I wake up every night with the same bad dream, the nightmare that this, all of this, is just an illusion.'

The interviewer sat dazed, enveloped by his gaze. As the echo of Jack's words died in the room, she came back to reality and turned to her cameraman.

'Harry. Tell me you got that?'

'Got it,' said the cameraman. He had just faded out to black on Jack.

'I'll do a voice-over just after he says that last line, the part about illusion, and we'll use it for the close. Maybe catch the setting sun, the green spark as it flashes on the horizon. Do we have any of that footage left over from Hawaii?'

'I think so,' said the cameraman.

'Good. We'll use it. They'll never know the difference.'

'Then you liked it?' said Jack.

'I loved it.' Jack and the interviewer stood in the center of the room and she took his hand. 'What's more, the audience is gonna eat it up.'

It was at that moment that Abby realized Jack was dangerous. He lied with a smile that paralyzed reason.

CHAPTER
TWENTY-NINE

Jack was due in the office in less than an hour and Carla was scrambling to get ready. With her assistant she was pulling together all of the last-minute bits of information that Bertoli had given her on marketing for the book.

Owens wanted to be the first to give Jack the good news. Agents always wanted to be bearers of glad tidings on the theory that the client would equate the news with the messenger.

'Do we have the figures on the television ad campaign?' asked Owens.

'In your folder,' said the secretary.

'And the "dumps"? The stuff on the up-front floor displays at the chains?' said Carla. 'Do we have the figures on that?'

'In your folder with everything else.' Jadra, Carla's assistant, was getting perturbed. Owens was always a basket case before meetings with important clients.

This time it seemed to be worse. For some strange reason, Carla was intimidated by Jack. She hoped he wasn't bringing the lawyer-consort this time. At their last meeting Abby seemed to be able to read Carla's mind, and Owens didn't like it. She was still working on ways to separate Jack from this troublesome woman. Give her time and she would figure it out. It was Abby Chandlis who had blocked her from selling more books to Bertoli, books that could have meant millions in commissions for the agency and put Jack in book bondage for at least five years. Control was the name of the game and right now Jack had it and Carla wanted it.

'Tell me about the dumps?' she asked the secretary. 'How many did Bertoli do?'

The assistant fished for a paper in one of the files. 'Five thousand.'

Carla whistled. She had never heard of a book with such a large purchase of up-front store space.

'Dumps' were shorthand in the industry for cardboard racks that the publishers provided to the book-stores. Each of these held twelve to fifteen books in a portable stand-up display, with a colorful riser showing the title and the author at the top, with all the hype that the publicity department could muster. Publishers had to pay to rent space in the front of the stores for their dumps. Space in a single chain of stores could cost a publisher thirty thousand dollars for a single week. For Jack's book, Bertoli would be spending nearly two hundred thousand dollars for space in the first sixty days. Without this, a book seldom, if ever, had a chance to become a bestseller. For this reason there was hot competition among publishers to get dump space.

It was only one of the things that publishers did to get an edge in the market. On the paperback side they actually rented the numbered racks in supermarkets across the country, numbers that had no real correlation to placement on any bestsellers list. For the right price you could buy number one. In commercial publishing, if you had enough money, you could create your own version of reality.

Bertoli had also purchased expensive print ads, full-page spreads in the *L.A. Times*, *Washington Post*, *New York Times*, and the *Chicago Tribune* as well as several high-circulation national magazines.

One of the chic tabloid magazines had named Gable Cooper among its fifty most beautiful people in America, right next to Mel Gibson and Antonio Banderas. Inside rumors were already circulating that Big-F had managed to influence this decision through its pricey print advertising buys.

In three days ads would go up inside all the New York subway cars with the title of the book, some appropriate hype, and best of all, Jack's picture. New York was a pressure point to establish buzz within the industry. Sample chapters of the book as a teaser were being delivered with selected copies of the morning newspaper on the day of publication. These would go to more than a thousand opinion makers in New York and Los Angeles, the A-list of the entertainment and publishing worlds. It was the biggest promotional push for a book in nearly ten years.

If Bertoli was successful, it would launch a career that most writers couldn't even dream of. The name Gable Cooper would be synonymous with hot books and even hotter movies. Anything penned under the name for the next twenty years would be gobbled up in Hollywood and New York. Carla knew this, so today she had a single objective in her meeting with Jack. Somehow she had to convince him that additional contracts now for more books were in his own best interest.

The com-line rang on Carla's phone.

'Oh shit.' Carla looked at the clock on the wall. 'He's

early. Jadra, finish up there quickly.'

Her assistant went into hyperdrive, slipping last-minute papers into folders, two sets of which sat on the conference table in Carla's office.

'And make sure we get coffee,' said Owens. 'And lunch. Call Da Umberto's and have them prepare something nice and have it delivered.' Carla had no intention of letting Jack get into a public restaurant where other agents might be courting introductions. His picture was already all over town.

The com-line buzzed again and Carla picked up the phone.

'There's a Mr Chandlis here to see you.'

'Who?'

'Mr Chandlis. Says he's related to an Abby Chandlis.' The receptionist sounded like she was about to hang up and throw him out the door. Strange people, some of whom wrote with crayons from institutions, often showed up unannounced at literary agencies. 'Do you want me to tell him you're busy?'

Carla thought for a moment. 'No.' She put her hand over the mouthpiece. 'Jadra.'

The secretary turned just as she was heading out the door.

'If Mr Jermaine shows up, entertain him for a couple of minutes. Tell him I'll be with him as soon as I can. Take him to the conference room.'

Jadra nodded, left, and closed the door.

Carla went back to the phone. 'Show Mr Chandlis in.'

Two minutes later there was a tap on Owens's door and another secretary opened it. 'Mr Chandlis.'

An instant later Carla got her first glimpse. Charlie had a head start on a five-o'clock shadow. His suit was wrinkled. He'd slept in it on the plane and had come directly by taxi from the airport to the office. He was carrying an attaché case. He looked like a salesman.

Carla rose from her chair and greeted him from on high, up on the pedestal behind her desk. She had no idea what the man wanted and figured a posture of authority was always safe.

'Mr Chandlis. Carla Owens. Please come in.'

Charlie seemed to look around a lot as he made his way between the door and Carla's desk. He had never seen an office as large as this or as elaborately decorated; purple plush carpets and smoked glass, a desk like a crystal altar. Charlie thought he'd died and gone to pimp heaven.

'Good to meet you,' he told her. When he finally arrived at the desk he handed Carla a business card. Charlie always did this with people he met. You could never tell when one of them might need a good criminal lawyer.

She looked at the card. 'What can I do for you?'

'It's about my wife,' said Charlie. 'Abby Chandlis.'

Carla nodded slowly but didn't say a word.

'You do know her?'

'I'm acquainted with an Abby Chandlis,' said Owens. 'She's your wife?' Carla didn't show it, but she was suffering a major adrenaline rush, visions of a peccadillo on the eve of publication with an angry husband who was a lawyer. Some authors drank. Some found other diversions. Maybe Jermaine's vice was married women.

'Actually we're not married any longer,' said Charlie.

'Ah.' Carla's heart dropped twenty beats a minute. 'Please have a seat,' she told him.

Charlie ascended, one giant step for mankind, and flopped into one of the tufted chairs across from Carla's desk.

'So what is this about Ms Chandlis?'

'I'd like to know where she is.'

'And why do you think I can help you with that?'

'You paid her a lot of money,' said Charlie.

Carla gave him big eyes, this was news to her.

'Well not exactly,' said Charlie. 'You wrote a sizable check to a mister –' he took a note from his shirt breast pocket and looked at it – 'a Mr Jermaine.'

He looked at Carla. Her expression at the moment was a stone idol. She was giving up nothing.

'This Jermaine endorsed the check over to my wife. A very large sum of money. This money was commingled with other funds and then the entire amount was withdrawn and the account was closed.'

The first crack in granite. Carla tried to hide it, but the news came as a major blow. Abby Chandlis had a stronger hold on her client than Carla realized. If she could get him to sign over a seven-figure check, getting rid of the woman might be more difficult than Carla thought.

'And what is your interest in all of this?'

'You can call me Charlie.' He smiled at her. Charlie sensed that she was hearing some of this for the first time. So was Charlie. He was making it up as he went. If he played his cards right, he might not have to tell her everything, especially the parts he guessed at.

'It's about community property,' said Charlie.

'I don't understand.'

'We have reason to believe,' said Charlie, 'that a portion of this money was in fact earned during the course of my marriage to Abby, Ms Chandlis. We have evidence that the funds were diverted to avoid a fair distribution at the time of the divorce.'

'We?' said Carla.

'I have a team of lawyers looking into this right now.'

It was Charlie at his bull-shitting best.

'I see. But you didn't have your lawyers call me. You came here yourself.' Carla had a well-trained nose for bullshit.

'I figured you're an innocent third party. No sense getting you involved in a messy law suit.' Charlie looked at her to see if he was making a dent. 'Unless it's necessary of course.'

Carla just smiled at him. Her lawyers could eat him for lunch. That is, if she didn't do the job first. Still, if this awful man knew Abby, maybe there was a silver lining here. Why be hasty?

'So you think your wife was hiding things from you during your marriage?'

Charlie made a face like this was a definite possibility.

Wait until he gets a gander at Jack, thought Carla. 'We would have a certain interest in this. Actually Mr Jermaine is our client. Our only contact with your former wife was through him.'

'I see. And you don't know where she is?'

'We might have some information,' said Carla. She knew of course that Charlie's story was gold-plated garbage. Publishers were up to their hips in friends, lovers, and former spouses, people who knew people, who were related to somebody who had a friend who wrote a big book. They came out of the woodwork with every hot novel. Charlie Chandlis had the classic look. His ex had gotten her claws into somebody who'd hit it big and Charlie now wanted a taste. He was probably jealous to boot. The whole thing smacked of sleaze, not the kind of publicity you wanted on a break-out book. She figured that's what this Charlie was gambling on.

'I'd have to check our records. I'd want to talk to Mr

Jermaine first. And of course we could not cooperate in any way if it meant trouble for him. You understand that?' said Carla.

'Of course,' said Charlie. 'I appreciate your position.' Charlie's own position at the moment was on his hands and knees. He was willing to agree to anything. Abby had disappeared like a puff of smoke. He had no idea how to find her. Without help from the literary agent he was up the proverbial creek with a broken paddle. He had a theory as to what was going on, but he wasn't willing to share it with Owens, not until he knew more. She might tell her client and Charlie would get zip. If nothing else, his theory had good nuisance value. And what was nuisance worth when you had a few mill in the bank, and a giant pain in the ass? Charlie didn't know, but he wanted to find out.

'What exactly is your relationship with this Mr Jermaine? I assume he's an author?' said Charlie.

He measured Carla's silence as assent.

'I suppose you wouldn't be paying that kind of money to someone who wasn't,' said Charlie. 'What did he write?'

'That's confidential,' said Carla. The use of a pen name made it awkward. If Chandlis really intended to make trouble and ended up suing Jack, it could look very bad; allegations of concealed money and an alias used on the book. There was probably nothing to it, but Carla wasn't willing to take the chance.

'Are you staying in town long?' she asked him.

'Just long enough to find out where my wife is.'

The phone rang on Carla's desk. Instinctively she knew what it was. She measured in her mind the next move.

'One moment,' she told Charlie. Carla picked up the receiver.

It was Jadra. 'Mr Jermaine is here. I've got him in the conference room. Do you need more time?'

'Ah. Yes. Hold him out there for a moment. I'll be right out.' She hung up the phone and smiled at Charlie. 'A matter I have to attend to. But if you can wait a moment, I'd like to talk to you further.'

'No problem,' said Charlie.

Carla quickly left the office and closed the door behind her. She headed down the hall. On the way she mussed her hair a little and took on a frantic appearance so that by the time she reached the conference room out front she looked like someone had raped her, at least mentally. She opened the door and rushed through.

Jack was drinking a cup of coffee, one cheek up on the conference table talking to Jadra, who didn't seem to mind the duty.

'Jack! Jack! God, I'm glad you're here. Jadra, could you excuse us for a minute.'

The secretary stepped outside, and as soon as the door closed Carla returned her full attention to Jack.

'We've got a major problem,' said Owens.

'What's the matter?' Carla's panic was becoming contagious. Jack's eyes took on an anxious look.

'There's a guy in my office. A lawyer. He says he's married or was married to Abby.'

Jack studied Owens's face.

'He says he's looking for her. That he has a team of lawyers ready to bring legal action. That she's been concealing community property from their marriage. He says his lawyers are looking at the present time to find out if you're involved. He's got some bank records. I don't know what it's all about, but it sounds serious. I shudder to think what Bertoli would do if he found out. This kind of scandal on the eve of publication. I don't have to tell you.'

'Where is he? This guy?'

'He's in my office right now.'

Before she could stop him Jack was out of the door. Carla was behind him like a shadow. 'Where are you going?'

'To talk to him.'

'Wait.'

Jack turned and stopped.

'Let's discuss this before we just blunder in there,' said Carla.

Maybe she was right. Jack listened.

'I don't know exactly what your relationship is with Ms Chandlis. And believe me, it's none of my business. But we're at a critical point. For the next several weeks we don't need any problems, especially problems like this. My advice,' said Carla, 'is to distance yourself. If there's a problem between the two of them, don't get in the middle of it. If you have to, stay in New York. We'll arrange accommodations. Alex and I can provide cover. Think of your career,' she told him. 'Let them sort it out. It's their mess.'

'Right,' said Jack. 'Good advice.' He turned and headed down the hall again like he hadn't heard her.

For Carla it gave her the excuse she needed to drive a wedge between Jack and Abby. 'I know what you're thinking,' she told him. 'You're thinking he's probably out to get whatever he can. He found out about your good fortune with the book and he's using Abby to shake you down. You're probably right. But there's no reason for you to get involved. If you do, you could end up flushing the entire deal.'

'I want to talk to him.' Jack had a problem. He'd never met Charlie. Abby had talked about him a few times, but he had no idea if Charlie might know something. Maybe Abby had said something about the book, or worse, about her plan to market it under a pen name from deep cover. If the truth about the book were leaked to Carla or Bertoli before publication, the book could be dead on arrival at the bookstores. Big-F might get nervous and pull the plug.

'What are you going to say to him?' said Carla.

'I don't know. But I want to talk to him alone. Find out what the hell's going on,' said Jack.

'You're not going to hit him or do anything stupid?'

Jack looked at her over his shoulder like who, me?

'Jack, use your head. Don't do anything foolish.'

By the time they got to the door to her office, Carla was beginning to think that maybe she'd made a mistake. She managed to wiggle around him and get in front before they reached the door. Carla took the lead into her office. They caught Charlie standing up on the pedestal behind Carla's desk reading her private papers.

'What are you doing?' said Owens.

'I thought maybe you might have an address for my wife,' said Charlie.

Carla started thinking that maybe it wasn't such a bad idea if Jack was to hit him.

'Mr Chandlis, this is Mr Jermaine. I talked to him about your problem and he agrees that the questions that you raise are matters between your former wife and yourself. He's willing to put you in touch with your wife so that you can obtain whatever information is required and this matter can be resolved. Now I think that's reasonable.' She turned and looked up at Jack to see if this would be alright.

Jack let it stand.

'Fine by me,' said Charlie.

'First I want to talk to him alone,' said Jack.

'Listen, anything said here is in the strictest confidence,' said Carla.

'Alone,' said Jack.

Owens gave him a look like maybe she should pat him down first before agreeing to this. Jack seemed to calm down a little too quickly.

'You can talk right here. I'll just step outside,' said Carla. 'I'll be right outside the door.' She made a point of it. 'Call me if you need anything.'

'We'll call.' Jack smiled at her. As soon as she closed the door behind her Jack turned and smiled at Charlie, a big blustery grin.

'It's good to finally meet you,' said Jack. 'Abby's told me a lot about you.'

'She has?'

'Oh yeah.' Jack extended a hand behind his broad smile and quickly closed the distance, climbing up onto Carla's platform. The move made a handshake a measure of manhood, so that Charlie had no choice but to step around the desk. As soon as their hands met, it was like lightning. Charlie wondered where his arm went, what it was doing up behind his back, and why his nose was suddenly pressed into the In basket on Carla's desk.

'Now let's talk.' Jack was up close in his ear, whispering so that Carla couldn't hear. 'What do you want?'

'I want to talk to Abby.'

'She's busy.'

'What the fuck is this? Ahh!'

Jack used a little leverage on the arm.

'Keep your voice down or I'll unscrew it and you can carry it home in a case.'

'Ahh.' Charlie whispered in pain.

'Now what is this about community property?'

'I had to say something,' said Charlie.

'So there's no team of lawyers hatching a law suit?'

'No.'

'What else did you tell Owens?'

'Nothing.'

Jack pressed on the arm a little more.

'Ahh! Ahh!' Charlie sounded like he'd stepped on hot coals.

'I swear I didn't tell her anything. I don't know anything.'

'But you've got some educated guesses, right?'

Charlie didn't say anything.

'Right?' Jack now had the back of Charlie's right hand up against the nape of his neck, a move that only the double-jointed could make without severe pain.

'Right! Right!' said Charlie.

'Well? Tell me.'

'I figure either you wrote a book together or you stole the book from her. That Abby's got a piece of it.'

'And what led you to that conclusion?'

'She's always writing.'

'So?'

'I figure it's a big book. Worth some money. That's how she got all that money in the account.'

'What if I told you I wrote the book?'

'Then why did you give her the money?' said Charlie. 'I know my wife,' said Chandlis. He was now breathing heavily. 'She suffers insecurity. She might have you stand in. You know. To do all the public stuff.'

Charlie was right. He knew Abby. Jack had a problem.

'You sure you didn't share any of this with Ms Owens?' Jack pressed on the truth lever a little more.

'No. No. I wouldn't do that. Why would I do that?'

'So what do you want?'

'I just want to talk to my wife.'

'You want to ask her for a little money, right? Shake her down?'

Charlie's head went sideways on the desk, just a little. It was the kind of shrug you might do if your face was pressed into the top of a desk and somebody was kneeing you in the ass.

'The thought had crossed your mind?'

'She had a lot in the bank. I thought I might talk to her.'

'And if she doesn't want to give you any, what then?'

'Nothing,' said Charlie. 'I just want to talk to her.'

'For old times' sake?' said Jack.

'Yeah. Yeah. For old times' sake.'

Jack slowly let him up. He thought about his options. He couldn't allow Charlie to stay in New York. Carla and Bertoli would pump him for information.

As soon as his arm was released, Charlie swung it around like an empty sleeve and grabbed it with his other hand. He cradled it like it was broken.

Jack turned him around and straightened the lapel on his suit coat while he talked in his face.

'What are we gonna do with you?' said Jack.

Charlie looked at him. For the first time there was real fear in Charlie's eyes. It was almost easier when he was in pain, looking the other way.

'Let me ask you,' said Jack. 'Why do you think I would endorse all the money over to Abby if we co-wrote this book?'

Charlie hesitated, but he had a theory on this, too.

'I don't know. Maybe you were hiding money from an ex. So you transferred it all to Abby?' Charlie looked at him, a question mark.

Jack didn't say a word but just looked back.

Charlie figured he wasn't far off the mark. It was precisely what Charlie would have done if he was in similar circumstances. As far as Charlie was concerned, it was a badge of honor. A male bonding thing, another way of cheating on your wife. All he wanted was a little piece of the action.

'I'll tell you where you can find her,' said Jack. It was the only safe course open to him; send Charlie down to the islands and let Abby deal with him. Maybe she could keep him quiet, or at least give them time to figure out what to do. In any case, Charlie would be out of New York, away from Bertoli and Carla. Jack would have to call Abby and give her a heads-up, that Charlie was on his way down.

He scrawled an address on a slip of paper from Carla's desk and handed it to Charlie.

'Do you know where this is?'

Charlie looked at the paper and shook his head.

'The Caribbean. You fly through Miami. Do you have a passport?'

'Back at my office.'

'Have 'em send it overnight express to this hotel, make a reservation there for tonight.' Jack scribbled the name of a cheap hotel near the Miami airport. 'In the morning you get your passport and you get your ass down there and you talk to her. You don't bother her. You don't make a pest out of yourself. Do you understand? And you wait there until I get back. Then we can all talk. There's a place called the Buccaneer. You present yourself at the desk and give them my name. The manager's a friend. He'll get you a room. And if you're smart, you won't say anything to Ms Owens or anybody else on the way out of the office.'

405

Charlie gave him a look like maybe he would and maybe he wouldn't. He was still massaging his arm to get circulation flowing again, flexing his hand to see if he could get the feeling back into it.

'If you say anything you're going to kill the goose,' said Jack. 'There won't be any more money for anybody.'

Charlie understood this.

Jack grabbed him by the ear like a school boy and led him to the door.

'Open it slowly,' said Jack. 'We wouldn't want Ms Owens to topple over and break her nose.' He guessed Carla had her ear pressed to the door.

'No, I think we can work this thing out.' Jack's tone was suddenly warm and loud very amicable, so Carla would have time to get up off her knees before the door opened.

'You go on down and talk to Abby, and I'm sure she'll explain how the whole thing happened.'

As the door opened Carla was framed in it, trying to look casual. Jack made a play of harmony and took Charlie's hand, shaking it while he looked at Owens. 'All a big mistake,' said Jack. 'Damn banks, they screw everything up. We'll have to sort it out. I'm sure Abby will be able to get to the bottom of it.'

Charlie even smiled, something sinister. His game was never physical. Jack was a Neanderthal. Charlie would use his brain. With Carla in the picture, he now had leverage. Jack couldn't afford to beat on him anymore, not in front of Owens anyway. There was something Abby and Jack didn't want her to know. All Charlie had to do was figure out what it was.

'You're not going to leave us so soon?' said Carla.

'He's got a plane to catch,' said Jack.

'Can I show you the way out?' Owens wanted to get Charlie alone for a couple more minutes.

Jack gave him a look to kill and Charlie declined her offer.

'I can find my way,' he said. 'But it was nice to meet you. Maybe we can get together again sometime.'

'Absolutely,' said Carla. 'Give me a call.'

'I'll do that.'

Charlie would have the last laugh. He had found the point of control.

CHAPTER
THIRTY

The phone rang but he finished typing the sentence into the word processor before he picked up the line.

'News room.'

'Is this Robert Thompson?'

'Yes. Who is this?' Thompson was the reporter for *The Intruder* and at the moment he was on a deadline.

'Nevermind who this is. Are you still interested in that piece involving the lawyer Abby Chandlis?'

'It's you again.' It was the second phone call that Thompson had received concerning Chandlis. 'Who is this?'

'Someone who is willing to give you information if you're smart enough to listen.'

Thompson shut up and listened.

'You were on a hot story. You shouldn't have quit so easily. It's much bigger than you could have guessed. One of the giant publishing houses in New York is about to publish a major blockbuster, a novel, except there's a scam going on with the book and they don't know it.'

'What's it all about?' said Thompson. 'I'm tired chasing shadows.'

'The book's going to be huge. The agent who handled

it doesn't know about the scam, either.'

'What's the title?'

'Later,' said the voice on the phone.

'At least tell me the publisher or the agent.'

'Not now. For now, all you need to know is that the lawyer Chandlis knows what's going on.'

'Listen, unless I have more information . . .'

'Film rights have already been sold on the book for three million dollars.'

Thompson stopped asking questions and started penning notes.

'The producers of the film don't know, either. Everybody's in the dark except Chandlis and a couple of people she's working with.'

'Why are they doing it?'

'That's for you to find out.'

'This sounds like a publicity stunt,' said Thompson.

'The police don't get involved in publicity stunts.'

'What are you talking about?'

'The Seattle police are trying to find Chandlis to question her.'

'Why?'

There was a brief silence on the phone as if the caller was trying to collect thoughts, wondering exactly how far to go.

'There have been two murders. Her roommate and her roommate's husband. There's a lot of unanswered questions.'

'They think Chandlis had something to do with this?'

'They want to talk to her.'

'What does this have to do with the book?'

'Talk to Chandlis.'

'I'd like to. I don't know where she is.'

'Try St Croix, the Virgin Islands. A house on Shoy

Beach Road just outside of Christiansted.'

'What's she doing there?'

'Avoiding you. And if my information is correct, hiding from the police back in Seattle.'

Thompson began to salivate. A scam on a book was one thing, murder was another.

'Give me something I can check, something I can confirm with another source besides Chandlis.'

'Why?'

'Because my editor's not going to let me waste any more time on this unless I can show him something concrete.'

There was another pause, breathing as if the voice on the phone was measuring how far to go.

'The victims' names were Jenrico. Theresa and Joseph Jenrico.'

'And these deaths are connected to the book?'

'The cops are looking for Chandlis. That's all I can say.'

'How do I confirm any of this?'

'That's your job.' The voice on the phone provided a number with an area code for the Virgin Islands. Thompson was told that the number would ring at the house on Shoy Beach Road.

'Who are you?'

'Nevermind that.'

'Just a second,' said Thompson. He fished in the drawer of his desk for the micro-cassette recorder and the little suction cup microphone that he used on the phone. It was highly illegal, but every reporter in the world had one. Thompson wanted something on tape that he could take to his editor.

'That's all I can tell you.'

'Hold on just a second. I'm making notes.' Thompson

licked the suction cup and stuck it on the outside of the earpiece of the phone.

'When did this murder happen?'

'A few months ago.'

'And Chandlis is involved.'

'I told you the police are looking for her.'

'And she's hiding in the Virgin islands?'

'What is this, are you hard of hearing? Enough. Check it out if you don't believe me.'

'Just one more question.'

The line went dead.

Thompson quickly played back what he had on the tape. It wasn't much, but it did mention murder and the fact that Chandlis was hiding from the police.

He punched out his piece for deadline and five minutes later dropped downstairs to a payphone in the lobby of a building a half-block away. He checked the phone book, the area code for Seattle: two-oh-six. Then he dialed long distance information.

'Can you give me the number for the Seattle Police Department? No, it's not an emergency.' He wrote the number down and dialed it.

A second later a female voice answered. There was a periodic beep on the line so that Thompson knew that he was being recorded.

'Hello, I'd like to have the name of the officer who's handling the Jenrico murder investigation? My name? My name is Bill Robinson. I'm a reporter for the *New York Daily News.*'

It took less than a minute before Thompson had the name and telephone extension of Lieutenant Luther Sanfillipo.

'Can you tell me, is he doing both murder investigations, Theresa and Joseph Jenrico? He is. Thank you.'

Thompson hung up. He didn't like dealing with the police. He never knew whether they had caller I.D. on their lines to trace the number of incoming calls. For this reason whenever he had to call them he always used payphones in one of the busy Manhattan office buildings, where there were a gazillion people roaming in the lobby.

In less than two minutes he had confirmed one part of the anonymous caller's information. The Jenricos were both murdered. But the caller could have gotten that information from anywhere.

He picked up the phone and dialed again, reading the number off the note he had just taken.

A man answered the phone. 'Homicide.'

'I'm calling for Lieutenant Sanfillipo.'

'I don't know if he's here. Let me check.'

Thompson heard what sounded like a hand being cupped over the mouthpiece. 'Anybody seen Luther?' He couldn't hear what came back by way of an answer.

'Think he's out to lunch.'

'I'm calling in regard to the Jenrico investigation.'

'Yes?'

'Do you know whether Lieutenant Sanfillipo is still interested in talking to Abigail Chandlis in regard to that matter?'

The hand went back over the phone and there was a lot of hushed conversation. Thompson couldn't make out what was being said.

When the voice came back on the line it was more subdued. 'Who's calling?'

'I'd rather not give that information. Can you tell me whether your office is still looking for Ms Chandlis, in connection with the Jenrico murder investigations?'

'We have some questions we'd like to ask her.'

It was all Thompson heard because an instant later he hung up the phone. It was all he needed. Chandlis was wanted in a murder investigation involving a book worth 'boo-koo' bucks.

For three days Abby juggled Charlie and kept him occupied with an open tab at the Buccaneer and a cover story that she couldn't agree to anything financial until Jack, her partner, returned from New York.

The ante to keep Charlie quiet seemed to go up when he saw the sporty little Bimmer, the Z-3, parked in the driveway under the palm trees in front of Abby's house with its top down. As far as Charlie was concerned, Abby was living the good life and he wanted a piece of it.

He spent his time partying at the Buccaneer on Jack's open tab, hitting on 'babes' at the beach as Charlie referred to them, and zipping around the island in Abby's little car.

Charlie didn't seem to pay much attention to the fact that Abby was working feverishly on another book. To Charlie all that mattered was that money was flowing freely. For him there was no correlation between hard work and its reward. He didn't believe in personal responsibility and knew that somewhere embedded in the Constitution was the absolute right to a free ride. Charlie was a life-long Democrat.

His first night in Christiansted he tried hitting on Abby. He wanted to spend the night, but she was having none of it. Their conversation was civil and short. Her mission was to not piss him off but to keep him in the islands until she could figure out what to do.

Spencer was due in St Croix that afternoon. He might have some ideas. She couldn't wait to see Morgan, somebody with a level head. She liked Jack, but he was like a whirling dervish moving in a dozen directions at once. He was a bundle of energy she couldn't seem to control. She'd watched him on the morning talk shows. He'd hit two of the networks in a single morning and did the third one the next day. According to plan, Jack lit up the screen, flashing teeth, sparkling blue eyes, and timing that was meticulous.

The magazine show they'd filmed on the beach aired the night before so that you couldn't turn on your tube without seeing Jack's picture. Even *Entertainment Tonight* had picked up on the buzz surrounding the book, a dividend they hadn't counted on. There was a synergy to this stuff. It seemed to feed upon itself like an atomic pile.

Abby was mid-paragraph and rolling at the little computer in front of the window facing the sea when the phone rang. Still typing with her left hand she reached for the receiver with her right.

'Hello.'

'Abby.' It was Jack. 'I don't have much time, but I wanted to call you.' There was an edge to his voice.

'What's wrong?'

'Not a thing. I'm a little tired. Bertoli called and got me out of bed this morning, early.'

'What did he want?'

'He wanted to tell me that we hit the *New York Times* bestsellers list.'

Abby didn't say a word. She was numb. She had conditioned herself to wait at least two weeks before asking when they might hit, if at all. It had been almost three years of hard work, writing, plotting, and planning. Now the news came like a thunderbolt. Her eyes began to water, and when she finally did speak, her voice broke. 'Jack, you'd better not be putting me on.'

'I'm not. It's true.'

'But we've only been on sale for three days.'

'I know,' said Jack. 'The book's flying off the shelves all over the country. Bertoli says it's on after-burner, incredible sales velocity. The hottest thing he's ever seen from a first-time novelist. His words. It'll appear on the list a week from Sunday.'

It was the practice in New York to provide publishers with a heads-up when one of their authors hit the list. The news was given out ten days before the list actually appeared in the paper.

'That's the good news,' said Jack. 'Now do you want the great news?'

Abby was trying to collect her thoughts, still recovering from the fact that her book had now made it. 'What, there's more?'

'You're number four,' said Jack.

'You're kidding.' Abby had always had a hard time celebrating. But at the moment she couldn't restrain herself. There was a whoop like a war cry from Abby's end of the phone. It almost pierced Jack's eardrum. Half a week of sales and they had catapulted inside of five.

'We won't know for another week, but they're pretty sure we'll go higher. With that kind of velocity, we can't help but climb. Bertoli says he might want to reconsider our offer, more books based on time and placement on the list.'

'I'll bet he would,' said Abby. Like placing a bet after the horses were out of the gate.

'They're making a lot of noise, both he and Carla. They want to see the outline for the sequel,' said Jack. 'The quick success has made both of them real antsy.'

'Tell them they can wait.'

'I have. But you should see the claw marks on my body. I can't hold 'em off much longer.'

'The answer's no. Tell them not 'til the manuscript is finished.' Abby was adamant. There were a lot of reasons, some of them having to do with film. Abby didn't want the storyline shopped around Hollywood before the book was finished. She knew the outline would wind up out on the coast the minute it landed on a desk in New York. When it came to feature film and hundred-million-dollar movie budgets, promises to keep a secret were worthless. If Jack thought he had scratches now, he would be flayed to the bone if the film people got their hands on the story and started lobbying for changes while Abby was writing.

'We'll talk about it when I get back,' said Jack. 'There's so much I need to tell you. Things breaking every minute.'

'Fill me in.'

'I can't,' said Jack. 'I'm off to another studio for an interview. I've only got a minute. Besides, I want to know what's happening with your husband.'

'Charlie's off somewhere in the car. I can handle him,' she said. 'Besides, Morgan's due in sometime this afternoon. He'll have some ideas on what to do.'

'I should be there when he arrives.'

'What for?' said Abby.

'To protect myself.'

'Give him a break. Morgan's only doing what he thinks is in my best interest.'

'Yeah, bad-mouthing me,' said Jack.

'He doesn't bad-mouth you. He gives me advice.'

'Yes but why does all of it involve taking my name in vain?'

'You're paranoid.'

'You know what they say about every paranoid's delusions possessing a kernel of truth. With Morgan I think I could make popcorn,' said Jack.

'He's coming down for business. Besides, I told him Charlie was here, that I've got a problem. I'm hoping Morgan will take him back in tow and deal with him in Seattle until this is over.'

She could hear Jack fuming on the other end.

'I saw you on *Good Morning America* yesterday. You were great.'

'You liked it?'

'It was wonderful. I thought of going out and buying the book myself.'

'Why didn't you?'

'I'll wait for the paperback,' said Abby.

Jack laughed. 'Still, it's easy to sell a great book.' They were getting into bilateral back-slapping now. Kudos all around.

'It's good of you to say,' said Abby.

'I mean it. I only wish I'd written it,' said Jack.

'Don't tell Charlie that.'

Jack laughed. 'It would light up his day. He thinks he has his teeth into you now. How did you ever pick such a loser?'

'He wasn't always this way. There was a time,' said Abby. Then she stopped herself. 'It's a long story. I'll tell you about it sometime.'

'Listen, there's other information I should be passing on to you. Bertoli's given me a ton of stuff on sales. I've taken notes but I can't remember all the details.'

'Where are you now?'

'Carla's office. They're waving to me from outside. I'm gonna have to go in a second,' said Jack. 'But I'll be back down there in two days,' he told her. There was a break in his schedule before he headed out on the fourteen-city tour. 'We'll crack a bottle when I get down there,' he said. 'I'll bring the champagne. We'll bodysurf in the buff, and get drunk. How does that sound?'

'Like shark bait,' said Abby.

'We'll be numb. Won't feel a thing. Gotta run.' They were waving at him again. 'The car's double parked downstairs. See you in a few days. Love ya,' said Jack.

Before she could say another word she heard the click on the line as he hung up. For a moment Abby dwelled on his last words.

Jack was at the top of his form. She could envision him running with the celebrity set in New York, flashing infectious smiles at camera lenses, and dashing through packed bookstores at autograph parties. He was a natural, show-boating in a stretch limo, doing the night spots of Manhattan after a busy day writing the name of Gable Cooper inside the covers of a thousand books.

At the moment even Abby, the soul of reserve, was caught up in the rush of a natural high. She picked up her can of Diet Coke from the desk and tapped it against the edge of her computer screen, then took a drink as if in toast of her own accomplishment. She had come from nowhere to write a novel that had fought its way onto the toughest bestsellers list in the world, a rocket that had landed inside of number five. It was no mean feat. For Abby only one thing took the edge off of absolute euphoria: the knowledge that her success had required so much deception. Bertoli and his pack in New York would never have allowed it had they known the truth; that Abby was the author. To anyone who cared, she was still a writer with a failed track record. Men still looked at her with a lustful gaze when she walked past, but that was not good enough for Bertoli. As far as he was concerned, she was over the hill.

Her gaze returned to the small computer screen, seven and a half inches of blue iridescence. For the next four months it would define the entire cosmos of her universe. It was a painful reality, but if her plan was to work she would have to stay the course and live with it.

The phone rang. Abby reached for it. Jack must have remembered something else.

She picked up the receiver. 'Don't tell me we climbed to number one already.'

'Excuse me?' It wasn't Jack's voice on the other end.

There was a cold moment of silence on the phone before she spoke. 'Who is this?'

'I'm looking for Morgan Spencer.'

'He's not here yet.'

'Can you give him a message?'

'Sure.' Abby reached for a scrap of paper and a pencil. 'Tell him the ship is the *Cuesta Verde*, in San Juan.'

Abby wrote it down. 'That's all?'

'Yeah.'

'May I ask who's calling?'

'He'll understand the message.' Whoever it was hung up.

Abby put the phone down for only a second before it rang again. It was driving her nuts. She thought about unplugging it, but it was her only lifeline to the outside world.

'Hello.'

'Am I speaking to Abby Chandlis?' It was a deep male voice, but she didn't recognize it.

All of a sudden everybody had her number. She had gone to great lengths to make sure the phone was unlisted. 'Who is this?'

'We talked once before, my name's Robert Thompson,

The Intruder. You didn't tell me you were moving.'

A chill ran down Abby's spine. How could he have found her? Her mind raced. 'How did you get this number?'

'It wasn't from information,' said Thompson. 'You're a difficult person to find.'

'I don't have time to talk right now.' Abby tried to figure some way to get off the phone gracefully.

'I'd give you my number, but somehow I don't think you'd call me back,' said Thompson.

'I have to go,' said Abby.

'I think you might want to talk to me. I'm much more pleasant than the police in Seattle.'

Abby's mind now went into hyperdrive.

'If I wanted to make trouble I would simply have told them where to find you. But I didn't do that.' He made it sound like he deserved a medal.

'What do you want?'

'I'm not trying to cause you any problems.'

'You said that already. How did you get my number?'

'We have our sources. They seem to have provided some accurate information.'

'What do you mean?'

'The phone number was right.'

Abby didn't say anything.

'And the police are looking for you.'

'How do you know that?'

'They told me so.'

'You talked to them?'

'Relax. I didn't tell them anything. They don't even know who called. I protect my sources.' He was cultivating Abby, trying to turn her into one. He guessed that she was a fringe player, a lawyer with information. If there was something scandalous happening, it was probably with a client, or somebody her client dealt with.

'We have a pretty good idea what's going on. It would be to your interest to make sure that we have your side of the story before we go to press.' Thompson didn't have shit and he knew it. But he was hoping that Abby would panic and start talking.

At the moment she was scared. She was also smart enough to know that scared people make mistakes. One of them is to talk too much.

'Some of our sources.' Suddenly they were multiplying, thought Abby. 'Some of our sources are telling us that you're involved in some rather strange dealings on a big book.'

'I don't know what you're talking about,' said Abby.

'Why don't you tell us what's going on? We don't think you're involved in anything criminal,' said Thompson.

'I'm glad to hear it,' said Abby.

'Who was Theresa Jenrico and why was she killed?'

There was a long breathless pause from Abby's end. She wondered for a moment if she should just hang up. But Thompson had already talked to the cops once. What if he got angry and called them back with an anonymous tip? They'd nail her at Immigration trying to get through the airport.

'She was a friend,' said Abby. 'And I don't know who killed her or why. I wish I did.'

'Why do the police want to talk to you about it?'

'I don't know.'

'Why aren't you talking to them if you're not involved?'

'Because right now it's not convenient.'

'I'm told that her death has something to do with the

book,' said Thomspon. It was a guess, but not a far stretch. The voice on the phone had mentioned the murder and the book in the same breath.

'Then you've been given misinformation,' said Abby.

'Then there is a book?' Thompson was sly.

'Why don't you ask your sources?'

'Why did you run from Seattle?'

'I got squeamish about staying in a house where my best friend was murdered.'

'And that's the only reason?'

Abby thought about answering him with a lie, but figured why bother. 'This conversation is going to end,' she told him. 'I have work to do.'

'What kind of work? What are you doing down there?'

'It's been nice talking,' said Abby.

'Can I call you again? At a more convenient time?' He sounded like a suitor, someone desperate for something. Abby was hoping it was information. Maybe he didn't have anything. Maybe he was just bluffing.

But Abby didn't want to take the chance. 'I can't tell you anything. But if you want to call I can't stop you.' She left him a glimmer of hope. It would at least buy her time.

'Is it something that's protected by attorney-client privilege?' asked Thompson.

Abby imagined a mental buzzer in her mind – *Wrong*. 'I can't discuss it.' She allowed him to form his own conclusions. If they were the wrong ones that was fine with her.

'When's a good time to call?' he asked.

'Early afternoon. Before two.' This was when she walked on the beach. Abby figured she'd get his message on her tape. At least she'd have some warning before she talked to him again. He wouldn't catch her flat-footed. 'But I'm telling you there's nothing to talk about.'

'The police think there is,' said Thompson.

Abby couldn't tell if he was trying to extort information or just keeping her like a bird on a wire in hopes that sooner or later she would tell him what he wanted to know.

'Somebody's getting you into a lot of trouble.' He made it sound very ominous, but then he would if he didn't know anything.

'I've got to go.' Without another word Abby hung up.

At the other end Thompson listened to dead air as it hissed on the line before he hung up. He toyed with copies of several clipped newspaper articles in front of him on his desk as he moved them around to see how they fit. They'd been sent from a clipping service earlier in the day. One of them showed a three-column photograph, a picture of a large green zippered bag on a barge, a bag containing the body of Joey Jenrico.

CHAPTER
THIRTY-ONE

Two main streets run through the center of Christiansted; King Street going east, and Company Street going west. These are flanked by Government House and a myriad of colonial buildings, most of them Dutch in their design. When tour ships are in, these streets are body-to-body with shoppers all looking for bargains in clothing, jewelry, and liquor, even Cuban cigars on the underground market.

Abby noticed that there were very few street signs and virtually no street lights left in the town. These had fallen victim to a hurricane a year before, and had not yet been replaced.

A few days earlier she had tried to take pictures of the damage done to Government House, mostly windows blown out, but a guard had chased her off. There was a virtual conspiracy to keep the outside world from learning of the damage, that the phones didn't work and that accommodations in some places were marginal at best. If you called from the States they wouldn't tell you. Tourism was too important to the island's economy.

As Abby walked past the old scale house toward King's Wharf, she could hear the drone of the motors, the twin engine Seaborne Vista Liner. It taxied over the choppy harbor toward its mooring station on the docks. The plane carried nineteen passengers and formed a transportation link with St Thomas and the other islands. Morgan had managed to catch a flight to Charlotte Amalie on St Thomas that morning and was now on the last leg of his trip to hook up with Abby.

She saw him getting off the plane, the perennial briefcase in hand. For Morgan this was like an extra appendage, what a pouch is to a kangaroo. He was holding a wide-brimmed straw hat on his head with the other hand, keeping it on as it flapped in the prop wash from the plane.

She smiled at him and waved. Abby had long since forgiven him for his indiscretion in spending her money on the little sports car. It had served a purpose, if nothing else to occupy Charlie.

'How was the trip?' She hollered over the drone of the engines as the plane revved up and prepared to depart with another load of passengers.

Abby's shoulder-length hair, which was now bleached by the sun, blew in the wind as Spencer looked at her and then gave her a peck on the cheek. He was dressed in a white linen suit, something comfortable for the tropics that she would not have guessed Morgan had in his closet. She wondered if he bought it for the trip. 'All you need is the whip and the gun,' she told him.

'I could have used those with Cutler. He didn't want to let me come. I told him I had a meeting with an old maritime client in San Juan.'

'He bought it?'

'It's true. Hey, listen, any lawyer who can't come up with a reason for business someplace in the world in fifteen minutes has no business practicing.' Morgan smiled at her.

'Besides, the guy's file's been on my desk for two years. It's about time I got around to it. Of course I could have done it by mail. I called him, set up a meeting for next week. We'll do some business, go to a bar and have a few drinks, and I'll send the bill to Cutler.'

Abby laughed, then led him away from the noise and hustle of the docks toward Company street, past the white wood-framed church with its tall steeple. They talked as they strolled along the covered sidewalk.

'So how much does he know?' Morgan looked tired and drawn after flying all day. He was talking about Charlie, who was off on a frolic somewhere on the island in Abby's car.

'He's making noises about staying down here,' said Abby. 'That's all I need. And he knows enough to make trouble if he decides to.' But Abby was worried about more than Charlie.

Around the corner and a block up from the old apothecary was Indies, one of the better restaurants and watering holes in Christiansted. It served exotic cuisine to the strains of music that owed its tempo to West Africa and its lyrics to Latin America, all spiced by the hot beat of steel drums. It was a good place to talk because people couldn't hear you, and Charlie wouldn't waltz in on them.

The entrance was a wrought-iron gate that led into a bricked courtyard. There were hanging carriage lanterns and a kitchen behind an arched stone doorway. Built in the 1700s as a carriage house, the courtyard was covered with a series of translucent roofs under which were tables and a bar against one wall.

The maître d' led them to one of the tables and a

waiter took orders for drinks, a mai-tai for Abby, and a beer in a tall frosted pilsner glass for Spencer.

There were tanned tourists all around, a lot of young women on bar stools, so that Spencer had a hard time keeping his eyes and his attention on business.

'I will say Jack found you a gorgeous spot.' Apparently he approved of St Croix. 'But it's awfully damn hot.'

'Thick blood,' said Abby. She tapped her drink to his. 'Take off your tie and drink some of that. It'll thin it out.'

Spencer was a fan of the Northwest. He was used to rain that was cold. Still, the bodies on the stools were a definite attraction and Abby smiled as she watched him stealing glances. It seemed as if Spencer never got away for much fun. Even with her problems she planned to show him a good time while he was down here.

'Before I forget,' said Abby. 'Somebody called for you the other day. Left a message.' She pulled the note from her purse, the one with the name of the ship, the *Cuesta Verde* – San Juan. 'He didn't tell me who he was. He said you'd know what this meant.'

Morgan read the note and laughed. 'Cummings. You'd think he still worked for the F.B.I. He's an investigator. Never wants to leave a name. Just tell 'em only what they need to know. Loves to be mysterious,' said Morgan.

'He succeeds,' said Abby.

Morgan pocketed the note.

'Now tell me about Jermaine. What's he up to?'

'Jack's still in New York. He'll be down in a couple of days.'

'Good. Then we can talk. Is he living at the house with you?' Morgan's eyes darted and he took a sip as if to cover the question.

Abby didn't like it, but she answered. 'He has a place at the Buccaneer. It's a resort down the road.'

'He's staying there?'

'That's what I said,' said Abby.

Morgan looked at the bubbles rising in his glass before he spoke. 'He's wrong for you. You know that.'

'How is it that everybody else knows what's right and wrong for me,' said Abby, 'when I don't even know myself.'

'There's just something wrong about him,' said Morgan. 'Call it intuition.'

'Yeah. He says the same thing about you.'

'What does he say?'

'He says you're a humorless tight-ass. And if you keep asking questions like this I'm inclined to agree with him.'

Morgan smiled. 'O.K. But he is trouble.' He raised his hand before she could respond as if to say it was the last word on the subject.

'Listen to me. You're getting deeper and deeper into trouble here,' said Morgan.

'I'll tell you what trouble is. Trouble is all of these distractions. Until two days ago I was flying through the manuscript on the sequel. Then Thompson calls and I haven't written a word since. He's given me a terminal case of writer's block. You'd think the man has nothing better to do in life but to track me down. You'd think it was Watergate,' said Abby. 'What I can't figure out is how he found me. What do we do about him?'

'A problem,' said Spencer.

'Tell me about it.'

'No. I mean bigger than you know.' Morgan was trying to figure some way to break it to her so that she would believe him.

Abby looked across the table at him.

'I think I know how he found you.'

'How?'

'Listen, I know what you're thinking. I'm jealous. Vindictive, whatever. But I think Jack told him.'

'Give it a break,' said Abby. She reached for her hair and pulled it, shaking her head at the same time. She was getting angry at their constant backbiting. If they didn't quit, Abby was of a mind to disappear where neither of them could find her until the book was finished.

'Think about it,' said Morgan. 'Who else knew where to find you? Who had your phone number? I mean, besides you and me.'

'For one, there's Charlie,' said Abby.

Morgan made a face of dismissal. 'Why would he call the reporter? He wouldn't even know the guy's name. How would he have found him?'

Morgan was right. Charlie didn't know that Thompson was chasing Abby on a story. Jack did.

'Admit it,' said Morgan. 'He's gotten to you. He's playing you like a piano, and the tune right now is not sounding good.'

'Stop it.' Abby didn't want to hear it. 'I'm starting to feel like a scrap of meat being fought over by two dogs.' She turned sideways in her chair so that she didn't have to look at him anymore and sipped from the drink that she now held in her hand. There were icy drips off the bottom of the glass onto her legs that were now darkly tanned. They contrasted nicely with the tight white shorts that she wore.

'I'm sorry you feel that way,' said Spencer. 'But somebody has to tell you. I think you're in danger.'

When she glanced over her shoulder at him, Spencer

had a look of seriousness that Abby could not ignore.

'Think about it,' he said. 'Think about your conversation with Thompson and what he said when he called.'

'What do you mean?'

'Did he say anything about Jack or Gable Cooper not being the author?'

Abby thought for a moment. 'He didn't seem to know the title of the book or the author.'

'Precisely. Because it wouldn't serve Jack's purposes to give him that information. What were the questions he asked?'

'He talked about the murders, Theresa and Joey. He linked them to the book. And he knew the police were looking for me.'

'Someone had given him that information along with the implication that maybe you were involved.' Morgan thumped the table with two fingers to make the point. 'It's just the kind of stuff someone might like to see in print if they wanted to discredit you. Now think, who would have a motive to discredit you? Who would gain if you were linked with some scandal just as you were trying to go public on the book?'

'What are you saying?'

'I'm saying look at the facts. Open your eyes.'

'Are you trying to say that Jack killed Theresa?' Abby now turned and looked at him across the table squarely.

Morgan's silence answered the question.

'I don't believe that. No. He wouldn't do that.'

For a moment she said nothing. Morgan allowed the silence to erode her convictions.

'What would he gain by her death?' said Abby. They were back to logic, Morgan's court.

'Theresa knew about the book,' he said. 'She knew you were the author. That would be a threat if he were making a move on the book. Don't you see it?'

'And Joey?' said Abby.

'He screwed with the movie rights, remember. Put himself in the middle. And Jack knew that, too. Remember? He was blind but he still covered it in New York with Carla. That cock-and-bull story about his old drug-induced friend who was passing himself off as Gable Cooper.'

Abby thought for a moment. 'No. I can't accept that. He wouldn't kill two people. Not over something like this.'

'What, over seven million dollars in advances and royalties. I've got relatives who would kill *me* for that. People who actually like me,' said Morgan.

'So what are you saying? He's going to steal the book?'

'We've tied it up in a nice package for him already,' said Morgan.

'But you've got him nailed seven ways from Sunday,' said Abby. 'Signed contracts and copyrights.' She looked at him, but Morgan didn't say anything.

'Well, you do, don't you?'

'Yes we've got contracts. We have a copyright. But the publicity has a life of its own. I've never seen anything like it. It's huge. Jack's face is all over the airwaves. Every twenty minutes I'm seeing ads on T.V. You've been down here. I don't think you realize . . .'

'That was the plan,' said Abby.

'Yes, but you don't understand. Jack and the book have become the same thing. I don't know how to explain it.' Morgan started talking with his hands, for once at a loss for words. 'Celebrity has a dynamic all of its own. Once it's out there, it's like the genie out of the bottle. The atom out of the bomb. How do you corral it?

Control it for your own purposes?'

Abby listened to him. She didn't like it, but she had to admit that he was right.

'It's gonna give Jack a big stick to use on us,' said Morgan. 'It puts the publisher in a hell of a position to scream fraud if they don't like it when you tell them the truth, especially if you're being questioned by the cops in a murder investigation at the time . . . Well. Jack's got extra leverage, doesn't he?'

'But I have an alibi. I was on a plane.'

'Tell it to the cops. He doesn't care. Besides, people have been known to hire other people to kill,' said Morgan.

'But why? Why would I kill Theresa? She was my friend.'

'Friends kill friends all the time. That isn't going to sway the police. We made a tactical blunder,' said Spencer. 'We should never have allowed him to bring you down here. It made it look like you were running. Evidence of flight. Guilty conscience,' said Morgan.

'I had to get away, you know that. The police would have been all over me, asking questions about the book.'

Still Abby knew he was right. Her plan had succeeded at a level far beyond her wildest dreams. She had underestimated the buzz on the book and the public's ready acceptance of Jack. She had started a small fire to warm her career, and now it was threatening to burn her alive.

What they couldn't control was the spin when Abby came clean. When she went public with the truth about the book. Was fame transferable like a children's game of tag? Or would the spin take a darker turn toward scandal? Neither of them had any answers.

Morgan took another swallow of beer before he spoke.

'I have something here that may change your mind. I didn't want to tell you over the phone. Jack is not the innocent you think he is.'

'I never said he was innocent.' Abby could have said innocents don't carry guns, but why throw fuel on Morgan's fire.

'I mean in the literary sense,' said Spencer. 'He's written a book.'

'I know. He's got a trunk full of unpublished manuscripts. He's shown them to me.'

'Did he show you this one?' Morgan fished in his briefcase and pulled out the book from the used book store. He passed it over to Abby.

She was now stone silent. She read the name of the author on the spine, Kellen Raid, the same name Jack had used on the false passport at his house.

She gave Morgan an incredulous look like she didn't believe this.

'How do you know it's his?'

'Look at the dedication,' said Morgan.

She opened it and read. The look on Abby's face when she finished was one of sheer pain, the realization of betrayal.

'Why?' she said. 'Why didn't he tell me?'

'If he had, would you have used him?'

'I don't know.' At the moment, it was the only honest answer she could give. The fact that Jack was published would have spelled trouble. If Bertoli had known, he would never have agreed to the big book budget. In publishing circles, with its idiotic rules, the sheen would have been off the package if he couldn't present Jack, his major find, as a virgin author.

'That's why he didn't tell us,' said Morgan. 'And it gets worse.' He disappeared back into his briefcase and a moment later came up with some folded pages. He passed them to Abby.

'Read and weep,' he told her.

Abby didn't know if she wanted to. Everything was coming apart.

'I stopped in South Carolina on the way down.' Morgan talked without looking at her, his head cast down at the table as if muses were speaking to him from his glass of beer.

'I went to Beaufort. It was a long shot, but I figured it was a small town with a newspaper. I thought maybe the fact that a local resident had published a book might be big news in a small town. I was right. I found this in the paper's morgue. The piece was done almost nine years ago. Jack was a lot younger.' He pointed to the picture on the first folded page. It was a photocopy, but still it was clear enough for Abby to recognize Jack's beaming smile as he sat at a desk and held up a copy of the book: The title and his name were in the cutline underneath.

'Apparently his editor did a lot of work on it. Cleaned it up,' said Morgan. 'But their timing was off. It was a military thriller published a little more than a year before military thrillers hit it big. They talk in there about military stories having no future. Even so,' said Morgan, 'it hit the regional bestsellers list in Atlanta. That was the hook for the news story.'

Abby felt like she'd been sucker-punched. She picked up the pages and read while the sharp timbre of steel drums and the hum of human voices blended in the open courtyard.

The portrait drawn by the article was of a young

435

writer obsessed by the bestsellers list. When the book hit the regional list, Jack had taken a mortgage on his house and had spent all his savings trying to promote the book onto the national lists. He bought advertising space in newspapers around the country and went on tour. He even tried selling the book out of the trunk of his car. But he had failed. It was a testament to the dynamics of distribution and marketing. Without a push from a big publisher and their network of contacts, he had wasted his money, and lost his dream.

When she finished reading she dropped the pages on the table and stared off into the distance, right through Morgan as if he wasn't there. She was in a state of shock, her stomach turning over. She didn't know whether to be angry or to cry. She couldn't believe that Jack hadn't told her about this. They had talked about his manuscripts. He wanted her to help him get them published; eight of them, and one other that he had mentioned but declined to discuss. Now she knew why.

'How could he?' Abby thought she loved him. She had trusted Jack, told him things she had never told anyone, not even Morgan. The sense of betrayal was overwhelming.

'Listen to me.' Morgan tried to get her to focus. 'We can deal with Charlie. We can even deal with this reporter. You can move again if you have to. Find another location. There's a million islands. We can lose him again. Right now our biggest problem is what to do with Jermaine.'

Abby's first reaction was to call him in New York and scream at him over the phone. Morgan talked her out of it.

'We know he's lied to us,' said Spencer. 'What else

he's done or planning on doing we don't know. We still have leverage.'

'What?'

'You haven't shown him the outline for the sequel?'

She shook her head.

'Or any of the manuscript?'

'No.'

'Smart girl. From everything we know the guy's land-locked when it comes to a keyboard. He can't write and he knows it. That's our trump card.'

'He could find a ghost writer,' said Abby.

'Not if he doesn't know what the story's about.' They were both confident that Jack would never be able to come up with a story line that would track well on the first book. Not something that would satisfy Bertoli or Carla. For the moment they still had a leash on Jack.

But Abby was troubled by something else. 'Do you really think he killed Theresa?'

Spencer looked at her but didn't speak. His eyes said it all.

'Don't tell him anything. Keep him in the dark. Don't say anything about this.' Morgan tapped the cover of the book on the table. 'At least until we can figure some way to move him out of the picture. To take control.'

'How?'

'I don't know. Give me some time and I'll figure it out. I've been thinking,' said Morgan, 'about leaving the firm. We could go someplace. Get away from all of this. Jermaine. These games. Live a real life. Maybe go to Europe. You and I.'

Abby was stunned. She had known for years that he was attracted, but she never thought he would actually bring himself to say 'Let's go away.'

'I can't.'

'Why not?'

'What are you suggesting?'

'I'm not suggesting anything,' said Morgan. He was silent, just looking at her for a moment, and then popped it. 'I'm asking you to marry me.'

Abby didn't say a word, not with her lips. Her answer was conveyed more by the look she didn't give him. Eyes off to the side, she refused to make contact, looking for a graceful way to say it. The man Abby loved had betrayed her. The man who loved her was a friend. Friends and lovers were two different things, like night and day.

'I know you've had a bad marriage,' said Morgan.

'It's not that.'

'Then what?'

'I value your friendship. Enjoy being around you,' said Abby.

'But?' said Morgan.

'But there has to be something more than that.'

'There could be if you give it a chance.'

'We've known each other a long time,' said Abby.

'But not in the way that I mean.' He was pleading, and it made it all the more difficult.

'I can't marry you, Morgan.'

'Why?'

'Because I don't love you.' She finally said it.

Morgan looked at her across the table, eyes that were filled with hurt. It almost brought tears to her own so that she ended up looking away. He was saying nothing. Abby finally turned to him, reached across and touched his hand. 'Friends?' she said.

For an instant, it looked as if he would pull his hand away. Then he left it, lifted his eyes, and said: 'Friends.'

CHAPTER
THIRTY-TWO

The dance floor overflowed with couples moving to the beat of steel drums, as Abby, Jack, and Morgan arrived at the terrace bar of the Buccaneer for dinner.

Jack had flown in a few hours earlier, expecting them to be throwing parties over the book. Instead, Abby was cool and withdrawn. Morgan had set up in the guest room at the beach house with Abby. Jack's things were back in his room at the Buccaneer.

Jack had whispered in her ear that he wanted a moment with her alone. She told him that anything he had to say he could say in front of Morgan. She said it loud enough that Spencer could hear. At that moment, Jack knew something had happened. He was in trouble.

He ordered drinks from the bar and waited as the bartender mixed them. Maybe a little alcohol would ease the tensions and loosen tongues.

Back at the table, Spencer tried to keep Abby from saying too much. 'When he comes back, let me do the talking. Whatever you do, don't mention his book.'

She nodded. For a woman with a novel high on the bestsellers list and an audience that was growing from thousands towards millions, Abby was remarkably subdued. Suddenly none of it seemed to matter. Abby's mind was occupied by a single thought: whether Jack had anything to do with Theresa Jenrico's death.

She kept trying to convince herself that it wasn't possible. She wanted to believe that her instincts weren't that flawed, that she could never feel the way she did about a man who would do such a thing. But the questions kept coming, the kind that lawyers deal with when they have a client they don't trust; mostly motive and opportunity.

Abby tried to remember where Jack was when Theresa was killed. She tried to piece it together. He had left New York ahead of her. Business at Coffin Point, he'd told her. But Jack had turned up in Seattle, unannounced. Abby's mind was working overtime, tortured by the possibilities.

She watched as Jack leaned on one of the brass elephant heads that graced the bar railing, waiting on the bartender.

A young woman with long dark hair and curvaceous moves boogied to the edge of the dance floor, gyrating to the sounds of the music. She took a good look at Jack. She seemed to undress him with her eyes as she did the bump and grind. Jack offered one of his enigmatic smiles in return. Connery as Bond. The girl displayed the pouting look of erotic arrogance that pretty young women seem to own.

Jack raised a glass in toast to her as he headed back to their table with two drinks. Abby was abstaining. Morgan had ordered scotch and soda.

The soft breezes of the eastern trade winds wafted through the open air of the dining room under the barrel-vaulted ceiling with its fans like wounded birds.

Some of the paddles were missing, victims of last season's hurricanes. The pungent odor of Cruzan rum filled the place along with strains of music.

Without asking, Jack took Abby's hand, and before she knew what was happening she found herself on the dance floor in his arms. They went cheek to cheek. She was stiff and uneasy.

Jack had lied to her. He never told her about the book he published. Now she was left to wonder what else he might have done, about Joey Jenrico, and whether Jack had killed him. The vocalist tortured lyrics, 'knock, knock, knockin on devil's door.' The words of the song echoed in her ears, and Abby wondered whether she had not made a deal with her own kind of devil.

'Why don't you pitch it in for the night and join us with a drink?' said Jack. As the music ended, he ran his hand up Abby's arm and rested it on her shoulder, a gesture of intimacy. She froze.

'I have a book to write, remember?' She forced a smile and took her seat at the table.

Jack pulled up a chair. 'Where's Charlie tonight?' He looked at Abby, but Spencer answered.

'We don't know.'

'Putting mileage on my car and his body,' said Abby.

'Shacked up somewhere,' said Morgan. 'Maybe he'll catch the clap.'

'Now there's poetic justice,' said Abby. Charlie hadn't returned the car in three days. The last time she drove it, there was a pair of woman's panties in the glove box.

'Well, I hate to throw hot water on a cold party,' said Jack. 'But assuming he doesn't drive off a cliff of contract a quick social disease, has anybody considered an alternate plan for dealing with him?'

'We have,' said Morgan.

'Well, is somebody gonna tell me?'

'We're providing him with a financial incentive to cooperate,' said Spencer.

'Is that lawyer-speak for buying him off?' said Jack.

'If you like.'

Jack raised an eyebrow and looked at Abby. 'You do what you want,' he told her, 'but I think you're making a big mistake.'

'We've already discussed it,' said Spencer. 'We made a decision and it's done.'

Morgan had drawn a line in the sand that was hard for Jack to miss even though he'd only been back on the island for two hours. Spencer was in charge, and it didn't seem like there was much Jack could do to reach Abby.

'I take it you've already told Charlie you're gonna pay him?'

'Not yet, but we have every reason to believe he'll accept,' said Spencer.

'Oh yeah. Like Dracula taking in a bleeder,' said Jack. 'How much are you going to offer?'

'That's not for you to know,' said Spencer.

'Does he know you wrote the book?' Jack was trying to draw Abby out, but Morgan answered.

'Not unless you told him.'

'I didn't tell him a thing.'

'He doesn't know,' said Abby. 'He thinks we wrote it together. If he knew it was mine, the price would go up. He figures he has no claim on your part of it.'

'That's decent of him,' said Jack.

'Decency doesn't enter into it. You'd know that if you knew Charlie.'

'And you've agreed to all of this? Paying to keep him quiet even though he's stumbling around and doesn't know squat?'

She nodded.

'Stumbling around he could cause a lot of trouble,' said Morgan.

'If it were my money, I wouldn't pay him a dime.'

'It's not your money,' said Abby.

'You're right,' said Jack. 'Your money. Your mistake.'

'Jeez, you're a hot shot, aren't you?' said Spencer.

'Morgan, don't!' Abby tried to stop him.

'No. No. I want to hear what he has to say. How he'd handle it. Tell me. I want to know. What would you do?'

'I'd talk to him.'

'Just like that.'

'Yeah.' Jack shrugged. 'Just like that.'

'And what would you say to him? What magic words would you use?'

'I'd reason with him.'

Morgan smiled, then he laughed. 'You'd reason with him.'

'Yeah. He's a very intelligent guy. We reasoned in New York,' said Jack.

'You make logic sound like a four-letter word,' said Spencer.

'Jack can be very persuasive,' said Abby. 'I saw him reason with some people in San Juan.'

Jack looked at her. 'They aren't asking you for money anymore.'

'One of them isn't asking for anything anymore,' said Abby.

'What the hell happened in San Juan?' said Morgan.

'Nevermind. I'd rather pay the money.' Abby'd had enough of the conversation.

'And what's to stop him from coming back for more?' said Jack.

'There won't be any more, because by the time he gets

around to spending what we give him, it'll be over,' said Abby.

'What are you gonna do, give him your bank card?'

'No. We're moving the schedule forward,' she told him.

'What are you talking about?' Jack looked at her.

'I mean we're not waiting for paperback publication to tell Bertoli that I wrote the book.'

Jack looked dazed. He had expected a lot of things, but not this. 'But it's going great in New York.'

'Charlie brings a new dimension,' said Abby. 'We can't keep him quiet forever.'

'Besides, some other things have come up,' said Morgan.

'What things?'

'You don't have to worry,' said Morgan. 'You're going to get your share. That's all you need to know,' he told Jack.

'No. What I need to know is what's going on. When are you going to tell Bertoli?'

'We're going to give it a month on the list,' said Abby. 'By then the hook should be set.'

Jack shook his head like he couldn't believe it. 'When you start something, you should finish it.' This was aimed at Abby. 'I didn't mind playing your games. Going to New York and doing the Alex and Carla show. In fact, for a while diddling corporate America was sorta fun. But these people are playing real business with real money,' said Jack. 'They made promises and they've lived up to them. You can say what you want but they delivered, which is a hell of a lot more than you've done.'

'They got what they bargained for,' said Abby. 'They got you.'

'Yes, and now you want to screw with their hardcover campaign,' said Jack. 'In the middle of it you want to jerk the carpet out from under all of us.'

'What's wrong,' said Morgan. 'You don't think the book will continue to succeed without you?'

'I put myself on the line,' said Jack. 'That's what wrong.'

Abby looked at him. 'What are you talking about?'

'You sent me up there alone and told me to wing it. So I did. I made a promise.'

'What kind of promise?' said Abby.

Jack hesitated for a moment. Then he spoke. 'I told Bertoli that from what I could see he'd delivered on his part of the deal. I told him we'd deliver the outline so he could see where the sequel was going. I thought that was fair.'

'You thought it was fair?' said Abby.

'You're on the list inside of five. When's the last time that happened?'

'You had no right,' said Abby. 'I told you on the phone . . .'

'And I told you we'd talk about it when I got back,' said Jack. 'I come back to find that you're getting ready to pitch me out onto the street.'

'There's nothing to talk about.' Abby was furious. She had visions of the outline landing in Hollywood before she could finish the manuscript. Morgan was right. Without her realizing, Jack was taking control.

The maître d' came over. Their table in the dining room was ready. Abby was angry. Her face was flushed.

Jack was the first one out of his chair. 'I gave them my word.'

'I guess you're just going to have to tell him you made a mistake,' said Abby.

'A mistake?' said Jack.

'Fine. Tell them you lied. I don't care what you tell them. They're not seeing the outline.'

'Well. I guess you've made your decision.' Jack froze Abby with a look and then turned a hard gaze on Morgan.

'Enjoy your dinner.' Without another word he turned and headed off in the other direction, toward the stairs and the path that led to his room down on the water.

A few tables away in a dark corner of the bar, an African American dressed in a sport coat and tie sipped what looked like bourbon as he read a newspaper. The drink was iced tea and the newspaper was three days old.

His eyes kept wandering over the top of the paper, looking at the three people at the table thirty feet away. They were engaged in a heated argument, but Logano couldn't hear a word. The music was too loud.

What the people at the table couldn't see was that on the table behind the newspaper was a photograph. It was a picture of Abby, mildly distorted by the electronic transmission that had sent it from Seattle to the Patrick Sweeny Police Headquarters in St Croix.

It had taken Sergeant Logano four days to locate the woman. The island was not large by U.S. standards, with only two sizable towns, but there were a thousand secluded houses along the shore and more up in the hills. She could have been staying in any one of them. Logano felt fortunate to have found her at all.

If you knew the island, there were only three or four places where you went to look for tourists. The bartender at the Buccaneer was one of them. He recognized Abby's photograph. Logano staked the place out for three nights running. Tonight he got lucky.

He continued to watch them while he wiped the sweat from his forehead with a handkerchief.

He pocketed the handkerchief and studied the two men with her. One of them had to be the lawyer. Which one Logano wasn't sure. He didn't know who the other one was. The Seattle homicide detective who gave them the information said nothing about a second man. But they had tailed the lawyer to the airport. After he boarded his plane, the Seattle police had talked to the airline clerk and discovered that he was headed for St Croix via South Carolina. What he was doing in the Carolinas they didn't know.

For Logano it was a sensitive assignment, one that required discretion. Seattle didn't have a warrant for the woman's arrest, though they were working on it. Right now they wanted to talk to her. Logano and his department were performing a professional courtesy. His job was to find her and call Seattle.

Logano was no fool. He knew that the woman was as good as cuffed and on her way to the States. When the Americans got their teeth into something, they were relentless. They might pick her up on a technical violation, Customs or Immigrations, but they would get her, of that he was sure.

He lowered the paper onto the table and covered the photograph. He felt the bulge under his left arm, the Smith & Wesson three-fifty-seven magnum with its four-inch barrel. Logano was of the old school. No semiautomatic spray and pray for him. He didn't want to shoot anybody, but if he had to, he believed that doing people should be like elephants; one shot with something that would bring them down.

He lifted a copy of the faxed report from Seattle out of

the inside pocket of his coat and glanced at it while he watched them.

According to the report, they didn't think she was armed, but they couldn't be sure. They wanted to talk to her regarding a double homicide. Logano wasn't going to get his ass shot off performing a professional courtesy for anybody.

As he put the report back in his pocket, the maître d' approached the woman's table. He couldn't hear, but Logano assumed that they were being told that their table in the dining room was ready. It seemed the maître d' had interrupted their argument.

One of the men, good-looking and tall, stood. They had some words, then he turned and headed for the stairs and the parking lot. The woman and the other man got up and headed for the dining room.

For a moment, Logano thought about following the man down the stairs, then settled back in his chair. Right now his job was the woman walking to dinner with her companion. Lose her and he might not be so lucky again. He had to find out where she was living and call the information to the police in Seattle. There was no hurry. He could always pick up other threads later, after he had the place where she lived under surveillance.

Cheeseburgers in Paradise was an open-air restaurant with live music on weekends and a bar that served anything you wanted to drink. It was a hangout for the young set, and lately Charlie was feeling particularly young.

He hit on a sweet little thing sitting on a bar stool. She was wearing a short skirt like a cheerleader, a tight pull-over top that showed her tits. Charlie was big on tits. He bought her dinner, a burger and fries, while he was busy throwing back shots of Grand Marnier with tequila chasers.

The girl was talkative, tanned, and vivacious. She was living on a small boat with a friend who had sailed to another island for a few days, and now she had no place to stay. Charlie couldn't believe his good luck. She was freckled and athletic. Charlie figured she could screw like a bunny.

About eleven-thirty he took her to his car to impress her and found her boyfriend waiting for them. They rolled him in the dirt of the parking lot, took his wallet and watch, and left Charlie in some tall grass to sleep it off. They were too smart to take his car. Where do you go on an island with a stolen car?

He woke up in the weeds a little before four in the morning, staring up at a sky full of stars that all seemed to have twins. Charlie's head felt like a balloon. Slowly he sat up.

The lights from Cheeseburgers in Paradise were out, and the parking lot was empty, except for Abby's little blue sports car. Charlie couldn't remember what happened. He had only vague recollections of his face being pressed between two breasts when the lights went out. The girl's face was a hazy memory.

He got to his knees, and found his keys in his pocket, then stumbled to the car. When he looked at his hand he found there was blood on it. Charlie felt the back of his head. There was a knot the size of a baseball and when he touched it everything above his shoulders throbbed. He wondered what they'd hit him with.

He went to check the time and realized for the first time that his watch was gone. 'Shit.' He patted the seat of his pants and realized they'd gotten his wallet, too. 'Son of a bitch.'

He hoped he wouldn't get stopped by a cop on his way back to the Buccaneer. It took him twenty minutes weaving all over the two-lane road. He was lucky there was no traffic.

Even the guard at the gate had gone home. The barricade was up so Charlie didn't have to pass muster. He drove up the hill past the main building and down toward the bungalows on the water, then parked the car in front of his room. For a few minutes he thought about sleeping right there, behind the wheel, then finally cleared his head enough to fish for the room key in his pocket. They had left this and a little pocket change.

He didn't bother to lock the car but made his way to the short path leading to his room. Nothing was going right tonight. The light over the door had burned out and Charlie couldn't seem to find the keyhole in the door. It was probably just as good he hadn't gotten her home. He probably couldn't have found that hole, either.

He missed three times with the key when he heard something thrashing in the brush behind him and started to turn.

'What the fu . . .' Charlie didn't feel anything, but he couldn't understand why his words no longer had sound.

CHAPTER
THIRTY-THREE

It was early morning, just a little after six, when Abby burst into Morgan's room. She threw open the door so hard that it slammed against the wall and came back at her.

'Get up. Get out of bed!' she yelled. 'Jack's left the island.'

Spencer rolled over in the bed and lifted his head, sleep still apparent in his eyes.

'What?'

'He's gone.' She grabbed his feet at the bottom of the bed with both hands. 'And he's taken my outline with him.'

'What are you talking about?'

'I left it on the table next to the computer last night and this morning it's gone. I called Jack's room at the Buccaneer. They told me he left for the airport early this morning.'

'Where's he gone?'

'They didn't know, but if I had to guess I'd say New York.'

Morgan wiped sleep from his eyes sat up and shook his head. 'He checked out of the room?'

'No.'

'You said he wasn't scheduled to go back to New York for three more days,' said Morgan.

'I know. It looks like you were right. He's making a move on the book.'

Morgan got out of bed and started looking for his clothes, stepped into the bathroom, and they talked through the closed door while he changed from his pajamas.

Abby had turned the house upside down, but there was no sign of the outline to the sequel. Apart from the copyright, it was her only remaining point of control. She remembered leaving the outline on the table by her computer before going to dinner the night before. Now it was gone.

'You heard him last night. Something's going on in New York. He's cut some kind of a deal with them. He intends to deliver the outline. So what do we do?' she asked.

'We don't panic,' said Morgan.

'He'll deliver the outline. Maybe he already has. He could have faxed it this morning for all we know,' said Abby.

'We need to think. The important thing now is how to deal with the publisher,' said Morgan.

'That's going to be tough with Jack in the middle,' said Abby. Morgan came out of the bathroom with his clothes on, looking for his socks and shoes.

'That's why we took precautions,' said Morgan.

She looked at him.

'The documents. The registration of copyright and the contracts we had him sign. It's time for plan B,' said Morgan.

'What are you talking about?'

'I guess it's O.K. to tell you now. You promise you won't kill me?'

'Kill you for what?' said Abby.

'I never trusted him from the beginning,' said Morgan. 'I was worried he had too much control. So I contacted another lawyer in New York, with a major firm that specializes in publishing matters, First Amendment, copyright infringement, that kind of stuff. I knew sooner or later there would be a problem with Jack. So I wanted to flank him.'

Abby gave him a look. 'What about this firm?'

'I figured they would give us credibility if we got into a showing match with Jermaine. It's a large firm, one that publishers deal with all the time. I put them on retainer about two months ago and made arrangements with one of the partners. Kept 'em in my hip pocket,' said Morgan. 'I hope you don't mind. I used your money.'

Abby smiled at him. Morgan was always two jumps ahead. It was the reason she valued him. His mind was like a taxi meter, running twenty-four hours a day. If his billings had kept pace, he would have retired as a millionaire ten years earlier.

'How much have you told these lawyers in New York?'

'They know Jack didn't write the book. At least they have my word for it. The trick now is to get to them with the documents, the copyright, and the contracts that Jack signed. To have them finesse it with the publisher so as to minimize damage.'

'Minimize damage hell,' said Abby. 'I want to kick his ass.'

'Trust me,' said Morgan. 'Damage control. That's the key right now. Otherwise we run the risk of scaring

Bertoli. If he sees a protracted court battle with all of its bad press, he's gonna pull the plug on the book. That leaves you and Jack fighting over a bag of bones. This is business. We'll get even later.'

Morgan was hopeful that they could keep the ball rolling on the book without missing a beat. Simply have the publisher make Jack disappear. That would be much easier with a powerful New York law firm that talked the publishing language. Their lawyers could nail Jack's feet to the floor with one hand while they finessed Bertoli with the other.

'We can forget about waiting thirty days to tell Bertoli the truth,' said Abby. 'Jack made that impossible. Everyday we wait gives him more time to erode our position.'

'So what now?'

'First we've got to get the documents, the contracts, and the copyright, and then we've got to get to New York.' Abby's brain was in hyperdrive. 'If we're lucky, we might be able to do that by tomorrow morning.' It was now Sunday.

'They're in a safe deposit box at the bank. I didn't trust Cutler. He's probably been going through my files at night. No. I'll have to get them myself.'

He laced up his shoes. 'I'll call the airline and make reservations.'

'What do we do about the outline?' she asked.

'Do you have an extra copy?'

'In my computer.'

'Print it out. In the meantime, you package up your computer and your printer. See if you can find a box for shipping, we'll send them directly to the firm in New York.'

'What for?'

'Evidence,' said Morgan. 'You produced the outline

454

with that equipment, didn't you?'

Abby nodded.

'A good expert can probably prove it. One more piece of evidence for our side,' said Morgan.

It hit Abby like a thunderbolt. 'Oh my God!' The missing typewriter from her house. She looked at Morgan sitting on the bed lacing his shoes.

From her expression Morgan knew that she'd finally figured it out.

'That's why it was missing. Jack took it. How long have you known?'

'I didn't want to say anything,' said Morgan. 'I had no proof. But when we couldn't find it, you had to figure whoever demolished your house also took the typewriter. Ask yourself one question: why take an old manual typewriter and leave a perfectly good television set behind?'

'Because the manuscript had been typed on it,' said Abby.

'Precisely.'

A sober look came over Abby as she stood at the edge of the bed. 'And the accident with the electrical box.'

'It was intended for you,' said Morgan. 'Theresa just showed up at the wrong time.'

'And he killed Joey,' said Abby.

'One more loose end.'

'Aw God! I'm gonna lose it,' she told him. Abby felt sick, nauseous. She turned away and nearly retched thinking about it. She had made love to the man and all the while she was sleeping with Theresa's murderer.

'I never loved him. Never.' As if by saying it she could erase the intimate moments they'd spent together. Abby also knew it was a lie. She started to tear up.

Morgan reached out for her, but Abby was too angry

to be held. She wanted to lash out. 'I'm sorry,' she told him. 'I'm going to the police.'

'With what?' said Morgan. 'There's no evidence. What are you going to tell them, that Jack stole your outline?' He was right. She had nothing.

'I don't know. But I have to tell them something. At least point them in the right direction.'

'That's what he wants you to do. While we're trying to explain to the police, he's going to be selling the outline to Bertoli. He's probably already making plans to revoke the power of attorney.'

She looked up at him. She had forgotten about the power of attorney, the document that directed Bertoli and the film producers to send the royalties and advances to Morgan's office. Now that he'd broken from them, Jack, with a single stroke of a pen, could divert the stream of money to himself.

'He's going to have problems when he tries to write the book. I've seen his writing,' said Abby.

'For a quarter of million he can find somebody to ghost it. That leaves him with four or five million and change,' said Morgan. 'Not bad for a day's work. And right now he's got the only commodity that counts.'

Abby looked at him, a question mark.

'The name you gave him, Gable Cooper,' said Morgan. He was right. Bertoli's ad campaign had turned it into gold.

'I wanted a commercial book. I guess I got it,' said Abby.

'The question is how to keep it. If he cuts off our stream of cash, starts getting his hands on the advances and royalties, he'll be using your money to fight you in court. Where do you think Bertoli will come down if Jack gets his own army of lawyers?'

'I don't know,' said Abby.

'I don't want to find out,' said Morgan. 'We got to move fast. Oh, shit I forgot!'

When she looked over, Morgan was looking at the ceiling.

'What's the matter?'

'I'm supposed to meet with the client in San Juan tomorrow. The maritime case I told Cutler about.' He made a face at Abby, a lot of consternation.

'Break the appointment,' said Abby.

'Don't worry. I'll find some way to get out of it,' said Morgan.

He headed for the kitchen and the telephone. Morgan called the airlines, looking for reservations while Abby packed a bag, and boxed up the computer and the printer. Fortunately she'd kept the boxes she'd bought them in.

When she came into the kitchen Morgan had his hand over the mouthpiece of the phone and a dour look on his face. Things were not going well.

'Next flight doesn't leave until seven tonight.'

'Book it,' said Abby.

'Problem is they've only one seat available.'

Abby thought for a moment. 'You take it. You've got to get to Seattle and then back. I can catch a flight in the morning and go directly to New York. We can meet there. Is there anything open on the morning flights?'

Morgan went back on the line.

'They've got open seats tomorrow. Early morning flight.'

'No problem,' said Abby.

Morgan hesitated. 'I don't like it.'

'Why not?'

'What if Jack comes back?'

'Why would he come back?' Abby shook her head. 'By tonight he'll be having dinner with Carla and Bertoli. They'll be working changes into my outline and suggesting casting for the film. He's not coming back.'

'I don't know,' said Morgan. 'I don't feel comfortable.'

'What choice do we have?'

Morgan had no answer for that. He got back on the phone and ordered the tickets using his credit card, then hung up.

'We can pick them up at the airport tonight. Deliver the computer and printer for shipping at the same time.'

'I wish I knew where Charlie was,' said Abby.

'Yeah. Then we'd have your car.'

'Not that,' said Abby. 'I just don't want to leave him here alone. I know he doesn't deserve it, but I'd like to give him a heads-up. Tell him to get off the island.' While she was telling Morgan that Jack wouldn't be back, Abby was worried. She remembered Joey. He knew very little about the book, but if Morgan was right, he was killed because of that knowledge. Charlie was in danger and he didn't know it. She remembered Jack's comments about reasoning with him and the fight in San Juan. True, it may have been self-defense, but Jack thought nothing about leaving a bleeding body in the street.

'Leave a message for him at the Buccaneer,' said Morgan. 'Something discreet. Tell him to get back to Seattle. Tell him there's a pile of money waiting there for him. He'll know what to do.'

They spent the rest of the morning and the afternoon planning their moves in New York. Spencer called and left a message on voice mail with the lawyers in New York, telling them that things were now on a fast track and that a meeting was necessary Tuesday. Then he made reservations for two rooms at the Hilton in Manhattan for Monday night. Morgan, if he was on time, would come in Monday afternoon. He checked the flights between Seattle and New York and made another set of reservations. He would be flying through the night.

About six o'clock Abby called the cab while Morgan made a note with the law firm's name and address on it and taped it to the outside of the boxes with the computer and printer inside.

Ten minutes later they were on their way to the airport. Morgan gave the driver twenty bucks to forget all the speed limits. They raced through Christiansted and out toward the north end of the island. They headed west and got to the airport with only a few minutes to spare.

Morgan got the tickets at the counter, separated them, and handed Abby hers.

'I don't like this at all,' he told her. Morgan didn't want to get on the plane without her.

'There's nothing to worry about. He's in New York. I'll be out of here first thing in the morning.' She checked her ticket. 'Seven-fifteen sharp,' she told him.

'Transfer in San Juan, then to Miami, hold over for an hour and to JFK.' He repeated her itinerary as if it wasn't on the tickets.

'Now listen to me.' Morgan had a stern look on his face, all business. 'After I leave, take the package to air express and as soon as you're finished, go back to the house, go inside, and lock the doors. Don't let anybody in. Catch a cab in the morning and come right back here. No other stops, do you understand?'

She nodded dutifully and gave him a mock salute.

'I'm not kidding.'

'I know. I'll be fine.'

'I'll call you tonight, from San Juan.' He looked at his watch. 'I should be there in about an hour and a half. Stay by the phone.'

'I will.'

'Then I'll see you in New York Monday night.' He paused. 'When I asked you to come away with me, this isn't exactly what I had in mind.'

Abby smiled. 'I know. I have no right to ask this of you.'

'You didn't. I offered. Friends, remember?'

He kissed her on the forehead, then the cheek, then disappeared through the gate.

Abby went back to the taxi and told the driver to take her to air freight. There was a line, and by the time she finished, it had taken almost forty minutes to process the packages, and more than a hundred dollars to send them. She put it on her debit card.

On the drive back in the taxi she actually fell asleep so that the motion of the car stopping in front of her house woke her. When Abby opened her eyes the driver was waiting with his hand over the front seat for the fare. She collected herself, looked at the meter, then fished in her purse and came up with the money.

The cab drove away and left her standing out on Shoy Beach Road. She turned and started down the dirt driveway. It wasn't until she was halfway down that she saw it. The little blue BMW with its top down was parked in the carport next to the house. Charlie was back. At least she wouldn't be alone. She moved quickly down the driveway to the house. The front door was unlocked. She thought Morgan had locked it, but she couldn't remember.

'Charlie.' She called his name. There was no answer.

She checked the kitchen, then walked through the hall to the bedrooms. He wasn't there. She opened the sliding glass door and looked out on the beach. It was getting dark and the sand was deserted. Stars had begun to emerge in the night sky. A fingernail moon was riding a ridge of clouds on the horizon.

Abby closed the sliding door and locked it, then looked at the clock on the wall in the kitchen. Morgan's plane would be approaching San Juan. He would be calling in half an hour.

'Charlie. Don't play games with me.' Her tone was now that of a mother giving a final warning to a child. She had visions of Charlie drunk, hiding in the house, getting ready to jump her bones as she got ready for bed. It was the kind of thing Charlie would do, especially with a few drinks under his belt. Tonight he would get all he was looking for. Abby was already on edge.

His fingers moved deftly to sever the line at one of the fittings. He used two adjustable wrenches, one to hold the pipe and the other to turn the fitting. He covered both on the inside with cloth to dampen any noise and avoid scratches on the fitting. Scratches on an old pipe might be something investigators would key on.

He loosened the pressure fitting until he heard the hiss of gas. It would look better that way, something that worked its way loose. It would also give him more time to finish the job before the air in the crawl space became unbreathable.

He made his way to another junction in the line. This one led to the kitchen and up through the floor to the propane stove.

He had already smothered the pilot light for the furnace and disconnected the electronic ignition for the stove. He didn't want any unintentional accidents.

There was an open chase four feet away that led from the crawl space under the floor along an outside wall to the attic above. This was used as a passage for plumbing and electrical lines.

He fed a plastic tube he'd brought with him up into the chase measuring off twelve feet. The polyurethane tube would begin to melt at three hundred degrees. It would vaporize at the temperatures ignited by a large propane fire. They would find none of it when it was over. He opened the other fitting, and using duct tape fastened the open end of the tube to the leak in the line. It wasn't a hundred percent efficient, but it would work. Gas began to move through the tube into the attic where it would lie like a deadly fog until it was time.

A bby checked the two bathrooms. There was no sign of Charlie. Finally she went outside to the carport. The keys to her car were in the ignition. They were still on the ring with a little piece of red ribbon around it, just as they had been when Jack took them out of the envelope at the front desk of the Buccaneer the day they arrived. So much had happened since then. It seemed like another lifetime.

She removed the keys from the ignition and put them in her pocket. Abby looked around to see if maybe Charlie had taken a walk, perhaps to have a cigarette outside, but there was no sign of him.

Maybe he'd gone back to the Buccaneer. Knowing Charlie, that was it. To get a drink or carouse on the dance floor until they closed up. Half of her wanted him to stay there, to work off his horny attitude on somebody else. Half of her wanted him to come back to the house, if for no other reason than to give her someone to talk to.

Still her mind kept picking at something that didn't fit. If he wasn't here, what was the BMW doing in the carport? Maybe Charlie'd had a sudden pang of conscience? She thought about it. Not Charlie.

Abby went back inside and remembered Morgan's advice. She locked the front door and put the chain on. Then she went around the house and checked all the doors and windows. She felt paranoid, but she did it anyway.

Trade winds and open windows were the only air-conditioning the house had. The night was warm and muggy, and within a few minutes the house began to feel uncomfortable. Abby felt dizzy. She didn't know why. The accumulation of the day's heat trapped in the attic was now finding its way out down through the ceiling. There was a cool breeze outside on the beach. But tonight Abby would have to try to sleep with the windows closed.

She stepped into the bathroom, dropped her clothes on the floor, and climbed into the shower. She allowed cool water to run over her body for ten minutes, keeping track of the time on her waterproof sports watch. She didn't want to miss Morgan's call. If she failed to answer, he would panic and think something had gone wrong. He would be back on the next flight. Abby knew Spencer.

With five minutes to spare before his plane was scheduled to land in San Juan she turned off the water, toweled herself dry, and threw on a robe. She continued to towel her hair and grabbed a diet Coke from the refrigerator. Then she picked up around the house. The place was a mess. Abby had no idea when or if she would be back. She thought about arrangements to have the car shipped to Seattle and how much it might cost. She hoped Charlie had enjoyed it. Between Charlie and Jack she had only been behind the wheel twice. Men were such pricks.

It would take only a slight spark, the completed synapse of an electrical circuit to ignite the gas. He pulled himself through the small hole at the side of the house and out from under the crawl space, then took his first deep breath in several minutes.

Quickly he moved to the little metal box nailed to the siding. He lifted the cover and attached two fine lead wires to the copper terminals inside, then looked at the wire going from the box along the side of the house. It joined the power lines at the corner near the front and from there disappeared into a plastic conduit for the journey underground.

In the islands burying utility lines was the least of two bad options. Hurricanes blew down power poles and surge tides flooded underground lines.

He wired one of the fine lead wires to the end of a small spark plug and wrapped the other around the metal tip near the gap. Then he tossed the spark plug as far as he could through the hole into the crawl space.

He sniffed the fumes of gas that were now surging under the house. With every cycle a new spark would bridge the gap in the plug. He couldn't imagine that it would take more than one or two.

Abby had laid her airline tickets on the kitchen table when she entered the house, and now she picked them up to place them in her briefcase so she wouldn't forget them.

It was getting too hot. Advice or no advice, she needed some air. She opened the sliding door and stood there facing the ocean. Cool currents washed over her, blowing open the folds of her robe and bracing her naked body in the crisp salt air of the sea.

She drank her Coke and remembered the first nights on the island when ignorance was bliss, before she knew about Jack and all of his lies. Thoughts flooded her mind, all the things she had to do before morning. She remembered her manuscript, the hard copy of which was printed and piled on her work table in the bedroom. Without her computer she was out of business, at least until she got to New York.

She took another sip of Coke and looked down at the tickets in her other hand and suddenly, as if the drink had done something for the mental synapse of her brain, it hit her like a lead weight. Her passport! Abby didn't have it. It was locked in the ElSafe in Jack's room at the Buccaneer. She had forgotten about it. Where was her mind? Without it she couldn't get off the island.

She headed for the bedroom. A cold sweat broke out on her forehead. Somewhere she had a key to Jack's room, one of those plastic coded cards with holes drilled in them. But where was it? Abby hadn't used it in weeks. She couldn't remember the combination for the safe. Jack had asked her for her birth date that day she put the passport and the second debit card in the safe, and Abby had lied. She couldn't remember what she'd told him, the year. What if he'd changed the combination, or destroyed the passport? She would be trapped on the island with no way off, not before filling out a flood of forms and the bureaucracy. A million worries flooded her brain.

She headed down the hall to the bedroom. The first

thing she needed was clothes. She opened the closet and as she did, something caught her eye in the corner of the room. It was a jacket, one she had seen before, Charlie's jacket. When Abby turned her head to look for her slacks her heart nearly stopped.

'Oh shit!' It was fright on the edge of pain, like ice in her veins.

'Damn it. Jesus, Charlie.' She turned and walked away. She was gasping for air, deep breathing and feeling dizzy.

'The next you do something like this so help me!' She felt her pulse pounding in her chest. Her hand, still clutching the airline tickets, was in the opening of her robe above her breast. For a moment she thought she was actually going to pass out.

'Damn you, Charlie.' She struggled to catch her breath. She was doubled over, one hand on her knee. Charlie wasn't saying a word.

'If you ever . . .' It took a couple of seconds for her pulse to steady, and then anger started to take hold. She stood up straight, stretched the muscles of her rib cage, and took a deep breath. As she did this, Abby stared directly into the mirror over the dresser drawers.

Charlie was still in the shadows of the closet. He hadn't moved. He was wearing some artsy tie-die shirt, white with a brown-red blaze from shoulder to waist. No doubt some hot threads for the clubs, she thought.

She looked in the glass without turning around and suddenly realized that Charlie seemed to have legs of rubber. His knees were splayed akimbo like some puppet, his shoes lost in the hanging garments at the rear of her closet. It was a posture that defied gravity.

His expression was of the queerest smile, and when Abby turned she saw the reason. The black wire of a coat hanger was coiled around his neck and wound over the clothes rod that held up his body. The rust-colored hue of Charlie's shirt took on new meaning.

Abby's hands went to her mouth, but the scream never came out. She ran headlong down the hall. Two strides and a piercing screech that she hardly recognized as her own echoed off the walls. Like water finding the course of least resistance, she erupted into the living room and saw only one thing – the open sliding door to the deck. In an instant she was though it into the darkness beyond, bare feet over rocks and marsh grass, not feeling the broken conch shells like knives cutting her flesh.

She was twenty feet from the house, breathless, and frantic, out of her mind when she heard it. The ringing of a telephone somewhere in the distance behind her. It stopped her dead in her tracks like she'd been hit by a bullet from a rifle. Morgan! He was calling. She turned and took one step back.

The next chime of the phone was seared in her mind by the heat of the blast. It lifted her off of her feet, and toasted the front of her body as the concussion of the shock wave threw her ten feet onto her back in the sand. It was like a surreal dream. The fiery mushroom jumped a hundred feet into the night sky, its brilliant orange and yellow flare obliterating the stars. The roof of the house actually lifted skyward and buckled in mid-air. An instant later it disintegrated into a million flaming pieces.

Abby scrambled to her feet and ran, then dove for the sand as burning embers and fiery shards of wood descended around her. There was a secondary blast and the remains of a water heater bounced with a dull thud on the ground twenty feet from where she lay. One hand went to her face and she felt the warmth of blood. A tiny piece of glass was embedded in her cheek just below her right eye. She plucked it out and lay there dazed. A corner of her robe was on fire, still burning. She finally gathered enough sense to sit, and managed to pound out the flames on her clothing in the sand.

Then she crawled toward the beach under the shelter of a young tamarind tree. She pulled the robe tight around her naked body and looked back toward the house. The walls and roof were gone. All that remained were the flaming innards fueled by the night air, and flickering embers on the dark ground like stars as far as she could see.

In the glow of the burning house a solitary figure was silhouetted on a bluff above the house near the road. For an instant, Abby started to get up to run toward it. Then she froze, trained her eyes to the night sky, took a closer look and realized – it was Jack.

CHAPTER
THIRTY-FOUR

Abby was naked except for the short terrycloth robe. Everything she owned on the island was now either cinders or burning. The remnants of the small sports car, its fuel tank blazing, was a burned-out hulk in the carport.

On the hill, silhouetted in the headlights of a vehicle, Jack stood looking at the devastation. At this moment the only advantage that Abby possessed was the fact that he thought she was dead.

She lay huddled in the darkness under the tamarind tree, waves crashing on the beach behind her. The white water lapping at the shore took on a fluorescent quality in the dark crescent shape of the cove. It was a rising tide and the foam washed up on the sand just a few yards from her feet. In the distance, she could see the indistinct outline of dark cliffs at the point near the Buccaneer. Abby could hear the loud music from the bar, but the building was around the point. There was no way they could have seen the blast. It was more of a whoosh than an explosion. She doubted if they heard it.

She had no money, no clothes. Her purse with the debit card now lay in the burning ashes of the house.

Jack had been thorough. His only mistake was one of timing. Charlie had saved her life. The last act of a dead man.

She wondered if Jack had used some kind of a clock or watch to set it off, or if he had detonated the explosion by remote control. This sent a shudder through Abby. The flash that singed her body seemed to come from the back side of the house toward the beach. She guessed he had wired the large propane tank near the kitchen. There was nothing left to indicate that the tank even existed. The police would think it was an accident.

When she looked back at the bluff, Jack was gone. She sank further into the shadows, wondering if he'd left, or was he searching? Maybe he had seen her running from the house. She looked for a path of escape. The only way out was the beach behind her.

She heard footsteps in the grass. Abby pressed herself against the trunk of the tree. When she peered between two branches he was standing less than fifty feet away. He had one arm extended out in front of his face to ward off the heat. Still, Abby could see every crease and shadow, the face that launched a million books. He edged around the flaming ruins closer to where she was hiding, then stepped on something. He looked down, stooped, and picked it up.

Abby couldn't tell what it was.

She looked at the road. Someone had to see or hear the blast. Even so it would take time before the authorities responded. They were miles from Christiansted and the nearest fire station. There was no one staying in the large estate house at the end of the road, and the other small houses were vacation spots mostly empty this time of year. The Buccaneer might send security, but by then, if Jack found her, it would be too late. For all intents the house on Shoy Beach Road was the perfect place for an accident, and Jack had picked it.

He turned and looked toward the water. Abby clung to the base of the tree, motionless and perspiring. He was holding something in his hand, a piece of singed paper that he'd picked up. He looked alternately between this and the beach. Suddenly Abby realized, it was the folder with her airline tickets. She had been holding them in her hand when she found Charlie's body. With the shock of the explosion, the blast that threw her to the ground, she'd dropped them.

Like radar, Jack's eyes scanned the distance to the beach, looking first in one direction and then the other. He looked back at the flames as if he couldn't quite piece it together.

It was Abby's last chance. Any second he would come up with a theory and start looking for footprints in the sand.

She slid down the incline to the water. The robe was now soaked as well as singed. She stripped it from her body, balled it up, and carried it under one arm so that Jack wouldn't pick up on the white terrycloth against the dark water and the night sky. She ran through knee-deep water and thanked God for the clouds that covered the moon.

The surf washed away her footprints, and the sound of the waves swallowed the noise from the patter of her feet. She ran more than a hundred yards down the beach, then darted up toward the marsh grass still carrying the robe under one arm. Abby huddled behind a bush long enough to don the robe and catch her breath. She was still stunned. It all seemed like a nightmare, as if at any moment she would rouse herself from

471

a fitful sleep. But the pain, the cuts on her face and feet, and the blood on her cheek were real. She would not wake up from this dream and she knew it.

She climbed up onto the bank above the beach and looked back toward the burning house. She could see Jack's car still parked with its headlights on. She ran across the broad expanse of grass toward the road. There was a small vacation house set back on its own driveway, deserted and locked. Abby huddled near the deck at the back of the house behind a lattice grille work with a gate in it. The lattice concealed a storage area under the deck. She opened it and slipped inside. She hid there in the darkness for several minutes, listening for sounds, trying to catch her breath and stop her heart from pounding.

The space under the deck was cluttered with cast-off lawn furniture, and children's toys, and infested with spider webs. Abby hated spiders.

There were rubber rafts and paddles, and a small canoe. Inside the canoe she found a pair of water shoes. She shook these out to make sure there was nothing making a home inside. They weren't much. Abby managed to stretch them onto her feet. It was better than being barefoot.

Suddenly she heard sirens off in the distance, slow, lumbering, more than one. Fire trucks. Someone had called it in.

She crawled out from under the deck and ran as fast as her feet would carry her. It was a long way to the road, and it took her more than two minutes to get there, dodging around boulders and bushes, scrambling up a steep incline.

The first engine came barreling over a rise and nearly ran over her. She waved but on the dark dusty road they never saw her. Another pumper truck followed. Abby was left choking in its dust.

She started to run after them, then realized there were lights coming on behind her. She turned, this time in the center of the road, and waved one arm while the other held the bathrobe closed around her body.

It was a police cruiser, a white sedan with a light bar flashing red and blue overhead and siren screaming. It came to a screeching stop and the driver tried to wave her out of the way. Abby refused to move, and instead launched herself at the hood of the vehicle, and then stepped around to the driver's window.

He didn't look much like a cop. He was heavy-set and wore a faded black T-shirt soiled by sweat and a pair of black chinos. Around his chest was a black nylon shoulder holster with a chrome revolver the size of a bazooka.

'What's you doin', lady? You gonna git yourself killed. Get the hell outta da road.' He waved at her like some angry midwife.

Abby stammered for words, then finally found them. 'Someone's trying to kill me. Please help me.'

'What you been drinkin', lady?'

'Listen to me. Someone fire-bombed my house.'

For the first time the driver looked at her as if she might be telling the truth.

Abby couldn't see the man in the passenger seat, but he appeared to be better dressed, a sport coat and slacks. The passenger door opened and the other man got out. He was a tall, slender African American, and he seemed to take a close look at Abby over the top of the vehicle when he stood.

'What's your name?' he asked her.

She had soot on her face and dried blood under one eye. Her hair was a tangled web of wet ringlets.

Abby didn't answer him. It was the look in his eye that troubled her, as if the cop recognized her.

Sergeant Logano reached for a flashlight in the car and shined it in Abby's eyes.

She shied away and held up a hand.

He reached back inside the vehicle and opened a large folder that lay on the seat next to the driver. As he did, a four-by-five photograph of Abby spilled out of the folder onto the floor of the car. In that instant, their eyes met over the top of the vehicle and Logano blinked.

Another pumper truck pulled up behind the squad car and Logano told his driver to pull over to the side of the road so that the fire truck could get by. For a fleeting instant he reverted to traffic cop directing the truck around the car on the narrow road. The car pulled over, the truck roared through, and when Logano looked back, Abby was gone.

She had no idea why the police would have her photograph, but she wasn't waiting to find out. If they had her picture, it was for a reason. The police would never buy her story. She had no evidence that Jack blew up the house. It was her word against his, and there was a dead man in her closet.

In the passing dust and confusion of the truck, Abby lost herself in the brush and shadows at the side of the road. Then quickly she retreated from the road, putting distance between herself and the squad car. She could see the two cops with flashlights beating the brush and hear their voices. She listened to them talking for sometime until the tall one in the sport coat pitched it in.

'Nevermind. She can't get far. Dressed like that she stands out like a sore thumb. Put out an APB. If we don't get her tonight they'll pick her up in the morning.' They got back in the car and drove toward the ebbing glow that had been Abby's house.

She watched as the taillights disappeared over a rise and then she moved, parallel to the road, as fast as she could. It took her several minutes to make it to the security gate at the Buccaneer. There were two men talking downstairs inside the stone tower.

Abby watched for some time and a third man joined them, part of the maintenance crew. They were gossiping about all the excitement, loud voices and animated gestures.

Abby shielded herself behind a couple of small utility vehicles on her side of the road and headed up the hill toward the main building. She didn't go inside but stayed on the road, passed the parking lot at the rear and the second-story veranda where the bar and restaurant were located.

With all of the excitement, explosions and sirens, the band at the bar hadn't missed a beat. She could hear the crowd clapping their hands and shouting to the hypnotic beat of steel drums and guitars.

Abby hustled down the road toward the sea and the bungalows on the beach. She kept a wary eye on the road, any sign of Jack returning, but it was dark, and except for the music on the knoll she was alone.

Toward the bottom of the hill was a paved parking lot with spaces marked in front of the rooms. Most of the rooms were dark. Abby knew some of these were vacant. Other tenants, she figured, were either out partying or asleep.

Jack's room was the second from the end near the beach. She had no idea how she was going to get inside. All the room doors locked automatically and used punched card keys. She had one of Jack's keys, but by now it was melted plastic in the ashes of her purse.

There was a small building across the parking lot from the bungalow set into the side of the hill and lights were on inside. It was some kind of a utility building. Abby had seen maids coming and going from this the day she and Jack checked in. A door was open on the side of the building and a light was on inside. She made her way to it and looked in.

There was a woman ironing what looked like uniforms. A large industrial dryer was tumbling sheets and pillow cases. The woman was listening to her own music being pumped into her ears by a headset from a CD player strapped to her waist. She had her back to Abby, who could have fired a cannon and not been heard.

Against the wall just inside the door were a set of lockers, maybe a dozen in all. These each had padlocks on them, except for one that was open. Abby watched from the open door as the woman finished ironing one of the uniforms, placed it on a hanger, and hung it on a bar against the far wall with others. She returned to the ironing board, took another from a hamper, and started again.

Abby looked down at her terrycloth robe. It was burned and had blood on it in two places. By daylight she would be a walking neon sign saying 'Arrest Me.' She had to find something to wear. She looked at the open locker, and the woman ironing, her rear end gyrating to the rhythm of the music in her ears.

Abby slipped through the door, across the concrete floor to the open locker. Inside were two maid's uniforms, a pair of jeans, and a top. The jeans and top were too small. The pants would have been four inches too short. She grabbed one of the uniform dresses. It should have been mid-calf but went almost to her knees. She took it anyway. There were no shoes.

Abby looked back at the woman. She was wearing white running shoes. They wouldn't have fit Abby in any event. She was stuck with the swimming shoes. The woman finished ironing half of the uniform and flipped it over on the board.

Abby saw a purse on the shelf of the locker. She grabbed it and looked inside. There was a wallet with two dollars in cash, some cigarettes and keys. She didn't want to do it, but she took the money. If nothing else she could get change and make a collect call to Morgan. She was putting the purse back when she saw it, a card key, probably a master for maid service. It was sitting on the shelf under where the purse had been. She grabbed it and put it in the pocket of her robe, then moved quickly across the room and out the door.

In the shadows outside she changed, took the key from the pocket, and threw the robe in a trashbin. She still had no underwear, but the dress would draw less attention than the burned and bloodied robe.

Now she moved quickly across the parking lot to Jack's room. The outside light was on over the door, but the bathroom window was dark, and there was no car parked in front. She took a chance, held her breath, and used the key. She was inside in a matter of seconds, closed the door behind her, and stood quietly in the darkness. She listened for any sounds but could hear only the clicking of the clock, its luminous dial visible on the dresser drawer in the bedroom.

The room was empty, but Jack's suitcase, still packed from his trip, lay at the foot of the bed. She hesitated to turn on a light, but she needed to see. She flipped on the lamp at the bedside table and quickly moved to the hall that separated the bathroom from the sleeping area.

Here there was a closet with louvered folding doors. She opened one side. The ElSafe was mounted on a wooden platform on the floor.

Abby kneeled down on the floor and tried to remember the combination. Jack had asked her for her birth date and she had lied to him. But she couldn't remember what year she'd used. It was part of the combination he had punched in. She prayed that he hadn't changed it. She did trial and error on the safe, punching in the month and day and then trying several different years. Finally she heard the hum of the motor and saw the word 'Open' in red letters appear in the window on the door. She pulled the latch with her fingers and it opened.

There were a number of items inside, envelopes and papers, a set of car keys that must have belonged to Jack. Then she saw it in the back. The dark blue cover of a passport. She picked it up and opened it. It was Jack's. She dropped it on the floor and frantically tore through the safe. Under a stack of papers on the bottom Abby saw another blue cover. She opened it and her pulse quickened. Inside was Abby's picture. She breathed a sigh of relief. She picked up Jack's off the floor and dropped them both into the large patch pocket of the uniform dress. Jack would have trouble following her off the island without a passport.

There was some loose cash inside. She grabbed it and counted: one hundred and seventeen dollars. This joined the passports in her pocket. Then she found the second debit card with her name on it. She took that too, then closed the safe door and pushed the lock button. The motor hummed again.

Abby went into the bathroom but didn't turn on the light. This would been seen from the parking lot outside.

She washed the soot and blood off of her hands and face, found a brush on the sink and brushed her hair so that she at least looked human again.

Then she went back to the closet. She opened the other side and surveyed the hanging clothes for anything she might use. Jack's pants and shirts were all far too big. She was better off in the maid's dress. She would use the automatic teller machine in Christiansted for cash as soon as she got there, and in the morning she would hit one of the many shops in town for the clothes she needed. Then somehow she would get off the island as quickly as she could.

On a hook in the corner of the closet she saw the blue fanny pack, the one Jack used to carry the pistol. The flap was unzipped. She lifted it. The pack was empty. The gun was gone.

She went back out into the sleeping area to the dresser and rummaged through the drawers. There was nothing she could use. She found a white pair of sports socks and wondered if she could fit them on under the swim shoes. She dropped them into her pocket.

She had just finished and was closing the drawer when she heard tires moving slowly on the gravel out front and saw the glare of headlights as they streamed through the window of the bathroom. Abby dove for the light on the night stand and turned it off just as she heard the motor die and the *thunk* of a car door being closed out front. An instant later there was the sound of a card key slipping into the lock of the door.

Abby dashed across the room in the dark toward the patio door, but it was too late. A shaft of light penetrated the room from outside and Jack came through the door.

Abby darted back, to the other side of the bed, scrambling on her hands and knees and lay on the floor. She lifted the bed covers. The mattress was on a platform. There was no place to hide underneath.

She lay stone still.

He came in and turned on the light next to the bed, then slumped onto the edge of the mattress. The springs groaned and Abby nearly screamed. She could hear his breathing, things being emptied from his pockets onto the nightstand on the other side. She prayed he would take a shower, comb his hair, anything to give her two seconds to get to the patio door.

He flipped a shoe onto the other side of the bed and it almost hit her. She held her breath for fear that he might try to retrieve it. He didn't. The other one followed, and then his socks.

He got up off the bed and she could hear the bottoms of his feet making suction on the tile floor as he walked to the bathroom.

Abby got up and dashed to the door. There was a simple turn-key lock under the handle. She turned it gently to avoid making any sound, then looked back toward the bathroom.

It was then that she saw it. On the floor behind her was one of the passports. It must have slipped from her pocket when she was crawling across the floor.

Suddenly she heard the flush of the toilet, Jack coming back. She looked at the passport, and the shaft of light from the bathroom door, Jack's shadow on the wall as he approached down the short hall.

Abby took the only option open. She stepped out onto the dark patio and eased the door closed. It was still moving when Jack turned the corner, but he didn't see it. She could see him moving in the bedroom ten feet away and prayed he wouldn't see the passport on the floor.

The urge to run was overwhelming, but she kept her head and checked the pocket of her dress, opened the single passport that remained and saw Jack's picture. There was nothing she could do. She was trapped on the patio. She would run if he found it. Otherwise she would have to wait and hope that he would go back in the bathroom or leave. It was her only ticket off the island.

Fortunately the passport was out of Jack's line of sight, around the corner of the bed. If he went there he would step on it, but there was no reason to go.

He picked up the phone and dialed. She heard him talk to the overseas operator, then wait on the line. He sat on the edge of the bed. He looked tired and worn. Killing people must be hard work, thought Abby. She couldn't see a spot of blood on his clothes. He must have showered and changed after slaughtering Charlie. If she had his pistol, Abby thought she could have shot him at this moment as he sat on the bed.

'Jess. Jack here. Listen, I need your help.' Jack stood, turned his back, and lowered his voice. Abby couldn't hear what he was saying now. They talked for several moments and all she could pick up was the hum of Jack's voice without the words. Then he turned toward her.

'No, I think she's still alive. I can't be sure. I'm looking.'

He listened while Jess said something on the other end.

'No. No. Don't give me any crap. I gotta nail Spencer. First I gotta find him. And I need help to find her before she gets off the island.'

Jess said something.

'Get out of it. I don't care what you do, but get down here.'

Jess was now doing all the listening. 'I'll call and have a ticket waiting for you at the airport, at LAX. I'll try for a flight tonight.' It was four hours earlier out on the coast.

Jess was arguing. He was probably getting ready to hump some starlet.

'Sleep on the goddamned plane,' said Jack. 'You gotta hit the ground running when you get here.'

Jess said something.

'Good. Listen, I owe you. See you in the morning.' Jack hung up. He wandered aimlessly in the room for a moment as if he was thinking. Then he glanced down at his suitcase still unopened on the floor at the foot of the bed.

Abby looked at the passport. Jack would see it if he grabbed the suitcase. In a moment she would run. Her heart was pounding. They were planning to kill Spencer. If she couldn't get off the island, she could at least call and warn him.

Halfway to the suitcase, Jack stopped as if he remembered something, thought for a second, turned, and headed for the bathroom. Like that he was gone. She could still see the shaft of light. The door to the bathroom was open, but she had to take the chance.

Quickly she slipped back in through the patio door, four steps across the room. Abby picked up the passport, turned, and in an instant was gone.

The door to Jack's room clicked shut as it closed. He heard it and stepped out of the bathroom. Instantly he knew what it was. He ran to the patio, threw open the door. There was no one there. He looked at the two-foot stone wall leading to the patio next door and the sea of bushes beyond.

CHAPTER
THIRTY-FIVE

The only thing she possessed of her own was the watch on her wrist. Abby had worn it into the shower before finding Charlie's body. She looked at it nervously several times as she sat in the back of the cab and wondered how she was going to get off the island and how long it would take.

Jack had her ticket for the morning flight. He would be watching the airport as would the police if they were looking for her.

It was a ten-minute drive to Christiansted. She told the driver to let her out near the shopping district at Gallows Bay and paid him with some of the cash taken from the safe in Jack's room. After seeing her on the road, the cops would question every cab driver who was anywhere near the Buccaneer. This way the driver wouldn't know where she went.

She walked the distance into town. It took her almost a half-hour. There she rented a room in a small hotel near King's Wharf. The clerk looked at her strangely, swim shoes and a wrinkled maid's uniform. But he took her money and didn't ask any questions.

She went up to the room and immediately made a

long-distance call to Morgan's house in Seattle. She knew he wouldn't be there, not yet anyway, but she left a message on his answering machine. She tried to mask the panic in her voice. There was nothing Morgan could do from Seattle, but she wanted to warn him. Jack and now Jess were after him. Morgan had suspicions, but he had no idea of the danger he was in.

It was nearly three in the morning by the time she peeled off the swim shoes, set the alarm, and collapsed on the bed. She didn't bother to take off the dress. She thought she would sleep immediately, but she didn't. Instead her mind turned over with thoughts of Theresa and Jack. The man she loved had murdered her best friend. The man who she thought loved her had just tried to end her life. She hugged a pillow to her chest, wrapped her arms around it, and began to sob. She cried herself to sleep.

It was light streaming through the window and not the alarm that woke her three hours later. Abby rolled over and rubbed her eyes, got up and looked out the window. Her mouth had a taste like she'd swallowed a rhinoceros. And she was hungry.

A few merchants were stirring on the wharf. Trucks were parked in the lot next to the hotel, their drivers already making the rounds delivering goods and groceries to the shops and restaurants that honeycombed the area around the docks.

In a few hours the place would be teeming with tourists, the first flood of the day from the cruise ships, and Abby would lose herself in the crowd.

She took a shower, tried to fix her hair as best she could, and slipped down the back stairs of the hotel so that she wouldn't be seen in the lobby. She was glad of one thing. When the police questioned her on the road, she was still wearing the soiled terrycloth robe. This would likely be included in any description of her. They wouldn't be looking for a maid's uniform, not for a few hours anyway, and once they figured it out, the dress, too, would be in a trash bin in Christiansted.

She scurried four blocks through alleys, staying close to buildings and watching out for the police. In five minutes she made her way to one of the banks on King Street and used the debit card to withdraw a thousand dollars in cash, all in twenty-dollar bills. She folded it and put it in her pocket, then crossed the street. She ordered coffee and a pastry from a small vendor and disappeared like a mouse under one of the trees in the public market a few blocks away. The market was only open on Saturdays so the stalls were all empty. Dressed as she was in the maid's uniform, Abby blended in with the few locals who wandered through the area on their way to work.

She killed an hour while she continued to watch the streets at the south end of town. Slowly they started to fill with shoppers. The covered veranda of the sidewalks started to crowd up, and people began to jostle for position in the doors of the shops.

Abby joined the human tide. First she went to Java Wraps. She bought underwear, two pairs of slacks, a pair of boat shoes and four tops, a light jacket, and a canvas bag to put it all in. On a coat-tree display she found a large straw hat with a broad brim and a polka-dot red ribbon for a band. She paid cash for everything. This way she didn't have to sign her name using the debit card. If the police questioned the clerks, at least they wouldn't have a name they could check.

Next she hit one of the perfume shops where she purchased makeup, a brush for her hair, and other toiletries. She walked two blocks through the crowded streets to Little Switzerland, where she found a pair of designer sunglasses.

Abby disappeared into a ladies' room in the lobby of one of the hotels near the wharf and by the time she emerged half an hour later, she looked as if she'd walked off the pages of a woman's fashion magazine.

Her hair was pulled back and piled on top of her head underneath the straw hat set off by its broad red-ribboned band. The white slacks were well creased and the blue sleeveless top was casual and cool.

The white boating shoes made it look as if she was headed for her yacht anchored off shore. Over her arm was the stylish canvas bag with her other purchases, the debit card, all the cash that was left, and the passports. She would dump Jack's in a trashcan once she got off the island and let him think up some stories to tell Immigration. She looked the part of the rich tourist. The only panic was in her eyes, and these were hidden behind the large oval dark glasses.

She melded with the tourists in King's Alley and went into one of the open-air restaurants, where she ordered a Long Island iced tea and took a table. It was a place where she could sit, collect her thoughts, and survey her options.

In the hotel lobby Abby had grabbed some tourist literature, folders on charter boat rentals and private air excursions. She looked through these trying to figure if any of them might get her to San Juan. Most of them only ventured as far as a few of the smaller off-shore islands.

One of the brochures caught her eye. It featured a sleek twin engine float plane, the Seaborne Vista Liner. It was the one Morgan had taken to get to St Croix from

St Thomas. She wondered if the police would be looking for her there. It all depended how wide they had thrown their net, how badly they wanted her. On that score Abby didn't have a clue, though with the discovery of Charlie's burned body in her closet their interest would no doubt be heightened.

She couldn't go to the airport. They were sure to be laying for her there. A small charter boat would take days to get to San Juan and by then they would be waiting at the docks. She had to move quickly. Abby figured at most she had a brief window of opportunity, a few hours, before the cops got their act together, or worse, Jack found her. In three or four hours the tour ships would pull out, leaving Abby alone on the streets of Christiansted looking like Audrey Hepburn in *Breakfast at Tiffany's*.

She sipped the last of her tea and merged with the sea of bodies on the street again.

Tickets for the float plane to Charlotte Amalie on St Thomas were sold through the window of a little building on the dock. The next flight departed just before one in the afternoon. There were a few seats open. She checked her watch, a little over an hour. Abby didn't like it, but she had no choice. She bought a single one-way ticket, then she headed for a payphone that she'd staked out earlier in the lobby of one of the hotels. It was one of those English telephone booths you might see in pictures of London, red with a door and little pane windows all around, a lot of privacy.

She stepped inside and dialed the overseas operator. Abby gave her the area code for Seattle and the number for Morgan's house. After four rings she got his message machine again. She didn't leave another message. Abby wondered if he hadn't arrived there yet, or if he'd come and gone. Maybe he was already on his way to New York. She called the law office. It was just after eight in the morning on the West Coast and Abby was hoping one of the receptionists would be answering the phone.

On the second ring they picked up. 'Starl, Hobbs & Carlton.'

'Hello. I wonder if Mr Spencer is in?'

'I'm afraid he's out of town.'

Abby hesitated for a moment, then figured she had nothing to lose. 'This is Abby. Abby Chandlis.' She thought she recognized the voice on reception, Janice, a girl she'd gone to lunch with a few times.

There was a momentary pause on the other end.

'Abby. Where are you?'

The question sent a shiver up Abby's spine. It was a little too pointed. No 'How are you?' – 'What are you doing these days?' – The woman only wanted to know one thing: where she was. Abby wondered if the police might have paid them another visit after Spencer left to come to the islands. With Morgan away from the office, the cops might have talked to Cutler. If that was the case, Abby was not on friendly ground. She could envision the frantic snapping of fingers by the receptionist as she tried to get the attention of a co-worker, perhaps to call the police, not that it would do them any good.

'Do you know where Morgan is?'

'Let me see. I think we have a message here. He called in over the weekend. Just a moment. I'll see if I can find it.'

Abby thought about hanging up. She wondered if the police might have put some kind of a tap or a trace on the line. Maybe they were taping her words as she spoke. She looked at her wrist watch. Fifteen seconds, twenty seconds, half a minute. The woman was still looking.

'Ah. Here it is. He called from San Juan, Puerto Rico. Says he's going to be a few more days. Some business down there. Where are you?'

Abby ignored the question. 'When did he call?'

'Let's see. The message was left on our machine early this morning. About six o'clock.'

Morgan was closer than she thought. But why hadn't he gone on to Seattle to get the documents? Maybe he couldn't get out of his meeting in San Juan? No. It didn't make any sense. He knew what was at stake.

'Are you sure it was Morgan's voice on the tape?'

'I didn't listen to it. Someone else cleared the machine. But who else would it be?'

'Did he leave a phone number?'

'No.

'Any address where's staying?'

'Not that I see on the slip. Where are you, Abby?' The perennial question.

'Nevermind. I'll call later.' She hung up. She actually wiped the telephone receiver clean with one of the new tops from the canvas bag and rubbed across the buttons on the phone. She wasn't sure why, whether it was a nervous gesture or something she'd seen in a movie. As she walked away from the booth, Abby tried to make sense of Janice's information. Why hadn't Morgan left San Juan? Maybe his office wasn't telling her the truth? But why would they make up something like that? Maybe Jack had already gotten to Spencer. Just like he'd gotten Charlie. If that was the case, Abby was now all alone.

She racked her mind trying to remember the name of the ship in San Juan that the caller had given her over the phone the day he called for Morgan. She'd written it down and delivered it to him at Indies over lunch, and now she couldn't remember. *Cuesta, Cuesta, Cuesta* what? Her mind was a blank. It was the only lead she had for Morgan in San Juan. Whatever his business was, she guessed it had to do with this ship. They should know where he was.

She headed toward the dock. Abby's mind was lost in thought and she was looking down at the ground. She let her guard down for an instant and it cost her.

From across the open pavilion near the old Customs House Jack zeroed in on a large straw hat. It wasn't the face, because he couldn't see it. The woman was hidden behind a pair of oversized dark glasses. Instead it was the way the woman carried herself, straight and tall. She stood out among the mostly elderly cruise passengers milling around the shops.

Abby didn't see him until he was within a hundred feet. By that time Jack was on the run, coming right at her. Abby panicked, adrenaline flooded her body, fight-or-flight. She turned and ran, pushing her way through the crowd. She clutched the canvas bag like it was a life line. She drew the ire of several tourists, nearly knocking down an old man. They hollered at her, but Abby didn't stop. She headed down King's Alley and went left on King Street. Jack was right behind her. She went around the corner of Church Street, and a half-block down darted into Little Switzerland.

There was a mob scene inside. People jostling in front of display cases, looking at watches and rings, comparing prices. The store was on two levels, jewelry and pens out front, and other gifts and sundries up two steps in a larger area of the store at the rear.

Abby managed to maneuver her way through the

crowd without drawing too much attention. She removed the straw hat and put it in her bag, hoping that Jack would be keying on the hat. She slumped down several inches and merged with a group of women ogling a necklace of Columbian emeralds. She kept one eye on the two doors at the front of the shop, the only way out onto the street.

A few seconds later she saw Jack push his way through the sea of humanity outside, past one door and then the other. She almost darted for the door, but before she could he was back, looking in one of the doors.

Abby slumped down further and looked at her watch. If it was on schedule the plane would be taking off in less than ten minutes. She would have gotten down on the floor and crawled if she could. But it would have drawn attention.

She peeked over the shoulder of one of the shoppers. He was still standing in the door scanning the crowd inside, looking off in another direction at the moment. He was wearing the little blue fanny pack off to the side on his hip, and Abby knew what was inside. Sooner or later he would see her.

From where he was standing he had both doors covered. If she made a move, he would grab her.

She thought for a moment, looked down into the canvas bag, and had an idea.

There was an Asian couple looking at the display case containing watches.

Abby moved over to them and spoke to the woman. 'Excuse me.'

They looked at her.

'I'm trying to decide whether to buy this hat, but I can't tell what it looks like from a distance.' Abby was holding the straw hat in her hand now.

'I wonder if you'd mind just for a moment walking up onto the stairs over there and putting it on?' Abby wasn't sure if they understood English, but the man seemed to. He explained to his wife, and she gave Abby a broad grin, bowed a little, then took the hat.

She walked twenty feet through the crowd with her back to Abby and her husband before she put the hat on her head. Then she climbed the two steps so that Abby could get a better look. When the woman turned, she was surprised to see her husband standing there alone. She was more surprised to see a tall man wearing a blue pack on his side pushing through the crowd, knocking people over, coming on like a locomotive, almost on top of her.

He didn't stop until an instant after she turned and he saw her face. It registered like a jolt of electricity, as if she'd lit him up. Then his eyes got big. He turned and looked at the door, but it was too late.

Abby made it past the crowds and to the corner by running down the middle of the street. She dodged two cars. One of the drivers leaned on his horn and came to a screeching stop.

Abby brushed by his fender and kept going. People were now looking at her. She ran down King's Alley towards the docks. She could hear the drone of the motors. The twin-engine sea plane was revving up. She ran as fast as her legs could carry her past tourists and carts with vendors selling their wares on the street. As she reached the end of the alley, Abby saw the plane still tied to the dock. But a crewman was starting to remove the gang plank leading to the door.

Abby shouted and waved her arms. The man looked at her, then lowered the plank back into place.

She fumbled in her bag for the ticket, handed it to

him, and stepped aboard. She found a seat by one of the windows on the dockside just behind the wing and one of the rumbling motors. She sat down and strapped herself in. If she could have she would have helped them close the door.

Abby turned to the window and searched the dock for signs of Jack. He couldn't be far behind. She looked back down the aisle of the plane. What was taking so long? There was a conversation going on at the door. The guy at the gang plank was now talking to one of the plane's crew, slapping him on the back and laughing.

She turned the other way, looked out the window again, and saw him. Jack had tracked her to the end of the alley where it met the dock. Now he saw the plane. It registered instantly. He started running. The door finally closed. The engines roared, and the plane started to drift away from the dock. As Abby looked out the window, Jack was standing screaming in her face less than twenty feet away. His hands were cupped to his mouth and he was shouting something that she couldn't hear. She couldn't read his lips, either, and she didn't want to. She turned her head away and his words were swallowed by the roar of the engines. One of the dock crew was trying to pull him back away from the prop-wash of the propellers and the tail of the plane as it turned and headed for open water. The engines revved higher and Abby finally caught her breath as the window next to her was covered by spray off the surface of the bay.

On the dock, Jack tried to ignore the crewman pulling on his arm while he shouted at the top of his lungs. 'Spencer did it! Abby, listen to me. It was Spencer!'

CHAPTER
THIRTY-SIX

'We don't have time to talk right now,' said Jack. 'Maybe on the plane.'

'But I just landed.' Jess looked tired and confused.

Jack took him by the arm and led him toward another gate. They passed through the metal detector and had their bags checked. The clerk asked if they had passports. Jess started to reach for his, but Jack stopped him and merely said 'yes.' Immigration wouldn't check them here departing from St Croix, but in San Juan when they landed. Jack would worry about it then.

'Where are we going?'

'I'll tell you on the plane,' said Jack. 'Did you get the bag I asked you for?'

Jess had made a detour to Coffin Point on the way down. He pointed to one of the pieces of luggage he was hauling toward the tarmac.

'Let me give you a hand.' Jack took the one piece and felt around inside the bag as they walked quickly across the taxiway.

The plane was fueled and waiting, Enrique Ricardi's sleek Gulfstream. The swept-wing executive jet sat whining like a cougar in heat. The words 'Ricardi

Spirits' in script were over the door.

'Hurry up.' Henry was waving them on from the top of the stairs. 'They've just given us clearance. We must take off.' If they moved they might be able to get to San Juan ahead of Abby. The unscheduled private jet gave them an edge.

They raced up the stairs and into the cabin, stowed their luggage, and took seats in plush swivel chairs. Henry went into the cockpit and told the pilot to take off.

'Now tell me what's going on,' said Jess.

'Spencer tried to kill Abby. She doesn't know it, and she's running right to him.'

They felt the wheels roll and a couple of minutes later the acceleration pressed them back into their seats. Twenty seconds and they were airborne. Cruising at five hundred and twenty miles an hour, it would take them less than one hour to get to San Juan. Henry had already given instructions to have the plane taxi to the American Airlines concourse. He was guessing. It was the major carrier between Puerto Rico and the Virgin Islands. The odds were with him that Abby would be coming in that way.

He also called ahead and alerted authorities to try to stop her at the gate if she got there ahead of them. To hold her if necessary. If they missed her there, Customs or Immigration would get her when she showed her passport.

'Sounds like you got it covered,' said Jess.

'I thought I had her covered in Christiansted,' said Jack. 'She ran my ass ragged and stood me up on the dock for a salt-spray shower.'

'How did you find about the lawyer?'

'There was a note under my door when I got back

from my trip,' said Jack. 'Saturday evening. It said Abby wanted to see me at the house at eight-thirty that night. Something about an explanation and a big mistake. Fortunately for me I was running late. The note didn't tell me it was a barbecue.'

Jess gave him a questioning look.

'He tried to get us both when he torched the house. She thinks I did it. It's a long story.' Jack reached into an inside coat pocket, pulled out an envelope, and handed it to his brother. 'It's where I went when I left the island on Saturday morning. Washington, D.C. To do a little research.'

The copyright office was closed on Saturdays, but the Library of Congress had a computer system. If you had the title of a manuscript, or the author's name, you could pull up the copyright registration on the screen and print it out.

'I was looking for the copyright on Abby's book. The one she had Spencer file for her months ago. The problem was I didn't have the title. I tried the one it was published under, but I only found the second registration, the one filed by Bertoli's lawyers. So I figured Abby must have used a working title for the earlier registration, something Bertoli wouldn't trip over when he went to file his. So I tried Abby's name.'

'And you found this?' Jess held up the envelope.

Jack shook his head. 'I found nothing. Oh. I found her earlier books alright, but not this one.'

Jess opened the envelope and removed a single sheet of paper. It was a dot-matrix copy, the registration of copyright for a novel entitled *Every Dangerous Dream*. It was stamped with the date of receipt, and at the top it listed the owner of the copyright: Morgan Robert Spencer.

'It was a hunch. I searched the computer under Spencer's name.' Jack shook his head. 'She never asked him for a copy. She trusted him.'

Jack wanted to get out and push the plane. Moving at the speed of a bullet it wasn't going fast enough for him.

'My guess is his name is all over those contracts I signed.' He was talking about the ones Morgan had him sign at his house that day.

'I never read them. Never got copies. Not that it would have done any good. Unless I miss my bet, he structured the signature pages so they could be removed and added to another set of agreements later. Ones that had his name on them. We were fools, both of us, Abby and I. He had total control, over the money, over the documents. Abby was busy writing. I was busy pretending. And Spencer was busy minding the store. The only thing wrong, he had his own name in the window.'

'How do you know he's in San Juan?' said Jess.

'I don't. If she gets away from us at the airport, we're screwed.' Jack sat shaking his head, powerless to do anything about it at the moment. They flew on in silence for twenty minutes.

There were so many signs, and Jack and Abby had missed them all. The typewriter they couldn't find, the one Abby used to write the book. Who but a lawyer would think of that? Possession of the writing instrument if a dispute arose could be used as evidence. An expert could match the keys on the typewriter to the manuscript pages.

Joey may have been the initial source for Thompson the reporter, but Jack guessed that Spencer had picked up this ball and run with it after Joey's death. How else would Thompson have found Abby in the islands?

'My guess is he's getting ready to tell Bertoli that Abby was his lawyer,' said Jack. 'That she died in a tragic accident along with yours truly. That we were just friends who agreed to help in the promotion of his book. He will apologize for the charade, and in the face of tragedy he'll come clean, or at least look like he is. He'll tell the agent and the publisher that he wrote the book. And who's gonna question him,' said Jack, 'when he's got everything – including Bertoli by the balls?'

It was true. With Jack and Abby dead, Bertoli had a winning horse and nobody to ride it. That gave Spencer all the leverage he needed. Nobody was going to rock a boat when it had that much money in it. In terms of commercial fiction, Gable Cooper was a name that was now made. Armed with that and Abby's outline, Spencer would find a ghost writer for the sequel. The publisher could help him with other stories later. They called it editing, and for the next ten years people would be reading books by Gable Cooper without a picture on the cover, and Morgan owned the franchise.

Henry came back into the cabin.

'We'll be starting our descent into San Juan in about five minutes. How are you feeling?' He looked at Jack.

'I'm fine.'

'My people will be there to help,' said Henry. He possessed a small army of security to protect his business as well as a personal body guard.

'I owe you,' said Jack.

'For nothing.'

'Can I ask you for one more favor?'

'What is it?'

'I had to leave my pack back in St Croix.' It was a code word and Henry understood.

'There was no time to send a package,' said Jack.

Henry smiled. 'And too many metal detectors at the airport?'

'You always understand,' said Jack.

'My security people will get you something when we land.' Henry spoke as if they were going to mix him a casual drink instead of delivering a deadly weapon.

'Besides myself, you're the only two people who know her on sight. If she gets loose in San Juan and finds Spencer, well . . .' Jack didn't have to finish the thought.

'How did you know Abby was alive after the explosion?' asked Jess.

'I wasn't sure, not until this morning, when I went into the safe to get my passport. She took it while I was getting ready to shower last night.'

Jess looked at him, a kind of wise-ass smile. 'She's got your passport?'

Jack nodded.

'Who's gonna vouch for you at Immigration when we land?'

'Not to worry.' Jack reached into his coat pocket and pulled out a blue passport cover and opened it toward his brother. 'Meet Kellen Raid.'

It was like the origami paper bomb. Jack never wrote about anything unless he tried it at least once. A kind of literary license.

When she saw Jack's face looking up at her from the shadows, Abby's heart skipped two beats. The drone of the jet engines had put her to sleep. When she opened her eyes he was staring at her, from the seat next to her, and the chair across the aisle where the woman had laid the book down and gone to the restroom.

Jack's ever-present dark and brooding face was everywhere, staring back from the cover of Abby's novel, the name Gable Cooper emblazoned on the front. She had seen at least half a dozen of them being plucked from knapsacks and book bags as she boarded the plane. It was surreal. He was stalking her, trying to kill her, and his picture was everywhere. She couldn't tell a soul, not without sounding crazy. Who would believe her? The only one was Morgan.

It was dark by the time the wheels hit the runway at Luis Munoz Marin International Airport. The shock of the tires on hard ground jolted Abby back to her senses. She blinked several times as the lights in the cabin came on and people started reaching for their luggage underneath seats. Abby was busy looking out the window, praying that Jack wouldn't be able to get off of St Croix without his passport. Abby had bought time.

In her mind she kept playing with the name of the ship: *Cuesta Cuesta*, *Cuesta* what? What was the rest of it? The name in Spanish that the man had given her over the phone. The message left for Morgan.

Once she found him she would be safe. They would go to Seattle, gather what they needed, and lay it on Bertoli's desk in New York. There would be nothing Jack could do at that point. In two days, the nightmare of the last twenty-four hours would be over. They would arrest Jack and it would all end.

Henry assembled his employees near the lounge by the gates. Most were engaged in security work for Ricardi's rum distillery. Together with Jack and Jess they fanned out to cover the incoming flights. Jack was worried they might have already missed her. There was one in-coming flight that had already landed. The passengers had cleared Customs and were gone. Jack prayed she wasn't on that flight. They searched the lounges in case she was waiting for a connecting flight.

He gave Henry's men a description of Abby, and hoped she hadn't changed her clothes or colored her hair while she was waiting for her flight in St Thomas. She would be nervous. He told them this and instructed them not to chase her. If they saw her, they were to follow and observe, and call Jack on walkie-talkies that the security people had provided.

If Jack approached her in a group, in a public place, maybe she would stop long enough to listen. All he had to do was get close enough to hand her the copyright. Once she saw it, she would understand. The pieces would fit like a puzzle. Jack was sure of it. His biggest worry now was that she had already slipped the net, that somehow she was on her way into San Juan to meet up with Morgan.

The plane pulled up to the gate, the jetway rolled out, and a moment later the door opened. Abby had no luggage, just the canvas bag. But she didn't want to be the first one off the plane.

She waited, then merged with the army of people jamming the aisle. Abby's only zone of comfort came from crowds. She immersed herself in them, submerged in anonymity. If Jack couldn't see her, he couldn't kill her.

They did the duck waddle down the aisle, carrying suitcases and packages, inching their way toward the door of the plane.

Abby was all darting eyes and wary looks from behind her sunglasses. No one seemed to notice, even though it was dark outside.

'Please watch your step.' A flight attendant was at the door. A tall, good-looking blond man with epaulets on his shoulders stood in the open door to the cockpit behind her.

'You coming to the party at *Isla Verde* tonight?' He was talking to the stewardess.

Abby thought about going to a party. It sounded good. Anything that hinted of a normal life sounded good. Then somehow the words clicked – *Isla Verde*. That was it. *Verde*. The rest of the message from the man on the phone. The name of the ship was the *Cuesta Verde*. Now all she had to do was find it.

Abby stepped through the door and out onto the jetway. She was halfway home. She could almost reach out and touch Morgan. Maybe she would call and try to find the ship. The harbor master would know where it was. She could call from a payphone.

She started to make the turn to go up the ramp, and she saw him.

Jack was at the top by the door leading into the lounge like a gatekeeper. He was looking the other way. She recognized Jess standing next to him. They were waiting for her.

Abby tried to go back, but she couldn't. She was being washed along by the sea of people coming off the plane.

She looked up the ramp again, and this time Jack saw her. He grabbed Jess and they started coming. A clerk tried to stop them, but they pushed their way through the door and waded into passengers exiting the plane.

There was a door that led from the jetway down some stairs to the tarmac. It was open. There was a man with a headset on and yellow overalls standing in the way.

Abby ran for the door, and the guy grabbed her.

'Not that way, lady.'

She kicked him as hard as she could in the leg and he let go. Before he could recover, she was out the door and down the stairs.

She ran under the wings of planes in front of giant tires that stood nearly as tall as she did. She was clutching the canvas bag.

Jack threw open the door at the top of the jetway and Abby saw him. He was down the stairs in less than three seconds, one of the flight crew yelling at him.

Abby saw an opening in the building and headed for it. It was a service area with vehicles coming and going. Little tractors towing trailers filled with luggage.

Abby got behind one of these and kept pace, running alongside until she was in the building.

This left Jack looking underneath and jumping to see over the top. One second he saw a pair of feet under the luggage cart on the other side, and the next they were gone. He ran the gauntlet of vehicles, and by the time he crossed the threshold under the terminal and inside the service building she was gone.

Jess caught up with him. 'Did you see which way she went?'

The police were coming with one of Henry's security people.

'In there somewhere. Take some of Henry's people. Cover the exits.'

They fanned out. Henry told the cops in Spanish so they would understand that Abby was neither armed nor dangerous. He told them she was a material witness so they wouldn't shoot her if she ran.

The people inside the service area wore various uniforms, from the bright yellow reflective overalls of the ground crew, to khaki work pants and shirts.

The cops covered the exits from the maintenance area.

There were only two doors, but once through them a person could move directly to the main lobby, bypassing Customs and Immigration. The doors were not locked from the maintenance side but secured by coded push-button locks from the public concourse inside. Jack combed baggage handling, while Jess searched the maintenance area.

There was no sign of Abby.

Jack checked the conveyor belt that carried bags to the level above where they were collected by passengers. It was possible that she could have jumped on the belt and gone up with the bags. But she would have caused a stir when she arrived, drawn a lot of attention. Airport security would have nailed her. Besides, she would still have to clear Customs and Immigration from that point.

He turned his attention to the baggage itself, big boxes and crates, anything she could hide behind or in.

In the meantime, Jess and two cops worked their way to the locker rooms, where several employees were changing their clothes, either coming on or going off shift. They did a careful search and found nothing. They were three minutes too late.

She was sweating under two layers of clothing in the tropical climate. Perspiration ran down her face. Her hair was piled up inside the construction hard hat as Abby made her way up the stairs and found the ladies' room near the ticket area in the terminal. No one except a little boy with big brown eyes seemed to pay much attention to the woman dressed in the bright yellow jumpsuit.

Abby hung the hard hat on the hook inside the bathroom stall, stepped out of the jump suit, and retrieved the canvas bag that she'd hidden inside one leg in order to get past the cop at the door. Then she straightened her clothes, and a minute later was headed through the front doors to the terminal.

Jack had given up on the crates and boxes. If Abby was there, she wasn't going any place. He left the cops to check them and headed out one of the exits with Jess right behind him. They climbed the stairs up to the terminal. Jack's fear now was that she had somehow slipped away. They moved quickly down the concourse to the public area out front.

Jack wanted to get his people onto the street in front of the terminal where they could watch for her. The net was widening and Jack was worried.

Out on the street Abby saw a string of cabs and made a beeline. A group of drivers were standing and talking twenty feet from the first cab in line. They seemed in no particular hurry, though one of them eyed Abby and gave her a lascivious smile.

She motioned to the taxi, and he held up a hand as if to say 'just a moment.' The drivers weren't quite through with their conversation.

Abby was looking over her shoulder, standing by the door to the cab. She wasn't certain which one belonged to the driver who waved at her. He was still trying to tear himself away, talking with his hands as much as his mouth, laughing and arguing.

Jack came out of the terminal door a hundred feet away. Abby saw him instantly. She opened the door to the first cab in line, an old blue Fairlane, and nearly dove onto the floor in the back seat, closing the door behind her. She pushed the button and locked it, then slumped down so that she couldn't be seen through the window.

She could hear the drivers talking in Spanish, one voice getting louder and laughing as he came closer. Finally the driver came around to his door, climbed in behind the wheel, and looked over the seat. At first he couldn't see her.

Abby was lying on the back floor.

'Are you alright?'

'I'm fine.'

'Where you want to go?'

'Old San Juan, near the docks.' Abby looked up at him from the floor.

The driver turned around, shrugged his shoulders, and the cab pulled out away from the curb.

Jack quickly keyed on the cabs. If you were throwing a net, this was the outer perimeter. He saw one pull out of line and he ran for it. He tried to stop it but couldn't. The driver didn't see him. In that instant, Abby sat up in the seat and looked out the back window. Their eyes met, and Jack shouted.

The taxi merged with traffic and headed for the highway.

'Fifty dollars extra if you take me by the scenic route,' said Abby. 'By way of the back streets past the El Condado.' She didn't dare tell him she was running from someone. He might stop the car and tell her to get out. If Jack followed her, she wanted to get off the highway as quickly as possible. They could lose him in the traffic of the downtown streets.

The driver looked in the mirror at her like she was crazy.

'And do it quickly.' The contradiction of taking back

roads and getting there quickly didn't seem to bother Abby. She was busy looking out the window behind. A second later she passed a twenty-dollar bill over the seat as an incentive.

'Sí, señora.'

Abby's car was out of sight by the time Jack flagged a cab. Jess was right behind him.

'Talk to the drivers over there,' said Jack. 'Find out if you can get the number of the cab or the driver's name.'

Jess took off and Jack climbed into the front seat of the taxi next to the driver.

'Out to the highway, fast!' Jack started peeling off bills and told the driver to step on it. He was using fives and tens, dropping them on the seat like an accelerator. He told the driver he'd take care of any tickets. The guy was doing eighty out the airport parkway, until he hit traffic backed up on the highway.

Jack figured Abby had to be caught in it as well. They started weaving around cars. More money on the seat. The taxi had two wheels in the median, going around cars in the fast lane, while Jack leaned out the window trying to look over the top of other vehicles to find Abby's cab.

He was just about to tell the driver to forget it when he saw the blue Fairlane. It was eight or ten cars ahead, stalled in traffic.

'Go around!' Jack almost grabbed the wheel from the driver, pushing toward the center of the highway, squeaking between cars in the fast lane and the concrete median barrier. You couldn't slip a finger between the side of the taxi and the wall that separated them from oncoming traffic.

They were now only four cars back behind Abby. Jack

could see her through the back window.

Abby's car was crawling at twenty miles an hour.

Through the rear window she saw him coming on in the outside lane. Abby looked ahead. There was an off-ramp.

'Get off here.' She screamed at the driver and he nearly jumped out of his seat.

'El Condado is two miles up.'

'I don't care. Get off here.'

The guy shrugged his shoulders and pulled to the right without signaling. There was a blare of horns as they dropped off the highway into the squalor of one of the outer districts of San Juan.

Jack was trapped in the fast lane. He grabbed the wheel and tried to pull to the right. Horns blared. The fender of the taxi caught the bumper of another car as they passed. The driver of the other vehicle threw his brakes on. The car went sideways in the lane, crossed over, and two other cars hit it. The chain that followed was like a train going off the rails, cars everywhere. Jack's taxi rolled past the off-ramp as a mass of vehicles piled up behind them. There was no way back.

Jack threw open the door and raced toward the cyclone fence that flanked the highway. In one leap he threw himself halfway up the fence for a view. Abby's taxi took a left-hand turn at a crossing intersection and disappeared.

CHAPTER
THIRTY-SEVEN

In the dust of headlights and the rantings of angry Puerto Rican drivers, Jack hopped the cyclone fence that bounded the highway and ran two blocks to the intersection where Abby's car had disappeared. There was no sign of her.

He used the VHF walkie-talkie and called Henry. Ten minutes later a large dark Mercedes pulled up at the intersection. Henry was in the passenger seat. One of his security men was driving, and Jess was in the back.

Jack climbed into the back seat next to his brother and the car sped off.

He had taken more lives than some serial killers; six people in all. Still Morgan didn't see himself in that way. One was an accident; the crewman on the *Cella Largo*. Two others were the moral equivalent of crushing cockroaches; Joey Jenrico and that leach of a husband Abby had married. Jack and Theresa were necessary. They knew too much.

The only real regret was Abby. He couldn't deny it. He loved her, bared his soul to her, and she had rejected him. He tried not to think about it and instead busied himself with the task at hand.

The secret was to use the minimum of materials. In this case, that meant two eight-foot lengths of detonating cord. The det-cord looked like heavy poly-plastic clothesline. But instead of nylon strands inside, it contained a seam of high explosives. It was flexible, extremely fast, and powerful. Wrapped around the base of a small tree and set off, it would sever the trunk in the flash of an eye without much noise.

Morgan used a linoleum knife, a wicked instrument with a short scimitarlike blade that was razor sharp. Carefully he cut a length of the cord and examined the water intake line that ran along the ship's plates.

The *Cuesta Verde* was old and rusted out. That she hadn't been delivered to the scrap yard years before was a testament to the owner's patience and the unusually high limits of their insurance policy.

He had agreed to perform this last job months earlier, before Abby's book shot through the roof on the list. Morgan no longer needed the money. He would have sidestepped the job if he could. But the owners of the *Cuesta Verde* were not the kind of people you crossed. They would become suspicious, start to wonder if maybe he was setting them up, perhaps working a sting with the insurance company. Morgan looked at the job as a kind of sending-off party, his final fling before retirement. The owners would make a killing on the insurance, and Spencer would quietly slip away to a new life of luxury, preferably in some cooler northern climate. Morgan mopped sweat from his brow as he considered Ireland. They had no income tax on writers, and with the money from the books he could probably afford a castle.

He wiped his gloved hand along the pipe looking for

lettering that indicated 'water.' The ship was so badly maintained that most of the markings on the pipes had long since worn off. Still there should be some indication. He grabbed a rag and wiped oil and dust from the surface of the metal. There was nothing. He was sure it was a raw water line for cooling the steam turbine. He had traced it to a point in the boiler room where it disappeared between the boilers and the inside of the hull.

He wrapped a single strand of det-cord around the large pipe three times. When it blew, the sea would flood the boiler room and the bilges below. There was fifty feet of water beneath the ship.

He looped the ends of the det-cord in a loose knot, then slipped an electrical detonating cap between the cord and the pipe.

He moved to the other side of the ship and repeated this process. This time the pipe was clearly marked as a water line by white lettering, chipped and faded but still visible. If it was done right, the two blasts would occur simultaneously. All that would be heard above decks was a sharp crack, nothing that could be described as an explosion.

Morgan took the drop wires, a hundred feet of number fourteen electrical wire. He attached the ends to the two detonators and retreated through a door in the bulkhead into another compartment near the boiler room.

Henry's driver took a circuitous route doing sixty down alleys and back streets. Jack could see the amber luminescence of old San Juan against the night sky as they approached. They took a wide, sweeping arc on two wheels around the plaza and stopped on Calle

Marina, directly in front of the cruise ship terminal.

There were two police cars parked at the curb, and between them was the blue Fairlane cab – but Abby wasn't in it.

Henry's car pulled up alongside and Ricardi got out. 'Let me handle it.'

The taxi driver was standing beside his vehicle being questioned by the cops. Henry approached them and identified himself.

The driver and Henry talked for a couple of minutes, then Henry returned to the Mercedes. He got in and looked over the back seat at Jack, knitted eyebrows and serious expressions.

'He says he dropped her off back by the warehouses on Fernandez Juncos. About a mile from here.'

'Did he see where she went?'

Henry shook his head. 'But he says she stopped to make a phone call before they got down here. He doesn't know who she called, but he heard her say something over the phone. Does the name *Cuesta Verde* mean anything to you?'

Jack shook his head.

'Nor to me,' said Henry. 'But it's what she was looking for. She asked the driver to take her to the warehouse district near the docks. He let her out and that's the last time he saw her.'

'A cargo ship?' said Jack.

'That would be my guess.'

Henry said something in Spanish to his driver and the Mercedes left rubber on the road. It took them less than two minutes.

The commercial waterfront area of San Juan was not large or sprawling. It covered only a few blocks and was dingy and poorly lit, with dilapidated metal buildings and no sidewalks. It was bounded by alleys with a lot of potholes and gravel.

Henry had his driver prowl these with their headlights on high beam looking for any sign of Abby. All they saw was a mangy dog, its eyes illuminated like amber in the headlights, and its ribs showing like washboards.

Most of the buildings sat behind cyclone fences with barbed wire or coils of razor wire on top.

They wound through alleys and up dead-end streets, but there was no sign of Abby. In fact, there was no one walking on the streets at all. At night this was no-man's-land.

Henry got on the car's cellular phone and made a call. A few seconds later he hung up and turned around to Jack in the backseat.

'There is a ship,' he said. 'The *Cuesta Verde*. It's waiting for repairs near the dry dock. Just over there.' He pointed down one of the dark alleys. Henry had called the harbor master's office.

Jack turned to Jess. 'Where's the bag?'

His brother handed it to him, and Jack looked inside. There was an old starlight scope and some tools inside.

'You keep looking,' he told Henry. 'Check all the streets.' Jack started to get out of the car.

'Not without me.' Jess followed him.

'One more thing,' said Henry.

Jack stood near the passenger window at the front of the car.

'Here, take this.' Henry handed him a matt-black semiautomatic pistol, a nine millimeter Beretta just like the one Jack was forced to leave in St Croix.

In Jack's grip it felt like an old friend.

'Thanks.' Then he and Jess disappeared down the dark alley toward the docks.

It had taken her almost a half hour, but Abby finally found a gate that was loosely chained. She threw the canvas bag over the top, then managed to squeeze her head and shoulders through the gate. She was struggling with the rest of her body when she saw headlights approaching the intersection a half-block away. Abby prayed that the car wouldn't turn into the alley. It didn't. Instead it stopped at the intersection.

Two men got out of the back seat and a chill raced up Abby's spine. One of them was Jack.

Abby pushed at the gate and strained to get through. They were talking to someone in the car. At any moment they would turn. She had time in the darkness, but only if she moved.

Abby caught her arm on a sharp piece of wire, flinched, and the gate rattled. She stopped for an instant, hoping they didn't hear her. Then she struggled, tore flesh, and finally pushed her way through.

The car was turning, its headlights making an arc toward the alley.

Abby got to her feet and ran. She literally dove into the shadows next to some pallets. She rolled onto her side and lay motionless on the ground. The lights surged over her like a cresting wave, then swept the area as the car continued its turn. In the inky darkness she got to her feet and ran.

She was forty feet from the gate behind some containers when she finally stopped and looked back. She pulled one of the blouses from the canvas bag, tore a portion of it, and wrapped the frayed cloth around her arm.

She was busy doing this when Abby heard the hollow wail of feet against cyclone fencing. She moved for position and saw them. Jack and the other man, bare outlines in silhouette, scaled to the top of the fence. She heard metal snipping and a second later the four strands of barbed wire on top coiled away. Jack slipped silently over the fence and dropped down on the inside. He was joined a few seconds later by the other man. She had no idea how they'd found her. Maybe they were looking for Morgan.

They were close enough now that Abby could see their faces. It was Jess. Jack pulled something from the back of his pants and examined it in dull light. It was a pistol. He checked the clip, sliding it from the handle, then jammed it back in and pulled the slide, chambering a round.

Abby didn't need to see anything more. She disappeared into the shadows and huddled in the dark among pallets and metal containers. As they moved closer, she retreated to the other side of the pallets, out closer to the edge of the dock. She was running out of ground.

In the distance she could see the large concrete dry dock floating next to the pier. Just this side of it was a ship, and on the stern was the name *Cuesta Verde*. The paint was chipped and rusted. Abby watched as they approached from the fence. If they got between her and the vessel, she would be trapped on the dock.

She ran for the ship. Giving up cover she raced for the stairs leading from the dock up the side to the top deck. She hit the first step and her feet clattered on the expandable metal. Abby was afraid to look back. She had to find Morgan now, before they did.

Jack heard footfalls on metal and followed the sound. He cleared the corner of one of the large green steel containers, and for a fleeting instant he saw her. Abby was climbing the stairs. She ran across the scaffold at the top and disappeared through the gunnel and into the shadows on the deck.

Jess was behind him. He started to give chase and Jack grabbed him by the arm, held him still, and listened for footfalls on the deck above.

Jack knew that by the time they got there she could lose herself in a million places on the ship. They would have no idea where to look.

Now unless he missed his bet, Abby was getting close to Spencer. Jack could smell him, the acrid odor of death.

There was nothing but silence from the deck above.

Jack found a ladder propped against a stack of containers and silently climbed to the top. He crawled to a place where he had a vantage point down onto the deck of the ship, then fished in the bag and pulled out the cylindrical black tube. He removed the old starlight scope and began searching for thermal images on the deck.

Minutes passed in silence as Abby huddled in the dark. She was scared and alone, stalked by two armed men. She couldn't be sure that Morgan was even on the ship. For all she knew, she was there alone, facing death. If she showed herself, she knew that Jack and Jess would kill her in an instant, just like Jack had killed Theresa and Charlie.

Then she heard a whisper, raspy and harsh, like someone trying to shout but under his breath.

'Abby. Come out where I can see you.' It was Jack's voice.

'Listen, Abby. It was Spencer. He set fire to the house. Can you hear me?'

Several seconds passed in silence, Abby motionless in the dark.

'If you don't want to say anything, just give me a signal.' His voice was coming from out in the shadows, somewhere above her, looking down on the deck.

'Just give me a signal, Abby. Something I can see or hear. I can prove what I'm telling you is the truth. Give me a chance.'

He was lying. Abby knew it. Jack would tell her anything to get his hands on her. Then he would find Spencer and kill them both.

'Throw something. Toss something out. Anything. Just so that I know you can hear me.' His voice sounded so plaintive, so familiar, the same tones he had used when he told her that he loved her.

She thought about that warm day, the beach on St Croix, as they floated in the surf, Jack's arms around her, the feel of his lips on her neck and shoulders. How he could always make her laugh. Dancing with him on the terrace at the Buccaneer, the intimate moments they had spent, the things they had said to each other. Then she remembered Theresa's lifeless body on the gurney.

She saw something flash, the glint of light on glass. It came from the top of one of the giant steel containers on the dock. Abby retreated deeper into the shadows and the thought dawned: Jack had a scoped rifle. She would be dead in an instant if she stepped into the light. Abby would never hear the bullet that killed her.

She watched and listened, straining her ears for the slightest sound. There was only the rasping of her own breath. She remained huddled in the dark as minutes ticked away.

Abby fought the conflicting emotions of rage and fear. She was scared and shaking, but she was also furious, at herself for being so foolish to fall in love with Jack. He had murdered her best friend, and butchered Charlie. While she didn't have much use for Charlie, he didn't deserve to die that way. If Abby had a gun at that moment, she wouldn't have asked a single question or said a single word. She would simply have fired at the reflection of the glass on the container. She would have killed Jack without a second's hesitation, because he deserved to die. Rage boiled over in her and fed an adrenaline rush.

Suddenly there was clatter on the stairs, not footsteps but something else. Abby froze, listened for a moment, heard it again, and ran. She ran like the devil was after her. Any instant a bullet could rip through her body. She raced toward the front of the ship, toward the superstructure looming three stories above, and into the companionway that passed beneath it on the port side.

She tried several of the steel doors. They were locked and the latches bolted tight.

She heard muted footfalls behind her, turned and looked. They were coming, already at the top of the stairs, running. Suddenly she realized they were shoeless on the steel deck and much closer than she thought.

Abby raced down the companionway. Twenty feet on she found another door. This one was open. She stepped across the threshold and tried to close it but couldn't. She looked and saw the hook on the back, released it, and slammed the steel door shut an instant before Jack's hand reached the opening.

He would have yelled but Jack was afraid Spencer would hear him. They pounded with their hands against the hard steel and kicked at the door with bare feet.

Abby had managed to turn the friction handles on the

inside, sealing it tight. They fought with the latches and Jess managed to open the bottom two. Jack was having more trouble with the ones up top. It was as if they were spring loaded. Every time he got one open it would snap back to a locked position. He could feel her hanging on the metal latches from the inside, pulling down with every ounce of strength she could muster, leveraging the force of gravity to her advantage.

He tried to whisper through the door, a half-inch of steel, but it was useless. Either she couldn't hear, or didn't want to.

They fought with the handles and finally they got three of them open. They pushed on the door, but it wouldn't give, not with the last latch in place. Jack fought a losing battle. Somehow she had managed to jam it from the inside. The latch wouldn't budge. Jack gave up. 'Come on. Let's find another way in.' They headed down the companionway.

Spencer attached a set of the wires to one of the terminals on the battery and looked around for a good place to shield himself. Tempered steel was like glass. It could fracture into a million pieces and fly in as many directions.

He found an old mattress in one of the compartments and carried it to the area by the boiler room. He propped it against the bulkhead near the open door.

There was one last chore. Morgan was four levels deep in the ship, inside a dozen watertight doors. He wanted to make sure these were open not only to flood the ship but to secure a path of escape.

He climbed three levels and checked each door. He had worked his way to the outside, one level below the main deck, when he heard footsteps running along the companionway overhead. There wasn't supposed to be anyone on that level. They had assured him – only a skeleton crew on the bridge. Someone had screwed up. Quickly he headed back down.

Morgan had to move. He slid down the ladder, ran for the opening in the deck, and dropped quickly two more levels into the boiler room. He raced past the cold boilers, through the bulkhead door and the machine room, and into the small compartment where the mattress blocked the door.

There was no time to connect the detonating switch. He could hear someone descending from the ladder above. He grabbed the loose drop wires and touched them to the empty battery post. A spark arced from the battery, and an instant later a blast roared through the compartment, a flash of light, fire and smoke.

The explosion threw Morgan halfway across the room onto his back on the steel deck. For an instant he lay there dazed. The only thing that shielded him from the blast and flames was the mattress. It had saved his life. Instinct told him immediately what had happened.

Spencer had severed a fuel line. Barrels of bunker oil were blazing, mixing with sea water rushing into the forward compartment. He got to his feet, shielded his face from the flames that licked through the open doorway. He tried to close the steel door but couldn't. The pressure of incoming water and the heat from the burning oil forced him back. Flames floated on water over the threshold. Morgan retreated to the ladder and climbed for his life.

Abby lay sprawled on the hard steel deck. It was dark with the acrid odor of smoke. A klaxon echoed in her ears, its cadence in time with the flashing red light over the door, the one she had just jammed shut with the broom handle.

She was stunned, her senses paralyzed, mind numbed, as sensations of heat from the metal deck embraced her in the folds of its comforting warmth.

Slowly, in a daze, she dragged herself to her feet and stumbled to the door. She removed the broom handle and tried to turn the latch. It wouldn't move. The explosion had twisted the bulkhead and sprung the steel door in its frame. Abby was trapped.

There was only one way out: toward the smoke and the heat. She covered her face with her arm and headed into the darkness.

The blast caught Jess on the ladder and sent him sprawling to the bottom. He landed fifteen feet down on a steel catwalk and gripped his leg in agony. Excrutiating pain shot through his calf below the knee, and when he looked down he could see the jagged end of bone protruding through the flesh. It had ripped through his pant leg and blood was spurting.

Jack scrambled back along the catwalk to his brother and made a quick assessment. Jess was going into shock. Jack removed the belt from his pants and fashioned a tourniquet above the knee using the case from the starlight scope to turn it. He tied it off and raced back up the ladder.

On the outside deck he found a fire hose in a glass cabinet, smashed the glass, unreeled the hose, and dropped it back down the ladder. He flew down the rungs to his brother, lashed the hose under Jess's arms, and tied it off like a safety harness. It took him nearly three minutes to hoist his brother to the outside deck. All the while the ship was settling in the water. Flames billowed from one of the stacks overhead. He propped Jess against the railing, then lowered his head for shock.

'I've got to go back down to find Abby.'

'Go.' Jess waved him off. 'I'll be alright.' He was breathing heavily but conscious.

Jack turned and headed back down the ladder.

Spencer entered an open metal bridge-work that spanned the area over the boilers. Flames floated on water and had risen halfway up the boilers. He started across the bridge.

'Morgan.' The voice seemed almost etherial. It came from somewhere above, surreal, something from the grave.

For an instant Spencer actually thought he might be dead. Heat waves wafted off the plates of the giant ship. Maybe this was hell.

He turned and looked up. There on the ladder, descending, was Abby. He rubbed his eyes and fear took hold. Apparitions from beyond the veil. She was coming to claim retribution. Her face was covered with soot. Her hands were bleeding and her clothes were singed. She dropped from the ladder and he grabbed her, almost as if in a reflex. Morgan was stunned. She was flesh and bone.

She hung on him, her arms draped around his neck as she tried to catch her breath. The air over the boilers was filling with smoke. It was stiffling and fouled with the odor of burning oil.

'How did you find me?' It was all Morgan could think to say.

'I found the ship. The message on the phone. Remember?'

The look on Morgan's face said that he did. The

question now was what to do with her. He looked over the edge of the railing at the burning cauldron below and considered the possibilities.

'We've got to get out of here,' said Abby. 'He's up there.'

'Who?'

'Jack. He must have done something to the ship.'

Morgan quickly forgot the raging flames below. 'Right.' He tried to take it all in. More mistakes in a week than he'd made in a lifetime; missing Abby and Jack at the house and now a fire.

'He's armed,' said Abby. 'He has a pistol. I saw it. Maybe a rifle, I don't know.' Morgan had a faraway look. She wasn't sure he was hearing any of this.

'You think he did the explosions?' said Abby.

'Must have.' It was as if Morgan was trying to figure things out. 'Right now we've got to move.' He grabbed her hand roughly and dragged her across the steel bridge that spanned the boiler room two levels up.

There was a burning inferno at the bottom of the ship and the flames were rising, a floating hell. The heat was nearly unendurable. Torrid waves of air coursed up from the boiler room as the searing temperatures penetrated the layers of Abby's clothing. The rubber soles of her shoes went soft as gum starting to melt. It was like running on a griddle.

They raced across the bridge and through an open door. Morgan stopped and closed it behind them to seal off the heat. He swung one of the latches closed.

Abby screamed.

When Spencer turned he saw Jack. He was standing six feet away at the foot of a ladder, the only way out. Jack reached for the Beretta and pulled it from the back of his pants. He aimed it at Morgan.

'Abby, step over here.' He was watching Morgan's hands every second. Taking a double-hand hold on the pistol, his eye aligning the sights on Morgan's chest.

Spencer moved behind Abby until a part of her head was framed in the front sight.

Jack moved a few inches, searching for an angle of fire if he needed it. They did a deadly minuet.

'Listen to me. Get away from him.'

Abby froze.

'Don't move.' Morgan was behind her, his hands on her shoulders as if for support.

'You don't understand. He tried to kill you on the island,' said Jack. 'It was Spencer who blew up the house.'

'Put the gun down, Jack. There's no need for this.' Abby tried to reason with him.

'If I put it down, he'll kill us both,' said Jack.

'You're sick, Jack. You need help. The police will understand.'

Morgan got up in her ear and whispered, 'You're right. He's out of his mind.'

'What's he saying?' Jack waved the point of the pistol as if he was trying to move them apart.

'I'm telling her to stay calm. Don't you think we should all get out of here?' Morgan looked over the edge of the railing. So far the flames had been confined to the forward area behind the bulkhead. But the metal plates were creaking, expanding. Morgan knew that any second the ship could explode. His grip became firmer on Abby's shoulders until they began to hurt.

'Abby, listen to me. I have proof.' Jack took one hand off the gun and tried to unfold the piece of paper from the envelope, but it wouldn't come. Heat from the ship's bulkhead was turning the area on the catwalk into an oven.

'Help me.' Jack held out the paper, but she wouldn't move toward him.

'Don't go. Stay still,' said Morgan.

'Don't listen to him. He tried to kill both of us at the house,' said Jack.

'He's sick.' Morgan was feeling the heat as it radiated off the plates of steel. 'He would tell you anything, Abby, anything to get you over there. Then he would kill you. He murdered Theresa and Joey, slashed Charlie's throat. You can't believe anything he says.'

In that instant as Jack's gaze met hers, Abby knew. It was in the aspect of his eye and the crooked angle of his head as if Jack were saying, 'See, there it is.' He held out the paper, but Abby didn't need it. How would Morgan know Charlie's throat was cut – unless he did it himself?

She tensed and he felt it. Suddenly Morgan realized what he'd said. In a single fluid movement he brought the glint of steel from the inside of his boot to Abby's throat. The razor-sharp blade of the linoleum knife, its needlelike point drew a pimple of blood from her neck.

'Move and I'll kill her. I mean it,' said Morgan. 'I didn't want to do this, but you forced it.' He was talking to Abby, a scolding father, the blade to her throat. 'You wouldn't listen to me. I tried to warn you. I told you he was no good. But you wouldn't believe me.'

Imperceptibly, leaning, Jack edged a few inches sideways on the catwalk, angling for a shot.

Morgan saw him and adjusted. He pulled Abby into Jack's line of sight. 'I swear I'll kill her.'

'Is that how you did it with Charlie?' she said.

'It was more than he deserved. He never knew what hit him. He didn't feel a thing,' said Morgan. 'There was no pain. No suffering. He would have bled you dry. You're a lovely woman, Abby, but you have lousy taste in men.'

'Almost as bad as my taste in friends.' She tried to pull away from him, but Morgan pushed the blade tighter to the flesh of her neck and she stopped.

'Throw the gun over here.'

'Not a chance,' said Jack.

'I'll kill her if you don't.'

'You'll kill her if I do. This way I get the pleasure of blowing your ass over the railing the second you move,' said Jack.

Morgan knew he meant it. Mexican stand-off. The heat was rising.

'If we stay here we're all gonna fry,' said Morgan.

'Throw the knife over and let her go,' said Jack.

The steel around them creaked.

It came from the bowels of the ship, the deep roar of an explosion that shook the vessel to its keel. One of the main fuel tanks. It lifted the three of them off their feet and dropped them onto the expanded steel of the cat-walk like sacks of cement. Morgan hit the metal first.

Jack landed on one shoulder and the pistol bounced on the catwalk and slid. A second explosion racked the ship and Abby slipped over. She dangled by fingers on the edge of the catwalk, hand slipping.

Jack clung to the grating of the catwalk and lashed out with one arm reaching for her. Caught her by a wrist, sliding to hands, sweaty palms, he held tight.

The steel walls below them buckled. Flames and water poured into the level below as Jack struggled to get another hand on Abby's arm. He swung her like a pendulum once, twice. Her leg hooked the edge of catwalk and Jack pulled her up onto the grating, her bare arms hitting the searing steel.

'You should have let her go.' Morgan was standing there, looking at them, holding the pistol trained on Jack.

Abby rolled a few inches over onto something hard on the expanded metal, and buried it under her side.

'Get up. On your feet.' Morgan started to wheel around, toward the ladder where Jack had come down.

They looked at the pistol. The safety was off. One shudder from the ship and it would go off.

'Move,' said Morgan. 'Or I'll kill you both right where you are.'

Jack got to his knees and stood. He helped Abby to her feet. She held one wrist to her chest as if there was something wrong with it. Together they inched their way around toward the closed bulkhead door. The one Morgan had secured with a single latch.

Abby could hear the steel around them expand with heat, creaking under the pressure of water and fire. She heard the hiss of hot metal and the vibrations of the ship as it came apart. The *Cuesta Verde* was going down.

'Move,' said Morgan. 'Now.'

Jack and Abby took a few more steps until they were in the corner, near the hinges of the iron door.

Morgan looked up. There was another watertight door on the level above. He could leave them, close it, and they would die in a blazing tomb, a solution to all of his problems.

Spencer got to the foot of the ladder, one hand up.

'If he gets there, we're dead,' Jack whispered in Abby's ear.

'I know.' She looked down at her chest and Jack saw it, the shiny glint of steel concealed between her wrist and the tattered cloth over her breast. She followed

Jack's eye to the sealed latch on the door.

'It didn't have to be this way.' Morgan looked at her, and with the pistol in one hand he started to climb.

Jack made a move. Morgan pointed the pistol right at him and Jack froze.

Morgan looked back for the next rung on the ladder and began to reach for it. Just as he did, Abby grabbed the blade of the linoleum knife between two fingers and flung it at him.

It was a reflexive action. Morgan moved a hand off the ladder to ward off the flashing blade of the knife, and for an instant he was suspended in midair.

Jack grabbed Abby with one arm, pulled her into the corner behind the steel door, and with the other he jerked the searing steel of the latch.

The superheated air of the boiler room expanded with an explosive force. The door shot open like a cannon. A dragon's tongue of fire lashed the catwalk incinerating everything in sight, catching Morgan in mid-flight and turning him into a human torch.

Screaming, in flames, he fell from the ladder, pulling off rounds from the pistol. They ricocheted off steel as Jack embraced Abby in his arms behind the shield of the iron door.

Morgan raced toward the railing of the catwalk, his body fully engulfed in flames, his brain ablaze. He plunged over the edge and into the swirling flame-filled water pouring into the ship.

Jack kicked the door closed, then tearing strips from his shirt he wrapped his hands and sealed the latch. He gave Abby strips of cloth to wrap her hands and they climbed the ladder.

Water was rising fast behind them. By the time they reached the open deck it was lapping at the bottom of the railing near Jess. Jack grabbed him by one arm. Abby took the other and they eased him over the side.

As they cleared the ship they could see the lights of the Mercedes on the dock, and police cars around it. Henry and one of his security men were running toward a wooden ladder that ran down from the wharf.

The salt water burned as it found every cut and burn on Abby's body. They floated among the debris and watched the flames as they raged beneath the surface of the harbor fed by air trapped in the compartments of the *Cuesta Verde*.

EPILOGUE

Abby and Jack sat quietly, relaxing at a sidewalk table in Fairhaven a block from Village Books. They were far enough away that no one seemed to notice, just two tourists sitting and talking. Today there was a lot of excitement in the village. Fairhaven was the historic section of Bellingham, not far from the Canadian border in western Washington.

Portions of Abby's big book were set here, and now scenes for the film were being shot just a few blocks away. There were cameras and trucks, and most of the people were busy gawking.

The producers had hired Abby as a consultant. They now knew the truth, and so did Bertoli. It didn't seem to matter.

Today she had come to autograph books. Lines were wrapped around the block. Abby's sequel was out in hardcover.

She and Jack were the hottest story in America, but not for the reasons that she'd planned. It was Morgan's effort to claim the book, the calculated murders, and his attempt on their lives that made it front-page news from coast to coast. No doubt audiences warmed to Jack's good looks, but their attention was riveted by the age-old forces that invariably weld curiosity to any story: a fascination with the tempest of violence and the forces that drive it. With all of Abby's meticulous planning, fate still played the trump card.

For the first time in her life Abby walked in the publishing sunlight, acknowledged as the author of her own work, Jack the rugged face on the dustcover standing beside her. The story of how they did it now assumed mythic proportions in the press, boosting sales to record highs, levels beyond Bertoli's wildest dreams. The book showed no signs of coming off the list. It swept the globe. Foreign sales were soaring. The novel had been translated into seventeen languages, and the numbers were growing. *Gable Cooper* was a brand-name.

Bertoli, in a master stroke of marketing, delayed publication of the paperback for Abby's first book and instead brought out the hardcover of the sequel. The two novels would now duel toe-to-toe for the top spot on the hardcover bestsellers list.

And yet with all of her success, it was a bitter-sweet moment. Morgan was right about one thing. Theresa had died because of the manuscript. She was in the way. She knew too much. Morgan had to get rid of her.

Jack lifted his cup and sipped. After nine months his hands still showed some signs of scarring from the white hot metal of the bulkhead door. His thick mane of dark hair floated in the breeze. It was one of those bucolic days on the Sound, what the natives had called the Salish Sea; wafting currents of salt-tinged air.

'I don't know if I told you. Sanfillipo called,' said Jack. 'They found your typewriter.'

Abby lifted her gaze from the surface of the table where she was lost in thought.

'It was in a small storage shed,' said Jack. 'Morgan rented it under a false name. They found everything. The forged contracts, certified copies of the copyright.'

The police actually found it two months earlier but had sealed the evidence until their investigation was complete. They also discovered the outline, the one Abby was sure Jack had taken from her desk that night in the islands. They found it in a hotel room in San Juan, along with Morgan's briefcase and a suitcase filled with his clothes.

'Why did he do it?'

'Seven million dollars is a strong incentive,' said Jack.

Abby shook her head. She could never bring herself to accept the obvious answer.

She wondered if Morgan had made the decision that very first day, when he discovered *she* was Gable Cooper. Sitting in his office looking at her across that vast gulf that separated them, did Spencer somehow realize what she did not; that the book was more than a dream, that it had a destiny. Perhaps he was grasping for the last straw of the desperate soul, a man beyond the pale of his career. For all of the violence, Abby knew in her heart that Morgan loved her. She was sure that he had pitched into that fiery grave knowing it himself.

Abby could not help but dwell on the chain of fury that she'd set in motion. It was a violence born of unrequited love, a senseless lashing out at the things that hurt him. At Charlie who had once possessed her and Jack who now did, but most of all at Abby, because she never understood his need.

There was evidence that Morgan had been burning his clients' own ships for some time to keep the wolf from his door, pyrotechnic skills he employed on Abby's beach house. This was something the police had now confirmed.

The registration of copyright, the document that Morgan made out in his own name, now languished, as Abby had originally intended, in the bureaucratic dustbin of the copyright office. It was not likely anyone would ever look for it again.

In the flush of excitement, Bertoli never noticed when Abby scrapped the outline to her sequel, and instead crafted a substitute.

Jack left a tip on the table and they headed down the street toward the crowds milling in front of the bookstore. As they drew closer, scores of curious eyes took a bead. Then there were hushed whispers, and a subtle motion rippled through the line like a Chinese dragon. People further back stepped out of line to get a glimpse. It was like a crafts fair for the famous; the star of the movie on one street, Jack and Abby on the other.

There were whispers and a few screams as the two of them came into view. Then quickly they were escorted past the crowd and through the door.

Inside there were stacks of books, windows piled high, everything Abby had ever written. On the table in front of her was the sequel. It bore the name Gable Cooper on the cover, and Abby's picture on the back, Jack's rugged countenance beside her, a partnership bound by love.

It was the story of a down-and-out writer, a woman approaching her middle years who crafted the novel of a lifetime, a terror-ridden tale in which she used a handsome and dangerous male face to sell her novel, a book entitled – *The List*.

Critical Mass

This book is dedicated to the selfless men and women of science who work to combat the dangers of nuclear proliferation, and, in particular, the people of the Russian Republic who have managed, against impossible odds, to keep the deadly genie in its bottle.

ACKNOWLEDGEMENTS

A great many people provided encouragement and support in the writing of this manuscript, including my family and a good number of friends. Among these were my publisher, G.P. Putnam's Sons, who showed grace and patience in waiting for the manuscript; my editor, Stacy Creamer; and my literary agent, Robert Gottlieb. Thanks for their encouragement and support. In particular, I thank my wife, Leah, for her ready ear in listening to my words as they were read and for her sharp eye in reading the early versions of the manuscript.

I would, however, be remiss if I were not to call out for special acknowledgement and thanks to those people at the Monterey Institute of International Studies and the Center for Nonproliferation Studies at Monterey, California. In particular, I wish to thank Dr Adam Bernstein, who has since joined the Sandia Laboratory. The center and Dr Bernstein are in no way responsible for any of the specific material appearing in the book, since they had no hand in writing any of it. For any errors in this regard the author is solely and entirely responsible.

Dr Bernstein was of considerable assistance in guiding me through some of the technical pitfalls of radiation poisoning and detection. I am also indebted to a number of people at the center for their advice concerning the thorny questions of global nuclear security and in particular for their insight into the selfless dedication of nuclear scientists and leaders in the Russian Republic, who against difficult odds have been able to assure that the story of *Critical Mass* remains one that is firmly fixed in the realm of fiction.

Steve Martini
April 1998

There were people in Hiroshima whose shadows were printed by the blast on the concrete walls of buildings and pavement. These shadows can still be seen. Some of the bodies that made them were never found, it was as if they never existed. There are those who have seen these shadows scorched on the hard ground, to whom they are mere curiosities of history – images of a time that has passed. If that is all they have come to be, then they are indeed the angels of apathy.

PROLOGUE

West of Cape Flattery and Strait of Juan de Fuca

The *Dancing Lady* was not a thing of beauty. She was sixty-three feet of welded steel, much of it dripping rust down her sides like dried blood.

Her raised forecastle deck and flaring prow were plowing the dark waters west of Vancouver Island at seven knots. She climbed the swells and plunged into the deepening troughs, straining to make headway in weather that was quickly turning foul. Her usual crew of five was down to three – the skipper, Nordquist, his son, and one other crewman who was like family, and like the family was now working for nothing.

The boat was a durable stern trawler with twin diesels designed for deep water. On her aft deck was a massive reel, and wrapped around it was a half-mile of open mesh netting, window dressing for this cruise.

The *Lady* was a bottom fisher, a work boat as common as ten penny nails in these waters. It was the reason they used her. She wouldn't be noticed even by overhead surveillance.

She rolled in the swells and wallowed in the troughs.

1

Hydraulic fluid seeped from the hoses that drove her massive boom, and one of her engines was a thousand hours past a needed overhaul, but Nordquist didn't have the money for the repairs. Working eighteen-hour days in bone-numbing cold water and ice-covered riggings, Nordquist was going broke. His wife was doing her shopping at the food bank, and loans were overdue on the boat. And still, the federal government did nothing to stop the Canadians from overfishing the areas west of Vancouver Island. They had killed the northwest salmon runs and were now busy taking everything they could find off the bottom. Nordquist and his compatriots couldn't afford the campaign contributions necessary to bribe their own government into action.

He looked out over the prow from the raised wheelhouse. She kept losing RPM on the starboard engine. Nordquist had to fight to hold her steady in the increasing swells. They rose up in front of him like ominous mountains, there one instant, and gone the next. The *Lady* was starting to pound. The weather was getting worse.

His son was straining to find a horizon through the fifty-power binoculars, eyes fixed to the west.

'Oh, shit.' The boy didn't have to say more.

Nordquist looked over his shoulder and saw it; a thirty-foot wall of water rushing down on them, on their starboard beam. He spun the wheel to the right, and thirty years of hands-on experience brought the bow of his boat like a knife toward the mountainous wall of water. It cascaded around the wheelhouse and shuddered the *Lady*'s steel to her keel. She plowed through and came out, plunging down the back side of the wave.

The wave had knocked the kid to the deck. He sat there in amazement, looking at his old man and marveling at his power to focus, even in the face of death.

*   *   *

2

The *Isvania* was a rusted-out hulk, a remnant of the once powerful Soviet fishing fleet. She'd been condemned for scrap the year before, but like everything else in the new Russia, even this was behind schedule. Heading for the boneyard, she was on her last voyage. She crossed the Bering Sea, threading her way through the Aleutians and the Gulf of Alaska, then down the Canadian coast. Her holds, fore and aft, were empty except for a light load of scrap metal. In the captain's safe were papers transferring the ship's title to a scrapyard outside of Bangkok. She ran with a skeleton crew of seven and made only one brief stop at Prince Rupert on the Canadian coast to pick up a small load of lumber which now rested, stacked on her decks. This was a cover in case she was stopped and boarded by coastal authorities, her justification for crossing the Bering Sea and hugging the American coast. Bills of lading showed the lumber to be delivered to Oakland, California, though her captain had no intention of going there. The lumber would be thrown overboard once *Isvania* dropped its real cargo. Then the ship would head west and south, toward the Indian Ocean and its final resting place.

The helmsman brought her five degrees to port as her captain, Yuri Valentok, strained his eyes through binoculars for anything on the horizon. The *Isvania* was taking on water in the forward hold and getting sluggish in the deepening troughs. The bilge pumps were handling it for now, but Valentok wasn't sure how long they would hold up. He couldn't see a damn thing through the binoculars. Drops of rain, driven by the wind, pelted the windows on the bridge like bullets. Only one of the wipers was working, and that was useless. The wind-whipped mist and froth from the waves created an impenetrable haze. Valentok could scarcely see the prow of his own ship. To make things worse, his radar was out. It hadn't worked since leaving Vladivostok. Twice they'd had to come to a dead stop in shipping lanes for fear of hitting other vessels. They laid on their fog horn and hoped the other ships could see them on their own radar. *Isvania* was like everything else in their crumbling country: coming apart with no money for repairs.

Valentok carried onboard one other waybill for an additional piece of cargo, but it was only to be used in the event of an extreme emergency, if his ship was forced into port. This particular waybill was forged. If the item was discovered, the captain would argue that he didn't know the nature of the cargo. Whether it would work with the American authorities he doubted, especially given the nature of what he was carrying. He would spend a long time answering questions, perhaps a long time in jail. He wondered if American jails were better than those in Russia.

He went to his charts on the table and braced himself against one of its metal legs. He checked the ship's position one more time. If his calculations were correct, they were precisely one hundred and twelve nautical miles due west of the Strait of Juán de Fuca, the passage to Puget Sound and the U.S. city of Seattle beyond.

Isvania's captain had never been to the U.S., though he had friends who sailed there recently, in a ship not unlike his own, a rusted-out scow ready for scrapping. It was becoming a common practice for Russian fishing vessels. They would clear customs and immigration, and as soon as the American officials left the ship, the entire crew including her captain would go over the side to start a new life, in a new land. They let the Americans deal with the scrap metal. Valentok thought he would like to go there himself one day, perhaps to Seattle, when this was over.

F our miles to the east in driving rain and surging seas, Jon

Nordquist gripped the wheel of the *Dancing Lady* with a firm hand. He used the leverage of his body to fight off the force of a giant rolling comber as it slid under the hull and slammed against the rudder. The boat listed heavily to port. For an instant he thought perhaps she might not come back. Then she responded to the helm, slowly.

'It's turning to shit out there. Can't see a damn thing.' Ben had his face pressed tightly into the covered scope of the ancient Furuno radar screen. 'How the hell are we supposed to find it?'

'Keep looking.' Nordquist cast a quick glance at his son and then back out to the mountainous wave that loomed before them, dwarfing the sixty-foot vessel. Their boat was like a matchstick in a flood.

The towering waves created vaporous green images on the radar screen like islands thrust up from the bottom of the sea. On the next sweep of the radar beam they were gone.

'She could run over us, and we'd never see her.' Ben was scared and it showed. He'd sailed in heavy seas, but nothing like this.

The thought of collision had entered Nordquist's mind, but it remained for his son to say it. For the moment he was more worried about broaching, or pitchpoling down the face of one of the waves, nosing in, never to come up again. There were a million ways to die at sea.

'Nothing.' Ben pressed his head closer to the radar screen until the pressure against his forehead actually hurt. 'Besides, even if we find 'em, how the hell are we supposed to bring the thing on board in this?'

'One crisis at a time,' said his father. He checked his watch. From his pocket he took a small black plastic object, not much larger than a calculator. With his teeth he pulled out the three-inch antenna and pressed a couple of buttons, then waited, one eye on the sea, the other on the portable global positioning satellite (GPS) unit in his hand. Two sets of numbers appeared, one over the other for longitude and latitude. The pocket GPS unit was not as reliable or accurate as its larger cousins that ran from fixed computers on bigger ships, but still it was not likely to be off by more than a few hundred feet. At this location the Russian ship should be no more than a quarter-mile off their starboard beam, that is, if it was on time and hadn't gotten lost.

There was no way to communicate by radio. Other ships were certain to pick up the signal, perhaps the Coast Guard. They patrolled the waters, even at two hundred miles out, the limits of their jurisdiction. They had satellites and planes and used both to interdict drugs and track vessels carrying human cargo, seeking to deposit their huddled masses on American soil. Two vessels meeting in open sea were not likely to go unnoticed. For this reason a careful procedure for drop and recovery had been worked out. But would it work in this weather? Nordquist didn't know. No one had anticipated the fucking storm of the century.

H e turned his ship into the weather.
'All ahead slow.' Valentok couldn't wait. Besides, the cargo he was carrying was not something he wanted onboard an instant longer than was necessary. Let the Americans find it, he thought. He had been paid handsomely to carry it, but it was their problem now.

He gave orders to raise the cover on the aft hold and swing the crane over the opening. He sent his first mate aft to supervise and watched from the outside starboard wing of the bridge as the cargo hook slipped into the hold and disappeared. He waited two anxious minutes. It seemed an eternity. The hook rose on its steel cable. Valentok saw it. It was attached to a heavy metal ring. Connected to the ring was a net, ringed with three large floating buoys. The entire package looked like a pouch closed by a drawstring at the top. Inside the net was an object wrapped in a canvas tarp. It wasn't large, about the size of a washing machine, and heavy for its size. Though it was no problem for the massive cargo crane of the factory ship. It was lifted easily over the deck and swung toward the stern of the *Isvania*. Slowly it slipped into the water, the cable descending.

Valentok had his back to the bow of his own vessel, watching the action, when he heard a scream from the wheelhouse. He turned, and in a flash of lightning from the darkening sky, he saw it. Barreling down the face of an oncoming wave was a sixty-foot stern fisher, the glass on its forecastle windows gleaming in the flash of lightning.

'Hard to port.' Without thinking Valentok gave the order to turn. His ship was still in the trough of the wave.

The helmsman didn't question, but spun the wheel.

Isvania began to heel to starboard. She listed as the luminous green and white wall of water hit her on the curve of her prow like a tidal wave. It washed over the forward deck and slammed into the windows of the bridge twenty feet up, blowing out glass like an artillery shell.

A thirty-foot wall of water swept down the companionway on port side, slamming men and machinery into the bulkhead and washing them over the side. Like Niagara it swept toward the yawning uncovered hatch of the open aft hold. Thousands of tons of green water cascaded over the edge, down into the ship's belly.

Valentok's grip on the rail was the only thing that kept him from being ripped over the side by the onrushing water. Like steel his fingers bit into the railing as he found himself contemplating the strange sensation of being totally submerged in the sea while standing on the deck of his own ship. He was waiting for the wave to pass, waiting for an eternity. He held his breath until his lungs felt like fire, until he realized that neither he nor his ship was coming up.

She turtled in front of his eyes. There was a flash of barnacled keel and two mammoth bronze propellers still turning as the ship rolled over. Then, before Nordquist could blink, the Russian ship was swallowed by the sea.

He stood motionless at the wheel, stunned, his knees locked as cold sweat ran down his face.

He was quickly jarred back to reality by the pounding of the *Lady* as she plunged to the bottom of the wave's trough. He held his breath, wondering if the wall of water rising in front of him held a deadly surprise: a hundred tons of twisted Russian steel tumbling just under the surface.

He gripped the wheel, white-knuckled, and waited for the screech of metal ripping metal. The diesel engines lugged down as the *Lady* climbed the face of the wave and seemed to pass harmlessly up and over.

It shot from the depths directly in front of him, and Nordquist caught only a glimpse before he felt it slam against the hull a stack of lumber still bound by its metal bands. It rolled under the hull of the *Lady* like a giant square log. Nordquist threw the engines into neutral, trying desperately to save the props. He felt the lumber bounce along the bottom and watched as it drifted to the surface behind them.

He had his back turned, so he got only a fleeting glimpse when he turned. There in the white-tipped froth on the crest of the next wave were three large orange buoys.

They slid from view down the back side of the wave.

'Did you see them?' Nordquist pointed for the kid to look.

His son's attention was focused toward the stern, to the place in the sea where the Russian had been swallowed.

'Shouldn't we go back?' He was looking now at his father.

'What for?'

'Maybe some of them are alive.'

'None of them are alive,' said Nordquist.

'How can you be sure?'

'Could you survive that?'

The answer was obvious to them both. Still the kid wanted to do the right thing.

'We could look,' he said.

'For what? To make ourselves feel good?'

'If it was us . . .'

'It wasn't us. They knew the risks.' Nordquist had no love for the Russians. His boat had been nudged twice in the last year by larger Russian trawlers seeking an edge in the good fishing grounds. They brought their huge factory ships in and took what they wanted. They would slice you in half if you got in their way.

'Don't argue with me. Turn that thing on.' The old man gestured with his head toward a drab green metal box mounted on the boat's console as he struggled with the wheel.

In the mounting seas the kid had to fight his way back across the wheelhouse to the radarscope and the metal box mounted next to it. He flipped the switch and the screaming signal nearly pierced his eardrums. He reached for a knob on the side and squelched the noise. The subsonic transceiver was Russian military surplus, part of the deal. It could pick up a signal a hundred miles away. This one was coming from a transmitter very close. It could not be heard on normal marine radio bands. The transceiver was a backup in case the two vessels missed each other in the open ocean. The buoys were designed to float for four days, then to sink with their cargo if no one picked it up. The subsonic transmitter would beam its signal for the entire period until it went down. Then the pressure of the deep sea would crush it.

The signal was confirmation. Somehow they'd delivered before they went down.

'How . . .?' The kid looked at his father.

Nordquist shook his head. He wasn't sure.

The *Lady* mounted the next wave and Nordquist saw them again. He was drawing up on the orange buoys quickly. If he wasn't careful he would run over them, foul his prop in their lines or net. Without power, in heavy seas, they would quickly join the Russian at the bottom.

'Get to the winch. Tell Carlos to come up.'

'What about the pumps?'

'Forget the pumps. Right now we got to get it onboard.'

Nordquist's son headed out the cabin door toward the open aft deck.

The old man brought the bow of the *Lady* into the wind and reduced power just enough to hold her in the heavy seas. It gave him lateral maneuvering with little or no headway. He would wait for the sea to bring the buoys to him.

They would have only one chance to pick them up. If they missed, by the time he came about in these seas, they would lose visual contact. Then they would have to track the package using the subsonic signal. Nordquist had been warned to get it onboard as quickly as possible and to turn off or disable the device. While the Coast Guard might not pick it up, American submarines, the so-called 'killer subs' that hunted their Russian counterparts, listened on these frequencies. If they got curious, they might take a look.

Nordquist saw them on the crest of the wave bobbing like orange barrels. Tethered beneath them in the depths probably fifteen feet down was the cargo, wrapped in a net. He had no idea of its weight or size. The fact that the Russian had rolled made him wonder if the load was heavy. Maybe that and the fact that a wave had hit them on the beam with so much weight over the side had caused them to capsize. If the Russian couldn't handle it, how could he?

Nordquist maneuvered using the wheel, as well as the throttle controls for the two engines. He guided the *Lady* so that the package would pass on her starboard side. Nordquist alerted the two men aft using the boat's bullhorn, then looked over his right shoulder and saw his son leaning over the side, straining for a view. The men swung the boom over the side and with a long gaff guided its cargo hook toward the buoys as the current carried them along the side of the boat. Nordquist could hear the cable of the net's line scraping the hull as the load passed beneath them.

Suddenly he felt the *Lady* heel over heavily to starboard. The hook had snagged the buoys. The drag caused the *Lady* to make a slow lingering turn in the trough, a ten-degree list, fifteen. This was what the old man was worried about; getting caught in the trough of one wave and hit from behind by another. The classic broach. She would roll and capsize.

He goosed the controls for the starboard engine, giving her more thrust on that side, then brought the wheel to port a few degrees. This brought the *Lady*'s bow into the wave at a forty-five-degree angle. The engines strained as she climbed the wall of water dragging her cargo along side.

The two crewmen struggled with the winch controls and finally swung the boom around the stern. They kept the load amid-ships and in the water, neutralizing its weight until they could get a break between seas to try to lift it onboard.

Nordquist tried to steady the boat as he looked out one of the stern portholes from the wheelhouse. He saw smoke and steam rising from the winch drum. The load was too heavy. Even over the howl of the wind he could hear the screeching of the winch's clutch as it struggled to catch and pull the cargo up out of the water. He could see the tethered cables below the buoys as they rose slowly from the depths.

Another wave, and Nordquist had his hands full. He could only hope that the weight of the load wasn't out of the water yet. His eyes to the front, he deftly handled the engine throttles and wheel to keep the boat balanced. The cargo dragging in the water acted like a sea anchor and actually helped him. For now it was a friend. The moment they got it out of the water, it would be another matter. If a wave struck, the load would begin to swing like a pendulum. Its weight could bring them over.

The boat seemed to settle in the water. The winch was cranking again, smoke rising from the drum as it turned slowly. Nordquist got the first glimpse of the tethered net. It rose slowly, dripping seawater over the stern. The canvas wrapping around the cargo had opened and filled with water, adding to the weight.

Slowly it came up until it cleared the transom and hovered over the stern. Another wave hit the prow of the *Lady*, and the load began to sway with the motion of the sea. The kid didn't wait. He panicked, pushed the winch lever forward and the entire weight crashed down on the afterdeck. There was a thunderous roar as the weight buckled one of the deck plates. Splintered wood and tons of seawater spilled out of the canvas cover as it ripped along one side. A small silvery sphere the size of a grapefruit rolled out of the smashed container and across the steel deck. It hit the gunnel with a deadening thud, and began to roll back the other way with the motion of the ship.

Stunned, the two crewmen were frozen in place, their gaze glued to the object now loose on the *Lady*'s deck.

From the wheelhouse Nordquist could see it.

The men moved, trying to corral it, but they were too slow. The *Lady* heaved forward over the crest of a wave, and the heavy metal sphere rolled along the passageway, beneath the forecastle deck and out onto the prow. Over the steel deck, it sounded like a bowling ball. Nordquist could hear it slamming against equipment and metal bulkheads. The only thing keeping it onboard was the boat's high gunwales. It careened around the boat like a pinball, slamming into a hatch cover. Nordquist could tell that it was dense and very heavy. He didn't know precisely what it was, but he had a good guess. The guys from Deming and Sedro-Woolley hadn't told him everything, but they'd given him hints, enough to put him on guard. He tried to warn his son with frantic hand signals. Finally he got to the microphone and pushed the button for the bullhorn.

'Stay away from it. Get clear.' His words echoed from a loud speaker mounted atop the wheelhouse.

The boy looked up at him, anxiety written in his eyes. They'd ridden heavy seas for days, survived a near collision with the Russian, and managed to snatch the buoys from the teeth of the storm. He wasn't going to lose it now.

The boy dove onto the deck trying to trap it between the steel gunwale and his outstretched hands. He got his fingers on it and held on, as Carlos came in on top of him.

'No!' Nordquist screamed into the bullhorn.

They managed to subdue it, trap it against the gunwale. With their bare fingers underneath, rubbing and chaffing at the sphere, it seemed to coat their hands with something like shimmering chalk. The powdery substance filled the air and drifted against the steel bulkhead beneath the wheelhouse window. The sphere was like a magical substance, and very heavy. Neither of them had ever seen anything like it before.

13

From the wheelhouse above, Nordquist looked on, slack-jawed, from under dark, furrowed brows. For some strange reason he didn't have to be told. He knew that his son was as good as dead.

CHAPTER
ONE

Friday Harbor, WA

Burned out at thirty-two, she'd had enough.

They knock L.A., but it isn't the place. It's the people. Too many of them. Lincoln talked about the better angels of our nature, but even angels have limits. Put them in a congested maze, pump in heat and foul air, and you can watch while they rip off each other's wings. Joselyn Cole's were long gone.

Two years ago she pitched it in, sold her furniture, listed the condo at Marina Del Rey, and started looking for a life. She headed north, up the coast, and kept driving, reading population signs as she went. In three weeks traversing back roads and taking her time, she found she had gone about as far as she could without leaving the country. So she left the road and took a ferry. At her first port of call she stopped, looked around and decided she was home.

Friday Harbor in the San Juan Islands was a ninety-minute boat ride from Anacortes in Washington State. It may as well have been the back side of the moon. The island was small and the town was smaller. Some say it is like a scaled-down version of Martha's Vineyard. Joselyn would have to take their word for it, never having seen that other place. What she discovered was that it was quiet, and the people, for the most part, were friendly, while they minded their own business. Once the islanders realized that she was there to stay, she became a local. Acceptance was automatic. Within a week the clerks at the little grocery store were all calling her by her first name.

It took a few months to hurdle the Washington State bar exam. Once she did, she hung out her shingle:

JOSELYN COLE
ATTORNEY AT LAW

Those who have known her for more than a week, call her 'Joss'. Business was slow. There were some drug cases, mostly marijuana grows, nurseries in houses and old barns run from generators big enough to light a small city. The Feds could detect them with thermal-imaging devices that picked up heat from the grow lights through a six-inch wall.

There are more than four hundred islands in the San Juan chain. Some of these are nothing more than a few rocks that disappear at high tide.

But with an international border only a few miles across open water, Victoria to the west, Vancouver to the northeast, the islands were a smuggler's paradise. Joss thanked God for small favors. With the small-time daily case, the occasional DUI (driving under the influence), and a few divorces, it kept the wolf from her door, even if her door wasn't much.

She learned that it was possible to survive without a VCR or, for that matter, a television. On Friday nights she found her feet tapping the floor to the strains of Jimmy Buffet off a hi-fi she bought when she was a kid. She was slowly reading her way through volumes from the local library. Occasionally, she would lose all sense of economic perspective and buy a new paperback.

In winter it was dark by four in the afternoon, and the streets of Friday Harbor were usually empty. Most of the summer businesses shut down for the season. Like bears, the fishermen and blue-collar types would hole up in any cave they could find, mostly the few dimly lit bars that form hangouts for the locals. The winter was when you found out who was hardcore.

Joss stared across her desk into the face of one of these hardcore types. Weathered like leather, its only soft aspect were two brown, basset-hound eyes looking back at her.

'There oughta be something you can do. I mean at least get 'em to pay the doctor bills.' George Hummel was smiling at her, but she could tell that he was scared. George was not exactly a picture of health. He had some signs of bleeding at the gumline. His hair was falling out like dry straw. Hummel was a fisherman, or at least that was what he did for a living when he wasn't too sick to take to the water. He was a client, one of five sport fishers trying to get the state to pay disability benefits for what they claimed was an industrial-related illness. All five men had the same symptoms, red blotches on the skin, loss of appetite, bleeding gums, hair loss. George had become their spokesman.

'I know damn well it's industrial,' he said.

'You don't have to convince me, George.'

'Fine, then do something. I'm running out of money.' His savings were nearly gone. His wife and kids had to eat.

From his lawyer's expression he could tell that the prospects were not good.

'What are the doctors saying?' She took notes on a legal pad at her desk, George's file spread out in front of her. Its contents were meager except for her own unanswered

17

correspondence, mostly to doctors and state agencies that were not much help.

'The doctors. They don't know from nothing. They want to send me for tests to Seattle.'

'Do it,' she told him.

'It costs money. My health insurance won't pay. They say its to pursue litigation, not for treatment.'

The great insurance-circle jerk. What the politicians, for a hefty campaign contribution, called 'managed-care'; a panel of physicians under the insurance company's thumb saying 'no' to anything that costs money. They had now managed to drive the system down the public's throat.

George told her that the insurance company was stalling, waiting for him to die. 'Then it won't cost 'em anything.'

'I need medical records,' said Joss. 'I can't do anything without a diagnosis.'

For the state to pay disability, she had to show some industrial connection, some job-related cause for George's condition. For this she required a medical expert to go out on a limb, to tell her in medical terms the probable cause of George's illness, exactly what he had.

'We all know what it is. It's the damn cheese-heads.' This was George's unflattering term for his neighbors across the border to the north.

'They been pumping raw sewage into the Sound at Victoria forever. They take our fish, now what's left all has three eyes. I got one the other day,' he told her, 'was startin' to grow front legs like a dog.'

The fight over diminishing salmon runs had taken on the specter of a war. Ferries stopping at Friday Harbor and headed for Sidney on Vancouver Island had been blockaded by fleets of commercial fishing boats in protest and held for hours at the docks. The Canadians had retaliated by blocking the Alaskan ferry up north. Indian nations had gone to court to uphold fishing rights granted in treaties with a term that were supposed to last 'as long as the grass grows and the winds blow'. Unfortunately, the salmon couldn't breed fast enough to cooperate. There were too many fishing boats chasing too few fish.

'It's a good theory, George.' She was talking about the charge of Canadian pollution. 'But I need evidence, medical records I can take to the state.'

'I'll bring 'em the fucking fish,' said George. 'The one with the two front legs.'

They'd had this conversation before. It was becoming circular. His hands were trembling. He was scared. He had slipped markedly since their last meeting two weeks earlier.

'They gave me a transfusion. Did you know that?'

'No, I didn't.'

'Well they did. Last Thursday. They told me I'm anemic. Red blood count is low.'

There might be something new in his medical records. Joselyn made a note. 'They didn't say anything about what might have caused this anemia?'

'Not to me,' he said. 'They asked me if I'd been around any chemicals.'

'That's a start.'

'You would think they would suspect something.'

Doctors didn't usually like litigation, even if it wasn't aimed at them. Their suspicions don't often end up in their notes. She didn't tell George this. It would only make him feel more forlorn. She made a note to get the latest medical records.

'I gotta leave something for the family,' he told her.

When she looked up from her pad, she could tell by his expression that George was thinking cancer. He had crossed

19

the great divide. He knew he was dying. Joselyn knew he was right.

She told him not to give up hope, tried to cheer him up. 'It may not be as serious as you think.' They both knew she was lying.

'I'll talk to the doctors. Try to get them to pressure the insurance company to cover the tests. Rattle their cage with threats of a bad-faith claim for withholding coverage. It might get their attention.'

'Might?' said George.

'There are no easy answers.'

'I don't know how long I can last.'

She told him to hang in, to come back in a week. 'I may have something by then.' Their meeting was over.

'You will call me?' He looked at her with that hopeful basset-like gaze.

'As soon as I know something.'

'You'll call the doctors?' He moved reluctantly toward the door.

She was up from behind the desk, moving with him now. 'This afternoon. I'll follow it with a letter.' She took one of his hands. It was shaking, like palsy.

George's wife was waiting in the outer room. He refused to allow her to attend these sessions, afraid she would only become more depressed.

There was another guy sitting in the reception area eyeing George as he stepped through the door. The man tried to be discreet, but couldn't help looking. George was one of those sights that no matter how hard you tried, you just couldn't divert your eyes. Like the man without legs propped against a building wall selling pencils from a cup. He made you feel uncomfortable, but you had to look.

The other man was well-dressed: cashmere sweater and Boston loafers. He had a lean face, sandy-colored hair and deep-set eyes. There was that serious business look about him, something that said no-nonsense. He wore an expensive wristwatch and a tan with that glow of humidity that screams the tropics. Just sitting in the chair, he looked like money. Not one of her usual clients.

She could feel his eyes move over her as the man's gaze left George.

George tried to put a brave face on bleak circumstances for his wife. 'Ms Cole's gonna help us with the doctors. Gonna get insurance coverage for the tests.'

He was making promises Joselyn might not be able to keep.

George's wife smiled. 'I knew she could help us.'

'You will call me?' said George.

'Don't worry, George. I said I'd call, and I will.'

'Good.' George shook her hand. His wife slipped an arm under his, more to help him than to be escorted, and they were gone, through the door and out to the parking lot.

When Joss turned, the man in the chair was now on his feet, blocking her path back to the office.

'Joselyn Cole?'

'Yes.'

'Dean Belden,' he said extending a hand as if she was supposed to know who he was.

'Have we met?'

'I was referred by Dick Norman down at the bank.'

She searched her memory. Then she remembered. She'd met Norman once at a Chamber of Commerce meeting.

'Well, if he's sending me business maybe I owe him a lunch.'

'I'm sure he'd enjoy it. Your office is pretty new.' The guy was looking around, appraising the empty walls and the reception cubicle with its frosted-glass window, closed and dark.

21

'I haven't had time to get a receptionist yet.'

'Good help is hard to find.' He looked at her and smiled.

Belden was a quick study. He knew instinctively it was not time, but money that was the problem.

'Your client there looks pretty sick.' He gestured toward the door through which Hummel had just disappeared.

'Yes.'

'You gonna be able to help him?'

'I hope so.'

'Is it serious?'

She gave him a shrug.

'Sorry, I shouldn't pry. Too nosy sometimes. Suppose you couldn't say even if you knew. Wouldn't be kosher.'

'No, it wouldn't.'

'Still I hope it's nothing contagious.'

The thought of catching whatever George had never entered Joss's mind, not until that moment.

'I think we're safe. What did you say your name was?'

'Belden. Dean Belden. You can call me Dean.'

'Well, Dean, what can I do for you?'

'Handle a little business,' he said.

'Let's step into my office.' She moved around him in that direction and he followed her.

'I'm trying to set up a small plant on the island.' He talked while they walked, not one to waste time.

'What kind of plant?'

'Assembly.'

'Have a seat.'

'High-end items.' He sat in one of the client chairs as if he intended to all along, never missing a beat. 'Electronics. Mostly switches used in industrial computers. It's not high volume, so transportation is not a major consideration. You might be wondering why I picked the islands?'

'Not really,' said Joss. 'Would you like some coffee?'

'No thanks. We have a contract to supply another company up in Canada, so the location works well. I need to incorporate in Washington State. Get a business license. Comply with the taxing authorities. Employer I.D. number. The usual stuff,' he said.

Joss was getting coffee for herself from the machine in the corner and wondering if maybe the guy at the bank had her confused with somebody else in town. Business law was not her usual fare, and as she turned back to her desk she ended up wearing the thought on her face.

'You can do this kind of thing, can't you? I'd be willing to pay a sizeable retainer.'

For the first time, he had her undivided attention. The sound of money.

'Oh, I could do it. I mean, incorporate a small business, pretty straightforward. It's just that I'm . . .' She was thinking of ways to cover the blank expression on her face. 'I'm pretty busy right now. But I could probably squeeze it in.' She picked up her calendar book from the desk and opened it, shielding the empty pages from his view. 'I could move this around, and cancel here until next week.' She looked up at him. 'I could fit it in.'

This could cut into reading time at the library and the parrot-head music hour at night.

He smiled like maybe he knew B.S. when he heard it. 'And what's your usual fee?'

Before she could say a word, he said: 'I'm assuming a hefty retainer against an hourly fee.'

Belden must be flush. What Joselyn knew about business law she could write longhand on the cuticle of one fingernail. But it would include the fact that corporate documents were usually done for a flat fee. A few thousand dollars at most, depending on the complexity. In some places it could be done mail order.

'I guess I'm just curious. Don't get me wrong,' she said. 'It's not that I don't want the business. But why didn't you just hire one of the big business firms down in Seattle?'

'It'd cost me more,' he said.

'Maybe,' said Joss.

'Besides, if I'm going to live and do business in the islands, I thought it would be best to have somebody here. I'm going to need somebody local on a regular basis for other matters.'

Joselyn didn't want to press the issue and lose a client.

'What kind of matters?'

He offered a thoughtful expression. 'Foreign licenses. Mostly to do business across the border. Pretty easy stuff. You've never done it?'

'No.' She wasn't going to lie to him.

'I'm sure you're a fast learner. It's pretty simple. Like piloting a plane, once you've done it.'

'I don't fly,' she told him.

'I do.'

'Why am I not surprised?'

He looked at her and they both laughed, like breaking the ice.

Belden was not unattractive. Closely cropped hair graying at the temples. He was over six feet and athletic in build. He wore a polo shirt, and stretched it in all the right places.

'Are you interested?' he asked.

Definitely, thought Joselyn. 'I think I can put the documents together for you.'

'No. No,' said Belden. 'I'd want to give you a retainer to serve as counsel to the company.' He smiled and bared even white teeth that could be an ad for the dental association. There was a twinkle in his eyes, which were a shade of green she had never seen before.

24

'We could end up buying a substantial amount of your time,' he told her.

'My professional time is for sale.'

'But you are not.' The way he said it was more of a statement than a question. She answered it anyway.

'I enjoy working for myself.'

'Good. An independent woman. I understand. Of course it could cut into the time available for your other business.' He looked at her and smiled a little as if perhaps he knew this was not a problem.

'I'll worry about that.'

'Good. Then it's agreed.' He reached into a pocket and came up with a checkbook and pen. 'What kind of a retainer do you usually take?'

'On the island I don't usually see a retainer.'

He looked up from his checkbook.

'Most of my clients are local,' she explained. 'I bill them, and they pay. When they can.'

'How about ten thousand?' he said.

It was a good thing her chair didn't recline any further. She would have been on the floor.

'And for an hourly fee?' He looked up again.

She was having a little trouble catching her breath, but thought quickly: 'How about two hundred an hour?' It was more than she charged her other clients, but it looked like Belden could afford it.

'How about three?' he said.

'You should be my business manager,' she told him.

'I always like to think my lawyer will take my phone calls when I have a problem.'

He had a light leather folder that he'd placed on the floor next to his chair. Now he reached into it and pulled out a manila letter-sized envelope, then started to write the check.

25

'I think all the information you'll need is in here.' He nodded toward the envelope. 'If you have any questions, my business card is there as well. Just give me a call.'

'In the interests of full disclosure,' she said, 'I think there's something you should know.'

He didn't look up. He was too busy putting all the zeros in the right places on the check.

'I know,' he said. 'You don't have an extensive practice in business law.'

'Is it that obvious?'

'No.'

'Then how did you guess?'

'The banker told me.' Now he was looking at her across the desk, a piercing green gaze over an in-your-face smile.

'But you said he recommended me?'

'Oh, he did. Very highly. I asked him if there were any good-looking women lawyers in town.' He was stone serious with only that little smirk. 'It was a short list,' said Belden. He said it shamelessly, so that she couldn't help but laugh.

She was still laughing when he passed the check across the desk, along with the file of information on his corporation.

She stared at it for a while.

'Like I say, it would cost me at least as much down in Seattle.'

From all appearances, Belden was a man who was used to getting his own way. There was something military about him, like he was used to giving orders, and having them followed. She wasn't sure she liked it, but she liked the money. Maybe that's what bothered her, the feeling that she was selling out, trading her independence for a check.

'You've got the retainer, all the information. Then we're agreed.'

She looked at the check again. 'I suppose.'

'Don't look so sad,' he told her. 'Having money should not make you depressed.'

'Oh. It doesn't.' She put a face on it and smiled.

'That's good. Now tell me. What brought you to the islands?' He made it sound like business was over, pesky stuff out of the way. He knew what he wanted, and was almost a little too focused and fast.

'What makes you think I wasn't born here?' she asked.

'You don't have the look.'

'There's an island look?'

'A slight gathering of moss on the Northern exposure,' he told her. 'You look . . .' He considered for a moment. 'Like California.'

'It's that obvious? I suppose the moss hasn't had time to form.'

'That and the license on your wall.' He nodded toward the certificate from the California Bar framed next to the one from Washington State.

'You have sharp eyes.'

'Wait 'til you get to my teeth,' he said.

That's what she was afraid of.

'What are you doing for dinner?' he asked.

'Sorry. I've got plans.' Once she cashed his check, a nice steak and Jimmy Buffet, thought Joselyn. He was moving much too fast. She wanted to do some checking around town. See if anybody knew him.

'Maybe some other time.'

'Perhaps. When do you want this done?' She tried to get back to business, tapped the envelope on her desk.

'Oh. I don't know. How long do you think it will take – without rushing?'

'A week, maybe ten days, if I don't run into any problems.'

'Then I'll see you in a week.'

He was up out of his chair. 'No need to show me to the door. I can find my way. Next week then.'

'Next week.'

CHAPTER
TWO

Santa Crista, CA

G ideon van Ry rocked lazily back in the old office
swivel chair. It was ungainly and undersized for his
tall, lanky body. In front of him the government surplus
desk was stacked high with papers; three weeks of unread
correspondence and reports. Van Ry was part of a U.N.
arms inspection team and had just returned from the Middle
East.

He was a product of the Cold War. Gideon had been born
in Holland but raised in later years in the Soviet Union. His
mother was Russian, his father Dutch. They had met after
the War in the university, but the marriage was not to last.

Gideon learned his English, as every school child does,
in the Dutch public school system and his Russian during
summer vacations living with his mother in Moscow. His
university education came there, where he showed a flair
for the sciences, and was climbing through the hierarchy in
the academic world of physics when the old Soviet Empire
collapsed. His specialty was nuclear magnetic resonance.
He had spent two years in Southern California at CalTech,

where he did not take a degree but learned everything there was to know about nuclear weapons design.

He had always been mechanically inclined, even as a child. He had taken his family's grandfather clock apart when he was eight. It had never maintained accurate time since. But his parents didn't have it repaired. His mother considered it a remembrance of his childhood.

Anyone watching might have feared that Gideon's slouching six-foot-five-inch frame would go over backwards in the chair, except that his long legs served as a counterbalance. He turned a little to face the window as he studied the document in hand and ran long fingers through long, wavy blond hair. He had blue eyes, dimpled cheeks, and fair skin.

'You have read this?' He spoke with a slight accent. He was talking to the woman standing in the doorway to his office.

'Yes.' Caroline Clark was a graduate student from Britain via Princeton University, where she took her undergraduate degree in physics. She was one of four interns assigned to work with van Ry on analysis and reporting.

There was a veritable stream of young interns who passed through the institute, remaining for anywhere from six months to two years. When they returned home, many of them, in time, went on to play prominent roles in the weapons control programs and policies of their own countries. It was one of the principal goals of the institute to plant that seed in fertile multinational ground.

'Have you shown this to anyone else?' asked Gideon.

'Not yet. I was going to if you didn't get back today. I didn't think it should wait.'

'You're right.'

The note was cryptic, typed quickly on an old typewriter. It was a note from an old friend of Gideon's, a fellow student from his days in Moscow. Gideon had maintained correspondence with him for several years during his studies at CalTech, but had not heard from him in more than a year.

Uri Valnick worked deep in the bureaucracy of Russia's nuclear industry, one of the many bureaus that issued statistics and records on what was becoming a burgeoning business behind the old iron curtain, the dismantlement of nuclear armaments.

The Institute Against Mass Destruction (IAMAD) had gone to great lengths to maintain contacts with people who worked in this field. It fostered communication across national boundaries, all with a common purpose: the dismantlement of weapons of mass destruction, the science of nonproliferation.

IAMAD had endeavoured to avoid being accused of fronting for any government. Its information was available to the world. Anyone with the price could log onto its database, one of the most extensive lists of nuclear, biologic, and chemical weapons in the world. Its purpose was to shine light into a dangerous crevice, the deadly and growing commerce in weapons of mass destruction.

Founded in the late 1980s, the institute had sprouted like a field of wild mushrooms until it now occupied a sizable Spanish colonial bungalow in the historic area of old Santa Crista. It was a deceptively tranquil location for activities that took its resident scholars and graduate students to some of the hottest spots on earth – the Middle East, the volatile republics of the former Soviet Union, and the fractured former Yugoslavia, ethnic hotbed of the Balkans.

'What do you make of it?' he asked her.

She shrugged, a sign that she couldn't be sure. 'It's possible it's just a bit of poor record-keeping.' It sounded a lot like wishful thinking.

31

'You know the problems over there. Limited staff, no money. Items get misplaced all the time.'

'True.' Still Gideon knew it had to be checked out.

'Could they have been dismantled?' he asked.

She shook her head. 'If so, the Pu_{239} from them would have shown up in the stockpile of raw materials. It doesn't.'

It was like the daily tally of cash drawers in a bank. If significant amounts of plutonium or highly enriched uranium showed up missing at the end of a month, alarms would sound off all over the institute and the information would be beamed around the world on its database.

Gideon checked his watch. There was eleven hours' difference. 'I don't think this can wait. If we have no one in place, I am going to have to call the director, get authorization for travel.'

'You're going to Sverdlovsk?'

'I'm the only one who could gain access,' said Gideon.

He was right. Sverdlovsk was one of four nuclear dismantlement sites in Russia. Each was heavily guarded. None admitted observers from the West. But Gideon was Russian. He had been raised largely in Russia at least in his later years, and had contacts in the Russian government, people who if he approached them in the right manner might allow one of their fellow countrymen access.

'It could be a mistake,' said Caroline. 'Someone could have transposed a number. You know how they're overworked.' She was talking about the Russian nuclear technicians, scientists, and military men, most of whom hadn't been paid in months.

'In which case we will not embarrass ourselves with an erroneous report to the international community.'

She looked at him as if she was not sure what to do.

'What if it's not a mistake?' Gideon knew that as things grew more desperate in Russia, the risk of a guard being paid to look the other way, or a technician to smuggle a few kilos of uranium from a facility, grew with each passing month.

'When did you get it?' he asked.

'Two days ago.'

'Then figure two weeks,' said Gideon. The question was, if the items were taken, when was it done? Operating on the principle of the worst possible scenario, Gideon was already working backwards to determine how long thieves may have had to transport the materials across national borders.

'As it stands we either have a mistake,' said Gideon, 'admittedly a rather gross one . . .'

She agreed.

'. . . or loose nuclear devices or dismantled devices with weapons-grade material on the loose. In any event if we've caught it, the Russian authorities have had enough time to discover the same discrepancy. Check and see if there are any signs of an investigation.'

Russian language analysts, either at the institute, or at the Defense Language Institute, would be scanning newspapers and radio news reports from the region. They would check to see if these were reporting anything unusual.

'Then you don't want me to check directly with Russian authorities?'

'Not yet.'

Uri Valnick had written to him in confidence. If the institute checked with Russian authorities directly, they would want to know the source of the institute's information. It was important for Gideon to protect his source. He would have to make discreet inquiries, use what contacts he had to gain access without causing alarm in the Russian nuclear community. If he wasn't careful all the doors would slam in his face while an internal investigation was conducted. He was half Russian, but he had lived for years in the West. It would require some diplomatic skills.

Caroline made a note. She had met some of the Russian scientists and technicians on a tour the year before. They were dedicated people, and she found it difficult to believe that any of them would sell nuclear materials on the black market.

Gideon scratched his chin. 'What troubles me is that two items are missing. Why would they take two?' He looked at her.

'In for a penny, in for a pound? That is, if there is a theft.'

He shook his head. 'Yes, but it increases the risk of detection.'

There had already been several documented cases of black marketeering, mostly low-grade fissile materials being smuggled from former satellite countries into Afghanistan and peddled with indiscretion so that the perpetrators were quickly caught. The usual pattern of theft was in the nature of pilfering; a few grams of low-grade uranium, not weapons grade, taken over an extended period until the thieves possessed a kilogram or so. It was stuff that might be used for a 'dirty bomb', something that would never reach critical mass for a chain reaction, but might produce a toxic effect and could, with enough high explosives, contaminate a considerable area.

But the information Gideon had before him was something different – two intact nuclear weapons with detonators. This was on a scale so bold as to be unbelievable. It was the reason Caroline did not buy it, and Gideon knew he would need more information to convince others, if it was something more than a mistake.

'What do we know about the items?'

She had the file in her hand, working notes that included information that was not usually entered on the institute's database. This was stuff not generally for public consumption. For reasons of security IAMAD did not usually identify the precise location of weapons storage facilities or the items contained in them even if they knew. This would only serve to mark them as targets for terrorists or the Russian mob.

Caroline fingered quickly through hand-written notes in the file.

'The missing items are from Sverdlovsk-forty-five. The facility was renamed about a year ago. It's now called Lesnoy, a principal location for dismantling warheads in the southern central part of the country.' She pulled a printout of a map from the file, walked over, and set it on the desk in front of Gideon.

'Here.' She pointed to the location on the map.

'It stores both plutonium and weapons-grade uranium. According to our information, it's one of Russia's largest weapons dismantling sites. About fifteen hundred a year.'

'Sounds like a good place,' said Gideon, 'if the plan were to lose something. They are no doubt backed up with business.'

She agreed.

'Inadequate storage facilities. It might take them a while to discover that something was missing. Do we know their security status?'

'It's unsafeguarded.'

The Russians didn't have the money to meet international standards for security. In some places, there were holes in chain-link fences through which children routinely climbed to play, where only meters away were earthen bunkers of plutonium-filled canisters behind rusting iron doors. It was a prescription for disaster, one that was getting worse, not better.

'According to information from Valnick, it looks like the two items in question were scheduled for dismantling.'

'Do we know what they were?'

'It looks like they were relatively small, core assemblies

35

complete with detonating devices for two field tactical nuclear artillery shells. One-hundred-and-fifty-three millimeter. Assembled in the sixties.'

'So no PALS?'

She shook her head. 'No.'

PALS were shorthand in the trade for 'permissive action links', the security mechanisms for nuclear devices that would prevent their detonation without approval from multiple levels of government control. Many of the devices made in the early 60s both in the U.S. and the Soviet Union lacked such controls. This made them prime targets for terrorists. The weapon of choice if they could get their hands on them.

The look on Gideon's face said it all. Devices that could be hidden anywhere and detonated without much difficulty. A terrorist's dream. The question was whether they would work.

'Do we know the yield?'

She shrugged, shook her head. 'According to the book, eight-tenths of a kiloton. Of course the book is notoriously understated.' During the Cold War both sides lied regularly regarding the potentcy of their weapons in order to gain an edge in arms treaties.

'If they're similar to comparable U.S. weapons,' said Gideon, 'they are probably somewhere on the order of between two and five kilotons.'

This would make them small, easily transportable, and nearly as powerful as the devices that devastated Hiroshima and Nagasaki. Alone, either device could take out the downtown section of a sizeable city. Detonated in tandem, they could destroy Manhattan and kill a million people instantly, leaving another half-million to die of agonizing radiation poisoning.

He picked up the receiver from his phone and punched

a two digit number on the com-line. 'Sally.' It was his secretary. 'See if you can get a meeting with the director for me early this afternoon. Tell him it is very important. Cancel my afternoon appointments. If you need to reach me, I will be at home.' Gideon would have to pack. He didn't know how long he would be on the road.

He put the phone in its cradle, picked up his briefcase, and made sure his passport was still inside.

'Get me a flight, as direct as possible,' he told Caroline, 'from San Francisco to Moscow.' He knew he would have to wait until be got to Moscow to make connections over the Urals into Siberia. He had never been to that forbidding place, and the thought sent a chill through his bones.

CHAPTER
THREE

Deer Harbor, Orcas Island

The 79 Ford pickup crabbed its way up the dusty road, its ass-end off to one side like a dog whose hind quarters had been run over. It was splattered with so much off-road mud that dirt would no longer stick. In the rear window was a placard the size of a license plate:

How's My Driving
Call 1–800–Eat–Shit

The truck skidded to a dusty stop in front of the lead-gray metal building. Oscar Chaney got out and slammed the door.

Another man stood in front of the building next to a pile of stomped-out cigarettes.

'You're late.'

Chaney shot him a look. 'Send me a bill for your time.'

'Why all the games with these redneck idiots? I don't get it. Why's the colonel using code names. It's like we're dealing with a legit government.'

'Exactly for the reason that they are idiots,' said Chaney. 'Sooner or later, they will make mistakes. He doesn't want those mistakes to take us down. It's the reason you're to have no contact with them. Understand?'

The guy nodded. 'Fine by me. Where did you get the truck?' Chaney's colleague looked at it unimpressed, taking in all the dents and dirt, something from a destruction derby.

'My contribution to local color,' said Chaney. 'It makes me look like one of them, don't you think?'

'Fuck local color. I just want to get this over with and get home.'

'Patience, Henry. With the money we're getting for this job, you can take a nice, long vacation.'

They had worked together for nearly five years. The colonel had kept them together ever since their time in the Caucasus under U.N. auspices, where they'd met as part of a peace-keeping force. Peace keeping. It was a joke! They were professional soldiers and they weren't even allowed bullets for their weapons for fear they might create an international incident. The four of them had mustered out, Fritz from Germany, Oscar from the U.S., Henry from the U.K., and the colonel who'd taken his training in South Africa but packed a British passport. Now they were on their own. In the last two years, they'd made a small fortune hiring out their services.

'What's it like inside?' Chaney gestured toward the building.

'Four walls and a roof.'

Chaney took a few steps and pushed his way past and through the half-open door. He took a quick survey of the building.

Inside was an empty concrete floor heavily stained in places by oil and grease. There were a few pieces of scrap metal in one corner and a workbench against the far wall. On it was an electric grinding wheel, bolted down, and a vice. There were a few soiled rags lying about on the bench and a handful of discarded hand-tools, assorted wrenches and a pair of pliers.

A spray of light flickered through the metal roof where somebody had missed a few screw holes and the sun had blistered away the caulking.

'Has it got sufficient power for the arc welder? I'll need a big welder.'

'Yes. Plus running water and lights. There's a latrine out back.'

Against one wall of the building was a large sliding door, suspended from a metal runner. Chaney walked over, grabbed the door and gave it a hefty push. It rattled open, sliding along the outside of the building, and stopped with a thud. The opening was about twelve feet wide and ten feet high, more than enough for the job he had in mind.

'Who owns the place?'

'A woman in a place called Kirkland. Over on the mainland. Her husband used to use it to do what he called "parting out" cars, taking the parts from stolen vehicles and selling them separately.'

'Ah.'

''Til one of the cars fell off a jack,' said Henry. 'Crushed his leg.'

'Bad luck,' said Chaney. 'It will do nicely. Secluded. Out of the way. This car-parting business. Were the police involved?'

'No. I checked. The man was taken to another location before the ambulance was called. They dumped a car off a jack out on the highway and called them. Then they took their time and got rid of what was here. The police have never seen the place.'

'Good. That is good.'

'What do you know about the people who own it?'

'The guy walks with a limp. The woman has money.'

'Are they likely to come over here looking around?'

Henry shook his head. 'No. I did what the colonel said. Told them we would pay cash every month. It's twice what they could get in rent from anybody else. I told them that we needed lots of electricity. He has to be thinking drugs,' said Henry. 'That we are putting in lights for a marijuana grow. A sizable nursery. They didn't ask too many questions after that. I think the old man figures the less he knows, the better. So that if the government comes calling he can say he didn't know. That way they can't confiscate his property.'

'Good. We chain off the road out there. Post some big "no trespassing" signs, and get a couple of mean dogs. I am talking something that will rip the ass out of anything that moves. Chain them to the outside of the building and make sure they can reach both doors. And somebody's got to be here all the time. Sleep here at night.'

Henry nodded, taking it all in. 'How much time do we have?'

'Enough,' said Chaney. 'But just barely. The colonel told me this morning that the government is poking around, issuing subpoenas. They're looking for organization.' He laughed a little. 'Fortunately for us, they are sniffing up a road which is about to become a dead end.'

He took a final appraisal of the building. 'I'd say to be safe we have ten days.'

'Can we do it in that time?' asked Henry.

'I can do the truck. I've got the frame and bed already. There's an old fertilizer tank on a farm on the other side of the island. I found it last week, talked to the owner. I can buy it and use it to fabricate the container on the back. The problem is the technical stuff. Handling it, and making sure we don't end up glowing like fireflies.'

'I know,' said Henry. 'I don't like dealing with that stuff.'

'Let Thorn worry about that. Besides the Russian is supposed to handle all of that. He is well trained. Knows what he is doing.'

'Yeah. So well trained he's sitting in some county jail as we speak.'

'The Russian's my problem,' said Oscar.

'Your problem?'

'Thorn has a plan to get him out.'

'He'd better do it quickly. I'm not handling that bomb.'

'You worry too much.'

'That's what they said in Chernobyl. Now they're all producing children with four legs and a single eye in the middle of their forehead. It's just that I would like to have at least one more child,' said Henry. 'And not be shooting blanks into the wife.'

'We'd be doing posterity a favor,' said Oscar.

They both laughed. Henry would have laughed harder if he wasn't so concerned about the risks.

'In the meantime, as the good old boys say over in Deming, "get me two ass-chewin' dogs". Got it?' Oscar mimicked the tough talk of the rednecks who believed they had hired him.

Henry nodded. The meeting was over. Oscar headed back toward his truck.

'Ah.' He turned around. 'I almost forgot. We are going to need some raw sewage. Get somebody to bring in one of those portable latrines. You know the kind? Set it up out front there and tell everybody in here to use it. Better yet, lock the latrine around back so they don't have a choice.'

'What for?'

'Never mind. Just do it.'

* * *

43

Oscar Chaney knew he was going to get it, one way or the other; either an exploding dye pack or the infamous electronic wafer.

After he'd gone fifteen blocks and nothing blew up inside his car he figured it had to be the wafer.

There were a lot of stupid crimes but none quite as witless as bank robbery, and Chaney knew it. Still, he had no choice. It was the one sure way to get busted by the Feds. Bank robbery was a federal offense. They would lock him up at Kent. The federal government had a contract with the county to house its prisoners at the Kent jail pending trial. The Russian was there and Chaney had to get him out before the FBI discovered who they had.

Chaney had warned Chenko to keep a low profile. Instead the Russian started visiting the red light district downtown. Three days ago Chenko tried to use Russian rubles to pay a hooker for services rendered. He had gotten drunk and abusive. The woman made a scene, and her pimp got involved. Chenko got a cut lip. The pimp ended up looking down the business end of a Taurus .45 automatic. Fortunately only loud words were exchanged, no gunfire. But by then cops showed up. Chenko and the pimp were both taken into custody. A check with immigration showed the Russian was in the country illegally. That and the weapons charge landed him in the Kent jail.

Chaney kept looking at the brown paper bag on the front seat next to him. He had allowed the teller to pick and choose. He knew that she'd given him one of the 'bait packs'. They were usually stacks of hundreds, something a robber wouldn't turn down. The old technology was the dye pack;

an exploding bundle of bills containing an indelible dye, usually a bright neon color, orange or green, with a little tear gas mixed in for measure. If it exploded it would be all over Chaney as well as the inside of his car. It was the kind of forensic evidence a prosecutor loved. Tell your lawyer to explain that to the jury.

The dye pack had one drawback. If it exploded early, inside the bank, an edgy robber with a gun could panic and take hostages or, worse, start shooting.

The newest rage among the law enforcement set was the electronic wafer. Pasted between two hundred-dollar bills, the credit-card-sized transmitter was triggered by the spring-loaded wheel of the cash drawer. As soon as the teller pulled it out, the transmitter started sending a silent signal that the cops could track.

Chaney figured they were already behind him, a train of unmarked cars following slowly in traffic. Why do a high-speed chase when you could beat the suspect and meet him at his house? The cops operated through a Violent Crimes Task force, a mix of local, state and federal agencies, a SWAT team packing automatic weapons. For this reason Chaney didn't carry a gun. He figured the teller wouldn't ask to see it if he put his hand in his pocket and threatened her. The idea was to get busted and booked into the Kent jail, not to get shot.

He had only two days to find the Russian and get him out. Without Chenko the entire plan would have to be called off. Only the Russian could assemble the device and make sure it would work.

Chaney turned the corner and saw the lights. Blue, red and white flashing from five patrol cars at the end of the street. They had it barricaded off. Shotguns and rifles pointed.

Three more cars screeched up behind him and blocked the intersection. With their doors open for cover, the cops took up positions with weapons drawn and the bullhorn came out.

'Step out of the car with your hands up. Where we can see 'em. Now.'

Chaney had all ten fingers out through the open window of the car before they finished talking.

CHAPTER
FOUR

Friday Harbor, WA

When Joselyn got to the law office in the morning, she noticed that Sam's car was already in the garage. Sam was early. Samantha Hawthorne was her landlady and her best friend on the island.

Sam was hardcore. She was immune to island fever, a survivor who could find a niche in hell if she had to. She had been in Friday Harbor for fifteen years and, therefore, was almost a native.

Samantha was forty-five, and looked thirty, buxom and brunette, too mean to be married, a person to be reckoned with. On her office door was a wooden placard, carved and painted. Under her name were the words:

COUNSELOR AND HYPNOTHERAPIST

When Joselyn headed down the corridor to her office, she saw Sam's door open. Sam was sitting inside behind her desk and a large pile of papers.

'Glad you could make it,' said Sam. 'Sleep in, did we?'

Joss looked at her watch. 'It's only nine o'clock.'

'Yes, and some of us have been working. Heavy date last night?'

'Right. With a corporate form book.' Joselyn had spent the evening until the wee hours working up the documentation on Belden's corporation.

'You're phone's been ringing off the hook all morning,' said Sam.

They shared a telephone system that Sam had installed when she moved in. She was hopeful of picking up a few more tenants so that they could soon share the cost of a receptionist.

'I finally answered it in self-defense,' she said. 'Couldn't get any work done.' She pushed a pink telephone slip across the top of her desk. Joselyn walked in and picked it up.

'Cup of coffee?' she asked.

The telephone message was from Dean Belden.

'No. I had some on the way in. Was it urgent?'

'Hmm?'

'The message?' Her week to get the job done not yet passed, and he was calling already.

'Not what I would call desperate,' said Sam. 'Just judging from the tone of voice, I would say he's not the type to panic.'

Sam was a quick study, even with only a voice on the phone to work with. She poured herself a cup of coffee from the machine on the credenza behind her desk.

'Yeah. But did he say what he wanted?'

'We didn't get that intimate.' She sipped her coffee and looked at Joselyn over the top of the mug. 'He wants you to call him. What is he? Domestic? Criminal?'

'Nothing you'd be interested in.'

'How do you know? He sounded pretty good on the phone.'

'He's a business client. And he pays up front.' Joss shot Sam a wicked grin.

'Then I'm definitely interested. Business is always filled with stress.' Sam winked across the desk at her. 'Perhaps he could use a little counseling.'

'Don't get your hopes up. Dean Belden doesn't seem like the kinda guy who lets a little stress get in his way. What are you doing for lunch?'

'Give me a call,' said Sam.

Joselyn headed to her office, opened the door and dropped her purse and briefcase on the chair. She dialed Belden's number. On the first ring, he picked it up.

'Yeah.' The tone was somewhat more harsh, less refined than their last meeting.

'Mr Belden. Joselyn Cole. You called.'

'Ah. Ms Cole.' His voice turned softer, more polished. 'I have a problem,' he said. 'I have to see you today.' It was more like a command than a request. Belden seemed used to telling people what to do.

'As soon as possible,' he said.

He wanted his money back. Joselyn could smell it. He'd found another lawyer.

'I've started work on the documents,' she told him.

'That's good.'

'Filed for corporate name identification already. I've reserved the name.'

'Excellent,' he said.

'I thought we were going to get together next week. Everything should be done by then.'

'This has nothing to do with that. Something has come up.'

'I see. Well when do you want to meet?'

'Right now. I'll be in your office in twenty minutes.'

Before she could say another word, he hung up.

Fifteen minutes later, Joselyn heard footsteps on the landing outside her office. The door to reception opened and closed.

'I'm in here.' She yelled through the closed door to her office.

Belden poked his head through a couple of seconds later. 'I hope I'm not interrupting your day too much. Thanks for meeting me on such short notice.'

'It's all right. Come on in. What's the problem?'

'I don't know how to explain it,' he said. 'I'm a little embarrassed. I've never had anything like this happen to me before. Not even a traffic ticket in ten years.'

'What is it?'

He sat down in one of the client chairs across from her desk.

'Yesterday I was in my office, finishing some paperwork. This man walks in. He was dressed in a blue suit and black cowboy boots. He had a big handlebar mustache. Anyway, he was somewhat disheveled. He asked me if I was Dean Belden. Looking at the guy, I wasn't sure if I should say yes or no. You understand?'

She nodded.

'He was big. Not very polite, pretty beefy, mostly around the middle. Like a potted-out policeman. I told him I was Belden. What else could I do?'

'And?'

'And he hands me this.' Belden reached into his inside coat pocket and pulled out an envelope. 'Then, just like that, the man turned and walked out of my office.'

He reached across the desk and handed her the envelope. It was already slit open across the top by something sharp.

Joselyn pulled a single folded piece of paper from the inside, and spread it out on her desk.

It was wrinkled and folded and had several coffee stains

with the round imprint of a mug where it was picked up and laid down on top of the paper. Some of the typed letters were smudged.

'What in the world happened to this?'

'I got a little coffee on it,' said Belden.

'A little? I can't read the date of the appearance,' said Joselyn.

'Wednesday,' he told her. 'I assume you're free?'

She looked at her calendar but didn't answer the question.

'So I guess the guy was a process server,' said Belden. 'How was I supposed to know?'

'Either that or a U.S. marshal.' She tried to read between the lines of what was on the page, as well as what was on Belden's face, in his eyes. The paper was brief and his expression an enigma.

'What's it about?' she asked.

'Search me.'

'I mean, you must have some idea why they want to talk to you?'

'I don't have a clue.'

She was not sure she believed him.

He put two fingers up like some kind of Scout. 'I swear.'

Typical of a federal grand jury, the subpoena compelling Belden to appear in Seattle disclosed nothing about the substance of the government's inquiry. In this country, a federal grand jury probe is the closest thing to Courts of Inquisition or a Star Chamber that exists. There are few rights, nothing that comes close to cross-examination, and no right to counsel inside the jury room. There are no real rules of evidence. The only thing they can't do is torture you, and on that you must take the government's word.

'Was there anything else inside the envelope?'

'Like what?'

'Like a letter? Any instructions?'

United States District Court

<u>Western</u>   District of   <u>Washington</u>

TO: Dean Richard Belden
     Route 12, Box 32
     Friday Harbor, WA. 98250

**SUBPOENA TO TESTIFY
BEFORE GRAND JURY**

SUBPOENA FOR:
X PERSON __ DOCUMENT(S) OR OBJECTS

YOU ARE HEREBY COMMANDED to appear and testify before the Grand Jury of the United States District Court at the place, date, and time specified below:

PLACE	COURTROOM
U.S. Courthouse Western District of Washington 1010 Fifth Avenue Seattle, WA. 98104	Grand Jury Room-3rd Floor

YOU ARE ALSO COMMANDED to bring with you the following document(s) or Object(s):

         None Specified

This subpoena shall remain in effect until you are granted leave to depart by the court or by an officer acting on behalf of the court.

CLERK

Howard E. Davies

This subpoena is issued on application of the United States of America
 	
William P. Wainright
United States Attorney
	By: **ASSISTANT U.S. ATTORNEY**
	     Thomas McCally, AUSA
	     Western District of Washington
	     P.O. Box B 135874
	     Seattle, WA. 98104

'No. Just what you see.'

'That's probably good news,' she told him.

'Why?'

'There's no target letter.'

'What's that?'

'If you were the target of their investigation, they'd have to notify you, give you what is called a target letter. Informing you of your rights. Mostly the right to remain silent. The fact that you didn't get one probably means they're looking at somebody else. You're just a witness.'

'What should I do?'

'First thing is not to discuss the subpoena with anybody else. You haven't, have you?'

'No.'

'Good. If you were a target I would advise you to take the Fifth Amendment. Make an appearance so they can't hold you in contempt, but say nothing. You can still do that of course, and it might be prudent.'

'Won't they think I'm guilty of something if I refuse to cooperate?'

'What they think can't hurt you. Only what they can prove.'

The problem with a federal grand jury probe was its range. Irrelevance was a concept that did not exist. They could turn your life upside down, subpoena all of your neighbors and business associates, spend a year defaming you by inference, and produce nothing but a sizable grease spot on your good name.

'In searching for someone else's crime, they may find one of your own,' she told him.

'I've never done anything wrong.'

'Saint Belden,' said Joselyn. 'I see.' She looked at him, her own dark eyes matching the emerald look that stared back from across the desk. 'And your tax returns,' she said. 'I suppose all of those are up to snuff too? Never claimed any deductions you can't justify?'

He looked up almost whimsically toward the ceiling. 'Ah, now let me see.' He thought for a moment. Put a single forefinger to his lips. 'I don't think so. No. I'm sure of it. My only offense is one of lust, and that, unfortunately has been committed only in my heart.'

Joss couldn't help herself. She fought back laughter.

'Please,' she said. 'This is serious.'

'I know.'

'If you want to cooperate with them, that's fine. But I would get something in return.'

'I'm trying,' he said.

'Please, Mr Belden.'

'Call me Dean,' he told her.

'Dean. You could get in real trouble. A good lawyer would demand immunity, just to be safe.'

'If that's what you think we should do.'

'If you're not a target, the government shouldn't care about granting you immunity. Perhaps use immunity.'

'What's that?'

'As opposed to transactional. What it means is that the government can't use anything you say before the grand jury to prosecute you, as long as you tell them the truth.'

'The trouble you can get into just doing what the government says. What's it all about?' said Belden. 'I mean what are they looking for?'

'You don't have any idea?'

He shook his head.

'They must think you have information they want.'

'What information?'

'Think,' she told him. 'Anything to do with your business?'

He shook his head slowly, as if searching his memory for some clue.

'What kind of business were you in before you came to the islands?'

'Electronics. It's always been electronics. I've never done anything else. It's my business. All I know.'

'Maybe someone you did business with?'

Suddenly there was a glimmer of light in those green eyes. He slapped his forehead with one hand. 'Of course! Why didn't I think of it?'

'Think of what?'

'Max Sperling. That's it. It has to be.'

'Who's Max Sperling?'

'I had some business dealings with him two years ago. Or was it three?' He thought for a second. 'Yeah, probably closer to three. He was a supplier of electronic parts out of the Silicon Valley. I heard he had some trouble with the law about a year ago, dealing in some stolen microchips or something. I didn't pay much attention at the time. I wasn't doing business with him anymore.'

'What did you buy from him?'

'Microchips.'

Bells started going off in Joselyn's head.

'How many?'

'Oh, I don't know. Couple of hundred thousand dollars' worth. It was a small order. He was a small supplier among independents. Moved up and down the coast.'

She had visions of this guy selling out of the trunk of his car, and wondered what Belden really knew.

'He traveled. His warehouse was down in the Bay Area. At least that's what he told me. At the time chips were hard to come by, especially the items he had.'

'What made these chips special?'

'They were for switches, specially designed stuff for certain kinds of electronics.'

The next question she framed with extreme delicacy.

'At the time that you bought these chips from Mr Sperling, you didn't have any reason to suspect that they were stolen?'

She led him with a wink and a nod. You never want to know with absolute certainty that your client committed a crime, especially one with as many avenues of escape as receiving stolen property.

He shook his head solemnly. 'No. Never. Not the slightest hint.'

'Let's talk about the price you paid for these chips,' she told him. What Belden thought was one thing. What a jury might think was something else.

'Did you pay a normal price?'

'It was a good buy.' He conceded this like a wily businessman. 'I wouldn't call it extraordinary. As I remember, it was on the low side of competitive,' he said.

'How far on the low side?'

'I mean it was within reason.'

She sighed. A request for immunity may not be an idle act after all.

'Was Mr Sperling selling chips to anybody else at the time?'

'Oh sure. Everybody in town.'

'To your knowledge were you one of his major buyers?'

'I don't know. But I wouldn't think so. There were others.'

'Who?'

'Off the top of my head, I don't know.'

'So you might have been one of his major buyers?'

'Could have been,' said Belden.

'But it's your position that you had no reason to suspect or believe that anything was wrong in these transactions? That they could have involved stolen merchandise?'

'Absolutely not. I was simply doing business. He was selling, and I was buying.'

'That is usually the case with stolen property,' she told him. 'It's what you reasonably believed that's important.'

'I reasonably believed that these were legitimate,' he said.

'Do you have any records of these transactions? Receipts? Purchase orders?'

'I might. I'd have to look.'

There was a moment of silence as she studied the subpoena once more.

'What's wrong? Is there something there?'

'No. It's what's missing that I'm worried about.'

'What's that?'

'Well, you would think that if your dealings with this Sperling were the issue, the government would be asking for your business records. Any evidence of your dealings with him.'

He looked at her and shrugged. 'I suppose.'

'But they didn't.'

He shook his head. 'I don't know. My dealings with Sperling are the only thing I can think of.'

'Well, if that's what it is, I would say you probably don't have anything too much to worry about. I think they probably just want to know what you know. But to be safe you should demand immunity.'

There was a palpable sigh of relief from the other side of her desk.

'I would go, make the appearance, answer any questions truthfully, but only if they give you immunity, otherwise remain silent and take the Fifth.'

'What do you mean? You're not going with me?'

'I don't know that it's necessary.'

'Well I do.'

'It will cost you a good deal of money.'

'I don't care. You're my lawyer.'

'They're probably on a fishing expedition, and your name

appeared on a document, or was mentioned by another witness.'

'That's probably it,' he said. 'Still, I want you to be there.'

'If you insist.'

'I do. Name your fee.' He reached for his checkbook again.

'I'd have to charge you for travel time.'

'That's all right.' He started writing before she could say anything.

'Have you ever done this before?' he asked.

'Not before a federal grand jury. But I've had clients indicted by the state.'

'I'm not sure that's a recommendation.' He looked up at her, and they both laughed.

'There's no need to pay me now.'

'Nonsense.' He continued writing.

'I'll call the U.S. Attorney's Office. My guess is they won't tell me anything over the phone, but I can try.'

'Sure. Try.'

'Really there's no need for another retainer. I'll bill you.'

He smiled and kept writing. 'You've been too good to me. I don't want to stiff you on the fee.'

'You're not going to be stiffing me.'

'Trust me,' he said. He finished writing, tore out the check, and slid it across the desk.

She was looking at the $5,000 written in the 'amount' space when he said, 'You know where Roche Harbor is?'

On an island, you tend to know where everything is. She nodded. He was moving toward the door.

'I'll meet you there on the dock Wednesday morning, seven o'clock.'

'Wait a second. Are you sure that'll give us enough time to get down to Seattle?'

'Not to worry,' he said. 'See you then,' and he was out the door.

CHAPTER
FIVE

Yekaterinburg, East of the Urals

It was six hours by air from Moscow, and Gideon was having a hard time sleeping. The climb over the Urals was like riding a sled down a rock-strewn mountain. Aeroflot did not use its European Airbuses on this route. Those were reserved for national face-saving to Paris and London, or overseas flights to America.

On the Siberian runs, they used their aging fleet of Tupelevs, heavy lumbering planes that looked as if they would defy the physics of flight. Sometimes they did. There were no oxygen masks overhead, and only the foolhardy wondered if the seat cushions would float.

Gideon was used to all of this. He had spent his early life bumping around Europe between his father in Amsterdam and his mother in Moscow.

But he had never been to the eastern part of the old Soviet Union, beyond the Urals. Here there were pine-covered slopes, millions of square miles of trackless forest, a region rich in mineral wealth where Stalin housed his Gulags and subsequent Soviet leaders hid their nuclear arsenal. It was an area that could swallow Western Europe whole and never belch.

It had taken him three days trekking between various bureaus and departments in Moscow, using every chit and button-holing old friends to obtain government clearance just to get through the gates at Sverdlovsk. He was to be met at the airport by a government car and driver.

As the plane began to descend through the clouds, Gideon could see a strange and surreal landscape, a green carpet of pine and birch, spreading east as far as the eye could see. Periodically strands of paved road would appear like curving ribbons out of the trackless forest only to disappear once more, into the verdant sea of pines. He could see no traffic, even where the roads were visible for long distances. It was as if the plane was descending onto some vast uninhabited planet.

Gideon knew better. Yekaterinburg was a city of two million people, one of the fastest growing and most prosperous regions in the Russian Federation. Named for Catherine the Great, it was a fur trading town when Jefferson crafted the Declaration of Independence. Gideon had seen pictures of mansions built by the fur czars, massive Georgian structures that still dotted the central area of the city, though they were now dusted by the soot of industry.

During the Bolshevik period the city got a new name – Sverdlovsk after Yakov Sverdlovsk, first secretary of the Communist Party's Central Committee. The Bolsheviks were anxious to wipe the name of Yekaterinburg from the map for a single reason. During the early morning hours of August 16, 1918, in the basement of one of its larger homes, an appalling act of murder was committed that stained Russian history. Nicholas and Alexendra, the czar and czarina, along with all of their children, the last of the Romanovs, were shot to death. Their bodies were trucked into the forest and buried outside of town.

As if continuing some thread of history, nearly seventy years later the city gave up another of its citizens to lead the country. Before becoming Premier of the Russian Federation, Boris Yeltsin had been mayor of Yekaterinburg. One of his acts while in office was to demolish the house where the dynastic executions took place, an act he later claimed to regret.

In the early 1990s, with the fall of Communism, the city reclaimed its heritage and once again became the City of Catherine.

So much of Russian history had played out here that Gideon had an abiding interest to see the place. As the plane dropped lower, he could see a sprawl of dismal white buildings on the horizon, an industrial complex that he knew only from photographs taken by satellite. It had been numbered during its heyday, and known only as Sverdlovsk-45. The areas around it were highly secured and soviet citizens were required to possess special passes to travel in the area around Sverdlovsk.

The plane dropped below the sea of pines, and its wheels skidded on the tarmac, the engines reversed, and the old Tupelev shuddered to a slow roll down the runway.

It took Gideon more than an hour to collect his luggage and find his driver and the government car in front of the terminal building. Fifty minutes later he was passing through the gates at Sverdlovsk-45.

It was an immense dingy complex of buildings, the kind you see in every developed nation where industrial decay starts to nibble at the fringes of a community. Here it was gnawing. Flat roofs and broken windows seemed to predominate, though there was none of the graffiti that marked similar sites in the West.

Everywhere there was activity, heavy vehicles pulling trailers, men in overalls wearing hard-hats, guards with

Kalashnikovs. The driver pulled to a stop in front of an aus-tere building just inside the gates. There were two Russian-built cars, Ladas with considerable wear, a lot of dust and a few dents in them: and next to them, a spanking new Mercedes SL convertible, a gleaming powder-blue.

The parking lot was strewn with the remnants of rusted-out sea-going containers too large to be carried away and steel bands that had probably encircled wooden crates long since transformed into ash in some enterprising worker's fireplace. Gideon assumed that the building adjoining this parking lot must be the administrative center.

Gideon knew that the bunkers that lay buried in the incline of gently rolling hills beyond were the focus of this enquiry.

It was known that there were 30,000 nuclear devices in storage or on launch pads in the Russian Federation. In addition to these, there was more than a thousand tons of highly enriched uranium and in excess of a hundred tons of plutonium in the country. It was these raw materials for bomb making that had most worried nuclear experts, both those in the West and their Russian colleagues.

There had been several episodes of smuggling in Germany and Italy, as well as other places in Europe and the new eastern republics. In all, about fifty cases documented so far. Almost all of these involved low-grade materials, some of it approaching weapons-grade, but in very small quantities.

It was not the first time that a nuclear device or raw materials had shown up missing on paper in one of the institute's reports. Almost invariably these turned out to be record-keeping errors. In this case, however, it was the nature of the missing items that caused concern. Two small devices that might be easily transported would be at or near the top of any terrorist shopping list.

Gideon was familiar with tactical field nuclear artillery. These had been items of discussion and negotiation in treaties.

The United States had developed an eight-inch nuclear artillery shell in the early 1950s. Over the years, they had perfected and increased its destructive capacity by reducing barrel length and tamper bulk and by adding beryllium reflectors and more powerful high explosives to trigger the chain reaction. In their final incarnation, these shells measured no more than three feet in length, eight inches around, and weighed less than 250 pounds. Yet in this compact package, they could unleash ten kilotons of destructive force.

These were meaningless statistics until applied to the real world. The Oklahoma City bombing which took 162 lives, would have leveled three square miles of the central city if one of these shells had been detonated instead of fertilizer and diesel oil. The death toll would have been measured in hundreds of thousands instead of hundreds.

If a nuclear shell had been detonated at the World Trade Center instead of a conventional truck bomb, the lower part of Manhattan would have disappeared; everything from the Financial District to Gramercy Park would have been totally destroyed.

The Soviets had developed similar artillery shells. This was what Gideon was looking for, hoping and praying to find at Sverdlovsk, two small packages lost in a monumental accounting glitch.

Gideon showed his pass to a guard at the door who passed it to an officer inside. Two minutes later he was led into a small waiting room where he took a seat on a hard wooden bench and waited.

He checked his watch. Ten minutes passed. Finally the door opened and a tall slender man, balding and with glasses, came out. He was holding the pass in his hand and spoke in Russian. Gideon answered him.

'I am Mr van Ry.'

The Russian looked him up and down. 'What is this about?'

Speaking perfect Russian Gideon gave him a business card from the institute and watched to see if the man could read the English printed on it.

The Russian's eyes darted between the business card and Gideon's face. The next words he spoke were in halting but clearly discernable English. 'What is this about?'

'I am authorized by authorities in Moscow to speak with your director. He is available?'

'He is very busy,' said the Russian.

'I think he will see me. Please tell him I am here.'

The Russian looked once more at the business card, then the signature on the security pass from Moscow.

Gideon could read his mind. He was wondering what a Russian citizen was doing working in the United States for an institute that dealt with nuclear weapons.

'Wait here.' The Russian turned and closed the door behind him.

Gideon looked at the clock on the wall, turned, took a seat, and waited. A few moments later the door opened again, and the Russian stepped out. 'Follow me.'

The Russian led the way down a long corridor and through a rabbit warren of small offices and cubicles, most of which were empty and looked as if they hadn't been cleaned in months. A uniform film of dust covered the floors.

Their feet left concrete, and suddenly Gideon found himself walking on carpet. A few steps further on, they stopped in front of a set of double wooden doors. The Russian opened one of them and stepped to the side for Gideon.

As he entered the room, he saw another man, seated behind a massive mahogany desk. There were pictures on the walls and several pieces of African art, masks and carvings of some expense, that seemed out of place against the stained acoustic ceiling tiles and drab walls of the office.

The man behind the desk stood to greet Gideon. He was

dressed in a suit and tie. Well-pleated shark skin, not something from Russian clothiers.

'Dimitri tells me you are from the institute at Santa Crista.' He was smiling and held Gideon's card in one hand.

'Yes. That's correct.' Gideon planted his best smile, crossed the office, and extended a hand that was eagerly taken by the Russian.

'We are not used to visitors here,' said the man. 'Please have a seat. You must be tired. Dimitri tells me you have come all the way from Moscow.'

Gideon nodded.

'How is the weather there?'

Gideon sat down and Dimitri closed the door, leaving the two men alone.

'The weather was pleasant,' said Gideon.

'You see what we have here. Overcast. Always overcast,' said the Russian. 'You must have some beautiful weather in California?'

'It can be nice.'

'You know I've always wanted to visit your institute. You must tell me how you obtained a position there. It is on the Central Coast, correct?'

'Yes.'

'Is it close to Hollywood?' The man spoke perfect English.

'No,' said Gideon.

The Russian seemed disappointed.

'You must excuse me,' he said. 'Where are my manners? I am Yuri Mirnov, director of Sverdlovsk. Or what is left of it.' He rolled his eyes toward the ceiling. 'You have already met twenty percent of my staff.' He was referring to Dimitri. 'But then you know the difficult times we are having here.'

'I am very much aware,' said Gideon. 'It must be very hard.'

'You have no idea,' said Mirnov. 'Dimitri hasn't been paid in two months. I myself have had to endure three salary reductions in the last year. And the work, it just keeps piling up.' He gestured toward stacks of paper on the floor strewn around his office.

Gideon was wondering who, under such conditions of austerity, owned the Mercedes outside in the parking lot. But he possessed sufficient diplomacy not to ask.

The area around Sverdlovsk was like few others in Russia. Since the fall of Communism, there had been a crippling crime wave. Those who did not know Russia attributed this to political dislocations for a nation trying to find its way. The fact was that crime flourished in the Soviet regime, particularly from the 1960s on. Artificial shortages of everything from sugar to nuts were state-manufactured in order to establish a thriving black market which in turn was controlled by bureaucrats and other high-level party functionaries. They mingled freely with an underworld that was inbred in the Russian culture. Three hundred years of oppression had made the children of Mother Russia adept at avoiding the strictures of the law. Beneath the statue of Lenin, under the banner of Socialism they created shadow capitalism to avoid the failures of their own planned economy and proceeded to line their pockets.

With the demise of Communism they were now free to come out into the open, a new age of robber barons, applauded by the West. It was a free-for-all on the order of Tombstone in the 1880s. There were a dozen shootings a day in Moscow, 'businessmen' assassinating their competition. The only place where things were rougher was Sverdlovsk.

Here was a land of wide open opportunity if you had a private army and were willing to look under your car with a mirror every morning before leaving for work. What made it even more dangerous was that the region possessed thousands of nuclear, chemical, and biologic weapons, a veritable bazaar of mass destruction.

Mirnov swiveled around in his chair to a credenza behind him. 'Can I offer you some mineral water?' he asked.

Gideon was thirsty and tired after the long flight. 'Yes. Thank you.'

The Russian lifted two clear plastic cups from a sizable stack on the credenza and reached down somewhere below, where Gideon couldn't see. He came up with a large liter bottle, not the cheap stuff from a Russian bottling house but *Monteforte* from Italy with a fresh seal on the cap.

Gideon seemed surprised to see that the bottle was already chilled and frosted and that Mirnov had no trouble finding ice cubes where he found the bottle.

The Russian noticed his expression.

'We still have a few conveniences,' said Mirnov with a smile.

Gideon grinned and took the glass.

The Russian lifted another bottle containing a clear fluid and merely held it up as if there was no need to identify its contents, offering some to Gideon.

'None for me. I'm fine.'

Then Mirnov poured a little vodka in his own glass and stirred it into the charged water with a swizzle stick.

'Now what can I do for you?' he asked.

'As you know,' said Gideon, 'the institute gathers data on nuclear materials; civilian power plants, military fissile materials when we can.'

'I am familiar,' said the Russian.

'It has come to our attention that there may be some materials missing from your facility.'

Mirnov's look suddenly went dark. His expression dour.

'It may not be accurate information,' said Gideon. 'Still, because of the specific nature of this information we thought it best to check it out, as discreetly as possible.'

'You have told authorities in Moscow this information?'

'No,' said Gideon. 'We did not want to cause undue concern or alarm until we had a chance to talk to the people in charge on site. As I said, it is entirely possible that our information is wrong.'

'What is the source of this information?'

'I would rather not say. If it is inaccurate it does not matter. If on the other hand . . .'

'I see.' Mirnov sipped from his plastic glass.

'A quick look at some of your records should clarify the matter,' said Gideon.

'We would be happy to comply,' said Mirnov, 'though I am a little short-handed at the moment. Perhaps if you could give us a little more direction, narrow the area of your inquiry?' He was fishing for specifics.

'Two field tactical artillery shells, nuclear,' said Gideon,.

'I see.' Mirnov sat up straight in his chair and put his glass down. 'We wouldn't want such misinformation to be reported.'

'That's what we were thinking,' said Gideon.

'I appreciate your concern for accuracy,' said Mirnov. 'I assume this error has not spread too far.' He arched an eyebrow. The Russian was clearly referring to outside intelligence agencies, particularly in the U.S.

'The information has been maintained in-house,' said Gideon. 'There is still time to correct it.'

'Good.' There was a sigh of relief from Mirnov. 'Of course, we will be happy to cooperate in any way we can. Where would you like to start?'

'Your own inventory numbers should make it very easy to check,' said Gideon.

'True,' said Mirnov. He punched the intercom key on his phone and picked up the receiver. 'Dimitri, would you come in here please?'

A moment later, the assistant entered.

'Dimitri. I would like you to pull these files.' Mirnov made a note pointing to a circled item. The assistant dutifully took the sheets and left the office.

'It shouldn't take him long to find them.'

'Good,' said Gideon. 'I have a plane to catch back to Moscow.'

'When do you leave?'

'About three hours.'

'We should have you back at the airport in plenty of time. I can have one of my people drive you,' said Mirnov. 'I'm sure Dimitri would love to do it. He has a large new Mercedes,' said Mirnov.

Gideon looked at him, wondering how a man who hadn't been paid in two months could afford this.

Mirnov could read his mind. 'Dimitri is also an entrepreneur. He has a small business on the side.'

In Russia this had become a euphemism for many things. 'What does he do?'

Mirnov shrugged like he wasn't sure. 'There are many business opportunities in the new Russia. I myself will have to investigate them, when I have the time,' said Mirnov.

Gideon smiled but felt a sick feeling in his stomach. 'Thank you for the offer, but I have a car and driver.' He took a sip from his own glass.

'I trust that the people at the institute are not too concerned about this mistake. They do happen,' said Mirnov. 'I myself have found records from our own facility where overworked employees have entered incorrect numbers.'

'I am sure the people at the institute will be relieved as soon as I can call them,' said Gideon.

'If it is our mistake, it reflects poorly on us,' said the Russian. 'As the manager of this facility I am responsible. We would not want the institute to have a bad impression of us. We do our best.' He was now talking somewhat nervously.

They both noticed that minutes were passing, and there was no sign of Dimitri or the files.

'Of course,' said Gideon.

'Either way,' said Mirnov. 'The information will be quickly corrected. We completed a fresh inspection only yesterday. So our records are accurate, up to the minute.'

They waited while the Russian tapped out a pattern of thumps on the surface of his desk and Gideon emptied his glass. Finally Mirnov got tired.

'Let me check and see.' He picked up the phone and dialed a number on the intercom. There was no answer. He dialed another number. This time it was picked up, and Mirnov spoke in Russian.

'Is Dimitri there?

'What do you mean he left?

'I see.

'I see.' Finally he put the receiver down.

'Excuse me for one moment,' said Mirnov. He rose and left the office, closing the door behind him. Gideon listened. He couldn't make out words, but he could hear voices rising in volume outside the door.

A moment later, Mirnov re-entered the room. His face was ashen. There were beads of perspiration on his forehead.

'You will have to excuse me,' he said. 'We seem to have a small problem.'

'A problem?' said Gideon.

'Dimitri has left the building. My staff is looking for him now.' He wiped his lip with a handkerchief and took a deep swallow of vodka and water from the glass on his desk.

'Have they found the files?' said Gideon.

'No. That is part of the problem. It seems the records for the two items in question . . . They are missing,' said Mirnov.

'And Dimitri has left to look for them?'

There was a blank expression on the Russian's face, followed by a slight shrug of the shoulders.

Gideon got out of his chair and headed for the door. He retraced his steps back out to the long corridor, followed closely by Mirnov. The two started at a walk and then a slow jog until they were running headlong toward the parking lot outside.

Gideon threw open the door. The Mercedes was gone.

CHAPTER
SIX

Padget Island, WA

He was short with dark brown hair, thinning on top, and soft brown eyes, the son of a Kansas banker. Scott Taggart had been many things in the space of his forty-two years. In his youth, after an argument with his father, he left home and drove a truck for a local freight company to put himself through college. He worked nights busing tables in a restaurant to finish graduate school.

Scott's field was American History, and he wanted to teach. Jobs were hard to find, but what he lacked in credentials he made up for in persistence. He found a job at a small college in western Washington State, first as a teaching assistant, then as a part-time faculty member. It was there that he met Kirsten.

She could have been the poster girl for Norwegian beauty. When she ended up in one of his lecture series, Scott couldn't keep his eyes off of her. The feeling seemed to be mutual. The college had strict rules against faculty dating undergraduates, and for nearly a year he fought off the urge to ask her out.

The school solved this problem for him in the early spring when it passed him over for a tenured position. It seemed they wanted someone with an Ivy-league pedigree. Taggart was forced to move on. But in the summer, he struck up a relationship with Kirsten, and when he moved, he didn't go alone. They lived together for five months and were married the following November. Together they started over, this time in eastern Washington where Scott found another teaching assignment. It was a step down, only a community college, but he liked the work and enjoyed the students, though most of them were not as serious as he would have preferred.

To make ends meet, Kirsten started a small bookkeeping business. She had studied accounting in college, though she hadn't finished her degree. A year later they had their first child, a boy they named Adam, after her father. Kirsten's business grew rapidly. She was affable and outgoing, as blessed with social skills as she was with numbers. In less than three years her business had blossomed so that by then she employed two other people.

It was about this time that the trouble began. It came in the mail, with a return address to the Internal Revenues Service in Ogden, Utah. Kirsten and her business were being audited. She couldn't imagine why. She'd made money, but not that much. She looked at the notice and discovered that they'd made a mistake. The notice of audit contained her name and the name of her business all right, but the employer identification number was wrong. It seemed that they had mixed up her business tax records with someone else's.

She called the telephone number on the notice, but no one could help her. They told her to tell her story to the auditor when he arrived. She didn't know whether to gather receipts and ready her books for audit or not. She assumed that when they discovered their mistake they would go away, leave her alone. She was wrong.

A month later, her first meeting with the auditor did not go well. The revenue agent was a middle-aged woman worn down to a humorless nub by years of civil service. When Kirsten suggested that they'd made a mistake, she was informed that: 'The service did not make mistakes'.

When she tried to show the woman the erroneous information on the notice, the auditor merely gobbled up the document, told Kirsten she would review it, then demanded to see Kirsten's business ledger and receipts.

The audit dragged on for months with an ever-increasing demand for more documents, more receipts. When Kirsten insisted that they had made a mistake and wanted to know why the notice listed someone else's identification number, the revenue agent lost her temper. She told Kirsten that if she wanted to be difficult, her business would not be audited for one year, but for two. Within days, a second formal notice of audit for an additional year had been issued. That would teach her to question the authority of the auditor. A level of personal venom now seemed to be driving the audit.

Scott tried to console his wife. He told her not to worry. Sooner or later it would be straightened out. They would discover their mistake, and it would be taken care of.

But for Kirsten there was no peace. The IRS gave her thirty days to gather her records for the entire additional audit year. Meeting the quixotic and ever-changing demands of the auditor became a full-time job for Kirsten. She no longer had time for business or for her family. She was forced to let one of her employees go. Her business suffered, and her income dropped. For seven more months, it dragged on with no indication from the government that they were getting any closer to the end. Kirsten still did not know what the IRS was looking for, whether she owed back taxes, interest, or penalties. Whenever she met with the auditor the woman was unpleasant. Nothing Kirsten seemed to say or do was ever the right thing. The auditor would tell her nothing. Whenever Kirsten asked a question, the auditor would take a note and tell her she would get back to her with the answer, but she never did. It was as if Kirsten's every inquiry was met either with open hostility or it disappeared into the vast black hole of government bureaucracy. Whenever the auditor called, it was always the same thing, a constant and unceasing demand for more records.

Now the government's search had led the auditor into Scott and Kirsten's personal tax returns. To Kirsten it seemed that the failure to find anything amiss only fueled the auditor's hostility. The IRS agent now had to justify an audit that had dragged on for fifteen months.

The auditor demanded an extension of the statute of limitations so that she could go back farther into their records, beyond the three-year limit. When Kirsten objected, the auditor told her that if she didn't agree to the extension, the IRS would file a tax deficiency with the courts, and they would be required to hire a lawyer. At one point the auditor even hinted at criminal penalties. Kirsten wanted to know what she had done wrong. The auditor wouldn't tell her.

Kirsten was losing weight. It seemed a day didn't go by without the auditor calling and demanding something. Kirsten couldn't sleep at night. Scott was worried about her. He tried to intervene with the IRS. He called the auditor and tried to discuss it with her. The auditor took a dodge. She told Scott that since the original audit was for his wife's business, he was not the taxpayer. She could not discuss the matter with him and promptly hung up.

Every time the phone rang, Kirsten feared it was the auditor with demands for more documents or, worse, the addition of still another audit year. Life was becoming unbearable.

Now when Adam cried at night Kirsten became irritable. Nothing Scott said or did seemed to reach her. There was no easing the constant anxiety.

Still, Scott made the best of it, trying to ease his wife's anxiety, until one Friday afternoon when he came home early from work and told Kirsten that his teaching contract had not been renewed for the following year. Without notice, the IRS had attached his wages for the failure to pay unspecified back taxes. The college received government grants, and its students applied for government guaranteed loans. It couldn't afford for its faculty to have problems with the Internal Revenue Service. The federal government was crushing Scott and Kirsten Taggart's lives.

The agony of the audit dragged on for two more months with no word as to closure. Scott and Kirsten received a foreclosure notice on their home. Without Kirsten's income they were now unable to meet their mortgage payment.

On a Saturday morning in June, shortly after the end of the school year, Scott took Adam to the park for a ride on the swings while Kirsten cleaned out her office. Word of her troubles with the IRS had seeped into the local accounting community. Her last client had departed two weeks earlier, fearful that Kirsten's problems might be contagious.

At two-thirty in the afternoon Scott returned home and called his wife at the office. There was no answer. Thinking that she might need help carrying boxes to the car or comfort in a moment of emotional anxiety, he left Adam with neighbors and headed to Kirsten's office. Inside, he found her at her desk, head slumped on the blotter as if she were taking a nap. It wasn't until he saw the thin line of spittle, a milky froth running from the side of her mouth that he realized something was wrong. Kirsten had taken an entire bottle of prescription sleeping pills.

She survived on a ventilator for sixteen days, until the doctors determined that there was no hope. Kirsten was brain-dead.

At her funeral, Scott wanted to crawl into the grave with her and pull the dirt in on top of both of them. He was racked by grief. With Kirsten he could bear anything, surmount any problem, deal with any questions the IRS could throw at him. He could have found another job, started over. Without her, he couldn't find the will or the strength to get out of bed in the morning. He didn't know what to do with Adam. He finally took the child to Kirsten's parents in Seattle while he regrouped and tried to find a reason to live. Strangely enough, it was the IRS that gave him that reason.

Three months after Kirsten's death, Scott received a computer-generated letter; the IRS advised Kirsten Taggart that the agency had made a mistake. Somehow a keypunch operator had entered the wrong employer I.D. number on Kirsten's estimated quarterly tax payments, crediting them to another taxpayer's account. Kirsten showed up as delinquent in their computer. She owed no taxes, interest or penalties. The government, rather than investigating Kirsten's information that it had made a mistake, assumed that she was lying, that she had received income, and that she had failed to make estimated quarterly tax payments. For this, Kirsten had been badgered and pursued until ultimately she took her own life. Scott had lost his family, his career, and his home and his infant son had no mother.

Scott Taggart didn't bother to inform the government of the price that he and his family had had to pay for bureaucratic arrogance. He would deliver the message in his own time – and in his own way.

The Victor Portable was a honey of a torch. Chaney had picked it up at a tool shop in Everett for five hundred bucks. It came in its own handy carrying case, the size of a large attaché, with two spare tips. He had ordered an extra bottle of acetylene, fearful that he might run out.

The torch was specifically designed for working in small places where a full-sized cutting torch wouldn't reach. It could cut through inch-thick case-hardened steel in a matter of minutes.

He had spent two days with a team of hand-picked militiamen setting the mission up, finding out where the Russian national Grigori Chenko was housed at Kent, and sizing up the jail. It was a two-story brick structure in an area of light industry on the fringes of town. The building didn't look like a jail. The architects had done what they could to mask it in order to avoid public controversy in its placement. Fortunately for Chaney, they had also compromised its security.

There were no high chain-link fences surrounding the facility topped by rolls of concertina wire. Instead, the unit where Chenko was housed backed up to a street used mostly by trucks during the day to make their deliveries to warehouses in the area. At night, the road was mostly deserted. The jail was pleasantly bordered by a ten-foot strip of well-manicured grass with shrubs planted against the exterior brick walls. From the outside, it was designed to blend in. It looked like most of the other commercial buildings in the industrial park.

It was only two years old, and on the inside it was like a country club. Those in custody were usually held here only a short time, pending trial. If convicted, they would be transferred to one of the permanent state or federal prisons to serve their time.

There was a large day room on the ground floor with a thirty-inch television set bolted to supports suspended from the second tier balcony. A ping-pong table and six stainless steel tables with fixed benches all bolted to the floor did double duty for cards and meals. There was exercise equipment, a weight machine, and two-and-a-half-pound barbells for running in place.

Within minutes of being booked, strip searched and given orange jail togs and rubber thongs for his feet, Chaney was issued a blanket and marched through the day room to a cell up on the second tier.

The Russian saw him when he came in behind the guard. Chenko was playing ping-pong.

Chaney waltzed into the cell.

'You get the upper bunk.' A grizzled loser with a gut like a canvas water bag was lying on the bottom bunk with his bare feet, toejam and all, poking up toward Chaney.

'Not to worry, hotshot, I won't be here that long.'

'Right. You're really with the Secret Service. They just put you in here for training.'

Chaney ignored him and threw his blanket onto the empty bunk up top and disappeared out the cell door. He headed down the stairs to the day room and caught Chenko's eye. The Russian immediately put the ping-pong paddle down and walked away. He and Chaney found a quiet corner.

'Who's in the room at the end of the corridor?' Chaney nodded with his head. 'On the left. Down there.' There was a short hallway with cells on both sides, each with a solid steel door and small observation window of wired plate-glass for the guards to look through.

'That's Tattoo and Homer,' said Chenko.

The Russian's cell was up top, on the second tier, just like Chaney's.

'Get 'em for me.'

'Who?'

'Homer and Tattoo.'

'What do you want them for?'

'Just do it.'

The Russian hesitated. 'Tattoo is very ugly guy.'

'Fine. Tell him I want to kick his ass. He might see it as an opportunity for upward mobility.'

The Russian looked at him, shrugged as if to say 'your funeral' and did the jail-house strut, cool and casual, over to two men working up a sweat on the exercise equipment. One of them was stripped to the waist, with more tattoos than the lady in the circus. The Russian said a few words in his ear, and the guy with tattoos started giving Chaney mean looks. He draped a towel around his neck and flexed his pecs like Rocky Balboa, then led the way over to Chaney, followed by another misfit who Chaney figured must be Homer.

'My man here says you wanna kick my ass.'

'As soon as I figure out which end it's at,' said Chaney.

It took the synapse in his brain a moment to make the connection. Then Tattoo's expression went lethal.

'No skin off my ass you wanna die,' he told Chaney. 'But just so I understand. Why?'

'Ugliness offends me,' said Chaney. 'I like to stamp it out before it can breed.'

The Russian was looking at him like he was out of his mind.

'Where ya wanna do it?' Tattoo got up close now, right up in his face, a show of prison manliness. Chaney's face didn't seem to flex a muscle as his knee shot up like a spring-fired catapult into the guy's groin. Tattoo's eyes dilated like two glass marbles as his testicles were pulverized. Chaney's right hand moved so quickly that the Russian wasn't sure he actually saw it. What he was sure of was that Tattoo couldn't speak any longer, and both of his hands were occupied feeling his Adam's apple, making certain it hadn't been forced up, and out through his mouth.

Tattoo slid to his knees, coughing as he went.

Homer stood transfixed, either terrified or fascinated. He'd never seen someone disabled so quickly, especially someone as fit as Tattoo.

Chaney slapped Tattoo on the back a few times as the other man coughed his guts out kneeling on the floor.

'What's goin' on over there?' One of the guards saw him down on the floor and started to come over to investigate.

'Something went down the wrong pipe,' said Chaney. 'He's all right.' Chaney slapped him a few more times on the back, put his hands under Tattoo's armpits and lifted him to his feet before the guard could cross the day room floor. As he did it, he whispered something in Tattoo's ear. Then pulled his lips away.

Tattoo's hand went up, and he waved the guard away.

Chaney was now back in his ear whispering again, then pulled away. 'Understand?'

Tattoo couldn't talk, but he could nod, and he did it eagerly.

'Good man.' Chaney slapped him on the back again. 'Do it now.'

Tattoo's face was a shade of reddish purple. Tears ran down both cheeks. His hands were now busy holding his groin. He turned and waddled away toward his cell at the end of the hall. Homer wasn't sure if he should follow him.

'You're moving out of your cell,' said Chaney. 'You got a problem with that?' Homer was a short-timer. He didn't know why they wanted the cell, and he didn't care. He was due to be released in ten days. He smiled and disappeared down the hall.

'You could have given him cigarettes? A few dollars?' said the Russian.

'Like feeding fish to seals,' said Chaney. 'He'd be knocking on the door all night for more.'

'Now he may turn us over to the guards.'

'By the time he lowers his balls back into place, we'll be gone. Get your stuff. Your blanket and whatever else. We'll be bunking at the end of the hall. Down there.' Chaney pointed toward Tattoo's cell.

The guards didn't care. As long as there were two warm bodies in each cell when lights went out, prisoners could wheel and deal for accommodations. One of them had even worked a deal with the guards to sleep out in the day room at night, when the jail was overbooked.

Five minutes later Chaney and the Russian, each with a handful of possessions, toothbrush, soap and blanket were setting up house-keeping in the ground floor cell at the end of the hall.

This was critical to their plan. Each cell had a window, not large, but big enough for a man, if he wasn't too fat, to slip through.

On the inside, the windows were covered by a half-inch screen of solid acrylic, bolted by six heavy screws to the masonry wall. The screw heads were fitted with a special slot that permitted them to be tightened, but not unscrewed.

Beyond the acrylic screen was a light shaft that ran at a slight upward angle, so that the prisoners couldn't actually see out to the street or get their behinds up high enough to moon the public as they drove by outside.

Eighteen inches beyond the acrylic barrier, set far enough inside the window shaft to be unnoticed from the outside, were four one-inch steel bars. These were made of case-hardened tool steel. They could probably be cut with a hacksaw, if you had a month to do it and an inexhaustible supply of blades.

For Chaney, time was essential, not only because they needed Chenko to assemble the device, but because the longer they took to engineer the escape, the greater the chance of discovery.

He set to work immediately. Chenko hung one of the blankets over the window on the cell door and cut a deal with another inmate for cigarettes to sit outside the door and tap out a warning if anyone headed down the corridor.

The most critical obstacle was the acrylic screen. Unless they could get that off there was no way they could work on the bars.

Chaney had planned ahead. He spent ten minutes taking a dump in the single open commode and on the fourth push, heard a splash in the stainless steel bowl.

He stood up halfway and looked down into the commode. Mission accomplished. Delicately he fished something out of the toilet. The rubber prophylactic was still smeared with KY Jelly and sealed at the open end with a rubber band. He unwrapped this and shook the package until a piece of metal about four inches long, the size of a fountain pen, dropped out onto the cement floor and bounced with a metallic clank.

The Russian caught it on the second bounce. Both men held their breath and looked nervously at the door for several seconds, until it was clear that no one had heard it.

In Chenko's hand was a small tungsten carbide chisel, flattened with a sharp hatchet-like edge at one end.

'You got a hammer up there, too?' said the Russian.

'I'm gonna use your fucking head,' said Chaney. He was not happy that Chenko had put him through this. Right now

Chaney should have been back on the island, putting the final touches on the truck, welding the steel tank onto the bed. As it was, he would be up for three nights running in order to finish the job. That was if they could get out.

Chaney told the Russian to sit tight. He left the cell for a minute, and when he returned he was carrying one of the iron two-and-a-half-pound molded barbells from the set in the exercise room. He wrapped it in a piece of Chenko's blanket off the bed and went to work with the chisel.

It made quick work of the six screw heads holding the acrylic screen in place. The heads popped off neatly and bounced on the floor. Using the sharp edge of the chisel, Chaney levered the acrylic screen until he could get his fingers under the thick panel. He lifted it off the broken screw shafts that were still sticking out of the concrete wall.

He reached up and grabbed hold of the iron bars in the window well. They were secured solidly in the concrete walls surrounding the window.

Carefully he then put the acrylic window back in place. He retrieved the screw heads from the floor, and, using small amounts of chewing gum, stuck the heads back in place so that if the guards checked during the day, the acrylic would look as if it had never been removed.

'Now what?' said the Russian.

'Now we wait.'

CHAPTER
SEVEN
_____

Yekaterinburg

To Gideon there was a certain irony in all of it, as if this place with its soil poisoned by the bones of the murdered czar was now playing out one more fateful hand in the game of history.

He had spent three days in a dingy hotel room guarded by security police. They did not allow him to make phone calls or post e-mail to the institute in Santa Crista. If Caroline didn't hear from him soon she would be calling the State Department. Like the surrounding landscape, his face took on the appearance of a sprouting forest, a two-day growth of stubble under eyes that were bloodshot pools clouded by sleep deprivation.

For someone who had worked in the vineyards of nuclear control as long as he had, it was a depressing scenario. Gideon felt like a prophet wailing in the desert. The Cold War was over. The precarious balance of power that governed the globe for fifty years had been swept away. The two sides were awash with awesome weapons that could, in a single ignition, take a million lives. And now, one of these powers lacked the means to secure these tools of death.

At eight o'clock in the morning Gideon had been roused from his hotel room by two stern-looking guards carrying Kalashnikov automatic rifles. For a while, in the back seat of a car with one of the guards, the thought actually crossed his mind that they might be taking him into the forest to be shot. The forest around Yekaterinburg held many dark secrets.

But ten minutes later they pulled into the parking lot outside of Mirnov's office and led him down the familiar long corridor. When he walked through the door of Mirnov's office, he could see that the Russian was himself a wreck.

Mirnov had been up all night. He had informed his supervisors in Moscow only that morning of the possibility that two nuclear devices were missing. He had waited as long as he could, hoping his staff would locate the two artillery shells. Instead what they found was more ominous.

Reports and allegations of missing devices had been made before but never by someone with Mirnov's position and access to information. The authorities took it seriously. Mirnov's boss was now on his way from the capital with a team of Russian experts, apparently to close the barn door after the horse had escaped. They would be looking for a scapegoat, someone to take the fall if the incident became international. Mirnov knew enough about the Russian bureaucracy and human politics to see himself being sized up for this role. He had begged them for more staff and better security. But the government in Moscow pleaded poverty.

'You look awful,' said Mirnov.

'You should see yourself.'

'Yes, well I have a reason. I have been working. Around the clock.'

'Yes. Well I haven't been sleeping too well. I'd like to get to a phone. I have been asking for hours now to make a phone call,' said Gideon.

'In time, my friend. Sit down, please.' Mirnov gestured to one of the chairs in front of his desk and Gideon sat down.

'It is ironic, is it not?' said Mirnov.

'What's that?'

'That for fifty years we were at each other's throats, that the only thing that kept us from destroying one another, was the threat of mutual annihilation. What was it the Americans called it?' He touched a finger to his nose as if it would come to him through the alcohol haze. 'The doctrine you called MAD?' said Mirnov.

'Mutually assured destruction,' said Gideon. 'Part of game theory.'

'That it is,' said Mirnov. 'Leave it to the Americans to come up with some catchy letters, an acronym they call it. That is why their culture is dominant. They did not conquer the world with armies, but with words, with their motion pictures and movie stars, McDonald's and Disneyland. But you are Russian.'

'And Dutch,' said Gideon.

'Ah, the Dutch. They are wonderful people. I have been to the Netherlands you know. Oh, yes. The Hague.'

'Let me make a phone call to my office,' said Gideon.

'My superiors will be here shortly.' Mirnov issued a broad, beefy smile. 'I am sure they will be able to answer all of your questions.'

Mirnov did not want to incur the wrath of Western nations. There might be an international incident that would only worsen the publicity when van Ry was freed. There would be more blame for Mirnov.

'Please,' he said. 'Relax. Bear with me just a few more moments. A few more questions.'

Gideon settled back against his chair, having no other choice.

'This game theory – is there a strategy to retrieve devices if they fall into the wrong hands?'

'That depends.'

'On what?'

'On what their goals are. The West might be able to purchase the devices off the underground market, that is if the objective of whoever took them is purely economic, to obtain the highest possible price. If on the other hand it is political . . .'

'The West would submit to this?' said Mirnov. 'Purchasing the weapons even though they had no hand in losing them?'

'I do not speak for any government. But I believe they would do whatever is necessary to take them off the market. As I am sure your government would. The other side of mutually assured destruction,' said Gideon, 'is mutual self-interest.'

'And what if whoever has them has no goal other than to use them. What does this game theory say about that?'

'We find them, before they can use them. We are no longer talking theories at that point.'

Gideon's words seemed to sober the Russian, who looked at him across the desk as if they had perhaps reached some spoken watershed. There was a long period of silence as he studied the Dutchman.

'I can tell you a little,' he said.

Gideon's ears perked up.

'We know that the devices do not show up on our current inventory. Your information is accurate,' said Mirnov.

'I assumed that when I came here.'

Mirnov's eyebrows arched a little. 'Then your people in

California, they have reason to believe that this was no error in paperwork?'

'If I don't contact them soon, you can be sure of it.'

Mirnov was spurred on. 'The two devices in question are not in the bunker where they were supposed to be stored.' He took another sip of coffee as if this was needed to strengthen himself for what was to come.

'Can I have a piece of paper and a pen?' said Gideon.

Mirnov thought about it, then figured it was better not to have mistakes of memory made. He handed over a sheaf of paper and a pencil, and Gideon set up to take notes on a corner of the desk. At least for the moment he was not demanding to leave.

'It's possible, I suppose,' said Gideon, 'that they could simply have moved the two devices to another location inside the facility.'

'I don't think that is likely,' said Mirnov.

'Why not?'

'The movement in this case does not appear to be an inadvertent act.'

'What do you mean?'

'First, there is the question of their disappearance from our inventory records,' said Mirnov.

'Surely it could have been an error in counting.' Gideon had learned by sorry experience that the Russian's system of accounting for these weapons was primitive. There were no computerized bar codes as on the U.S. inventory of weapons, so they could not be tracked with a master computer as in the West. Here they did it the old-fashioned way, by finger count, if they did it at all. For more than two years, national security experts in the U.S. had feared the worst. Nuclear accounting in Russia was abysmal. The Russians had no firm idea of the precise quantity of fissile materials in their possession. So how could they know if any was missing? What Gideon was coming to realize was that their accounting for tactical weapons was also flawed. From the perspective of terrorists, why get materials if you can have the bomb instead?

'If it were only the inventory records, you would be right,' said Mirnov. 'But there is the more troubling matter of the facsimile shells.'

'What facsimile shells?'

'We found two dummy devices in the bunker, empty shells, made to look like the real thing. We do not know how long they were there. It would appear that this is the reason we did not pick up the error in the count of the bunker's weapons.' The Russian gave a heavy sigh.

'I don't understand,' said Gideon. 'Why would anyone go to the trouble of replacing the real thing with dummies and then simply drop them from the count on the inventory sheets?'

'I can think of only one reason,' said Mirnov. 'There was no need to continue with the deception, because the devices had been removed and were beyond our reach.'

The Russian's cold logic sent a chill up Gideon's spine.

'Then let's start with one assumption,' said Gideon. 'Someone took the trouble to maintain false inventory records at least until they didn't need to cover their tracks any longer.'

'That appears to be the case,' said Mirnov.

'Who had access to these records?'

'That is the problem. Only two people. Dimitri and myself.'

'That's it?'

'Yes.'

'Where's Dimitri?'

'We have been looking for him since he left the facility. His apartment. Places where he has been seen. We have not found him. But we are still looking. Unfortunately, it appears that Dimitri is involved,' said Mirnov.

'Obviously,' said Gideon.

'I have called my sister to see if she has seen him.'

'Why your sister?'

'Dimitri is my brother-in-law.' Mirnov said it like Gideon should have known. No wonder he was doubling up on the shots of vodka. One thing was clear. Gideon had to get whatever information he could from Mirnov before his superiors got there. Once they arrived, the Russian was likely to be removed, taken someplace for debriefing and Gideon would not see him again.

'We don't have much time. You know that, don't you?'

'Yes.' The Russian said it with soulful eyes.

'Then you've got to tell me everything you know.'

Mirnov looked at him for a moment and thought. He had worked for nearly five years at a salary that barely provided a subsistence for himself and his family. For months he had not been paid at all. His family was not eating well, and his children had holes in their shoes. Mirnov had done it out of duty to his country and a belief that Russia alone was responsible for its weapons of war. It had built this arsenal, and national pride dictated that it should control it. He could have done as Dimitri had and taken money. There were many in Russian crime who would pay handsomely for nuclear and chemical materials smuggled from Sverdlovsk. But Mirnov had never taken a ruble.

He looked at Gideon and wondered if the governments of the West were any better than his own. He had heard about politics in Washington on CNN, about a government run by and for the people 'inside the beltway', about endless scandals over money. Still, under the skin, he felt some kinship with this man. Gideon was not part of any government. He did not have to travel all the way from California to Moscow and Sverdlovsk to double-check on an error in paperwork. The people at the institute could have simply published the information and garnered international headlines, but they did not. There was something in that act of caution, a respect for the truth that impressed the Russian.

'If I were to tell you what we know, it would remain confidential?' said Mirnov.

'I would have to tell my people at the institute,' said Gideon.

'Of course. But would it go any farther?'

'That would depend. If there was a bona fide threat, authorities would have to be notified.'

'I understand,' said Mirnov. 'But you would not go to the press? You would not identify me as being the source of this information?'

'No.'

'There would be no public disclosure? The Western governments would treat it as confidential?'

'I believe I can assure you that the information would be treated at confidential as long as public safety can be protected. No one wants a needless panic. And in any event, you would not be named as the source.' Gideon could not control what would happen if the information was disclosed to the authorities. But he could protect his source.

'We have discovered two forged waybills,' said Mirnov. 'A man named Grigori Chenko, a technician who worked at Sverdlovsk prepared both of the documents. The first about four weeks ago. The second about two weeks after that. Each document listed machine parts that were crated and shipped east to the port of Vladivostok.'

'How do you know these were the bombs?'

'We don't,' said Mirnov. 'Not with certainty. However,

before they were shipped, the two crates were weighed. Each time the weight was precisely the same, a little over one hundred and four kilos. Accounting for the weight of the wooden crates themselves, it is almost precisely the weight of the two field artillery devices.'

'You say the first one was shipped a month ago?'

'Yes,' said Mirnov.

Gideon corrected a note and looked at the scrawl he had written quickly underneath it as Mirnov spilled out his information. 'This man Chenko. Where is he?'

'That is what causes us concern. We don't know. Shortly after this shipment was made he disappeared. He simply stopped coming to work.'

'And you never checked?'

'We assumed he found a better job. It is not unusual,' said Mirnov. 'I have lost more than half of my staff in the past year. If you don't pay people, they stop coming to work. If I stopped to check with each of them I would never get anything done. Do you know that months now go by and the military isn't paid? Soldiers and sailors, who were once gods, are now treated like trash,' said Mirnov. 'When a government starts doing that, they are asking for trouble.'

He was right. What's more, Gideon knew the Russians weren't alone in this. Both sides were guilty of the sin of denial. The danger lay in the fact that it had become politically unfashionable to worry about the bomb. Nuclear winters and atomic holocausts were the phobia of the 60s and 70s, no longer chic in the world of the Internet and the global economy. Why should politicians warn their citizens that nuclear annihilation was still a possibility? Why trouble them with such negative thoughts? After all, the Cold War was over. In the West, they were closing military bases, wallowing in the peace dividend, appraising with new capitalist vigor the expanding world markets. The president of the United States and the premier of Russia were friends. Why worry people with reports that their cities might be incinerated by an errant nuclear bomb? This, even as daily intelligence reports told world leaders that Russia was losing its grip on the atomic genie. And what if the unimaginable happened? Gideon had no doubts. The American president would declare a national emergency, call out FEMA, and tell the survivors that he felt their pain. It was what passed for statesmanship at the end of the millennium, a poor cry from Roosevelt and Churchill.

'What type of work did Mr Chenko do?' asked Gideon.

'As I said, he was a technician. He was employed in disassembling the devices.'

'The warheads themselves?'

'Yes.'

'So he would know how to assemble them as well?'

'Of course.' The Russian answered without any hint as to the gravity, though he obviously had considered the significance of this himself. Someone with these skills would be sought after by governments outside of the nuclear club or by 'subnationals', one of the euphemisms in the intelligence community for terrorists.

Gideon looked at his notes, underlined several items, and went over them again, committing the details to memory, then asked Mirnov for a match. In front of the Russian, he put the single sheet of paper with his notes in a large ashtray on Mirnov's desk, struck the match, and set an edge of the paper on fire, then watched it burn until there was nothing left but smoking cinders.

'One last question,' he said. 'What was the final point of destination for the two shipments?'

Mirnov swallowed hard. His superiors would draw and quarter him. 'We have not had this conversation,' he said.

'Agreed.'

'We cannot be certain with regard to the second crate. We do know that it is no longer in the warehouse at the port in Vladivostok. But the first shipment,' said Mirnov, 'had what you call a paper trail. The documentation of marine transshipment was telefaxed to me this morning.'

He reached into his shirt pocket and began to unfold a piece of paper, spreading it out flat on the desk.

'No one except myself and the port administrator in Vladivostok have seen this, and he does not know the significance.'

'I understand,' said Gideon.

The Russian turned the paper around on the desk so that Gideon could read it and commit its terms to memory. The shipment was marked, at least on paper, for a destination in the United States, a company called Belden Electronics.

CHAPTER
EIGHT

Roche Harbor, WA

A thin vapor of fog rose like steam from the surface of the water, so smooth and mottled it had the appearance of a pane of windowed bottle glass. Joselyn could see wisps of smoke winding from the chimneys of homes on Henry Island, a mile away.

She checked her watch. It was now five minutes to seven. She was hoping they would make it on time. Federal judges have a bad habit of issuing bench warrants for the arrest of witnesses who fail to appear, warrants that, from time to time, may embrace a lawyer or two. It was her signature, under her letterhead, faxed to the court that had assured Belden's appearance.

She looked back from the dock toward the parking lot. There was no sign of Belden and no cars on the road winding down from the hill above the resort.

The white façade of the Hotel de Haro with its second-story balcony wrapped in vines looked like a wedding cake. Dating from the 1800s, it was built by a business baron who owned a limestone quarry. The quarry was closed forty years ago, but the hotel had found another heyday. With its adjoining restaurant, it was one of the most charming spots in the islands. Far from the glitz of San Tropez and the Costa del Sol, the rich and famous, the sultan of Brunei and the Microsoft king Bill Gates had been known to moor yachts in the harbor and to take meals at the restaurant.

She looked again at her watch as she heard the monotonous hum of an engine somewhere overhead. She feared her suspicion was correct. She turned to fix it low in the sky and approaching from the west. Perhaps it was the early-morning seaplane from Victoria. It serviced the island twice daily.

The plane swooped down toward the channel gliding just above the mist, between Henry Island and the harbor, then settled onto the water and skimmed across the glistening surface. It made a big circling turn and headed toward the dock, throwing up spray behind it from the prop wash.

As it approached, the roar of the big radial engine shattered the tranquility of the inner harbor. A small flock of Canada geese took flight, followed by three mallards.

Joselyn had never been this close to a float plane before – no more than a hundred feet away – when the pilot cut the engines. All she could see was the outline of a dark silhouette in the cockpit. The plane drifted in silence like some mythic bird of prey, its momentum carrying it toward the dock.

At the last instant, the door under the wing opened and the pilot gracefully lowered himself down, one hand on the wing strut, one foot on the pontoon. In a fluid motion, he stepped across onto the dock. As if by some magic of leverage, he brought the heavy plane to a stop without the pontoon even touching the dock.

Joselyn's fears were realized. It was Belden. She wasn't

hot to fly, even in commercial planes. Now this. The man was full of surprises.

'You were expecting me?' He looked at her and smiled.

'And we're going to fly down in that?'

'Unless you have wings.' He had that cocky grin, like Robert Redford in *The Great Waldo Pepper*.

She stood looking at him, her feet frozen to the dock.

'Come on. It's only about forty minutes by air to Seattle. Besides, you'll love it.'

Inside of Joselyn that voice that speaks to each of us silently was now spitting expletives. Taking her own name in vain for lacking the sand to tell him no. 'I don't get into small airplanes with men I don't know. In fact I don't get into small airplanes at all.'

'You are afraid?'

'No.' What made her say it, she wasn't sure.

'Good. Then hop in.'

Holding onto the strut of the plane, he took her briefcase and put it down on the dock, then helped her step across onto the pontoon.

'Use the step up.'

She placed her left foot onto a metal step built into the strut of the plane. She had visions of falling between the pontoon and the dock: FLASH! 'Woman Killed Falling from Plane.' Embarrassing details to follow.

Somehow in heels and a business suit with a tight skirt that ended up high around her thighs, she managed to pull herself up into the pilot's seat. When she looked down, Belden was checking out her legs, and from the expression on his face, enjoying the view.

'Let's change clothes and you can try it,' she told him.

He laughed. 'No. No. I'm sure it wouldn't be as fetching.'

She got up out of the seat, straightened her skirt and

stepped around the controls in the center console. There were six seats in the rear of the plane, two on either side and a bench across the back.

'Take the co-pilot's seat on the other side up front,' he told her.

'Are you sure?'

'Of course. That way you can see where we're going.'

'I may not want to.'

'You're going to love it.' He didn't give her time to argue. Instead he threw Joselyn's briefcase up to her. She caught it in mid-air and stumbled into the seat up front.

He pushed off before she had a chance to change her mind, and they drifted quickly away from the dock. He climbed up into the pilot's seat and closed the door, flipped a couple of switches overhead while he fastened a headset with a microphone over his ears. He flipped several more switches and turned a dial. Suddenly the propeller kicked over and the engine started.

Belden looked out the side window, watching to be sure that his wing cleared any obstructions on the dock. 'Have you flown in a seaplane before?'

'Never.'

'But you have been up in small planes.'

She shook her head as he watched her out of the corner of one eye, his hands continually messing with the controls overhead.

'Then it should be exciting.' He looked down at her skirt. 'Though you might want to buckle your seatbelt so it doesn't get too exciting.'

She buckled the single belt, low across her lap, fumbled with it until the ends snapped together, then pulled the strap until it was tight, pulling her down into the seat.

'There's nothing to worry about.' He looked over at her. He could smell fear. 'I've been flying planes for years.'

'I'm not scared,' she lied.

'Good. Then that makes one of us.' He gave her a smile, more Redford. Before she could say another word, he pushed a lever forward and the engine literally ignited in a burst of power. The plane lurched forward and into a slow turn, away from the dock and out toward the open channel.

Her knuckles were white from gripping the front edge of her seat. She looked over at him and the smile finally left his face. He was now all business, concentrating on the channel out in front of them.

The movement of the plane over the water picked up a rhythm, and she began to relax, to settle in. It glided smoothly, then hit a wake, probably its own from the trip in. The plane lurched a little.

Belden made a turn, and lined up in a straight path down the channel between the harbor and Henry Island. Without hesitation, he reached for the handle on a control that rested on the console between them. He pushed it forward and the plane began to move faster through the water, lurching over mild undulations in the surface of the sea. The noise and vibration of the engine increased until Joselyn could hear nothing but the rattle of metal and the pounding of pontoons on the water. The plane picked up speed as his hand pushed the control farther forward, and the noise became a roar that filled her senses, the vibration chattering her teeth and penetrating to the core of her body.

Belden's concentration was intense, eyes straight down the channel as they bounded over the water, until in one smooth motion he pulled back slowly on the wheeled yoke, and like Pegasus they broke contact with the shimmering surface of the sea and lifted skyward.

This was a new sensation for Joss, having never before

flown in a small plane. Unlike heavily powered passenger jets, they were buffeted by air pockets, and rocked by crosswinds. The sensation of perpetual climbing was strange, as if any instant gravity would reassert its power and pull them down into the sea.

Joss looked down at the islands of the San Juan chain, hundreds of them, spread out beneath them, verdant mountains rising from a carpet of blue water, shimmering in the morning sunlight. 'It's beautiful!'

'It's one of the reasons I like to fly. You can't see this in a jet. They get above the clouds too fast. Besides, I'm a control freak. When I'm going somewhere, I like to have my hands on the wheel.'

She nodded like she understood.

They continued to climb for several minutes as they circled over the islands then headed south, down the sound. The engine ceased its struggle as they leveled off and settled into a steady monotone.

'Why don't you take it for a second?'

'What?'

'The controls,' he said. His hands were off the wheel before Joselyn could say anything else. She grabbed the controls in front of her, and the right wing started to dip.

'Put your feet on the rudder controls.' He pointed to two pedals on the floor. 'Just keep them even. Keep the nose level with the horizon and you'll be fine.'

Joselyn found herself flying the plane, unable to speak, a cold chill running down her spine. It was like an out-of-body sensation. Pebbles of perspiration broke out on her forehead. Sheer fright.

'How do you like it?'

'Great. Take it back.'

'You're doing fine.' He started looking through some

papers he pulled from a pocket in the door, totally ignoring what she was doing at the controls.

'Aren't you afraid I'm going to fly us into a mountain?'

'Nope.' He didn't look up. 'The only mountain I have to worry about is behind us.'

'Good to know you have confidence in me.'

'I might even take a nap.'

'Don't you dare.'

He was smiling again.

Her eyes were darting from the dials and switches on the panel in front of her to the horizon and back. Terror ebbed toward discomfort as she began to get the feel of the controls.

'You're on a perfect heading. Another twenty minutes, and we should be over North Seattle.'

'This is no way to treat your lawyer,' she told him.

'Aren't you having fun?'

She wouldn't admit it, but actually she was beginning to.

'It's just like riding a bicycle,' he told her.

'Yes, but if I fall off a bicycle the ground is a lot closer.'

'The object here is not to fall. You're diving a little.'

'So what do I do?'

'See your airspeed?' He pointed to one of the gauges. 'Very easily pull back on the wheel just a little. That's it. Bring the nose up just a little.'

She stopped talking and concentrated on the controls. The horizon slowly leveled out across the bottom of the windshield and the airspeed indicator dropped thirty miles an hour.

'Good. Now let's talk about what I can expect at the courthouse today.' He had some papers spread out on his lap, like he was going to take notes.

'You're not going to be getting my undivided attention unless you take this back.'

He laughed and took the wheel, putting his feet on the control pedals. 'Relax. I've got it.'

Joselyn took a big sigh and stretched back in the chair feeling knots release from the muscles in her arms and shoulders where she'd stiffened up over the controls. She took a couple of deep breaths and then reached for her briefcase and the pad inside on which she had made notes. She flipped through some pages, and when she looked over his hands were off the wheel.

'Who's flying?'

'Autopilot,' he said. 'I'll keep a lookout for other planes. You tell me what I'm supposed to do when we get there.'

'If you say so.' She picked up her notes. 'First thing. We may get an idea of what they're looking for if there are other witnesses waiting when we get to the courthouse. You may recognize some of them. If so, it may give us a clue as to what they're fishing for. You have to tell me if you recognize anybody. There's still time to take the Fifth, to refuse to testify, but only if we have good reason.'

'I understand.'

'Once you get inside, the jury foreperson will swear you in. The prosecuting attorney in charge of the investigation, probably a deputy U.S. attorney will advise you of your rights. The right to counsel, the right to remain silent, so forth. They will probably warn you that because you are under oath, if you do not tell the truth, you can be prosecuted for perjury.'

'I understand.'

'At that point the prosecutor will probably tell you something about the nature of the investigation. This is a critical point. If there are any surprises, if in fact they are not investigating this guy Max Sperling, the one you told me about, take a break. Tell them you want to confer with your lawyer. They have to let you do it. Don't answer any questions until you come outside and we have a chance to talk. Do you understand?'

'Piece of cake,' said Belden.

'Let's hope so.'

'What happens then?'

'Once we get the ground rules nailed down, the prosecutor will start asking you questions. Think before you answer. Just answer the questions he asks. Don't volunteer anything. If you start giving long answers and getting into items he hasn't raised, it's just going to make the whole thing go on longer. That only serves to create more jeopardy for you. To open areas of inquiry the prosecutor hasn't thought about. Keep it short and sweet.'

'Got it.'

'Once you start testifying, tell them the truth. Don't hide anything.'

'But you just said I wasn't supposed to volunteer.'

'What I mean is that you have to answer their specific question directly and completely. But don't go beyond the specific question. Don't open the door on other matters. That's their job. The less you say, the faster you're going to be out of there. If you can answer a question with a single yes or no, do it.'

'Got it. Just a second.' He flipped a switch and a dial on something that looked like a radio overhead, then talked into the microphone fixed to his headset.

'I.L.S. control. This is J.N. eight-two-four-six. Coming in on vector . . .' He looked at his compass, and gave them a heading.

The tower talked and Joselyn could hear static but none of the words.

'Lake Union.' There was another pause.

'Thank you,' said Belden, then turned a dial on the radio.

'Sorry, had to clear for approach.' He flipped another switch and took the controls. She assumed he had turned off the autopilot.

'OK, so I don't give them anything they don't ask for.'

'Right.'

'I talk to you if there's any surprises.'

'Right.'

'What else?'

'I'm not precisely sure. Procedures vary from district to district. Some prosecutors allow members of the grand jury to question the witness directly once the prosecutor is finished. I don't know if that will be the procedure here or not. I'll try to find out before you go in. But if they do allow jurors to question you, be careful.'

'Why?'

'Because the jurors are going to look like ordinary folk. That's what they are. Most of them are going to be friendly and smiling. They're not going to be talking in legal-speak. They're going to sound like your neighbors. There is a tendency to let your guard down, to get into a conversation with them. Don't do it! The prosecutor's going to be listening to every word, and any door you open he's going to walk through. These are not your friends. They didn't invite you down for a social meeting.'

'I understand. The enemy,' said Belden.

'Don't be hostile, just be guarded.'

'Good. Does that cover it?'

'Pretty much. If you don't understand a question, get clarification. Don't hesitate to ask them to restate the question. And if you feel that you want to talk to me, tell them you want to take a break to confer with counsel.'

'OK.'

Joselyn could see houses spread out like a carpet on a field of green beneath them as they started to descend over the northern suburbs. The University District spread out along the western shore of Lake Washington.

'Tell me a little more about your business?' she asked.

This came out of the blue and seemed to surprise Belden.

'What's to tell?'

'Exactly what is it you make?'

'Switches.'

'I know. But what kind of switches?'

'The kind that turn things on and off.'

She looked at him, like give me a break.

'Right now we're actually into designing computer chips for voice-recognition systems. Used in security,' said Belden. 'It's like a fingerprint, only in this case what we're checking is a voiceprint. Somebody speaks into a telephone, or microphone, and the computer compares the voice to the voiceprint on record. If it matches, the door opens, or the lights go on, or an alarm is set. You can turn on your sprinklers or your lights long distance. If the voiceprint doesn't match, the person doesn't get access.'

'Fascinating,' said Joselyn. 'They can actually do that?'

'Accurate to more than ninety-nine percent. Almost impossible to fool.'

'And what if I have a tape recording of somebody's voice?'

'Even with a tape recording of the right voice, the chip will pick up background noise, the slightest gain from the microphone on the tape, and lock you out. The best systems use coded words. With the right words you could control the world.'

He swung the plane wide to the east and began his approach over the university, cutting power and dropping his wing flaps. He banked steeply to the right and dropped rapidly, so that Joselyn's stomach felt as if it was going to bounce off the ceiling. They picked up speed, with the engine almost at idle as they dove toward Lake Union, over the I-5 bridge with traffic backed up to a standstill.

As they approached Lake Union, Belden pulled back slowly on the controls and slid the throttle forward for a little more power. The engine lifted the nose momentarily.

Touchdown on the water was smooth and barely perceptible, but for the spray shooting up from the pontoons to the side and behind them, and some shudder in the plane as they glided across the water.

'There. I got you here in one piece.' He looked over at her.

'I never had a doubt.'

'Right,' he said.

He taxied the plane toward one of the docks. A large sign on a green building read 'Seattle Seaplanes'. There were flowers, a fusillade of color in wooden planter boxes all along the dock, and several small floatplanes tied up, one of them pulled up on a floating dock that was partially submerged under the load.

'I made special arrangements to tie up here. Just for a few hours. I don't come down that often to have a permanent berth. We can call a cab from inside.'

Joselyn checked her watch. He was right. They had plenty of time.

Ten minutes later, they were in a cab cutting through the downtown, heading up the hill toward Madison and Sixth, the United States Courthouse in Seattle.

CHAPTER
NINE

Culver City, CA

It was an absolutely wild scam, better than knocking over a bank, or using a pickup truck with a chain around the axle to pull an ATM machine out of a wall and haul it away. Nobody was going to get shot doing this one, and most banks didn't have this kind of cash on hand.

Besides, the tight khaki shorts made Buck's behind look real sexy. The little receptionist was checking him out as he stood at the counter and waited for her to finish her phone call. If she knew that the view was going to cost her employer a thousand dollars or more, she might have looked a little longer.

Buck Thompson lived in the small town of Sedro-Woolley in the extreme northern part of western Washington State. He was a lumberman by vocation, but he hadn't worked at it for three years. There were no jobs. He and most of his friends did whatever they could to keep their families together. From time to time, Buck took odd jobs in other states to make a few dollars. It was how he got in on this current thing.

He'd made a decent living for ten years until the last compromise between environmentalists and the White House on timber harvests for federal land closed all the mills. Since then, Thompson and most of his friends had been out of work. One of his boys dropped out of school a year ago, at age fourteen, to get a job. His wife held down two, cleaning offices at night and answering phones in a small brake shop during the day.

What made him mad was the constant drumming on CNN, telling everybody that the economy was just fine. The news media, or whatever they were calling themselves these days, had become nothing but a mouthpiece for the federal government, parroting press releases from the White House. If the president took a crap in public, they'd report that he shit gold bricks.

If Buck and his friends wanted to know what was going on politically, the only place the could get the truth was on the Internet. At least there they could pick their own bias, rather than having the news moguls spin everything for them.

Buck searched the web nightly when he was home, hitting all the familiar sites, Aryan Nation, The Brotherhood, a handful of tax protest sites, all the places where people with militia leanings hung out. They communicated on-line, using code words and aliases. The Feds were always listening, watching all the chat rooms.

Buck knew that jobs were being shipped to other countries in droves. The American trucking industry all along the Mexican border had been decimated. Unemployed truckers were big-time on the net. Companies that had flourished for generations went bankrupt within months of the U.S. entering into the North American Free Trade Agreement. It was an unholy alliance between the political parties, Democrats and Republicans, and big business to screw over working people. As far as Buck was concerned all politicians were a pack of pimps, anxious to sell their country to anybody in return for a quick campaign contribution, half the time from foreigners or foreign governments.

Buck thought the Justice Department was a joke. It did nothing but cover it all up. The FBI was interested only in chasing people like Buck, people who didn't fit the definition of being politically correct. Anybody who resisted taxes, made a critical comment about the IRS or criticized the president found that they were suddenly being investigated or audited.

It had gone full circle. America had destroyed the Soviet Union only to replace it as the world's biggest totalitarian government, run by crooked politicians, and their corporate friends in the media, and administered by corrupt bureaucrats. It was America's legacy for the millennium.

It was the reason Buck took so much pleasure in the latest scam, screwing over the phone company, dialing for dollars. It was certain to raise a lot of money in a very short time. Buck guessed that something big was up.

He wondered who thought it up. He'd been told it was a Russian, a mobster from Moscow who immigrated to the U.S. The Russians didn't rob banks or knock over liquor stores. They believed in making money the modern way, by reaching out and touching somebody. Surviving in the shadow of the Kremlin for seventy years, the Russian mob was more than a match for American law enforcement. In five years, the federal government would be wishing the Iron Curtain was back, trying to rebuild the wall in Berlin. America wanted to free the people of Eastern Europe. Be careful what you ask for, you may get it.

The scheme was brilliant. There were fourteen of them, all militia members, working it this afternoon. Each one wore the uniform of various delivery companies. They all carried a package under one arm and a metal clipboard with phony shipping receipts under the other. Though all of the guys came from the Northwest, today they worked the area around Culver City in Southern California, mostly light industry, a few warehouses and a couple of large retail outlets. They picked businesses that looked large, the kind of company that might not notice an extra thousand or two on their phone bill at the end of the month.

The little blonde receptionist was kind of cute. She reminded Buck of one of his nieces. She wore a headset like an airplane pilot and punched buttons on the phone's keypad like a pro. He was glad the money wasn't coming out of her pocket. She punched one of the buttons on her phone, looked up at Buck, and smiled. 'Can I help you?'

'Got a package for Mr Zinsky,' he told her.

The girl looked at him quizzically, like she didn't recognize the name. There was no reason she should. Zinsky didn't exist.

'You sure you have the right address?' she asked.

Buck read her the name of the company and the address from the shipping label inside its clear plastic holder on the package.

'Maybe he's new,' she said. She rifled through the roster of employees on the counter in front of her. 'Hmm.' Nothing. 'Why don't I take it,' she said, 'and I'll call your office if I can't find him.'

'I can't do that,' said Buck. 'He has to sign for it.'

'I can sign,' said the girl.

'Special handling,' said Buck. 'Requires Mr Zinsky's signature.'

'Well.' Now she wasn't sure what to do. 'I could call my boss.' She started paging through the printed roster one more time just in case she had missed his name. Still nothing.

'It's a priority overnight,' said Buck. 'Must be something pretty important.'

She offered a pained expression. She didn't want to get in trouble. But she didn't know what to do.

'Could you spell the name?'

'Harold Zinsky. Z-I-N-S-K-Y.'

She looked some more. There was nobody by that name. By now the phone lines in front of her were all lighting up, bells ringing everywhere.

'Just a second.' She answered one of the phones. 'Can you hold.' She went down the line. 'Please hold.' She did it six more times until all of the lines were flashing, but quiet.

'That's the right address, and our company,' she said. 'But there's no Mr Zinsky here.'

'Erm.' Now it was Buck's turn to looked troubled. 'I wonder if I could use your phone. Check with the dispatcher. It's an eight hundred number.'

'Sure. There's one at the end of the counter there. Just press nine for an outside line.' The girl went back to her phones, relieved that she didn't have to make a decision at least for the moment.

This one was gonna be a cakewalk. Buck sidled down to the end of the counter five feet from where the girl was talking on the line. He picked up the phone, dialed nine, and then the number. Only it wasn't an eight hundred number. He dialed nine-hundred and then the phone number. It was what is known as a 'pay-per-call' service, one of those numbers used by some legitimate businesses but known mostly as the telephone equivalent of the red light district. 'Call me. My name is Sherie. I'll tickle your dingle-dangle long distance with a feather for three dollars a minute.'

What the average phone user didn't know was that some telephone companies allowed businesses to charge as much as $250 per call when dialing a nine-hundred number.

The service provider, usually one of the big telephone carriers, would take a small percentage, or a flat fee per call, and would forward the rest of the money earned during the month to the customer possessing that particular nine-hundred number. In Buck's case this was the Western States Militia, a consortium of well-armed and organized patriots. Only they didn't use the militia name with the phone company. Instead they used something nice and respectable. 'Rock Island Finance and Investment.' They would change it next week when they moved to a different area of the country and did the scam again with a different number and corporate name.

Buck listened and waited for the taped message to end. It was very brief, something innocuous about financial planning, no more than ten words in length.

He hung up the phone without saying a word. The girl looked over at him. She was talking to somebody else on the switchboard.

'Busy,' Buck whispered to her.

She read his lips, nodded, and smiled like she understood. She kept talking, forwarded a call, and picked up another.

Buck dialed again. Did the same routine. By the time he was finished he had dialed the number five times: $1250 on the company's phone bill. The charges would be sent along to the receptionist's employer at the end of the month, and unless the company's bookkeeper was Ebenezer Scrooge, it would probably be paid without much question. The phone company in turn would send the money along to the militia under its corporate alias.

Buck could have done it four more times, but he took pity on them. Besides it didn't pay to be greedy with one pigeon. This was the land of opportunity. There were at least a dozen other good-sized businesses on this same street who wouldn't notice the charges on their phone bills for at least two or three months, if ever. He would hit them all within the next two hours. Then he would move a few miles away and start over again. Tomorrow they would pick up sticks and move out to Orange County and from there down to San Diego. Welcome to the electronic superhighway.

Buck walked back over to the receptionist. She looked up at him, still dealing with a caller on the line.

'Can you hold a moment?' She pressed the hold button.

'The line's busy,' said Buck. 'I don't seem to be able to get through. Tell you what. I'll check the information with my office from the cellphone in my truck. Have 'em run a trace on it and call the party who sent it out. They probably either got the name or the address wrong. We'll straighten it out, and if it's supposed to be delivered here, I'll come back and drop it by this afternoon.'

'That'd be great.' The girl flashed big pearly whites at him like he'd just solved a huge problem for her.

Always willing to help, thought Buck. After all he shouldn't be wearing their uniform unless he was willing to provide the service.

He turned and headed for the door. He could see her checking out his tight ass in the dark smoked glass of the front door just before he opened it.

He had done a quick calculation in his head before getting started that morning. If each one of the fourteen men working the scam that day averaged $1,000 a hit, and they could do five businesses in an hour, they were pulling down $70,000 an hour. Times eight hours, was $560,000 for the day. The militia would take ninety percent. The other ten percent would be divided among the fourteen men working the scam. Buck wasn't asking any questions. No matter which way you cut it, it beat the shit out of climbing trees and whacking off limbs.

Toothpaste and toilet paper did the job on the smoke detector in the cell. The smoke detectors were there so the guests wouldn't light up at night and burn the jail down.

Chaney molded a flat baffle out of a dozen pieces of the toilet paper and held it together with toothpaste and water. He fit it precisely over the smoke detector then used more toothpaste to seal it off.

Quickly Chaney moved to the window, removed the screw heads and lifted the acrylic screen off, setting it gently on the floor against the wall. Taking a single match he held it up as high as his arms could reach into the well of the window and allowed the match to burn like a candle for several seconds.

'What are you doing?' said Chenko.

'Shut up.'

They waited for almost two minutes. It seemed like a lifetime. Chaney was about to light another match when he heard the rustle of branches and noise outside. He looked up and saw a man's face beaming back at him from beyond the bars.

'What the hell took you so long?' said Chaney.

'There was a car coming. Here, take this.' The man outside was breathless. He passed Chaney a small walkie-talkie attached by wire to a headset.

'We got cars at each end of the street. They're both on channel seven. They see any movement outside, cars

118

coming by, guards nosing around, they'll let you know. Cover the flame. You got it?'

'Got it,' said Chaney.

'Here. Now don't drop it.' The guy outside carefully slid the carrying case with the Victor torch through the bars. He had tied the handle of the case onto a rope so that he could retrieve it if for any reason they weren't able to get out that night.

'If you need anything, holler into the headset. I'll be in the car at the corner.' Before Chaney could say anything the guy was gone.

He left the other end of the rope coiled on the ground outside and headed back to his colleague in the car. For this he walked a very careful route, one that they'd mapped out earlier in the week.

Outside the jail was a video surveillance system. Cameras mounted on rotating motors were erected under the eaves of the building and monitored by guards at a station inside.

The system had only one problem; a noticeable blind spot in the area outside of the ground floor cell that Chaney had muscled away from Tattoo and Homer. It might have been a relatively new county jail, but it wasn't Pelican Bay or the Federal Prison in Atlanta.

Chaney got the sparker out of the box, adjusted the oxygen and acetylene for the right mix, and sparked the torch. He adjusted the nozzle until there was a blue flame and the steady hiss of gas.

Inside the box were a set of welder's glasses. Chaney put them on and went to work. It was a long and awkward reach, eighteen inches up into the open well of the window. He stood on the rim of the commode that was directly beneath it, and several times almost slipped and stepped in the open toilet.

Chenko held a blanket over the window in the cell's

door so the flash of sparks from the torch cutting steel wouldn't be reflected outside into the partially dark corridor. Occasionally he peeked behind the blanket to ensure that the guard wasn't making his rounds.

Smoke from the torch began to waft back into the cell and up toward the ceiling. Chenko looked nervously at the smoke detector wrapped in toilet paper and hoped that it would hold.

'Are you almost finished?'

'Shut up and watch the door,' said Chaney. He'd cut through one of the bars and was halfway through another when the guys outside in the car whispered into the headset of the walkie-talkie.

'Cool it. Pedestrian coming up the street.'

Chaney removed the torch from the window well and held it down near the floor so that it wouldn't be visible from the outside. He waited a couple of minutes until he was given the all clear.

Chaney was hoping the guys outside had remembered to bring the pry bar. The plan called for Chaney to cut through each of the bars one time near the bottom. Using the pry bar, they would then bend the steel bars out of the way, enough so that Chaney and the Russian, using the bars as handholds, could shimmy up and out through the window.

He hadn't quite finished the second bar when the torch began to sputter and showed a yellow flame. The first acetylene bottle was empty. Chaney began to worry that maybe he hadn't brought enough. If they couldn't cut the other bars, he would have to push all the tools out through the window, have the guys in the cars pick them up, then put the acrylic screen back in place and wait until tomorrow night to finish. If the guards checked the window and saw the burned bars or checked the acrylic screen, it would be all over.

He disconnected the first acetylene bottle and hooked up the second, sparked a flame, and went back to work. Chaney was almost through the third bar when Chenko snapped his fingers twice. 'Guard.'

Chaney whipped the torch out of the window and doused the flame. He dropped the torch into its case and with one foot kicked the whole thing under the bunk.

The Russian pulled the blanket off the window and dove for the upper bunk as Chaney replaced the acrylic screen. He didn't have time to mess with the screw heads. He fell on his bunk just as the guard's flashlight beam reflected off the glass window in the cell door.

Chaney lay like a dead man in his underwear on the bunk as the guard's light flashed around the room and flickered off the acrylic panel in the window. He prayed that the guard wouldn't notice that the six screw heads were missing.

Chaney's head was turned away from the wall toward the door. His eyes were open enough for peripheral vision to pick up something on the floor. It was a loop of red rubber hose from the torch, sticking out from under the bunk.

The flashlight beam moved around the walls of the cell like Tinker Bell. Chaney flopped over on the bed as if shifting in his sleep, dangled one arm over the edge of the bunk, and with his hand scraped the floor catching the hose in a single fluid motion, sweeping it under the bunk.

The flashlight traced his movements just a half-second too late to pick up the hose which by then had disappeared under the blanket hanging over the edge of Chaney's mattress. He held his breath as the light swept the wall above the bunks. It passed over the toilet paper cocoon covering the smoke detector so quickly that the guard didn't notice. He also failed to pick up the hazy cloud of smoke that floated lazily just beneath the ceiling of the cell like mist over the Blue Ridge Mountains. The guy was either blind or going through the motions of a bed check while his mind was off duty, probably thinking about humping his wife or his girlfriend or somebody else's wife.

The light disappeared from the cell door window. Chaney and the Russian waited several seconds until they heard receding footsteps back down the corridor outside.

Chaney got up and checked the window. 'Go.'

The Russian grabbed his blanket, jumped off the bunk and covered the window again. This time he kept a careful eye peering behind it.

Chaney went back to work with the torch. 'Just one more.' He cajoled and coaxed the little torch, babying it to conserve fuel. He kept checking his watch. Eighteen minutes later, he was through the last bar.

'Done.' He whispered into the mouthpiece of the headset and a second later heard a car door slam some distance away outside. A minute later there was rustling in the bushes beyond the window and Chaney saw the business-end of a long steel pry bar poking into the window from outside. Using the hard frame of the masonry around the window, the man outside leveraged his weight against the cut bars one at a time until each of them were bent almost ninety degrees and lay nearly flat against the well on the inside of the window.

'Time to go,' said Chaney.

Chenko went first. He didn't bother with clothing. In his underwear he put one foot on the edge of the commode, then pulled himself up using the bars inside the window. He slid through the window easily and disappeared through the bushes outside.

Chaney started to go, then looked back. He stepped back down off the commode, disconnected the twin hoses from the bottles of oxygen and acetylene, flipped the bottles up and out through the window. Then he assembled the torch back in its box and placed it on top of the commode. Only then did he pull himself up through the window and out. He used the rope on the outside to lift the case with the torch out through the window. There was no sense leaving it behind for the cops to trace. A Victor Portable torch was an item that a hardware dealer would remember selling. He might remember Chaney's face. Why have a bad portrait hanging in the post office when you didn't have to?

CHAPTER
TEN

Yekaterinburg

I t appears the problem may be double what we originally
thought.' Gideon van Ry found himself shouting into
the mouthpiece of the telephone. 'No, I said double.' He
worried that his accent along with the bad connection was
making it more difficult for him to be understood back in
Santa Crista where Caroline was taking notes.

He also spoke in cryptic terms. He was sure they were
listening somewhere, probably down the hall from Mirnov's
office.

'Yes. Yes, that's what I said.' He hoped Caroline would
get the message without saying it; that whoever took the
devices took two of them. He worried that if he got too
specific, the Russians would cut the phone connection. He'd
already lost contact twice. Gideon waited for the deadening
click, but it didn't happen.

Mirnov looked at him from across the desk. Gideon
offered a harmless smile, shrugged his shoulders as if to
say 'bad connection'.

'Oh, they're being very helpful. The Russian government

is most cooperative,' said Gideon. He hoped this might buy more time on the line. For the most part, it was true. The problem was that in the new Russia no one quite knew precisely where to draw the line on security.

'The facility here is everything we thought it would be,' said Gideon.

This had a double meaning. He and Caroline had discussed what they knew about Sverdlovsk before Gideon left Santa Crista, and it was not good.

'Yes, you can put that in the report,' he told her.

Mirnov smiled at him, and Gideon smiled back. He would call her once he left Russia and edit the report before it was released, otherwise they would never allow him back in. Diplomacy was always important if you wanted continued access to information. While sunshine was the institute's business, they were not out to embarrass the Russian government. Poking the light of public awareness into dark crevices containing arsenals of mass destruction was the institute's stock in trade. There was nothing the Russians would hear or read that they did not already know. Parts of their weapons storage and disposal system were in serious trouble. The problem was that neither the Russian nor the American governments were telling their people about this.

'One other note,' said Gideon. 'The items in question. They were not taken at the same time.' He listened. They did not cut him off.

'That's right. Both of them shipped through Vladivostok. Right.

'Say again?

'No. No. Different bills of lading. Both labeled machine tools. Same ultimate point of delivery. Yes.'

Caroline was now probing him, trying to get everything she could. In an hour, the bare outline of information would be on their database. The details they could disclose publicly would follow in a few days. Clients around the world would be on the alert, mostly government security services. They would want as much information as possible. No doubt they would be querying the institute by phone, fax, and e-mail. It was a major story for a very select audience.

'Let me spell it. That's Belden Electronics. B-E-L-D-E-N. A Washington State address. Check with information,' said Gideon. 'It appears to be incorporated, if the address means anything. It's a P.O. Box. A place called Friday Harbor. Probably an address of convenience. You can be sure they did not ship the devices there. That's right.' He held one hand over his other ear to hear better over the faltering phone line.

'What? Say again?

'Do I know when the last device was taken?' Gideon looked over at Mirnov. His superiors had instructed him to cooperate as much as possible. The Russian shrugged his shoulders. He wasn't sure. Or perhaps he was just in shock. No doubt he would be on a plane to Moscow by nightfall to answer a lot of questions.

'We cannot be sure when the last one was taken.

'Specifications, you say?'

Caroline wanted to know precisely the type of devices missing.

'Artillery shells. One-hundred-and-fifty-three-millimeter artillery. Hello. Caroline, are you there?'

He listened for a second. 'Hello. Hello.'

Apparently he'd gone too far. He could hear clicking on the line. They'd cut him off.

He held the receiver away from his face for a second and looked at it as if Caroline might actually crawl through the wire. Then he placed the phone into its cradle on Mirnov's desk.

'Ah. Telephone service. What can I say?' said Mirnov. 'Like everything else in the new Russia. Only the new entrepreneurs have good phones.'

Gideon looked up at the ceiling in frustration and ran the fingers of both hands through long blond hair. It was usually parted in the middle and full. This afternoon it was a mess. He hadn't shaved or showered in more than two days. He and Mirnov had been camped at the Russian's office trying to assemble what information they could. Mirnov was constantly called out to confer with superiors. Gideon wondered if he was being told everything.

He worried that maybe the Russians would hold him, if not here, then upon his return to Moscow. The Russian government might be the least of his concerns. There were darker forces at work in Mother Russia. The Mafiya, as it styled itself, was more violent there than anyplace else on earth. They did not mind murdering foreigners, particularly those who threatened their interests.

Gideon pushed himself off the corner of Mirnov's desk where he'd been leaning on the edge since his call went through to Caroline.

'We'll have to wait and see if our people can put the call through again,' said Mirnov.

'Two devices,' said Gideon.

'Yes.' Mirnov lit a large Cuban cigar and offered one to Gideon.

The tall Dutchman shook his head. 'Both artillery shells,' he said. 'I understand why they would take two of them. They could sell them both on the black market, Libya, Iran, Iraq. There are plenty of potential buyers. But why ship them to the same point of destination? That does not make sense,' he told the Russian.

Even if there were two targets in North America, Gideon

was convinced they wouldn't send a second device by the same route. The risks of surveillance were too great.

'You would send them to separate destinations, so that if one was discovered, the other might get through.'

'Unless . . .' said Mirnov.

'Unless what?' Gideon looked at the Russian.

'These are old weapons we are talking about. Some of these artillery shells date back to the mid-sixties. Their nuclear cores are aging. The high explosives surrounding the plutonium pit are old. The detonators which are critical may not have been checked in years. They have been in storage for two, maybe three decades. We do not have the maintenance records. I checked. I suspect that Dimitri had looked as well.'

'What are you saying?'

'What you call nuclear shelf life,' said Mirnov. 'If you were purchasing a nuclear device on the black market, paying top prices, would you not want some assurance that it would function?'

'I would,' said Gideon.

'What better way than a second device?' said Mirnov. 'Remember they have Chenko.' Grigori Chenko was the Russian technician who disappeared about the same time as the first device.

'He would know if the first warhead was defective. Perhaps they found a problem after it was shipped. That would account for why they did not take them at the same time.

'With a second warhead, you have spare parts. Even if both were defective in some way, Chenko could probably make one good bomb. And perhaps increase its yield.'

There were two basic types of nuclear weapons, so-called gun devices that used high explosives to propel a projectile of highly enriched uranium into a larger core target of the same. The resulting collision, assuming there was enough velocity, would split the atom, releasing massive amounts of energy and setting off a chain reaction.

The second type was more sophisticated. The so-called implosion device was constructed of a plutonium sphere in thirty-two individual pie-shaped sections. This was used to surround a beryllium/polonium pit in the center. The entire sphere was wrapped in conventional high explosives, a form of plastique, and set off by multiple simultaneous detonators. The uniform force of detonation, critically timed to one-ten-millionth of a second around the entire outer portion of the sphere, would drive the plutonium into the beryllium core, setting off the nuclear chain reaction.

The implosion device was more powerful, generating more atomic yield. The two artillery shells in question were of this type.

The elaborate nature of the implosion design also presented a problem. It required more maintenance. The timing of individual detonations around the outer sphere required exquisite precision. Without this, all that resulted was a dirty bomb, radioactive debris blown into the air by the explosion. By itself this could kill a few thousand people if they inhaled the dust. But if there was critical mass, if there was enough plutonium for a chain reaction and the device worked as designed, then in the flicker of an eye a major population center, hundreds of thousands, perhaps millions of people would be incinerated in a matter of seconds.

'Am I correct in assuming there are no safety devices for these shells?'

'What you call permissive action links?' said Mirnov.

'Exactly.'

'No. They are too primitive for that.'

The devices in question were small, and old, with a definite shelf life. They were not something that would find its way onto the shopping list of some rogue state for their own arsenal unless they had no other choice. It would be easier and more effective to purchase fissile materials and design their own bomb.

The artillery shells in question would be the weapon of choice only for a calculated act of terror. They were easily armed and transported. Whoever had taken them had gone to the trouble of coming back for a second device, evidencing some concrete plan. Everything Mirnov was telling him led to one unassailable conclusion: whoever bought the weapons had a clear target in mind.

He looked at the scrap of paper in his hand, the notes he'd made for his phone call to Caroline. He could catch a flight east across the Bering Sea, make a connection in Fairbanks. In ten hours, maybe twelve, he could be in Seattle. He wondered how long it would take him to get from there to this place on the note – this Friday Harbor.

CHAPTER
ELEVEN

Seattle, WA

A sign on the wall with an arrow pointing left said:

GRAND JURY ROOM

Joselyn and Belden headed down the carpeted corridor in silence.

The place had a hushed feeling of unfettered power. Joselyn had never been partial to the federal side of the law, where cold formality seemed to hold sway. Just being here sent a chill down her spine, the kind experienced by nearly every citizen when you mention words, like 'Internal Revenue Service'.

Federal buildings were temples to power, where judges were appointed for life, and U.S. attorneys possessed the prosecutorial powers of warlords.

The reach of federal criminal statutes was troubling to Joselyn. They had become so broad that they virtually mimicked every state crime. The protection of double jeopardy had become a joke. If a defendant was acquitted at the state level, but the crime violated notions of political rectitude, the defendant would be tried again at the federal level. This was now done routinely in high-profile cases where political points could be made by a president or his attorney general.

While Belden may not have been concerned, Joselyn was. She knew that a determined federal prosecutor could indict nearly anyone they wanted for virtually any act of human conduct. Whether they could get a conviction from twelve unbiased citizens on a trial jury after they heard all the evidence, and not just hearsay that the government chose to dish up, which was the case before grand jury, was another matter. Even if you were innocent it could take a half-million dollars and two years of your life to prove it.

In the distance, she could see a blue-blazered security man sitting behind a desk, just beyond a door with a frosted glass sidelight. On the glass the words GRAND JURY ROOM were etched in black letters. There were a line of wooden chairs backed against the wall in the corridor, hard and foreboding.

Joselyn was hoping to see other witnesses, someone Belden might recognize, to confirm that it was as he said, Max Sperling and his escapades of larceny that had brought them here. She was disappointed. The chairs against the wall were all empty.

Joselyn took the lead as they entered the door. She talked to the guard. With a pleasant smile, she handed him her business card.

'I'm Joselyn Cole. I'm here with my client, Mr Belden. He's been subpoenaed to testify today.'

The guard returned the pleasantries, but his gestures and movements were automatic, like a robot. He looked at the card, then opened the desk drawer and pulled out a clipboard. He held it so that Joselyn couldn't see what was printed on the pages clipped to the board, then he checked something in pencil.

She assumed it was the witness list and hoped there were other names on it for this particular case. From what she knew of federal grand jury proceedings, they handled a vast mix of cases. The jury might hear bits and pieces of evidence on a dozen different and unrelated matters in a single day, most of it hearsay from government witnesses; the FBI, ATF (Alcohol, Tobacco and Firearms), Customs and Immigration, the IRS, and the DEA (the Drug Enforcement Agency).

Some of these might be long-term investigations involving complex criminal matters that could go on for months or even years. Some of them never resulted in indictments after prosecutors discovered that allegations were founded on nothing but rumors. Too often they made this determination after they called most of the target's friends and all of their business associates before the grand jury for a good grilling. The subject of the investigation might not be convicted, but their reputation would certainly be destroyed.

Other cases, the vast majority, were clear-cut; a bank robbery with a dozen eyewitnesses. These would usually result in an indictment after half an hour of testimony from two witnesses. Joselyn had no idea which of the two extremes might be involved in this case.

'I'd like to talk to the assistant U.S. attorney before my client testifies,' said Joselyn.

The guy looked at the clipboard again. 'That's Mr McCally. I'll see he gets the message.' He wrote a note on the back of Joselyn's business card.

They took a seat outside on the hard chairs and killed time counting the dimples in the plastered wall four feet away on the other side of the narrow hallway. A number of people filed by, looked at the two of them sitting there, passed through the door, said hello to the guard, and disappeared into the jury room. After the first few went by, Belden shot Joss a quizzical glance.

'Jury members,' she told him.

Another ten minutes passed, and a few more jurors arrived. A door opened behind the glass sidelight, and a shadow appeared on the other side of the frosted glass; undertones of a male voice could be heard talking to the gatekeeper at the desk. They heard Belden's name mentioned.

He got up.

'Sit down,' she told him. Joselyn stepped around the door and came face-to-face with a tall man in a gray pinstripe suit. He had dark brown hair with some gray creeping in above the ears and deep-set eyes behind angular wire-framed glasses. His complexion was pale, like someone who has been indoors squinting under fluorescent tubes too long.

'Mr McCally?'

'Yes.' There was nothing friendly about the man. The quintessential prosecutor. He was stone-faced, almost icy.

'I'm Joselyn Cole. Mr Belden's lawyer.' She smiled and extended a hand, hoping to crack the cold veneer.

It didn't work. He took her hand. 'How do you do?'

'Can we talk for a moment before my client goes into the jury room?'

'Sure.' He didn't move from the area directly in front of the guard's desk. The marshal just sat there looking at them, expecting to be the third set of ears in the conversation.

'I meant someplace private,' said Joselyn.

'If you like.' McCally had a file under his arm, quite thick with the edges of paper sticking out, but nothing Joselyn could read. He led her down a short hallway behind the guard's desk to a room, where he opened the door and flipped on the wall switch. Fluorescent lights flickered on and hummed overhead.

Inside was a small metal conference table with four chairs, two on each side, and a telephone on one corner of the table. The walls were bare, painted pea-green. It was very institutional.

They stepped inside, and McCally closed the door behind them.

'What is it you'd like to discuss?' He apparently had no intention of sitting down.

Joselyn was becoming concerned. If Belden was an uninvolved witness, the prosecutor's demeanor certainly did not reflect it. Maybe it was just the hard-nosed edge of federal authority showing, a display of who was boss, but Joselyn's antenna was up.

'My client received a subpoena to appear. He has no idea of the subject matter or what this involves.'

'Is that right?' McCally almost seemed amused by this.

'Yes, it is. It would be helpful if you would give us some indication of what this is about?'

'I'll bet it would,' said McCally. 'Have you ever appeared with a witness before a federal grand jury before?'

Joselyn squirmed. He was checking her credentials.

'Not federal,' she said. 'I've accompanied witnesses at the state level.'

'That's what I thought,' said McCally. 'Let me give you a little advice. I am not at liberty to discuss the subject matter or content of a grand jury investigation.'

'So this in an investigation, not an indictment, at this point?'

'At this time, that's correct.'

'Is my client a subject or target of the investigation?'

'Did he receive a target letter?'

'No. Not to my knowledge.'

'There's your answer.'

'That doesn't tell me much.'

'Sorry about that, but it's all you're going to get.'

'Can you at least tell me how many witnesses are being called besides my client?'

'No.'

'Are any charges pending against anyone in connection with the investigation?'

'You don't appear to understand English.'

'I represent a client who is being compelled to testify with no indication of the subject matter. You expect me to allow him to walk into a room without legal counsel to be grilled by God knows how many federal prosecutors and an army of grand jurors, and you won't give us a clue as to the subject matter?'

'Welcome to the real world,' said McCally.

'My client doesn't have to testify. He can take the Fifth.' She was testing the water, to see if she could walk on it. How badly did they want Belden's testimony? Maybe she could draw McCally into a discussion of immunity.

'He can take the Fifth,' said McCally. 'That's his right. However, I would point out that in long-term investigations it's often better for a client to stake out his turf before others give us their side of things. Mr Belden could come up on the short end.'

'What are you saying? That he is a target?'

'I didn't say that.'

'What are you talking about? You just threatened him.'

'I didn't threaten anybody. I just explained how the system works.'

'In other words if some other witness comes before the grand jury and lies through his teeth, you'll focus suspicion

138

on my client because he exercised his constitutional right to remain silent?'

'He has an opportunity to dispel any suspicion by testifying.'

'And if he doesn't?'

'Well. That's his decision, isn't it?'

Joselyn could feel the blood boil like molten lead in her veins, fired by the heavy hand of the federal government.

'You've already focused suspicion on him.'

'No, I haven't.' He smiled as if to say, 'prove it'.

'If you want him to testify, we want a grant of immunity.'

'Forget it.' He turned toward the door as if to leave, then turned to face her again. 'Tell your client he can expect some more mail.' He was clearly threatening a target letter.

'Wait.' Now he had her attention. 'You're telling me that if he doesn't testify you're going to aim this thing at him?'

'What I'm telling you is that he can help himself or hurt himself. It's up to him.'

'What kind of government is this? You won't tell us what the hell is going on, and now you're telling me that if my client doesn't waive his right to remain silent you're going to indict him.'

'I've got nothing more to say. Tell your client to make his decision.'

'Wait a second. There's no way we can talk about this?'

'That's the process. Take it or leave it.' McCally started for the door again.

'Let me talk to him.'

He turned. 'I would have thought you'd done that before you came here.'

Whatever McCally thought Belden had done, he clearly thought Joselyn knew about it. She bit her tongue, afraid that what might come out of her mouth at this moment would only cause her client more grief. It seemed he was already in trouble. Her advice would be that he take the Fifth. But she wanted to keep open the lines of communication with the prosecutor.

'I'll have to talk to my client.'

'Do it.' He looked at his watch. 'How long do you need?'

'I don't know. Give me ten minutes.'

McCally was out the door, leaving it open behind him and Joselyn in the room alone. She knew Belden was in trouble. What she didn't know was why. It wouldn't have been the first time a client had lied to her.

She waited for a moment, so that McCally would not be loitering in the hall when she talked with Belden. She heard the door to the jury room open and close. Then she went out past the guard station and through the frosted glass door to the row of chairs against the wall. They were empty. There was no sign of Belden. She looked down the long corridor: nothing.

She stood there frozen in place and for a moment wondered if McCally had pulled one on her, if during the confusion of their conversation he'd taken her client inside the jury room. Even the Feds wouldn't do that, she thought. Still she asked.

She turned to the guard behind her at his desk. 'Did Mr Belden go into the jury room?'

'No.'

'Do you know where he went?'

'He's not out there?' The guard looked puzzled, stood up and came to the door, took a look for himself.

'Maybe the men's room,' said the guard.

She turned and looked down the hall in the direction indicated by the guard. It was a long stretch leading to the solid oak double doors of one of the courtrooms at the other end.

'Unfortunately I can't check,' she told him.

He gave her a look, like he really shouldn't leave his post, but he did. He walked quickly down the corridor, with Joselyn following behind him. The guard went into the men's room, and the door closed behind him.

She waited outside pacing back and forth, running the fingers of one hand nervously through her hair. She looked at her watch. Seconds seemed like minutes. Finally the door opened. She spun around expecting to see Belden. Instead, it was the guard. He was shaking his head.

'Nobody inside.'

'Where could he have gone?'

'I don't know.'

'You're sure he didn't go inside the jury room?'

'Yeah. Mr McCally went in, but nobody else. You want me to check with him?'

'No.' That was one thing Joselyn didn't want. Next he'd be issuing a subpoena for her. McCally was already wound and wired for action. If he found out that Belden had gotten cold feet and boogied, it would only serve to confirm whatever suspicions he already had.

'Maybe he just went out to get a breath of fresh air,' she said. 'I'll check.'

Joselyn was getting that sick sense, the kind you get when you realize your client has lied to you. She wondered if there was a Max Sperling or if Belden had made him up. Still, why would he come all the way to Seattle with a lawyer and then run? It didn't make sense.

'Are you sure you don't want me to get Mr McCally?' The guard pulled her from her reverie.

'No. That's all right.' Joselyn quickly headed down the hall toward the elevators, leaving the guy standing outside the men's room door. All the way there she wondered what she should do. She could withdraw. After all, she hadn't made a formal appearance. It wasn't like a trial. She'd have to give Belden his money back, at least the part she hadn't already earned. If he wasn't going to tell her the truth, she couldn't represent him.

She could always buy time, tell McCally that her client had a change of heart. That he'd decided to assert his Fifth Amendment rights. Maybe McCally wouldn't ask to see him. If he did, she could tell him he'd already left the building. Still, that might infuriate the prosecutor. McCally gave all the appearances of possessing a short fuse. He might apply to the court for a bench warrant and have Belden arrested for failure to appear. In the meantime, Joselyn would have spun a yarn to a federal prosecutor. She wondered if that would constitute obstruction of justice? A million thoughts raced through her mind as the elevator seemed to stop at each floor to pick up and deposit passengers. Finally she got to one, stepped out and checked the lobby. There was no sign of Belden.

They had entered from the Fifth Street side of the building, so instinctively she went to that door.

Maybe he was outside having a smoke. Did he smoke? She couldn't remember. He chewed gum. He'd offered her a stick, outside the courtroom. It began to settle on her that she knew amazingly little about this man. He had paid her fifteen thousand dollars in retainers, and all she had was a post office box for an address, and a phone number someplace in Kent. It was funny the things that money made you do, like stop thinking. Joselyn had accepted him as legitimate. Why? Because he came up with the cash? So could most drug dealers.

Her mind began to reel with the possibilities. What if he disappeared? Then she'd have his money. She could write to the court and tell them she couldn't find her client. Yeah, given McCally's mind-set he'd believe that!

She looked at her watch. She had told McCally ten minutes. It had taken her almost five just to get to the Fifth Street entrance.

She stepped outside the door. It was like a meeting of the fallen angels at smokers anonymous, the acrid odor of burning cigarettes. A dozen people stood around, hands in their pockets, shuffling and looking down at stamped-out cigarette butts on the ground, as they added to the carnage in their lungs. None of them were Dean Belden.

Joselyn raced down the stairs toward Fifth Street, looking both ways. There was no sign of him. It took her five more minutes to wave down a cab. She looked at her watch as she climbed into the back seat, and gave the driver directions.

'There's an extra fifty bucks in it if you can get me there in under ten minutes,' she told the driver. By now McCally would be looking for her, asking the guard where she went.

The acceleration of the taxi almost gave her whiplash. It drove her back into the seat, her hands scrambling for the seatbelt. Fifty bucks was extravagant, but right now she was angry that Belden had misled her. She would pay some of his money for a fast taxi ride to rip into him. Why he had bothered to fly down she wasn't sure, but there was only one place he could be. If he got cold feet, he would go back to the lake and the plane. Joselyn hoped she could get there before he left.

The driver weaved in and out of traffic and took a course that looked nothing like the one she and Belden had taken earlier that morning. The taxi went under I-5 and climbed the hill on the east side. It took a left on a narrow residential street and then picked up speed. The taxi must have been doing seventy, the driver slowing to fifty for peripheral glances at the cross streets.

Joselyn was afraid to look. If anybody opened a door on a parked car it was likely to end up in the next county, along with the driver, or at least his hand. She was about to relent, to tell the taxi driver to slow down, when he took another left on two wheels, throwing Joselyn against the corner and the door.

Then she saw it, Lake Union. It was less than ten blocks away on the other side of the freeway.

They headed down the hill. Joselyn fished in her purse for the money and came up with three twenties, then looked at the meter and grabbed a fourth. She was going to make the driver's day. Joselyn had no time to haggle over change. She wondered how long it took to prepare a floatplane for flight. Maybe he'd have to refuel? That would give her plenty of time to catch up with him. She hadn't spent that much time talking to McCally. Even if Belden left the courthouse immediately after she'd gone into the room with the prosecutor he couldn't be more than ten minutes ahead of her. Unless his taxi driver had his own private turnpike, he couldn't have gotten to the lake any faster than she did.

They ran a red light and sped along the east shore of the lake.

'It's about a mile up. On the left.' Joselyn unbuckled the seatbelt and was leaning over, hanging onto the front seat as best she could. She saw the restaurant, Chinese, or Japanese, the words Kamon on the Lake in neon scrawled on a large sign. The seaplane dock was just beyond the restaurant. She remembered it.

'There.' She saw Belden's plane. It was at the dock, but somebody had turned it around, and the engine was running. She could see mild ripples on the water being churned from the prop wash. There was no sign of Belden, but he couldn't be far.

'Stop here. Let me out.' She almost threw the money at the driver. The car was still moving when she opened the door. It skidded to a stop on the graveled pavement of the parking lot and Joselyn jumped out. Struggling for a better grip on her briefcase and purse, she nearly tripped.

'You want a receipt, lady?'

She ignored the driver. Her thoughts were on the plane, its engine idling a hundred yards away at the end of the dock. She had to negotiate around a wooden planter box, through a white picket gate covered by an arbor.

Joselyn just cleared the gate when she saw him. Belden was putting his wallet in his hip pocket. She was right. He had to refuel. He was walking toward the plane as if he didn't have a care in the world. He'd stood her up, left her talking to an angry prosecutor at the courthouse, and now he was going to head home as if nothing had happened.

Anger flared like molten lava. 'Hey.' She yelled at the top of her voice, but it was swallowed by the rumble of the engine.

He stepped across onto one of the pontoons.

She yelled again, but he showed no sign of recognition, his back still to her.

She dropped her briefcase and purse on the dock and started to run, hands cupped to her mouth yelling for him to stop. The heel of one of her shoes caught in the gap between two planks on the dock and snapped.

'Damn it.' Her best pair of dress shoes. She took off the broken one, started to hobble, and nearly tripped. She ditched the good shoe, throwing it ahead of her on the dock, and ran in stocking feet, yelling Belden's name along with unmentionable epithets through cupped hands.

The constant rumble of the engine grew louder as she

drew near. She was sure he couldn't hear her. He loosened one of the lines securing the plane to the dock, and then for some unfathomable reason, Belden turned, his gaze rising to meet her on the dock.

Joselyn stopped in mid-stride, out of breath, the nylons on her feet shredded. Standing on one pontoon, directly below the plane's open door, Belden looked directly at her, a studied expression as if at first he wasn't sure it was her. Then the sign of recognition, he waved. The fucker actually waved at her and smiled. She couldn't believe it. There was no remorse, not the slightest expression of atonement for the fact that he'd left her holding the bag with an angry prosecutor at the courthouse.

She bent over, hands on her knees, still catching her breath. She was furious. She wanted to kill him. She looked down at the shredded nylon on her feet. Then heard the roar of the engine as it revved up.

Joselyn looked up, startled. He'd released the aft line, pulled himself up into the plane and was pulling away from the dock. After all of this, Belden was going to leave her standing there. Over her dead body. She grabbed the first thing she saw – her single good shoe on the dock – and ran headlong toward the plane. She reached the edge of the dock and threw the shoe as hard as she could. It struck the metal of aileron on the plane's tail and dropped into the water.

She stood there at the edge of the dock, perspiration running down her face, frustration boiling over. The bottom of one foot throbbed and bled where she'd picked up a splinter. She watched as the plane made a wide, sweeping turn beyond the boathouse at the end of the dock and passed out of sight. The roar of the engine was muted by the wooden façade of the building. Still she could hear him throttling up for the channel and his takeoff, and she could do nothing.

She walked slowly toward the end of the dock, furious. As she reached the corner of the boathouse, Joselyn heard the engine gain an octave in pitch and a hundred points on the decibel meter. Suddenly the plane emerged from behind the far corner of the building, tail down, engine at full throttle, it roared across the water.

Joselyn stood transfixed as if witnessing the emerging geometric shapes of a kaleidoscope, as the propeller shot forward and skipped across the water like a stone. The wings seemed to lift in a single unified piece, separated from the plane's fuselage by an emerging orange flash, a brilliant burst that seared the optic nerve, delivering intense pain to her eyes. An instant later, the pressure wave hit Joselyn, throwing her onto her back on the dock. Her last memory was one of intense heat as the shock wave passed over her body. The spreading flare of exploding aviation fuel shot a hundred feet into the sky. Small bits of the plane floated in the air like leaves in an autumn gale.

CHAPTER

TWELVE

Washington, DC

The White House Working Group had tentacles into the National Security Council, eyes and ears at the CIA, the FBI, the Justice Department, and a dozen other federal agencies. They were the clearing house for information on domestic terrorism. The group had been formed after the bombing of the federal building in Oklahoma City, and since that time had convened once a week in the Old Executive Office Building unless there was some urgent business, in which case they could be called together on a half-hour's notice. This was not a regularly scheduled meeting.

'What's this about?' Stuart Bowlyn was the chairman of what was known as the Working Group. Its more formal name was the Coordinating Subgroup on Counterterrorism. The panel was designed to try to ease the turf wars that erupted every time Congress threw more money at the war on terrorism.

The attorney general wanted to make sure the State Department wasn't sticking its nose under the lawyer's tent on matters of criminal prosecution. The State was perennially pissed off at the National Security Council for making foreign policy. The FBI and the CIA had their own forms of tribal warfare, and the Department of Defense had only one concern: that nobody, including the president or Congress, screwed with its budget. Dropping money into this pit was like chumming with bloody bait in a tank full of sharks.

Bowlyn had his work cut out. He was an assistant to the National Security adviser and closer to the seat of power than anyone else on the panel. Seated with him at the table were an assistant director of the CIA, a high-ranking official of the FBI, and an assistant attorney general. The other members came from military intelligence, Alcohol, Tobacco and Firearms, and the Protective Intelligence Division of the Secret Service. They all had high-security clearance.

The deputy director of the CIA handed Bowlyn a report in a folder marked TOP SECRET. Bowlyn opened it and read, then closed the file and looked up.

'Who's up and running on this?'

The CIA nodded toward a man in a naval uniform wearing the rank of captain on the shoulder boards of his white uniform dress shirt.

Bowlyn nodded. The officer got out of his chair and moved around the table toward a large map of the world that was pulled down in front of a chalkboard. He picked up the pointer.

'About a week ago, Naval Intelligence started picking up a lot of frantic transmissions between a Russian military installation in Siberia. A place called Sverdlovsk, here.' He pointed to a location on the map in central Russia. 'And their Pacific Fleet Command, here.' He pointed again. 'At the port of Vladivostok. We didn't think anything of it, but we continued to monitor. Most of it was encrypted.

But some of it wasn't. Some of it was over phone lines that weren't secure.'

'They were talking in the open?' Bowlyn seemed surprised.

'Yes. That got our attention too. It was as if they wanted us to listen in.'

Bowlyn nodded to him, a signal to go on.

'One word kept cropping up in the conversations and transmissions – *Isvania*. We weren't sure what to make of it. We pumped it into one of the military intelligence databases and two days ago we made a hit. The *Isvania* was a Russian factory trawler. According to our information, it went down in the eastern Pacific sometime earlier this month.'

The naval officer moved the pointer on the map again, this time to the U.S. side of the Pacific.

'It sank here, about sixty nautical miles due west of the Strait of Juan de Fuca, off the coast of Washington State. A Coast Guard C-130 spotted the oil slick about ten days ago. A Dolphin helicopter launched from the Coast Guard cutter *Regal* recovered small pieces of wreckage. A marker buoy, a floatation bag, and a partially inflated liferaft.'

'No survivors?'

'No.' The officer picked through a file he'd put on the table until he found the photographs he was looking for, then passed them around the table toward Bowlyn.

'Stenciled on the side of the raft was the name *Isvania*. According to the Russians, the ship was slated for scrap. It was supposed to be headed for Bangkok.'

'What was it doing off the West Coast?' said Bowlyn.

'We don't know,' said the officer. 'Neither do the Russians.'

'At least that's what they're telling us.' The man from the CIA apparently had his doubts about Russian candor.

The Navy man ignored him. 'There were heavy seas in

the area but no distress calls. The Russians acknowledge that it is possible the ship was involved in smuggling.'

'Smuggling what?' said Bowlyn.

'That's the part they're not telling us.'

'And we know why,' said the CIA. 'Because they know more than they're willing to admit.'

'The wreckage we recovered wasn't much,' said the Navy man, 'but it was enough to give us a hint that whatever it was, the crew of the *Isvania* didn't want us to find it. The marker buoy contained a marine transponder. It emitted a signal that could be picked up on a Russian military frequency. It's an older system. Had a range of no more than about a hundred miles. The flotation bag was the kicker. It was filled with a hundred gallons of diesel fuel.'

'What for?' said Bowlyn.

'A submersible lift, to assist the buoys. The buoys would float on the surface, one of them emitting the signal. Whatever the cargo was hung from a line below the bag of diesel fuel. You wouldn't be able to see the bag or the cargo from the surface. The whole thing was pretty ingenious. It was designed to go to the bottom if whoever was supposed to pick it up didn't get to it within a few days. There was a small valve on the flotation bag. And a timer set to open the valve. Once the diesel oil spilled out into the sea, the cargo would have pulled the buoys to the bottom. The only reason we got it was that the cargo had been removed. The buoys kept the empty bag near the surface.'

'Any idea what the cargo was?' said Bowlyn.

'It weighed roughly two hundred pounds.' Now it was the FBI's turn. 'Our lab analyzed the bag and the marker buoy. Assuming there were two other buoys. We found three severed lines. If they were the same size, and given the capacity of the flotation bag we worked backward and determined the weight of the load. And there's something else you should see.'

He passed a copy of the lab report to Bowlyn, who looked at it quickly, flipped to the second page, and stopped halfway down.

'You're sure about this?'

'Tested it twice.'

'What else do we know?' Bowlyn looked around the table.

'We've continued to monitor the Russian communiqués out of Sverdlovsk.' This from the CIA deputy director. 'We haven't been able to decipher all of them, but what we have indicates a considerable degree of anxiety at fairly high levels of the government.'

'This could come from the place Sverd—'

'Sverdlovsk,' said the CIA. 'Yes. Underground bunkers. We've got satellite photos if you want to see them.'

Bowlyn shook his head. 'You think something got away from them?'

'It would appear that way,' said the naval man.

'Tell me about this place Sverdlovsk?'

'Nearest city is Yekaterinburg. It has a highly developed criminal subculture. There has been considerable violence there in recent years, most of it by organized gangs. Several local officials have been assassinated. One of the key prizes between the warring underworld factions is viewed as the armaments facility at Sverdlovsk. The various criminal groups vying for dominance see the facility as vital turf.'

'That coupled with the fact that the place has piss-poor security,' said the CIA. 'From what we hear, the gangs in the area see themselves as major players in the world arms market. As far as they're concerned, the Russian

153

government is merely storing the stuff for them, until they can find buyers.'

'We know that the Iranians and Iraqis have been over there trying to shop,' said the Navy officer.

'Maybe they've made a purchase,' said the CIA.

'Is there evidence of state involvement in this shipment on the *Isvania*?' asked Bowlyn.

'Not so far,' said the Navy officer. 'But we're still looking.'

Bowlyn took a deep sigh.

'It gets a little worse,' said the CIA.

'What do you mean?' Bowlyn looked at him.

'Some of the encrypted transmissions between Sverdlovsk and Vladivostok have been decoded. A name has popped up.'

'What name?'

'A forged waybill for a shipment of machine parts out of Vladivostok, shipped by a Russian company called Blue Star Enterprises. The trawler *Isvania* left Vladivostok four days before the communiqués started flying back and forth.'

'Wonderful,' said Bowlyn.

'The CEO of Blue Star Enterprises is Viktor Kolikoff.'

Bowlyn's gaze suddenly went cold as steel. He said nothing but sat there looking at the CIA deputy director. This went beyond mere security clearances. They would have to clear the room before the discussion went any farther.

CHAPTER
THIRTEEN

Lake Union, Seattle, WA

Joselyn winced just a little as the emergency medical technician maneuvered his forceps and plucked another wooden splinter from her forearm. In reflex, she had shielded her face from the force of the blast. The plane's explosion had shattered a piece of wooden railing, showering her with small splinters.

Thankfully the front edge of the blast had put her down flat on her back on the dock so that most of the flying shrapnel and bits of debris from Belden's plane sailed past, embedding themselves in the wall of the wooden boathouse behind her.

'I hope you know you were very lucky.' The EMT didn't look at her as he continued his work.

'Lucky. Right.'

'Hang on. I've got a couple more here.' He gripped another splinter with the forceps and plucked it like a feather from a bird.

'Ow.'

'Relax. Just a few more.' The EMT held up the splinter.

It was half the size of a toothpick. 'I can leave 'em and let them fester. You won't like it much.'

Joselyn's arm looked like it had been peppered by a porcupine. 'Go ahead, just be a little more careful.'

'Maybe we can talk while he works.' McCally wasn't happy. He had arrived at the dock just forty-five minutes after the explosion. Now he was standing outside the back of the open ambulance with an FBI agent in a blue windbreaker, the letters stenciled across his back, and another guy in jeans, running shoes, and a dark sweatshirt with a hood.

'Tell me,' said Joselyn. 'How did you guys get here so fast?'

'We had your client under surveillance.' The guy in the windbreaker spoke before McCally could keep him quiet.

'Thank you, Mr Larkin,' said McCally. 'Why don't you go over there and look for pieces of Mr Belden before the seagulls find them all.'

The guy accepted the rebuke, looked down at the dock, but didn't move. Joselyn assumed that the other one in the sweatshirt was a federal agent as well. He was mostly bald and well built, like an athlete, with darting eyes that didn't settle on anything for very long. He had the wary look of some of the criminal clients she had represented down in California.

'You mean you had my client under surveillance the entire time he was under subpoena to appear before the grand jury?'

'Never mind that,' said McCally. 'You saw him get on the plane, is that right?'

'I already told the police what I saw. You can get whatever information you need from them.' Joselyn had identified Belden as being on the plane. As far as she knew he was alone.

'We'd rather get it from you. We've already talked to the police,' said McCally. 'According to them, you flew down in the plane with him. Why weren't you on it for the return trip?'

'You sound like you're upset that I wasn't.'

McCally said nothing. He looked at her, waiting for an answer.

'It so happens he didn't tell me he was leaving the courthouse. When I discovered he was missing, I knew he had to come back here. I took a taxi and got here just as he was pulling away from the dock. You can find the cab driver if you don't believe me.'

'We'll do that,' said McCally. 'Why would your client come all this way, fly down here, go to the courthouse, and then without talking to you, without any explanation, run?'

'Maybe he just got cold feet,' she said.

'Hmm.' His expression indicated he didn't buy it.

'Where did he get the plane?'

'How do I know?'

'You were his lawyer.'

'I suppose he bought it.'

'No,' said McCally. 'He didn't. We got a list of his assets. There's no plane.'

'You seem to know more about him than I do. If you were watching him so closely how did he get himself blown up?'

McCally looked at the other guy in the sweatshirt. It seemed neither of them had an answer for this.

'Why, if you'd focused so much attention on my client, didn't you send him a target letter?'

'You're not here to ask the questions,' said McCally, 'but to answer them.'

'Oh, am I? I was under the impression I was here to receive medical attention. If you had him under surveillance, we had a right to a target letter.'

'Maybe yes, maybe no,' said McCally.

'What's that supposed to mean?'

'It means maybe yes, maybe no,' said the agent in the sweatshirt.

'Does the name Harold McAvoy mean anything to you?' McCally changed the subject.

She thought for a second. 'No.'

'Or James Regal?'

'No.'

'What about Liam Walker?' This time it was the agent in the sweatshirt asking.

'What is this, twenty questions?'

'Just answer.'

'I've never heard of any of them.'

The agent and McCally looked at each other. They moved a couple of steps away and whispered to each other so that Joselyn couldn't hear.

'Tell me what's going on,' she demanded.

McCally looked at her as if it was against his better judgment. She heard the agent speaking to him. 'It's not likely we're gonna be getting any answers from her client. She's the next best thing.'

McCally thought for a second, then finally caved in.

'The three names are aliases,' he told her. 'Just like the name Dean Belden.'

'What are you talking about?'

'These are all names used by your client in various countries where he's worked over the last two years. He has at one time or another possessed passports under each of them.'

'Belden wasn't his name?'

'No.'

'And electronics wasn't his business,' added the man in the sweatshirt.

'What was his business?'

'He was a kind of specialist,' said McCally.

'You might say transportation is his main field,' said the agent. 'Though he's done other things over the course of his career. Usually whenever he showed up, people started dying.'

Joselyn listened but didn't say a word.

'He hired himself out to various clients. Businesses, sometimes governments, groups out of power who wanted back in. As far as we know this is the first time he's ever worked in this country.'

'You're telling me he was a hired assassin?'

'Nothing so modest,' said the agent. 'Mr Belden, or whatever name he was using on a given day, dealt in group discounts. Why murder one person when you can do a few hundred, maybe a few thousand.'

'What are you telling me?'

'The Kurds in northern Iraq. Your client provided some of the services.'

'And some villages in Croatia,' added McCally. 'He didn't use bullets or guns. No explosions. It was all very neat, except for the bloated bodies in the streets.'

'His specialty,' said the agent, 'was moving dangerous cargos. As far as we know to date, he'd confined himself to chemical weapons. What we're worried about is that he may have been branching out.'

'That's enough,' said McCally.

Joselyn guessed they were now getting into areas that might compromise the grand jury investigation.

'You still want to know why we didn't send him a target letter?' asked McCally.

'Given the outcome, it looks like we saved the taxpayers the cost of a first-class stamp,' said the agent.

'I suppose you had me under surveillance as well?' said Joselyn.

McCally didn't respond, but from the look on the other guy's face he didn't have to.

'You still haven't explained how, if you were watching him so closely, somebody was able to get to his plane with explosives.'

'Did they?'

'I'd say so.' Joselyn looked at the scattered pieces of debris out on the water.

'And who might they be?' said McCally. 'These other people who got to his plane?'

'How would I know?'

'You worked with him.'

'I was his lawyer.'

'Fine,' said the agent. 'And now he's dead, so you won't mind telling us whatever it is you know about his business dealings?'

'I don't know anything except what Belden told me. And according to you that is probably all a lie.'

'Humor us,' said McCally.

Joselyn looked at the two of them but didn't say a word.

'Maybe you'd like to lawyer up?' said the agent. 'Want us to read you your rights. Get you a lawyer.'

'Let me get this straight. Am I under arrest?'

'No,' said McCally. 'Not for the moment anyway.'

'Good. Then what I have to say is going to be very short and to the point. I don't know a thing about any of the activities you've mentioned. I don't know if Belden was his name or what he did for a living. All I know is what he told me, and if the two of you are telling me the truth . . .' She looked at them as if perhaps she had some doubts. 'Then the information he gave me was a crock.'

'And what was that?' said McCally.

'That he wanted to set up a business on the island.

Something about electronics and switches. He wanted me to form the corporation for this business. That's all I know.'

'And you didn't ask him anything else?'

'What else was there?'

'How did he pay you?'

'By check. Drawn on a personal account.'

'Did you ask him where he came from?'

'He told me somewhere near Seattle. Kent, I think. But if what you tell me is true, then he probably lied about that as well.'

The two men looked at each other, but from their expressions Joselyn could tell that what she'd told them was no help.

'Why did he pick you to do his legal work?' asked McCally.

'He told me it was a referral. A local banker.'

'What was the banker's name?'

'I can't remember. I might have written it down somewhere.'

'We'll need the name.'

'I'll look when I get back to my office.'

'How much did he pay you?' asked McCally.

Joselyn wasn't anxious to answer, but she knew they could access her bank records with a subpoena. 'A ten-thousand-dollar retainer for the business work. Another five thousand for accompanying him down here for the grand jury thing.'

The agent rolled his eyes. 'Is that normal?'

'Dream on,' McCally answered for her. 'And this didn't give you some clue that Belden might have problems? When did he call you on the grand jury subpoena?' He asked another question before she could answer.

'Late last week.'

'And what did he tell you?'

She told them about Max Sperling, though by now Joselyn was convinced that Belden had fabricated that as well.

'And you accepted all of this at face value?' said McCally.

'Why wouldn't I? A client comes to my door, tells me he needs legal services . . .'

'And pays you fifteen grand,' said the agent. 'Don't forget that.'

'What other records do you have?' said McCally.

'Wait a second,' said Joselyn. 'You think I'm going to turn over client records just like that?'

'Your client is dead,' said McCally.

'I'm not sure the privilege died with him.'

'We can debate the point in front of a federal judge,' said the prosecutor. 'Or perhaps the grand jury.'

'I'm not under arrest, just under suspicion, is that it?'

'You could cooperate,' said the agent.

'I have. I've told you everything I know.'

'Maybe Belden just liked lawyers who wore skirts,' said the agent.

'For most men it beats the alternative,' said Joselyn. 'No offense.'

'None taken,' said the agent. 'Did the two of you get it on?'

'Ask your people with the field glasses,' she told him.

'They say no.'

Now she was getting angry. 'There you go,' she told him.

'You are aware,' said McCally, 'that attorney-client privilege does not apply if you are in any way involved in furtherance of your client's illegal activities?'

'Why would I be worried about that? I've got the best alibi in the world. Just ask Peeping Tom there.'

'Hey. I can't vouch for your every minute.' The agent was

the kind of in-your-face civil servant that gives government a bad name.

'I see, just the bathroom and the bedroom,' said Joselyn.

'Enough,' said McCally. He gave the agent a stern look and the guy backed off.

'Then there's nothing else you're going to tell us?'

'There's nothing else I can tell you,' said Joselyn. 'I represented the corporation, Belden Electronics. While Mr Belden or whatever his name was may be dead, the corporation that he formed is not. My obligations as a lawyer runs to that corporation.'

'We've checked the listing of corporate officers,' said McCally. They already knew about the corporation.

'It shows Belden's name, yours, and a woman named Samantha Hawthorne. Who is she?'

'It's a usual practice,' said Joselyn. For purposes of formation, lawyers often listed themselves and their employees as corporate officers. Samantha, her landlady, had agreed to be listed. 'She and I were to be substituted out for other officers at the first meeting of shareholders.'

'I take it that never happened?'

'No.'

'Were there any other shareholders besides Belden?' This was something McCally couldn't get from public records, but he could subpoena it from her files.

'Not that I know of.'

Before they could ask another question another agent wearing a dark blue windbreaker, the letters ATF stenciled on the front and back, came up to McCally from behind, whispered in his ear, then handed him something. Joselyn couldn't see what it was, something small enough to be concealed in his closed hand.

McCally talked to the agent in street clothes. The three men took a few steps back so they could confer in private and not be heard. The EMT started to go to work on Joselyn with his forceps again.

'I think I'll keep 'em, as souvenirs,' she said. Before the guy could get a grip, she rolled down the sleeve of her blouse. It was torn and spotted with blood.

The FBI agent in the blue windbreaker was the only one standing close enough for idle conversation. His two colleagues were locked in some mortal disagreement. She could see the one in the sweatshirt waving his arms intensely. He was losing the argument with McCally. Joselyn guessed that the agent wanted to take her into custody.

'So tell me. How long have you guys been following Mr Belden?'

The agent in the windbreaker just looked at her, smiled and said: 'Right. Like I'm gonna tell you.'

McCally walked back toward them.

'Are you finished with me?' she asked.

'One more question,' he said. 'What do you know about this?' He opened the palm of his hand. In it was a small piece of white plastic about an inch square. It looked like a tiny white picture frame with what appeared to be off-colored gray paper in the center.

'What is it?' she asked.

'Agents found it floating in the water out there. You've never seen it before?'

'No.' Joselyn didn't recognize it until McCally put it up against the lapel of his suit coat, like a badge. Then suddenly it clicked. She'd seen them on the white coats of lab technicians in hospitals, people who worked in radiology.

'It's called a dosimeter,' said McCally. 'It registers doses of radiation, to make sure that people who come into contact with it don't absorb too much. Why would your client have one?'

'I don't know.'

McCally looked at her like maybe he didn't believe her.

'A word of caution,' said the prosecutor. 'Do you have any idea as to why your client was killed?'

'Not a clue.'

'If I had to guess,' said McCally, 'it's because we got a line on him. These are people who live in the shadows. Your client, Belden, whatever his name was, and his associates are people who live under rocks and slither out at night. When we subpoenaed him he was suddenly caught in the headlights. His friends saw him as a threat, a weak link.'

'What's that got to do with me?'

'Perhaps more than you think. Maybe you're telling us the truth. Maybe you don't know anything about your client's activities. On the other hand, it's not what you know, but what they think you know that could get you killed.'

'What are you saying?'

'I'm saying that if they'd put the bomb on that plane for your flight down, from the islands, we wouldn't be standing here talking now.'

It was something Joselyn hadn't thought about, until McCally said it.

'I'm telling you that if you know something, now's not the time to keep it to yourself.'

CHAPTER

FOURTEEN

Padget Island, WA

Scott Taggart stood on the dock and watched as the small boat cut a swath of white water across the San Juan Channel and toward the island. No one came to the island unless they were invited. There was no ferry service and no mail delivery. Letters were sent to the post office at Friday Harbor, a four-mile boat ride across tide-ripped waters.

The island was less than a mile from tip to tip and only seven hundred yards at the widest point. It had been owned by a sheep farmer at the turn of the century, a place where he could raise livestock without worrying about predators. In 1927, the island's only well ran salty, and except for a few seasonal streams there was no other water on the island. The rancher gave it up.

The next owners didn't worry about water. They shipped in whatever they needed by boat and made a fortune running Canadian whisky across the border during Prohibition. It was less than twenty nautical miles across the Straits of Georgia to the Canadian side. It was a feature that commended the island to Scott and his group.

They had set up in the old lodge house built by a bootleg baron in the early thirties. The ground floor was constructed of stone and heavy timbers. The house overlooked the dock from the crest of the hill.

It was guarded by men packing Barret fifty-caliber semi-automatic rifles. These were legal weapons unless converted to full-automatic. They were accurized and scoped for precision, some of them mounted on fixed tripods. Their bullets penetrated the sound barrier with a distinctive crack and struck with the impact of a small cannon shell. They could penetrate light steel armor as well as the more modern ceramic plate that was favored by the military for its light patrol boats.

The clips for these guns each held eleven rounds. There were hundreds of clips, all loaded and stored in bunkers around the island. Each bunker had a commanding view designed to establish a crossfire against anyone attempting to land on the island.

The committee had been here for nearly a month. It was one of the conditions that was laid down by the man who called himself Thorn. Their food was brought in on their own boat, and water was provided by a large catchment basin built in the 1980s by the island's current owner, a wealthy Belizean who Scott figured was probably heavily invested in narco-traffic. Thorn had made the arrangements. He seemed to be well connected internationally.

Scott watched as the boat slowed its speed and cut a wide 'J' through the tranquil water of the bay. It pulled alongside the floating dock and a single occupant got out. He grabbed a bag handed to him by one of the others and started walking toward Taggart at the other end of the dock.

They had met three times, twice in a cabin in the mountains of Idaho almost six months ago. Scott recognized the walk, like he had a ramrod up his ass. Thorn had a military bearing that was unmistakable.

'Mr Taggart, is it?' Eyes like an eagle, even in the half-light of dusk.

Through the mist, Scott could see the broad outlines of his face, a kind of coercive grin under sandy-colored hair. Thorn's military training came from South Africa. Scott had learned at least that much.

Thorn wore a neoprene dive suit, the hood folded back off of his head. As Thorn drew close, Scott could see the most distinctive characteristics of what was admittedly a handsome face; deep-set piercing green eyes. Thorn had used many aliases over the course of his career. The most recent was the name Dean Belden.

'I didn't expect you to be on the reception committee. You could have sent one of the men.' Thorn climbed the ramp from the floating dock made more steep by the ebb tide, lugging the heavy bag at his side.

'If there was bad news, I wanted to be the first to hear it,' said Scott.

'No bad news. You worry too much. You have to learn to be more positive. Look on the bright side. How many people would have given us even odds that we'd have gotten this far? You think you're federal government has any idea?'

'You tell me.'

'Not a clue,' said Thorn. 'As we speak, they are dredging the bottom of that lake for shards of metal no bigger than this.' He held his thumb and forefinger about two inches apart, like a caliper. It was what a pound of C-4 could do when it was properly placed near a tank of high-octane aviation fuel.

'As for the body, they'd do as well to look for the remains of the Lord Himself, all the good it will do them.'

'Good.'

'You have to learn to calm down,' said Thorn. 'You get too intense and it can take a toll on the ticker. Learn to savor the moment.'

'I'll savor the moment when we're done,' said Taggart.

'Oh no. You have to learn to take pleasure from each step along the way. For the time being take consolation in the fact that the only thing worse than being chased by your government is working for it.'

'How's that?' They started walking toward the house.

'Right now all those civil servants are up to their government service honkers in cold water looking for things that the fish ate two hours ago.'

Scott couldn't help but smile. There was something about Thorn, a certain affable gleam to his deadly edge.

'Now tell me about the accommodations,' he asked. 'I hope there's some good showers. I could dearly use one.'

'Good showers. As for the place, I'm hoping we won't have to be here that much longer.'

'Like I said, patience.' Thorn stretched his back as he walked and groaned a little. 'I'm getting too old for this. The ride was a little choppy. Hard on the low back and kidneys.'

'We would have sent a bigger boat, but we didn't want to draw attention.'

'Exactly right.' Thorn stopped, took out a pack of cigarettes and offered one to Scott.

'No thanks.'

He lit up and took a deep drag while he surveyed what he could see. 'How many men have you got?'

'Twenty-eight. Enough for around-the-clock shifts. Food

and water for eighteen days. That's what you said, isn't it? Eighteen days?'

'That's what I said.' He flicked a little hot ash onto the dock. 'Your people, you haven't told them anything?'

'They know something's up. They don't know what.'

'Let's keep it that way.'

'They're all handpicked,' said Taggart. 'Kept in the dark as to their destination until they arrived on the island. So their families don't know where they are. Only two of them are allowed off the island. I'll vouch for both.'

'Yes, you will.' Thorn looked at him. 'With your life if you are wrong.'

Scott didn't answer him.

'We did everything exactly the way you told us. We brought them in from different groups around the country. They are the cream. All have prior military training. Half of them have seen combat in the Gulf War, four of them in Panama. One is a former Navy Seal. We checked them out. None of them have been members of their units for less than two years. They are all committed. They will fight. If necessary they will lay down their lives.'

'Well, let's hope it doesn't come to that.'

Scott guessed that Thorn looked down his nose at these men. Thorn was a professional soldier, a hired mercenary with an obvious history of combat under his belt. Unless Scott was wrong, most of it paid for by the highest bidder. He came with the ordnance, the Moscow connection. If Scott and his group wanted the device, there was one condition: Thorn came with it. The sellers couldn't take a chance that some foreign government would trace it back to them. The cost in reprisal would be too severe. Scott had anticipated someone with a thick Russian accent. Thorn had none. His English was perfect, clipped and precise.

He had a number of aliases and could be contacted only

through a mail drop in Ontario, Canada. Even that was a forwarding address. Where he lived no one knew for sure. But he apparently lived well, if his fees were any indication.

'They will fight.'

'Hmm.' Thorn looked at him. 'Oh, I'm sure they would if necessary.' He didn't seem entirely convinced. It wasn't their bravery he was concerned with. It was their organization, and the assumption by Taggart that his ground had not already been penetrated by the government. The FBI had written the book on undercover ops. They had infiltrated the mafia with its culture of *omerta* – silence or death. An institution as old as the Borgias', in which blood kinship was the key to acceptance, had been riddled like Swiss cheese in less than a decade. They would have done it sooner except that J. Edgar Hoover had been on such friendly terms at the racetracks with some of the bosses. Thorn assumed that Taggart's organization was already compromised. He would operate on that basis. None of them would know what he was doing at any given time.

'You've said nothing to any of your people?' he asked

'Not a word.'

'Reduced nothing to writing?'

'No.'

'Good. There is no need for them to know what we are about. Their job is to maintain security on the island, simple as that. Yours is to wire the funds in the agreed upon amounts at the times stated, into the properly numbered accounts. If that happens, everything will go smoothly. The rest of the plan is mine. If you are taken by the government at any time, I reserve the right to terminate our arrangement. If the money is not wired at the times required our arrangement is terminated, all funds paid to that point are forfeit, and the device disappears with me. Do you understand?'

'We've been over all of that.'

'Yes. We have.' Thorn took a quick survey of the area around the dock, as much as the limited light of dusk would allow.

'Looks like you've got everything pretty well secured.'

'We got it covered.'

'I would throw up a few pine boughs for a blind. Your man out on the point there.' Thorn gestured with the glow of his cigarette toward the tip of land that jutted out into the channel. It provided a sheltered bay for the dock.

'You can see the cannon your man is carrying from a mile out. There's no sense advertising. You don't want some pain-in-the-ass member of the Audubon Society calling the Coast Guard to come and take a look. Bald eagles and all that.'

'I'll see that it's taken care of.'

'Good.' Thorn was smiling again. He put his arm around Scott's shoulder. He was now in charge, and they both knew it. Scott was the ideologist, the man that other true believers would follow. He'd spent three years after Kirsten's death in the mountains of Idaho, living alone in a cabin and making contacts with people who shared a single common interest – an abiding hatred of the federal government. Many of the people he met were racists. Scott did not encourage or participate in their rantings on this subject. There were times when he felt shame for listening and not speaking up as they lanced this boil and spread their poison.

But as months turned into years, Scott found himself talking more and listening less. He was steeped in the history of the country, better educated than any of the men with whom he associated.

He traveled the backcountry and spoke in barns and

metal buildings, to men in dirty overalls and cotton flannel shirts with frayed sleeves. The lucky ones wore the dust of their jobs on their faces. The rest looked for work in a lumber industry now decimated by federal timber policies.

They listened wide-eyed as Scott told them about Jefferson and the rights of man, the God-given prerogative to pursue their dreams free from the tyranny of an overbearing government. It was Jefferson who warned that 'the tree of liberty must be refreshed from time to time with the blood of patriots and tyrants'.

There was a moral reckoning to Scott's words, and the way he delivered them that erased any doubt as to the rightness of their cause.

In time these men came to trust him. Trust became leadership, not because he could handle a gun, but because he spoke to their concerns, their fears for the future. They viewed themselves the victims of a political aristocracy, a ruling class that had forgotten about its own people. Bureaucrats with lifetime tenure ran their agencies like warlords, unaccountable to anyone including elected officials.

Their view of the federal government was of a parent who devoured its own children. Its only real constituency was foreign governments or multinational corporations willing to pay for what was euphemistically called 'political access'. Good-paying jobs were shipped to Mexico or Asia where they could be downgraded to sweatshop wages while the president made empty gestures about job-training and touted the benefits of the global economy. It didn't matter whether they were Republicans or Democrats, they all sang the same song. Scott Taggart knew the melody and could explain the lyrics.

The two men, Taggart and Thorn, were now inextricably bound.

Thorn stamped out his cigarette. They turned and began

walking up the hill toward the house. Its windows had been blanked out by heavy drapes to prevent prying eyes with high-powered optics from observing the inhabitants or taking pictures.

'Where's the device?' asked Scott.

'In a safe place.'

'I thought we were in this together?'

'We are.'

'Then why the Chinese wall?'

'Because our success does not depend on your knowing where the device is. Suffice it to say that I do. And that it will be delivered to its ultimate destination at the appointed time. That is all you need to know.'

'And the detonation. How will you accomplish that within the stated time parameters?'

'Again one of those worrisome details that you need not trouble yourself with.'

'I always worry about the loose ends.'

'I can tell,' said Thorn.

'Like Belden Electronics.'

'They can rummage through Mr Belden's affairs all they want. They won't find a thing.'

'What about the woman? The lawyer?'

'She doesn't know a thing. But just to be safe, we're about to tie up that loose end as well.'

Scott looked at him.

'What do you mean?'

'There's no sense taking chances,' said Thorn.

'Is that necessary?'

'There are documents in her office that are best disposed of in the flames of a hot furnace. If we take them, she will notice. Then she will start thinking, putting two and two together.' Thorn stopped, turned and looked directly at Scott. 'You tell me. Is it necessary?'

Taggart hesitated only a instant. 'Yes. I suppose.'

'You sound reluctant.'

'I take no pleasure in killing innocent people. It's why I selected the time and place.'

'A virtue not shared by your government,' said Thorn.

Scott looked at him and wondered. He had never told Thorn about Kirsten or how she had died. Could he know? Thorn was not the kind of man with whom you wanted to share your most intimate secrets, the things that propelled you through life and motivated your actions. Whatever inhabited that dark space behind those cold eyes left little doubt that it would use such information for its own purposes. He wondered if Thorn knew about Adam and Kirsten's parents in Seattle. For the first time since starting down this twisting path, Scott Taggart began to question what he was doing.

'Not to worry,' said Thorn. 'The woman is not your concern. She will be taken care of.'

'When?'

Thorn looked at his watch.

'Soon.'

They walked on in silence toward the house. It troubled Scott that innocent people had to die. But there was no alternative. Scott was not a soldier, but he knew the lessons of combat. Whether the federal government knew it or not, they were now at war.

CHAPTER
FIFTEEN

Rosario Strait

E ven if Joselyn wanted to cooperate with McCally and the federal probe, she had a problem. She'd told him the truth. She didn't know anything. She searched her memory for bits and pieces of information, anything that Belden might have said in her office or on the plane. Joselyn was no legal virgin. She'd had enough criminal clients lie to her over the years to know that among the lies there were at times a few kernels of truth. Maybe in Belden's lies there was some thread of information, something she might key on.

His business was electronics, at least that's what he told her. Maybe the name Max Sperling was real, even if the story about him wasn't. She would look at her files when she got back to the office. Maybe there was something in her notes.

By the time McCally and his agent had finished with her on the dock it was dusk. She was dirty and tired. She had been standing for hours in the chilly air. Her arm was now throbbing where the medical technician had plucked splinters and wrapped her with a heavy gauze bandage. By this hour, there were no ferries to the San Juans from Seattle. The only regular service left from Anacortes, a ninety-minute drive north by car.

She called a cab and had the driver take her to the nearest discount store where she bought a pair of slip-on sneakers and some socks to replace her shredded hose and broken shoe. Then she went to a car rental agency. She had no choice. She would have to pay the hefty drop-off charge on the island and bill it to Belden's account.

As she drove, she wondered what she would do with the rest of his retainer. How would she return the unused portion? It was the kind of thing only a lawyer would think about. But she had a business to run. She would have to find some way to wind up Belden's corporation, to dissolve it, and to get her name off of the documents of incorporation. She thought about publishing a notice, going through the formality of searching for heirs. If McCally was right about Belden's past, it was not likely anyone would come forward. Presumably the money, any unearned fees, would escheat to the state after a period of time.

The concussion from the explosion had left an incessant ringing in her ears, and her body now started to feel the soreness of having landed on the hard dock after the pressure wave had knocked her off her feet. Her joints and muscles had the aching tenderness she'd experienced only once, following a minor auto accident.

Fifteen minutes after leaving the freeway, she rolled down the main drag of Anacortes, took a left at the light and drove toward the headlands. Sleep now began to tug at her sleeve. She passed through the residential area of town and hugged the bluffs above the water. She could see the lights of Guemes across the narrow inlet. Occasionally through a break in the trees, she could see the glow of the bright vapor lights from the ferry terminal as they bounced off the underside, a few wispy clouds floating overhead.

One of the ferries with its cavernous open car deck lit up, its portholes and windows aglow like a Christmas tree on the water, was making a wide turn as it approached the dock a half-mile out. Joselyn hoped it was the Ferry to Friday Harbor.

She wound down the steep grade toward the terminal and saw that the parking lot was nearly empty. Two truck and trailer rigs and a handful of cars waited in line. Whatever rushhour existed for the islands was over for the day, and the tourist season was still months away.

She paid for a ticket at the tollgate.

'What time's the next ferry to San Juan Island?'

'That's it coming in.'

A pickup with a camper on the back pulled up behind her, its bright lights beaming through the back window of her rented car. There was another big truck behind him. The last-minute rush. People in the islands lived and died by the ferry schedule. At night trucks often made their deliveries to avoid the heavier ferry traffic of the day.

The woman in the booth gave Joselyn the cash register ticket and her change and glanced back at the parking lot.

'Take lane four. They'll be boarding in just a couple of minutes.'

By this time in the evening the ferries were usually late, losing time on every run during the day. Joselyn knew they wouldn't waste any time at the dock. She pulled into lane four and went all the way to the front, turned off her lights and engine and waited. There were a few cars in the lane next to her, no more than a dozen in all. The ferry would be nearly empty.

She watched as the vehicles, their headlights gleaming,

streamed off the boat and passed her on the exit road heading up the hill. Traffic from the islands was mostly one-way this time of day, some late stragglers headed for home.

Five minutes later, they were waved onto the ferry. Joselyn drove her small rented car directly into the main bay and up to the bow. She could hear the wind whistling through the open car deck. When they landed she would be the first one off. She couldn't wait to hit the soft flannel sheets of her bed and pull the covers over herself, a refuge from the nightmare that had been her day. Sleep was fast overtaking her.

The few other passengers left their cars and headed to the upper decks, the cafeteria and the lounge. Joselyn pushed the toggle switch on the door that said 'lock' and the buttons on both doors snapped down. She pulled the lever on the side of the driver's seat and reclined until it wedged against the back seat. She closed her eyes and wished she had a blanket.

She drifted in another world, only vaguely aware of the boat's movement. The vibration of the massive diesel engines stirred her only a little. The gentle swaying in the troughs as the vessel glided out away from the dock acted as a sedative.

The wind picked up and whistled past the closed windows, causing the small car to shudder, as the ferry turned and headed out through the Guemes Channel and into Rosario Straits. Four miles of open water until they reached the narrows of Thatcher Pass. Wind whipped froth off the crest of small whitecaps. Occasional small waves crested and crashed against the steel bow of the ferry, sending droplets of seawater splattering against the windshield of Joselyn's car.

The noise caused her to open her eyes halfway, to gaze

up through the tinted windshield. It was a clear, brilliant night, the kind that bring the heavens to life with flickering stars, pinholes of light against the black backdrop of space. Joselyn drifted in that netherworld between sleep and consciousness. She gazed up through the opening between the wings of the passenger deck one level above. Tonight the two wings that projected out over the bow of the ship were empty. It was too cold. The few passengers on board were huddled inside, warming their hands around cups of hot coffee or sprawled out sleeping on the benches beneath the windows.

Somewhere in the Rosario Straits, Joselyn drifted into deep sleep, swayed by the gentle rocking of the great vessel and the occasional gust of wind that shook her small car as it swept through the car deck like a giant ghost.

She was lost in the rumble of the engines and dreamed of Belden and the small plane, the flash of brilliant light, and the explosive force that followed an instant later. Luminous, blazing lights, piercing the shield of her closed lids. Her eyes began to ache, and slowly Joselyn opened them to realize that she was not dreaming at all. Someone behind her in a vehicle had switched on their headlights, bright, piercing high beams. They filled the rear window of her car with a painful luminance like the sun. The reflection from her rearview mirror was blinding.

Joselyn shielded her eyes. 'Turn them off,' she muttered to herself, half-asleep. Then she heard the rumble of the engine, deep and guttural, a heavy diesel starting up. Maybe he needed to charge a battery, or refrigerate a load. She couldn't see a thing in the rearview mirror, the bright lights blinding her. She would wait a second and see if he turned them off and shut down. If not she would go topside to escape the noise and the lights.

Then she heard the grind of gears and an instant later the

hiss of compressed air. The driver had released his brakes. Joselyn looked into the rearview mirror in stark terror as the headlights behind her began to move, closing in on the rear of her car. Suddenly the bright beams were no longer in her mirror. They flashed over the top of her roof, and all she could see was the massive grille and the huge steel bumper, with its metal studs. It made contact with her car at the level of the trunk and instantly there was the grinding sound of metal crushing metal. The trunk folded up like paper.

Before Joselyn could think the truck driver gunned it. The car began to crumple like a crushed soda can. Joselyn went for the handle of her door. It wouldn't open. The frame of the car had bent. The door was jammed. She lunged for the door on the other side. Same story.

She heard the crunch of glass as the rear window exploded, shooting pellets of safety glass into her hair and over the front seat. The small car began to move relentlessly forward, its tires sliding on the ferry's smooth steel deck. The webbed safety net that spanned the ship in front of her car began to stretch, then rip as the diesel truck and trailer rig pushed her car like a steam-powered piston into the net. She could hear the driver double-clutching. This was no accident. Whoever was in the truck was trying to kill her.

Joselyn frantically looked up through the driver's-side window for help, her fingers pressed against glass. The ship's two passenger wings from the upper deck were nearly behind her now. They were both empty. No one could see her. She pressed the electric button, trying to open the driver's window. It didn't work. She pounded on the glass to no avail. Desperate, she swung her legs around the steering column and pressed her feet against the windshield. With her back wedged against the seat she pressed with all of her might, trying to break the windshield out. It didn't work. She was entombed in metal and glass, being crushed and pushed toward a watery grave.

Even with the brake set and the transmission in 'park' Joselyn's car was no match for the huge truck. The small Chevy moved toward the open bow and the deep, green water was now rushing toward her. She pressed on the brake pedal to no avail. The wheels continued to skid across metal. She laid on the horn. Finally, something worked. At least it made noise. Someone should hear it.

The safety net shredded, and the single steel cable across the top rode up over the hood of Joselyn's car, slid up across the glass of the windshield and onto the roof. Now there was nothing between her and cold, deep water of the sound.

She reached for the door handle one more time and laid her shoulder into the door as hard as she could, but it wouldn't open. She tried the electric opener on the window one more time then suddenly realized. She turned the key in the ignition, pressed the button, and the window began to come down. Wind rushed in through the opening.

Joselyn reached out with both hands for the roof of the car and turned her body sideways to pull herself out. The front wheels of the car went over the edge. The vehicle tilted forward, gravity taking hold, bumper down; the small car teetered toward the on-rushing water, white foam boiling off of the ferry's massive steel hull.

'S top all engines.' The captain of the *Tillicum* laid his hand on the red button on the console in front of him and leaned on it. The huge airhorn on the deck above the bridge pierced the cold night air like a knife.

The movement on the bridge was frantic. The first mate grabbed four levers on the console and pulled them back until they were straight up in the neutral position. The vibration of the engines stopped, but the ship continued gliding forward, cutting through the water, propelled by its own momentum.

'Hard to starboard.'

The crewman brought the wheel over hard, but without the propulsion of the engines forcing water over the control surfaces rudder, the ship turned but very slowly.

The captain watched helplessly as the massive weight of the diesel truck pushed the small car over the edge.

'Engines full back.'

With her last ounce of strength, Joselyn reached out, her body halfway through the open car window. The grip of one hand filled with nylon mesh, a piece of shredded safety net. The car tilted forward. A hundred tons of white water hit the hood, snapping the little car down into the sea. The violent force ripped Joselyn through the open window and left her dangling in space, her feet running along on air, just inches above the lapping bow wave.

She could hear the wail of the ferry's horn, and she twisted by a single hand from the frayed remnants of the nylon net. The joint of her shoulder was racked with pain. She couldn't hold much longer. Joselyn reached with the other hand, trying desperately to control her spinning body. She lashed out and felt the net with her other hand. She grabbed it and held for her life. Looking down, she saw the rush of white water under the bow and felt the momentum of the ship as it began to slow. It seemed to take forever. She got a single foothold and clung to the net, spinning in the wind, the icy sea lapping at her feet.

Ordinarily he would have reversed the engines to bring the vessel to a stop in the water, but he couldn't. The captain of the *Tillicum* knew that if he did, the small car would pass under the hull only to be shredded by the massive bronze propellers.

He prayed that there was no one inside the vehicle. He could hear it bouncing, metal against metal, under the hull as the ship passed over it. Air trapped in the vehicle would keep it near the surface, at least for a few seconds. The two men ran to the wing of the bridge and watched as the dark green water glided past the ship.

The captain grabbed the swivel light mounted on the railing, swung it around toward the water and flipped it on. A powerful beam of light penetrated the darkness, reflecting off the rippled surface of the sea.

The first mate ran back inside, grabbed the microphone for the hailing system. 'Man overboard. All crew to the railing. Man over.' He could hear the powerful speakers overhead echoing his voice. He repeated it two or three times, then hung up the mike. He'd barely returned to the wing of the bridge when one of the crewmen hollered from below. 'There off the stern quarter.'

The captain swung the light out, searched the water. Someone flung a life ring on a line as far out as it would reach. The captain followed it with his light until it hit the water, then kept moving the beam of light outward over the dark shimmering surface of the sea.

'There.' He steadied the light, though the continuous movement of the ship made it difficult.

Barely recognizable, the pulverized vehicle bobbed a few inches above the surface. It was the twisted and battered roof of the small car, held up by a bubble of air under its dome. The mangled metal danced just a few inches above the surface of the sea as water lapped greedily around the edges. A small ripple swept the water driven by a gust of wind, and from the open driver's window, there was a gush of bubbles. Suddenly the car was gone.

They swept the water with lights. Now three of them, powerful spots operated by the crew. There was no sign of anyone in the water.

The torn and tattered nylon mesh of the safety net hung over the front edge of the ferry like a broken spiderweb, and Joselyn hung from it. She looked up, wondering if the net would slip and drop her into the sea. The ship had slowed, but still it moved fast enough to take her under the massive hull if she fell. There were tons of water and cold steel, leaving her with little chance of being found in the dark water.

The wind whistled through her clothing, sending a chill through her body. Her hands were numb. Joselyn's grip on the netting was beginning to slip. In shock, she hung like a rag doll. She tried to clear her mind, to focus. Using her legs she tried to twist her body so that she would be facing the bow of the ship. She tried to reach with her feet for the steel plates at the ship's bow to get leverage. But the plates curved back and under the overhanging deck forming a prow, before plunging straight down into the water below. It was like trying to climb under an overhanging ledge on a sheer mountainside.

With one desperate grab, she reached up for a another piece of netting with her right hand and snagged it. Now she hung as if on a cross, her arms spread. Somehow she managed to hook her other foot through a piece of the open webbing. She clung there waiting for help, but no one came. It dawned on her that they couldn't see her. The crew and passengers were focused on the stern, looking for the car. No one paid attention to the ripped safety net. They were looking for survivors.

Joselyn could see reflections off the water, beams of light as they made a wide arc over the water and disappeared toward the stern. She could hear voices shouting. The onrushing water at the bow began to slack, as its momentum over the water slowed. The bow wave disappeared, and the rush of white water against steel slowly evaporated. The wind against her back slacked.

With her foot wedged firmly in the webbing of the net, Joselyn pushed with one leg and climbed hand over hand up the netting. A few passengers were now out on the wing over the car deck. She could hear their voices, asking each other if they could see anything. But no one looked down onto the car deck.

They were leaning over the railing looking to the starboard side of the ferry as Joselyn clawed her way onto the deck.

She lay prostrate and exhausted a few feet from the edge of the bow, her face turned sideways, her cheek against the cold steel deck. It took a moment to focus. Then the object she was staring at registered. What filled her line of vision was black rubber, the massive front tire of the diesel truck and trailer rig that had pushed her car into the sea. It was less than six feet away. She scrambled to her knees and looked up at the driver's door that loomed open, above her. Slowly she stood, eyes fixed on the open cab of the truck six feet up. There was no one inside, behind the wheel or in the passenger side. Whoever had tried to kill her had vanished and now mingled with the other passengers. As Joselyn stood gaping through the open door, she heard footsteps approaching on the deck.

She quickly moved to the other side of the truck and ducked down between two cars in the next lane.

Two crewmen started to examine what was left of the safety net. One of the other crewmen climbed up into the seat of the truck. 'No key.' He looked under the dash and pulled some loose wires down. Somebody had hot-wired the starter.

'Don't mess with it. Let's get the driver down here and see if he can back it up to balance the load. Did anybody call the Coast Guard?'

'They called from the bridge.' Several crew members now mingled and talked among themselves, taking charge. No one seemed to notice Joselyn.

She quietly started to walk up the car ramp to the staircase that led to the passenger deck. The concrete deck felt icy. Joss looked down and discovered she had lost her second pair of shoes while struggling to climb back up the safety net. Her purse and her briefcase were still in the car, sinking down to the bottom of the sound. Her clothes were torn where she had been peppered with the splinters from the explosion.

She opened the door at the top of the staircase, and saw the women's restroom right across the corridor. She slipped into a stall and locked the door.

Whoever drove the truck into the back of her car thought Joselyn was dead. Her mind was confused. She was still in a state of shock, but her better judgment told her, that at least for the moment, it was safer if she remained dead.

CHAPTER
SIXTEEN

Washington, DC

It was now after midnight. The Capitol dome was lit up. Bowlyn could actually see it from the office window that belonged to Sy Hirshberg in the White House's West Wing. Hirshberg was the national security adviser to the president. He had bags under his eyes and was wearing a black bow-tie and a tux as he slouched in his chair behind the big cherry wood desk.

Bowlyn had snagged him as he had headed home from a party at the Kennedy Center following a performance. He had thought better of discussing his problem with other members of the Working Group before giving his boss a heads-up. No doubt what Bowlyn was about to tell him was going to ruin Hirshberg's day.

'Can we make this quick? I've got a seven-thirty meeting tomorrow morning and a flight out to New York at ten.' Hirshberg was on his way to meet with some of his counterparts from Europe at the U.N. to discuss Bosnia and the Middle East.

Bowlyn took a long deep breath, then spoke: 'We have

information that Russian arms merchants may have shipped a nuclear device to clients in the U.S.'

Hirshberg sat on the other side of his desk, his gaze fixed on his assistant as if he were in a trance. The only sign that he was conscious were the deepening furrows over his brow that set like concrete. Before Hirshberg could speak, Bowlyn anticipated his first question.

'The device may have already been delivered,' he said.

By now he had Hirshberg's undivided attention.

'We think the weapon was transshipped by vessel across the Pacific. The ship itself sank, possibly in a storm. The Coast Guard has confirmed that much.'

'If the ship sank, how do we know the weapon didn't go down with it?'

Bowlyn opened his briefcase and pulled out a copy of the FBI lab report. He passed it across the desk to his boss.

Hirshberg opened it and read. It took several minutes to absorb the salient portions of the report. There were two key items of critical evidence. The first was that the tattered cargo lines that linked the cargo to the diesel-filled flotation bag above had been cleanly severed, probably by a knife, according to the laboratory report. This was a clear indication that someone had cut the cargo free from its flotation, probably after pulling it aboard a vessel, and then jettisoned the flotation bag and the buoys over the side.

The second finding in the report was vastly more critical.

'Refresh my understanding of physics. It's been a long time,' said Hirshberg. 'A *rad* as I recall is the basic unit of radiation absorbed by the human body.'

'That's correct.'

'And the outer skin of this flotation bag contained enough radioactive contamination to cause cancer in a thousand people?'

'According to the analysts,' said Bowlyn. 'As soon as they found out they shipped all of the recovered items from the *Isvania* to Oak Ridge for final examination and disposal. They had to decontaminate the lab at Quantico.

'Based on what they've seen, the device in question contains aging weapons-grade plutonium that has been exposed to the air for some time. It's begun to oxidize. Still, the physicists tell us that plutonium would not be emitting these high levels of gamma radiation. There is something else. We don't know what. The Coast Guard tried to decontaminate the chopper that picked the stuff up. When they couldn't, they simply pushed it over the side. Gave it to Davey Jones. The flight crew and everybody else who came in contact with the items have been quarantined. They're under observation.'

Hirshberg went back to the report. The analysts suspected that whoever took the device from the Russian munitions bunker had dismantled it before shipping. They had exposed the plutonium core to the air and possibly wrapped it in the deflated flotation bag before crating it up. The bag itself registered exceedingly high levels of radiation. He laid the report on the desk.

'Do they have any idea of the size of the bomb?' asked Hirshberg. 'Any sense as to its destructive force?'

'No. Only that there's a danger of contamination. Whoever shipped it apparently didn't know what they were doing.'

'Let's hope they're equally ignorant about detonation,' said Hirshberg. 'What are the Russians saying?'

'Dan Murphy at State has some of his people checking with their ministry of defense. The problem is that what little we know comes from intercepts, some of them on commercial telephone lines. We can't very well tell the Russians that we've tapped into their domestic phone system. We're not sure what they'll tell us publicly. We're hoping they'll cooperate. CIA has dispatched an agent to the facility in Siberia to see if he can find out anything. We've been working on decoding some of the intercepted transmissions, but so far nothing.'

'So what can I tell the president?' said Hirshberg.

'That's the problem,' said Bowlyn.

'What do you mean?'

Bowlyn took a deep breath. 'We have reason to believe that the weapon in question was obtained by the Russian Mafia, a group out of Yekaterinburg in Siberia. It was stolen from a government arsenal in that area. The documentation for a shipment of machine parts, which we think was the weapon, was made out in the name of a Russian corporation. That corporation is operated by Viktor Kolikoff.'

Hirshberg turned his face up toward the ceiling and paused a long moment before he exploded. 'Son of a bitch. I knew it.' He shook his head, got up out of the chair, and began to pace toward the big window with the Capitol view.

'We warned him. We told him not to get involved with the guy. And what does he do? He invites him to the fucking Oval Office and shakes his hand in front of cameras. Invites him to dinner, sits down with him at coffee klatches. Does everything but give him the key to the front door of the White House.'

'He gave the money back,' said Bowlyn, trying to look on the bright side.

'Yeah. Right. After the *Post* drove twelve inches up his ass on the front page.'

The problem was that the president had taken $240,000 in the last election, money that was ultimately traced to Kolikoff and was laundered through straw donors. When party officials got caught, they returned the funds. Kolikoff was a foreign national. To knowingly take political contributions from him was a crime. But they couldn't prove the president or any of his people knew the money was from Kolikoff.

'No one's going to prosecute him,' said Bowlyn.

'Certainly not that rube of an attorney general,' said Hirshberg. 'Besides, the president has sold the public on the principle that if it isn't a crime, it's fine, and even if it is, it might be OK,' said Hirshberg. He looked at Bowlyn. 'Don't you get it? The voters have given the president a complete pass on matters pertaining to ethics, both in and out of government. Now they may get a slow nuclear burn in their beds for the favor.'

Bowlyn looked nervously around the room, wondering if it wasn't bugged and cabled for cameras. He knew the White House Situation Room was. Hirshberg had a temper, and when he lost it, all judgement flew out the window.

'Problem is,' said Hirshberg, 'the public's bought off on all of it. This country's in for a hell of a future.'

'It's not the president. It's his political handlers,' said Bowlyn.

Hirshberg looked at him and arched an eyebrow. 'If you want my job you'll have to speak a little louder into the pen set on my desk,' Hirshberg told him.

Bowlyn's face flushed. 'You have to admit Williams is a snake. To get caught with some hooker while he's talking to the president and have the gall to continue offering advice as if he were indispensable . . .'

'I give you Williams and the rest of that nest of vipers.' Hirshberg lifted a glass of water from the desk and took a drink as if in toast. 'But I ask you, who is it? Have his lips wrapped around the flute playing music to coil by?'

Hirshberg looked at him through the glass of water. Bowlyn didn't have a reply.

'He was warned by the CIA and the State Department. Both told him before he ever met with Kolikoff that the man had ties to organized crime in Russia, that he had links in the illicit arms trade. Did he listen? No.'

Kolikoff had gotten more than the usual grip-and-grin photo session with presidential handlers telling him where to stand, like a cardboard cutout. He had spent days in the White House, filling the president's Rolodex with phone numbers and addresses of hefty contributors. The State Department and even the CIA had cringed. The president didn't care. All he wanted was the campaign cash, and he was willing to do anything to get it.

'Now if there is a weapon of mass destruction on U.S. soil and Kolikoff is involved, I guarantee you that our commander in chief is not going to want to hear about it.'

'He's going to have to do something,' said Bowlyn.

'I remind you,' said Hirshberg, 'this is the administration that led the charge against private ownership of guns, that made the NRA a four-letter word. Have you forgotten?' said Hirshberg. 'Our president is for children, education, and the environment, children! and social security, children and Medicare, and children.

'How can a man with that kind of a political mantra tell the public they might wake up tomorrow and find one of their cities missing, their children dying of radiation poisoning, that is if they weren't incinerated in their beds? Oh, and by the way, your president took money from, and shook the hand of, the man who delivered the device to your doorstep.'

CHAPTER
SEVENTEEN

Friday Harbor, WA

A ferry with an accident overboard is like a small village. The rumors quickly spread from the crew to the passengers. They couldn't find anyone belonging to the car that went to the bottom. Consensus was growing that there may have been a fatality.

Joselyn wanted to tell the captain the truth, but she had no idea who'd tried to kill her. Whoever it was was still on the boat. She'd be putting her life in the hands of an unarmed crew, perhaps putting them in jeopardy. It seemed much safer for the moment to remain dead.

The truck driver whose diesel had run her car off the ferry's bow apparently was having a cup of coffee up in the cafeteria when someone borrowed his truck. Five witnesses saw him there.

The ferry crew searched the water for twenty minutes with lights, until a Coast Guard boat showed up and took over. Two of the Coast Guard officers boarded the ferry to interview the crew and any witnesses. The *Tillicum* slowly picked up speed and motored for Friday Harbor. It took nearly forty minutes.

Joselyn waited in the restroom until she felt the ferry dock. Walk-on passengers were always the first off as the crew readied the car deck for off-loading. As she left the restroom, the passenger deck was empty. She quickly made her way down the stairs to the car deck. The crew was busy removing the chocks from the car wheels as Joselyn walked off the ferry. She held her breath, waiting for someone to call out, to try to stop her. No one noticed her.

The sigh of relief was almost palpable as she headed up the dock toward Front Street.

She hoped the Coast Guard wouldn't spend too much time out on the frigid waters looking for a body. Still she had no intention of being dragged in by the authorities tonight. She was exhausted, both mentally and physically. She would stop in the sheriff's office in the morning and tell them what happened. There would be plenty of time for them to pick up the pieces of the investigation then.

Joselyn walked quickly to the end of the dock and took a right toward the Spring Street Landing. Vehicles coming off the ferry would have to make a sharp right along Front Street for a block before making a left up Spring Street to pass through town. On the waterfront, it was a one-way street. They would have to drive under bright streetlights before heading up the hill. Joselyn could get a good look at the drivers and passengers under the lights.

She wasn't sure what she was looking for. She wished she'd had a pencil and something to write on. The only thing she had at the moment were the clothes she was wearing. She fished in her skirt pocket looking for change, something to make a phone call. Nothing. She would have to bum a phone call from somebody, maybe one of the restaurants down the street. Call Samantha to come pick her up.

She looked at her watch; nine-thirty. It was possible Sam might still be at the office. She often worked late.

Joselyn hunched down in the shadows under a tree and sat on the end of a wooden bench outside the offices of Western Princess Cruises. Everything in town was closed, except a few of the night spots. She could hear muted strains of music coming from a tavern down the street.

Slowly vehicles began to emerge from the ferry, one at a time as they cleared the checkpoint set up by the Coast Guard. This made it easy for Joselyn to study each of the cars and their occupants. She wasn't exactly sure what she was looking for, perhaps anything out of the ordinary, somebody that stood out, who wasn't a local, not that it would be that easy to tell. She had one advantage; there weren't many cars on the ferry. Whoever had tried to kill her was still onboard. Of that she was sure.

The first two vehicles had Washington plates, one belonging to a family with small children. The other was a pickup truck with a local business name and phone number on the door, a masonry contractor. She dismissed them both.

The third vehicle drew her attention. It was a late-model white sedan with two men in the front seat. They were dressed in business suits and the passenger was talking on a cellphone. It wasn't until they made the turn up Spring Street that Joselyn saw the federal license plate over the rear bumper.

She looked intently at the car for a moment as it disappeared up the street, then she dismissed the thought. If McCally was going to have her followed, the FBI wouldn't have used a car with government plates. Or would they? The two guys were probably agriculture inspectors here to roust some dairy farmer on the island.

Her attention was quickly distracted by the next car, an older-model sedan with a lot of rust and dents. It had seen better days. Joselyn squinted under the bright lights to get a look at the driver. It was an old woman, a lot of gray hair with a bandanna holding it in place. She took the next car in order. There were kids in the back seat.

In all she counted eighteen cars and the diesel truck. She saw the driver, got a good look at him. Maybe he was lying about being up in the cafeteria. Still, if what she heard on the ferry was correct, there were witnesses who saw him there.

Her thoughts returned to the car with the federal plates. If McCally had her followed, why didn't the agents help her? They must have been watching, unless they figured she couldn't go anywhere on a ferry and went upstairs to get coffee like everybody else. At the moment, she had a lot of questions and no answers.

Without wheels, Joselyn hoofed it toward her office near the courthouse. It was only a few blocks from the ferry dock through downtown Friday Harbor. She could hear strains of guitar music coming from Herb's Tavern on Spring Street, some loud conversation from a few patrons inside.

As she walked, her mind swarmed with a dozen thoughts, none of them related. Belden was dead. What few notes or documents she had concerning his grand jury appearance were now at the bottom of the Sound. There was probably nothing there. Still she would have killed to get one last glimpse at them.

She'd have to get a new driver's license, call the credit card companies and have them issue new cards. What else was in her wallet? Her state bar membership card. She made a mental note to call the bar.

She hoped Sam was at the office. At least she could get a ride home. She turned down First Street, past Christy's and the Clay Café, then left on Court Street, and walked quickly across the road and in front of the county courthouse. As she cleared a few trees and the corner of the building, she could see lights on upstairs under the covered walkway in front of Sam's office. She was in luck.

Joselyn picked up her pace and looked at the lights. She was halfway across the street directly in front of the office when she realized it wasn't Sam's office that was lit up – but her own.

She was sure she hadn't left the light on in her office. Maybe the janitor was inside cleaning.

Given the events of the day, she was taking no chances. She walked past the building and approached from the rear, through the small garage on the ground floor. It was deserted. Sam's car wasn't there.

Slowly and very quietly, she took the passageway that lead to the wooden landing and the stairs then began climbing, two half-flights, to the outside corridor that ran in front of the doors to the office suites on the second floor.

There was a beauty salon on the ground floor at the front of the building. Joselyn could see the reflection from a display of flickering lights in the window as they flashed on the grass and a few shrubs near the sidewalk out near the street.

She stopped at the top step, pressed her back against the stuccoed wall and took a deep breath, then a quick peek around the corner and down the corridor. The overhead lights were out. Usually they were left on all night. Joselyn realized that it was the dark corridor outside that made the light in her office so visible and obvious from the street. Why would someone go to the trouble of turning off the outside lights to break into her office and turn on the office light? It had to be the janitor.

For a moment, she hesitated. She thought about running down the stairs to the sheriff's office near the courthouse. Somebody would be on the desk. She could wait there for a patrolman to check her office. And what if it was the janitor? She'd look like a fool. Worse, she'd have to tell them what happened on the ferry; otherwise she'd have a hard time going to them with the truth in the morning. They'd haul her back to the dock and the Coast Guard and she'd be into it for a million questions. She'd spend half the night under bright lights. The U.S. attorney's office would get wind, and McCally would be in her face again. This time he'd be sure she knew something she wasn't telling him.

The thought caused her to edge her way past the last step, around the corner and down the corridor. She hugged the front wall of the building, so if there was anybody inside she'd see them first. She passed two locked office doors, came up to Sam's door and tried it. It was locked. There wasn't much chance she'd be inside with the lights out, but Joss had hoped.

She stopped and listened. She couldn't hear anything, but the door to her office was partially open, and light was streaming out onto the dark decking outside. It wasn't until she took another step that she felt something under her bare feet. Joss looked down and realized it was the crunch of glass. The lights overhead hadn't been turned off after all. They had been broken. At the same instant she lifted her eyes and saw the frame of the door to her office. The wood was splintered, and Joselyn could see the tool marks in the paint where a pry bar had been inserted.

With the realization, Joselyn started moving away from the open office door and the light. She retreated three or four steps, and felt the crunch of glass followed by a sharp pain in the heel of her right foot. She hopped, trying to catch her balance, and finally steadied herself against the wall. A razor-thin shard of glass from one of the broken bulbs had penetrated her sock and buried itself in her heel. She scratched gently with her fingernail, trying to pluck it out, and felt a warm trickle of blood on her fingers. A quick-moving shadow broke the shaft of light behind her.

Joss tried to run, but as soon as she put weight on her foot her knee buckled in pain as the glass was driven deeper into her foot. She collapsed on the wooden decking, turned, and saw the towering silhouette of a man backlit in the open door of her office.

'Don't touch me. I'll scream.'

'Please. Do not be afraid. I'm not going to hurt you.'

'Stay away from me.'

'Are you all right?'

'I'm fine.'

'Let me help you up.'

'Leave me alone.'

He ignored her and stepped forward, but instead of grabbing her, he reached gently for her foot with one hand. 'That looks bad. You are bleeding. Here, let me help you.'

The gentleness in his voice calmed Joss, but she was still wary. He was huge, at least six foot five, perhaps taller. In a single fluid motion, his arms were under her, cradling her back and under the bend of her knees. He lifted her as if she weighed nothing, turned toward the lighted doorway, kicked it fully open and carried her through into her own office.

He placed her gently on the couch against the wall in the reception area, then turned, and headed for the door. He started to close it.

'Don't,' said Joselyn.

He didn't turn around but looked at her over his shoulder. 'I thought you might be cold. I will leave it if you wish.' He left the door open and in three steps crossed the room to where she lay on the couch.

'That does not look good.' He was foreign, had an accent. Joss wasn't sure from where. The blood from her heel was soaking into her sock, turning it a bright red. 'I'll have to take that off to get at the glass.' As he gently removed the sock, he caught the edge of glass in the fabric and she winced in pain.

'Sorry. If you lie still I think I may be able to get it.' As he studied her foot, Joselyn got her first good look at the man. He had fair skin, and wavy blond hair, broad shoulders. The features of his face were sharp as if etched in stone; a straight nose, high cheekbones, full parted lips.

He reached into his pocket and pulled out a four-inch folding knife.

Joselyn's eyes went wide, but before she could speak he plucked a tiny pair of tweezers from the handle of the knife and laid it on the small end table at the foot of the couch.

He looked at her. 'Very handy little things,' he said.

Joselyn smiled nervously and nodded.

'Think about something pleasant and don't look at your foot,' he told her.

That was not going to be easy. She laid back and looked up at the ceiling. She felt the tweezers at work, but his large hands were amazingly gentle. Then sharp pain. Her leg jerked uncontrollably.

'Easy. I got most of it. Let me see.'

She looked down at him as he studied intently the underside of her foot.

'Did you cut your knee when you fell?'

'What?' Joselyn looked down.

There was blood running down her leg from her knee. The adrenalin rush on the ferry caused her not even to notice until now.

'An earlier accident,' she told him. Joselyn had cut her knee to the point of bleeding while clawing her way back onto the deck of the ferry.

'You lead a hazardous life,' he said.

'You have no idea,' she said. Joss was beginning to relax. If he wanted to kill her, he could have done it by now. 'What are you doing in my office?'

'This is *your* office?'

'That's right.'

'Then you are Joselyn Cole?'

'Who are you?'

He didn't answer her but adjusted the light from the table lamp at the end of the couch. 'One thing at a time,' he said. 'I should concentrate, or the glass in your foot may require a visit to the hospital.'

He picked at her again with the tweezers, and she flinched in pain, forgetting for the moment questions about the man's identity.

'There. I think that is all of it. That I can see anyway. You will know in day or two if I have missed any. It will begin to fester. Very painful,' he said.

'That's encouraging.'

'I'm not the one who was running through glass in my stocking feet.'

'Let's get back to what we were talking about,' said Joselyn. 'Who are you and what are you doing in my office?'

'Ah, yes.' He reached into an inside coat pocket and came out with a business card. He handed it to Joselyn.

'My name is Gideon van Ry.'

She read the business card. 'What is the Institute Against Mass Destruction?'

'We are what you call a think-tank dealing with international relations. Specifically the institute monitors fissile materials, missile systems, weapons of mass destruction. We publish reports, a database.'

She looked at him, taking it all in, nodding almost as if in a daze.

'Why did you break into my office?'

'Oh, I didn't.' He looked up and saw that she was focused on the door and its splintered wooden frame. 'I found it that way.' He raised one hand as if taking an oath. 'I was looking for you. Found your office. I discovered the door as you see it.'

'And you just let yourself in?'

'It was open. I thought perhaps someone was inside.'

'Was there?'

'No. Whoever did this had already left.'

'It's not going to be cheap to get that fixed.' Joselyn was looking at the door again.

'Unfortunately whoever did that did not stop there.'

'What do you mean?'

'The inner office,' said Gideon.

She tried to get up off the couch.

'Easy.' He pressed her back down gently, and dabbed the blood off the bottom of her foot with his handkerchief one more time, then tied it around the wound.

Joselyn swung her legs off the couch and stood. She took one step and began to hobble as if she might go down. He grabbed her arm and steadied her, helping her as she hopped on one foot to the door to her office.

When Joselyn got there, she just stood in the open doorway, looking. The desk was turned over. Her two filing cabinets had been pulled over on their face, the drawers pulled out and the contents thrown all over the floor. The glass in their frames holding her degrees and licenses had been smashed, though two of them still hung on the wall behind broken splinters. Whoever had vandalized her office had done a world-class job.

The light from the office's reception area and the open door offered a clear line of sight, even from across the street with the driver's window rolled up. With a rifle, he could have taken both of them right there. But Thorn insisted it had to look like an accident.

The car was rusted out, its motor idling. The driver reached up with one hand and grabbed the bandanna. The gray woman's wig slid off his head with it. His eyes never left the two figures standing, centered in the doorway of the second-floor office. He had to admit that from behind she had a nice body. She also had nine lives. He was sure he'd gotten her on the ferry. He wondered who the blond giant was standing next to her. He dreaded his next task; telling Thorn that she was still alive.

CHAPTER
EIGHTEEN

Washington, DC

Hirshberg reported to the president in a written memo, sealed and marked, FOR THE PRESIDENT'S EYES ONLY. The memo was brief, discreet, and factual, reporting only what had been confirmed so far; that a Russian ship had gone down off the coast of Washington State, that it was believed to have been carrying fissile materials, perhaps a nuclear device, and that the device or materials were unaccounted for. He held the information on Kolikoff's involvement to a single line at the bottom of the memo. It was sealed and hand-delivered to the president by one of Hirshberg's aids.

Three minutes after the president slit the envelope and read the memo he was on the phone to his national security adviser.

'Sy. Who else knows about this?'

'You mean the Russian ship, Mr President?'

'And Kolikoff's involvement.' The president cut right to the chase.

'CIA, FBI, and military intelligence know about the ship, the fact that it was carrying fissile materials.'

'And Kolikoff?'

'Only myself and the CIA deputy director.' Hirshberg could hear a palpable sigh of relief at the other end.

'Which deputy is that?'

'Malcolm Sloan,' said Hirshberg.

'Oh, yes. Sloan. He's a good man.' Interpretation: Sloan was ambitious and could be reached by the White House for the proper spin on the story if it became necessary.

'I'd like you in my office in ten minutes to discuss this.'

'Would you like me to call Sloan, or Director Gentry?' Kurt Gentry was director of the CIA, and Sloan's boss.

'No. I don't think there's any need for Gentry to know anything more at this point. He knows about the Russian ship, I'm sure. I'll call Sloan myself,' said the president. The president was busy trying to narrow the circle of knowledge. Information in politics was power, and compromising dirt on a president was the ultimate form.

'Don't talk to anyone about this. Do you understand?'

'Yes, sir.'

Forty minutes later, Hirshberg and Sloan had their preliminary rewards for silence and discretion. They were named to chair the special crisis task force appointed by the president to look into the ship *Isvania*, its cargo, and whether the incident posed any imminent threat to national security.

Assigned as staff were all of the people on Hirshberg's working group. Notably, their bosses had all been cut out of the loop. Hirshberg and Sloan were to report directly to the president. If their bosses, the directors of the CIA,

FBI, or joint chiefs of the military interfered, Hirshberg and Sloan were to report the matter to the president.

Both men were given special passes, issued by the president himself and authorizing them to interrupt presidential business if at any time, in their judgment, there was a need. It was something sure to cause rancor within the White House pecking order. The president's chief of staff, the principal gatekeeper, jealously guarded his prerogatives, foremost among which was access to the Oval Office. Now he would be left to stare at the president's signature on the special passes and wonder what it was that Hirshberg and Sloan knew that he did not.

To identify the group they borrowed an acronym from the FBI; ANSIR. It stood for Awareness of National Security Issues and Response.

The ANSIR team convened for their first meeting less than two hours after Hirshberg and Sloan left the Oval Office. Each one of the members was reassigned on a temporary basis to full-time duties with the ANSIR Team. Any questions on this assignment were to be referred to the White House – more fuel for the fires of political envy.

'We are going to have some structural and support problems,' Hirshberg told the group. 'None of the Cabinet secretaries have been told about this.'

Heads turned and looked around the table at one another. 'Why not?' Finally one of them spoke up.

'Those are our orders,' said Hirshberg.

'There's no sense starting a panic.' Sloan from the CIA put a better spin on it. 'The more people who know, the more chance of a leak to the press. If it gets in the media that we suspect a nuclear device is in the hands of terrorists in this country, all hell could break loose. It's on a need-to-know basis, and they don't need to know right now.'

Once the Cabinet-level officers became involved, the

bureaucracy would take hold. News would filter through the various agencies and before long mid-level bureaucrats would be talking over coffee about how the president compromised himself with Kolikoff. From there it was only whispering distance to the *New York Times* and the *Washington Post*. As a consequence, the limitations on the ANSIR group were severe.

Hirshberg sat at the head of the table, flanked by Sloan, who saw the entire exercise as a fast elevator to the penthouse of power. The very surroundings confirmed his sense in this regard: the White House Situation Room with its proximity to the president.

'Here are the ground rules,' said Hirshberg. He read from hastily written notes prepared during his meeting with the president.

'All discussion of the device, its alleged smuggling into the country, steps to discover its location, or to secure and disarm it if it was in the country, are to be confined to members of this group, at least until further orders.'

He looked around the table to ensure that this was understood.

'Assets for any investigation will include only military intelligence.'

Hirshberg tried to go on.

'Excuse me.' It was the representative of the FBI. 'The Bureau has principal responsibility for domestic terrorism. I can't just go behind my director's back. I would at least ask to get clearance. To discuss it with the director.'

'I'll look into it,' said Hirshberg. 'I'll talk to the president. But for the moment you are to say nothing. Understood?'

'Yes.'

'For the moment the president, as commander in chief, wishes to deal with this issue through the military chain of command. Therefore for the time being we are to rely principally on Naval Intelligence.' There was a muted but obvious smile from the naval officer at the other end of the table. What it boiled down to was that the people who already knew about the Russian ship, and the name Kolikoff, had now been effectively coopted by the president.

The FBI interceded again. 'The problem is we have contingency plans for these situations. This effectively makes those plans worthless.'

'Sorry. But that's the way it is,' said Hirshberg. 'At least for the moment.' Hirshberg agreed with the FBI. The problem was, the president saw it differently.

'What we can all do to alleviate the situation is to work quickly,' said Hirshberg. 'If we can confirm that there is no device in the country, that it went down with the ship, then there won't be any further need for this group to meet or for further action to be taken, other than perhaps to recover whatever is out there. For the moment, we can't be sure there was a device.

'If on the other hand a device is in the country, then I will prevail on the president to put all of our resources to work. I'm sure he will see the wisdom of bringing in the Cabinet and all the appropriate agencies at that time.' Actually Hirshberg wasn't sure of this at all, but he would do his damnedest to convince the man.

'Where do we go from here?' Hirshberg looked at Sloan.

'I think it would be best if we start with an analysis of what we already know. In the last twenty-four hours we've gathered new information which indicates that the device or devices in question . . .'

'There's more than one?' The FBI was asking questions again.

'We're not sure,' said Sloan. 'There may be.'

211

The FBI started searching other faces around the table for support but didn't get it.

'As I was saying, new intelligence reveals that the devices in question may have been paid for, at least in part, by a rogue state, possibly Iraq. According to our reports, they're keeping their distance. It's likely that the people involved at this end don't even know about the outside support. They're merely being used to achieve a mutual goal. If the reports are correct, the Iraqis may have put up considerable cash to obtain the device and are probably paying a middleman to facilitate assembly and transportation.'

'The middleman. Do we know who he is?' asked the FBI.

'No. Unfortunately we have no information, but we're following it up. We do have solid information that whatever it was that was shipped out on the trawler in question was obtained by the Russian Mafiya, specifically a corporation founded by KGB money as the Soviet Union collapsed. It is now run by former rogue agents. Its CEO is Viktor Kolikoff.'

Sloan shot a sideways glance at Hirshberg. He didn't intend to get into the finer details of Kolikoff, though most of the people in the room had read the newspapers and could fill in the blanks for themselves. The president's political predicament was going to make their job much more difficult.

'Do we know if there is verifiable state sponsorship for these activities?' It was the man from the State Department asking.

'You mean Iraq?' said Hirshberg.

'Yes.'

'Why?'

'If so, the administration is on record. It has not ruled out a nuclear strike in retaliation for such an attack.'

'And your point is?' said Sloan.

'It's vital that any foreign state actively involved with domestic terrorists understand the risks to themselves.'

'You're suggesting we contact the Iraqis?' said Hirshberg.

'If we have incontrovertible evidence of their involvement,' said the man. 'It's possible that we can peel them away from whoever they're dealing with in this country if the risks to themselves are made readily apparent. A full-out nuclear attack,' said the man.

Sloan looked over at Hirshberg and wrinkled an eyebrow. It wasn't a bad idea. 'Who knows, the Iraqis might give up whoever is working at this end if they know their own ass is in the flames,' he said.

'Thank you. We'll see if we can firm up the Iraqi connection.' Sloan made a note. The item was now firmly in his own quiver of ideas, the ones he would fawningly present to the president. Sloan wouldn't remove lint from the shoulder of a friend's coat unless he got credit.

'There's another aspect to this whole thing.' This time it was Navy Intelligence.

'What happens if a device is detonated in a major American city? How could we be sure some other power doesn't panic and launch a full-out pre-emptive strike out of fear?'

'Why would they?' said Sloan.

'He has a point,' said the man from the State Department. 'Another nuclear power, Russia, China. Even if they're not involved, if they think there's a chance we might suspect them, they could launch before we have a chance to quell their fears.'

'You really mean a full-out pre-emptive strike?' said Hirshberg.

The man from the State Department nodded his head. They all knew that the Cold War might be over, but the risks of nuclear annihilation were not.

'The problem with the Russians,' said the naval officer,

'is that their early warning system is shredded. There's no money for maintenance, and their stations in Latvia are gone. They're a nuclear giant stumbling around blind. If there's a detonation somewhere in a population center in this country, their first inclination may be a pre-emptive launch rather than wait to see if we sort things out.'

'That shouldn't be a problem,' said the FBI. 'The president made a statement six months ago that Russian missiles were no longer aimed at American cities.'

'They're not,' said Sloan.

'Then we would have time to contact them and give them assurances,' said the FBI.

'You don't understand,' said Hirshberg. 'Russia's nuclear missiles are configured in such a way that even if the Russians removed the targets from the missiles' computerized guidance systems, if they're launched, the missiles are programmed to immediately reacquire their last known targets.'

The president's assurances aside, they were living in a fool's paradise.

CHAPTER
NINETEEN

Friday Harbor, WA

Joss stood looking at the mess in her office, this time in the cold light of morning. If anything, it looked worse than the night before.

By nature she was not well organized. She generally worked from piles of papers that to the average eye might appear disheveled. It was her own kind of filing system. Usually these stacks rested on her desk and any other flat surface that was available. She knew where everything was and could usually stick her hand in any of a dozen of these document heaps and come up with whatever was needed. The problem now was the these stacks had been scattered all over the floor, some of them torn up.

'What in the world?'

Joss turned to see Samantha outside, standing in the doorway. She was examining the splintered wood around the lock of the office's front door.

'I had visitors last night,' said Joselyn.

'I can see.' Sam wandered in looking at the tall blond guy

standing in the reception area, holding some loose pieces of paper he'd picked up off the floor.

Joss made the introduction. 'Samantha Hawthorn, Gideon van Ry.'

They shook hands. Samantha eyed him, making a careful and slow appraisal, then looked around the office again. 'They really did trash the place.'

'Sam's my landlady,' Joselyn told Gideon.

'You have my condolences,' he told her.

'I hope insurance will cover this. What happened?'

'I came back from Seattle last night and found it as you see it. Somebody broke in,' said Joss. 'Trashed the place and left.'

'Kids, you think?' said Samantha.

'I doubt it.'

'You sound like you know who did this.'

'Not really,' said Joss.

'Have you called the sheriff?'

'A deputy just left. He took the report. Of course they'll investigate.'

'We'll need it for insurance if nothing else,' said Sam. She was still surveying the damage. 'Is anything missing?'

Joss gave her a shrug, like she couldn't be sure. She had also used the opportunity with the sheriff's deputy to report the incident on the ferry the night before. When she did, the cop looked at her askance, like this clearly wasn't her day. Still he didn't seem driven by the coincidence to link the two events or ask many questions. Joselyn was sure she would be hearing more from them, but at least for the moment they seemed satisfied.

Gideon had spent the night in a small motel by the airport just on the fringes of town. Given the events of the day they agreed that it was not wise for her to go home. She took a room just a few doors away.

Van Ry seemed a straight arrow. That morning Joselyn had slipped away from him long enough to call the phone number down in California that was on his business card. They vouched for him and provided information about the institute, which seemed to correspond with what he'd told her the night before.

Now he disappeared into her inner office and was lifting the two filing cabinets off the floor and positioning them against the wall where they belonged.

'Who is he?' Samantha whispered in Joselyn's ear.

'He's here about Belden's business.'

Sam looked at her as if the name didn't register.

'The guy with the desperate phone calls.'

'Ah. That one.'

Samantha craned her neck to peak around the doorway for one more look at Gideon. 'Not bad,' she whispered. 'You can send him to my office to clean up when he's finished here?'

'He's here on business. Belden's dead.'

This took Samantha's attention away from the doorway and the tall blond. She looked at Joselyn wide-eyed. 'How did it happen?'

Instead of answering, Joss unfolded a copy of the Seattle paper with the story on an inside page. It was sparse on details and attributed Belden's death to an accident that was still under investigation.

'You flew down on this plane with him to Seattle?'

Joselyn nodded.

Sam slumped into a couch in the corner. 'You could have been killed.'

'That's not the worst of it.'

Sam looked at her.

'His death was no accident. I can't tell you anything more. Not right now.'

217

'He was murdered?'

'It looks that way.'

Suddenly the light clicked on in Sam's eyes. 'You think this is connected?' She meant the trashing of Joselyn's office.

'I don't know.'

'You should go to the sheriff. You told them that he was murdered, didn't you?'

'No. I don't have any evidence.'

'Start with this, what happened to your office, the fact that your client is dead, the fact that you were on the plane with him earlier in the day. I think they'll be able to connect the dots.'

'I don't want to get into it right now. Can we talk later?'

'Sure, if that's what you want. But I'll tell you, I wouldn't wait. Can I help you clean up?'

'It's pretty much a one-person job. And I've got . . .' Joss gestured toward the door to her office and Gideon. She could hear metal drawers sliding into their hardware.

'Call me if you need me. I'll be right next door.' Sam took one last look at her, then slipped down the corridor to the next office.

Joss headed toward her inner office and the mess that was inside.

'I am just putting all the files in a stack on your desk.' Gideon looked up at her. He was on his hands and knees behind the desk.

'There's no need for you to do that.'

'As long as I'm here, I may as well be of some help.'

'Really.' She went over behind the desk and started taking the papers and folders out of his hand. 'I can do this. Please.'

He got up from behind the desk.

'Tell me,' said Joselyn, 'how did you get my name?'

He picked up her office swivel chair, which was flipped over behind the desk. 'You were listed as one of the corporate officers for Belden Electronics – with your State Department of Licensing.'

'Of course. The corporate formation.' Suddenly Joselyn started wondering. If van Ry could find her from the documents of incorporation, so could anyone else. Belden's associates, the ones McCally warned her about. Maybe that's how they found her on the ferry and located her office.

'I assume you were simply acting for your client?' said Gideon.

'Hmm?'

'In creating the corporation.'

'Of course.'

'So you weren't involved in any actual management activities?'

'No.'

'What do you think they were looking for? The people who did this?'

'I don't know. Maybe they weren't sure themselves.'

'Ah, what do you call it?' Gideon thought for a second. 'A fishing expedition.'

She nodded but didn't look terribly convinced.

'I would say you are in a great deal of trouble,' said Gideon.

'Why?'

'Because the people who did this are very dangerous,' said Gideon. 'I do not think they were on some idle search for the unknown in your office.'

'All of my papers relating to Belden and his business went to the bottom of the Sound with the car.' She had

219

told him about the incident the night before. 'Maybe that's what they were looking for.'

'It's possible, but I doubt it.'

'Why?'

'Put yourself in their shoes. You go down to represent your client Mr Belden before the grand jury. You would take the Belden file with you, wouldn't you?'

She nodded.

'They would figure that much out themselves. They attempt to kill you on the ferry. As far as we know, they are satisfied that they succeeded. You are silenced. The file was with you in the car. They can surmise as much. And still, they come here and do this.' He wrinkled his eyebrows. 'The question being, why?'

Joselyn shook her head. She didn't have a clue.

'Let's start with your client's business.'

Joss was no longer in the mood to protect client confidences. She wondered if she'd made a big mistake in refusing to cooperate with McCally. She wasn't going to make the same error twice.

'He said he was in electronics. I had no reason to question it.'

'What kind of electronics?'

'Something about switches. Programming for security systems or something. I don't remember all the details.'

'Did he ever take you to his place of business?'

'No.'

'Did he give you an address?'

'He said he was just getting set up. I'm not sure he'd found a place.' Joselyn slumped into the swivel chair behind her desk as Gideon pushed one of the client chairs into position across from her and took a seat.

'In other words, you're not certain he was in business at all.'

She shook her head. 'Why would he come to me to set up a business if he didn't need it?'

'Why indeed?' said Gideon. 'What did he look like?'

She gave him a quick description and then told him about the investigation by the U.S. Attorney's office and McCally's warning that Belden had used many aliases, that the government believed he was involved in moving dangerous munitions. Gideon took it all in, made a few notes, and didn't look up at her until she mentioned the small plastic device that the authorities found floating in the water at the site of Belden's plane crash.

'What did it look like?'

'Small white, about the size of a square wristwatch.'

'And they said it was for measuring radiation?'

She nodded.

'A dosimeter,' said Gideon.

'That's it.'

'Did you get a good look at it?'

'He showed it to me.'

'The paper inside the square,' said Gideon. 'Was it discolored?'

'I don't know. I don't remember. I didn't look that closely. Besides, they pulled it out of the water.'

'Yes. That could have affected it. Also the heat of the blast. You said the plane exploded?'

'The biggest damn fireball you ever saw,' said Joselyn. 'I got melted nylons to prove it.'

'So we are back to where we started.'

She shot him a quizzical look.

'What were they after? The people who did this.' Gideon was glancing around her office again like he coveted whatever it was they were looking for, the missing piece to a puzzle.

'Like I said, there was nothing here to find.'

'My guess is that if you did not know the item or items were significant, you would not have hidden them. They would have been in your files or on your desk.' He ignored this disclaimer and seemed to think out loud to himself. 'That means that whatever it is, they probably found it. So we are left with a simple process of elimination.'

'What are you talking about?'

'We account for all of your files and materials. And whatever is missing . . .' He looked at her from under arched eyebrows.

'Read my lips. There was nothing here. Besides, going through all the files would take all day.'

'You have other things to do today?'

Looking at the mess in her office, the answer was obvious.

'So the sooner we get started . . .' Gideon was back down on the floor, rummaging around, picking up files and loose papers from the floor, trying to figure out which papers went with which files.

She took them out of his hand and put them on the desk. 'You stack. I'll sort,' said Joss.

CHAPTER
TWENTY

Deer Harbor, WA

The pit was composed of less than thirty pounds of pure plutonium, surrounded by a casing. Grigori Chenko worked in a tent shrouded by heavy mil plastic. In the roof was a vacuum hose and high micron filter intended to create a slight negative air pressure inside the enclosure. This would keep any of the friable particles of plutonium from escaping, hopefully trapping them in the filter.

To protect himself the Russian wore a hazmat suit of yellow neoprene. It was equipped with a breathing apparatus containing fine micron filters. Chenko was sweating inside the hot suit, the plastic face piece continually fogging over. It was not the kind of forced-air breathing apparatus they used at Sandia and other high-tech labs but something Chaney acquired on the open market.

He took a break, stepped outside the tent, and removed the headgear so he could clear it to see. His hands were sweating inside the neoprene gloves, his back aching from bending over the small table he'd set up inside. The work was slow and tedious, punctuated by moments of intense anxiety as when he removed the plastic explosives from around the core.

The garage had been evacuated and Chenko's footsteps cast an eerie echo from concrete floor to metal walls as he paced about and stretched to loosen his body. The others waited outside until he was finished and the device was secured in its new metal casing.

Chaney had fabricated the casing from pieces of two old military fighter wing tanks that he found in a scrapyard on the mainland. Working from photographs of the original device Chaney demonstrated his skill with a welding torch, reshaping the metal and adding touches like rivets for realism. The Russian could not tell the reproduction from the original on display. They were peas in a pod from a large photograph that had been taken a month earlier and brought back to the island by Thorn himself. The plan was ingenious.

He donned the headgear and ducked back through the slit in the plastic tent. To the untrained eye the device on the table looked like a soccer ball. It was composed of thirty-two individual pie-shaped pieces of plutonium. Each was cut at a forty-five-degree angle. These were formed into a sphere and surrounded a beryllium/polonium core.

The entire package was wrapped in conventional plastic explosives that contained multiple detonators. It was this, the plastic explosives and the detonators that drew Chenko's attention. They were old and presented the greatest risk of failure. The simultaneous timing of the detonators was critical. The nuclear reaction was a given, an immutable matter of physics, but only if the plastic explosive that triggered it was timed to one ten-millionth of a second. The pressure giving rise to implosion would have to be precisely uniform around the entire outer ring of the sphere.

Only then would critical mass be achieved, setting up the nuclear chain reaction.

It was a small bomb, as nuclear devices went, but at its core, at the instant of ignition, temperatures would reach one million degrees, hotter than the surface of the sun. The high temperatures would release massive amounts of electromagnetic radiation. Objects in the immediate vicinity would be vaporized instantly.

The radiation would be absorbed by the air immediately around the bomb. This in turn would be heated to incandescence, creating a fireball that would expand at velocities approaching the speed of light until its temperature dropped below 300,000 degrees. Then it would slow to the point where the mammoth shock wave created by the compression of air in the atmosphere would overtake the fireball, flattening structures and knocking down trees. Within a second, the fireball would reach the same area, igniting every flammable surface, melting metal, and turning human bodies into instant steam.

The shock wave would travel more than two and a quarter miles in ten seconds and result in maximum devastation of the affected area. The luminosity of the fireball would fade. The violent overpressure of the shock wave would pass. Out of the violent sphere of fire, the forbidding mushroom cloud would raise its deadly head toward the stratosphere, cooling as it climbed, creating its own violent convections of air. There would be lightning from within, and if conditions were right, a deadly downpour of highly radioactive particles, a rain shower of agonizing death.

It took Chenko more than two hours to check and replace detonators. He did this by cannibalizing and using the spare parts of the other device, the first one the fishermen brought in, missing its deadly plutonium core.

He then took the assembled device and bolted it into

the open half of the bomb casing that Chaney had built. He stepped out of the plastic tent and lifted the hood of the hazmat suit from his head. Sweat dripped down his forehead into his eyes and ran in rivulets down his neck into the suit.

He walked toward the large sliding door of the metal garage and slid it open with a rattle. The men outside turned from their conversations to look. A few of them dropped cigarettes into the dirt and stamped them out.

Chaney and Thorn were off to one side, by the old battered pickup truck Thorn was using. The Russian joined them, unzipping his suit as he walked.

'It is finished.'

'Good,' said Thorn. 'And the lead wires for the electronic detonator?'

'As you requested. I have left them exposed through the small opening near the tail-fins. You can replace the hatch cover when you are finished, touch up the paint, and it is ready.'

'Excellent. You do good work.'

The Russian smiled.

They went inside, and Thorn went to work. He set up at a workbench against the back wall of the garage, opened a briefcase, and pulled out a small computer. He attached a microphone and began speaking into it, reciting only two words: 'Critical mass'. The sound of his voice was registered in spiked lines similar to a graph on the computer's screen. He did this several times until he got a voice test he wanted. Then he saved this onto a computer disk. He removed the disk and punched it into another small computer-like device known as a blue box. It had a keypad similar to a computer and terminal ports. Thorn punched the keys and delivered the information on the computer's disk to its destination. He then carried the small plastic package over to the device.

By now, Chaney was finished fastening the two halves of the bomb casing together. He and two other men had it on a hydraulic floor jack, rolling it on wheels toward the truck.

They stopped a few feet from the vehicle and Thorn did the final preparation. He connected the wires to a switching device capable of sending a powerful electric charge to the detonators set into the plastic explosives inside the bomb. The receiver and its wires were then carefully fitted into an area near the bomb's large square tail-fin assembly where the battery pack would also be placed before the device was delivered to its ultimate destination. The tail-fin assembly had been fabricated by Oscar Chaney using precise specifications from photographs taken of the original. Even the olive-drab paint had been matched with care.

'Done.' Thorn wiped his hands on a rag and turned to Chenko. 'You're sure the device is properly assembled?'

'Absolutely.'

'No last-minute adjustments required, anything like that?'

'No. Connect the lead wires according to the schematic I have provided, install the batteries, and it is armed.'

'Good,' said Thorn. 'Let's you and I go outside, have a beer.'

The Russian smiled.

'Oscar. Go ahead and get it inside the truck,' Thorn yelled to him across the garage, and Chaney gave him a thumbs-up.

Thorn and the Russian went outside to the old pickup truck, where Thorn reached into the back and opened a small cooler, pulling out two glass bottles of ice-cold beer. He twisted the cap off of one of them and handed it to Chenko, then opened the other for himself.

Inside the garage, Chaney was busy with two other men, rolling the large bomb across the concrete floor on a hydraulic alligator jack. They maneuvered it under the tank that Chaney had welded onto the bed of the truck. Then Chaney pumped the long handle of the jack, raising the bomb up into the opening under the belly of the tank. It was bolted into place and secured, and the false steel panel under the tank was put back in place.

In ten minutes they were finished, and Chaney began pumping raw sewage from the portable john into the separated upper compartment of the tank, in case they were stopped.

Chaney had welded a solid plate of steel, lined with lead, separating the truck's tank into two compartments; a lower section for the bomb and an upper section for raw sewage. Conventional satellite surveillance would be of little use in detecting the truck. Plutonium gave off only mild gamma radiation, that could be shielded by a piece of paper. Thermal detection at checkpoints, if the Feds had time to set them up, could be more problematic. Thorn had taken the precaution of having Chaney line the bomb compartment with a quarter-inch lead liner. The absence of any signature from the device, coupled with the obvious presence of actual sewage in the truck, should cause authorities to wave them through without much question. They were counting on the normal human reaction to recoil from thoroughly inspecting such cargo. Besides, who would suppose that a septic-tank truck would be hauling an atomic weapon?

Outside, next to the pickup truck, Thorn watched as Grigori Chenko twitched on the ground. He was in the final tremors of death. His eyes rolled back into his head like two cherries in a slot machine. Potassium cyanide worked very quickly, especially in a dosage as strong as that which Thorn had added to the beer he'd given to the Russian. Chenko's job was done; one more loose end eliminated.

CHAPTER
TWENTY-ONE

Friday Harbor, WA

It was after four in the afternoon, and they were both tired. Out of the corner of one eye, Gideon watched Joselyn Cole as she arranged the files on her desk. She was an attractive woman, blue-eyed with shoulder-length sandy-colored hair. Her body was well proportioned and curvaceous, and a tawny complexion that the tall Dutchman found pleasing.

She also had a core of iron. After the events of the previous day, many people would have gone to bed and pulled the cover over their heads for a week. But Joselyn remained focused on the job at hand.

She looked up at him. 'Thank you for your help today,' she said.

'I must admit to a certain selfish motive,' he told her.

'What's that?'

'You are the last lead I have for the two forged waybills.' He had told her about the shipments out of the port of Vladivostok. There was a grave tone in his voice. 'I cannot impress upon you enough the seriousness of why I am here.'

'Maybe if you told me a little more,' said Joselyn.

'If I am correct, your client Mr Belden was involved in a very dangerous matter, a matter that could have devastating consequences for your country, and perhaps for the world.'

'What consequences?'

What he had discovered at Sverdlovsk could start a public panic if it were published. The fear that a nuclear device might be in the country, in the hands of terrorists, could result in wild speculation as to a target and mass migration of hundreds of thousands of people clogging highways and overrunning airports.

'Until I know more,' said Gideon, 'I can't be sure of my information. I can tell you this much, what I know would seem to be consistent with the information given to you by the prosecutor in Seattle. It is possible that this man who called himself Belden was involved in transporting weapons of mass destruction.'

'And you think these weapons are here, in this country?'

'I don't know. Perhaps what they were looking for here in your office will tell us that.'

Joselyn returned to the documents on her desk, looking through each more carefully now, mystified by what could possibly be contained in her files that would confirm van Ry's suspicions.

'I was curious as to why you omitted to tell the local authorities that the incident on the ferry was an attempt on your life,' said Gideon. 'You told them it was an accident. Why?'

'Because I have no proof,' she told him.

He engaged her eyes from the other side of the room as he put the final touches on one of the filing cabinets, pushing it against the wall.

'Do you really think it is coincidence that your client is

killed in the afternoon and that night someone tries to push you and your auto off of the ferry?'

'It could happen.'

'I see,' said Gideon. 'And you attribute all of this sudden misfortune to an unusual episode of bad karma?'

She gave him an irritated expression but didn't respond.

'You might wish to check the alignment of the planets before you venture out onto the street again.'

'You seem to have all the answers. What would you have me do?'

'You could have told the authorities about your conversation with the prosecutor in Seattle, about Belden's death. The two incidents, the plane exploding and the fact that you were driven off the ferry only a few hours later. I suspect they might have seen some pattern here.'

'Fine. And what would have happened then?'

'I suspect they would have provided you with some protection.'

'Great. Wonderful,' said Joselyn. 'So they put a sheriff's deputy outside my office door. That's going to do wonders for my practice. "Mr Jones, I'd like you to meet Deputy Smith. He's going to be watching over us while we talk, just in case someone makes an attempt on my life during client consultation." To say nothing of the chilling affect it would have on clients in criminal cases.'

'They would certainly know you have influence with the sheriff's office,' said Gideon.

Joselyn stifled a laugh. 'Besides, if McCally found out about the ferry incident, he'd drag me before the grand jury for sure. Probably have me taken in federal protective custody.'

'Why not?' said Gideon. 'You would at least be safe.'

'Just what I need, cops outside my door, or a cell, courtesy of the federal government. For how long?' she asked.

'Until this is over.'

'And how long will that be?'

Gideon couldn't answer this. The expression on his face said as much.

'Precisely,' said Joselyn. 'In the meantime, whatever meager practice I have here disappears.'

'You would be alive.'

'You call that living?'

'It may be better than the alternative,' said Gideon.

Joselyn didn't argue the point.

'Why in the world do they want to kill me?'

'Because you know something.'

'I don't know a damn thing.'

'They think you do, and for the moment that is the same thing,' said Gideon. 'I suspect that the answer is somewhere there, in front of you.' He gestured toward the papers on her desk. She returned to the task, this time with more energy and interest.

'Is there anything this man Belden told you?'

'I've already been over all of that, with McCally and the FBI.'

'Yes, but their powers of perception may not be as finely tuned as mine.'

Joselyn looked up at him, cracked a smile, and they both laughed.

'OK, Sherlock. What do you want to know?'

'When did Belden first come to you as a client?'

'Less than two weeks ago.'

'And how did he find you?'

'A referral from a banker in town. At least that's what he told me. It was probably a lie.'

'I suspect you are right,' said Gideon. 'Did you have any special expertise that he might have been looking for?'

'We talked about that,' said Joselyn. 'In fact, it was just

the opposite. He could have hired a hundred lawyers down in Seattle who knew more about business law than I did and not paid them a dime more in fees.'

'So we know that he wanted something else,' said Gideon. He looked at her with an appraising eye, so that she could read his mind.

'I don't generally discuss my sex life with strange men, but if you have to ask, the answer is no, we didn't. Not even close,' said Joselyn.

'I didn't think so,' said Gideon.

Joss feigned hostility. 'And why not?'

Now his face turned a shade of red she had not seen before.

'It's just that . . . ah . . . Belden being a client and all,' said Gideon.

'What's that got to do with it?' She looked at him steely-eyed, unwilling to let him off so easily.

'All I meant was that it wouldn't be the professional thing,' said Gideon.

'And you see me as the consummate professional, is that it?'

'Absolutely,' said Gideon.

'Gid. Can I call you Gid?' said Joselyn.

'Whatever you want to call me is fine,' he told her.

'If that's the case, then for the moment I'll just call you a bullshitter.'

Gideon tried to maintain composure but could not. The red veins in his neck began to stick out, and he started to laugh. 'What is it they say? Takes one to know one.'

'That's what they say,' said Joss.

He settled into one of the client chairs across from her desk. 'We know one thing.'

'What's that?'

'There is clearly some connection between what happened in Sverdlovsk and whatever is going on with your grand jury down in Seattle.'

'Why's that?'

'According to the prosecutor, your client, Mr Belden or whatever the latest name he is using, was expert in the handling of certain large-scale weapons. It cannot be a coincidence that fissile materials are missing from a Russian storage facility, traced to the port of Vladivostok, and that forged waybills show a shipment to Belden Electronics. I would think the prosecutor knows something.'

'Maybe he does, but you can be sure he's not telling us.'

'Perhaps not,' said Gideon. 'But he might tell someone else.'

'Who?'

'His own government.'

She looked at him quizzically.

'We have some contacts in the intelligence community. I will call my director at the center and see if perhaps we can float some balloons, do some checking. If it is a matter of national security, the Justice Department might contact the National Security Agency.'

'What good would that do us?'

'At least we would know that intelligence agencies are, as they say, in the loop. And after all,' said Gideon, 'we do have information to trade.'

She looked at him questioningly.

'What I learned in Sverdlovsk,' he said. He clearly had more confidence in government than she did.

Joselyn was holding a single piece of paper in her hand, searching the surface of the desk for the appropriate file as he spoke. She had been looking at it intermittently, trying to find the file it belonged to. Suddenly she realized the file wasn't on her desk.

She stepped across the room to the filing cabinet that Gideon had straightened against the wall. Joselyn opened the second drawer and thumbed through the files. She turned and looked at him, a troubled expression on her face.

'What is it?'

'Are all the files back in the cabinet?'

'Except for the ones on your desk.'

She retraced her steps and checked the surface of the desk one more time. It wasn't there.

'What is it?'

'It doesn't make any sense,' said Joselyn.

Seattle, WA

Thomas McCally flipped through the pages of the report. Only three pages long, it was lean on many details. The FBI was still investigating, but two federal prisoners awaiting trial had escaped from the Kent jail. One of them was of particular interest to McCally. Oscar Chaney was a bank robber with no prior criminal history but a colorful military record. He had been trained by Army Special Forces in what was euphemistically called 'special ops' and had participated in what the report called 'operations other than war'. McCally was no military tactician, but he knew what this meant. These were insertions into other countries that were never publicly reported, sometimes into hostile Third World countries, sometimes into the territory of allied nations. The purpose might be to gather intelligence on the ground or deliver arms to insurgent movements or to destroy some strategic facility, a radio station or fuel depot. The people who did this work were highly trained. Oscar Chaney had done this and was also active in the Gulf War. He'd cashiered out of the military, and for the past five years he had lived abroad. According to the State Department, he traveled in Europe, Africa, and Latin America. More important, information obtained by the FBI from European intelligence sources indicated that Chaney had been involved with Harold McAvoy, alias James Regal, alias Liam Walker, alias Dean Belden.

The report provided clear evidence of outside help and extensive planning in the jailbreak that sprung Chaney. The FBI had already arrested one of the men assisting from the outside. The man arrested had extensive contacts with a local militia group.

'It looks like they wanted Chaney out, and they came well prepared.' As McCally read the report, the FBI agent who delivered it paced the office in front of his door. 'They cut the bars with a torch,' said the agent. 'We didn't find it, but the thermal marks on the steel are unmistakable. We also found a small portable wire transmitter. According to the one arrested, there were three others helping from the outside.'

'The one you picked up. Is he giving up any information on Chaney's whereabouts?'

'I don't think he knows. He says he was drafted for the job by higher-ups in his militia cell. He doesn't know the names of the others involved in the break. My guess is they all came from different cells, and if we go up the food chain, we're going to find out that the people who tapped them for the job don't know any more than they do.'

'How did we arrest the one guy?' said McCally.

'He was shootin' his mouth off in a bar about how easy it was, the jailbreak,' said the agent. 'Like he was looking for more clients.'

'If the information in this report is accurate, he's not

the kind Chaney would run with, or trust very far,' said McCally. 'Which brings us to the question of why Chaney was robbing banks.'

'And doing it so poorly,' said the agent.

'What do we know about the local militia groups?' asked McCally.

The agent gave him an expression as if to say, 'not much'. 'Mostly situated up north and on the other side of the Cascades. Rural counties. They operate in leaderless action cells – small, loosely organized units. There's not a lot of contact between the cells. Nothing you could call organized command and control. It's mostly a mixed bag of nuts, some with racial motives, some just hate the government, and a lot of wannabe soldiers. Almost all male. Mostly in their thirties and forties.'

'Have we been able to penetrate any of the cells?'

'Not a problem. Just go to weekend war games and bring your own rifle. Problem is because of the small size and lack of cohesion between the groups you'd need a thousand agents in war togs and face paint to cover them all. For the most part, the ones here in Washington have generally been satisfied with hating the world and shooting at cardboard targets. Not that violent.'

To McCally it sounded like the agent might want to join them.

'Define violent,' he said.

'Most serious is recreational explosives. Stealing a rifle from a National Guard armory's the equivalent of earning your bones in the mob. They consider it big-time. We can usually pick them up in a local bar bragging about it. Not what you'd call a well-planned conspiracy.'

What the government had learned in Oklahoma City is that intelligence against such groups was almost useless. The most dangerous among them often acted alone or with one or two other friends. The first wind of any activity came with the pressure wave of an explosion.

McCally thought for a moment. 'Doesn't sound like an organization that could get up to speed on weapons of mass destruction.'

'You thinking chemical or biological?' said the agent. 'Not unless they could make it in somebody's garage.'

'What I'm thinking of they couldn't make in a garage,' said McCally. 'I'm thinking nuclear. Remember the little piece of white plastic – the dosimeter we found in the water after Belden's crash?'

'I hear Russia is a major shopping center for nuclear arms. But how would they get the money? That would cost a bundle. Even Iran and Iraq haven't been able . . .'

'As far as we know,' said McCally. 'Let's assume for a moment they found an open channel for such a weapon. Then they would need help. Professionals who knew how to arm and transport such a weapon.'

'That would explain Belden and Chaney,' said the agent. 'But how would they get the money for a bomb, to pay people like Chaney and Belden?

'Raise it. They have a network. Bogus check-writing schemes, a little fraud here and there, sell securities in the Comstock Lode to the aged.'

'That might raise a few hundred thousand, maybe a million if they're playin' the market. But we're talking multiple millions here.'

'They could have a secret investor,' said McCally.

'Whaddaya mean?'

'I mean what if you were Saddam and you were itching for a little revenge, but you didn't want to be *it* in a game of nuclear tag?'

'A rogue state?'

'Working from the shadows. I can think of a half-dozen

regimes that would love to blow the shit out of a major American city, especially if they could deflect blame to one of our own homegrown groups. Such a government might come up with a little subsidy to make a device available.'

The agent thought about this.

'They might even steer a little technical help in their direction,' said McCally. 'Suddenly Mr Belden and his colleagues are knocking on your door courtesy of Saddam or Muammar.'

'You think . . .?'

'I don't know,' said McCally. 'But people like Belden, and Chaney, are here for a reason. It is possible that they came as part of a package, attached to some kind of a device.'

For a moment they simply looked at each other, each knowing the question but declining to put it into words: Was it already here?

'The militia groups up north,' said McCally. 'Are they at all tied in with the bunch out on the island?'

The FBI and Alcohol, Tobacco, and Firearms had identified a sizeable contingent of well-armed militia members on a small private island in the San Juan chain just south of the Canadian border.

'Not as far as we know. The group on the island came in from Idaho and Montana.'

'What are they doing out there?'

'We don't know, but they're armed to the teeth. ATF has spotted some major ordnance.'

'Anything we can move in on? Get a search warrant?' asked McCally.

'Not without the Marines.' The agent arched his eyebrows as if to emphasize the point. 'We don't know if the weapons are legal. We've taken some long-range photos, but we can't tell.'

'No full-automatic stuff?'

'Haven't seen or heard any bursts.'

Possession of fully automatic weapons was illegal without a special license issued by the federal government. Evidence of such might be enough for a search warrant.

'They're under twenty-four-hour surveillance?'

The agent nodded.

McCally took a deep breath. He knew they were on the edge of something, but what? Without a warrant he couldn't search the island, and without Chaney he had no one to squeeze for information. He didn't want to look like a fool by going to intelligence agencies, but he had decided one thing. It was time to share what information he had with superiors in the Justice Department. Let them make the call.

'Let's assume Chaney's involved with the ones on the island,' said McCally. 'The local militia could be providing logistical support. Helping to spring him.'

'That would demonstrate a lot more organization than we've seen before,' said the agent.

'Let's just suppose something big, very big is in the works,' said McCally. 'The people in charge have secluded themselves on the island.'

'Why?'

'To stay out of reach, to prevent us from infiltrating, from getting information until whatever it is they're planning is finished.'

'So why do they want Chaney out?' said the agent.

'Maybe he's key to their plan.'

'And who killed Belden?'

'I don't know,' said McCally. 'Maybe Chaney. He had a lot of explosives training in the military.'

'But why?' said the agent.

'What, do you think I've got a Ouija board?'

The agent sat in one of the client chairs across from McCally's desk and rocked his head back, counting ceiling tiles as the lawyer finished scanning the report on the jailbreak.

'What's this?'

'Hmm?' The agent brought his gaze down and looked at him.

'It says here this wasn't the cell Chaney was assigned to.'

'Yeah. Can you beat it? Jail staff lets 'em move wherever they want within the unit. Fucking five-star hotel, and we get handed the bill.'

'Who's this guy, Chenko?'

'He's the other one, got out with Chaney. We're probably lucky they didn't allow a slumber party in the cell. We'd be hunting for fifty of 'em,' said the agent.

'It wasn't Chenko's cell either,' said McCally. 'Says here he was in on an immigration violation.'

The agent shrugged his shoulders as if to say, so what.

'So what do we know about him?' Suddenly McCally sat upright in his chair.

'Nothing beyond what's in the report.'

McCally looked at him. 'You still don't get it?'

'What?'

'Why would Chaney rob a bank and accept a packet of bait bills from the teller normally reserved for the mentally impaired, then within twenty-four hours after getting busted pick up with some guy in the county jail who speaks pidgin English and who's in the country illegally?'

The agent shrugged his shoulders. 'I don't know.'

'They weren't after Chaney,' said McCally. 'Get me everything you can find on this guy Chenko. If you have to, contact authorities in Moscow. Do it. See if he has any prior record. Find out his occupation.'

Friday Harbor, WA

George Hummel's file was missing. Joselyn was back at the open filing cabinet, rifling through it for records relating to other fishermen.

'Who is George Hummel?' Gideon was behind her, looking over her shoulder.

'He's one of my clients. There are five of them,' said Joss. 'All local fishermen with similar medical symptoms. I was looking for some kind of industrial causation, a link that would explain the condition and provide some financial recourse.'

What Joselyn held in her hand was a medical report. It had come into the office late the previous week. She hadn't had time to file it or to call Hummel. She had thrown it into a basket on her desk. Whoever trashed her office apparently had missed it, but the Hummel file was gone; so were the files of the other four fishermen.

'Can I see that?' Gideon gestured toward the paper in her hand, and Joselyn gave it to him. It was no time to make a stand at the bulwark of client confidence.

He read it quickly then looked up at her. 'When did these clients first come to see you?'

She thought for a moment. 'I don't know, maybe two months ago.'

He looked at the medical report, the brief description on the piece of paper under the heading SYMPTOMS: *Initial nausea and vomiting, anemia, rapid hair loss, intermittent and repetitive bleeding mostly from the gums and mucous membranes, periods of unquenchable thirst.*

'Where do these people work?'

'They're sport fishers. Some of them own boats; others work as chartered skippers.'

'They all work here on the island?'

'As far as I know.'

'And the boats, where are they kept?'

'Docked down at the harbor,' said Joselyn. 'Why?'

'Your clients are suffering from radiation poisoning,' said Gideon.

'How would they . . .?'

'I don't know. But you said this man Belden came to you out of the blue. You said you wondered why he hired you, why he picked you when he could have gotten a more experienced business lawyer down in Seattle.'

'That's right.'

'Maybe he didn't want an experienced business lawyer,' said Gideon. 'Maybe there was something else you had that he wanted – information about these clients. Maybe what he wanted to know was whether you had discovered the source of their illness.'

Joselyn thought about it. She remembered that Belden had asked her questions the first day she met him. George Hummel was in the office, and Belden saw him. He asked her about him, and tried to pry for details.

In an instant their eyes locked. 'We take my van,' said Gideon. 'I have some equipment.' Before he finished the words, he was headed for the door with Joselyn on his heels.

CHAPTER
TWENTY-TWO

Washington, DC

The president put the pen to paper and formed a single letter of his name. The motorized clicks of a hundred cameras echoed like crickets in the Oval Office.

With a smile he handed the pen to one of the congressmen standing behind his chair, picked up the next pen, and repeated the performance. The last pen was presented to the attorney general who thanked the president graciously, stepped back, and began the round of applause that brought the chief to his feet with a broad grin and handshakes all around.

'Mr President, if you have a moment when we're finished,' Abe Charness, the attorney general, whispered in his ear. He got a smile and a nod from his chief.

The little performance was the final chapter in a legislative package that did virtually nothing but was being hustled to the public as the administration's centerpiece for campaign finance reform. It would give folks back home the cozy feeling that something good was happening in Washington.

At the moment, the president was riding high in the polls, taking credit for an economy over which he had virtually no control. As a politician, he followed the first rule of medicine; do no harm. He coupled this with a lot of smiles and promises of vague new programs.

Two of his military aides and a couple of White House ushers herded the press toward the door. After they left, the president took a couple of minutes and chewed fat with some congressmen. Photos were taken of them shaking hands with the president in front of his hand-carved cherry desk. They would use the pictures in their upcoming campaigns. The last congressman smiled, then took his leave. Finally they were alone.

'Have a seat, Abe.' The president loosened his tie and undid the top button of his shirt. He was back in his doughnut phase, having put on twenty pounds since the last election.

'Someday I'd like to get a golden screen,' said the president, 'so I could lounge behind it in pajamas like the Empress Dowager, and whisper what I wanted done to some eunuch out front.'

'I'll build you the screen, Mr President. But I draw the line at cutting off my pecker.'

The president laughed. It was what he liked about Charness. What little ceremony the man stood on was grounded in some crude Georgia clay. They were both sons of the South, raised in families that eked out a living on the upper edges of poverty.

'Sit. Sit,' said the chief. They took up the same ends of opposing sofas across the coffee table in front of a fire that was still crackling.

'How's Jenny and the kids?' asked the president. The two men hadn't seen each other in three weeks. Charness had been at the Hague for a conference and had traveled trough Europe meeting several of his counterparts.

'Oh, they're fine.'

'I imagine the kids are getting big.'

'John's taller than I am,' said Charness.

'Makes us all feel like we're getting old.'

'You bet.'

'Well, what is it?' The president could tell something was bothering Charness.

'It's, ah . . . It's one of my assistants. Jim Reed. I think you know him.'

The president arched an eyebrow and thought for a second.

'Tall man, slender. A little sparse at the tree line,' said Charness.

'Oh, yeah. Sure. You brought him by for a cabinet meeting a few months ago.'

'That's the one.'

'Is there some problem?'

'I don't know. It seems Jim has been assigned to some team or special task force during the time that I was away. No one back at the office seems to know much about it, and when I talked to Jim he indicated he wasn't at liberty to discuss it.'

'What kind of team?'

'From what I understand,' said Charness, 'it was authorized by you.'

The president looked at him, an expression of surprise on his face. He shook his head as if he was at a loss.

'I think it operates under an acronym, ANSIR. I don't know what it means,' said the attorney general.

'Ah. That,' said the president. Suddenly he was filled with recognition, and a hearty smile, a lot of bluster. 'I didn't know what you were talking about. I'd forgotten all about it.'

Charness looked at him, an expression of interest filling his eyes. 'I figured there would be some explanation, Mr President. You can imagine my surprise when he told me he wasn't authorized to discuss it with me.'

'Oh, it's nothing. Nothing,' said the president. 'Probably be wrapped up in a week or so.'

'Can I ask what it's about?'

'Oh, one of the national security types brought something to his boss. It required a number of reviews including legal. I figured your people would be the best for the job, so I just told them to tap whoever they needed. I guess this Reed fellow was drafted.'

'It would have been nice if maybe I'd gotten a memo or something,' said Charness.

He was worried about turf, the eternal battle of every bureaucrat. 'Yeah, well I borrowed a few people from a dozen agencies. If I took the time to send memos to all of them, the task would be done before the memos went out. If your man Reed is taking too much time off the job, I'll tell them to let him go, find somebody else.' The president started to get up off the couch.

'No. No. That's not necessary, Mr President. I mean, if you need him, that's fine. Not a problem. We can pick up the slack.' What Charness really wanted to know was what was going on.

'Well, good.' The president wasn't telling him. 'Listen, we're gonna have to get together for dinner over here, just the two families,' said the president.

'We'd love it,' said Charness. The president had changed the subject, leaving his attorney general with nothing but heightened curiosity. He would have to pump other cabinet members to see if they knew anything, who on their staffs had been tagged for the ANSIR group.

'Is there anything else?' asked the president. He smiled.

The last one he needed with his nose under this particular tent was the attorney general. He was already aware of the president's false steps with Kolikoff, the acceptance of campaign money and the photos in front of his desk. Knowing Kolikoff, those pictures were probably already being used on labels to hustle some cheap brand of Vodka in Moscow.

Charness looked at the floor, then at his hands that were on his knees. He was hoping that if he sat there long enough the president would tell him why he was using one of his assistants.

The president looked at his watch. 'Got a reception in half an hour. Jesus, I wish I could get that screen. You sure you won't reconsider?'

Charness laughed and got up off the couch. The two men moved toward the door, the president with his hand on the attorney general's shoulder, making sure that he kept moving in the right direction.

'There is one other thing,' Charness added, as if he'd just remembered it himself.

'What's that?'

'It's probably nothing,' said Charness. 'Something that crossed my desk this morning. A report from my office in Seattle. Seems they've got an investigation going, dealing with some militia groups out in the northwest.'

'What else is new?' The president edged him toward the door, trying to get rid of him.

'This one may be a little different,' said Charness. 'There seems to be some basis to believe these people are shopping for weapons, something big, maybe out of the FSU.'

Like a flashing red light, reference to the term – Former Soviet Union – stopped the president in his tracks.

Suddenly Charness could tell that he had the boss's undivided attention. There was finally something he had that the man wanted to know.

'Like I say, it's probably nothing,' said Charness.

'No. no. Tell me about it.'

'Not much to tell. Just a brief report.'

'What did it say?'

The attorney general scrunched up his face like he was trying to remember. 'Oh, some group is holed up on an island. They seemed to be armed and waiting for the second coming. Probably just another group of nuts. As long as we don't overreact, wait them out, I'm sure it can be handled.'

'Is there a Russian connection?' said the president.

'Not with their government,' said Charness.

'That's not what I meant. You said there was information that this group might be trying to get weapons out of the former Soviet Union?'

'Well. Yeah, there seems to be some information that some of the people involved might be hired professionals.'

'What kind of weapons are we talking about?'

'One of these people, a mercenary of some kind, was killed in a small plane crash. They found a small item floating with the wreckage. Something called a dosemeter.'

The president gave an expression as if it meant nothing to him.

'It's what radiologists wear. That little piece of plastic with paper in the frame that they wear on the lapel of their lab coats. It's used to measure doses of radiation,' said Charness.

The president nodded.

'Like I say, it probably means absolutely nothing, but it was passed up the chain, and I thought I'd mention it.' Charness started to move toward the door.

'Maybe I should see the memo,' said the president.

'I can send it to NSA,' said Charness. He was talking about the National Security Agency. 'I don't want to bother you with it.'

'I think it might be a good idea. Why don't you send it over here. Fax it back when you get to your office. I'd like to look at it before we forward it on.'

'Sure. If you think it's important enough.' Charness opened the door and was headed out, past the little cubicle occupied by the president's press secretary.

'And, Abe.'

The attorney general turned around. The president was standing in the open door.

'Keep me posted if you hear anything more about this.'

Friday Harbor, WA

It was now dark. The only light came from a few vapor lamps that threw a yellow haze over the mist as it rose from the still waters of Friday Harbor. The ferry-boat dock was empty. There was one late-night run, but it wasn't due for more than an hour.

Over the last decade the commercial fishers had been decimated by fished-out salmon runs and large factory trawlers that prowled off the coast. The few sport fishing boats that were left clung to docks in slips out at the end, beyond the pleasure boats with their bright canvas dodgers and gleaming fiberglass hulls.

Gideon parked his van at the end of Front Street, across from the small building with a sign over the door; PORT OF FRIDAY HARBOR. The building was dark, except for one light outside over the door.

'These fishing boats that belong to your clients. Do you know where they are moored?'

'A general idea,' said Joselyn. She started to open the door to get out.

'Let me do this.'

251

'Why you?' said Joselyn.

'Because it may be dangerous.' Gideon moved quickly out of the vehicle and around to the other side.

'Tell me what you think is out there.' Joselyn wanted to know what they were facing.

'I don't know. I can't be certain.'

'But you have some idea.'

'It is based only on the information I have from my travels in Russia.'

Joselyn looked at him, waiting for an answer.

'We may be dealing with old nuclear devices. If I am correct, they date back to the early nineteen-sixties. Such weapons can be very dangerous.'

'You're talking about an explosion?'

'It is not what I am worried about.' Gideon knew that if some group intent on an act of terror had gone to the trouble of smuggling nuclear weapons into the U.S. they were not going to waste them on some isolated islands in Puget Sound. They had a more strategic target in mind. The question was where?

'I am concerned about oxidation,' he told her. 'Plutonium, when it is exposed to the air, turns to a fine powder. This powder is very toxic. It can be very dangerous.'

'And yet you're going to go out there.'

'I know what I am looking for. Besides I will take precautions.'

He opened the sliding door to the van. He had borrowed the vehicle from a friend who worked for the University of Washington, someone in the radiation lab he'd met years before. With the information he had gathered in Sverdlovsk, he knew he might need the equipment, and it was the only local source. Inside were a number of large metal boxes. On a hook was a yellow suit with a hood and what appeared to be a breathing apparatus that attached to the face mask.

'I only have one of these,' he said, pointing to the suit. 'Besides, if I get into any trouble out there, I will need someone back here on the docks to call for help.'

Joselyn looked at the boxes and the suit inside the van. She didn't like it, but what he said made sense.

'I'm coming at least inside the gate on the dock. I want to get as close as I can.'

'I want you out of harm's way,' he told her.

'I can't help you if I can't see you.'

Gideon agreed. Then he opened one of the boxes and took out a flashlight and another small device. Joselyn instinctively knew what it was, even though she had never seen one up close; a Geiger counter. He slung it over his shoulder by the strap attached, then grabbed the suit off the hook, and slid the door to the van closed. He started to walk toward the dock.

'What about the suit?' said Joselyn. 'Aren't you going to put it on?'

'Not yet.' He headed across the street and Joselyn followed him.

Washington, DC

It was nearly one in the morning when Sy Hirshberg reached the security kiosk leading to the West Wing of the White House. The uniformed secret service agent waved him through, and Hirshberg parked his car and walked quickly to the entrance.

There were a few lights on, even in the middle of the night. The West Wing never shut down completely. Hirshberg didn't stop at his office but headed to the southeast corner of the ground floor. A secret service agent stepped from the shadows of a room directly across from the Oval Office. He recognized Hirshberg, greeted him by name, but stood in the way until he checked a clip-board showing appointments for the president. This one showed that the president himself had cleared the appointment an hour earlier. The agent tapped on door to the Oval Office.

'Yes.'

The tone in the president's voice was not pleasant. Hirshberg had detected an air of crisis when the president called him at home after midnight. He sensed that whatever it was, it was important, and probably not good.

'Mr President.'

'Sy. I'm glad you got here.'

The agent stepped outside and closed the door to the office. Hirshberg had expected to find a dozen people, high level advisers closeted in crisis-mode inside the Oval Office. Instead the president was alone, sitting in front of the fire, reading papers, and making notes on little Post-its.

'What is it, Mr President?'

'A problem. A big problem.' Without looking up at Hirshberg, the president flipped a piece of paper from the top of the stack to the other end of the couch. Hirshberg crossed the room, picked it up, and read. It didn't take long.

'What I want to know,' said the president, 'is why I have to find this out for myself. You've got a team of people, all the resources of intelligence, the military, and law enforcement, and I have to find out by myself about this band of crazies holed up on an island in Washington State shopping for nuclear bombs.'

'Where did you get this?' said Hirshberg.

'From the attorney general. Seems they've had an investigation going on out in Seattle for some weeks now, based on information that home-militia groups were attempting to obtain a weapon of mass destruction and that criminal elements in Russia were attempting to fill the order.'

The president had a pile of paper in his lap. 'Grand jury transcripts,' he told Hirshberg. 'It makes very interesting reading. It's too bad the various agencies of the executive branch aren't sharing information. It's just a goddamned good thing I happened to meet with the attorney general today.'

Hirshberg bit his lip. He wanted to defend himself, to tell his boss that if he hadn't been so intent on covering his tracks following the embarrassment with Kolikoff, the cabinet would have been alerted. The Justice Department through the attorney general would have known about the sinking of the Russian ship off the Washington coast, the suspicion that it might have been carrying one or more weapons, and no doubt would have linked it with the information in their grand jury probe. Hirshberg looked at the date of the Justice Department report. They had now lost vital time.

'I want you to get your people on this now,' said the president. He lifted the mass of transcripts so that Hirshberg could gather them up. They were trailing paper onto the floor.

'Does this mean that we can come out in the open, involve other agencies, local government?'

'Hell, no,' said the president. 'I want you to read this stuff before morning. Call in whomever you need from your team. I want a briefing at eight o'clock in the morning, here. I want to know if Kolikoff's name appears anywhere in that transcript. Do you understand?'

Hirshberg was stunned. They were confronted with the possibility of a nuclear device loose somewhere in the United States and the president's first concern was whether it might lead to a political scandal in the White House.

'Mr President, I think we have to call in all of the appropriate civil authorities. There is a protocol that's been established for this very kind of situation.'

'No.' He looked at Hirshberg through intense, narrow slits of eyes.

'But, Mr President, knowing what we now know there is a good chance that these people have in their possession . . .'

'I said no. I'll be damned if I'm gonna have this thing splashed all over the front pages and played on an endless tape every half-hour on CNN. We don't know any such thing. All we know is that Justice has some kind of investigation going on out on the coast that may or may not lead anywhere. It's under investigation.'

'Mr President, we know that wreckage from the Russian ship was highly radioactive. We know that it went down somewhere off the coast of Washington State. We know from Russian sources that there has been a tremendous amount of radio traffic from this Siberian arms depot to Moscow and back. Now we have this.' Hirshberg cast a glance at the reams of paper that were now weighing him down. 'I think that we can be reasonably well assured that there is cause for serious concern. That some action is essential. At least let's find out what this militia group is doing out on the island.'

'You think the weapon might be on the island?'

'It's a possibility.'

'We need a map.' The president was up off the sofa, grabbed the phone and dialed the number for the Situation Room. 'Who's the duty officer tonight?' He spoke into the receiver, then waited a second.

'Monagan, this is the president. Get me a map. I'm in the Oval Office. I'm looking for area around the North Puget Sound in Washington State. There's an island.' He snapped his fingers twice and pointed to the papers in Hirshberg's arms, the grand jury transcripts, then put his hand over the phone and spoke to his national security adviser.

'The name of the island? It's in the transcript. I marked it with a purple margin sticker.'

Hirshberg fingered through the pile of paper until he found the marker. 'Padget,' said Hirshberg.

'Place called Padget Island,' said the president. 'Get me everything you can on it and deliver it here in five minutes.' He hung up the phone and headed back to the sofa.

'We gotta be careful here, Sy. I don't want to go off half-cocked. We can't even be sure there is a device.' The president was in denial.

'According to Oak Ridge there was enough contamination on the junk from that Russian ship to keep the glow on Yeltsin's nose going for the next thousand years,' said Hirshberg. It was a hard fact to ignore.

The president looked down at the carpet and took a long deep sigh. 'OK. All right. We'll put the island under surveillance.'

'Watching it through binoculars is not going to tell us what's going on,' said Hirshberg.

'What do you recommend?'

'We need to get somebody on the island. Eyes and ears,' said Hirshberg.

'I don't want some shootout, another Waco or Ruby Ridge.'

'I understand,' said Hirshberg. 'But if we don't move now and they have a device and they move it . . .' He didn't have to finish the thought.

They had worried for years about people like Saddam and Qaddafi getting their hands on weapons of mass destruction. Sail it into Seattle on a cargo ship or, better yet, up the East River and park it just off the U.N. Plaza and you could destroy half a city and cut off the head of

United Nations at the same time. Such a message would have a clear impact on world policy and the willingness of nations to form a united front.

The maps came from the White House Map Room, and a military aid spread them on the president's desk.

The president thanked the aide, and the marine left the room. The president and Hirshberg scanned the map and found Padget Island.

'It's not very big,' said the president. The map did not show any structures or streets. 'We could get aerial surveillance, some satellite photos.'

'It wouldn't do us any good. If the device is there, it's probably pretty small. Not likely we'd be able to see anything. And it would take time, and that we don't have. If the device is there we have to confirm it quickly and bottle up the island as fast as possible.'

'So what do we do?'

'I would suggest, Mr President, that we send in a small contingent, a platoon. Probably Navy SEALs,' said Hirshberg. 'We have them plant listening devices and cameras and then we take them off. A quick insertion, in and out. If it's done right, the people on that island will never know we've been there. Then we'll know what the hell's going on.'

The president had a long, drawn expression on his face. If shooting broke out on the island, he had visions of news crews with live cams on yachts taking it all in for CNN and the networks. Things could get quickly out of his control. Congress would start asking questions, and before he knew it Kolikoff's name would surface in connection with a nuclear bomb. Considering the lack of alternatives, however, there wasn't much choice.

'I don't want to go through the Joint Chiefs on this,' said the president. 'All we need is a story about some loose nukes in the country, and the Pentagon will be using it to beat me over the head with Congress to reinstate budget cuts.'

The administration had spent four years reducing the defense budget and closing bases around the world. Since the collapse of the Soviet Union, the military brass had been forced to sit quietly on the sidelines and take it. But there were those among the Joint Chiefs who would relish the opportunity to roast the administration for its lack of readiness. They would serve the president up on a platter to the press if they had a chance.

'This insertion on the island. Can you arrange it through your Navy rep on the ANSIR team?'

Hirshberg didn't like it. Presidential concerns over a scandal were now driving military policy. What if shooting did break out? What if it turned into a rout on the island and Navy SEALs were killed? The military leadership in the Pentagon would be outraged, and rightly so.

'The man's only a captain,' said Hirshberg.

'That's all right. I'll give him whatever authority he requires.'

'We'll need the cooperation of the SEALs down at Coronado. SEAL team one,' said Hirshberg.

'That can be arranged.' The president had him boxed. It was against Hirshberg's better judgment, but it was either avoid the normal chain of command, or do nothing. They had to find out quickly if the devices were in the country and, if so, where.

'If we're going to do it, we need to go in and set up intelligence on that island in the next twenty-four hours,' said Hirshberg. 'I don't know if they can be ready.'

'Let me handle that,' said the president.

Time was running. If there was a device, and the militia

group on the island had time to move it, the chances of finding it again were slim.

The president looked at him with a reluctant expression, took one more deep breath, then nodded. 'Then we're agreed. Twenty-four hours,' he said.

CHAPTER
TWENTY-THREE

Friday Harbor, WA

The damp night air seeped through Joselyn's clothing and chilled her to the bone as she and Gideon made their way to the gate leading out onto the floating dock at Friday Harbor.

Gideon kept a close eye on the Geiger counter's meter and listened for the telltale clicks of danger. So far all he got was mild background radiation, nothing that would indicate the presence of fissile materials.

At the gate, he stopped her. 'I want you to stay here.'

'The boats are way out there.' She pointed out into the dark distance. 'You won't know which boats to look for.'

She had given him the names of the vessels and a general description of their location on the docks. They would be with the sport and commercial fishers out near the end, near open water.

'It is too dangerous,' said Gideon. 'This is my job.' He was adamant. 'There is a cellular telephone in the van. If I am not back in ten minutes, call this number.' He pulled a card from his pocket and circled one of the telephone numbers on it with a pen.

'It is a special twenty-four-hour number at the institute. Use my name. Tell them what we know, about the sick fishermen and the boats. They will know what to do. Then call the police and have them cordon off the docks. Tell them not to allow anyone on or off and to wait for help.'

'But you'll be back by then,' said Joselyn.

'Perhaps.'

The way he said it caused Joselyn to think she might not be seeing him again. There was more danger than he was admitting.

'If you have to wait for these people from the institute to come up from California that could take hours,' said Joselyn.

'Trust me. They will know who to contact up here.'

'Shouldn't the sheriff come out and get you?'

'No. Just do as I ask. Please.'

'I will.'

'If I do not come back immediately, it may be because I do not want to spread further contamination. Not to worry,' he told her. 'I will move away from the source and wait for help. No one should be allowed to enter or leave the dock until the decontamination team arrives. Do you understand?'

'Yes.'

'Good.' He flipped on the flashlight and checked it. Then he looked at her one more time. 'If there is no problem, I will be back as quickly as I can.'

He headed down the ramp toward the slips farther out in the harbor. In his hand he held the list of the fishing vessels' names, printed in pencil by Joselyn on a scrap of paper she found in the van during their ride to the docks: *Martha's Desire*, *Skip Jack* and *Float Me A Loan*.

Joselyn stood on the dock, watching as he disappeared into the darkness beyond the reach of the big vapor lamp on the power pole overhead. When she could no longer see him, she began to pace the dock and wrapped her arms against her sides, hugging herself against the chill of the damp night air. Every few seconds, she would stop and strain her eyes for any glimpse of Gideon among the forest of masts and sea of boats. Less than a minute had passed since he left the gate and already it seemed like forever.

She looked at Gideon's van parked at the curb and tried to remember if they had left the door unlocked. If not, she would have to find a pay phone.

She looked at her watch again. She was worried that he would get lost out on the labyrinth of floating docks. She wondered why he hadn't put on the protective yellow suit before he headed out onto the docks.

She tried to take refuge in the fact that he knew what he was doing, that if there was anything out there, the Geiger counter would pick it up. By now, if there was radiation on the docks, the instrument should be recording something.

She waited a few more seconds then looked at the van. She checked her watch. Three minutes had elapsed. She could hear nothing except the creaking of the docks, the straining of mooring lines, and the occasional clang of hardware or the gong of a small bell somewhere in the distance as the boats bobbed in their berths.

The docks formed a labyrinth of dead-ends out on the water. Anchored in place by old wooden pilings, they rose and fell with the tide. What light existed was cast by the few boats that were live-aboards, inhabited year-round by their occupants. For the most part, the floating docks were lost in pools of darkness.

Gideon's flashlight had begun to flicker, perhaps the batteries were bad. He stopped for a second and checked the Geiger counter. It was still reading only mild background radiation. He tried to get his bearings and wondered if maybe he made a wrong turn at one of the intersections where the floating docks joined. He seemed to be mired in a sea of tall masts from sailboats, and large, extravagant crafts, some of them more than fifty feet in length. Most of the boats were dark, though in the distance he could hear the sound of a television set and see muted light from a salon below decks. It gave him a sense of confidence that at least he wasn't totally alone on the docks.

He looked back toward the port building. Situated as he was, behind a row of boats, he couldn't see the gate where he'd left Joselyn, though he could see the halo of light from the large overhead streetlamp.

He checked his watch. He had six minutes to find the boats or else get back to her before she called the institute. He tapped the flashlight against one of the pilings, and it flickered a little brighter.

He slung the yellow neoprene suit with its hood over his free shoulder. He wouldn't put it on until he had to. The hooded visor limited visibility and would quickly fog up with exertion. If he stepped off the dock in the dark it would fill with water quickly and take him to the bottom.

Gideon moved as fast as he could down the dock, counting boats as he went, straining his eyes, searching the distance. When he got to eighteen, the beam of his light ran out of concrete and suddenly reflected off of water. He'd come to the end. There were no sport fishing boats on this dock, and none of the vessel names he was looking for. He had to go back.

He checked his watch. Five minutes to go. Nothing on the Geiger counter. Gideon began to run, stepping over power lines that fed heat to the boats and kept them from freezing in winter. At a dead run he jumped the small cracks between the floating sections of dock and in less than a minute found himself at the main crossing dock.

Now he could look back up the dock and see Joselyn. She was still at the gate, though now she was pacing, not looking in his direction. He tried to catch her attention with the flashlight, but it was flickering, the batteries quickly dying. He turned it off to save power, then looked in the other direction out into the dark distance. The docks seemed to stretch forever before disappearing into inky blackness. Beyond, he could see the lights of houses on Brown Island, tiny and flickering in the cold night like stars in the heavens.

For a moment he hesitated, wondering if it wouldn't be wise to return to Joselyn up on the docks. He could get batteries for the flashlight and tell her to give him more time. The thought died in his mind as he transferred the strap of the Geiger counter from one shoulder to the other. The instrument suddenly picked up a slow rhythmic click as it cleared his body. The reading was coming from somewhere out in the darkness, toward the end of the dock.

By now Joselyn was freezing. She kept a constant eye on her watch. If he didn't return in four minutes, she would make the call. She assumed Gideon was looking at his own watch, that he knew how much time had elapsed and that if he didn't find anything he would come back before she called. That was a big assumption, and Joselyn knew it.

She looked at the gate leading down the ramp and toyed with the latch. Maybe she should join him on the docks? She hesitated. He had told her to wait. The tall Dutchman seemed to know what he was doing. If she went out there, she would only end up putting both of them in danger. She was torn. Joselyn wanted to help but couldn't. She was getting more angry with herself by the minute. Why hadn't she seen through Belden? He was the kind of man every woman should be able to read like a book; full of hype, full of himself, full of lies. God knows she'd had enough clients who had lied to her over the years. She should have seen Belden coming in a minute. He was too good to be true.

Suddenly Joselyn realized what it was that she liked so much about the tall Dutchman. She had known him for little more than twenty-four hours, but the difference was like day and night. Gideon van Ry was the very antithesis of Dean Belden: self-confident without being arrogant. He took the time to explain to her what he was doing and why. He didn't tell her what to do and try to manipulate in the way that many men do but reasoned with quiet persuasion, the kind of logic that could not be denied. It was not his looks so much as the way he treated her that made her suddenly wish he was standing back here on the docks next to her again.

She strained her eyes for any glimpse of the moving flashlight out on the docks. 'Where is he?' Without thinking she spoke the words out loud to herself and heard the echo of her voice off of the wooden siding of the port building. It was followed an instant later by what sounded like leather scraping gravel. She turned and looked toward the building, but couldn't see a thing. Bathed as she was in light from the vapor lamp, the building was lost in shadows. She shaded her eyes but still couldn't see anything.

'Hello.' She waited an instant. Nothing. 'Is somebody there?'

No one responded. Like a child in the dark, her imagination was now playing tricks.

She turned and looked back down the dock for Gideon. He was out there somewhere. She checked her watch; two more minutes and she would make the call.

The register on the Geiger counter was now giving up a steady stream of clicks, getting louder and more constant as Gideon moved down the dock toward open water. There were sleek pleasure crafts, gleaming *Grand Banks* and *Island Gypsies*, a large *Ocean Alexander* that rested at the dock and looked like the *Queen Mary*. There were private yachts that Gideon could not even dream of owning. As he moved further out the dock, they gave way to small craft, working boats with wooden hulls stained by rusted bolts and aging fittings. The floating docks changed from concrete to wood, some of the planks split and stained by oil. The neatly coiled power cables disappeared, as electric power was no longer present to fuel the boats' heaters. Most of the vessels were small, under forty feet in length, many of them with open cockpits and large live-bait tanks centered in the stern.

The meter on the Geiger counter was now registering a virtual constant flow of ionizing radiation. Gideon had to turn the volume down to hear himself think.

He was in little danger, at least for the moment. There were three principal means of protecting himself: time, distance, and shielding. He had the protective C-suit, which would provide shielding if he needed it, so now he had to factor in the other two – time and distance. Looking at the gauge on the Geiger counter, Gideon estimated that he should spend no more than four, possibly five, minutes in the area.

The radiation seemed to get more intense as he moved

toward the end of the dock. Now, even in the darkness, he could see the last four boats, each tied neatly in its slip. Across the long end of the dock on the outside, as if crossing the T, was a larger commercial fishing boat, a steel vessel that Gideon estimated to be close to fifty feet long.

The first boat in the slip to his right caught Gideon's eye. It was backed in and tied securely with spring line. On its stern the name in stenciled black letters: *Float Me A Loan*.

Gideon spun around and quickly looked at the small boat in the slip across from it: *Martha's Desire*, and next to it a small vessel, barely twenty feet long, the name *Skip Jack* lettered on the bow.

By now the Geiger counter was clicking incessantly, its meter tripping at times off the top end of the scale as Gideon moved it around over the surface of the dock. There were significant traces of radioactive contamination on the wooden dock itself. Gideon knew that the levels of radiation being recorded on the Geiger counter were not coming from plutonium. There was something else on the boat. Something emitting deadly levels of radiation that compounded the dangers of the device. He did not want to stay here long.

He moved the instrument toward the stern of *Float Me A Loan*. He was surprised when it failed to measure any increase in the count. Gideon moved along the side of the boat on the slip and the reading on the Geiger counter actually diminished.

He moved back toward the center of the dock and tapped the flashlight on wood trying to obtain light to read the meter. He got a flicker, a weak beam of light and moved toward the other two boats. Neither vessel seemed to register higher readings as he moved toward the slips and between them. Then the needle soared as Gideon came back onto the main dock and took a few steps toward the end. He looked up. There in front of him was the steel fishing trawler, her name etched in chipped and faded paint on the bow: *Dancing Lady*.

J oselyn was freezing. It had begun to drizzle, and she'd taken refuge under the eaves of the port office building. She strained for any glimpse of Gideon out on the dock but could see nothing except a forest of aluminum masts swaying in the quickening breeze, their halyard lines clanking against metal as the boats rocked. She had been here long enough to get the feel of the islands. A weather front was moving in.

She looked at her watch. Twelve minutes had now elapsed. She had given him two extra minutes. She prayed that he would come back, that she wouldn't have to make the call. She wanted to shout, to pull him back.

Joselyn was beginning to feel incredible guilt. There was no way she could have known Belden was involved with nuclear weapons. Still, she had allowed him to use her name and the address of her law office and in this way Gideon had been bound up in Belden's web.

Now whatever was out on that dock was Joselyn's fault. She had through her own stupidity and greed, brought whatever it was into the quiet tranquility of Friday Harbor.

She checked her watch once more, then reluctantly headed toward the van and the cellular phone. She turned one last time in the hope that maybe she would see him coming up the dock. Her mind was filled with thoughts of regret. I'll give him one more minute, she thought. Then I'll give him a piece of my mind. He had no right to put himself in danger. There were people who were paid to do this, people who worked for the government. The thought had barely entered her mind when regret followed it. She was thinking of these as nonentities, people who worked in dangerous jobs to protect the rest of us. They had families, too, people who cared for and loved them. She could feel the pulse in her throat and the pounding in her ears. Sensory perceptions were dulled by the feelings that raged within her so that she failed to comprehend the movement of shadow behind her, just beyond her shoulder at the corner of the building.

G ideon stepped over the railing near the stern of the *Dancing Lady* and onto her deck. A huge reel of netting occupied the fan-tail, and overhead two large booms forked high in the air and flared to either side of the vessel.

The meter on the Geiger counter spiked as Gideon moved forward around the wheelhouse. He took two more steps toward the forecastle area up on the bow, all the while watching the meter closely. The Geiger counter was now pulling in consistently high radiation readings. The audible clicks were rapid, constant, and loud, even with the volume turned down. Something had happened on this part of the deck that had turned it into a hot zone. If the device was armed with a plutonium/beryllium core, the radiation readings he was picking up from the boat were from something else. There was something besides the nuclear core with that bomb.

Gideon backed away, turned off the flashlight and set it on the deck, then began to put on the yellow C-suit. It was arranged like a jumpsuit. Gideon stepped into the pants, then pulled the top up and slid his arms into the sleeves. After he wrestled it over his shoulders he zipped it up the front, then finally put the hood over his head, sealing it with strips of Velcro around the neck.

The suit was not one of the more advanced models with a self-contained air supply under pressure. Now breathing became an exercise in endurance. Every breath had to pass through the fine micron filters that were built in to the face mask. Carbon dioxide had to be expelled and oxygen forced in. Gideon began to sweat, and the visor in the face mask began to fog.

There was a single hatch cover, closed and latched on the forecastle deck. Whatever was in there, or had been in there, was the source of radiation. Gideon was sure of it.

He looked down, searching for the flashlight he laid on the deck. Visibility through the mask was now a problem. There was no peripheral vision at all. He stooped over and felt around with his hands on the deck and finally located the flashlight. He pressed the button to turn it on and got nothing, then tapped it hard on the stainless steel railing in an effort to revive it.

That was when he heard it: a metallic clank that echoed his own, like something hitting against the hull of the boat. He stopped in his tracks, stood still, and looked back at the wheelhouse. He couldn't tell the direction from which the sound came. He struck the railing with the flashlight again and within three seconds heard a reply. This time it was sharper, more pronounced, metal-on-metal coming from the aft part of the vessel somewhere below decks. On the back side of the wheelhouse, facing the aft deck was a cabin door. He guessed that this led down to the engine room and whatever accommodations passed for living quarters.

Quickly he moved to the cabin door, opened it, and shone the feeble beam of the flashlight on the Geiger counter. It was registering only half of the radiation he'd picked up on the forecastle deck. Here he was shielded by the steel structure of the wheelhouse. Inside was a ship's ladder, leading down into the bilge and engine room.

Gideon cast the beam of the light down in the direction

of the ladder and peered into what seemed a bottomless pit. Between the faltering batteries of the flashlight and the fogged face mask, he was nearly blind. He gripped the railing on the ladder, stepped over the threshold, and began to climb down. He went down only one step and turned, then felt around with his hand on the inside of the bulkhead near the door. If there was a light switch, it would be here. He found it mounted on the bulkhead and turned it. Nothing.

Someone had either turned off the gen-set, or else it had run out of fuel. Without a generator or shore power, there were no lights. Gideon knew just enough about boats to know this was trouble. If there were no lights, there was no power for the bilge pumps. Vessels always took on water somewhere, slow leaks in the packing around the drive shaft and through the hull fittings. Depending on how long the power had been out, the bilge and lower holds could be filling with water.

Blinded and weighted down by the suit could be a problem. He looked down the dark ladder and then proceeded slowly, a step at a time. He held the flashlight out in front of him, not that it was much use.

A dense cloud of blue vapor danced in the beam from his light and settled just under the overhead deck. Gideon put the Geiger counter up toward it and took a reading. The needle on the gauge didn't move. It was holding steady in the low to mid ranges, nothing as hot as the forecastle deck and the sealed hold up front.

Tentatively Gideon broke the seal on the Velcro around his neck and lifted the lower flap of the hood. What he breathed was not fresh air, but it was more cool than the CO_2 trapped under stifling hood. It was tinged with a foul stench of diesel fumes.

He lifted the hood off his head and directed the beam of

his flashlight down the ladder. It shimmered off the surface of oily water.

'Hello. Is anybody here?' Gideon's voice echoed off the walls of the steel chamber.

Instantly the reply came, again in the clang of metal against the steel hull. It emanated from somewhere behind him toward the stern.

He stepped down into the water, still clinging to the ladder, standing on rungs. With the light, he could see only a few feet out in front of him. Gideon looked down onto the oily surface but couldn't tell how deep it was. Now the neoprene suit presented a hazard. If he slipped, and fell in over his head, or stepped into an open and flooded hatch, the suit would quickly fill with water. In the dark, without a clear sense of direction, weighted down by the suit he could quickly drown.

He stepped down one more rung, still no bottom, then another. On the third step down, he finally hit a flat surface. He was now well above his knees in water. With one hand still clinging to the railing of the ladder, he took a tentative step away. He appeared to be in a narrow companionway that spanned the center of the vessel from bow to stern.

Gideon took a chance, let go of the ladder, and began sloshing toward the stern, down the short companionway in the direction of the last metallic echo on the hull.

'Hello.' He listened. The signal of clanging metal was now being repeated as if in desperation, though the rhythm seemed erratic and without energy.

'Here.' Gideon could hear a voice, weaker than the beam of his own flashlight but still audible.

'Where are you?' he called back.

'Here.'

Gideon took a reading on the Geiger counter. It was well below what he'd received on the forecastle deck; still time was running. By now Joselyn should have made the call. He'd been wise to leave her behind. Help was on its way.

To the right along the companionway was a cabin door.

'Keep talking so I can hear you.' Gideon listened. Nothing.

He looked with the flashlight as far as he could see down the companionway before the beam disappeared in a film of fumes and darkness.

'Here.' The voice was breathless but close. It came from further down the companionway. A few feet farther on was an open door. Gideon peered inside and flashed the light around. It was a small galley, a table that was just above water and a propane stove with two burners. Water sloshed around inside, and remnants of food, some waterlogged slices of bread, floated on the surface.

He headed back down the companionway. Within five feet he came to another door. This one was closed. He tried the handle. The water had swelled the wood in its frame and jammed the door. He put his shoulder into it and heard the wood panel in the center of the door begin to splinter. He hit it again, this time with his full weight. The door buckled and broke. His foot hit the threshold and Gideon nearly fell through the opening into the water on the other side. Somehow he managed to stay upright and flashed the light inside. He peered through the darkness. In the distance, against the bulkhead on the far wall, was a double bunk bed, upper and lower. The lower bunk was several inches under water.

As he watched through the flickering beam of light, a form moved under the blanket on the top bunk. Quickly Gideon stepped over the threshold and sloshed his way across the cabin.

He held up the flashlight and lifted the blanket back. Gideon wasn't ready for the vision that awaited him. It was only arguably human. The hair was completely gone from the head and lay in tufts like molting fur on the pillow. There was a stench emanating from the bunk that overpowered even the fouled air of diesel fumes. Gideon wanted to put the hood back over his head, but he knew if he did he wouldn't be able to see.

The pathetic form on the bed was bleeding from the mouth and nose, dark frothy blood that Gideon knew was coming from deep in the lungs. It formed a pool on the mattress in which the man now rested.

His eyes looked pleadingly up at Gideon. 'Water. Water.' He seemed able to repeat only the one word.

Gideon was no physician, but it did not require a medical degree to tell that this man would never make it to a hospital. He was dying. Gideon knew he had no more than a few minutes.

'Who are you?'

'I need a drink. Water.'

Gideon looked quickly around the cabin. In one corner was a table, high enough to be above the water. On it was a stainless steel pitcher. He made his way to it around a pillow and small stool floating in the water.

Suddenly he felt a lurch as the vessel tilted toward the stern, the weight of the engines drawing it down. She was taking on more water. The *Dancing Lady* was slowly sinking.

There was no water in the pitcher. Quickly Gideon made his way through seawater that was now creeping up his thigh. He moved from the cabin down the companionway and back to the boat's galley. The fresh-water tanks should still be watertight, he thought. The question was how he would get water without a functioning pump. He turned the tap and gravity emptied enough water from the pipes into the pitcher to put about three inches in the bottom.

It was not much more than a small glass. More than that would probably kill the man in any event.

Gideon made his way back to the cabin. When the man saw the pitcher of promised water, he expended his last spark of energy, straining toward the pitcher, trying to raise his body.

'Easy. Easy,' said Gideon. 'Slowly.' He knew the man would choke to death if he swallowed too quickly, and there was no more to give him once this was gone. He held the man's hands down and fed him a few drops of water slowly from the pitcher.

The man began to hyperventilate and cough.

Gideon removed the pitcher from his lips just in time to prevent being flooded with a froth of dark venous blood.

This dripped down the man's chin, and Gideon wiped it gently with a corner of the blanket.

'Who are you?' asked Gideon.

'My name is Jon Nordquist. My boat,' he said. He was breathless. 'Water.'

'In a moment. Where is the device? Is it up forward in the hold?'

The man used what energy he had to turn his head slowly from side to side only once. 'It's gone.'

'Where?'

'I don't know.'

'What happened?' said Gideon.

'It . . .' His voice faded. He regrouped. 'It opened. The casing.'

'The fissile materials were exposed to the air?'

The man lowered his chin as if to nod. 'Yes.'

'They took it in that condition?'

'Water.'

Gideon was now using the pitcher as incentive, trying

to keep the man alive long enough to find out what had happened. He gave him a few more drops of water.

The man choked them down, and coughed up a little more blood.

'Did the men who took the device handle the fissile materials inside?' If they had, Gideon knew they would be in the same condition as Nordquist, perhaps a few days less advanced, but dying none the less. If they were lucky, any plan they had for a bomb might die with them.

'Did they handle it?' Now Gideon pressed.

'No. Over the side,' said Nordquist. 'My son put it over the side.'

'Where?'

'At sea. Broke open on the deck,' said Nordquist. 'My boy is dead.'

It was a cryptic picture, but Gideon understood. Somehow the casing of the Russian artillery shell broke open. Plutonium, along with the beryllium reflectors inside the bomb, had toppled out onto the deck. Beryllium was a magic metal, lighter than aluminum, stronger than steel, and very expensive. It was prized for its role in inducing critical mass in a nuclear weapon. A beryllium reflector used to surround the plutonium core would reflect neutrons back toward the core, multiplying the chain reaction and hence the power of the bomb.

They were only fishermen, with no training in the handling of nuclear weapons. Beryllium dust in the lungs was deadly. It resulted in berylliosis, in which the lungs closed down and the victim choked to death. Under the circumstances, the fishermen had the presence of mind to do the only thing they could. They put the nuclear core over the side.

'Is that why the forecastle is radioactive?'

'Rolled around,' said Nordquist.

That explained part of it. The device had probably already started to oxidize in the bunker at Sverdlovsk. Once it was free, rolling on the deck, abrading against the rough surface of the wooden deck, it would have left a trail of plutonium dust like a snail's track. The crew had breathed it in, along with beryllium dust, trying to catch the elusive silvery sphere as it rolled around the pitching deck. But there was something even more deadly present. No amount of salt water or solvent could cleanse the boat, not with the readings that the Geiger counter had detected.

'More water,' said Nordquist.

'Was there a second device?' said Gideon.

'Water.'

Gideon gave him a little more, and Nordquist lurched into a coughing spasm. For a moment, Gideon thought he would expire. He put one hand behind the man's back and eased him up so that gravity might help clear his lungs and the blood might run to his stomach. It took several seconds but it worked.

'Were there two bombs?' asked Gideon.

The man was breathless, his eyes glazed. Gideon had seen the pallor of Nordquist's face only once in his life, on a cadaver in a science course in college.

'You must tell me. Was there a second bomb?'

Nordquist struggled to breathe, speaking only as he exhaled, between parted and parched lips the word that Gideon dreaded: 'Yes . . .'

'Where is it?'

Nordquist was suddenly silent.

Gideon moved the pitcher to his lips, but the water merely formed a rivulet down the man's chin onto his chest. Van Ry studied the man's open eyes and realized that he was staring from the fixed gaze of death.

*   *   *

She had given him almost twenty minutes. Joselyn couldn't wait any longer. He had a watch and a flashlight. She had to assume that whatever he found out on those boats was not good, otherwise he would have signaled her from the docks or come back. She was worried that perhaps she had already waited too long.

She turned and headed for the Dutchman's van at a run. She skipped over the curb and passed the corner of the port building. The only sensation was the sweep of air an instant before the leaded-leather sap connected with the base of her skull. Joselyn never felt the impact of the concrete as her head hit the sidewalk.

CHAPTER
TWENTY-FOUR

Inbound, San Juan Archipelago

Captain William Conners didn't like it. The orders had not come down through the SOC (Special Operations Command), the normal chain. Instead they had been routed out of Washington, high up in the Pentagon.

Conners had never seen anything like it before. In his view, it was not only unusual but dangerous. Still, nobody was asking for his views. He wondered who in the chain of command knew what was happening.

He and the other four men on his team would have no real logistical support. There would be no patrol boats for insertion and extraction. A slow fishing trawler was supposed to pick them up, a vessel that couldn't move faster than nine knots if it came under fire.

Conners looked at his watch. The Lockheed C-130 Hercules was five hours into its mission, out of the Naval Air Station in San Diego. Three of his men were asleep in reclining flight chairs, the same kind used on commercial jets, only in this case they were bolted to the floor up front in the cargo bay, down under the ladder leading to the flight deck.

Another thirty-five minutes and they should be over the drop zone.

'What's the weather looking like?' Conners cupped a hand to his mouth and shouted over the roar of the four huge Allison turboprops.

The flight engineer had just come down the ladder. He was doubling as load master for this trip and getting things ready for the drop.

He gave Conners a thumbs-up. 'Clear. Light winds at the surface. Shouldn't be any problems.'

That was easy for the flight crew to say. They didn't have to jump out into a jet-black sky at twenty thousand feet over open water cold enough to induce hypothermia in a matter of minutes. If his men couldn't find the inflatables in the dark sea, they would drown, even with tanks and fins and clothed in wetsuits. Whoever planned this one had shit for brains, and Conners knew it.

The so-called HALO (High Altitude-Low Opening) jump was something that might provide great cinematic effect in a James Bond flick. But Navy SEALs who put their bodies on the blocks in combat knew it was insane, especially at night.

'What are you calling light winds?' said Conners.

'Five, maybe seven knots,' said the engineer. He was now busy with the gear, unlashing it and getting it near the rear cargo ramp.

Conners followed him. 'Seven knots!'

'Tops,' said the guy.

Conners knew that this could be enough to whip up whitecaps on the surface. He checked his tide charts. The northern reaches of Puget Sound could be treacherous. The tidal pull in the narrow channels between the islands could suck a man out into the Pacific quicker than some cruise liners.

Calculating the tides and currents and the wind drift during freefall, Conners estimated their drop point to be a quarter-mile west of Padget Island. If they hit it within half a mile, they would consider themselves lucky.

The island was a dot of land, a half-mile wide by a mile long. There was a single rocky beach on its western shore. The other three sides faced the water with sheer cliffs that would require climbing gear. This was not included in their equipment or their briefing, leaving little margin for error.

The plan called for using the tidal flood to reach the island. Motors were out; too much noise. Timing was critical. The incoming tide would last for only two more hours. If they missed it and failed to reach the island before the tide turned, the out-going flood would pull them toward the Strait of Juan de Fuca. There would be no way they could paddle fast enough to stay out of its grip. Beyond the strait was the North Pacific, one of the roughest bodies of water in the world. It was not something you wanted to ride in an open inflatable raft.

'What's the drop altitude?' asked the engineer.

'Seventeen thousand,' said Conners.

'And your opening?'

'Three hundred feet.'

'They couldn't pay me enough,' said the engineer. He adjusted the altimeter on the large cargo parachutes, so that they would trigger to open at five hundred feet. Deploying at five hundred, the chutes would not open fully for another two hundred feet. If the loads hit the water too hard it would dislodge the flotation, sending the packages to the bottom, perhaps leaving the men to die in the water.

In the dark, dropping like bullets through the cloud deck, none of them would know where the rest of the team was. Breathing from their scuba tanks, they would freefall at speeds approaching one hundred and thirty miles per hour for more than a minute and a half. At three hundred feet they would pop their chutes and drop into the sea. They would have just enough time to slow their descent before hitting the water. They would be visible in the air for less than ten seconds. The plan was intended to minimize the chances of detection by sentries on the island. It also increased greatly the team's risk factor. Night drops into the sea often met with casualties. Usually these were the result of accidents rather than combat.

The cavernous cargo bay was nearly empty, except for the two small pallets containing the inflatables and the listening gear along with cameras to be planted on the island. There were small arms, automatic weapons, and supplies of ammunition in the event of trouble, though Conners had been briefed. He knew that in a fire fight they would be outgunned. The men on the island had fifty-caliber weapons. It wasn't known whether they were full automatic.

The pallets were dragged to their position near the rear ramp. The men themselves would jump from one of the two doors on either side of the aircraft behind the landing-gear fairings.

With eight minutes and counting, Conners got his men up and started final checks on their gear, the regulators on their tanks, the seal around their face masks.

At six minutes, the warning light on the cargo bay bulkhead went on and the flight engineer donned his face mask for oxygen. The team would breathe from their compressed-air diving tanks.

Conners tapped the altimeter on his wrist and checked his compass.

At three minutes, the whine of hydraulic motors kicked

in and a yawning ramp at the rear of the plane opened. As the shape and control surfaces of the giant C-130 changed, it began to buffet, porpoising through the thin, high atmosphere.

The flight engineer opened one of the side doors and removed it. Now the rush of wind filled the cargo bay. Conners lined his men up at the door. Then the green light. One by one, they jumped from the door, falling like stones through the cold night air.

Conners was the last. He felt the cut of air like a dozen knives as it hit the flesh of his face and forehead between the diving mask and the hood of his wetsuit. He tried to breathe normally from the mouthpiece as his body experienced the giddy weightlessness of freefall. In the dark, with no point of reference, it was easy to relax, to go too far and blow past the safety point. If it happened, the jumper would never know it. Hitting the water at more than one hundred miles an hour, the human body would explode like a water balloon hitting concrete.

Conners kept a tight eye on his altimeter. He heard the pop of a chute, like a rifle shot, as he flew past and continued to drop. If his altimeter was working, they were at two thousand feet. They hadn't hit the water, and already there was a problem. He wondered if it was one of his men or one of the giant cargo chutes.

He dropped through the cloud deck, and suddenly there were lights. In the distances he could see the glitter of a small town spread out in front of him. He checked his compass. He was facing east. He bent his knees and dropped his torso, spinning his body half a turn. Now he was facing Padget Island. All he could see below was the darkness of the sea. Off in the distance were lights of a large refinery. That would be ARCO. It was a marker for the pilot.

Six hundred feet. He put his hand on the ripcord. Three seconds later he pulled it. The black Jedi Knight chute exploded above his head, jerking his body to a stop like a rag doll. The delta canopy overhead, with its steering shroud lines, allowed him to maneuver if only for a matter of seconds. Conners used the time to orient himself toward the island. He was looking at his compass, then suddenly saw the fluorescence of the sea an instant before he hit the water.

He went under immediately. The trick now was not to get tangled in the chute or the shrouds. In the water, with any kind of current, it could drag you down. Even with the right gear, using engineered releases, it was possible to be dragged through the water by tidal rips and towed into deep, pressure-crushing trenches by falling cold water currents.

Conners hit the release on his harness. It popped open. Quickly he swam away from the lines. The chute was weighted around the seams so that it would slowly sink.

Conners got to the surface and cleared his mask. He tasted the brine around his mouth as he spit the mouthpiece out and bobbed in the water. There were small whitecaps forming, wind blowing in a westerly direction. He could hear one of the men calling. Each of them had a small light mounted on the shoulder of their suit. It emitted an intense halogen beam. Conners could see two flickering beams, like Tinkerbell bobbing in the distance. He lowered his mask and bit into the mouthpiece, then lowered his face in the water and began to kick. It took him several minutes swimming against the current to reach the other two men. They were struggling with one of the floating cargo pallets. It was still attached to the cargo chute.

Conners lifted his face mask and spit out his mouthpiece.

'What's the matter?'

'We can't get it to release.'

The parachute had filled with water and was acting as a massive sea anchor. It was going down and hauling their gear with it. The men were hanging on, trying to buoy it.

Conners pulled his diving knife from a sheath on his ankle, grabbed some of the shroud lines in a bundle, and cut them. The chute immediately released its load of water, like a sail spilling wind, and the floating pallet righted itself.

One of the SEALs opened a canister and removed the metal oars while Conners cut the line binding the inflatable raft and the other man popped the pin. In less than a minute, the raft filled with compressed air.

By now they were all bobbing in the sea, whipped by wind-driven whitecaps. Two of the men tumbled into the raft while Conners lashed the floating pallet with the gear to an aft line and climbed aboard. They stowed their tanks in the bottom and removed the fins from their feet while they continued to scan the sea for the other two men.

There was nothing but the dark sea and the black night sky. Conners looked at his watch.

'How long can we wait?' one of them asked.

'We can't,' said Conners

'But they're out there somewhere.'

'I know.'

'They could be in trouble.'

'I'm aware,' said Conners. He looked in the direction of the island. He could see a dim outline in the distance and hear the crash of a mild, wind-driven surf on rocks or a beach. Soon the emerging rays of dawn would silhouette the island and light up the surface of the sea.

'If they're behind us, we can't get to them. If they're between us and the island, they should be all right.' Even without the raft, Conners was confident they had come very close to the drop point. They could swim to the beach if they had to.

They continued to scan to the east for flickering signs of the halogen shoulder lamps. But there was no sign.

'We can't stay here, and we can't go searching for them.' Conners knew they would only exhaust themselves paddling against the tide, searching in the dark. When the sun came up, they would be caught out on open water. If the men on the island were as dangerous as Conners had been led to believe, three divers in an open raft would be dead meat. The rest of the team would have to find the other raft and make it on their own. The three men in this raft were now a SEAL team, and they had a mission.

'We'll find 'em on the beach,' said Conners. 'Now let's paddle.'

San Juan Channel

Joselyn was bleeding from the nose, and the base of her skull had a lump the size of a goose egg. Even without touching it she could feel it as her head bounced against something hard. She came to in the bottom of a small boat running at high speed on choppy water. Her hands were tied behind her back, her eyes covered by a cloth blindfold that did not entirely do its job. She could peek under the corners and get glimpses of the dark space into which they had jammed her body, a kind of cuddy cabin below decks. The pressure of the knot from the blindfold at the base of her neck caused even more pain in her head.

Periodically she could hear male voices somewhere outside, shouting above the roar of the engine as it churned and whined through the swells.

Joselyn had lost all sense of time. She had no idea how long she'd been unconscious. She was lying in bilge water and breathing gasoline fumes. Between the throbbing in her head and the ceaseless motion of the boat, nausea began to overtake her. Joselyn was ready to retch when suddenly the engine eased and the boat begin to surf in its own wake. A couple of seconds later there was a solid thud against the hull. The boat stopped dead in the water, its only motion now caused by its own wake as it bobbed against a dock, or a larger boat. Joselyn wasn't sure.

'Where is she?' This time the voices came from outside the boat.

'Down below.'

'Bring her up to the house. We don't have much time. Only twenty minutes before Thorn and Taggart have to leave. Thorn doesn't want to go before he knows what's up.'

Joselyn heard something like a cabinet door open somewhere behind her, and suddenly the murmur of voices got louder. She went limp as if still unconscious.

Something poked or kicked her. It felt like a foot.

'Come on. Get up.' He poked her arm.

She still didn't move.

'She's still out. Sure you didn't kill her?'

'I didn't hit her that hard.'

'That's fine. You can carry her.'

Someone grabbed her around one ankle and dragged her several inches across the rough wooden bottom of the boat. Joselyn offered no resistance though the wood caused an abrasion on her arm.

'You get her arms. I'll take her feet.'

'Just pick her up. She can't weigh more than a hundred and twenty pounds.' The other voice sounded exasperated.

Suddenly Joselyn felt a strong set of arms behind her knees and across her back. She went limp in the man's arms, and he lifted her easily. She allowed her head to hang back, though the pain was intense. Her mouth was open, her eyes only partially closed under the cloth that covered them. As long as they thought she was unconscious, Joselyn sensed she was safe. They wanted her for a reason, information they thought she had, otherwise they would have dumped her body over the side out in the Sound.

Whoever was carrying her moved quickly. With her head hanging back, draped over the man's arm, she was able to catch glimpses of light and see figures passing as she heard his footsteps move along the wooden dock.

'They're waiting up at the house.'

'They're gonna need smelling salts.' The man carrying her was talking now.

'Maybe they got some ammonia.'

'Look and see.'

They started to climb stairs, stone or concrete, Joselyn wasn't sure, but they were steep and there were a lot of them. The man began to breathe heavily. She could hear more voices now, and see lights. Under a corner of the blindfold, she caught a passing glimpse of a porch under a roof and lighted windows, lots of windows.

Somebody got the door for them. She couldn't see who without moving her head, but when it opened the voices got much louder. There was a lot of shouting.

'Listen, don't you tell me. I was the one who said we should deep-six the trawler and the fishermen with it.'

'Yeah, right, Charlie.' Now that he was in the room, the guy carrying her was getting into it. 'You were the one said he drowned the woman here. On the ferry, remember?'

'I pushed her off. Whadda ya want?'

'Heaviest fuckin' ghost I ever saw.' The man carrying her was huffing and puffing.

'I got the goddamn car.'

'Well shit, let's call the auto club and report the crime.'

'Listen, asshole, I suppose you coulda done better.'

'My six-year-old niece coulda done better.'

'Now we got the Feds crawling all over the docks, talkin' to God knows who . . .' Now other men in the room were getting into it. Joselyn couldn't see their faces.

'We don't know it was the Feds.'

'Who the hell else would it be?'

'Where do you want me to put her?' The guy carrying Joselyn was still trying to catch his breath.

'Put her in the bedroom at the end of the hall.'

As he carried her down the hall, she could hear the argument continue.

'Why didn't they get the guy?'

'He was out on the docks.'

'What, you're afraid to go out there?'

'Damn right. Fuckin' stuff'll light you up like neon. You haven't seen the fishermen coughing up their lungs, have you?'

'Show some hair, why don't ya.'

'I don't mind showing it. I just mind losing it.'

'I told you we should have got some of those rubber suits.'

'You and your fuckin' rubber suits.'

'I'm telling you we ought to get the hell off this island before the Feds show up. You can be sure they know what's goin' on.'

'And how would they know that?' This time it was

a different voice. Suddenly there was silence in the room down the hall, like someone had thrown water on a fire.

'I just meant we should get off the island while we still had a chance.'

'You sound like maybe you know something the rest of us don't.' It was the voice that had quelled the argument. There was something strangely familiar about it. Joselyn couldn't see his face without moving her head to look down the hall. She was playing possum as long as she could.

'No. I don't know anything.'

'You seem to be awfully worried about the federal government,' said the voice.

'There is reason to be worried. This woman . . .'

'The woman is not with the federal government.'

'Yeah, but the guy with her.'

'I doubt if he's with the federal government either.'

'How do know that?'

'If the federal government thought there was a weapon of mass destruction out on that dock, do you think they would have sent one man to check it out, with a woman to stand guard at the dock?'

'I don't know.'

'Trust me. There would be two hundred armed troops on that dock and two dozen men in haz-med suits crawling all over every boat moored out there. What we have here is the stuff of amateurs.'

Now there was some chuckling in the room.

'You worry too much. You should learn to relax. You'll live longer.'

'Yeah, Charlie. Relax.'

The voices receded into the background as Joselyn was carried down what seemed like a long hallway.

The man wedged her body against a wall and leaned against her with his weight as he freed one hand and opened the door.

He crossed the room and dropped her on the bed like a sack of potatoes. She fell limp and loose, bouncing with the springs. She heard his footsteps recede across the room toward the door.

'You musta fuckin' brained her.' Another voice in the doorway. 'You better hope she's not dead. Thorn wants to talk to her.'

'Fuck Thorn and the horse he rode in on. I'm getting a little tired taking all his crap.'

'Well, maybe you should tell him.'

They closed the door, and Joselyn heard the key turn in the lock. She lay still on the bed for almost a minute, listening to the voices in the other room. Every once in a while, she could make out a word or two.

The room was dark. She could see little triangles of wallpaper and part of the ceiling through the space under the blindfold where her cheek met her nose. She lay motionless, listening for the sound of breathing to make sure she was alone in the room before she moved on the bed.

Finally satisfied, she rolled over, hooked one leg over the edge of the bed and with some effort sat up. By tilting her head back, she could scan the room from under the blindfold. It was a large bedroom, and whoever owned it had money. There was an adjoining bathroom and what looked like a marble floor.

Joselyn stood up. For an instant she began to weave in circles, dizzy from the blow on the head. She steadied herself by bracing her legs against the side the bed. She slowly took a step, then another. She made her way across the bedroom, her head tilted back, peeking under the blindfold so that she didn't run into a wall or trip over furniture.

She stopped in the bathroom doorway. She could see a light switch, a large plastic toggle with its own light built in so you could find it in the dark. She could have hit it with her shoulder, but they might see the light under the door or through the window on the porch outside.

Joselyn moved to the sink and turned her back. With tied hands she pulled open the top drawer. She fished around inside; a comb, a brush, something that felt like a mirror.

She turned around and peeked down into the open drawer. Somewhere there should be a pair of scissors, anything sharp to cut the cord around her wrists. She couldn't see well enough in the dark.

She heard footsteps coming down the hall. Joselyn slammed the drawer shut and in five giant steps raced back to the bed throwing her body onto it and turning her head to the wall an instant before the key turned in the lock. The door opened and a moment later the light came on.

'Leave me alone with her.' It was all he said before the door closed.

She waited. It seemed forever. Joselyn didn't move, but lay as if she was unconscious on the bed. Then she heard his footsteps moving closer to the bed. She felt his weight on the mattress as he moved behind her and untied her hands. She closed her eyes tight, and he undid the knot on the blindfold and slipped it from her face. It wasn't until he ripped the tape from her mouth that she moved.

'You can open your eyes now.'

That familiar voice. He knew she wasn't unconscious.

The game was up. She turned her head and squinted in the light, having difficulty focusing, and moved one hand up to shade her eyes. He appeared as a dark silhouette, the features of his face lost in shadows cast by the bright overhead light in the room.

She rubbed her eyes. He stepped back from the bed. Joselyn fought the dumbstruck expression as it crept across her face. He was staring at her with that same smile – the arrogant grin he had left her with on the dock as he climbed into the plane.

'You are surprised to see me?' said Belden.

'You were . . .'

'Dead?'

She nodded.

'The brain accepts what the eye beholds,' said Belden.

'But I saw the plane.'

'I had to do something. Your government had a great many questions to which I did not have very many good answers. You can appreciate my predicament. It seemed the easiest thing was to become dead.'

'But the plane?'

'A simple matter of electronics, some explosives. Of course I had to wait until you reached the dock. You did take your time. For a while there I was afraid you weren't going to come. It wouldn't do to have an explosion without a witness. Someone who actually saw me climb aboard, who could identify the victim for the police. Who better than my own lawyer?'

'That's why you hired me?'

'No. No. You should have a higher regard for yourself than that. I came to you because you were a good lawyer. In fact you were a little too good. You were getting a bit too tenacious on behalf of some of your clients.'

She looked at him with a puzzled expression.

'The fishermen. We knew they were sick. What we didn't know was whether they had information as to the source. Whether they knew about the *Dancing Lady*.'

'The what?'

'Of course,' said Belden. 'You don't know about that. No doubt, by now your friend out on the dock does, however. By the way, who is he?'

'Someone who is going to get you into a great deal of trouble,' said Joselyn.

'Oh. I am relieved. I thought perhaps he was trouble himself. No doubt, you heard our discussion in the other room.'

She shook her head.

'Oh yes. I forgot. You were sleeping.' He smiled at his own humor. 'Can I get you something to drink?'

She shook her head again, though she was dying of thirst.

'There is no need for us to make this unpleasant. Some of the men outside are, shall we say, not in a good mood. They have concerns about your friend, the tall blond one on the dock. I thought perhaps you could allay their fears.'

'No problem,' said Joselyn. 'He's with the marines. The rest of them were busy getting their helicopters warmed up.'

Belden gave her an expression of regret. 'Is he with the government?'

'Yes.'

He reached across the bed and slapped her across the face.

'No.'

He slapped her again with the back of his hand.

'Maybe.'

He slapped her again, this time much harder.

'Who is he?'

She didn't respond.

Belden sat on the edge of the bed, grimaced a bit, then reached into his pants pocket and removed a handful of items that had created a bulge; keys, a folding knife, some scraps of paper and a business card. He put these on the bedside stand.

'These other men outside. They are not as nice as I am. You should learn to trust me.'

'I see. They don't draw the line at beating women.'

'No, as a matter of fact they don't.'

'The last time I trusted you, you left me at the courthouse all alone talking to a federal prosecutor.'

'Yes, well, he had all those pointed questions,' said Belden. He looked at his watch. 'I would love to discuss this at length, but there really isn't much time.'

'And I suppose if I tell you what I know you're going to let me go?'

'No.'

'I didn't think so.'

'But there are many ways to die,' said Belden. 'Some of them are actually quite painless.'

'I'm sure you'd be the expert on that,' said Joselyn. 'So what are you saying? You're going to let me pick my own poison?'

'If you like.'

'Fine. I want to die in a plane crash by remote control.'

Belden laughed. 'Ah, if we'd only met under other circumstances. Another time, another place.'

'But you've got such a busy schedule, moving all those bombs.'

Belden looked at her. For the first time the smile was gone.

'Who told you that?'

Joselyn didn't answer.

'Your tall friend?'

She just looked at him.

'Or was it the federal prosecutor?' He leaned on the bed with one hand.

'Tell me.' His voice lifted a little at the end.

While Joselyn was still looking at his face, the back of his hand caught her full force on the cheek, snapping her head to the left. The pain exploded like a star burst. For an instant, Joselyn thought she might pass out. She tasted the salty tang of blood inside her mouth and tried to focus her eyes.

Now he was smiling again. 'You can tell me. After all, you are my lawyer,' said Belden. 'We really shouldn't have any secrets.'

She could tell he was starting to get off on it. Fire was forming in his eyes. Hitting women was something he enjoyed.

'After all, I did pay you a fee,' said Belden. 'Maybe it wasn't enough?' He caught her with the hand coming back the other way, and the pain in her head ratcheted up one more notch.

'Don't we have some kind of confidence or something here? Maybe I should file a complaint with the bar,' said Belden. 'My lawyer won't tell me what's going on.'

He reached over like he was getting ready to smack her one more time when the door opened. Joselyn looked through glazed eyes at the man standing in the open doorway. She could feel blood running down her chin from the corner of her lip.

The man in the doorway was small, with soft brown eyes and dark thinning hair. He was carrying a suitcase and dressed in a sport coat and slacks, like he was ready to travel. For an instant, his eyes met Joselyn's.

There was something in his expression that provided a sense of sanctuary, as if suddenly something human had entered the room. It was an expression of compassion. It was quickly coupled with regret.

Belden stopped in mid-slap and dropped his arm. 'Ah. Mr . . .' He almost said the name but then stopped. 'I'd like you meet my lawyer, Ms Cole. We were just having a frank exchange of views.'

'It's time to go.' The man did not acknowledge her presence but broke eye contact and turned away. At that moment, Joselyn knew she was dead.

Belden picked up the items from the bedside table, all but one. The business card he left, dog-eared and frayed, and replaced the rest of the items in his pocket.

'I wish it could have been longer,' said Belden. 'But all good things must come to an end.'

'Until the next time,' said Joselyn. Blood trickled down her cheek and fire filled her eyes. If he'd given her an opening, Belden would have been sporting permanent scars and speaking with a much higher voice. She might have paid the price, but he would have known he'd been in a fight.

'Unfortunately not,' said Belden. He took one last look at her, crossed the room in three strides, closed the door, and was gone.

CHAPTER
TWENTY-FIVE

Padget Island, WA

C onners could no longer feel the tips of his fingers. They were numb from the fifty-degree water. The three men struggled with the inflatable raft, pulling it up onto the rock-strewn beach. In the dark with no clear landmarks, Conners couldn't even be sure if in fact they had landed on Padget Island. He looked for landmarks. A jagged rock cliff on the left seemed right. The swale cut by a small creek that drained on the beach matched the map he'd studied on the plane.

The beach was nothing like the sandy dunes around San Diego where they trained. The three men slogged up to their knees through the mud of a tidal flat, their feet slipping on moss-covered boulders and slick seaweed. They struggled to pull the raft with its floating pallet of equipment above the incoming tide line.

Conners huddled with the other two men in the lee of a large boulder and scanned the beach with night goggles for any sign of thermal images.

'You think Scofield and Reams made it?' One of the others

looked at Conners. The kid was no more than nineteen years old. His first time in anything approaching combat, and he was scared.

'I don't know.'

'Shouldn't we look for 'em?'

'Break open the gear,' said Conners. 'Get me the radio.'

They took their gun-metal diving knives to the black neoprene cover over the pallet, sliced it neatly, and popped the lid off of one of the metal containers inside. Within a few seconds, they found the small handheld radio set. It had a range of only about a mile, but it used secure low-range frequencies.

Conners took it and checked the power switch, then hit the transmit button and held it down. 'Gopher, this is Gopher One, do you read?'

He let the button up. All he heard was static. He turned the squelch dial up to kill the sound, so sentries in the bunker on the bluffs wouldn't hear the noise.

'Gopher, this is Gopher One. Come in. Do you read?'

More static.

'Maybe we should check the beach for them. Maybe they got separated from the pallet and lost the radio.'

'We don't have time,' said Conners. 'If they're on the island, they'll find us.'

'If we stay here the people up there are gonna find us real quick.' The third SEAL was older, more experienced than either Conners or the other man. He had seen action in Panama and the Gulf. He knew what Conners suspected; a night dive over pitch-black water you could expect fifty-percent casualties to be delivered by the forces of nature, tides, weather, and the sea.

'Right now, we've got to find that sentry post up on the bluff,' said Conners.

'But Richie and Jason . . .'

'Richie and Jason knew what they were doing,' said Conners. 'We can't help 'em, and we can't go looking for them. Do you understand?'

The kid didn't like it, but he understood.

'According to the map, the militia has a fifty-caliber gun mounted in a bunker somewhere up here in these trees.' The three men looked for landmarks that offered some clue as to the location.

Normally SEALs would take any sentries out, either with a silenced round or a knife. But the rules of engagement in this case made that impossible. They were to fire only in self-defense. The mission was classified as an 'operation other than war', an event that if it went right, would never be reported. Their job was to get in, plant their equipment – miniature cameras and listening devices along with a small microwave transmitter – and then get out, and to do all of it undetected.

They opened the watertight arms container from the pallet and removed the small arms. Each pallet contained six weapons, two M-16s, an M-14 for distance and penetrating power, an MP-5 submachine gun and two handguns, nine-millimeter Berettas, each with a silencer. If they had to shoot, the plan was one shot, one kill. They would aim for the high chest or forehead. Unlike the movies where emptying a full clip in a single burst made for action, the SEALs had limits. Ammunition was heavy. Pulling too much of it behind you on a pallet in the open water was like dragging a sea anchor. Unless they got into a full-out fire fight, three round bursts were the limit.

There had been one M-60 light machine gun included with their equipment. Along with the loss of two of his men, Conners now discovered that the M-60 was missing.

'It musta been on the other pallet.'

'Check the electronic gear,' said Conners.

One of the SEALs popped the metal lid off the other container, while Conners and the other man checked the ammunition. Quietly they slipped loaded clips into the receivers and pulled the bolts back, chambering rounds.

Each man took a rifle. Conners took the MP-5 and tucked one of the Berettas into a pack.

Into the pack they loaded five small microphones along with miniature cameras, each with a fish-eye lens that would allow wide-angle shots at short distance.

Into a separate pack they loaded a base-station transmitter, a small metal box weighing fourteen pounds with its own collapsible dish. This would be put at a high remote point on the island, facing the southwestern horizon. It would transmit both audio and video signals on a special subsonic frequency to a satellite in space. In turn, this would be relayed to the naval base in Everett, forty miles south, where agents of the FBI and military intelligence would monitor the signals.

'Check the batteries,' said Conners.

The SEAL flipped a switch on the transmitter and watched as the tiny pin-head lamps flashed on. 'It's good.'

They cut the line tethering the equipment pallet to the inflatable raft, then punched holes in its rubber flotation wings with their knives. They stripped the flotation off the pallet and buried it in some loose gravel under a rock. Anyone finding the pallet would think it was mere flotsam, washed up on the beach.

Then the three men muscled the inflatable raft along with their air tanks and diving gear further up the beach. They hid the raft and tanks under some brush and cut a few low boughs from the trees to cover it all.

They smeared their faces and the back of their hands with jungle-green and black-sand-colored grease paint to repair the camouflage that had washed off in the water.

Conners checked his watch. They had less than two hours before the first rays of dawn crept over the mountains to the east. Using hand signals, he directed the man with the M-14 and the other silenced pistol to take point. The three of them began to scale the high bank toward the bluff.

Washington, DC

S y Hirshberg was camped in the Situation Room in the basement of the West Wing. He had been there all night, waiting for word from the naval base in Everett. It was now after seven in the morning on the east coast, and Hirshberg was worried.

'What are we hearing?'

Hirshberg turned and saw the president as he entered the room.

'Nothing. Not a word since the plane left the drop point last night.'

'It's still early,' said the president.

Hirshberg looked at his watch. 'We should have had radio communications by now.'

'You think something went wrong?'

'It's possible. I think we should have provided some contingency plans,' said Hirshberg. 'If those men get in trouble . . .'

'They'll be all right. The SEALs are the best,' said the president. 'I don't want to overreact. You remember what happened at Waco. We don't want a repeat.'

Hirshberg didn't like it. The SEALs were under-gunned, out-manned, with no backup or fast boats to extricate them if trouble developed.

'I think we made the right decision,' said the president.

Hirshberg grated in silence at the use of the plural pronoun. 'I'm sorry, Mr President, but I have to disagree. I think we should have sent in troops.'

'More troops just draw more attention. We'd need a staging area.'

Hirshberg knew the president well enough to know what he was really afraid of. The media would pick up on it.

'No. I'm satisfied that this is the right way to go about it,' said the president.

'And if it fails, we will have lost any element of surprise,' said Hirshberg. 'If they have a device and if it's ready to detonate, what then?'

This actually stopped the president for a moment as he considered the consequences. 'If it must be, better there than some major population center.'

Hirshberg couldn't believe what he was hearing. The expression on his face betrayed his thoughts.

'Listen, Sy, I'm not at all convinced there's anything to this. You want my personal view – I think we're all running around chasing our tails. I don't think there is a device. I don't think there ever was one.'

'What about the debris from the Russian trawler?'

'Yes, well, who knows where that came from. Maybe they used the ship to refuel some of their subs at sea. You know the Russians. They're not exactly careful the way they handle and transport the stuff. Stone-age safety systems. Remember Chernobyl?'

'Can we afford to take that chance, Mr President?'

'That's why we're sending in the SEALs. To check it out.'

Hirshberg knew what the president was afraid of. If he sent in forces he would have to explain why, the nature of the threat. This would be followed by a lot of questions from the press and Congress that would inevitably lead to

Kolikoff and his corporation, questions the president would rather not get into.

If anything went wrong, Hirshberg suspected that the White House was already prepared with the usual litany of lies for the public and the press. A tragic accident had occurred on the island during a training exercise. The president knew nothing about it, but was getting the facts. He would be calling the next of kin to commiserate with them. He and the first lady would be flying west to meet with the families in San Diego. It wouldn't be the first time some screwed-up covert ops got passed off as a wayward training exercise.

The question in Hirshberg's mind was what the president would do then. Would he agree to throw a ten-mile cordon around Padget Island and send in troops, or would he continue to deny everything until a mushroom-shaped cloud formed somewhere in the sky over the northwest?

'Mr President, we have to assume that if the people on that island have a bomb, they will use it. We may only have one chance to stop them and that's to act now, swiftly and with maximum force to seize the device before they know what hits them.'

'If the people on that island have a bomb, my first objective is to isolate it. Keep it where it is. Bottle 'em up, and then talk 'em to death,' said the president.

'Negotiate with terrorists?' said Hirshberg.

'I didn't say negotiate. I said talk, until we wear them down.'

'And what if we don't wear them down? What if they decide to push the button?'

There was a long deep sigh from the president. 'We're not talking New York or Boston or even L.A.,' he said. 'We will have confined the damage maybe to a single island.'

'That assumes the bomb is on the island.'

'That's why we sent in the SEALs, to find out. Now let's not argue about this anymore. I've made the decision.' The president wandered to a side table where there were some Danish pastries and a pot of coffee. He poured a cup and picked through the pastries. 'What is this – can't we get anything hot?' He looked at the marine aide who immediately took his order, bacon and eggs with toast.

'Sy, you want anything?'

'No, Mr President.' Hirshberg had lost his appetite. He was beginning to envy the litany of aides who had bailed out on the administration as it neared the end of its first term.

'Something coming in, sir.' One of the communications staff was talking to the officer in charge, a marine lieutenant.

Hirshberg got out of his chair and literally flew to the area over the soldier's shoulder, looking at the computer screen.

'Is it from Everett?' The president put a half-eaten pastry down on the side table as he chewed and swallowed.

'No, sir.'

He went back to his pastry.

'I think you better see this, Mr President.' Hirshberg was reading the screen.

The president grabbed his coffee and walked over toward the computer station.

There on the screen was a communiqué. It was not from the naval base at Everett, but from the Department of Energy, marked TOP SECRET, RD (Restricted Data) URGENT!

CIVILIAN SOURCES CONNECTED WITH THE INSTITUTE AGAINST MASS DESTRUCTION SANTA CRISTA, CA REPORT EXISTENCE OF HIGHLY RADIOACTIVE DEBRIS ON VESSEL, LOCATED FRIDAY HARBOR, SAN JUAN

ISLANDS. CONTAMINATION BELIEVED RELATED TO NUCLEAR DEVICE. REQUESTING DISPATCH OF NEST.

The acronym referred to one of four Nuclear Emergency Search Teams. Their role, though they had never been called up in an actual event, was to respond to nuclear emergencies, including terrorist devices brought into the country. The teams had conducted mock emergency exercises in the early 90s with less than satisfactory results.

'Did they find a bomb?' asked the president.

'Sir, it doesn't say. Only that they believe the contamination is related to a nuclear device.' The young Lieutenant at the monitor looked back over his shoulder at the president.

'Well, get some clarification. Call somebody at DOE.' The president's words sent the military aides in the room scrambling.

'Mr President, we can't afford to wait.'

'What?' The president looked at Hirshberg.

'It's no coincidence, sir. The militia on that island. The discovery of radioactive debris on a vessel.'

The president looked at a map of Puget Sound that was already projected on a large screen on the wall. Padget Island was circled by a slow flashing ring of light, indicating the area of operations by the SEAL team. Hirshberg grabbed a laser pointer from a podium below the map and hit Friday Harbor with a red arrow.

'It's less than twelve miles.'

Even in a state of denial, the president could no longer avoid the obvious.

'There's a small force of marines at Everett. They can be airborne in choppers in less than a hour.' Hirshberg had done his homework. He had, through the Joint Chiefs, put the marines on alert.

'Cordon off Friday Harbor,' said Hirshberg. 'Hit Padget Island with everything we've got and hope we find the device.'

'We should wait for confirmation,' said the president. 'What do we know about this institute? This place in California?'

'They produce a database. Information on weapons of mass destruction. Several of our agencies subscribe. CIA, DOE. Some of their people have participated on U.N. inspection teams.'

'Their information, is it usually accurate?'

'Yes.'

There was silence in the room, a look of grim resignation on the president. The ultimate fear of every man of power: his options had suddenly been limited by events he could not anticipate.

'Sir, the longer we wait, the greater the risk that they could move the device,' said Hirshberg. 'If they do, it could be very difficult to find it again.'

The president said nothing.

'Sir, the marines will need time to muster.'

San Juan Channel, WA

They turned toward Iceberg Point, and Thorn, alias Belden, pushed the throttles forward on the twin engine outboard. The bow lifted out of the water and the boat began to plane out across the Sound. The harbor at Cap Santé was at least an hour away even in good weather and top speed.

The sea picked up a chop as dawn approached. Taggart settled into the seat across from Thorn and zipped his jacket, turning the collar up against the cold, damp air.

His gaze fixed upon a distant island in a daze as if there were nothing there.

At the moment, his mind was occupied with thoughts of Kirsten. Increasingly, in the last days he had spent more time thinking about her and wondering what their lives would have been like had she lived. He could see the features of her face as clearly as if she were standing in front of him. At times when he was alone, he would actually speak to her, confident in the belief that she was with him wherever he went. And he worried about Adam who was now five years old. He wondered what kind of a world he would be leaving to his son.

'What time's your flight?' Shouting over the noise of the engines Thorn interrupted Taggart's thoughts.

He looked at his watch. 'Eleven-forty.'

'You'll have time to drop me off,' said Thorn. 'You've got your ticket?'

Taggart nodded.

'When you transfer planes in Denver, call for further instructions.'

'I know.'

'Use the cellular number.'

'We've been over all of that,' said Taggart.

'Just checking,' said Thorn. 'You've got the cellular number?'

'I've got it.'

Thorn was a definite A-type. He was neurotic. He believed that unless he said it out loud, it wouldn't happen.

Then out of the blue: 'You're not planning on contacting anybody else?'

'Who would I be calling?'

'Maybe not a phone call,' said Thorn. 'I was thinking maybe a letter.'

Taggart reached into his inside coat pocket. The letter he'd written the night before to his son Adam, something for the boy to read when he got older, some explanation from his father. The letter was gone.

When he looked over Thorn was holding the envelope between two fingers. It was stamped and sealed. At least he hadn't read it.

'Give it to me.'

'I took the liberty of checking your coat just before we left.'

'Give it to me.'

Thorn didn't say a word, but just held it up in the wind as the boat skimmed the water.

'I suppose you went through my bags as well?'

Thorn made a face of concession. 'I understand the urge to let your boy know something about his father. But I couldn't take the chance that you might have mentioned my name.'

'I don't know your name.'

'Good. At least something's secure. It's only natural,' said Thorn. 'You want to explain to him why you did what you did. Hell, if I killed a hundred thousand people and had my name attached to the act I'd want the entire world to know why.'

'My son's the only audience I care about.'

'It won't do to have this floating around in the mail.' With that Thorn let loose of the letter.

Taggart lurched from his chair and tried to grab it, but he was too slow. The envelope flipped up into the wind like a leaf, then landed on the churning prop wash behind the speeding boat. Taggart stood and watched as it disappeared in the distance.

'I wasn't gonna mail it now.' Taggart shouted above the wind and the noise of the engine.

Thorn was hunkered down behind the boat's windscreen.

'I was gonna wait until we were done. Until the last minute,' said Taggart.

'And when would that be?'

'I don't know. You haven't told me.'

'Precisely,' said Thorn. 'And for very good reason. The fewer who know the better. You would have mailed that letter from the target city. If the authorities got their hands on it before we had a chance to detonate the device, they would have been able to piece together the target and concentrate their forces. You don't give them an edge. Not if you're smart.'

'That assumes they would have been able to intercept the letter.'

'Oh, they'd have found the letter all right. Your boy is staying with relatives, right?'

Taggart didn't have to respond. Thorn already knew the answer from the address on the letter.

'Your wife's parents?' Thorn didn't wait for an answer. He knew he was right.

'You're not doing them any favors by sending them mail from the grave. The government will be all over them when this is over. Anybody you've ever talked to – your friends, family, girlfriends you haven't seen in twenty years. They will all be getting visits from the FBI. There will be search warrants for their homes, any property they own. They will ransack their lives looking for evidence. A letter like that will only cause your family more trouble.'

Taggart didn't say a word. Anger consumed him. Almost a minute passed in strained silence as the two men looked straight ahead through the windscreen.

'If you want to talk to the boy, leave a tape-recorded message.' Thorn reached into his pocket and pulled out a small microcassette recorder. He reached over to hand it to Taggart, who remained stone-silent, looking at the man who

313

had just destroyed the last words his son would ever receive from his father.

'Take it,' said Thorn. 'I'll see the tape gets delivered. In a way that the government doesn't find it, after this is all over. You can tape it in the car when we get to Cap Santé.'

'Why would you care about my son?'

'Call it an inoculation against disaster. Human nature being what it is.' Thorn shouted above the noise of the engines. He looked straight ahead at the swells as they slammed under the bow of the small boat. 'If I didn't give you a way out, you'd just write another letter.'

'How do I know you'll deliver the tape?' said Taggart.

'You don't. But you can be sure of one thing. If the government gets its hands on anything you write, you can be sure your boy will never see it. And they'll probably twist whatever you say for their own purposes.'

He had a point. The government probably already had Taggart's name on a list, taps on his in-law's phones, and court orders to monitor incoming mail. It was why the men on the island had cut themselves off from the outside world. Taggart took the tape recorder.

'Now tell me,' said Taggart. 'A question I've been itching to ask. How much are you getting paid for all this?'

'You ought to know. You're paying the freight,' said Thorn.

'Don't insult my intelligence. You're gonna tell me there was a white sale on nuclear bombs? You got a discount at the home show? We tried for three years to make contact, even to get a price. We never got close. Then you show up and, just like that, magic. For a long time we thought you were the federal government.'

'How do you know I'm not?'

'Because the radiation on those boats was real. As well as the guys coughing up their lungs.'

'Let's just say you've got friends,' said Thorn.

'Who?'

'Your government has managed to piss off half the world. Take your pick.'

'And how much are these people paying you?'

'You're being well subsidized. Don't tell me this offends you. Undercuts your pride of anarchism. You can be sure you'll get all the glory,' said Thorn.

'And what's in it for them?'

'Cover. It's very simple. Your goals are entirely mutual. You want to destroy your government. So do they. You want the world to know you did it. They want the world to believe it. To that end they will waste no resources, spare no expense. Witnesses, documents. It's all been arranged.

'All they want is to avoid retaliation,' said Thorn. 'Your government is on record. The use of weapons of mass destruction by a foreign state against U.S. interests will be met with nuclear retaliation. If on the other hand what is left of your government can be convinced that it was entirely a domestic matter what are they going to do – bomb Seattle?'

'So you just brokered the deal?' said Taggart.

'That's my business. I must admit, it is the biggest deal I've ever done. In the end, your government will thank us for blaming you.'

'Why's that?'

Thorn was amazed. As bitter as Taggart was, he was naive.

'You think the politicians are going to be anxious to start World War Three? Why do you think they centered on Oswald so quickly after Kennedy was shot, and why they insisted that he acted alone? They were shitting little green apples for fear that the Russians might be involved, and that they might have to do something about it.

'You pull this off, and they're not going to be looking very far for answers. They're gonna be bending over, grabbing their collective asses, and trying to figure ways to keep a grip on power. To demonstrate that they're on top of the situation. What they'll want are some heads they can roll quickly; I'm not particularly interested in offering mine, and if we're successful, yours won't be available. They'll take what they can find and call it justice,' said Thorn.

'Not if we're lucky,' said Taggart.

'And what's gonna stop them?'

'The people.'

'The people?' Thorn was now laughing out loud. His hair blowing in wind. 'Right. The people. I forgot about the people.'

'If they act quickly, they'll have a chance,' said Taggart. 'They'll respond.'

'That assumes they can find the off button on their remote controls. Within twenty-four hours, there'll be a thousand experts getting face time on the tube, all analyzing the nuclear cloud and offering bullshit as answers. Geraldo can show pictures of fried politicians with lard melting off their bones like a barbecued roast, and everybody can argue whether Democrats or Republicans smell worse when charred. Within forty-eight hours, the public will be bored with the story and flipping channels again. Take my word for it. The only thing this is going to do is up the ante in the ratings war.'

Thorn didn't have much confidence in 'the people'. He also knew that once they detonated the device there were not going to be a lot of places to hide. He had spent twenty years working for dictators in banana republics and kings who'd traded in their camels for an armored-plated Mercedes. This job was the capstone of his career, one final and great shake of the money tree. The men involved could never work again. They would be international outlaws. No country on earth would dare to give them asylum. It was why Thorn, in his incarnation as Belden, had gone to great lengths to die and to do it in such a public way. It was why the woman, Joselyn Cole, had to die to keep his secret.

Suddenly Thorn's gaze out through the boat's windscreen became focused and hard. He squinted into the early-morning dawn. Then without saying a word he turned the wheel and brought the vessel into a curving right-hand turn. They cut a wide arc, sweeping across the open channel.

Taggart was jostled in his seat and looked over at him. 'What's wrong?'

'I don't know.' Thorn was peering into the distance.

The water's surface took on a heaving silvery hue of mercury under the breaking dawn. For a second Taggart thought it was just the cresting tip of another wave. But as the water shifted, the object took on a permanence, dark and angular. It was something floating on the surface, caught in the pull of the tide, being carried toward the straits.

Within seconds the boat overtook it. Taggart grabbed a boat hook from a tray that ran along under the gunnel. He tried to snag whatever it was but missed.

Thorn maneuvered the boat in a wide turn to take another pass. This time he pulled alongside and cut the engines completely. He left the wheel and took the boat hook. He reached over the side and snagged a line.

It was connected by a metal hasp that joined a number of lines. The lines ran to the water and disappeared into inky darkness. Thorn knew instinctively what floated beneath the surface. Without saying a word he pulled a folding knife from his pocket and cut the shrouds to the parachute, then ripped open the protective rubber covering over the floating pallet.

'What is it?' said Taggart.

'It's trouble.' Thorn reached in his pocket for the cellphone and punched the autodial button for the number on Padget Island, then hit the SEND button. He had programmed the number on the island into the phone but never called it for fear that the government had a tap. Now he had no choice.

It rang once. Then again. 'Damn it. Pick it up.'

'Hello.' Finally somebody answered.

'Thorn here. You've got company on the island.' He could hear laughter and a lot of bluster on the other end. No doubt they were all in from their bunkers getting coffee and warming their feet in front of the fire.

'Quiet.' The man on the other end was hollering for them to shut up so that he could hear.

'Get the men into the bunkers,' said Thorn, 'and send out patrols.'

'Is it the military?' asked the voice on the other end.

'We got an M-60 machine gun floating in a package out here,' said Thorn. 'What do you think?'

The voice repeated everything he said at the other end and now the sounds coming from the house on the island were the sounds of panic.

'Get to those bunkers,' said Thorn. 'And listen.' He couldn't tell if the man on the other end had dropped the phone.

'Are you there?' said Thorn.

'Yeah I'm here.'

'The woman. Kill her. Now.'

CHAPTER
TWENTY-SIX

Padget Island, WA

Joselyn heard the phone ring. A moment later there was a lot of shouting coming from the other room. She was tied and gagged, lying on her side on the bed. One of the men guarding her had gone the extra yard of tying her feet and looping the rope through the one on her wrists, pulling it tight so that her body was now strung like a bow. He hadn't bothered to replace the blindfold. Joselyn took it as an ominous sign.

She struggled with the knot on her wrists, trying desperately to free her hands. She couldn't tell what was happening outside, but something was causing a lot of excitement. Men were running around, the sound of heavy boots on the wooden deck of the porch. Somebody was shouting orders from outside the window to the room.

'Who's got the B-A-R?'

'Tom, I think.'

'Tell him to get his ass down on the beach. How many Brownings we got?'

'Two. One of 'em's out of commission. Bent firing pin.

I been telling Thorn to get it fixed for a week. Where's Oscar?'

'He left this morning, right after Thorn.'

It sounded like two men had closed the distances, so that their voices now dropped to conversational tones right outside the window.

'That was Thorn on the phone. Says we got company.'

'Locals or Feds?'

'He found a pallet floating in the straits. An M-60 and a lot of other gear. You figure it out.'

'I'm surprised they waited this long. Do we know how big the force is?'

'No. I want you to get the men on the beach and keep 'em busy. Break out the two Brownings that are still working and make sure they got plenty of ammo. The Feds want fireworks, we'll give 'em a fifty-caliber light show, followed by one big fucking bang.'

'Where's the boat?'

'Tied up in the cove on the west end.'

'None of them know about it?'

'No. And let's keep it that way unless you want it to look like the Cuban boat lift. Thorn made it clear before he left. Any trouble, we get off the island, make for the truck, and get the thing moving. Oscar left early this morning. He's already headed that way. To get it ready.'

'What about these guys?'

'Dead bodies tell no tales.'

'What are you talking about?'

'Thorn had me wire the bunkers last night. Those crazy fuckers are gonna be shootin' from on top a pile of C-4. One round in those sandbags, and God's fringe element's gonna get some heavy reinforcements.'

'What about the woman?'

Joselyn stopped struggling with the ropes on her wrists and did some heavy listening.

'Like I said, the dead tell no tales. Now move. And if shooting starts don't go diving in any bunkers.'

Now she was frantic, struggling with the ropes. She heard someone come back inside the house. The front door slammed shut. There were footsteps, heavy boots on carpeted wood. Then she heard it; the slide and click of metal. Joselyn was no firearms expert, but she knew the sound of a gun being loaded with a clip and chambered with a bullet.

Now she could hear the creak of footsteps coming down the hall toward the room. She rolled on the bed toward the wall until her back slammed against it. She tried to wedge her body between the bed and the wall. A key turned in the lock. The knob moved, and the door started to open.

Joselyn wiggled her hips and pressed down hard with the weight of her body. Her eyes bulged as she saw the shadow come through the door. She never looked at his face. Instead she was mesmerized by the pistol in his hand, a semi-automatic with a bore the size of an elephant gun.

His head centered down the sights as he took aim.

She moved violently on the bed, trying desperately to made a bad target. Joselyn drove her hip into the crack between the wall and the mattress. Something moved.

She squeezed her eyes shut tight and prayed, an out-of-body experience, waiting for the bullet to rip into her.

The force of the concussion registered behind her, hitting the wall with a thud, a vibration that passed through her body. The blast resounded in her head, nearly puncturing her eardrums. It hit the wall like a bowling ball. Joselyn waited for the searing pain to register. A shower of dry plaster peppered her face.

When she opened her eyes she realized she was no longer

on the bed but down on the floor. Her last wild gyrations had shifted the mattress. Joselyn had gone between the bed and the wall. The bullet had hit just above the edge of the mattress, punching a hole the size of her thumb in the drywall.

Now she saw his face, flushed with anger.

'God damn it.' He took aim a second time. Leveled on the sights, she could see his single eye as he lined up and carefully angled the muzzle over the edge of the mattress. Joselyn was trapped, unable to move, wedged against the wall.

The explosion was muffled, almost quiet. It sounded like someone popping the tab on a beer can. A red dot appeared on his forehead just above the line of the sights on the gun. It expanded like red ink on a porous paper then ran down his nose in a rivulet. A quizzical and vacant expression spread across his face. His eyes open, the man with the gun toppled onto the bed and bounced on the mattress.

Joselyn issued a muted scream through the gag in her mouth. She lay trapped on the floor between the bed and the wall and watched in horror as the man's hand twitched on the bed just inches from her nose.

Suddenly there was automatic weapons fire outside the house. Glass shattered in the window, breaking the pane.

He was wearing a black neoprene wetsuit and came through the window, a single leg followed quickly by his head and shoulders. In a fluid motion, he hit the floor, turned, and began firing out through the broken window, rapid coughs from the tiny machine gun in his hand. It had a bulbous black cylinder over the end of the barrel. The shots came in staccato bursts.

Bullets punctured the wall around him and ripped through the wood frame of window. Several more shots punched through the shade. Exploding glass from the upper pane sprayed the room. The man dropped to the foot of the bed, and for an instant Joselyn thought he was dead. He turned his head and looked at her.

'You all right?'

All Joselyn could do was stare at him bug-eyed and nod. Quickly he got to his hands and knees, then removed the gag from her mouth, and in a single motion produced a knife from somewhere near his ankle and sliced the rope from her wrists and legs, freeing her body.

'I'm OK.' She rubbed the chaffed flesh of her wrists.

Another volley of bullets ripped into the window. This time the shade fell to the floor and sunlight streamed into the room.

'We can't stay here. Green Giant's gonna shred this place in a minute.' He grabbed her by the arm and led her across the floor, both of them crawling on their hands and knees as fast as they could go. Bullets punctured the wall above them and smashed into a mirror over the dresser. Shards of silvered glass showered down, catching in Joselyn's hair and nicking the flesh on her cheek.

'Who are you?'

'No time for that now,' he said.

She wiped the blood from her cheek absently with the back of her hand, then saw it. Joselyn crawled toward the window where the bullets were hitting.

'Not that way.'

She ignored him, then reached up and grabbed the business card Belden had left on the bedside table. Joselyn scampered back across the floor.

'Lady, you're out of your mind. You're gonna get shot.' He crawled toward the door, and she followed him. The man in the wetsuit opened it a crack and stuck the fat cylinder of a muzzle through, then peeked out. The fact that he didn't fire told her it was clear.

He threw the door open and crawled through. She followed him closely until they sat propped against the wall, shoulder-to-shoulder in the hallway outside. There were no windows here, no other opening except the end of the hall that emptied into the living room. He kept his gun pointed in that direction as he pulled a canvas bag from his shoulder and reached inside.

When his hand came out it was holding a pistol, small and black with a tube on the end.

'Have you ever fired a handgun?'

Joselyn shook her head.

'If I get hit, you may have no choice. Listen up.' He unscrewed the tube from the end. 'I'm taking the silencer off. It'll be loud. It's better. They're more apt to keep their distance.' He figured the chances of her hitting anything were slim. The noise might provide some cover.

'There's fifteen rounds in the clip. The little red dots on the side.' He pointed to them. 'When they're uncovered – when you can see them – it means it's ready to fire. When you can't see them, it means the safety's on.' He clicked the safety back and forth several times so she could see how it worked. Then he handed it to her.

'You got it?'

She nodded like she understood.

'When you put the safety on, the hammer goes down automatically. In order to fire, you just take the safety off, cock the hammer back, and pull the trigger. Aim before you do it. Every time you pull the trigger after that it will shoot.'

Joselyn was nodding at every word, but he could tell by the dazed look that she probably was not going to get it right. He pulled the slide back and chambered the first round, then handed it to her. 'Keep it pointed away from me.'

They were shooting up a storm outside, bullets hitting metal with a dull thud, the clink of broken windowpanes. The curtains in the living room danced as if inhabited by ghosts.

He checked his watch. 'There's a gunship coming in in three minutes. They're gonna shred this place. It's ground zero. We gotta get the hell out.'

'Who are you?'

'Navy SEAL. Time for introductions later.' He went into overdrive and started crawling on his hands and knees down the hall toward the living room.

Joselyn looked down at the gun in her hand, made sure she couldn't see the red dots, then followed him so that the highest points on each of their bodies were their hind ends, like two hounds sniffing the carpet.

'Colonel, please tell me what your plan is?' Gideon yelled over the *thwop-thwop-thwop* of the helicopter rotors as the chopper approached at slow speed, three miles out from Padget Island.

'We've got to wait until they soften the place up.' The marine officer in charge was juggling incoming messages from the other choppers in formation, a few Black Hawks, but mostly older HU-1 Hueys from the Air National Guard that had been grounded for inspections. They were now pressed into service by executive order, the only means of close transport that they had. The entire force had been patched together at the last minute. It was all they could assemble on short notice from Everett.

He'd managed to dig up two Cobra gunships, one of them an AH-1G left over from Vietnam, nearly an antique, to provide covering fire when his men hit the ground.

'We don't know what they've got down there. I'm not sending my men in to get killed on the ground. I've got a handful of noncoms with combat experience, and that's it. Most of these men have never seen any fighting.'

'Could you not get more experienced men?' said Gideon.

'There wasn't time,' said the colonel.

'I understand, but I am still worried about Ms Cole.'

'You think she's on that island?'

'That is my guess. The sheriff back at Friday Harbor found the piece of paper with the telephone number, the one I had given her before I went out to the docks. It was on the ground in the parking lot. He also found minute traces of blood next to it.'

'She's probably dead,' said the colonel.

'I don't think so.' Gideon had to shout to be heard above the rotor wash and the noise of the engine. 'Why would they carry away a dead woman? If they took her and if that island is the center of their operations, my guess is, she is down there.'

The colonel didn't turn to look directly at him, but Gideon could read his pained expression even in profile.

'I'm afraid I've got my orders, Mr van Ry. There are protocols for dealing with this kind of scenario, NBCs, nuclear, biological and chemical. That island is off-limits to anything that moves right now. Nothing goes in. Nothing comes out. And we're about to unleash hell on them.'

'What kind of hell?' said Gideon.

'As you can see, I don't have much by way of fire power with me. A few old choppers to transport my men. No artillery and no armed vehicles. I could use a couple of Bradley fighting vehicles, but getting them here and down onto that island in the face of fifty-caliber machine gun fire is another story. I've got to silence those guns before we do anything.'

Gideon shook his head and gave the marine a quizzical look like he didn't understand.

'We're lucky,' yelled the colonel. 'We had some equipment out here on the coast for testing.'

'What kind of equipment?'

'It's a palletized gunship. C-130. Those people down there are about to get a lesson in modern urban warfare. Hundred-and-five-millimeter howitzer rounds, precision-guided and very deadly. I've got to bust up those bunkers before we hit the ground.'

'I'm very worried about Joselyn Cole,' said Gideon.

'We will do out best to confine our shots,' said the colonel.

'Colonel.' The chopper pilot turned his head toward his commander in the jump-seat behind him. 'We got contact.'

'Lemme have the headset.' The colonel held the earpiece in place with one hand and talked into the mouthpiece.

'Able, this is Charlie. Where are you?' He listened for a second.

'Good. Test your guns out over open water, then check back. And don't sink any fishing boats out on the Sound.' He handed the headset back.

'Jolly Green Giant,' said the colonel. 'You know what that is?'

Gideon shook his head. 'I think you should wait, Colonel.'

'Why?'

'Because if one loose round hits that device you could get a very dirty explosion.'

The marine officer now turned and looked at Gideon over his shoulder with a quizzical expression. 'What are you talking about?'

It was the only reason he'd brought the Dutchman along. The NEST team couldn't move north fast enough. It would be three hours before they arrived at Friday Harbor with their equipment. Gideon was the only nuclear expert on site. The military needed him in case they found the device.

'That Russian artillery shell is very old,' said Gideon. 'It's a style of munitions made in the early nineteen-sixties. It contains conventional high explosives wrapped around a core of plutonium. We cannot be sure how old those high explosives are. They could be quite unstable due to age. If you hit them with a round, a piece of shrapnel, anything hot, they could explode.' The Dutchman said this in a matter-of-fact manner that caused the colonel to sit up and take notice.

'That'll set off a nuclear blast?'

'Probably not,' said Gideon.

'Then what's the problem?'

'An explosion like that could pulverize the plutonium core. It could turn it into dust and send it into the atmosphere. I would not want to be downwind if that happens.'

'Radiation?' said the colonel.

Gideon nodded.

'How far could it travel?'

'That depends on the prevailing winds, how high the dust is carried. It could certainly reach the mainland, parts of Seattle, Victoria, Vancouver, depending on the direction of the winds.'

This gave the colonel something to chew on. A possible international incident. He thought for a second. Then tapped the pilot on the shoulder. 'Gimme those photos.'

The pilot handed him a file from the rack on the inside of the door. The colonel opened it and looked at the pictures inside, satellite reconnaissance photos of the island.

'It's the only sizeable building,' he said. He showed the pictures to Gideon. If the device is on the island, chances are it's inside that house. They wouldn't put it in one of the bunkers unless they were crazy.'

'Perhaps,' said Gideon.

The colonel tapped the pilot one more time, then snapped his fingers for the headset.

He held it up. 'Able, this is Charlie. Change of plans. Scratch the house. Do you read?' He waited for the response, which Gideon could not hear over the engine and rotor noise.

'Do not hit the house. Everything else is fair game. Do you read?' He listened again. 'That's affirmative. You can go in but don't hit the house.' He handed the headset back to the pilot.

'That plane's got a palletized hundred-and-five-millimeter howitzer. Fires terminally guided munitions. It can put a round through a fart from ten thousand feet, before the gas comes out your ass.'

Gideon wasn't sure about the metaphor or the wisdom of man's actions. 'Colonel, if they took Ms Cole, she's alive and she's on that island.'

'That may very well be, Mr van Ry. But I've got my orders. I've got men on that island too. We're not going in there until we've pulverized those bunkers.'

'We'll leave the house alone and hope for her sake that she's inside.'

Altitude Fourteen Thousand Feet, San Juan Channel, WA

It emitted a streak of fire that looked more like a flamethrower. Four rounds thundered through the airframe of the reserve KC-130 in less than two seconds.

They tested the gun out over water. Four distinct plumes rose thirty feet in the air like white feathers all in a line, as the rounds hit the surface of the Sound and exploded.

The targeteer checked the coordinates from the global

positioning satellite, as well as the link to the mission data computer.

'We're set. Take her in on a left-hand orbit, maintain one-four triple zero.'

Flying at fourteen thousand feet in an orbit that would not cross over the island at any point, the men on the ground would never hear the plane. Their first clue would come in the form of bunker-busters, high explosive shells that could be pinpointed, designed to rip into revetments and tear up sandbagged emplacements. Not knowing where the rounds were coming from and with no enemy to shoot at, it was a prescription for panic. The ground war in the Gulf proved that even trained soldiers would throw down their weapons and run when faced with an enemy who was killing them with invisible precision.

Once this occurred, phase two would kick in. The bunker-busters would be followed by antipersonnel rounds. When these hit the ground, they would release small baseball-sized bomblets that would bounce ten feet up before exploding. Fired in rapid four-round bursts, they would spread a carpet of death, sending out thousands of ball-bearings, ripping into flesh and tearing up everything in a radius of hundreds of feet.

The gunship would take the starch out of anybody on the ground who wasn't sitting in a concrete bunker ten feet down. By the time the Hueys swung in over the beach to offload their troops, the people on that island would be running in panic, tripping over their weapons, and looking for anybody who would take their surrender without killing them. It was mismatch – a total turkey shoot.

A s the motor launch skimmed over the waters of the channel, Thorn stayed to the far side, away from the ferry landing at Anacortes.

'Here, take it.' They changed seats and Taggart took the wheel. 'Keep her straight down the channel.'

Thorn got the field glasses out of a case in the cuddy cabin. He trained them on the docks and focused. Two Coast Guard patrol boats were moored a hundred yards off the docks.

'What's wrong?' Taggart looked over at him.

Both of the state ferries were tied up, and a line of traffic snaked up the hill and out onto the highway.

'What do you make of that?' said Thorn.

Taggart squinted. Even without glasses, he could see the traffic. 'Pretty busy, even for a weekend.'

'Busy, my ass,' said Thorn. 'Take a better look.' He handed the field glasses to Taggart, who held them to his eyes with one hand while he steered with the other.

'What am I supposed to be looking at?'

'The shoulder of that road coming down to the ferry terminal.'

Taggart let go of the wheel long enough to focus the glasses. There, off to the right of the road, was a string of dark, olive-drab vehicles each with a distinctive white cross painted on the top and sides.

'Humves,' said Taggart.

'Not just any kind,' said Thorn. 'Military ambulances. Looks like they're expecting patients. And they've stopped all ferry service.'

'What do you make of it?'

'I'd say it's obvious,' said Thorn. 'They're not interested in having any civilians out on the waters in the San Juan Straits, at least not today. I'll bet there're military vessels patrolling. We might have just made it past them. They don't want the good citizens getting in the way, maybe seeing something they shouldn't.'

Thorn looked at his watch. His worry now was Oscar Chaney. If he was on schedule, he would already be onboard the *Humping Goose* along with the tanker truck. It would be an unremarkable sight out on the waters of the Sound; a small private working ferry with a septic pumper on its open deck, shuttling between the islands, or in this case between the island and the mainland.

Thorn unrolled a small laminated chart of the islands from inside the cuddy cabin. 'If he's on time, Oscar would be right about here, heading down the Rosario Straits.' He traced it with his finger on the chart. 'Two hours would put him off of Whidbey, another half-hour to Keystone.'

'If there are military vessels patrolling out there, there's a good chance he won't get through.'

Thorn knew that this was the most problematic part of his entire plan. Until he broke out of the Sound, onto the mainland with the truck and the device, he and his entire project were in peril.

'I'm banking that they've got their hands full, concentrating on that island for the next several hours. If your people hold up their end.'

'My people will hold up their end. They will die holding up their end.'

'Then by the time the Feds figure out the device was never there to begin with, it will be too late. Oscar will have the truck on the mainland. They won't know what to look for. A million miles of road to cover and a nuclear device they can't be sure where. With every hour, the circle to be searched will grow, and with every mile, the odds shift to our side. They have no description of the vehicle, and if they are lucky enough to corner him they have to worry whether he'll detonate it.'

'He won't, right?' Taggart was adamant. 'Not until we reach the target. This is not now some blind act of vengeance. We have a purpose, a goal. If we don't reach our objective we don't detonate. That was understood from the beginning.'

'Agreed,' said Thorn. 'But they don't know that.'

Taggart wasn't sure he believed him. The council, the militia leadership, had offered a bonus of a million dollars if Thorn met the target date. There was no way he could make the deadline. Taggart was worried that Thorn and his cadre might set off the device in some city or town along the way – cut and run. The group had lost financial leverage by transferring the final payment the night before they left the island. It had been done through numbered accounts in Europe and Thorn had confirmed the payment. Those had been his terms. He was taking no chances.

Now Taggart didn't have a choice. 'I am authorized,' said Taggart, 'to offer you an incentive to deliver the device to the appointed site even though you missed the date.'

Thorn looked at him but didn't say a word. The prospect of more money. 'I thought you guys were belly-up. Financially, that is.'

'We have half a million,' said Taggart.

'Oh.'

'A contingency fund.'

'And what exactly is the contingency in this case? You don't trust me?' He smiled.

Taggart didn't say anything.

'Half a million would buy some more trust, I suppose.'

'And how much trust is that?'

'Half a million's worth.' Thorn smiled and looked straight ahead down the channel. 'Half now, half when it's delivered,' said Thorn.

'All of it after it's delivered.' They had already been down that road.

Thorn laughed out loud, the kind of mocking chuckle a man makes when he's already had you once. Then he made a face of acceptance. 'That makes a bonus of a million and a half if I meet the target date.'

'Dream on,' said Taggart.

'The date has not yet come and gone,' said Thorn.

'Fine. A million and a half. We both know you're not gonna drive that truck across the country in three days.'

Thorn didn't say a thing, but merely arched his eyebrows as if this were a matter of opinion. 'Take my advice,' said Thorn. 'You should operate as if everything is on schedule.'

'Right. Even if it isn't,' said Taggart.

'You hired me to deal with the details.'

'I didn't hire you at all. You came with the device.'

'For good reason,' said Thorn. 'Learn to have some faith.'

Faith was not the first thing that came to Taggart's mind when he thought about Thorn.

'Don't go spending the bonus money,' said Thorn. 'I still have three days.'

Padget Island

Pinholes of light punched through the walls of the living room, as bright sunlight broke over the dock and the front of the house. The noise of the shots was distant but Joselyn could hear the distinct and repetitive impact of the bullets as they pierced the front wall of the house and lodged in the wall on the other side.

She followed the man in the wetsuit on her hands and knees, then took his lead and went to her stomach. They hugged the floor and shimmied along the back of the couch under a horizontal rain of death. Windows and mirrors shattered. A table lamp over her head disintegrated in a shower of clay shards. The paneling on the kitchen-cabinet doors came apart like tree limbs run through a shredder. The stacked dishes on the shelves exploded in a thousand pieces of fired ceramic.

He made it to the back door when it hit him, low in the back, lifting him off the floor and spinning him in agony. The wetsuit erupted in blood.

Joselyn was in shock. She dropped the handgun and crawled toward him.

'What can I do?'

The man didn't respond. All that passed from his lips was a groan of agony.

She lifted his head and looked down at his stomach. The bullet that struck him in the back had passed through his body. Blood was pulsing from the wound.

She crawled on her hands and knees without thinking, headed for the kitchen and the towel that was draped over the oven door. The snap of bullets breaking the sound barrier an inch from her head brought her back to her senses. She hit the floor and crawled. Joselyn grabbed the towel and three seconds later was back at his side. She pressed the towel to the open wound with as much pressure as she could muster lying on the floor.

She looked into his eyes. They were half-open, half-closed, staring at nothing. Though Joselyn had never seen the trance of death, she recognized it, held a finger to his nostrils in hopes of feeling some sign of breath. There was nothing.

Her hands were covered with blood. She looked around her on the floor. The pistol. She grabbed it. The man in the wetsuit said something about Green Giant. Gonna shred the place. Had to get out.

Joselyn reached up far enough to grab the knob on the back door. She turned it and opened the door an inch. Like an invitation to a convention of hornets, a score of rounds hit the door, turning what was left into splintered firewood.

Her face shielded in her hands, Joselyn looked at the small machine gun on the floor next to the dead sailor's hand. She didn't know if she could figure out how to fire it. She had seen him do it in the room. She picked it up and looked for a safety catch. There was a small lever on the side. She flipped it up and saw a painted red dot on the black metal. Now the question was: were there any bullets in it?

Carefully, as if not to hurt him, she pushed against the dead man and rolled him over, then eased the canvas satchel off his shoulder.

She looked inside. There were black metal clips like the one in the machine gun. Joselyn pulled one out. It was heavy and she saw the copper heads of bullets stacked inside. And there was something else, smooth and round, the size of a large metal egg. She had seen pictures of grenades that looked like pineapples. This was different. But it had a metal clip along the side and a pin connected to a round ring, holding the clip in place. She lifted it in her hand to get a sense of its weight, then wondered how anyone could throw the thing. It weighed as much as a cast-iron pan.

Carefully she put it back in the bag and moved the articles around with her hand. There was a compass, a shiny metal mirror, a drab green can of what looked like food. That was it.

She tried to figure out how to get the clip out of the machine gun. She pulled on it but it wouldn't come. She saw a button on the side, pushed it and the clip fell out on the floor. There were bullets in it but she couldn't tell how many.

Assuming the one from the bag was fully loaded she slid it into the gun and hit the end of the clip against the floor. It clicked into place. She flipped the lever on the side until the red dot appeared, then pointed the fat muzzle toward the wall on the far side of the room. She flinched and turned her head away as she squeezed the trigger gently. She was startled only by the near-silent vibration in her hands as a dozen bullets riddled the wall.

So much for target practice. She grabbed the satchel and edged her body toward the door. If the house was a target for something called Green Giant, she had to get out.

She flattened her body to the floor and with one hand swung the door open. Another flurry of shots round out. Bullets snapped the air in the open doorway. She slid the muzzle around the edge of the door frame, and without looking she pulled the trigger. Once, twice, three times. She tried a fourth but it wouldn't fire.

Joselyn pulled the gun back in before they shot it off. She pushed the button and the clip fell out. It was empty. She reached into the satchel and found another and slid it into the gun. Quickly she stuck the muzzle out the doorway and pulled the trigger. Nothing.

She looked at it, slapped it on its side, hit it on the floor, and tried it again. It wouldn't fire. If they realized she had a broken gun, they'd be on her in a second. She reached for the pistol in the bag and pulled it out.

Suddenly she remembered. The sailor had slid something back on the top of the pistol when he loaded it. She looked. There was nothing like that on the machine gun. Then she saw a small knob on the side. She hooked a finger over it, pulled hard, and slid it back. When it got to the farthest point, the knob slipped out of her finger and slammed forward. She reached for it again and without thinking squeezed the trigger. Bullets ripped the wall six inches away.

'Fixed.' It scared the hell out of her, but at least it worked. She stuck the muzzle out the door and fired again. Within seconds the clip was empty.

She couldn't hit a damn thing, and she knew it. Joselyn looked in the satchel. There were only two more clips, and the Green Giant was coming. She didn't have a clue as to what it was or how much time she had. For all she knew within a minute she would be lying dead on the floor next to the sailor.

She reached in the bag and felt around, found the small metal mirror. She loaded a fresh clip into the gun, then rolled over on her back so that she was flat on the floor with her head just inches inside the frame of the door. She held the mirror in her left hand and slowly eased it past the edge of the door. Finally she could see who was shooting at her. Four men behind a wall of sandbags, their rifles resting on top. They were maybe fifty feet away. Joselyn had been shooting into the dirt.

B uck Thompson had his own rifle, a 270 Winchester with a scope and a kick like a mule. A Remington bolt action, he couldn't fire rapidly, but he could thread the needle at two hundred yards. He had arrived from down in California only the day before, carrying a satchel of cash from their fundraising activities back to Taggart. Now Thompson was in the thick of it.

'How many you think are in there?' He looked at the guy next to him behind the sandbags.

'One. I think.' The guy was reloading a clip from an M-16, sitting in the bottom of the bunker with his back against the sandbags. 'There was another one, but I think we got him.' Thompson peaked over the top of the bags. He could see a bright reflection off a piece of metal or glass. 'Son of a bitch is checking us out with a mirror.'

The other man slammed the clip into his rifle and came up next to him. Soon there were four heads peaking over the top.

'He's laying with his head against the wall, just to the right of the door at the level of the floor. Let me have one shot at the mirror,' said Thompson. 'That'll force him to lie still, flat on his back. Give me a count of three, then concentrate your fire right at the level of the porch floor, just to the right to the door. Put enough rounds there, we'll get him in the head.'

Thompson slid the bolt back on his rifle and brought it up to the top of the sandbag.

She'd been looking at the image in the mirror for several seconds, taking it all in before it finally registered: the four men were standing in a bunker.

One of them took aim. Joselyn pulled the mirror in a half-second before he fired. The round smashed into the wooden threshold at the bottom of the door and a spray of splinters caught the back of Joselyn's hand. She grimaced in pain, and pulled it to her chest. She took one long breath and then, without waiting or looking, pulled two splinters as long as porcupine quills from the back of her hand. Searing pain ran up her arm, but the rush of adrenalin and the fear of death worked like a narcotic.

She rolled on her side toward the door. She remembered the two men she had overheard talking about the bunkers being wired for explosives. Forming a mental image of the sandbags and their location, she stuck the muzzle out the door, holding it higher this time, and pulled the trigger. A dozen rounds rattled off; nothing.

Bullets smashed through the wall an inch behind her head, shattering the maple leg of the end table under the window and slamming into the dead sailor. His lower body danced on the floor like a marionette pulled by invisible strings.

Joselyn lifted the muzzle higher and, pulled the trigger again, holding it down. She couldn't tell how many rounds she fired, but the gun stopped shooting just an instant before the concussion blew what was left of the windows out of the back of the house. The super-heated air of the blast rushed through the open door like a firestorm. Joselyn could feel the radiation on the side of her face. One of the sandbags came down, slamming through the roof over the porch. It landed with a thud two feet from the open door. Joselyn could see the scorched fabric of the bag still smoking.

Now there was silence, broken only by the crackle of flames somewhere outside. Carefully, Joselyn peeked around the door frame. The bunker was a scorched ruin. There was no sign of any of the men. She wasn't going to wait for their friends to show up. She dropped the pistol and the mirror into the satchel and picked it up. Then she scurried to her feet. She took one last look at the dead sailor on the floor, then ran as fast as she could out the door, headed for the wooded high ground behind the house.

CHAPTER
TWENTY-SEVEN

Situation Room, the White House

Hirshberg closed the door and left behind the acid odor of coffee having cooked too long over a heated plate. The corridors in the basement of the West Wing were now bustling with people as the work day moved toward noon. As he passed the White House Mess, headed for the small flight of steps and the president's office upstairs, Hirshberg yearned for a fresh cup of coffee. But he didn't have time.

Hirshberg climbed the stairs two at a time and headed down the crowded corridor. Young interns and secretaries parted for him like the waters the Red Sea. None of them knew precisely what was going on, but the president had canceled all of his meetings outside of the White House, and Cabinet secretaries and military personnel were seen entering and leaving the Oval Office all morning.

It was a busy time of year. Preparation was ongoing for the State of the Union address, now just a few days off. But events in the West Wing had the smell of an international crisis, not the usual domestic soothsaying of growth in the economy and fine times ahead.

Hirshberg was growing double bags under each eye to match the double chin his wife had been warning him about. He was no longer a kid, and staying up all night had long since lost the excitement it held in his youth.

He didn't bother with formalities but walked into the Oval Office and closed the door behind him. The president was huddled with General Richard Skzorn, Chairman of the Joint Chiefs, and two other military aides. They were seated on the couches near the fireplace.

The president looked up. 'Any word, Sy?'

'Yes, sir. None of it good.'

'Give it to us.'

'Coast Guard cutters a mile off the island report gunfire, and one large explosion.'

'How large?'

'Conventional,' said Hirshberg.

There was a palpable sigh of relief from the president. 'Any word from the SEALs? They're our eyes and ears. We've got to get information from them to know what to do.'

'We have nothing from them directly,' said Hirshberg.

'That means either the satellite station didn't function right, or maybe they lost it going in,' said the president.

'They could have gotten caught in a fire fight before they had a chance to set up,' said the general.

'In any event, we're blind,' said the president.

'That's not the worst part,' said Hirshberg. 'We now have casualties.'

'Who?' said the president.

'The SEALs did make contact with one of the Coast Guard cutters on a military frequency. It was very brief and sketchy before their signal broke up. They were calling

342

for boats to get them off. They were under fire. According to the information, two of the five-man team never made it onto the island. We think they were lost at sea in the night drop.'

'Jeez.' The president got up from the couch, hit his thigh with one hand, and turned his back to the men sitting across from him on the couch.

'How did we get in this mess? We shouldn't have gone in at night. That was a mistake. And there should have been a much larger force, more time for planning.'

'Mr President, you will recall that is what we recommended,' said the general.

'I know. I know,' said the president. 'I made the call. The responsibility rests here. It doesn't make the pain any less.' He turned to Hirshberg. 'Do we have ships in the water, searching for those men?'

'It's pretty difficult right now, Mr President. With incoming troops and a gunship in the air. Besides we're trying to screen vessels on the Sound. Private pleasure craft, commercial fishing vessels. Just in case they got the device off the island.'

The president took a long, deep breath and thought for a second. 'Has the Coast Guard seen any traffic coming from that island this morning?'

'Not since oh-five-hundred when the blockade was put in place.'

'Then let's forget screening the vessels. We can't cover everything on the Sound. Let's assume that the device is bottled up on that island,' said the president. 'Get what boats we can spare to search for those men.'

'Mr President, I don't think we can take that chan—'

'Don't argue with me, Sy.'

Hirshberg knew when it was useless, but he tried anyway.

'They couldn't survive in that water for more than two hours, Mr President. Even in wetsuits.'

A new taste of reality for the equation.

'They can survive,' said the president. 'They're Navy SEALs. They're the best in the world. I will not have it said that I did not give them every chance. Stop screening vessels and get those ships into search-and-rescue mode, every available ship that isn't needed for the blockade. Is that clear?'

'We're very likely to have more casualties before the end of the day, Mr President,' said Hirshberg.

'Let's hope they're all on the other side,' said the general.

'Hoping is not going to make it happen,' said Hirshberg. 'Most of our troops going in are green. Only the commanding officer and five of his non-coms have any combat experience.'

'We've got fire power and training on our side,' said the general.

'I certainly hope so,' said Hirshberg. 'Because we're going to need that, and a lot of luck, if we're going to find that bomb before they detonate it.'

'Sy, see if we can make contact with the SEALs on that island. Tell them that help is on the way.'

'They know that, Mr President. The Coast Guard told them to stay away from the bunkers, that they were targeted.'

'Good. That's something anyway.'

'I'd better get back and see if there's any more communiqués,' said Hirshberg.

'Let us know the second you hear anything,' said the president.

T he Coast Guard vessel was showing red and blue lights, flashing like strobes over the roof of the bridge as its bow cut across the wake of the slower-moving LSC and pulled in behind it. It closed the distance quickly. The *Humping Goose* was no match for the fast and nimble Coast Guard patrol boat.

Oscar Chaney saw it in the mirror of the truck as he sat behind the wheel. He rolled down the passenger-side window and leaned low over the seat in order to look up at the wheelhouse.

The skipper slid open the window.

'What do they want?' asked Chaney.

'They want us to stop so they can board and inspect.' Nat Hobbs leaned out of the wheelhouse window and yelled down to Chaney. Hobbs was wearing a Greek captain's cap that looked like it was molting little blue balls of fuzz. His face was smudged with oil and his jumper had seen enough sweat to stand in the corner without Hobbs in it.

Chaney looked at the ferry dock less than a quarter of a mile away. He noticed two State Patrol cars parked near the ferry building and what looked like an older blue Customs Department vehicle.

'I hope you're not on a tight schedule,' said Hobbs. 'I'm gonna have to stop.'

'Gotta do what you gotta do,' said Chaney.

'I could try and put in for the dock, but if I jack 'em around we may get the full nine yards. I'll be tied up at the dock for two hours for a safety inspection while they hassle the hell outta me with forms.'

To Chaney it sounded like Hobbs might not pass. He didn't say a word but rolled up the window as if to say the call belonged to Hobbs. At the same time, he reached under the seat cushion on the passenger side of the truck and slid the 45 semi-automatic across the seat and into the belt of his pants. He pulled his sweater down over the handle, then ran his hand along the back of his leg and into the top of his boot to feel for the hilt of the large Bowie knife inside.

He opened the door of the truck and stepped down. The Kalashnikov was under the seat, fully loaded with a fifty-round clip. It could be fired on full automatic, and there were six more loaded clips lying beside it, but it was no match for the mounted gun on the bow of the Coast Guard boat.

Chaney glanced with one eye behind the seat, just enough to catch a glimpse of the red metal ring attached to a light cable. The cable ran through a hole in the back of the truck's cab and from there into the welded tank on the back. It was connected to a timed detonator and eight pounds of C-4 plastique. This was mounted just underneath the device. If all else failed, Chaney could pull the ring. He would then have exactly ninety seconds to hit the water and swim as fast as he could, against the direction of the wind.

The explosion would not go nuclear, but it would blow the truck into the air, rupture the tank, and send highly radioactive plutonium dust into the wind. If he waited until the Coast Guard boat was tied up alongside, the ensuing chaos might give him time to get away. What he needed now was to stall for time, control of the boat.

Chaney closed the truck door but didn't lock it, then walked toward the stern of the *Humping Goose* and climbed the short ladder to the wheelhouse.

When he got there, Hobbs was on the radio.

'You guys just inspected me last month.' Hobbs let up on the button to the microphone and turned to see his passenger.

'We see one truck onboard,' said the Coast Guard. 'How many passengers?'

'Just one. Just the one truck,' said Hobbs.

'What's on the truck?' asked the Coast Guard.

'It's a septic truck. You wanna look inside?'

There was a delay, several seconds at the other end.

'We are under orders to board and search all vessels in this area. You are ordered to come to a dead stop and prepare for boarding. Is that understood?'

'Shit.' Hobbs didn't press the mike button, but said it to himself.

'At least let me clear the channel to the ferry landing,' said Hobbs. 'Unless you want an accident.'

Again there was a delay from the Coast Guard end.

'You better get down to your truck. Sounds like they're gonna want to look and see what's inside,' Hobbs told Chaney.

'Affirmative,' said the Coast Guard. 'We will follow you into the channel.'

Hobbs hung the microphone up on the radio receiver set, like he wanted to break off the knob that held it.

'Son of a bitch. They think I got nothin' else to do.' He was now talking to himself. 'I hope they bring their fancy white dress gloves.' He kicked the two throttle handles for the twin diesels from idle to full-ahead, while he steered the *Humping Goose* back out into the open channel. He didn't pay any attention to the fact that Chaney was still behind him. 'I guarantee you those dandies aren't gonna want to look inside your truck. One whiff and they'll take their starched uniforms back to their boat and disappear. In the meantime, I'll lose an hour screwing around.'

The squared-off bow of the *Humping Goose* was designed to drop like a World War II landing craft. It formed a hydraulic bridge that allowed cars and trucks to drive onto a beach or more usually a private boat ramp. The captain of the Coast Guard boat watched as it plowed the water in its own ponderous way back out toward the channel and the rougher waters that fed the Straits of Juan de Fuca from the North Pacific.

In five minutes, they had gone more than a mile.

'*Humping Goose, Humping Goose*, this is the Coast Guard. How far out are you going?'

The Coast Guard captain released the mike button and listened. There was no response.

'Private ferry, do you read? This is the Coast Guard.' The radio channel opened and all the officer heard was static. He was about to punch the button to speak one more time, when the frequency suddenly came to life.

'Coast Guard. This is the *Humping Goose*. I wanna get well clear of the channel,' the voice came back over the radio.

'You're now in safe waters,' said the Coast Guard officer. 'Cut your engines and prepare for boarding.'

Suddenly one of the enlisted men came onto the bridge. 'Sir, communiqué from Everett.' He handed the captain a slip of paper with a typed message.

The Coast Guard officer was still watching the stern of the old rusted-out LCS bearing the chipped green paint and the words *Humping Goose* across the broad transom. There was no sign that its engines were slowing.

The captain looked down and read the message in his hand, then fumed and shook his head. He opened the channel again. 'To the working boat, *Humping Goose*, do you read? There has been a change in our orders. We are being diverted to air-sea rescue in the north Sound. Thank you for your cooperation. You are free to put in at Keystone. Repeat. You are free to put in at Keystone.'

'Thank you, sir. I appreciate it,' the reply came back.

The Coast Guard boat cut a sharp swath across the wake of the *Humping Goose* and bounced into high speed as she overtook the slower vessel on her port side. The officers on the bridge didn't pay much attention to the working boat's captain with his greasy face and Greek sea cap as he waved and smiled at them from the open window of the wheelhouse. The Coast Guard boat sped away and cut across the *Humping Goose*'s course two hundred yards ahead before making the turn back north.

Oscar Chaney took the hat off his head and dropped it onto the deck of the wheelhouse as he steered a course south down the channel. Change of plans. He wasn't going to Keystone or any other public dock. They were looking for something, and Chaney knew what it was. He glanced over his shoulder at the river of blood that began to dam near the threshold of the wheelhouse door. The big knife had not only cut the jugular vein and carotid arteries, it had all but severed Nat Hobbs's head.

Padget Island, WA

The trees, large evergreens some of them ninety feet tall, looked like the charred masts of a wrecked fleet. They had been limbed, some of them snapped in half by the aerial howitzer rounds from the gunship. Every third tree seemed to be missing its top. Many of them were still burning.

The howitzer had not been as effective as originally believed. The dense foliage had caused many of the rounds to explode high in the trees. Still there were bodies everywhere.

Gideon counted at least eight dead in the fifty feet around the area cleared for the helicopter landing pad. He jumped out behind the colonel and ran at a crouch until they cleared the rotor wash.

'I want you to stay here, Mr van Ry.' The colonel turned and looked at him. 'I will leave one of my men with you. You do whatever he tells you. Do you understand?'

'Colonel, if the device is on this island, I would suggest that we get to it quickly.'

'I understand. You're anxious to get at it. But we haven't rounded up all the terrorists. There's still a pocket of resistance down near the beach. Until it's safe, I want you here.'

'What about Ms Cole?' asked Gideon.

'I've passed the word to my men to keep an eye out for her. I don't want to be worrying about you as well. So you will stay here.' It wasn't a question. It was an order.

Gideon nodded.

The marine colonel looked like maybe he didn't trust him. 'Corporal.' He turned to one of the young marines behind him. 'I want you to keep and eye on Mr van Ry here. If anything happens to him, I'm going to hold you personally responsible. Do you understand?'

'Yes, sir.'

'Good. Now let's get down to that beach.' The colonel headed out. 'Where's my radio man?' A clutch of armed troops followed him as another helicopter came in. Another young marine, with a radio strapped to his back and a coiled antenna looping over one shoulder like a wounded angel, loped up next to the colonel. He took the telephone receiver from the kid and started talking, but Gideon couldn't hear what he said. The sound of the rotors and the helicopter engine revving-up for takeoff drowned out everything else. Dust kicked up, and Gideon and the corporal turned their backs to the landing zone and covered their eyes.

The helicopter swung up over the trees and out toward the water. It was followed by another incoming chopper.

'I think maybe we should get out of here,' said Gideon.

The corporal didn't seem to object, so Gideon headed off toward a clump of burned-out trees on a high knoll overlooking the west side of the island. When he got far enough away that he was no longer deafened by the noise of the helicopters, he found a flat boulder, hefted the backpack with his equipment off of one shoulder, set it down, and sat on the rock. He checked his watch. It was now after noon, and his empty stomach was grumbling. He had not eaten since supper the evening before, with Joselyn at her house on San Juan Island. He wondered if she was alive or dead.

The distant sound of the helicopters was now punctuated by the periodic sound of gunfire, single shots and short bursts, the echo of what sounded like machine gun rounds, some of it heavier.

The corporal brought his M-16 up across his chest. An expression of concern suddenly crept across his face.

'What is wrong?' said Gideon.

The soldier was standing on an outcropping of rock closer to the edge of the bluff and looking down at something Gideon could not see.

'I don't like this. We're silhouetted up here,' said the marine. 'If there's anybody down there with a rifle, we'd make a pretty good target.' He pointed and Gideon got up to take a look.

Below, nestled in the embrace at the bottom of the bluff was a large building, the back side of which was still smoking. He could see no movement, no signs of life. Beyond the house was a cove and what remained of a small dock, shattered and gone in places, some of its pilings charred to the waterline.

'Is that the main house?' said Gideon.

'I guess so.'

'Do you have a map?'

The marine shook his head.

Gideon turned and looked in the direction of the gunfire. 'I take it the beach is on the other side of the island?'

'I think so.'

'Then we're probably safe here.' Gideon stepped back and reached into his pack. He pulled out the one piece of useful equipment he'd thought to bring: a small pair of binoculars. The field glasses were not the best. They were underpowered for the distance.

He trained them on the house and focused. The place looked deserted. He held them as still as possible and watched for any telltale signs of life, anything that moved. The only motion came from wisps of dense black smoke that floated across his field of vision.

'See anything?' asked the corporal.

'No. Would you like to look?'

The marine smiled, strapped his rifle over his shoulder, and took the field glasses. He started scanning from the corner of the house nearest the dock, trying desperately with compromised optics to check the windows for rifle muzzles. He did this slowly, scanning the house from one end to the other.

'Do you see anything?'

'No.' The corporal still had a troubled look on his face.

'Why don't we go down there and take a look?' said Gideon.

The marine gave him a sick laugh. 'No way.'

'Where is your sense of adventure?' Gideon smiled, the look of an older man challenging the other's manhood.

'I left it at home,' said the soldier.

He might be young, thought Gideon, but he was no fool.

There was a sudden respite from the noise as all of the helicopters moved offshore, a sudden lapse in the deafening sound that seemed to be replaced by a lot of shouting back in the clearing. The corporal turned to see what was going on, while Gideon took another look through the binoculars. When he turned, the marine was totally distracted, his back to the bluff.

'What's happening?' said Gideon.

'I don't know. Something's up.'

They could still hear more firing off in the distance. What sounded like heavier machine gun fire now.

Gideon turned and looked at the house once more. He wondered if Joselyn might be inside. He didn't know what other buildings existed on the island, but the house was definitely a candidate for the device. When he looked back at the corporal, the marine was now totally occupied with the scene back at the landing zone. If the kid had an antenna of his own, it was now definitely up. Something was wrong.

'Maybe we should go find out what's happening?' he said.

Gideon grabbed his backpack and followed the marine back to the landing zone. By now marines were coming up from the beach in groups of four and five, all with differing but dazed expressions on their faces. Some were running, others walking, but all conveyed a single uniform emotion – fear.

'What happened?' The corporal tried to stop one of them. The man ran right through his arms. 'What the hell's goin' on? Somebody talk to me.' Something had happened, and a contagion of fear was taking hold of the young marines on the hill. Now they were coming up from the beach in larger groups. It looked like a wholesale retreat.

Gideon recognized panic when he saw it. He grabbed one of them by the arm. The kid dropped his rifle and looked at him with a vacant stare.

'You!' He looked down at the man with as stern an expression as he could muster. 'Tell me what's happened?'

'Hisss . . . his head. It . . . it . . . it . . . it . . .'

'Whose head?'

'Co . . . Co . . . Colonel Simmons.'

'What about Colonel Simmons?'

'His head's gone.'

'What are you talking about?'

'The colonel's dead. They shot him in the head. It just . . . just . . . exploded.'

'Who's in charge?' said Gideon.

'I don't know,' said the marine. Gideon released his hold on the man for an instant to collect his thoughts, and before he could grab him again the kid was gone, leaving his rifle behind him in the dirt as he ran down the hill in the other direction.

Gideon reached down and picked it up. By now the corporal that Simmons had left to watch him was caught up in the general panic that was spreading like a rash across the landing zone. They were in trouble, and Gideon knew it. Shots were still coming from the beach, heavy gunfire.

'Where's the radio?' said Gideon.

No one paid attention to him.

'Who has the radio?'

CHAPTER
TWENTY-EIGHT

Denver International Airport

Scott Taggart reset his watch to eastern time, skipping the mountain zone since he would be there for less than an hour. He tried to calculate how many hours had passed since he dropped Thorn at the small private airport at Arlington in the Skagit Valley. While he wondered what Thorn was doing there, he knew better than to ask. Thorn was not one to share information unless there was a purpose. At that point, Taggart's job was to get to Sea-Tac and catch his flight to the east coast.

On a stopover in Denver, he found a bank of phones and placed the call as Thorn had directed. He dialed the cellular number and heard it ring twice before a voice answered.

'Yes.' It was Thorn. He was breathless, his single word muffled by what sounded like industrial noise in the background: heavy equipment, and the relentless peal of a safety bell as a truck or some other vehicle backed up.

'Taggart here.'

'I was beginning to worry,' said Thorn.

'I just arrived. The flight was ten minutes late getting in.'

'Then you don't have much time,' said Thorn. 'Check inside your briefcase. You will find a key stamped with a red number. It fits a locker on that concourse. Go to the locker. Everything you need as well as your instructions are inside. Do you understand?'

'Yes.'

'Follow the instructions precisely,' said Thorn.

'How will I contact you?'

'You won't,' said Thorn. 'Just follow the instructions.' The signal at the other end went dead. Thorn had punched the END key on the cellphone before Taggart could say another word.

He hung up the receiver, lifted his briefcase onto the flat stainless steel surface under the phone, then spread it open and looked inside.

The leather briefcase had not been out of his possession since he packed it the night before. But there in the bottom was a brass key, the number C-142 stamped in red plastic. Thorn must have dropped it into the case on the boat that morning, when they switched seats so that Taggart could drive.

He grabbed the key and began searching the concourse for lockers. The first set he found didn't correspond to the number on the key. He checked his watch. He had less than eighteen minutes to find the locker and catch his connecting flight.

Padget Island, WA

T wo helicopters were headed back in from the Sound toward the landing zone. Gideon could see them coming in low over the water. Only this time they were not the ponderous overburdened Hueys that landed Simmons and his troops. These were smaller, with a sleek, black profile. Gideon recognized their dark silhouettes from pictures he had seen in *Jane's Defence Weekly*.

The two Cobra gunships swept in low over the landing zone at high speed, causing the marines on the ground to flinch and duck. The two choppers swung toward the beach and the sound of the gunfire. It was clear that somebody in authority had found a radio.

Gideon didn't wait to find out what would happen. He knew that if he wanted to see what was in that house he would have to do it now. The corporal that Simmons had assigned to watch him was busy getting an earload; descriptions of death down on the beach.

Gideon picked up the marine's M-16 from the dirt where the panicky kid had dropped it. He slung the gun over his shoulder, grabbed his backpack of equipment and ran through a grove of burned-out trees down a dusty path that seemed to head in the right direction, toward the house on the cove.

In the star burst of figures fleeing the landing zone, Gideon was just one more running figure. In less than a minute, he had separated himself from the forces on the hill. He was alone, moving quickly down the dusty path.

He rounded a bend and could see the house, this time from a different angle. He stopped behind a tree and studied the front of the building again through the field glasses that he took from his pack.

Most of the windows across the front were shattered, blown out like the ones in the back that he and the marine corporal had seen from the bluff above.

What looked like fly specks all over the white paint under the overhanging porch on the front side, on closer inspection through the glasses, turned out to be bullet holes.

There had been a pitched battle at the house, and Gideon wondered what caused it. Simmons had ordered the building off-limits to the gunship and its howitzer.

He scanned the area in front of the house. A sandbagged bunker appeared to be empty, though he couldn't see into part of it because of a corrugated metal roof.

He dropped the field glasses back in his pack and started back down the path.

Thirty feet down, he crossed a small creek. The path suddenly descended precipitously. His feet hit loose gravel, slipping out from under him. Gideon grabbed the rifle and managed to keep it out of the dirt, but slid on his side and began to roll down the steep incline.

He lost control and tumbled. Items came flying from of his backpack. He lost his grip on the rifle. The sling wrapped around his arm, and halfway down the hill something hit the trigger. The rifle discharged. The shot didn't hit him, but the sound of the report close to Gideon's head nearly deafened him. He rolled down the hill but somehow managed to get control of the rifle again. He clung to it like a lifeline.

It wasn't until the tumbling stopped abruptly in the hollow of a small ravine that Gideon realized that he never checked the rifle to see if the safety was on or if it was loaded. The fact that he hadn't shot himself was a miracle, though anybody within a half mile of the house now knew he was there. He lay there dazed for a moment, trying to recover his bearings.

Gideon felt a burning sensation along the side of his leg and looked down. His pants were ripped, and the skin that poked through on the side of his thigh looked like raspberries that had been crushed in a blender. His right arm was scraped and scratched from the wrist to the elbow.

He tried to collect himself, looked back up the hill, and saw items of equipment from his backpack strewn over the steep path. The pack was still wrapped around one arm, its strap twisted around his wrist. He unwound the strap from his arm and set the bag carefully on the ground to check what was left of its contents. The heavy Geiger counter was still in the bottom, though Gideon couldn't be sure after the pounding whether it would still function.

The binoculars and compass were gone. He looked with a pained expression back up the hill. He did not have time to go searching for them now.

Carefully, Gideon checked for a safety on the rifle, and found what he thought was it. Even though he was a weapons designer, he had little expertise in firearms. He flipped the wedge-shaped metal catch back and forth several times, until he satisfied himself as to which position was on and which was off.

He fumbled with the gun for a few more seconds and managed to detach the metal magazine from the underside of the weapon. He checked this for ammunition. The clip appeared to be full. He took one of the bullets out of the magazine.

Five-point-five-six-millimeter NATO rounds. The Netherlands was one of the charter members of NATO, though Gideon knew more about its organization than its small arms.

It was a small bottle-shaped round with a bullet roughly the size of a .22, but heavier in weight and longer. Gideon guessed that the bullet was probably fifty or sixty grains in weight and steel-jacketed. The rifle would be accurate out to maybe two hundred yards, that is, if you were a good shot, which Gideon knew he was not. Perhaps he could hit a large, still target at a hundred yards, if he was lucky.

He hoped he wouldn't have to use the gun at all. If he did, he would fire one shot at a time, and hopefully come close enough to discourage anyone from investigating him at closer range. He had no desire to kill anyone, and even less to be killed himself.

He pressed the bullet back in the magazine and carefully slid the clip back into the gun. Then he checked the safety one more time, slung the rifle over his shoulder, grabbed his backpack and stood up.

With the first step he limped heavily on the injured leg. Blood was spreading through the material on his pant leg, though the pain told him that the injury was not serious. He had no time to take care of it. He gritted his teeth for the first few steps and slowly lengthened his stride as his limbs loosened up and the burning sensation in his leg began to pass. A few more paces, and he shook off the stiffness. He moved in the direction of the house. It was maybe fifty or sixty yards away, across a small meadow.

He felt the percussion of the bullet as it passed an instant before the sound of the shot registered. Gideon hit the ground like a sack of sand.

Denver International Airport

Taggart checked two more alcoves off of the main concourse before he found the locker with the right number stamped on the metal door. He slid the key into the lock, and it turned. Carefully, applying pressure with one hand while he pulled gently with the other, he opened the small metal door just a fraction of an inch, just enough to allow a sliver of light to penetrate into the dark confines of the locker. Then he looked to see if anyone was watching.

The busy concourse was filled with travelers, most of them in a hurry. No one seemed to be paying particular attention to anything going on at the bank of lockers.

Taggart peeked inside over the edge of the slightly open door. There was a piece of paper, what looked like a single sheet, folded inside on the bottom of the locker. It was a few inches back from the door. On top of it was a glass container, what looked like a classic bottle of men's aftershave. Next to these appeared to be a closed book of matches.

Taggart looked for wires or strings connecting the bottle to the door, any sign of a booby trap.

He had never trusted Thorn from the inception. The man had come into the deal, firmly attached to the nuclear device as part of the transaction. Taggart had never fully understood why, only that it was an immutable condition of the transaction.

The man had been paid a bundle of money by Taggart's group, money they had raised by highly intricate scams and a few violent robberies, mostly banks with large cash deposits.

For all Taggart knew the nuclear device that his group had paid for might well be resting at the bottom of the Sound, dumped there by Thorn at the first sign of trouble. He had seen the device only once, and then only briefly after being blindfolded and taken to an undisclosed location as a condition of payment.

If things had now soured, eliminating Taggart would be Thorn's first instinct. Why leave somebody behind who could identify him? After all, Thorn had killed the woman for the same reason.

Taggart couldn't see any wires or thin fishing filament

connected to the door or running from the back of the locker to the bottle.

There was one other possibility. The bottle was large enough to contain an explosive accelerant, nitro, or something else equally potent. It might be set up to detonate by a photocell. When the door opened, and enough light reached the bottle – BANG.

Taggart carefully closed the door and leaned against it with his shoulder to keep it shut against the pressure of the slight back-spring. He took the handkerchief from his pocket and wiped the perspiration from his brow, then checked his watch. He was down to eight minutes if he was going to catch his flight.

Quickly he lifted his briefcase and reached inside. He grabbed a thickness of pages eight-and-a-half-by-eleven sheets from a spiral notebook, and ripped them from their wire binding.

He dropped the briefcase and held the thickness of paper up to the edge of the locker door like a shield, then carefully opened the door, a fraction of an inch at a time.

Sweat ran down his upper lip. Finally with the door open just a crack he slipped the flat of his hand through, holding the thickness of paper between his thumb and his palm. He then shut the door against his forearm and tried to seal off as much of the light as he could with his shoulder.

Feeling around inside like a blind man, Taggart inched his hand toward the bottle, careful not to jar it or knock it over. He got a grip on it and wrapped the paper around it. He tried to feel for any protrusions in the glass that might indicate the existence of a thin photocell cemented to the outside. He felt only the smooth symmetrical shape of the glass.

Still he took no chances. Carefully he lifted the bottle out, still tightly wrapped in its paper covering. Then he grabbed the piece of paper that was neatly folded and lying on the bottom of the locker.

Using his lips and his free hand, he opened the note and read. It was typed and very brief. His brows furrowed, and a smile curled on his lips as he digested the message. It was so simple it was brilliant. It gave him a whole new sense of appreciation for Thorn.

He was no longer worried about the bottle exploding. He carefully unwrapped it from the paper, then checked its cap to make sure that it was sealed tight. He gingerly set the bottle into the bottom of his briefcase and propped a few items against it for safety, so that it wouldn't break or leak.

The last instruction in the note he followed to a tee. He placed the note back in the locker, then looked to make sure that no one was watching. He picked up the book of matches inside and without removing his hands from the locker, struck a match and set an edge of the paper on fire. Closing the door only enough to confine the smoke and look over the top, Taggart watched the paper slowly turn to ash as the flame finished its work.

A light haze of smoke curled from the locker as he opened the door. No one else seemed to notice. He reached inside and swept the ash out of the locker and onto the floor, then checked his watch. He had less than five minutes to catch his flight. Taggart picked up his briefcase and ran for the gate. Thorn was about to make his bonus money after all.

*　　*　　*

J oselyn edged cautiously toward the edge of the small grove of wind-dwarfed trees with the sound of the first shot. She had heard distant firing all morning, but this was different. It was much closer.

She waited and listened. She moved out of the brush, all of her senses sharpened like a cautious deer. Clutching the small machine gun from the dead Navy SEAL in her hands, she was now down to the last full magazine of bullets. She had stashed the satchel with the pistol and grenades in the hollow of a tree in the grove. It would be her last refuge if she were forced to retreat.

Joselyn had just cleared the edge of the small grove and was looking toward the path when she saw him, sitting on the ground a hundred yards away, looking at his pant leg, picking at it with the fingers of one hand. It was same tan pants and white shirt he'd been wearing the night before, when he left her standing on the dock in Friday Harbor.

The ungainly figure sitting on the ground looking at his leg was Gideon. She had no idea how he'd gotten to the island, and what's more, she didn't care. All she knew is that he had come for her, that she was no longer alone.

Without thinking, she dropped the gun and started to run.

Gideon didn't see her. He seemed focused on the backpack on the ground in front of him and the front of the house. He never looked toward the grove of trees set into the high bluff behind it.

Joselyn edged her way around giant boulders of sandstone, and into a small ravine running with water from a creek. She lost sight of him as she dropped down into the ravine and tried to climb up the other side. She couldn't. She kept sliding back down. She grabbed at some small roots growing from the side of the ravine, and they pulled loose in her hand. She turned and followed the ravine down, following the flow of the water, the course of least resistance.

She ran for what seemed like a minute, but was in reality only seconds. Her head surfaced just above the edge of the ravine so that she could see Gideon once more, walking through the meadow, limping toward the house.

Joselyn raised an arm and was about to call to him, when the shock of the rifle butt against the side of her face drove her to the ground and back down into the ravine.

She had failed to see the man wedged in the rocks just above her. Joselyn got only a fleeting glimpse of his face, hideous and seared, as she hit the ground and rolled on one shoulder into the shallow channel of the creek. The only force keeping her conscious was the shock of the icy water and the flow of adrenalin coursing in her veins.

Dazed, she looked up and saw him as he took aim.

Buck Thompson was a crack shot, but his rifle had taken a beating, bouncing on the ground after the explosion had thrown him out of the bunker. He centered the crosshairs of the scope on the man's chest and squeezed the trigger.

Unable to shake off the effects of the blow or to crawl to her feet in the trickling waters of the creek, Joselyn heard the sharp peal of the rifle as the shot reverberated through the ravine. A second later he was on her, the barrel of his rifle waving in her face as she got to her knees. Its tapered muzzle moving close to touch the side of her temple just below the hairline. Cold, hard steel.

He worked the bolt and ejected the round, seating another.

'Don't scream.'

She tried to open her mouth, but nothing came out.

'Don't.' His voice issued from twisted lips, burned crisp to a hideous black at one corner.

She knew from the way he fired, and leaped from the crevice in the rocks that his shot had found its mark. Gideon was dead. The thought made its mark on her consciousness, but acceptance of the fact as reality did not.

She began to scream. Joselyn couldn't keep her eyes off of the man's face. It embodied every grotesque event of the last twenty-four hours. She screamed in a pitch of fright and revulsion at the death that lay about her.

The man's right eye seemed to be gone, the side of his face had the texture and pallor of melted wax, part of it seared and blackened like meat that had been left too long on a spit.

Even in this form, she recognized him. It was the man with the scoped rifle, the one she had seen in the mirror, taking aim as she lay near the open doorway. How he'd survived the blast in the bunker Joselyn had no idea.

His one good eye darted between Joselyn and the edge of the ravine over which he could no longer see. He rapped her on the head with the barrel of the rifle, not hard, but with enough force to get her attention, to stop her screaming, which pierced his open sinus cavity like a knife.

Joselyn looked at him in stark horror, but she stopped screaming.

He lifted the muzzle of the rifle and grabbed Joselyn roughly by the arm, pulling her to her feet. Then he pushed her ahead of him, down toward the shallow end of the ravine, where it poured into the open meadow.

They entered flat ground near the side of the house, Joselyn in front, the steel barrel of the man's rifle in the small of her back.

Keeping her between himself and his dead quarry, the man kept peeking over Joselyn's shoulder with his one good eye, trying to locate the body on the ground. Grass and wild flowers now formed an impenetrable horizontal sea, a foot deep and a hundred yards wide across the meadow. Having given up the high ground the gunman could no longer find his target. He wanted to put one more bullet in him just to make sure.

As they walked along the side of the house, he pulled Joselyn in close to his body like a shield.

She could smell the odor of singed flesh hanging over her shoulder, the whistle of heavy breathing through the edema of burned airways.

'Slow down.' There was fear in his voice.

Joselyn knew that any second he could pull the trigger, sending a rifle bullet smashing through her body.

He held her tight in front of him as pressed his back against the wall at the side of the house, forming his own kind of human bunker.

'What was in that?' He whispered into her ear.

'What are you talking about?'

'The sandbags, behind the house? What was in them?'

'I didn't do it,' said Joselyn.

'Explosives?'

She nodded.

'Who?'

'The man they called Thorn,' said Joselyn. 'He had them wired.'

'Why would he do that?'

'He didn't want any witnesses. He didn't want any of you to survive.'

'I don't believe you.'

'Shoot into that one.' She nodded as far as he would permit her head to move, toward the sandbagged emplacement at the front of the house. It was no more than thirty feet away.

He glanced in the direction but held her close with a firm grip on her shoulder, as he pressed the barrel of his rifle against her back with his other hand.

'If you don't believe me, do it,' said Joselyn.

'I've got a better idea,' said the man. 'Get over there.' He let go of her shoulder and pushed the barrel of the rifle into her back, hard.

Joselyn staggered forward several steps and stopped.

'Go on.' He was breathless, almost panting.

Joselyn was thinking that if she could hang on, stall him just a few more seconds, he might pass out. She turned now and looked at him.

'You want to shoot me. Do it now.'

'No. I want you over there.' He motioned with the rifle toward the bunker.

'I told you the truth. I didn't do it.'

'You fired into it.'

'Only because you were shooting at me.'

'Move,' he said. Now there was anger in the single eye that peered out from the scarred face.

Joselyn backed up several steps, held her hands in the air, an emphasis that she was now disarmed. She could tell by the look on what was left of his face that it didn't matter. He knew the pain he was in, and he wanted revenge. She backed up a few more steps.

The barrel of the rifle began to wave in broad circles as he focused his good eye on her.

'More.'

She took two more steps back, turned and looked over

her shoulder. She was less than five feet from the corner of the sandbagged bunker.

'Get up against those bags.' He brought the rifle up to his shoulder and tried to sight through the scope. At less than thirty feet, it was a blur. Still, at this distance he couldn't miss the sandbags.

He brought the side of his body against the wall of the house for support and shielded himself from the blast behind the corner.

Joselyn backed up until the back of her legs and buttocks hit the bags. She pressed against them and prayed, Dear Lord, let it be done.

A thin splinter of wood split from the molding at the corner of the house just at the level of his eyes an instant before the sound of the shot echoed off the bluff. The gunman stood as if suspended by some unnatural force, his rifle barrel dipping six inches before it tumbled from his hands. His knees buckled. Joselyn watched as the rigid lines of his body turned fluid and collapsed into the dust by the side of the house.

She turned and looked behind her toward the meadow. A tall, slender giant stood halfway to his knees in grass and wild flowers, a rifle in his hands.

Gideon looked at the sky, and thanked God for a lucky shot.

CHAPTER
TWENTY-NINE

Padget Island, WA

A marine marksman examined the gunman's rifle where they found it lying in the dirt by the side of the house. He found that the scope had been jarred, probably by the explosion in the bunker, so that its mountings were forced slightly out of alignment. Buck Thompson's shot had missed Gideon by inches.

The marines, with Gideon in tow, searched every structure on the island for nearly three hours. The Geiger counter clicked with only periodic surges of background radiation, but nothing more. They could find no sign of the nuclear device. The NEST team showed up shortly after noon and took over the search.

Gideon and Joselyn were put onboard a marine helicopter and flown to the naval air station on Whidbey Island, where Gideon was taken in one direction and Joselyn in another.

Joselyn wanted to know why they were being held. No one would give her an answer.

She was allowed to shower and clean up at the base,

constantly under the eye of a female marine, then given a quick medical exam and treated for the multitude of bruises and abrasions.

The Navy doctor wasn't sure about Joselyn. He thought she might have suffered a concussion. The knot on the back of her head where the men had sapped her the night they took her on the dock, as well as the bruise on her cheek from Thompson's rifle butt, had swollen badly and was quite discolored. The physician wasn't sure about her ability to travel.

'Is it life-threatening?' asked a stone-faced FBI agent.

'Probably not, but I won't take responsibility,' said the physician.

'She can travel,' said the agent.

She was handed a blue Navy jumpsuit, in place of her soiled and torn clothing, and hustled aboard a small Air Force jet in the company of two agents. A moment later Gideon, also wearing a Navy jumpsuit and bent over so that he was nearly crouching half his height, entered through the door of the small jet. He smiled when he saw her, bandaged and scrubbed, and wearing a jumpsuit two sizes too big for her.

'Lovely. It's good they had one in your color,' he said.

'Sit down and buckle up,' said the agent.

Gideon took the chair next to Joselyn.

They talked for maybe an hour until the drone of the jet engine finally put them both to sleep, her head tilted over onto his shoulder, his head against hers.

Gideon was awakened by the gradual decline in altitude and air pressure. Instinctively he looked for his watch and only then realized that it was gone. He'd left it with his clothes back on Whidbey Island. He shifted in his seat. Joselyn blinked her eyes and woke. She stretched and yawned.

'I think we're about to land.' He told her. 'Do you know what time it is?'

She looked at her empty wrist. 'No.' Then out the window, but she couldn't see a thing. They were flying through cloudcover thick as soup.

Ten minutes later, they felt the wheels of the jet as they skidded onto the runway. The plane taxied to a stop near a large hangar. All they could see out of the windows were military planes, jet fighters, and transports, lined up along the runway.

Gideon craned his neck to see out of the low windows. There was another large plane, blue and white with gleaming silver wings parked inside a massive hangar a hundred yards away. On the tail section was painted a large American flag, just above the tail number 28000. The words UNITED STATES OF AMERICA, were stenciled in clear dark letters on the white upper portion of the fuselage.

'I think it is Andrews Air Force Base,' said Gideon.

A dark blue government van pulled up on the apron next to the plane. Gideon had to manually unfold his legs, and even then he walked like a stick figure once he cleared the low door on the small Air Force jet. He felt as if he was coming out of a sardine can.

Joselyn got to the bottom of the steps ahead of him. On solid ground now and rested, she became more assertive and turned to one of the agents. 'Where are you taking us?'

'You'll see.' He opened the sliding door of the van and motioned for them to get in.

She didn't move, and when Gideon tried to, she stopped him. 'Are we in custody?'

The agents looked at her, and then glanced at each other.

From the look, it was clear they weren't sure.

'If we're under arrest I want to see a lawyer, and I want to know what we're charged with.'

'Later,' said the agent.

'No, now.' She had been shot at and kicked, threatened with a rifle, and nearly fried by an explosion. She wasn't going to move until she got some answers.

Gideon took one look at the stern expression on the agent's face. 'I think that perhaps this is not the time to stand on legal principle,' he told her. He took Joselyn's arm and gently gestured toward the van.

'Where are they taking us?'

'I don't know.'

'Well I'm not going. Not until I get some answers.'

'I think if you do not, they may put you in the van forcibly.'

'Listen to the man,' said the agent.

'I want to talk to somebody in authority,' said Joselyn.

'That's where we're taking you,' said the agent. 'To see the man in charge.'

Joselyn looked at Gideon. She wasn't happy. She folded her arms and tapped her foot, but she didn't move

'We could always call the Dutch ambassador,' said Gideon.

She didn't look at him, but the stone slowly cracked around her lips; she laughed, and the resolve was gone. They got into the van. The agent shook his head.

It took an hour in thickening city traffic before they started to see familiar landmarks. The Lincoln Memorial, Jefferson's in the distance on the other side, and the tall obelisk of the Washington Monument. Joselyn had never been to Washington, DC before, and she hovered like a tourist at the darkened windows of the van as they sped past each site.

Gideon seemed to take it in stride. The adrenalin rush of the previous day left him weary, even with the fitful sleep on the plane. He was jolted into full consciousness when the van turned and pulled up to the black iron gates.

The expression on Joselyn's face said it all. 'Is this what I think it is?'

Gideon didn't say a word, but he was leaning forward, looking over the front seat between the two agents. In the distance, through the black wrought iron of the southwest gate, was the gleaming oval portico of the White House with its Doric columns.

One of the agents flashed credentials at a uniformed guard in the kiosk and they waited while a phone call was placed. Seconds later the iron gates rolled back. The van drove up West Executive Avenue and turned right, stopping in front of a basement entrance to the West Wing.

Without ceremony, the van door slid open and two men in suits looking suspiciously like secret service agents helped Joselyn and Gideon from the back of the van.

Neither of the agents said a word, but instead led the couple past a guard. They took the first right, down a few stairs. Joselyn could smell food. When they got to the bottom she could see the White House Mess, a kind of small cafeteria.

'Wait here.' One of the agents stayed with them while the other went over to a large locked door. A marine guard in dress uniform with a sidearm was stationed next to the door. The agent worked the coded keypad next to the door, opened it, and disappeared inside.

The cafeteria seemed to be bustling. Young men in rolled-up shirtsleeves and ties, and young secretaries in short skirts hustled back and forth on the stairs, each looking as if they were on a mission from God.

The plastered walls were painted a glossy white with colonial pediments over the doors.

No one seemed to pay much attention to Gideon or Joselyn. She felt like an itinerant in jail togs. She fussed with her hair a bit, wishing she had a comb and mirror and a little makeup.

A few seconds later, the door to the room opened again and the agent came out. He was in the company of an older man in shirtsleeves rolled to his elbows, his tie knotted halfway down his chest and glasses, narrow cheaters propped up on his forehead like a visor.

He took the glasses from his forehead and held them in one hand a second before he reached them.

'Ms Cole and Mr van Ry, I assume.' He extended his hand and the first smile either of them had seen from anyone in half a day.

'My name is Sy Hirshberg.'

Gideon recognized the name.

'I am the president's national security adviser. I want to thank both of you for coming.'

'I didn't know we had a choice,' said Joselyn.

He ignored her. 'Are you hungry? Would you like something to drink?'

'I'm dying of thirst,' said Joselyn.

'What would you like?'

'A club soda, if you have it.'

'Done. And you Mr van Ry?'

'Very good. Yes. The same.'

With a look from Hirshberg, the secret service agent was suddenly transformed into room service. 'And while you're at it, see if they can put together a couple of sandwiches.'

'No meat,' said Joselyn, as the agent turned and headed for the Mess.

'If you'll come this way,' said Hirshberg. 'We have a lot of questions, and not much time.'

He led them back to the door with the combination on it. Hirshberg opened the door and ushered them in. It was a conference room surrounded on three sides by two small offices, computer workstations, and little warrens filled with communications equipment. The main conference area was small and gave the appearance of being cramped, every inch being employed in some functional use.

There was a map projected on a screen hanging down from one wall. It was large-scale and very familiar. It showed in detail large sections of the North Puget Sound, the area embracing the San Juan Islands.

There were a series of tables arranged in a rectangle with an open area in the middle, a few men and two women sitting around it. Some of men were in uniforms.

There was intense conversation. They were in the middle of a meeting. A few people looked up, but no one paid particular attention to Joselyn or Gideon.

Gideon immediately recognized one of the women. Sheila Johnstead was the U.S. ambassador to the United Nations.

Joselyn's eyes were fixed on the man seated at the far end of the room. She couldn't help but stare, in the dim pools of light, at the president of the United States.

He didn't smile or acknowledge their presence, in fact he barely looked at either of them. He was locked in conversation with a man seated directly in front of Joselyn with his back to her.

'I cannot emphasize how important this is,' said the president.

'Sir, I can appreciate that,' said the other man.

She couldn't see his face, but the voice had a familiar ring. Joselyn thought maybe it was someone she'd heard interviewed on television.

They were ushered into chairs against one wall just inside the door. The room was crowded to the point of overflowing. Young aides stood against the walls with pads and pens, periodically scribbling notes. An air of tension hung over the place as palpable as smoke.

'Sir. I realize it is important, but evidence before a grand jury, if it is to mean anything must be maintained in confidence.'

'We have a crisis here,' said the president. 'Don't you understand?'

'Yes, I do.' It was that familiar voice. Joselyn tried to edge around to see the profile of his face, but she couldn't.

'Then help us out,' said the president. 'You are the only one who has reviewed all of the evidence in this case. I am asking you in my official capacity, as president, to tell me everything you know concerning your investigation of this matter.'

'With all due respect, sir,' said the man, 'Rule Six of the Federal Rules of Criminal Procedure makes no exception for disclosure of grand jury information pertaining to national security.'

It hit Joselyn like a lightning bolt. The man sitting in front of her was Thomas McCally, the assistant U.S. attorney from Seattle, the man she'd left waiting in the courthouse the day Belden ran.

'Well if the law doesn't provide such an exception, it should,' said the president.

'That is a matter, sir, between you and Congress,' said McCally.

Joselyn arched an eyebrow. McCally was clearly swimming in deep political waters.

The president flipped a pencil into the air. It landed in no-man's-land between the tables

'He's yours,' said the president. 'You deal with him.' He turned to Abe Charness, the attorney general, who was seated two chairs away.

Charness offered an uncomfortable smile to McCally and

ran one hand through his thinning gray hair, disheveled and falling out faster by the minute. His shirt showed signs of perspiration under the arms, where it was bunched up by the thick suspenders that looped over his narrow shoulders.

He was not a big man, but Charness mustered all the authority he could in his voice. 'Son, we don't have the time to go through the grand jury transcripts. We assume that if you had uncovered anything regarding the smuggling of a nuclear device into the country, you would have alerted all of the appropriate agencies, the National Security Council and the military.'

McCally nodded.

'So we assume that you did not uncover such information.'

'That's correct.'

'Fine. The president has a simple question. It goes to issues of policy concerning this administration. We need to know whether the name Viktor Kolikoff ever surfaced in connection with testimony by any of the witnesses in your investigation.'

'That I cannot tell you,' said McCally.

Charness looked at the ceiling and fumed. He did not want to get into the specifics, not in front of staffers and military brass. Members of the Cabinet knew or guessed what the problem was. The president couldn't be sure if Kolikoff's name had surfaced. If it had, and if indictments were later handed down in connection with militia activity in Washington State, and if Kolikoff was involved in brokering a weapon of mass destruction to the group, nothing the president could do would keep it under wraps.

If on the other hand Kolikoff's name had come into the investigation, then a low-profile search for the bomb might be in order. If they could find it quickly and quietly, Kolikoff's connection to the device might never become public. The president's acceptance of campaign contributions would be a minor blip on the screen.

'Are you telling us that you don't know?' said Charness.

McCally said nothing.

'Are you telling us that you can't remember whether you ever heard that name in connection with the investigation, Mr McCally?'

'I'm telling you that I will not get into the substance of grand jury testimony in a room filled with people who are not authorized to receive that information.'

'Then you would be free to tell the attorney general what you know concerning this matter in private?' said the president.

McCally paused for a moment and took a deep breath. 'If I were assured that it would go no farther and that the disclosure were for legitimate law enforcement purposes,' said McCally. 'Solely for purposes of investigation and prosecution of crimes.'

The president looked at Charness and smiled. Finally they were getting somewhere. Charness could go into a closed room with McCally, get the information the president wanted, then come out, and spill his guts to the president in private.

Charness did not look happy. Clearly what the president had in mind was the commission of a felony and the use of the Justice Department to do it. He had to know where Kolikoff was in the entire scheme of things before he charted his course and decided how aggressive to be in the search for the device.

'I'm going to suggest, Mr Charness, that you confer with Mr McCally in private.' The president nodded. 'You can use one of the small conference rooms.' He pointed to what looked like a closet just off the Situation Room.

McCally saw Joselyn for the first time when he got up. He swallowed hard and found it difficult to maintain eye contact. Both of them knew the government's investigation was about to be compromised, that unless Charness was made of steel, the president would vacuum him like a rug for information the second they emerged from the conference room.

Joselyn had a whole new respect for people like McCally, working in the trenches.

She leaned into Gideon's ear. 'Who is this guy Kolikoff?'

When she looked at him he had an enigmatic smile.

'Arms merchant,' he whispered. Kolikoff's name had appeared enough times in reports from the institute in Santa Crista that he was well known in circles concerning arms control.

Joselyn looked up at him. 'Nuclear?' she whispered.

Gideon held one hand just off of his lap and waffled it a bit as if to say anything was possible.

'What about this other lawyer?' said the president. 'This woman, what's her name?'

'Joselyn Cole,' Hirshberg spoke up.

'Yes, Cole. Has anybody heard from her?'

'She's here, Mr President.'

'Oh.' Suddenly the president perked up, looking around the room for a female in a business suit. 'Where?'

Joselyn tentatively raised her hand. After seeing what happened to McCally, she wasn't sure she wanted to do this.

'Oh.' He looked at the way she was dressed, the bruises on her face, then whispered to a man at his right shoulder, who passed him several sheaves of paper and a small box. The president listened and nodded while he looked at Joselyn, the way people do when you know they're talking about you.

The president's brows arched and his forehead furrowed, some hint of surprise registering in his expression as he listened to the quick briefing. The aide straightened up, and the president squared his chair to the table again.

'Well, young lady, you've had a very harrowing couple of days. Please move up to the table. Gentlemen, make room for her. Find her a seat.'

The waters parted. Suddenly she found herself headed for McCally's vacant chair. She balked and wouldn't go without Gideon.

'Is that your friend?' said the president.

'This is Gideon van Ry,' said Joselyn. 'He's the reason I'm here. Otherwise I would be dead.'

'Please come forward. Mr van Ry. You, too.'

One of the men seated at the table got up and gave Gideon his chair. They moved forward into the chairs and sat down at the table.

'I trust you both understand the seriousness of the situation?' said Hirshberg.

'I think so,' said Joselyn. 'We don't know everything.'

'I dare say you probably know a damn sight more than we do,' said the president. He smiled, and there was some light banter around the table.

'That's why you're here. We need your help. We understand, Ms Cole, that you represented this man, Dean Belden, before the grand jury in Seattle,' said the president.

'If that was his real name,' said Joselyn. 'It appears he told me a good many things that were not true.'

'I'm told that you believed he was dead, killed in a plane crash.'

'That's correct.'

'It seems that both you and the U.S. attorney were taken in by this.'

'Yes.'

'But he wasn't killed?' said the president.

'No. Somehow he managed to stage his death for my benefit, so that I would tell the authorities. You see, he used me to identify him. He wanted to be officially dead, so that the government would stop looking for him. It was the only way he could finish whatever it was he was doing.'

'And what was that?' said Hirshberg.

'I'm not exactly sure. He tried to kill me twice, the first time, the night that his plane crashed. I'm certain now that he tried to push my car, with me in it, off of a state ferry into Puget Sound.'

'And the second time?' said Hirshberg.

'On the island,' said Joselyn. 'He left orders for me to be killed. The only reason I'm alive is that a Navy diver saved my life, and he paid with his own. A good many men died on that island. I saw the bodies.'

'Yes. I know.' The president seemed very uncomfortable with the thought. 'These people. The people on the island. They may have a nuclear device. You understand that?'

She nodded.

'Do you have any idea where it is?'

'No.'

The president looked at Gideon, who shook his head.

'You, sir. You're with the Institute Against Mass Destruction in California?'

'That is correct, Mr President.'

'I want to thank you for your help. We have been in touch with the director at your institute. He has been exceedingly helpful, very cooperative. We're aware of your travels in the former Soviet Union and of the information you turned up there. That was exceedingly useful, and we are all very thankful.'

'Not useful enough, Mr President.'

The president looked at him as if he didn't understand.

'To keep the device out of your country,' said Gideon.

'Oh, yes. Indeed.'

Hirshberg interrupted. 'Ms Cole, you were on the island with these men. They took you captive, is that correct?'

'Yes.'

'While you were there, did you hear anything?'

'I saw Belden. He came into the room where I was being held. I believe he went by another name as well.'

'Yes?'

'Thorn. The men on the island referred to him as Thorn.'

Notes were being scrawled on pads around the table.

'He seemed to be in charge,' said Joselyn.

'We're trying to identify the bodies on the island now,' said Hirshberg, 'to see if he's among them.'

'Don't waste your time,' said Joselyn. 'You won't find him there. He left the island with another man before the raid.'

Joselyn's words inspired a flurry of eye contact among the men around the table, along with more intense note taking.

'We have a picture of the man we believe you call Belden,' said the president. 'Would you look at it for us and identify him?'

Joselyn nodded and an aide handed her a file with the photo in it. She opened it and looked.

'That's him.'

'Good. Send that photo out to all state and federal law enforcement agencies,' said the president. 'Say that he is wanted for . . .' He looked down the table at the attorney general's empty chair.

One of his assistants stepped up from against the wall, looked at the president quizzically, and said: 'Kidnapping, murder of a federal officer, assault on federal officers.'

'That's enough,' said the president. 'Let's not put anything in there on the nuclear device. At least not for now. We don't want to start a panic.'

'Be sure and let them know he's extremely dangerous,' said Hirshberg. 'And if state or local authorities see him, no attempt should be made to take him. They should call the FBI immediately.'

'Good,' said the president. He turned back to Joselyn. 'You say that he left the island with another man. Can you describe this man?'

Joselyn thought for a moment. 'He was short, maybe five-foot-five, five-six. Thinning hair, brown, dark eyes, dark complexion. A kind of sad face.'

'Could you help the FBI artists prepare a computer composite of the man?' This question came from an intense-looking man along the right side of the table.

'I could try.'

'You say he was dark,' said Hirshberg. 'Could he have been a foreign national?'

'He didn't speak with any apparent accent.'

'You heard him speak?' said the president.

'A few words. They were in a hurry. He came to the door of the room where I was and told Belden it was time to leave. That's all I heard.'

'You were bound, gagged?' asked one of the other men.

'Tied up, on a bed. Belden had torn the tape from my mouth. He was questioning me.'

'What did he want to know?'

'He wanted to know what I had said to the authorities after the plane crash. Who Mr van Ry was. They had seen him down on the dock, by the boats at Friday Harbor the night I was taken. They thought he might be with the government.'

'What did you tell him?'

'Nothing. There was nothing I could tell him. I didn't know anything. He already knew about my clients, the fishermen who had become ill. We thought it was an industrial injury of some kind.'

'And what was it?' asked Hirshberg.

'Radiation poisoning,' said Gideon. 'The military confirmed that the docks and several of the boats were contaminated.'

'How?' said the president.

'The device. The outer casing split open. The plutonium core somehow got loose on the deck during a storm. It abraded.'

'What's that?' said Hirshberg.

'Plutonium is very soft,' said Gideon. 'If it is rubbed on a rough surface, it will turn to dust. If that gets into the lungs, it is usually deadly. But I do not think that was the only problem here. There was too much contamination on the boat that I found. I believe there was something else.'

'What?' said the president.

'I believe that whoever engineered the device had in mind something particularly deadly. I believe they have combined the nuclear device with a quantity of cesium-137.'

'Explain,' said Hirshberg.

'Cesium is a particularly toxic material. A by-product in the refinement of plutonium. It emits very strong gamma radiation. It must be carefully handled in order to shield anyone from uncontrolled exposure. At room temperature it is a liquid, but it reacts violently to contact with other materials. It is soluble in water and a big worry for those who must dispose of it.'

'Why would they be bringing what is basically a nuclear waste product on the boat?' said one of the military men.

'As insurance,' said Gideon. 'In case the device itself

failed to reach critical mass, in which case there would be no nuclear chain reaction. Then at least the conventional explosive around the core of the device would vaporize the cesium, releasing it into the atmosphere. In sufficient quantities, it is very deadly. Carried on the wind, it would have killed thousands, perhaps tens of thousands.'

'If nothing else,' said one of the other military men, 'it would have been a hell of a message from Saddam or Muammar.'

'If that's who really is behind this,' said Hirshberg.

'I believe there was a quantity of cesium on that boat, and that some of it spilled.' Gideon ignored their obsession with fixing blame. The nuclear genie was coming home to roost.

'So essentially we have a dirty bomb?' said one of the military men.

'No,' said Gideon. 'A dirty bomb relies solely on nuclear fallout for its destructive force. I believe this is a nuclear device with cesium to make it more deadly. Wherever it is detonated, that place will become a toxic wasteland and deadly for decades.'

There was silence around the table, deep lines of concern etched in the president's face.

'It is the only thing that can explain the levels of con-tamination on that boat,' said Gideon.

'How far would this fallout travel?'

'It would depend on the wind,' said Gideon. 'Whether there was rain.'

'Where is this boat now?' asked the president. 'The boat that was contaminated.'

'It has been towed out to sea, along with several of the other fishing boats.' One of the military men answered the question. 'They are decontaminating the dock. They may have to remove part of it.'

'Have they analyzed what was on that boat?' said the president.

'I don't know,' said the man in the uniform.

'Well, find out.'

'Ms Cole. Did the men on the island ask you any other questions?'

She shook her head slowly. 'Not that I can remember.'

'Do you know how Belden and the other man left the island?'

She shook her head and thought for a moment. 'It was a boat. I think the other man said something about a boat.' She couldn't remember now whether she'd heard it or simply assumed it.

'Did you hear a boat leaving?'

She shook her head.

'Did they say anything about a destination?' asked Hirshberg.

She thought again. 'No. Just that time was getting short. That they had to leave.'

'Anything else? Any other names?' said Hirshberg. Joselyn searched her memory, racked her brain. 'No. But the two men on the porch. They mentioned names.'

'What men?' said the president.

'I don't know. I could only hear their voices, outside when the shooting started. They mentioned a name.' She thought for a second. 'Oliver. Edgar.' She looked down at the table top. 'Oscar.' Suddenly she looked up. 'That was it. Oscar. I remember because they said he'd left the island earlier that morning as well.'

'With Belden and the other man?' said the president.

'I don't think so.' Suddenly a look of revelation came over her face. 'Oh, my God.'

'What is it,' said the president.

'They were talking about the bomb,' said Joselyn.

'What? Where?' said the president.

'The two men. They were out on the porch. There was a lot of confusion. Shooting. They had a boat tied up in a cove somewhere on the island. They were talking about escaping. It's how I heard about the bunker's being wired for explosives. They said Thorn had ordered it done. They mentioned Oscar, said he had left that morning and that they were supposed to get off the island if anything happened. The two men. They were supposed to go to a truck. And get the thing moving. Those were their words.'

'Does that island have ferry service for vehicles?' said Hirshberg. He looked at the people around the table. They were all scratching their heads and looking at each other.

'It did not.' The voice that spoke up was Gideon's.

'How do you know?'

'I checked before I flew out of Friday Harbor on the marine helicopter. I was supposed to help search for the device. I did not want that weapon placed on a car-carrying ferry in the Sound as we approached. There was no public ferry service to the island.'

'Then it was never there,' said the president.

'No,' said Gideon.

'The Coast Guard threw a blockade around the island,' said Hirshberg. 'There's no way they could have gotten it off once the assault started.'

'Unless the man Belden took it out on the boat with him.'

'No. Not on a small boat,' said Hirshberg. 'Satellite surveillance would have picked up a vessel that big coming from the island. Especially if it was on a truck.'

'That leaves one other matter,' said the president. He

opened the small box that had been handed to him by the aide when he first called Joselyn's name. He lifted the top and poured the contents out onto the table.

Gideon immediately recognized the wristwatch as his. Joselyn's was next to it. Everything from the pockets of their clothing including wallets, scraps of paper, and change were lying on the table. Someone had gone through their wallets; driver's licenses and credit cards landed on the table in small heap.

'We have checked everything,' said Hirshberg. He was speaking to the president. 'There are only a few items that we have questions about. I hope you understand.' He looked at Joselyn and Gideon.

Joselyn was angry. The authorities had gone through their clothing at the Air Station on Whidbey Island, searching through their wallets and pockets for information.

'It would have been nice if you asked,' said Joselyn.

'There was no time,' said Hirshberg.

'There was what, four hours on an airplane crossing the country?' she told him.

'Nonetheless, we have a few questions,' he said. 'These notes, the name Grigori Chenko in your wallet, Mr van Ry. What is it?'

'Ah. Notes I took at Sverdlovsk, Russia.'

'Ah yes. The information I believe came to us from the institute?' Hirshberg was checking with one of his assistants who nodded.

'Ms Cole. These phone numbers on a note from your wallet.'

'Those are friends down in California.'

'I see. We can check them out.' He handed the note to one of his assistants. He didn't believe her. She was now burning at the tips of her ears.

'And this?'

She looked at what he was holding in his hand but couldn't make it out.

'It's a business card,' said Hirshberg. 'Port-a-John Sanitation Service, Oak Harbor, Washington.'

He drew a blank stare from her. Then suddenly she remembered. The business card that Belden had left on the bedside table. The one she picked up as the Navy SEAL tried to get her out of the room.

'I forgot all about it,' she said. 'Belden left it behind, in the room.'

CHAPTER
THIRTY

Oak Harbor, WA

The FBI had had the business card from the pocket of Joselyn's blouse for nearly seven hours by the time she reached Washington, DC. They had wasted no time checking into it as a lead.

Two agents drove to the small town of Oak Harbor on Whidbey Island only a short distance from the base. They found the owner of Port-a-John Sanitation Service. The man was able to identify Belden from a photograph, as one of several men at a site near Deer Harbor on Orcas Island. The man had rented them a portable toilet and delivered it, the kind usually used at construction sites and outdoor events.

'The reason I remember is 'coz they were a little strange.'

'In what way?' said one of the agents.

'There was a building there. You know. One of those fabricated metal jobs over a concrete floor. It was all closed up. When they heard me drive up, one of them came out through a side door and told me where to set the unit down.

'When I finished, I realized I'd forgotten to have him sign the paperwork. So I went in the door. Knocked on it, but nobody answered. I guess they didn't hear me. So I let myself in. I thought they were gonna kill me.'

'Why?'

'I don't know. But two of 'em grabbed me and forced me back out the door. Roughed me up. I had a good mind to put the unit back on the truck and take it away.'

'Could you see what was inside the building?'

The guy made a face, like not much. 'Some tools. A cutting torch. They pushed me outside real quick. They signed the papers and I got the hell outta there. These guys were on the thin edge. You know what I mean? Why are you interested in them?'

The agent ignored the question. 'Could you see what they were working on?'

'Oh, yeah. It was a truck. They were welding something on the back of it.'

'What kind of truck?'

'Search me. I was busy being pushed out the door. But it looked like a tank.'

'You mean an armored tank?'

'No. Like a small tank truck, the kind they use to haul chemicals. Like I say, I damn near put the john back on my truck and left. Not that they would have missed it.'

'What do you mean?

'There was a perfectly good bathroom in the building. It was right by the door. I heard it flush when I was outside.'

Deer Harbor, Orcas Island, WA

 score of high-powered rifles with expert marksmen

from the Skagit County Violent Crimes Task Force, along with FBI agents and sheriff's deputies from Island County surrounded the place.

It was a fabricated metal building just as the man had described. Once they were set up with positions for covering fire, the tactical squad moved in. They hit the side door with a battering ram. The metal door took two shots before it gave, and officers with M-16s went inside.

They were there less than a minute before one of them came back to the door and gave them the all-clear sign. Handheld radios on secure frequencies announced that it was secure, that nobody was inside.

The FBI agents in suits moved in. The Tac-squad started to cordon off the building and the driveway around it with yellow crime-scene tape.

The building was deserted. There were a few tools scattered around on the concrete floor, what looked like an expensive portable torch and some wrenches. There was a makeshift bench set up near the center of the floor.

They were inside only long enough to take some quick pictures and get a reading on a Geiger counter. Radiation levels were high.

'I want everybody out now,' said one of the agents. 'Call the NEST team. Tell them we need them over here now.'

The men started to move out. One of the agents kicked something with his foot, and it slid across the concrete floor.

It was a metal sign, the kind with magnets on the back used to display the name of a business on the door of a vehicle. He walked over and slipped the blade of a small penknife under the face of the sign and flipped it over so that it was face up. On the other side was the name: A-One Septic, Denver, Colorado, Luck. # CZ 14869.

T he Justice Department was picking up the tab for accommodations, at least until they were released. Gideon and Joselyn were driven to the Hay-Adams Hotel on Sixteenth Street, not far from the White House. They were given fresh overalls, this time with 'FBI' printed on the back, clean underwear, toothbrushes, a few toiletries, and adjoining rooms with two agents camped outside.

'For house arrest, it isn't bad,' said Joselyn. She grabbed the robe from the back of the bathroom door as she talked to Gideon through the partially closed adjoining door to his room.

'I'm going to take a shower. Change my jailhouse jumpsuit. The sooner I get out of here, the better.'

'Don't you like the White House?' said Gideon.

'The place is fine. I can't say as much for the people in it,' said Joselyn. 'That's why I need a shower.'

She disappeared into the bathroom, dropped her clothes on the floor, turned up the hot water, and allowed it to run over her body, like a waterfall.

With her eyes closed, the pelting beads of water hitting her bruised face, the events of the past twenty-four hours played themselves back in her mind like a bad dream. She couldn't get the dead Navy diver out of her thoughts. Five minutes under the spray and she began to shake and cry uncontrollably.

The reality of what had happened suddenly hit home. It came with a force and permanence that Joselyn never expected. It wasn't a film or make-believe. A young man with his entire life in front of him had died before her eyes. His wife, if he had one, would never feel his arms around her again. His mother and father would in this world never set eyes on him. She did not want to think about whether the man had children. In less time than it took to blink, his life had been snuffed out by a bullet as he tried to save hers. She was crying not only from grief but guilt. She was alive, and he was dead. If she hadn't been there, he might never have entered the building. He might still be alive.

The water poured down her body, mixed with her tears until she was drained. Exhausted, she leaned against the tile wall, steadied herself, and turned off the water.

Quickly she toweled herself dry, put on the clean underwear, a tee-shirt in place of a bra and the terrycloth robe. She wrapped her hair in the towel turban-style and walked back out into the bedroom.

'How was it?' It was Gideon. He was standing in the door between their rooms.

'Great. I didn't realize how tired I was.'

'Your eyes. They are very red.'

'Oh.' She took the pointed end of the towel that hung down from her head and wiped them. 'I got soap in them.'

'Ah. I see.' Gideon could tell she had been crying. 'Are you hungry?'

'Not really.'

'We could raid the mini-bar,' he said.

'What's in there?'

'Let's see.' He took the key from the top of the bar and opened it. 'We have peanuts, M&Ms, a chocolate bar.'

'Sounds awful.'

'How about something to drown your pain?' When he stood up he was holding three tiny bottles with seals around their caps.

'Now that sounds good.'

'Vodka, whiskey, or Scotch?'

'Scotch. With a little soda if there's any in there.'

'Just the thing.' He came up with a can of club soda.

'If we were in Amsterdam I would give you something a little more potent. Something from one of the brown cafés.'

'What's that?'

He thought for a moment while he popped the can and opened the bottle.

'I suppose you would call it a pub, or tavern, maybe a coffeehouse. All three. They are very old. Some of them have been open for hundreds of years. You can find them on every street in the old part of town. And their walls on the inside are very brown. They are never cleaned or painted. They serve wonderful blends of coffee – along with mind-altering drugs.'

She looked at him and laughed.

'What's the matter, you don't believe me?'

'No. I believe you. It's just that I can't see you doing drugs.'

'It's the Dutch national pastime,' said Gideon. 'By American standards we are a sinful people. Very permissive. At least in Amsterdam. Drugs are considered a recreational necessity.'

'Try selling that one to the group we met with today,' said Joselyn.

'Free sex is regarded as a constitutional right.'

'We are different,' said Joselyn. 'Over here it's just one of the perks of public office.'

'Aw, empty.' Gideon picked up the ice bucket, opened the door to the room, and stuck his head out.

'Excuse me, gentlemen.'

One of the agents came to the door.

'I think the ice machine is on the next floor. We are getting drunk. Would you mind?' He handed the bucket to the FBI agent and closed the door.

He turned, folded his arms, and leaned against the door. 'Well. We have some time to kill. What shall we do?'

'I'm sorry, but I'm a little too tired. You'll have to exercise your constitutional rights with someone else tonight.'

Gideon laughed and blushed a little.

'I could mine your thoughts,' said Gideon.

'You mean pick my brain.'

'Yes.'

'That would be poor pickings indeed, at least tonight.'

'You are not convinced that Denver is the target?'

The call from the FBI at Deer Harbor had come in when they were in the White House.

'It was that obvious?' said Joselyn.

'Well, when you told the president that he had his head wedged securely up his rectum . . .'

'I never said that.'

'No. But the implication was quite clear.'

'Well, if the hat fits,' said Joselyn.

'How can you be so sure?'

'Because the Belden I knew is not a man to make mistakes. Not like that. A sign left on the floor?'

'As I recall, Denver was the scene of a major trial for domestic terrorism.'

'Very convenient,' said Joselyn. 'I'm sure Belden thought of that. In the meantime, the FBI spends its time combing highways that cover half of the western United States, searching for a truck that may or may not exist.'

'Ah. But the witness they talked to saw the truck.'

'But did he see what was in it?' said Joselyn.

'A septic truck would be a perfect cover. Who is going to want to search it?' said Gideon. 'And the tank on the back can be lined with lead. You are not going to pick up any emissions from the device, even if you run it through a portal monitor.'

'Maybe,' said Joselyn. 'But if you want to know what I think . . .'

'I do,' said Gideon.

'I think Belden's not that stupid. I don't think he's the kind of man that makes that many mistakes. First the business card on the table, then the sign in the garage. Why did he leave them?'

'Maybe they meant nothing. Maybe they were in a hurry.'

'No. He took everything out of his pocket because he wasn't comfortable sitting there slapping the hell out of me on that bed. He put it all on the side table, and when he was finished he carefully picked everything up, except the business card. He leaves that there.'

'He was finished with it,' said Gideon.

'He was finished with me, but he wasn't gonna leave me lying around.'

'You could identify him.'

'So could the man who rented him that portable john.'

Gideon thought for a moment. She had a point.

'Think about it. According to the agents, this guy drives up to the building and they immediately come outside. They don't stay with him and keep an eye on him. They don't ask if he has a receipt or anything to be signed. They tell him where to put it and then they back go inside. When he knocks, they don't answer. But when he opens the door, they allow him to come inside just long enough to see the truck before they make a big scene and throw him outside.'

'What are you saying?'

'I'm saying that Belden wanted him to see that truck. The same way he wanted me to see his plane go up in smoke. To serve a purpose. Our port-a-john salesman just did. He has the federal government looking in all the wrong places.'

'You have a very devious mind,' said Gideon. 'Are you always this paranoid?'

'Only after I've been pushed off a ferry, kidnapped, beaten and shot at.'

'Are you sure it wasn't simply because the president dismissed your views about Mr Belden and his plans?'

'I grant you the president doesn't have a very high opinion of women or their views.' They wouldn't listen to her, and she was angry. They weren't interested in her judgment, only the information she could give them. But she had dealt with Belden first hand, the only one in the room with that experience. Joselyn was convinced that she was right.

There was a knock at the door. Gideon opened it.

'Thank you.' He took the ice bucket from the agent, closed the door, and walked over to finish mixing the drinks. He handed Joselyn hers.

'Thanks.' She sipped slowly from the plastic glass.

'It doesn't matter anyway,' said Joselyn. 'Tomorrow I'm outta here. It's their problem.'

Gideon arched his eyebrows. 'There's a nuclear bomb loose in your country and you don't care?'

'You haven't heard. Apathy in America is chic. As long as they don't set the thing off under my bed, it's none of my business.'

'You really believe that?'

'Why not?'

'I don't think you do.'

'What makes you think so?'

'Because I saw the way you looked when you talked about that sailor. Tonight when you told them how he died. I think it is easy to be apathetic when we think about death in the abstract. But a two-kiloton nuclear weapon is no abstraction. It would kill thousands of people. It would

403

make what happened on that island seem tame. Entire families would cease to exist. They would die horrible deaths.'

Gideon took a drink from his glass, swallowed it, and then chewed on a small sliver of ice.

'You know,' he said. 'There were people in Hiroshima whose shadows were printed by the blast on the concrete walls of buildings and pavement. These shadows can still be seen. Some of the bodies that made them were never found. It was as if they never existed. There are those who have seen these shadows scorched on the hard ground, to whom they are mere curiosities of history – images of a time that has passed. If that is all they have come to be, then they are indeed the angels of apathy.'

CHAPTER
THIRTY-ONE

Seattle, WA

Oscar Chaney pulled to the curb in a loading zone and turned off the diesel engine and the headlights. He sat quietly behind the wheel for almost a minute, checking the rearview mirror to make sure no late-night strollers or homeless vagabonds were wandering in the area.

It was now after midnight. A solitary streetsweeper, its emergency light dominating the deserted lanes, was doing doughnuts down on Fifth Street cleaning the pavement, while the stop lights flashed red at the intersection.

Chaney could see the federal courthouse two blocks away. Its five story block monolith was dimly lit by security lights as janitors finished up their nightly chores.

With gloved hands, Chaney checked the passenger door on the truck to make sure it was locked, then opened the driver's door, stepped down onto the running board and from there to the curb. He checked the street one more time. The last thing he wanted was someone who might be able to link him to the truck.

He checked his watch. The metermaids wouldn't start

patroling the streets until just before rushhour. A large truck in a traffic lane, even at a loading zone, would be an item to draw their attention. Chaney wanted to make sure that they didn't simply tow it away to the city's impound yard.

He reached behind the seat and grabbed the two magnetic signs. They were identical to the one he'd left on the floor of garage at Deer Harbor. The only difference is that these identified A-One Septic as being located in Bellevue, Washington. He pushed the locking button down on the driver's door and closed it, then placed one of the magnetized signs on the door. He went around the truck and put the other sign on the passenger door.

Chaney already knew that the authorities had raided the empty garage. One of his crew had stayed behind to observe and report the intelligence.

He knew that the minute the metermaids reported the vehicle for towing, police computers would go nuts. They would match the name on the truck with the name on the sign from the garage. The Feds would stop wasting their time and resources searching the highways between Washington State and Colorado, and turn their attention instead to Seattle. They would waste several more hours clearing the area and bringing in experts to check for radiation before they took the first tentative steps to disarm the device. It would be mid-afternoon on the west coast before they realized their mistake.

Chaney crossed the street and headed down toward the corner. He walked two blocks and allowed at least four cabs to pass, before raising his hand to flag one down. When it pulled over, he opened the door, slid into the back seat and told the driver: 'Sea-Tac Airport.'

Joselyn heard a light rap on the door. It sounded distant and roused her only slightly from slumber, so that the voices of the men talking seemed like a dream, laid over sleep. She rolled over on the bed in the dark hotel room and looked at the illuminated digital clock on the night stand. It was after ten. She assumed it was morning, though with the heavy drapes pulled she couldn't be sure.

She sat up abruptly in the bed, suddenly concerned that she might have slept away the day. She stumbled to the window with the comforter from the bed wrapped around her body, and pulled back the heavy drapes. The brilliant sunlight blinded her, forcing her to turn her back and cover her eyes.

She had a massive headache and wondered if there was any aspirin in the small bag of toiletries the agents had given her the night before. Joselyn had killed all four of the tiny bottles of Scotch from the mini-bars in both rooms. She drew the line at the whiskey and left the vodka for Gideon. She fumbled through the bag in the bathroom and found nothing that would take the edge off her head. She was headed to the mini-bar to see if there was anything there when Gideon came through the adjoining door.

'I thought I heard you moving around. Did they wake you up?'

'Who?'

'The agents at the door.'

'That's who it was?'

'Yes. They are leaving. I've got your wallet, cash and credit cards along with my own, and the keys that were in your pocket.'

'Then we're free to go?'

'No. They have asked us to remain in town until further word, in case they have more questions. But it appears that they believe everything you told them,' said Gideon. 'More important, they have found the truck.'

Joselyn was on her hands and knees rummaging through the mini-bar on her quest for aspirin, the thick comforter wrapped around her like a bear skin. She turned and looked up at him, the obvious question written on her face.

'They found it in Seattle,' said Gideon.

'Seattle?' Joselyn was surprised.

'The bomb?'

'They are working on it now. The agents didn't have many details or if they did they weren't talking. It appears the authorities got some readings off the vehicle. High gamma radiation. Beyond that they don't know anything more. It looks like you were wrong,' said Gideon.

'Do you have any aspirin?' she ignored him.

'No. But I can run down to the package shop in the lobby and buy some.'

She shifted the bedcover around her, adjusting it from under where she sat. 'While you're at it, get me some new clothes and a bra, and some make-up.'

'We can go shopping after,' said Gideon. He could tell that her mind was on other things. 'I wonder why they would go to all of that trouble to drive the device down to Seattle?'

She looked at him and nodded from sleepy eyebrows. 'I just hope the people across the street are wondering the same thing.'

T here was an air of celebration in the Situation Room when the president came through the door and even some brief applause.

'Let's not get carried away,' said the president. 'We still have a lot of work to do. What have we heard from emergency team on site?'

'They have relatively high gamma readings but nothing above safe tolerances that would be injurious to passers-by, people who came in contact with the truck. They think the device is shielded, probably inside a lead container in the tank.'

'Do they have any estimates on how long it may take to defuse it?'

'They haven't actually gotten to the bomb itself. Right now they're trying to clear the area.'

'They haven't made a public announcement?' said the president.

'No. No. We are telling the public that we have a gas leak in one of the major mains in the area. We're evacuating eight square blocks. It's gonna take time. We've shut down I-five at the interchange and we've ordered all civilian aircraft out of the area.'

'Good,' said the president. 'We don't need any pain-in-the-ass television crews in choppers over that truck.'

The president didn't leave the doorway to the room but stood against the closed door, a sign that he wasn't going to be there long.

'Mr President, I'd like to talk to you in private if I could.' Sy Hirshberg had been trying to get into the Oval Office all morning. The president had been taking written communiqués from Seattle all morning from military aides but, other than that, had been incommunicado. He had been locked up, in preparation for the State of Union that evening. There had been a constant shuffle of Cabinet secretaries into the Oval Office all morning, each trying to get last-minute items into the president's speech or to make sure that nothing from their A-list agendas had been taken out.

'Can this wait, Sy?'

'I believe it is important, Mr President.'

'Is there something having to do with the current situation I don't know?'

'No,' said Hirshberg. 'But something that we should talk about.'

The president looked at his watch. 'I'm sorry, but it's gonna have to wait for now. I've got at least two more meetings. These fanatics with their bomb could have waited a few days. It would have been a great deal easier to deal with. Education is due in my office now. The staff is waiting to put the final touches on the speech. And I need at least two hours to go over the final draft.'

He looked at his watch. 'I'll have some time around four-forty.'

Hirshberg knew that he would get the president's divided attention at best. 'I'm only gonna have about five minutes,' he told him.

Hirshberg nodded. He suspected that given the momentum of events what he had to say to the president was likely to fall on deaf ears.

CHAPTER
THIRTY-TWO

The National Mall, Washington, DC

Scott Taggart sat on a bench and watched as young people jogged along the broad gravel path that looped around the National Mall. Behind him was the Hirshorn Museum and beyond that, across the curving street, was the red sandstone castle, the headquarters of the Smithsonian.

Its myriad museums, like copies of the acropolis, spread out in every direction. At one end, sealing off the Mall was the U.S. Capitol Building with its imposing dome.

Less than a mile away, to the west, and across the Ellipse, was the White House.

Taggart put down the newspaper and checked his watch. The museum had been open for a little more than hour. He got up from the bench, pulled a pair of heavy leather gloves from his pocket and put them on, then put his gloved hands into the pockets of the heavy navy pea coat. He started to walk in the direction of the Capitol. He crossed Jefferson Drive at Seventh Street and walked one block to Independence Avenue, where he turned left. Halfway down the block, he climbed the stairs in front of

411

the massive building with its two story glass front and followed a line of school children on a field trip into the National Air and Space Museum.

Directly in front of him was a large information desk, and behind that, in the distance, a display entitled *Milestones of Flight*.

For a weekday in the middle of winter, the place was crowded. The usual tours of children mingled with the retired and the growing number who took vacations in the off-season.

To the right, *Space Hall* was cordoned off in preparation for the party that night. Tables had already been set up and a raised dais was in the process of being erected.

Over Taggart's shoulder was the Wright Brothers' plane from Kitty Hawk, and just beyond it was the *Spirit of St Louis*, hanging from wires in the ceiling.

But today Taggart wasn't interested in history. The thought that preoccupied him at the moment was of a massive building three hundred yards to the north and a little west, well within the zone of maximum destruction. The Offices of the Internal Revenue Service were across the Mall, wedged in behind the Museum of Natural History, and the Head-quarters of the Justice Department. Within hours, all of these would take on the appearance of the burned-out concrete remnants of Hiroshima and Nagasaki after the blasts.

Taggart convinced himself that he harbored no ill will against the people who worked in these buildings but rather against the institutions themselves. It was the reason why the cesium was so important. Computer records and documents for every agency in the federal government would be instantly transformed into nuclear waste. There was no more effective way to kill the beast than to destroy the information that fed it.

The government was entrenched behind a Constitution

that could not be amended by the people and that the politicians used at every turn to increase their own power. It could only be interpreted and constrained by judges who shared in the federal spoils system that was now expanding faster than the universe. The government grew like a tumor, engulfing everything in its path.

In Taggart's mind, America had reached the end of the line. It had killed Kirsten and given rise to a perpetual political class that was arrogant in its views and brazen in its corruption – a political aristocracy that displayed an indifference and contempt toward the public that was stunning. Now they would pay the price.

At the main concourse, behind the information desk, Taggart stopped for a moment, took a small vial from his inside coat pocket. Fumbling with his gloved hands he removed a small capsule from the vial and placed it inside his mouth, between the cheek and gum. He threw the vial in a trash can, then turned to his left and walked past the history of *Early Flight* and *Jet Aviation*.

He strode with a purpose through the thronged gallery, passing the ghosts of another era – the airships that carried America to world power. They were old now and obsolete, like the generation that made them and the men who flew them, symbols of past glory and honor that no longer had a place in America. They and he were irrelevant to the corrupt politicians who took money from foreign countries that were our enemies.

Taggart's mind raced as he walked, his hands plunged deep into the pockets of his coat. He walked with purpose, looking through people as if they weren't there. His focus was centered on the object in the far corner, on the north side the building toward the Mall.

There were only a handful of tourists and sightseers gathered beneath the gleaming sheets of metal with their aviation rivets and the number '82' stenciled just under the huge nose canopy.

Like a laser, Taggart's concentration was fastened on the cylindrical object beneath the mammoth airframe near the open bomb-bay.

Through the thickness of the gloves, he felt deep down in his pocket for the glass bottle, the one that Thorn had left for him in the locker at the Denver airport.

The bottle contained hydrochloric acid, with a dye capable of etching metal and staining it a blood-red color.

Taggart edged his way toward the barricade beneath the huge fuselage. He stopped and looked around to make sure that no one was likely to get in his way. Then without hesitation he stepped over the metal railing.

One of the guards, forty feet away, saw him. He started to react, but it was too late.

Taggart closed the distance quickly to the green metal cylinder under the fuselage, then pulled his hand from his pocket and flung the bottle at the olive-drab cylinder.

The glass shattered against the sheet-metal casing, exploding in a fusion of blood-red dye that covered the side of the cylinder and ran down onto the floor. Taggart covered his face to escape the vapors rising as the acid ate into the metal.

'America is a nuclear murderer!' Taggart shouted at the top of his lungs as tourists retreated from the airplane and guards moved in. They watched his hands for signs of a weapon but saw none.

The acid from the bottle was beginning to eat a small hole in the side of the metal display.

Taggart continued to shout. 'America is a nuclear killer.'

He lashed out with his foot, kicking the metal cylinder, and smeared the dye with his gloved hands.

Though seemingly hysterical, he possessed the presence of mind to strip the gloves from his hands before the acid could penetrate and dropped them onto the floor.

Before he could kick the metal side of the cylinder again, two of the security guards were on him. They wrestled him out beyond the barricade and within seconds managed to cuff his hands behind his back.

Before the guards could even lead him away, the staff of the museum had moved in to assess the damage. The gleaming fuselage, perhaps the most significant icon of the age of air power, was untouched. But the acid on the metal cylinder beneath it continued to send off noxious vapors.

Quickly two maintenance men bent low under the fuselage and pushed with their hands against the tail-fin. Using the rectangular wheeled dolly that was part of the display and all of their strength, they maneuvered the green metal casing out from under the giant body of the *Enola Gay*. They wheeled the dolly toward the open door at the rear shop entrance to the museum and watched as the acid ate and etched the metal of the faithfully authentic replica of *Little Boy*; the atomic bomb dropped on Hiroshima.

Oval Office, the White House

The president looked up from the thick sheaf of papers spread out before him on the desk. He was crossing out words and lines and inserting others with a pencil. Sy Hirshberg was standing in the open door to the Oval Office.

It was nearly five o'clock in the afternoon. 'What is it, Sy? I don't have much time.' The president was only four hours from the State of the Union address, and butterflies were beginning to gather in his stomach.

'Anything new from Seattle?' he asked.

'Not yet. They're trying to figure out how to get into the tank without applying heat to cut the metal. They've tried X-rays to see inside, but there's a lead shield.'

'Can't they just move the damn thing? Tow it onto a boat and take out into the ocean.'

'They're concerned that it might be booby-trapped.'

The president took a deep breath and looked at the ceiling. 'How in the hell am I supposed to go before two hundred million people and talk about the state of the nation while on the other coast we have men trying to disarm a nuclear bomb?'

'That's why I wanted to talk to you, Mr President.'

The president looked at Hirshberg.

'I think you should cancel the speech.'

'What?'

'Just postpone it, Mr President.'

'What the hell. I can't do that. Not now. It's too late. We've given embargoed copies of the speech to the press. Do you have any idea what they would say if we canceled it? They'd want to know why.'

'Maybe we should tell them.'

'No!' The president was adamant. He swiveled around in his chair, so that Hirshberg was presented with the high leather back.

'There's no reason to cancel,' he told Hirshberg. 'If that bomb is safely disarmed, why should we needlessly alarm the public? And if it's not, canceling the speech isn't going to do a damn bit of good.'

'And if it goes off during the speech, Mr President? What then?'

'At least the president will be seen as engaged in the country's business, even in the face of a crisis,' said the president.

'There is another possibility,' said Hirshberg. 'Much more serious.'

'What's that?'

'That the device isn't in Seattle.'

The president wheeled around in his chair to face him again. 'What are you talking about? They found the truck.'

'Yes. But they haven't gotten inside of it.'

'They have radiation readings.'

'That's true. But that doesn't necessarily mean that the device is inside. Remember, Mr President, that there were much higher radiation readings on those fishing boats, the ones the Navy hauled out of Friday Harbor and sent to the bottom in the North Pacific. It could mean that the truck was used to transport the bomb. It is possible that the device could have been removed before the truck was ever driven to Seattle.'

'What are you saying?'

'That the truck could be a decoy, Mr President.'

'Bullshit,' said the president. 'We have the device, and you know it. And if your people were smart they'd get it the hell out of that city before we have an accident.'

'An accident?' said Hirshberg. 'This is no accident. They are people bent on mass carnage. If there is a chain reaction, fifty thousand people could lose their lives. Maybe more.'

'I thought you evacuated the area.'

'Twelve blocks, Mr President. If that device goes off, the fireball will take out the entire metropolitan area of downtown Seattle. The shock wave would cross the Sound in less than three seconds and take out the eastern waterfront of Bainbridge Island, a major residential community. That would be awful,' said Hirshberg. 'But what if the bomb isn't there?'

'If it isn't there where would it be?'

'Need I remind you, sir, that in four hours you are going to be assembled in the same building with every member of Congress, the Cabinet, except for a single member, the Supreme Court, the Joint Chiefs of Staff, the entire federal government under one roof.'

'You've been talking to that woman,' said the president. 'What's her name?'

'Ms Cole. No, I haven't seen her since she left the Situation Room yesterday. But I will tell you that what she had to say about this man Belden has been troubling me ever since. Why did they make the truck so easy to find?'

'It may have been easy to find,' said the president, 'but they sure as hell haven't made it easy to get into it.'

'No. Perhaps that's by design,' said Hirshberg. 'To keep us looking in the wrong place just long enough.'

The president thought about what he was saying. 'You think I should cancel the speech?'

'I do.'

'What do I tell Congress?'

'Tell them you'll deliver it next week.'

'Then what do I do, leave town?'

'That would be advisable. Perhaps Camp David,' said Hirshberg. 'Or some other secure military base.'

'You haven't told the Secret Service about your concerns?'

'No.'

'Thank God. They'd be hauling me away with a rope.' The president held the pencil between two fingers and drummed the papers in front of him. It was a no-win situation. If he left the Capitol and didn't tell Congress why, and word got out later, they would cut his political legs out from under him, even members of his own party. He would become known as the president who left the entire government sitting under the Capitol dome to face a nuclear holocaust while he trekked off to Camp David to save his own ass.

'Jesus, Sy, if you thought this was a possibility it would have been nice if you'd mentioned it a little earlier.'

'Mr President, until yesterday we thought that the device, if there was a device, was on that island. Now it appears that it was never on the island, and we don't know how long it's been on the loose. They could have had time to transport it.'

'Maybe it doesn't exist,' said the president. 'Have you ever thought of that? After all, no one has actually seen it, have they?'

'No.'

'Not the woman. Not her friend, what's his name? The Dutchman.'

'Van Ry,' said Hirshberg.

'Why don't you talk to them again? See if maybe we've missed anything.'

Hirshberg could tell he was being sent on a mission of distraction, something to get him out of the president's hair so that he could avoid a decision.

'There is another possible way out. You could become ill at the last minute,' said Hirshberg.

'No!' He exploded, dropped the pencil on his desk and stood. 'That's all I need. Speculation that I've had a stroke or a heart attack. Hell, if I was the president of Russia, I could just tell them I was drunk, or better yet let the press figure it out.'

'It doesn't have to be a stroke,' said Hirshberg.

'You don't cancel the State of the Union for a cold. No. It's too late to cancel,' said the president.

'But . . .'

'No. Now I've made a decision and it's final.' He looked at his watch. 'Is there anything else?'

'No, sir.'

'Then if you don't mind,' said the president.

Hirshberg turned and left the office.

The president's gaze returned the papers on his desk, but his thoughts did not.

Near Silver Hill, MD

He had been in the air, on an off, for more than fourteen hours. The vintage DC-3 was slow and flew at a low altitude, but it was nothing if not reliable.

Thorn taxied up the runway in front of several small hangars. No one paid particular attention to the old plane, even in mint condition. Vintage planes were more common here than perhaps anywhere except the annual Oshkosh Air Show.

The airport was only a few miles from Silver Hill, the home of the Paul E. Garber Restoration, Preservation and Storage Facility. It was the repair center and principal storage area for the Air and Space Museum.

Sitting on twenty-one acres and comprising more than forty thousand aviation artifacts, the Garber facility had a full-time paid staff and an army of volunteer aviation buffs, people who encompassed every aspect of construction and repair from the space shuttle to planes dating back to Kitty Hawk.

Thorn was counting on this volunteer spirit and the loose arrangement that existed between the museum and people who donated their time, some of whom worked at the Garber facility.

Before the plane's wheels even stopped rolling, a truck pulled out from behind one of the hangars. It was thirty feet long with a cargo box on the back, the kind of truck that furniture movers use. It pulled alongside the cargo door of the DC-3.

Thorn cut the plane's engines. Oscar Chaney jumped down from behind the wheel of the truck and threw two wooden chocks in front of the plane's wheels. He arrived at the rear cargo door just as Thorn opened it.

Chaney looked at his watch. 'Right on time.'

'Let's move,' said Thorn. 'We've got a lot to do.'

Chaney backed the truck around until its rear-end lined up perfectly with the cargo door of the plane. He lowered the hydraulic Tommy-lift on the back of the truck so that it was out of the way, sliding easily under the fuselage of the plane. He climbed up into the DC-3 and, together with Thorn, fitted a heavy wooden ramp that had been pre-designed to level and bridge the brief span between the slanting body of the plane and the bed of the truck.

In less than five minutes, using gravity and leverage, they rolled the cargo on its rectangular dolly and metal wheels over the ramp, and into the truck.

Thorn donned a pair of blue overalls and a baseball cap with a logo above the bill that read 'I'd Rather Be Flying'. He dropped down onto the concrete apron, then closed and latched the plane's cargo door from the outside.

Seconds later, he was in the passenger seat of the truck as it headed out toward the road that ran in front of the airport.

They stopped at the front gate. Thorn got out and ran across the street to a pay phone at a gas station. He was inside the phone booth less than a minute. When he came back Chaney had the radio on, tuned to NPR.

In less than three hours the president will address Congress and the nation. Among the items to be covered will be a major push toward national standards for education . . .

Thorn and Chaney looked straight ahead through the murky

film on the windshield as the sun moved low in the sky. They followed the signs toward the interstate, onto the on-ramp heading northwest under the green highway sign that said 'Washington, DC'.

Chaney put his arm out the window, signaling to the merging traffic, then allowed it to dangle, his fingers just inches above the magnetic metal placard on the door: Paul E. Garber Facility, Silver Hill, MD.

The director wanted the smoldering display of *Little Boy* off the museum grounds before guests began assembling for the party that night. They were the overflow crowd, the people who couldn't get seats in the gallery above the House of Representatives. Nonetheless, they were VIPs. Many of them were large contributors to the Smithsonian. Some of them were on the A-list in Washington, rollers and shakers, but simply not quite high enough this year to get one of the coveted seats under the dome tonight.

They would watch the speech projected on a large sectional television screen in *Space Hall*, then drink cocktails and eat hors d'oeuvres. Afterwards, the president's chief of staff and several other notables would visit, though the president himself had other plans.

'I want that thing out of the parking lot now. I don't care what you have to do with it. Call the Army and have it hauled away.' The museum director was up to his ass in alligators and someone was letting more water into the swamp. He had a thousand guests to worry about, and less than three hours to get ready. He was standing just inside the barrier looking at the rust-red stains on the concrete floor.

'Will those come out?'

'We don't know.' It was one of his maintenance supervisors.

'Well, don't make them any worse. Try to get something to cover it, just for tonight. And get that thing out of the parking lot.'

'What are we supposed to do with it?'

'I don't care. Just move it. I don't want people who park there looking at it.'

'We can't roll it into the shop. It's putting out some pretty heavy fumes.'

'Is it toxic?'

One of the workmen looked at the other and wrinkled his eyebrows in a questioning way. 'Not if you don't touch it.'

'Is there any damage to the fuselage?' asked the director.

'No. Just the stains on the floor.'

'Cover them and get the ropes back in place. People are going to want to tour the museum after the speech. They're going to want to see *Enola*.'

The director turned and headed back toward his office. He had a million things to do to get ready. Now they were having problems with the wiring on the big screen.

'What are we supposed to cover it with?' said one of the workmen.

'Search me. Keep working and I'll see what I can find.' The supervisor disappeared in the direction of the shop.

The men continued to run wet mops over the floor, but the rust-red color wouldn't come out. It didn't look as bad as the blood-red dye on the casing of *Little Boy* itself, but still it was noticeable.

'What do you think that guy was on?'

'Who? The director?'

'No. The nut who did this.'

'I don't know. But he's lucky he didn't splash some of that shit on himself.'

'Yeah. Phantom of the fuckin' opera,' said the other guy with the mop.

'Hey, hey, you guys.'

They turned and leaned on their mops to see the super coming back from the direction of the shop.

'What's up?'

'We're in luck. Somebody got hold of the facility out at Garber. Guess what? Seems they've got another one out there.'

'What some fucking nut?'

'No. Another mock-up of *Little Boy*.'

The two guys on the mops looked at each other. 'What are they doing with two of them?'

'I don't know. I don't care. All I know is it's on a truck and it's headed this way. According to Robbie, who took the phone call, the restoration people out there got the shade of green paint on the first *Little Boy* they did a little off. I can see why, not havin' the real thing and all. Anyway, they threw the fabricated casing in a warehouse out there.'

'Maybe it's pee-green,' said one of the guys.

'Hey, right now I don't care if it looks like puke. It'll cover that stain on the floor.'

'Shouldn't we tell the director?' said one of the workmen.

'Why? He told us to cover the floor with something. That's what we're gonna do. Besides he's up to his ass. We'll tell him later. Right now we gotta push that thing in the parking lot outta the way, make room for the truck comin' in. If we're real lucky we can get 'em to haul that smoldering pile of crap outside back to Garber before OSHA declares this place a toxic waste dump.'

The truck pulled up to the back door of the Air and Space Museum ten feet from a pile of something that seemed to be smoking under a black plastic tarp. There were two smiling workers standing beside it.

Thorn looked over at Chaney behind the wheel.

'Looks like Taggart did a real fine job,' said Chaney. 'Wonder where he is now?'

'Not to worry,' said Thorn. 'The man was a true believer.' He got out of the truck and smiled at the men by the plastic tarp.

'How ya doin'? I guess we got what you're lookin' for.' Thorn nodded toward the box of the truck, and pretended like he was chewing on gum. 'How do you wanna get it inside?' he asked them.

'You can back up to the dock there,' said one of the men. The other one went around to open the large overhead door.

Chaney backed the truck up to the dock.

'Any chance of getting you guys to take this one away when you go? Take it back out to Garber?' said the supervisor.

Thorn and Chaney looked at each other. Thorn smiled. 'Sure. Why not.'

It took the four of them to roll the display out of the truck, groaning and grunting every inch of the way, even with the tommy-lift to make a smooth ramp down onto the loading dock.

'Jeez. This one weighs a ton,' said the super. 'Why's it so heavy?'

'Musta' used a heavier gauge metal,' said Thorn.

'Yeah. And put concrete inside,' said Chaney. The four of them laughed.

Once it hit the floor the metal wheels of the dolly began to roll with ease.

'Tell you what,' said Thorn. He looked at the supervisor. 'Why don't you help my friend George here?' He looked at Oscar. 'He'll move the truck and the two of you can use the tommy-lift to load the other one in the back of the truck. That way we can get outta here.'

The supervisor was happy to oblige. In the meantime, Thorn and the other man rolled the mock-up of *Little Boy* out of the shop area and across the floor of the museum. By now the Air and Space Museum was closing, people milling toward the exits. Some of them watched as the bomb rolled down the concourse toward the gleaming B-29.

'Damn shame,' said Thorn. 'You spend a lotta money doing all this, and some idiot with a loose wire comes in and tries to ruin it. Takes all kinds.'

'You bet,' said the other guy. 'Shoulda' seen our director. Mad as hell. If he got his hands on the guy I think he'd kill him.'

'Hmm.' Thorn just looked straight ahead and smiled as they pushed the dolly toward the gleaming belly of the *Enola Gay*.

He could see the two-story windows looking out on the Mall, the only thing standing between ground-zero and the Capitol Building.

The fireball would race down the Mall at the speed of light. It would vaporize every living thing within two hundred yards, and melt the bronze statue on the dome of the Capitol. An instant later the blast would rip the copper sheathing off the roof and ignite every flammable surface inside. Temperatures would reach two thousand degrees within seconds.

The White House would be blown off its foundations. Even the underground bunkers would be heated to temperatures approaching incineration.

Thorn wondered whether Scott Taggart would feel any of it, or whether Taggart had discovered the other item that Thorn had dropped into his briefcase along with the key; the small glass vial with a single capsule of cyanide inside.

CHAPTER
THIRTY-THREE

Hay-Adams Hotel, Washington, DC

Gideon and Joselyn spent the afternoon shopping, getting some clothes, the bare essentials to get themselves home. They caught a movie in the late afternoon and unwound in the cool dark theater, some place where they didn't have to answer questions or look over their shoulders to see if they were being followed by the FBI.

Joselyn wondered if the government would pay for her air fare back to Seattle. It seemed the decent thing, considering the fact that she hadn't asked to come here in the first place.

By the time they got back to the hotel it was almost eight o'clock. She dropped her shopping bags on the bed in her room and kicked off the new pair of shoes she had purchased. They were killing her feet.

Gideon rapped on the adjoining door. She walked over and opened it.

'I'm going to take a shower,' he told her. 'You want to get some dinner once I get out?'

'I'm exhausted. I'd rather eat in the room. Just relax tonight, get to sleep early.'

'Why don't you order room service. Get something for me. A steak, medium rare and a small dinner salad.'

'Where do you want to set up, my room or yours?'

'Doesn't matter,' he told her, then disappeared to take his shower.

She studied the room service menu and called down for dinner. Gideon left the door to the adjoining room open, in case she had the waiter deliver it to his room. She could hear when he knocked on the outside door.

Joselyn wondered if she might be able to get a plane back to Seattle in the morning. She had talked about it with Gideon. One of the agents had told him that the FAA was screening flights into Sea-Tac, diverting some into other airports, until they were able to defuse the device in downtown Seattle. They were using the cover story that maintenance on one of the runways was causing a problem.

She could hear the water running in the shower, and Gideon singing. He had a pretty good voice, though his tune at the higher register was a little off.

She smiled to herself and dropped onto the bed, grabbed the remote off the nightstand and turned on the tube. She checked out the pay-per-view movies. It was a wasteland. She surfed the channels, CNN and the weather. She found the local news, neighborhood shootings in the District, and the plight of city government on the financial edge.

They were trying to buy off the mayor, to keep him from running for another term with a six-figure appointment as professor emeritus at one of the universities. Joselyn was glad that she lived on an island.

She was about to turn off the set when they switched stories:

And there was a great deal of excitement at the Air and

Space Museum today. For that story we go to Charlene Williams . . .

An attractive woman with a microphone in one hand and a notepad in the other appeared on the screen. She was standing on steps in front of a wall with large metal block letters: NATIONAL AIR AND SPACE MUSEUM.

Yes, Charlie, there was a great deal of excitement here today. Police arrested a man inside the museum after he threw a container of acid on one of the displays.

No one was hurt, but an undisclosed amount of damage was done to a replica of the first atomic bomb dropped on Japan. A reproduction of the atomic bomb known as Little Boy, *resting under the fuselage of the famous B-29* Enola Gay *was doused with acid. It had to be removed from the museum because of highly toxic fumes and damage.*

A woman inside at the time of the incident caught these pictures on videotape, moments after the man was hand-cuffed by police, and just before he was led away.

The image on the screen broke up in diagonal lines for a second as the videotape began to play. Joselyn was lying on the bed with her head on the pillows, her mind beginning to wander, thinking about dinner, when she saw his face on the screen. Her eyes opened wide in disbelief as she sat up on the bed.

She only saw his face for a second on the screen before he was hustled away by police, but it was a face that was engraved on her mind's eye. It was the same face she had seen in the house on Padget Island. The man standing in the doorway that morning telling Belden that they had to leave. She had described him to the president, and to the FBI, who were working on a composite drawing.

429

She reached for the TV controls and turned up the volume.

And the mystery deepens tonight. Police have reported that the man (she looked at her notes) *Scott Evan Taggart, died of an apparent heart attack shortly after being taken into custody. Police are saying nothing more about the incident, only that it is under investigation.*

They cut to the anchor:

Charlene, do authorities have any indication as to why the man did what he did?

Not at this point, Charlie. The matter is being handled by the Metropolitan Police as a case of vandalism. You will recall that three months ago there was a similar incident at the National Museum of Art. They are trying to find out if the man had a medical history that might account for his sudden death. Other than that, all they will say is that it is under investigation.

It was as if Joselyn was shell-shocked, sitting on the bed hyperventilating, her brain running at warp-speed.

'Oh shit.' She was talking to herself.

'Oh my God.' She got up from the bed and began pacing, looking at the walls, frantic, trying to figure what to do. The only calming sound filtering through the strains of the television was the constant force of the water hitting the bathtub in Gideon's shower and the occasional sound of his voice as he sang.

She ran to the adjoining door, into his room and straight toward the bathroom. She didn't bother to knock but opened the door. She crossed the steam-filled room in two strides and pulled back the shower curtain.

Gideon stopped singing in mid-note, a bar of soap in his hands and his head covered with suds. He looked at her, bug-eyed, his Adam's apple still bobbing in place.

'Get out of the shower!'

'Excuse me?'

'Get out of the shower, now!' She grabbed a towel from the rod and threw it at him.

He caught it but didn't bother to cover himself. It was a little late.

Joselyn walked out into his room and began pacing by the end of the bed.

He opened the bathroom door. 'Would you mind throwing me some underwear.'

She found a package of new jockey shorts on the bed and carried them over, handing them through the sliver of an opening in the door.

'What's the matter?' said the Gideon.

'The man, that, that . . . guy. The one in the hallway outside of the room on Padget Island. I just saw him on television.'

'Did they catch him?' said Gideon

'They did,' said Joselyn. 'Here in Washington.'

Suddenly the door swung open and Gideon looked at her. He was standing in his underwear, toweling himself.

'What are you talking about?'

'I just saw him on television. They arrested him someplace. The Air and Space Museum,' she said.

'What was he doing there?'

'Throwing acid on a replica of an atomic bomb.'

Gideon stopped toweling and looked at her intently. 'Are you sure it was him?'

'Positive.'

Gideon started pulling on his pants. He slipped his shoes on without socks. Rivulets of water were running out of his hairline at the temple and coursing down his neck into the sparse forest of chest hair.

'And there's something else,' said Joselyn. 'He's dead. They're saying it was a heart attack. Like hell. Where is the Air and Space Museum?'

'On the Mall, near the Capitol . . .' Gideon didn't finish the sentence. They simply looked at each other for a split-second before he dived for the phone. He picked up the receiver and looked at her. 'Who do I call?'

'Nine-one-one. No. That's the police. It'll take an hour to explain it to them,' said Joselyn. She looked at the clock on the table. They were less than forty minutes from the opening of the president's speech. 'We don't have that much time.'

They had been watching snippets all day on the news, every fifteen minutes, political teasers about the president's State of the Union address.

Joselyn raced to her room and ripped open one of the shopping bags. Inside was the FBI jumpsuit she'd put in the bag when she changed to street clothes at the store. She rummaged through one pocket then tried another and came up with a business card. It was Sy Hirshberg's. He had given it to her when she left the Situation Room, just in case she remembered anything else.

By now Gideon was standing in the doorway to her room with a polo shirt in one hand and a towel in the other.

She dialed Hirshberg's number at the White House. It rang twice. A woman answered: 'NSC.'

'Mr Hirshberg please.'

'Who's calling?'

'This is Joselyn Cole. I was there yesterday meeting with the president and Mr Hirshberg. This is an emergency.'

'Just a moment please.'

The line went dead. She was put on hold. Joselyn looked at the clock.

'Is he there?' said Gideon.

'I don't know.'

'Tell them the bomb is in Washington, DC. Tell them we think it's at the Air and Space Museum.'

The woman came back on the line. 'I'm sorry, but Mr Hirshberg has already left the office.'

'I need to reach him immediately. This is an emergency,' said Joselyn.

'What did you say your name was?'

'Joselyn Cole. Is there anybody else there that I can talk to?'

'Just a moment.' The line went dead again.

'Shit,' said Joselyn. She wanted to slam the receiver against the glass surface of the nightstand.

'Let me have it,' said Gideon.

She handed him the phone, and searched for her shoes, sat on the edge of the bed, and slipped them on.

When the voice came back on the other end it was a man this time. 'Hello.'

'Who is this?' said Gideon.

'Who are you?'

'My name is Gideon van Ry. I am with the Institute Against Mass Destruction in Santa Crista, California. I was in the White House Situation Room yesterday with Mr Hirshberg and the president. I have information that there is a nuclear bomb in Washington, DC, somewhere near the Capitol Building.'

'Who is this?'

'Where is Mr Hirshberg?' said Gideon.

'He's with the president. On his way to the Capitol.'

It was too late. By the time Gideon and Joselyn got to someone in authority and explained what they knew, Washington, DC would be a flickering cinder.

'Listen to me. Do you have a pencil and a piece of paper?'

'Yes.'

'Take a note,' said Gideon. 'I don't care how you do it, but get in touch with Mr Hirshberg, immediately. Do you understand?'

There was silence at the other end of the line.

'Tell him that Joselyn Cole and Gideon van Ry called.'

'Give me those names again, slowly,' said the man.

Gideon spelled them for him.

'Tell him that we are on our way to the Air and Space Museum. Listen to me, and get this right. He will know who we are. Tell him that the nuclear device is not in Seattle. Tell him that we believe it is at the Air and Space Museum, and that the president should not speak tonight. Do you understand?'

'I think so,' said the man.

Joselyn was watching the television. The pre-game show was already starting, political analysts were getting face time on the tube, and reporters were interviewing members of Congress under bright television lights. The coverage was live.

'Did you get all of that?' asked Gideon.

'Yes.'

'Now do it,' he told the man. He hung up the phone and grabbed Joselyn, nearly pulling her off her feet. He opened the door to her room just as the waiter was arriving with dinner on a rolling cart.

'Out of the way,' said Gideon. He pushed the cart and the waiter against the wall.

'Just a minute,' said the waiter.

They squeezed by the cart as the door to the room closed behind them.

'Leave it by the door,' said Gideon.

'Hey. Who's gonna sign for this?'

'The government,' said Joselyn. She looked over her shoulder as Gideon pulled her along down the hall.

Gideon got his hand, all the way up to the wrist, into an elevator door just as it was closing. The doors slowly opened. An older couple dressed to the nines looked at them wide-eyed, with more than a little disapproval. Gideon's hair looked like smoke in a wind storm, and Joselyn was winded, with a wild expression in her eyes.

'That's a good way to lose a hand,' said the man.

'If that is all I lose tonight I will consider myself fortunate,' said Gideon.

There was nothing else he could do in the elevator but wait. Gideon ran the fingers of one hand through his hair in a losing effort to make himself more presentable. He reached in his pocket and found his wallet. He had thirty dollars in cash. Enough for a taxi.

When the door opened, they nearly ran over a man and woman standing outside. They hurdled across the hotel lobby, Gideon actually jumping over a small bench. A hundred sets of eyes were drawn to them like doppler radar to a fast-moving object.

Receptions were forming up all over town tonight and the Hay-Adams was no exception. Gideon and Joselyn had to negotiate their way through a crowd at the door. When they got to the curb there was already a small mob waiting for cabs.

Gideon stepped in front.

'You'll have to wait your turn, sir.' The doorman put his hand up and tried to push him back into line.

'We don't have time,' said Gideon.

'What's your problem?'

Gideon thought for a second. 'My wife. She is very ill.' He put his arm around Joselyn and squeezed her shoulder. 'I think she has food poisoning. Something from room service.'

A look of some anguish came over the doorman's face. The crowd began staring at Joselyn. She began to look ill, holding her stomach.

The doorman wasn't in the mood to perform a diagnosis, not with a crowd watching. He blew his whistle and stepped out into the street. A second later a cab pulled up and he ushered Joselyn and Gideon into the back seat and closed the door.

'The Air and Space Museum,' said Gideon. 'And there's an extra twenty in it for you if you get us there in under three minutes.'

'Can't do that, but I can get you there in five,' said the driver.

'Let's not negotiate. It's yours,' said Joselyn.

The acceleration forced them back into the seat. It was a wild ride through the downtown streets of Washington, many of which were one-way. Gideon looked for his watch, which they had returned to him with his wallet. Unfortunately, he'd left it behind in the hotel room.

'What time is it?'

She looked at her watch. 'Eight-forty. Can we get there in time?'

'I don't know.'

'What do we do when we get there?'

'We'll have to find some way to get into the building. If we have to, I'll throw something through a window.'

'That should get the attention of the cops,' said Joselyn.

'Let's hope we can get inside before they arrive. At least we can lead them to the device. Maybe if they see it, at least they'll call for help. If it's not too late,' said Gideon.

The cab raced down H Street and took a left on Seventeenth, passed along the side of the Old Executive Office Building and the Ellipse then headed for the Tidal Basin.

Joselyn could see the Washington Monument off to the

left, its red beacon flashing in the night sky. They swung in a wide arc around the monument, passed the Sylvan Theater and on to Independence Avenue. The cab shot by art galleries and museums, passed behind the back side of the Smithsonian Castle. It was approaching the Transportation Building on Seventh Street when they ran into thickening traffic, red brake lights as far as they could see.

'What is it?' said Gideon.

'I don't know, man. Something's going on.'

Within a hundred feet, the cab was stopped dead in traffic. Joselyn could see stretch limos and large town cars, women walking on the sidewalk in evening gowns and furs, and men in tuxedos, all walking in the same direction.

'How far is the museum?' asked Gideon.

'It's only a block up.'

Gideon looked at the meter. It showed eight dollars. He took the thirty out of his wallet and threw it over the front seat to the driver, opened the door and got out. Joselyn followed him.

They hustled along the sidewalk, passing women in three-inch heels with their gloved hands through the arms of formally attired men. Some of them were wearing military dress uniforms. They were all heading to the broad terrace of stairs leading to the Air and Space Museum.

'At least we won't need to throw anything through the window,' said Gideon.

'How are we going to get in?'

'I don't know.'

The place was lit up like a church on Christmas Eve. There was a vintage searchlight on the street out in front, its beam scanning the night sky. A sign on it read: Relic of the London Blitz.

Docents were handing out programs with maps of the museum printed inside. Gideon saw a man get one and immediately drop it into a trash can. He went fishing in the can as the docent watched him with a sick expression.

'What are you doing?' asked Joselyn.

'Once we get inside there, we are not going to have time to go on a hunting expedition. The display that this man threw acid on. Do you remember the name?'

She looked up at the sky and thought. 'I wasn't paying that much attention.'

'Think,' said Gideon.

'Boy . . . Boy. Something boy.'

'Little Boy,' said Gideon.

'That's it.'

Gideon's eyes found the words *Enola Gay* on the schematic of the museum floor-plan like a magnet. It was isolated in the northwest corner of the building, on the ground level. He oriented himself and the map to the front of the building as an army of guests climbed the stairs toward the gleaming glass façade.

'What do we do now?' said Gideon. 'Go up to the man at the door and tell him there's a nuclear bomb inside?'

'Not unless you want to spend what is left of a brief life in the back of a paddy wagon,' said Joselyn.

Suddenly she saw it. 'Follow me.' She grabbed Gideon by the hand and led him toward the stairs. They merged into the crowd, Gideon trying to be as inconspicuous as a six-foot-five man can be, when he is improperly dressed and his hair is messed.

Several people looked at them. Joselyn didn't pay any attention. Her focus was on the man in front of them in the wool top coat, the one with the large square envelope holding up the flap on the pocket on his coat.

A women in a flowing mink coat wearing diamond earrings gave them a condescending look and continued to stare.

Gideon smiled. 'I see you are a fan of animal rights.'

The woman diverted her eyes and whispered to the man whose arm she was on.

They got to the terrace, leading to the museum, and the line stalled as the people piled up at the door trying to get in. They all seemed to have invitations in large envelopes, passing these to two staff members on either side of the door as a guard looked on.

Joselyn peeked around a shoulder and through an opening in the crowd. Slowly they inched their way forward. Ten feet from the door, the man in front of them stopped dead in his tracks. He began frisking himself, slipping his hand into his inside coat pocket, then unbuttoned it. The woman with him looked at him.

'I swear I put them in my coat.'

Joselyn neatly stepped around him and pulled Gideon after her. They reached the door ten seconds later where the white-gloved attendant looked at them, then reached out and took the engraved invitation from Joselyn's hand.

'You know it is black-tie?' said the man.

'We'll sit in the back,' said Joselyn.

Before he could say anything, they stepped through the door and into the lobby of the museum and kept walking.

Gideon took a brief sideways glance over his shoulder and saw the attendant talking to guard, who was now looking at them with sufficient intensity to burn a hole through their backs.

'I'd ask you how you did that,' he told her, 'but we don't have time.'

The man who had lost his invitation was at the door, still patting his pockets and now talking to the attendant.

At a near run, Gideon and Joselyn headed across the lobby, dodging around guests with champagne glasses in their hands. Gideon tried to make himself ten inches shorter so that he wouldn't be seen above the crowd.

With his long legs he gobbled up the sixty feet of the lobby passing the information booth, but not before a member of the staff behind the desk saw them. The woman picked up a phone and punched a button.

Joselyn tried to keep up with him. The leather soles on her news shoes slipped like ice on the smooth concrete floor. Now they were in full stride, left past the *Milestones of Flight* and down the main gallery past the escalators that led to the second level.

When Gideon looked over his shoulder, he saw them. Emerging from the crowd like destroyers under full steam were three armed guards. They were soon joined by a fourth, one of them with his hand already on the handle of his holstered revolver.

As they left the last cluster of wandering guests behind, Gideon and Joselyn stood out like two doughboys in no-man's-land.

Gideon broke into a full run. Joselyn followed him. They darted behind a temporary display in the center of the broad concourse and crossed over to the north side of the building.

For a second Gideon lost sight of the guards. When they popped out from the other side of the escalator, one of them was talking with his chin pressed down into a microphone clipped to the lapel of his uniform shirt. Gideon saw the guard pop the safety snap of the leather holster from across the hammer of his gun, and draw the pistol, holding the muzzle toward the floor with both hands as he ran.

He grabbed Joselyn and pushed her out in front of him, shielding her with his body, and propelling her down the concourse toward the *Enola Gay*. They ran between the last stairwell in the center of the building and past the final partition separating the displays.

There in the gallery to the right was the gleaming fuselage of the B-29. Without its wings, which could not be assembled in the confines of the building, it looked like a mammoth silver cigar. The giant nose wheel was turned just a little as if the plane had just taxied to a stop on the runway. The bright overhead lights of the display reflected off the Plexiglass bubble of the bombardier's station up front.

Under the body of the *Enola Gay*, halfway back toward the tail section, was the ominous green cylinder with its bulbous nose and square tail-fin – the paradigm of the atomic age, the full-sized replica of *Little Boy*.

For an instant Joselyn and Gideon stood transfixed, knowing that what they were looking at was no mere model. Unable to speak, they looked at the bomb for what it was; two kilotons of radioactive death capable of rising in a death-head mushroom more than nine miles into the stratosphere above the nation's capital.

The clatter of feet on concrete, approaching from the main hall, brought them back to the moment.

'What do we do?' said Joselyn.

Gideon turned toward the hall behind them, the footfalls closing. 'Quick. Get inside the railing, under the plane,' he told her.

They ran across the deserted gallery and jumped the railing, then moved under the belly of the plane, careful not to jostle the bomb or its rectangular steel dolly.

Gideon scanned the green metal casing looking for a small covering panel with screws or an area of rivets, anything that would provide access to the device inside.

Even if he found one, he had no idea how he would pry it off. He had no tools.

The guards reached the corner of the partition leading into

the gallery housing the *Enola Gay*. Joselyn saw one of them poking his head around the edge of the partition.

Another guard sprinted across the opening into gallery and took up a position on the other side. Both had their guns drawn.

'Come out now, with your hands up,' said one of the guards.

'We are not armed,' said Gideon. He was breathing heavily, winded from their run down the concourse.

'Show your hands and come out,' said the guard.

Gideon could hear movement in the shadows where the tail section of the huge bomber disappeared behind the walls of the exhibit. He knew that police or guards were moving in from that direction. In seconds they would be on him. Anything he said would be lost in the din of a scuffle that would soon be over.

They could hear the sound of the giant television as suddenly it was piped into the speaker system of the museum.

Any moment now the president will be announced by the sergeant-at-arms of the House. There we see Secretary of State Knowland coming in. He is followed by the attorney general . . .

'Listen to me,' said Gideon. 'The man who threw acid on the model of *Little Boy* this morning. He was part of terrorist group. This casing, the one under the plane, contains a nuclear device. It was substituted sometime during the day. Call Mr Hirshberg, the president's national security adviser. Tell him that Gideon van Ry is here at the museum. He will vouch for me.'

'Put your hands up where we can see them, and come out now.'

There was more shuffling and movement and now

whispering in the shadows where the tail of the plane disappeared into darkness.

You know, Tom, we do see the Secretary of State. But you know who we don't see is Sy Hirshberg, the president's national security adviser. If he's not here tonight that will indeed fuel rumors that perhaps Mr Hirshberg is on the out with the administration. There have been rumors . . .

Two uniformed guards rushed out of the shadows behind them. They flung the full force of their bodies into Gideon, one high and the other low. They sent him sprawling across the floor under the plane.

A third guard emerged from the darkness and grabbed Joselyn before she could move, throwing her to the floor and placing his knee with the full weight of his body in the center of her back. It felt as if the man broke her spine, the pain nearly causing her to black out.

As Gideon wrestled on the floor, the two guards rolled him so that he was face down. As they held him, two more guards jumped the railing to help.

With his face pressed to the floor and turned to one side, Gideon saw it. There was a small panel, roughly four-by-ten inches on the underside of the casing. It was held in place by six small screws. Looking from the top of the bomb as it rested on the dolly, the panel was impossible to see.

He struggled to get free, but the guards only increased the pressure on his arms as they were forced up behind his back. Gideon was rangy and powerful. One of them applied a wristlock. Gideon closed his eyes in pain. They watered. He tried to focus on the metal panel under the bomb, as if by sheer force of mind he could will it open.

'Get off of them.' It was a voice from out in the gallery, spoken with authority. 'Did you hear me? Let them up now.'

Gideon lifted his head and saw the lanky frame of Sy Hirshberg just beyond the railing. For an old man, Hirshberg was nothing if not agile. Balancing himself with a single hand on the railing he threw one leg over, and then the other and within three seconds had his hand on the shoulder of one of the guards.

They didn't look at Hirshberg but at the man who was with him, tall, in formal attire.

The museum director nodded, and the guards released their hold. The one kneeling on Joselyn's back immediately got off of her. He reached for her arm and tried to help her up, but he had knocked the wind out of her.

Gideon got up off the floor, feeling his wrist to make sure it wasn't broken. He looked at Joselyn, but there was no time.

'I need a screwdriver.' He scrambled over to the bomb and looked underneath. 'Phillips-head,' he said. Then he got on his back as if he were getting ready to crawl under a car.

The guards hesitated.

'What are you waiting for?' said Hirshberg. 'Now.'

Two of the guards scrambled into the darkness.

By now Joselyn had made it onto her knees. Holding her stomach with one hand and struggling to get air into her lungs, she crawled toward Gideon and the bomb casing.

Hirshberg moved in and got down on one knee next to them.

'How much time do we have?'

'Where is the president?' said Gideon.

'He's getting ready to speak,' said Hirshberg.

'That's the key,' said Gideon. 'If I am correct it will be detonated by radio signal as soon as the president appears on the floor of the Congress.'

Hirshberg turned to an assistant who was behind the railing. 'Can we reach the president's secret-service detail on their radio frequency?'

'No,' said the young man. 'I don't think so.'

By now some of the guests had wandered down, drawn to the commotion at the other end of the museum. They stood riveted as the tall slender man lay on his back looking up at the bomb.

'If we can't reach them by radio,' said Hirshberg, 'call the White House detail. Tell them to keep the president off the floor of the House. I don't care what they have to do. Hell. Tell them there's a bomb about to go off near the Capitol.'

With those words a ripple of panic started to move through the crowd beyond the portal to the gallery.

'What did he say?'

'He said there's a bomb.'

People started to move toward the lobby. The news traveled with them like a wave. In less than a minute, it reached the front doors and people started streaming out onto the street.

Hirshberg's assistant punched keys on a cellphone as Joselyn watched him.

One of the guards came out of the shadows with a small toolbox. Hirshberg and Joselyn fished in it until they found a Phillips screwdriver.

Considering the trauma to his wrist, Gideon worked with deft fingers to loosen the six screws on the metal cover. There was no time for finesse. He could only pray that Belden and his people had not taken the time to install a tripwire on the panel. Intuition and experience told him that this was unlikely. A tripwire trigger would make transport of the device more difficult, unless they had time to arm it after it was in place. In a public museum with staff watching that was not likely.

He held his breath as he pulled the last screw from its hole, then slowly slipped a fingernail under the edge of the panel. The panel cover was heavier than it looked. Without the last screw it fell off in his hands. Gideon flinched and squeezed his eyes shut tight. When he opened them, he was still there.

Joselyn could feel her heart thumping like a steam engine.

He dropped the metal panel cover onto the floor and looked inside. It was a maze of wires, different colors going in every direction.

Somebody handed him a small flashlight. He shot the beam inside and moved it around looking for something.

'Damn.'

'What's wrong?' said Joselyn.

'I don't see any receiver. There should be a small box. A battery power pack.' He traced the wires with his eyes. 'There is no clock or timer switch that I can see.' He was now breathless.

'It has to be remote detonation,' he told them. 'They would want to be far enough away not to be caught up in it. That would require a good-sized receiver,' said Gideon. He was breathing hard, perspiration pouring down his forehead as he flashed the light through the small opening in the casing, frantically searching for something that wasn't there.

He could see the spherical core of the nuclear device up near the nose of the bomb. It was only a fraction of the diameter of the bomb casing that disguised it, a twisted testament to the progress of man in the twenty years after the end of the war.

The core rested in what appeared to be a cradle of molded styrofoam, designed to buffer the device and its multiple detonators during transit.

Something wasn't right. Around the core fastened to the inside of the casing were a number of small metal tubes, the size of a fire-extinguisher, the kind you might carry on a small boat. Gideon counted nine of these.

Sweat was streaming down his forehead and into his eyes.

He wiped them with the back of his hand, and continued to flash the beam of light through the hole.

For a second, he thought the device was thermonuclear. Instead of two kilotons, Gideon wondered if he was looking at five megatons. If it was, it would take out the entire District, part of Maryland and the northern reaches of Virginia.

Suddenly it settled on him as he looked at the wiring. It was not thermonuclear at all. The metal tubes were filled with radioactive cesium.

'Get everybody out of here,' said Gideon.

'It's too late if it goes off now,' said Hirshberg.

'It may be too late even if it doesn't go off,' said Gideon. 'Get them out now.'

Hirshberg got to his feet. 'Out. Everybody out,' he said.

The guards began herding the few people who remained toward the main hallway and the exit.

'You, too,' said Hirshberg.

'I'm not going anywhere,' said Joselyn.

'Take her out of here,' said Gideon.

Joselyn fought with the guards and wrestled with Hirshberg. They dragged her toward the railing, out from under the *Enola Gay* and finally Hirshberg managed to calm her. She looked at Gideon lying on his back, his face nearly under the bomb, shining the small flashlight inside.

'I won't go,' she said.

'You must,' he told her.

'No.' Tears streamed down her face.

'Mr Hirshberg.' It was Hirshberg's assistant.

'I can't get through. The phone lines at the White House are jammed.'

'What do you mean, they're jammed?'

'They're all busy.'

'There's two hundred lines over there,' said Hirshberg.

'The circuits are jammed.'

447

It settled on her like ether, looking at Gideon lying on the floor. The cellular phone and the assistant. The jammed lines.

'It's not a radio receiver,' said Joselyn. She called to him, tried to run back to his side, but they stopped her. 'It's a cellphone.' Two of the guards lifted her over the railing as she fought them, struggled, using both hands.

Gideon, on his back, shot a glance in her direction. She was hysterical, being carried away.

'It's a cellular phone,' she told him. 'That was Belden's business. Voice identification. Look for a cellular phone.' She pounded on the guard's back but to no avail. He carried her slung over his shoulder toward the main hall.

Almost as her lips said it, his eye caught it, not a phone, but a single wire, gray in color and oval, heavier than the others. It was ordinary telephone wire. It ran in one direction and disappeared under the core of the device, where it rested in the styrofoam cradle. In the other direction, the wire passed through what appeared to be a white cloth shield that sealed off the tail of the bomb toward the square metal tail-fin.

Gideon looked at the metal covering plate resting on the floor. It was lined with lead. He flashed the light just inside the hole and scratched the inside surface of the casing with his fingernail. It was lead. The entire casing of *Little Boy* was lined with lead to shield anyone handling it from the deadly radiation of the cesium.

He was now alone under the still and looming body of the B-29, the only sound the distant scream of Joselyn as they carried her toward the exit and the television feed from the giant screen.

Gideon took a deep breath, then stuck his hand and his bare arm into the opening in the case of *Little Boy*. All the way to the shoulder. He felt the cloth shield that sealed off the tail section and the telephone cable that passed through. He pushed the shield with his fingers. There was resistance, but it was not solid. The shield was made of canvas, surrounding a lead liner. He punched it with his clenched fist and the duct tape holding it to the inside of the case ripped. He hit it again harder, and the shield collapsed into the tail of the casing.

When he pulled his arm out and flashed the light back inside, he saw it. Fastened to the inside of *Little Boy* with black electrical tape was a small cellular phone. Completing the circuit, the phone cable plugged into the bottom of it. It had been necessary to get the cellphone outside of the lead shield in order to ensure a signal reception to the phone.

Gideon guessed that at the other end of the phone cable, under the nuclear core, was a computer chip programmed with the verbal code. This would be attached to the principal detonator. From there, the current would fan out to multiple detonators planted in the high explosive surrounding the plutonium core.

He looked at the containers of cesium then without hesitation he put his arm back into the casing of the bomb, all the way to the shoulder. He reached for the cellphone taped to the side of the casing, but he couldn't free it from the tape. He needed a knife.

He slid the toolbox closer and with his free hand he felt around inside. Something sharp. It was the flat blade of a screwdriver not a knife, but it would have to do. Quickly he maneuvered it into the casing and tried to cut the tape with the metal end. Belden had secured it well.

Suddenly he heard footsteps running toward him. It was Joselyn. Somehow she'd gotten away from guard. She jumped the railing and ran to him, slid on the floor on her knees until her head and upper body landed gently on his chest.

'You should be out of here. Please.' He pleaded with her.

'I won't go. I won't leave you.'

'You don't understand,' said Gideon.

'I don't care. I'm not going,' she told him.

They didn't have time to argue. Gideon struggled with the tape on the phone and finally got an edge loose.

He grabbed the phone as it dangled from the remnants of sticky tape and pulled until it came free.

'Please don't get close to me,' he told her. 'Move away to the other side of the bomb.' If he couldn't convince her to leave, he could at least put the shield of the casing between Joselyn and himself. His body was now heavily contaminated by radiation, and Gideon knew it.

She looked at him with eyes that told him she would go that far, but no farther.

Carefully he withdrew his arm until his hand, with the phone in it, slipped through the opening of the casing. It was still trailing the telephone cable connected to the detonator. He considered cutting the wire but wasn't sure if this would set off the device. Even if Belden had used a verbal code to arm the device itself, Gideon couldn't be sure whether he'd wired the cesium with a separate explosive in the event that someone tried to sever a circuit.

Joselyn looked at the small phone, her gaze seeming mesmerized.

Ladies and Gentlemen, the president of the United States.

The sound system in the museum erupted with applause, as the giant screen played to an empty room. The crowd of more than a thousand people dressed in tuxedos and evening gowns, streamed out onto the street.

Women were falling down the stairs in their heels, others dropped their sequined bags, men stepping on them, running, visions of the carnage in Oklahoma City playing in their minds. They had no idea that the bomb was nuclear.

*   *   *

U nder the belly of the *Enola Gay*, the phone came to life in Gideon's hand. It rang, and the liquid crystal screen lit up.

Gideon didn't hesitate. There was no time. He reached up with his fingers and pressed the clip on each side of the wired fitting at the base of the cellphone. The end of the cable disconnected from the phone.

It rang again. As he looked at Joselyn, her eyes peering over the top of *Little Boy*, the same question crossed their minds; with the phone locked away inside of the casing, who would have ever answered it?

The solution came with the third ring. Suddenly there was the hiss of an open line. They could hear someone breathing at the other end. Belden had programmed the phone with an answering chip.

He said only two words, but his voice carried crystalline and clear. 'Critical Mass.'

Gideon looked at it for a moment, then held the mouthpiece of the phone to his lips.

'I'm sorry. You have the wrong number.' Then he pressed the END button.

CHAPTER
THIRTY-FOUR

Bethesda, MD

T he ward at Bethesda Naval Hospital was quiet, almost deserted. This section of the floor was now off-limits to all except a handful of doctors and specially trained nurses.

Joselyn had been coming by for three days, camping there most of the day. Still they wouldn't let her see him.

'Why not?' she said.

The doctor shook his head.

'Why can't I see him?'

'Because he's very ill,' said Hirshberg.

It was the look that passed between the two men that told her it was much more serious than she had been led to believe. She had thought it was for security. That they were debriefing him.

'He's not going to die?'

Hirshberg and the doctor merely looked at each other, but neither of them spoke.

Then finally Hirshberg reached out and placed his hands on her shoulders. 'He's absorbed a tremendous amount of radiation.'

'We were all there,' said Joselyn.

'His arms, inside of the casing, were exposed for too long,' said the doctor.

'There must be something you can do?' She looked at him with pleading eyes.

The doctor shook his head as Hirshberg released her and turned away.

'I want to see him now,' she told them.

'That's not a good idea,' said Hirshberg.

'I'm going in there.'

She turned toward the room and one of the guards started to move toward her.

'That's all right.' Hirshberg shot him a look, and the guard backed off. He looked at the doctor.

'Only if we set up a shield. And then only for a couple of minutes,' said the physician.

Joselyn waited outside the room in the hall while a device like a small dressing screen was rolled down the hall and into the room. A few seconds later the attendant, wearing a lead vest, came back out and nodded.

'You can only stay in there for two minutes,' said the doctor. 'I will be watching you from the control booth. You have to stay behind the shield. And whatever you do. You are not to touch him.'

The guard opened the door, and Joselyn looked inside. It was dark. There were no windows. It was a large X-ray room. She saw the doctor walk quickly into a booth from another entrance somewhere down the hall. She could see his shadow moving in the booth through a thick glass window the size of a postcard.

She entered the room, and the guard closed the door behind her. For a moment, she stood looking at the hospital bed rolled against the far wall, just beyond the X-ray table. She could hear his rasping breath and see his

454

long form under the single white sheet that covered his body.

'Please get behind the screen.' The doctor talked to her from beyond the shielded booth where he watched.

She walked over behind the shield that stood at the head of the bed. Tears began to well in her eyes. She could see his arms resting on top of the sheets as she approached, bleeding and blistered. They appeared to be covered with some kind of a gel.

Joselyn turned toward the booth and the doctor inside. 'Can't you do anything for his arms?'

'We're making him as comfortable as possible.'

With the sound of her voice close now, just beyond the shield, Gideon slowly rolled his head toward the side of the pillow and looked at her face through the specially shielded glass, a small window in the screen.

'Hello.' Joselyn tried to smile.

'Hi.' Gideon's face was marked with lesions and his lips were blistered and broken.

She wanted to reach out and grab him by the hand, pull him from this cave of a room out into the bright sunlight where life was fine and the world continued. Her hand hit the screen as she leaned forward.

Instead all she could do was look at him. 'How are you feeling?'

'Oh.' He was breathless, tried to smile, but started to cough. His respiration was ragged; his chest rose beneath the single sheet as he fought for breath. A trace of frothy blood formed at the corner of his lip.

Gideon's golden hair had turned to straw, and lesions had formed under the skin on his forehead.

She tried to keep herself from crying. She didn't want him to see her that way. Quickly she brought a hand up and rubbed her eyes with the back of it.

'I had to see you,' she said.

He smiled. 'You did the right thing,' he told her. 'If you had not told me about the phone, I would never have looked for it, and we would all be dead.'

'Oh, God.' Now she looked at the ceiling, tears streaming down her cheeks.

'It's not your fault,' he told her. 'There was nothing else we could do.'

'We could have run,' said Joselyn. 'We could have left this place.'

'No,' he said. 'No, we couldn't.' He smiled at her, his soft blue eyes, the only part of him that seemed untouched, melting her soul.

'I love you,' she said. Joselyn had no idea where the words came from, only that she could not control them.

All he could do was smile.

'Oh, God. I'm gonna lose it,' she said. She turned away so that he couldn't see her face. She ached to touch his hand, to hold him in her arms and comfort him. She was two feet away and it was as if for all the world he was alone.

'No.' He was breathing heavily. 'Don't. Don't. Please.' He was hyperventilating, struggling for breath as he spoke. He knew time was short.

'You must not feel this way,' he said. 'We did good.'

As she turned back to him, his blistered face the picture of serene acceptance, Joselyn suddenly realized that it was not her actions or her words that night that brought him to this place, but what Gideon himself believed in. 'Yes. We did good.'

'You know,' he said. 'We never did get to exercise our constitutional rights.'

She smiled, laughed, with tears running down her face.

It was the last thing she heard as the monitor above his bed began to scream, and the blip on the screen ran to a flat line.

Doctors and nurses in heavy lead vests streamed into the room, pulling a crash cart behind them.

Before they could hook up, the doctor in the booth stopped them. He shook his head, and slowly they filtered out of the room, leaving Joselyn alone, standing behind the screen, looking at Gideon's smile and his lifeless blue eyes.

CHAPTER
THIRTY-FIVE

Andrews Air Force Base, MD

Sy Hirshberg made the arrangements to fly Gideon's body home to Amsterdam, aboard an Air Force jet with a full honor guard.

Joselyn was at Andrews Air Force Base when the hearse arrived.

The United States government paid for the special lead liner and coordinated with the Dutch government for burial. But the hearse itself bore a simple wooden coffin that had been requested by Gideon's parents.

Joselyn had never met them, but she wanted to. They spoke by phone the day after Gideon died and agreed that in the summer they would meet. She had much to tell them about how their son had lived his last days. They had a lifetime of stories to tell her.

Hirshberg had arranged for a separate plane to take Joselyn back home to Seattle. They met on the tarmac and watched as the coffin was carried from the hearse with military precision. The flags were folded, Dutch and American.

They offered the stars and stripes to Joselyn. She took it, but later handed it to Hirshberg with a request that it be given to Gideon's mother. The final tears made their way down her cheeks as the casket was slowly lifted and finally disappeared into the cargo hold of the big jet.

Hirshberg sighed. He choked. His voice cracked as he turned toward Joselyn. 'I am sorry that this had to happen.'

She looked up at him without missing a beat. 'It didn't.'

'I know. You're angry. You're bitter. You have every reason to be.'

'No. He had every reason to be.' She pointed to the open cargo door on jet. 'Tell him that you're sorry.'

Hirshberg didn't know what to say.

'You know, I read in the paper that there was an *incident* at the Air and Space Museum.' She looked at him for a few seconds to allow the word to sink in.

'There was nothing on the news about a nuclear bomb. Nothing about Belden or Taggart. He died of a heart attack,' said Joselyn.

'We know it was cyanide,' said Hirshberg.

'Well. Now that's a start. Have you found Belden?'

'No.'

Belden had called two more times to the cellphone at the museum, uttering the same message each time, before he realized what had happened. The NSC was able to trace the last call to a pay phone in Augusta, Georgia. By the time authorities got there, there was no sign of Belden.

'You don't understand,' said Hirshberg. 'There are important policy issues here. Matters of immense strategic concern.'

'I would hope,' said Joselyn. 'The man tried to kill a few thousand people in your city. Hell. He tried to destroy the entire government. He managed to kill some good people on that island. And . . .' She looked at the Air Force plane with its cargo door still open.

'I don't understand, how you can just let him go?' she said.

'We are not letting him go,' said Hirshberg. 'He is as good as dead.'

'Really.' Joselyn looked at him, incredulous. 'What's he going to die of, old age?'

A chill wind swept across the runway as jet engines screamed their high-pitched whine in the background.

'Why haven't I seen his name in the papers? A picture? You have one. Or has the president lost it?' said Joselyn.

Hirshberg took a deep breath and stared off in another direction. She was waiting for an answer.

'There once was a man named Dean Belden, or Thorn, or a dozen other names, none of which we're sure of. But he died in a plane crash near Seattle.' Hirshberg found it impossible to look at her as he said it.

It was breathtaking. She stared up at the side of his face as he looked off into the distance at nothing in particular, then spoke the only words she could think of. 'I don't believe it. You people are incredible.'

'Joselyn, you have to understand what is happening here. The men on that island in the Sound may have paid for Belden's services, but they didn't hire him.'

Joselyn looked at him.

'There is no way they could have raised the money needed to pay for an intact nuclear device,' said Hirshberg. 'Maybe some fissile materials, a chemical bomb, but not a nuclear device. Not with the expertise needed to make sure that it would function as designed. Gideon knew that,' he told her.

'Then who?'

'That's the question no one wants to answer,' said Hirshberg.

'I don't understand.'

'The United States government has a long-standing policy of maximum retaliation,' said Hirshberg. 'Any foreign nation that employs or attempts to employ a weapon of mass destruction on U.S. soil would face retaliation of a similar kind.

'Don't you see? We're not anxious to find Mr Belden. At least not through any public channels of law enforcement. If we do, we run the risk of discovering the link between Belden and whoever sponsored his activities.

'If the government ever made a public acknowledgment that it knew who was behind that device, who paid for it and who hired the man you knew as Dean Belden, then national honor and credibility would require that we do something about it.'

'What if the bomb had gone off?' said Joselyn. 'Would you continue to stick your head in the sand?'

'If the bomb had gone off, it would have become someone else's problem,' said Hirshberg.

'So we have a policy that we're afraid to carry out.'

'The consequences for this nation and the world were that to happen are too horrific to contemplate,' said Hirshberg. 'In such cases ignorance is bliss.'

'And in the meantime, Belden just walks away,' said Joselyn.

'I would not wish to be in his shoes,' said Hirshberg. 'Whoever hired him, he took their money, and he failed. What's worse for Mr Belden, he is now a very dangerous loose end in a game of nuclear brinkmanship. If he were to fall into the wrong hands and if his story were to be made public, in ways that it could not be denied . . .' With his furrowed brows, Hirshberg put an expression on the face of the obvious.

'His employers are not going to be anxious to have him wandering around. No,' said Hirshberg. 'If I were Lloyd's of London, I would not be writing any policy on Mr Belden's life.'

EPILOGUE

Chiapas, Mexico

I t was a small café with three tables in the sun out near the street. There were strains of mariachi music in the distance, signs that a wedding had just concluded at the catholic church two short streets away.

The man had a growth of beard and straggly hair, an old Mexican blanket cut at the fold and worn so that his head went through the hole in the center and the blanket rested on his shoulders.

He had weathered three attacks on his life in the last month, killing one of them with a knife and another with his hands. The third assassin planted a bomb that did not go off until he found it under the seat of his own car.

He carried a pistol tucked in his belt under the serape, and his gaze never rested in one place for long.

He had friends, but they no longer slept near him at night or rode with him in the same vehicles.

The Americans were relentless. They had eyes and ears everywhere. They may not have maintained diplomatic relations with some of the countries of the Middle East, but a note detailing his whereabouts, they would willingly slip under a door.

He would have to leave Mexico soon, and he knew it. His funds were running out, and the local guerrillas were not going to hide him for much longer. The numbered accounts in Europe had been frozen. He saw the deft fingers of the American State Department visible in this.

By now he should have been lying on a private beach in Bali sipping coconut milk and rum, earning thirty percent on his money. Instead they were hunting for him, his dreams of retirement if not destroyed certainly deferred.

He opened the U.S. newspaper. It was yellow with age, a copy of the *Santa Crista Herald*. It was three months old and spattered with oil from a hundred baked tortillas. Some of the pages were missing and others were torn, but he carried it like a relic.

He slapped it on the table as he ate and looked at the photo under the fold on page three. It was not much of a story, only four inches, along with a two-column photo of a group of people standing in front of a bronze plaque embedded in the wall of a Spanish Colonial bungalow.

It was a monument to a Dutchman named Gideon van Ry, awarded by an organization known as the Institute Against Mass Destruction.

He was not interested in the plaque, or the story that was sparse on details, but in the woman standing on the chair, lifting the cloth that had covered the bronze shield.

The image of her face was grainy and smaller that the nail of his small finger. The tips of her blond hair danced just off her shoulders in the wind as her eyes darted toward the lens, as if the photographer had caught her by surprise.

It wasn't much of a picture, but there was not a doubt in Thorn's mind that it was Joselyn Cole.

She had walked away from the house on Padget Island;

how he would never know. Thorn had left her for dead on two occasions, and twice she had come back to haunt him.

His gaze burned a hole through the yellowing photograph on the table. She had cost him twenty million dollars and a life of ease. Now he would have to work again and watch his back while he did it.

He chewed with determination as he looked at the photograph and tried to imagine the expression on her face if she ever saw him again.

The Arraignment

Steve Martini

When a lawyer friend, Nick Rush, is killed along with a client in a hail of gunfire outside the federal courthouse, attorney Paul Madriani is determined to find out the truth behind the double murder. Tortured by the possibility that he himself had been marked for death, only to have a friend die in his place, Madriani casts a suspicious eye in all directions – at Rush's business associates, his clients, even the beautiful widow and her mysterious new companion.

As he investigates, Madriani rides the crest of a dangerous wave of international drug deals and people who murder for money. In a quest that takes him from California to Mexico, he discovers that, while the motive to kill may be driven by events taking place thousands of miles away, the killer lies much closer at hand . . .

Don't miss Steve Martini's previous bestsellers, which have been warmly praised:

'Compelling indeed . . . a terrific debut' *Sunday Telegraph*

'Nice insider touches, and a hard-punching climax' *The Times*

'A tense and gripping story' *Books*

'Fascinating trial scenes and legal insights' *Washington Times*

'Thoroughly absorbing' *Literary Review*

0 7472 6610 7

headline

Now you can buy any of these other bestselling books by **Steve Martini** from your bookshop or *direct from his publisher*.

FREE P&P AND UK DELIVERY
(Overseas and Ireland £3.50 per book)

The Arraignment	£6.99
The Jury	£6.99
The Attorney	£6.99
Critical Mass	£6.99
The List	£6.99
The Judge	£6.99
Undue Influence	£6.99
Prime Witness	£6.99
The Simeon Chamber	£6.99
Compelling Evidence	£6.99

TO ORDER SIMPLY CALL THIS NUMBER

01235 400 414

or visit our website: www.madaboutbooks.com

Prices and availability subject to change without notice.